PROTECTORS 2
HEROES

PROTECTORS

2

HEROES

EDITED BY **THOMAS PLUCK**

TABLE OF CONTENTS

FOREWORD

Thomas Pluck

These stories are not all about protecting children, but this book is.

Protectors 2: Heroes exists to fight for children by supporting PROTECT, a non-partisan anti-crime pro-child lobby whose sole focus is making the protection of children from physical, sexual, and emotional abuse a top political and policy priority at the national, state, and local levels. The people who work for PROTECT and the contributors to the Protectors anthologies are so different that we might react like matter meeting antimatter, but we work together for this important cause because we share one belief: *children deserve our protection from emotional, physical, and sexual abuse, and exploitation of any kind.*

PROTECT is two separate and distinct, but united-in-purpose, initiatives. PROTECT PAC is a political lobby, a 501(c)(4) organization. Its victories include the Circle of Trust Law which closed New York State's infamous Incest Loophole, striking down a law that served as a "Get Out of Jail Free" card for predators who sexually assault victims in their own families. Their nonprofit arm, The National Association to Protect Children, funds the H.E.R.O. Child-Rescue Corps, a joint program between PROTECT, USSOCOM, and Immigration & Customs Enforcement which trains wounded veterans to join state-level Internet Crimes Against Children task forces across the country, where they assist local law enforcement in identifying online predators and rescuing their victims.

The abuse of a child goes against our nature so deeply that we often refuse to think about it, but we must. Fighting child abuse is necessary to our survival, and predators who hurt our children are truly civilization's greatest threat. When early humans sat around campfires outside their caves, they invented monsters; today, to quote contributor Andrew Vachss, "We make our own monsters. The formula is frighteningly simple: Take child abuse or neglect, especially at the hands of those constituted by the laws of man and nature to protect their own, and let the government either ignore or exacerbate the situation." [1]

PROTECT chooses to stand together and fight for children, and all proceeds from the sales of this book will be donated to PROTECT PAC, our political lobby. The first Protectors anthology contained forty-one stories; this volume contains contributions from fifty-six authors, artists, poets, and illustrators. Counting the people who designed the cover and the print and electronic copies of the book, the number is fifty-nine.

You can make that number an even sixty by joining PROTECT. Learn more at their website, www.protect.org

You can support PROTECT's cause whether you purchase the books or not, by requesting that your local library order the Protectors anthologies.

Thank you for your support.

Keep Fighting,

Thomas Pluck, July 2015

YOU CAN FOLLOW OUR DONATION RECORD
AT WWW.PROTECTORSBOOKS.ORG

---

[1]   "Today's Victim Could Be Tomorrow's Predator," by Andrew Vachss. Originally published in *Parade Magazine*, June 3, 1990. © 1990 Andrew Vachss, all rights reserved.

PROTECTORS

2

HEROES

EDITED BY **THOMAS PLUCK**

THE QUESTIONS

Alison Arngrim

At first, I didn't tell anybody. Who would I tell? And what on earth would I tell them? And if I could possibly even bring myself to describe it, what could they do about it?

Then later, when I tried to tell people, everybody asked me questions.

Did you enjoy it? Have you forgiven him? Did you climax? Have you asked God to forgive you for your part of the sin? Did you get pregnant? Is he sorry? Is this a "recovered" memory? Do you hate men now?

When I got finished staring at them as if they were insane, I realized that all of their questions had the same answer. "Um . . . *nooo*."

So for awhile, I stopped telling people.

Then PROTECT called me. They didn't have so many questions. Just two, really.

"Would you like to be on our board?"

"How soon can you start?"

Nobody at PROTECT asked me "what happened?" or "what was it like?" or "why?" They didn't need to. PROTECT was full of people who either had it happen *to them*, or had spent the last several decades putting the kind of people who made it happen *in jail*. They already knew *exactly* what happened and precisely what is was like. And they didn't give a damn "why".

They didn't want me on the board because of what happened to me. They wanted me because of who I was. They knew that not only was I famous from being on TV, but that I had used it before to publicize worthy causes with excellent results. I was experienced in giving interviews and wasn't scared of a camera.

It turned out, one of the first things they asked me to do was help change a law in California, the Incest Exception, a law that allowed people who sexually assault children they happen to be related to, to get *less* jail time than someone who sexually assaults a child they're *not* related to. Or even *no* jail time at all. Simply because they're related to the victim.

Surprisingly, getting legislation passed to fix this totally bizarre loophole that only benefitted predators, turned out to be harder than it looked. Some of the people who had originally put it on the books over 20 years before were still in office and they had absolutely no intention of changing anything. They completely stonewalled us at every turn. Some of them were quite rude about it too. They didn't like being the ones questioned.

The only way to get any traction was to take the fight to the public, many of whom were completely unaware that their elected officials, some of who they had happily voted for, were fighting to keep incest offenders *out* of jail.

As a result, I wound up being interviewed on everything from Larry King Live and Showbiz Tonight, to Fox & Friends and Bill O'Reilly.

It got quite surreal. Some of them asked some of the old stupid questions— and even came up with some new ones nobody had been rude enough to ask before. But then they let me talk.

About the law. About how convicted sexual predators were able to take advantage of legal loopholes all over the country to completely avoid jail, even after sexually abusing multiple victims for years. About how this was happening even in California—*especially* in California and how all their elected officials knew about it. How the police knew about it, the judges knew about it, the prosecutors, the defense lawyers—everybody. Everybody except the voters, the people at home watching the show I was being interviewed on. But now they all did.

And then the questions they were asking me changed. "*How on earth was this allowed to happen?!*" "*Who did this?!*" "*How can we make it stop?!*"

I was quite happy to answer them. And the viewers wasted no time in contacting their elected officials. They asked them lots and lots of questions. Some of them quite loudly.

When we went back to Sacramento, the mood had definitely changed. A few of the real diehards put up a fight, of course, but eventually they passed the legislation striking down the incest exception.

Later we went to New York. And did the same damn thing all over again.

When I first "went public" I was afraid. I was afraid that if *everyone* knew, then everyone would ask me the same horrible stupid questions. That going public would make it all worse.

But it didn't.

I now think that there are some people who ask abuse survivors horrible, rude, insensitive, personal questions—that they wouldn't *dream* of asking anyone else—I think they ask them *not* to get an answer, but *to make them shut up*. To intimidate them into keeping silent, into protecting the abusers.

Because after I started talking about sexual abuse and incest in public, after I started fighting for PROTECT, for the rights of victims, I'm hearing much fewer stupid questions.

Everyone has suddenly gotten *way* more polite or I've scared the bastards off.

Either way is fine with me.

I'll be asking the questions now, thank you.

WHEN!?

Linda Sarah

when,
oh when,
oh when,
oh when,
oh quand,
oh quand,
oh when,
oh when,
. . . .

← IRRELEVANT
BADLY DRAWN
TESLA FAN GIRL INTERLUDE

...hate is learnt,
not innate.
If we value our young,
love, protect and respect them,
then will maybe the
tides of violence
turn back?
You Know

♡

These kinds of
questions...

W
H
Y
?

why are
young people
still the most
abused, invisible,
afraid, neglected,
ignored, unrespected,
silenced ....etc.
members of society when,

no wonder
there's so much
anger and
hate —
albeit
misplaced
sometimes... maybe

Will we start
asking the
right questions ??

It's proven.
Completely.
Research
and everything!
Child Abuse,
whether physical,
emotional, sexual
damages young
people

not only are
they the most important
for our future,
but also the most
powerless, voiceless,
smallest and vulnerable

CITY WATER

Allison Glasgow

My friend Paul drowned at school during beginners' swim class. He drowned but he didn't die. He stays at Bethesda General, tied to machines that do the things his body can't do anymore, like breathe and eat. Most things, they say, he won't ever do again. Like open his eyes and see me, or understand my words as I say them.

When I visit Paul, his mother is always there, except when she has to work or visit her own mother who lives in a nursing home. Ms. Kimberly does a lot of bedside sitting. I feel bad for Ms. Kimberly, and Paul probably appreciates me being a comfort to his mother, but it's weird, like I'm visiting her, not him. Like Paul himself is a monument of Paul in the bed between us. When Ms. Kimberly's there, I can't do the things I do when it's only us, things I wouldn't do if Paul was awake. Sing to him, or hold his hand. And she doesn't either. When I'm around, she sits with a daily paper she borrows from the gift shop, scrutinizing the pages, looking for Paul.

Today, Ms. Kimberly sits with the *Free Press* spread over her lap like an old lady blanket. When I say hello, she replies, as if we've been in the middle of a conversation for some time: "You know what they are saying, Lil'Bit? They're saying this is an accident. An *unfortunate incident*. This isn't no accident. Babies dying at school is *murder*." Her eyes are demanding, not leaving my face, feeling like a teacher calling on me, waiting for an answer to something I should've already learned.

What I want to say is, "Paul's not dead." Because he's not. I hear the gasping suck of the respirator, followed by its slow hiss, and the steady smooth electronic beat of his heart. When I was born, I lived on machines at Bethesda too. Nanna says I was born only a feathery package of soft bones, a baby bird tumbled out of the nest. She called me Elizabeth. Mom wanted to call me

Grace, but Nanna said little girls ought to have little girl names, not expecta-tions of goodness. I've not seen a birth certificate to know how they settled, but everyone calls me Lil'Bit. I never did grow into much of a girl, good or otherwise. I'm so small, I'm my own species.

People say you're not supposed to remember being born, but I do. I remember everything that ever happened, though I don't talk about it much, because I'm pretty sure no one believes me. All I have to do is think of a color, or a song, and I pull out memories from this big file in my brain, starting from day one. That's how I remember the sounds and smells of Bethesda, the first of my life. I remember kind ladies in green smocks loving on me. They sang lullabies, and stuck latex hands into my box, to stroke my bird body. Ms. Kimberly says, "There's nobody who cares about people like us, Lil'Bit. Not a one." But she's wrong. Those ladies cared about me the way I want to care for Paul. Paul would cringe if he caught me whispering pop lyrics into his cheek, or smoothing his eyebrows with my fingertips. I don't care. If I rose up, what's to say he won't?

I wait out Ms. Kimberly's stare and return it just the same. I won't talk to her as if Paul's already dead. No one misses Paul more than I do, though it's hard to imagine the pain Ms. Kimberly's feeling. I think hurt and missing must be different things. Since I remember everything, there's an awful lot to miss. But hurt, like hunger, is something I don't recognize. I don't know if I've never been hungry, or am always starving to death.

The city is waiting for Paul to do something. He's updated in the paper every day. Ms. Kimberly doesn't have internet, and it's a good thing because sometimes I Google his name in the library at school and the whole *country* has ugly things to say about her mothering. Like how come we live in the state of Great Lakes and she never taught him how to swim? Paul was in swim class when he drowned. I wonder if Ms. Kimberly knows how to swim herself. Besides, you don't know what a Great Lake is when you're from the skirts of Detroit without a car—forget living in the Motor City. These are only words, anyway. Car. Lake. Detroit. The country talks about us like we're spectacles, Detroit's a big joke. Paul's part of that story now, where before, he was just a kid.

Worse is when they call Ms. Kimberly a gold-digger because she says things like "murder." There've been a lot of men and women in dark suits and tidy hairdos sniffing at the hospital, offering Ms. Kimberly legal advice. In the end they have to wait on Paul, like the rest of us. Wait and see what he's gonna do.

Although I don't like being in the hospital with Ms. Kimberly, as mothers go, I think she's doing fine. There's an expectation of mothers, that they gotta love stronger and harder than anyone else, and it seems to me that Paul is loved. Ms. Kimberly has always had room for me, and my baby brother. Paul and I grew up next door neighbors, a thin wall separating our apartments. Ms. Kimberly's door is always open, she says, I just got to knock. Before my brother was born, I might have stayed a whole week, sleeping in the upper bunk of Paul's bed, eating breakfast with the pair of them, and walking with Paul to school. My own mom is seldom found, and I don't care to speak of her, except hers is a sneaking memory, refusing to stay filed. I have more reruns of Mom than new episodes. Honestly, I don't think much about mothers, but I have some ideas about family. Paul's my family.

There's a chance Ms. Kimberly will pull the plug. The papers and people at school talk about it, supposing what they would do if they were her, but Ms. Kimberly hasn't asked me once what I think. That's the difference between real kin and not. Paul has moved to past tense. I wonder if I am on my way to past tense too, fading from Ms. Kimberly's present.

But he's not past. He's lying right here. Not murdered. Not dead.

When she says murder, I know she's going to start asking me the *hows*. Ms. Kimberly asks me every time I see her, then again when I give her the answers, as if my explanation couldn't be heard. I don't blame her. The answer's not satisfying. Paul drowned because we couldn't save him. There wasn't anyone who could help.

This is how I tell her: Paul was standing on the diving board over the deep end, the kids taunting him to jump in. He stepped off and began to panic when he couldn't touch bottom, reaching and hollering for any of us to hold him up. The teacher was sitting at the top of the bleachers, talking up the girls on their periods. He was a substitute, been there giving "free-swim" time for the better part of two weeks. The whole time he subbed, he never put on swim trunks, never put a toe in the water. And he didn't come when we called for help.

The cops determined it was nine minutes before someone, a classmate, got the attention of the security guard in the hallway. Nine minutes of us struggling to keep him afloat, Paul, frantic, clawing at my body. He'd grab my shoulders, trying to rocket himself above the surface, heaving up and down, swallowing and erupting water after every submersion, until he just stopped, and in slow motion, drifted down. We couldn't dive get to him, none of us good enough swimmers. We couldn't sink, like Paul, though we tried. Our bodies were buoys propelled to the surface. The deep end is ten feet, but he could have been on the moon, he was so far. I don't know how to explain this to Ms. Kimberly, even though it's the most important part.

Finally the security guard arrived. He sent a call from his radio to the main office before crashing into the water. Mr. Johns, the freshman Biology teacher was on his heels, diving in without hesitation. I'd never seen anything like that man, suit coat and tie and dress shoes, run right up to the lip of the pool, his arms pointed over his head like an arrow. He broke the water with his fingertips first, and his body slipped right in. Mr. Johns pulled Paul up like it was nothing. Together, with the security guard, the men delicately slid him onto the deck. They went to work with CPR, but by then Paul's lungs couldn't catch.

I tell Ms. Kimberly all these things, all except the fact that I gave up trying. I felt so worn out, eventually there wasn't any more diving down, or reaching to him. Only a sudden, terrible stillness and waiting, our heavy breaths echoing on the walls. But those men, like giants or gods, managed so easily. I can't make it sound reasonable to Ms. Kimberly. Paul was rescued. He *could* be rescued. And if he *was* rescued, but then why is he gone?

At school, we're not supposed to talk about the incident. The adults love to talk about Paul, but not about what happened. He's the great unknowable. The security guard just up and quit, and Mr. Johns disappeared. I haven't seen that sub again, but swim class is canceled, and the pool's been shut down. When the cops came to do interviews, the faculty stepped back with their hands in the air. Nanna warned me, cops can't talk to minors without a guardian present, but the cops ask questions and the teachers slink sideways out of the room. The kids were the witnesses, anyways. The kids have the answers. The adults have lawyers.

There's a bathroom down the hall of the ICU that I excuse myself to, saying bye to Ms. Kimberly. She won't let me leave without a hug, and as she pulls me into her mattressy form, I say a silent goodbye to Paul. I pass the words into his mind through the will of my own, like a prayer. It's too embarrassing to say it out loud in front of Ms. Kimberly, but I can't leave without offering him a piece of my presence. That bed must be so boring.

In the bathroom, I open my backpack and unload eight plastic water bottles. I fill each one up with water from the sink and recap them and pile them back into my bag. The heft with my schoolbooks is almost undoable. I imagine I am strong, but I'm small. A preemie still. I swing the backpack over my shoulders and begin walking around the perimeter of the hospital. Outside, to the left of the ambulance port is a loading dock with a garage door half rolled up. I duck down and take a peek inside. "Hello," I call, not too loud. No one hollers back, so I shift under the garage door and see exactly what I am looking for: stacks and stacks of water jugs. The big ones, for office coolers. I pull one down to the concrete floor and tip it onto its side. I push it gently and it starts rolling and I guide it with kicking nudges out of the garage and onto the sidewalk. It's going to take a while to get home, but this is how I go, real slow, pushing the water jug in front of me with my feet. No one stops me. No one ever does.

I scoot the water jug about three-quarters of an hour to Nanna's rented townhouse. The city turned the water off a few weeks ago, for bills past due. Nanna can't say what she owes, she says she's never seen a water bill in her life, that's the landlord's business. Why we gotta suddenly pay for water, she says. So I bring the water home. Even this big jug won't last very long. We need water for everything, but you don't notice until it's gone. To wash, to cook, to bathe. Nanna will probably use most of it to bucket flush the toilet.

"Why don't you come out and help me," I yell to my uncle, Howard, who is sitting in the living room like he was built out of couch-stuffing. I can see the back of his head through the large screen on the window. Howard's common-law periodically kicks him off his own couch. And like a hermit crab, he wanders over here, wearing our couch as his new home. I give the jug one last push into the brick steps leading to Nanna's door. I step over it and climb into the house. "Where's Nanna?" I ask Howard, panting a little and relieving my bag with a thud onto the floor. "I brought water."

Howard moves his eyes over me slowly. "Damn, Bit. When you gonna hit puberty so's I can tell whether you're a boy or girl?"

I ignore him and move into the back hallway. "Is that Dave?" I say, hearing the unmistakable chatter of my little brother traveling from the back rooms. "Dave!" I call, and he hoots in response from the bathroom. I find him sitting in his diaper, in the empty tub, a couple chew toys from the dollar store squeaking in his ferocious little fists.

"Howard! Where is Nanna?" I scoop up Baby Dave, about as angry as I can be, the heat igniting in my collarbone and consuming my face. Baby Dave's diaper is light and papery, not wet, at least. But, maybe he's not eaten. Got nothing to eliminate.

Nanna's nowhere. Not home.

"Howard," I say, wasting my breath, "how is it I'm thirteen years old and I take better care of a baby than you? You're a grown man, you can't leave a baby in the bathtub, empty or not."

I have to be careful with the lectures, Howard might cry, and I can't stand to see it. Last thing I want to see for the rest of my life is my mother's lump of a brother crying when I yell at him.

"He's not my kid," he sulks.

"He's nobody's kid," I say, and try to heft my backpack off the ground, but it's too heavy to carry with the baby too. I set Baby Dave down and unzip the bag, furiously dumping the water bottles onto the stained, scarred floorboards, where they roll to all corners of the room. "Here's the damn water. Tell Nanna, I'm about done with her shit."

I start walking with Baby Dave, not sure where we're going, but I meant it when I said I was done. Nanna knows Howard is incompetent, if not dangerous, but I've come to think Nanna's the same, same as Howard, same as Mom. The same repeated all the way down the line. Same as me, maybe. Maybe.

Baby Dave rides like an animal on my hip, chirping and blowing bubbles cheerfully, his strong little hands snatching at my ears and mouth. Sometimes he really hurts me, grabbing at me like that. Not enough to complain about, but I'm surprised at his strength, his insistency, unignorable. Baby Dave's not the same. Dave's not even made one promise yet. We walk down East Canfield toward the church and the park with the baby swings.

There's quite a crowd gathered outside the church, some with picket signs and a caravan of cars lined along the curb, their back hatches open and people unloading large plastic jugs. But something is off, the people halfway unload and then reload the jugs back in. Then I see a man with a camera balanced on his shoulder, directing the action. Reverend Michaels is there, chatting with a woman holding a microphone. Around the block, I notice the news truck, a spirally tower sprung out of its roof. I cross close enough to hear the conversation. Canadians from Windsor have brought the water over the Ambassador Bridge and they are telling the world that water is a human right. They've called the United Nations. They've called the President. Detroit is in a State of Emergency.

Lots and lots of people have lost their water, thousands even. Who shut it off, I wonder? God? Is that why they are here at the church? I imagine a giant hand of God reaching down and turning off the spigot on the whole lot of us. God does these things, these simple, game-changing things. On or off, here or gone, alive or not. I'm not hurt, though. Who's hurt at God? Besides, I know where there's water.

I take Baby Dave across the street to the swings and we swing for a little while until he starts fussing. I remember he's probably hungry. We walk to the corner store and buy a banana and a baby jar of carrot mush, a box of milk and a pink popsicle with my lunch money. Baby Dave's got dirt all over his hands and I forgot to ask for a spoon. I give him the popsicle to calm him as we walk back over to the church to see if Reverend Michaels will let us wash up.

Most of the commotion has quieted, the news crew is gone. The Canadians are carrying water jugs through the heavy wood doors that have been propped open for the procession. I squeeze past them into the chapel. Baby

Dave's made good work of the popsicle and his face is a sticky disaster, rivets of pink streak down his forearms and then my own arms as I lug him around.

I don't really know Reverend Michaels. I've come to church some with Paul and Ms. Kimberly, but not for a while. I am surprised by his smile when he sees me, and he says "Elizabeth" kindly, like my favorite teachers. I am a little intimidated to ask to use the bathroom, I don't want him thinking I don't have water. Reverend Michaels always felt, to me, like a celebrity, standing on the big stage in front of the congregation, talking with a voice so loud without shouting. Everyone always wants to shake his hand and now he's going to be on the news.

"The church got a kitchen?" I say, awkwardly shifting Baby Dave on my hip while I try to show him the jar of carrots I have in my fist. "I'm looking for a spoon."

Reverend Michaels pops an eyebrow up on his forehead. "Why don't you follow me. I've been meaning to come find you and Ms. Kimberly for some time."

We go down to the basement, which is finished with carpet and some rec room stuff, like plastic lawn tables and fold-up chairs and a ping pong setup. The walls are lined with cabinets and even a sink and a dishwasher. Reverend Michaels wets a paper towel and delicately cleans up Dave's face. He says, "May I?" and takes Dave from me. I roll my shoulder with the relief of the weight and finally regain enough dexterity to put down the banana and milk and carrot jar. I sit in a chair at one of the tables and wait. Reverend Michaels runs the water from the tap and sets Baby Dave on the counter, his dirty toes in the sink. With a steadying hand on Dave's back, the man soaps up his little legs and arms and fingers and cups the water in his free palm to rinse the suds away. Baby Dave doesn't mind that Reverend Michaels is a stranger. It's always been that way with Dave. He's happiest when someone's holding him, little matter who.

The process takes a few minutes, and all the while I'm sitting there watching the Canadians lug water jugs down the stairs, listening to their accented chatter, laughs and happy commotion. They sound so different for just living over the bridge. They finish bringing the water down as the Reverend bathes Dave. They line up to pat his back, his hands full of my brother, and offer encouraging words about his role in their efforts. One girl with a long yellow braid sets down a two-liter water bottle and comes over to me shyly. She says, "I want you to know, I wish you good luck." I look at her with what I think is politeness, but the bridge of my nose pinches accidentally.

"So," Reverend Michaels says, when everyone has left and he is patting Dave dry with more paper towels. "We need a spoon." He hands Dave back to me and I prop him on my knee while Reverend Michaels fishes in a drawer under the counter. "This," he says revealing a giant wooden spoon, "is too big!" but he hands it to Dave anyway, who begins gleefully smacking at the table and squealing. He then pulls out a normal-sized spoon and hands it to me. Somewhere in the maze of cabinets, he emerges with a sippy cup into which he pours the carton of milk and Baby Dave drinks eagerly.

I feed Dave the carrots and mashed banana by the spoonful and Reverend Michaels sits next to me watching. "I wanted to ask you about Paul," he says.

"What about him?" I say.

"Well, I wondered how you were doing, with all of this? How you are feeling?"

I scoop a little bite of banana on the spoon and smush it with my thumb before offering it to Baby Dave's gummy mouth. Reverend Michaels continues to wait for my response and I eventually shrug. "I feel okay. What's there to feel?"

"Sad? Scared, maybe? Let down?"

"Why would I be let down? Paul's let down. I'm the one who couldn't bring him up."

Reverend Michaels holds out his hand for Dave to play with, and Dave grabs onto the man's finger and tries to shove it in his mouth.

"Well, the city has filed charges against that substitute teacher, you know," Reverend Michaels says. "There's going to be a trial."

"So, Ms. Kimberly is right. It's murder," I say.

"No. Gross negligence. The substitute couldn't swim. He lied on his resume that he was a certified lifeguard and the school did not look into it appropriately. *You* were let down, Elizabeth. Paul was let down, but it wasn't your fault. That man should not have been teaching the class. He didn't know how to swim."

I had sort of heard this before. Some kids who were at the pool that day told the cops that the teacher said he couldn't go in for Paul because he couldn't swim, but I wasn't sure I believed it, or understood how that could be possible. Knowing this truth doesn't diminish the *how*. There were so many ways in which Paul couldn't have drowned, so many ways in which he is saved. Like, say we'd already learnt to swim over the summer with the kind of kids who practice on trips to a Great Lake. Or the substitute is a great swimmer and gets into the pool to teach us properly. Or Paul never steps into the deep end because he's not so brave or tough. Or Mr. Johns dives in nine minutes earlier. Or I am born bigger and stronger and I just lift him out.

"This trial, it might be hard. Some of the students may need to testify," Reverend Michaels says. "I want you to know, you can always come here, for water, for rest, for talk. Whatever you need."

"Ok," I say, shuffling Baby Dave back onto my hip and standing up and handing Reverend Michaels his spoon.

"Before you go," Reverend Michaels returns to the tap and wets a towel to yet again attend to Baby Dave's newly messed face. "Tell Ms. Kimberly we're praying for her."

"What about Paul?" I say.

He smiles. "Him too."

We step outside the church and the street is dark, like night is a flip of the lightswitch. On then off. I wish Baby Dave could ride piggy back, rather than side saddle, he just gets heavier. We're going to need a diaper or two. There's a pharmacy on Gratiot that doesn't have any cameras. Behind new packages of diapers on the shelf, I have hidden an open package, from which I sneak loose ones, only a few at a time, and stuff in my pants while the counter guy is busy. There are two left back there, I notice. Time for a new plan, Baby Dave. Maybe potty training. I buy a bag of chips for myself and we head back towards Nanna's.

But we aren't going home. I pass Howard's bald head, framed in the illuminated window like a still-life at the museum. When we were eight, Paul taught me how to open his door without a key and since then I always carry my library card inside a plastic sleeve in my pocket. I slide it in between the door jamb, retrieving the memory of Paul's instruction from his file in my head. I hear him say, "Just wiggle down, wiggle up, down, down, turn and pop. Open sesame!" The door opens exactly as it should. Ms. Kimberly's house is dark, she's still with Paul likely, where she'll stay until her night manager shift begins, restocking groceries at Family Dollar.

I change Baby Dave's diaper on the floor of the bathroom, laying him on a towel, and cleaning his privates with a nearly dried-out package of baby wipes. Ms. Kimberly has rash cream too that she bought when Mom left Baby Dave with Nanna. Just in case, she whispered to me, when she showed me where the supplies were kept. I long used up all her extra diapers, not replaced since Paul's drowning. I open the toilet lid and there's water. Ms. Kimberly still has water. Maybe they forgot to turn her water off because now that Paul's gone, she's never home. No one lives here anymore.

Or maybe Ms. Kimberly does the right thing, all the time. Maybe she takes care of motherless babies with extra diapers and breakfasts and places to sleep when they can't go home. Maybe Ms. Kimberly is the best good person, a good neighbor, and this place still swallowed up Paul, swallowed him whole.

There's no one who cares, she said. I still don't believe her, there's so much caring in this house.

I take Baby Dave to Paul's room. We don't turn on any lights, we don't touch anything on our way. I want to climb to the top bunk, my bunk, like I used to do, but I'm afraid Dave will roll off, so we curl into Paul's bed, on the bottom. It doesn't feel like Paul's in here, his smell a brighter version of this room. I might never smell Paul again, because the Paul at the hospital is plasticky and disinfected, like mouthwash. His pillow smells like Ms. Kimberly, vanilla and nutmeg. It smells like she's been sleeping here too.

When I say I remember everything, I mean it. I remember being a baby at Nanna's, myself naked in the empty tub, alone for so long.

I sing pop songs to Dave, stroking his muscled and tough little body with my fingers until I hear sweet snores. He's not the same, this one, not yet. I can't know all that Baby Dave will remember, but if I hold him all he wants, carry him forever, feed him, bathe him in church water, and offer him faces of grace and light and love, I can be sure he remembers this.

BLACK AND WHITE AND RED ALL OVER

David Morrell

You probably read about me in the paper this morning. Fact is, if you live near the corner of Benton and Sunset, I'm the kid who normally delivers it to you. Course, I couldn't bring it to you today, being in the hospital and all with my arm busted and my skull what the doctor says is fractured. My dad took over for me. To tell the truth, I kinda miss doing the route. I've been delivering three years now, since I was nine, and it gets to be a habit, even if I do have to wake up at five-thirty, Christmas and New Year's and every day. But if you think I slept in this morning, you're wrong. The nurses wake you up early here just the same as if my mom was nudging me to crawl out of bed and make sure I put on my long johns before I take the papers 'cause it's awful cold these snowy mornings. You have to walk the route instead of riding your bike, and that takes a half hour longer, especially with the sky staying dark so long, and sometimes you can't see the numbers on the houses when you're looking for where a new customer lives.

The way this works, the *Gazette* has this guy in a truck come along and drop a bundle in front of my house, and my dad goes out to get the bundle and fold the papers in my sack while I get dressed. A lot of times, there'll be this card with the name of a new customer or else the name of a customer who doesn't want the paper anymore, and then my mom and I'll have to add or subtract the name from my list and figure out how much the customer owes me, especially if he's starting or stopping in the middle of a week. It's pretty complicated, but my dad says it teaches me how to run a business, and the extra money comes in handy for buying CDs or playing video games, even if I do have to put a third of what I earn away in my bank account.

Heroes

But I was telling you about my customers. You'd be surprised how close a kid can feel to the people he delivers the paper to. They wake up early and rush to get ready for work or whatever, and I figure the only fun they have is when they sit down at breakfast to read what happened while they were sleeping. It's sorta like catching up on gossip, I guess. They depend on me, and I've never been late delivering the papers, and the only times I've missed are when I was sick or like now from what happened yesterday morning. The bandages around my head feel itchy, and the cast on my arm's awful heavy. The nurses have written lots of jokes on it, though, so I'm looking forward to going back to school in two or three weeks, the doctor says, and showing it to all the kids.

You get to notice things about your customers, stuff a guy wouldn't think of unless he delivers papers. Like after a big football game you can't believe how many people are awake with all the lights on before I even get there, waiting for the paper so they can find out something new about the game they already heard or went to or watched on TV. Or like this house on Gilby Street where for a week or so I had to hold my breath when I came up the sidewalk past the shrubs because of the worst scuzzy smell like something really rotten. Even when I held my breath, it almost made me sick. Like the bad potatoes Mom found in the cellar last month. Nobody was picking up the papers I left. They just kept piling up beside the door, and after I told my dad, he looked at my mom kinda strange and said he'd better go over to see what was wrong. I could tell he figured maybe somebody was dead, and I guess I wondered that myself, but the way things turned out, those people were just on vacation, which is why the papers kept piling up, and the smell was only from these plastic bags of garbage they'd forgotten to put out and some dogs had torn open at the side of the house. That smell really made me nervous for a while, though.

And then there's the Carrigans. He lost his job at the mill last summer, and his wife likes fancy clothes, and they're always yelling about money when I'm next door playing with Ralph or when I come around to collect or even at six in the morning when I bring them the paper. Imagine that, getting up way before dawn to argue. Or what about old Mr. Blanchard? His wife's old, too, and she's sick with what my mom says is bone cancer, and I haven't seen Mrs. Blanchard in a couple months, but old Mr. Blanchard, he's up when I put the paper under the mat. I can see through his living room window where the light's on in the kitchen, and he's sitting at the table, hunched over, holding his head, and his shoulders are shaking. Even out front, I can hear him sobbing. It makes my throat tight. He always wears this gray old lumpy sweater. I'd feel sorry for him no matter what, but he cries like it's tearing his chest apart.

And then there's Mr. Lang. He's got this puffy face and a red-veined nose and squinty angry eyes. He's always complaining about how much the paper costs and claims I'm cheating him by coming around more often than I should to collect, which of course I've never done. Two months ago, he started swearing at me so I'm afraid to go over there. My dad says it's the whiskey makes him act like that, and now my dad collects from him. The last time my dad came back from there, he said Mr. Lang's not bad if you get to know him and realize he doesn't like his life, but I don't care. I want my dad to keep collecting from him.

I guess I was spooked by what you read about that happened in Granite Falls two months ago when Mr. Lang swore at me. That paperboy who disappeared. His parents waited for him to come home from his Sunday-morning route, and after they got calls from customers wanting to know where the paper was, his dad went out looking and found his sack full of papers a block away in an empty lot behind some bushes. You remember how the police and the neighbors went out searching, and the paper he worked for put his picture on the front page and offered a reward if anybody knew where he was, but they didn't find him. The police said he might've run away, but that didn't make any sense to me. It was too darn cold to run away, and where would he go? My dad says he read how the police even seemed to think the parents might have done something to him themselves and how the parents got so mad they wanted to sue the police for saying that. One man was cruel enough to phone the parents and pretend he had the boy and ask for money, but the police traced the calls, and the man didn't have him. Now the man says it was just a joke, but I read where he's in lots of trouble.

Granite Falls. That's not too far from here. My dad said some nut from there could easily drive to other towns like ours. I wasn't going to give up my route, though, just because of what happened there. Like I said, I'm used to the money I make and going downtown on Saturdays to buy a new CD. But I felt kinda fluttery in my stomach. I sure didn't want to disappear myself. I'm old enough to know about the creepy things perverts do to kids. So my dad went with me the next few mornings on my route, and I took a flashlight when I started going alone again, and I delivered the papers fast, believe me. You can't guess what the wind scraping through bushes behind you in the dark can make you feel when it's early and there's nobody around to shout to for help. But after a month when nothing happened, I started feeling easier, ashamed of myself for getting scared like I was a little kid. I slipped back into my old routine, delivering the papers half asleep, looking forward to the homemade Orange Julius my mom always has waiting for me when

Heroes

I get back from the route. I read the comics in the *Gazette* before I catch an extra hour of sleep till it's time for school. After being out in the snow, those blankets feel great.

Three weeks ago, another paperboy disappeared, this time right here in Crowell, and you remember how the neighbors searched the same as in Granite Falls, and his picture was in the *Gazette*, and the parents offered a reward, but they didn't find him, only his sack of papers stuffed behind some bushes like the last time. The police said it looked like the same MO. That's fancy police talk for "pattern." But heck, you don't have to go to police school to figure out that both kids disappeared the same way. And one kid might have run away, but not two of them, leastways not in the snow.

Oh yeah, that's something I forgot to mention. Both mornings when the kids disappeared, it was snowing real hard, so there weren't any tracks except for the neighbors searching. No kid runs away in a blizzard, I'll tell you. The rest of us paperboys nearly went on what my dad calls a strike. Actually it was our parents wanted us to quit delivering. They demanded police protection for us, but the police said we were overreacting, we shouldn't panic, and anyway there weren't enough police to protect us all. The *Gazette* said if we stopped delivering, the paper would go out of business. They asked our parents to keep a close watch on us, and they made us sign a contract agreeing to give up seventy-five cents a month, so the paper could insure us in case something happened to us on the route.

Well, that made my dad twice as mad. He told me to quit, and I almost did, but I couldn't stop thinking of all the money I like to spend on Saturdays. My dad says I was born a capitalist and I'll probably grow up to vote Republican, whatever that means, but I told him I won a ribbon last year on the sixth-grade track team, and I could run faster than any pervert, I bet. Well, he just laughed and shook his head and told me he'd go out with me every morning, but my mom looked like she was going to cry. I guess moms are like that, always worrying. Besides, I said, I only have to worry if it's snowing. That's the only time the kids disappeared. My dad said that made sense, but all my mom said was "We'll see," which is always bad news, like if you ask for a friend to stay overnight and your mom says "We'll see," you figure she means "no."

But she didn't. The next morning, my dad went with me on the route, and it was one of those sharp, cold times when your boots squeak on the snow and the air's so clean you can hear a car start up three blocks away. I knew for sure I'd hear any pervert if he tried sneaking up on me, and anyway my dad was with me, and all the other carriers had it as easy as I did. Still, every morning I got up praying it wasn't snowing, and often it had snowed in the night but stopped, and when I saw the house across from ours clear in the streetlight, I felt like somebody had taken a rope from around my chest.

So we went on like that, getting up at five-thirty and doing the papers, and once my dad got the flu, so my mom went with me. You can believe it, she was nervous, more than me I guess. You should have seen us rushing to finish the route all the time we were looking over our shoulders. Mr. Carrigan was yelling at his wife like always, and Mr. Blanchard was crying for his own wife, and Mr. Lang was drinking beer when he opened his door and scared me, getting his paper. I almost wet my pants, no fooling. He asked if I wanted to step in and get warm, but I backed off, saying, "No, Mr. Lang, no, thank you," holding up my hands and shaking my head. I forgot about his stairs behind me. I bet I'd have broken my arm even sooner than now if he'd shoveled them. But the snow made them soft, and when I tumbled to the bottom, I landed in a drift. He tried to help me, but I jumped up and ran away.

Then last Sunday I woke up, and even before I looked out, I knew from the shriek of the wind that it was snowing. My heart felt hard and small. I almost couldn't move. I tasted this sour stuff from my stomach. I couldn't see the house across the street. The snow was flying so thick and strong I couldn't even see the maple tree in our front yard. As warm as I'd been in bed, I shivered like I was outside and the wind was stinging through my pajamas. I didn't want to go, but I knew that'd be all the excuse my mom'd need to make me quit, so I forced myself. I dressed real quick, long underwear and the rest, and put on my down-filled coat that almost doesn't fit me anymore and my mitts and ski mask, and it wasn't just my mom or dad who went with me that time, but both of them, and I could tell they felt as scared as I was.

Nothing happened, as far as we knew. We finished the route and came home and made hot chocolate. All our cheeks were red, and we went back to sleep, and when we woke up, my dad turned on the radio. I guess you know what we heard. Another paperboy had disappeared, right here in Crowell. That's an MO if I ever heard of one. Three carriers gone, and two of them from town, and all three when it was snowing.

The storm kept on, so this time there weren't even any tracks from the police and the neighbors searching. They couldn't find his sack of papers. A couple of people helping out had to go to the hospital because of frostbite. The missing boys didn't live on our side of town, but even so, my dad went over to help. With the streets so drifted, he couldn't drive—he had to walk. When he came back after dark with his parka all covered with snow, he said it was horrible out there. He couldn't get warm. He just kept sitting hunched in front of the fireplace, throwing logs on, rubbing his raw-looking hands and shivering. My mom kept bringing him steaming drinks that she called hot toddies, and after an hour, he slumped back snoring. Mom and me had to help him up to bed. Then Mom took me back downstairs and sat with me in the living room and told me I had to quit.

I didn't argue. Crowell's got forty thousand people. If you figure three-quarters of them get the paper and most of the carriers have forty customers, that's seven hundred and fifty paperboys. I worked that out on my dad's pocket calculator. Kinda surprising—that many paperboys—if you're not a carrier yourself. But if you're on the streets at five-thirty every morning like I am, then you see a lot of us. There's a kid on almost every corner, walking up somebody's driveway, leaving a paper in front of a door. Not counting the kid in Granite Falls, that's two missing carriers out of seven hundred and fifty. That might make the odds seem in my favor, but the way I figured it, and my mom said it too, that many paperboys only gave the nut a lot of choice. I like to play video games and all, but the money I earned wasn't worth disappearing the way those other boys did with my sack of papers stuffed behind some bushes, which by the way is where they found the third kid's sack like the others, when the snow stopped. After we put my dad to bed and my mom looked out the living room window, she made a funny noise in her throat. I walked to her and saw the house across the street, all shimmery, covered with snow and glinting from the streetlight. Any other time, it would've looked peaceful, like a Christmas card. But I felt sick, like all that white had something ugly underneath. I was standing on a vent for the furnace, and I heard the gas burner turn on. Warm air rushed up my pajama leg. All the same, I shivered.

I quit, I said. But my dad says we've got something called a body clock inside us. It comes from being used to a regular routine, like when you know even if you don't have your watch on that it's time for your favorite TV program or you know you'd better get home 'cause your mom'll have supper ready. I wasn't going to deliver papers, but I woke up at five-thirty the same as usual, even if Mom didn't wake me. For just a second, I told myself I'd better hurry. Then I remembered I wasn't going to deliver the papers anymore. I slumped back in bed and tried to go back to sleep, but I kept squinting at the digital clock Mom and Dad gave me last Christmas, and the red numbers kept changing, getting later. Five-forty. Then five-forty-five. At last I couldn't bear feeling guilty, like I'd done something wrong even though I hadn't. I crawled from bed and opened my curtains and peered at the dark snow in our driveway. I could see the tire tracks on the street where the guy from the *Gazette* had pulled up and thrown my bundle. It was all by itself in the driveway, sunk in the snow. It was wrapped in a garbage bag to keep it dry, this big black shape with all this white around it.

I kept staring at it, and the *Gazette* office hadn't been open the day before, on Sunday. Even on Monday, they're not open till eight, so there wasn't any way for the paper to know I'd quit. I kept thinking of my customers getting up, looking forward to reading the paper at breakfast, going to the door, not finding it. Then I thought of all the calls we'd soon be getting, forty of them, wanting to know where their paper was. The more I thought about it, the more I felt worse, till I reminded myself of what my dad always says: "There's only one way to do a job, and that's the right way." I put on my long johns, my jeans and sweater and parka. I woke up my dad, whose face looked old all of a sudden, I guess from being out in the storm searching the day before. I told him I had to deliver the papers, and he just blinked at me, then nodded with his lips pursed like he didn't agree but he understood.

My mom made a fuss as you'd expect, but my dad got dressed and went with me. I wasn't sure if I was shaking from the cold or from being scared. It wasn't snowing, though, and even shivering I knew I'd be all right. We hurried. We'd started a half hour late, but we got the papers to every customer without seeing any tire tracks in their driveways to tell us they'd left for work already. A couple places, we met a customer shoveling drifts, puffing frost from his mouth from the work, and every one of them looked glad to see me, like they'd been sure they weren't going to get a paper and here I'd been as dependable as ever. They grinned and promised me a tip when I came around next time to collect, and I guess I grinned as well. It made me feel warm all of a sudden. Even Mr. Lang, who's normally so hard to get along with, came out and patted me on the back the way the track coach sometimes does. My dad and I did the route the fastest we ever had, and when we got home, my mom had pancakes ready and syrup hot from the Radarange. I guess I'd never been so hungry. My dad even gave me a little coffee in a glass. I sipped it, feeling its steam on my nose, actually liking the bitter taste. Then my dad clicked his cup against my glass, and I felt like I'd grown in the night. My chest never felt so big, and even my mom had to admit it, we'd done the right thing.

But that didn't change what had happened. At eight, just before I left for school, my mom phoned the paper and told them I was quitting. When I went outside, I felt relieved, like something heavy had been taken off my back, but that didn't last long. A block from school, my stomach started getting hard, and I couldn't stop thinking I'd lost something or like the track season was over or I'd missed a movie I was looking forward to. It's funny how you get used to things, even a job which I know isn't supposed to be fun, that's why it's called a job, but I liked being a paperboy, earning money and all, and I could tell I was going to feel empty now from not doing it.

Heroes

All morning, I couldn't concentrate on what the teacher said. She asked if I was sick, but I told her I was only tired, I was sorry, I'd be okay. I tried my best to act interested, and when I got home for lunch, my mom said the paper had called to ask if they could send somebody over to talk to us around suppertime. She'd done her hardest to tell them no, but I guess they insisted, 'cause someone was coming anyhow, and I ate my hamburger fast from being curious and I'll admit excited from getting attention.

The afternoon was the longest I ever remember. After school, I didn't care about hanging around with the guys. I just stayed at home and played video games and watched the clock on the TV recorder. My dad came home from work a little after five. He was just opening a can of beer when the doorbell rang. I don't know why but my arm muscles hurt when he went to the door, and it was Sharon from the paper. She's the one who came to the house and explained how to do my route when I first got started. Lots of times, she stopped at the house to give me extra cards for figuring out how much my customers owed me. Once she brought me the fifty dollars' worth of movie passes that I won from going around the neighborhood and convincing the most new customers than any other carrier in town to take the *Gazette* in the morning instead of or maybe as well as the *Chronicle* from Granite Falls, which is the evening paper, but you know that, I guess.

Sharon's younger than my mom. She's got a ponytail and rosy cheeks, and she reminds me of the student teacher from the college here in town that's helping my regular teacher. Sharon always shows more interest in talking to me instead of to my parents. She makes me feel special and grown-up, and she always smiles and tells me I'm the best carrier she's got. But last Monday she wasn't smiling. She looked like she hadn't slept all night, and her cheeks were pale. She said so many carriers had quit and no new carriers wanted to take their place that the paper was worried, like it might go out of business. She said her boss had told her to go around to all the carriers that had quit and tell them the paper would pay them three dollars extra a week if they stayed, but my mom wouldn't let me answer for myself. My mom said no. But it was like Sharon hadn't heard. She said the *Gazette* would promise that any morning it snowed the papers didn't have to be delivered, and I could see my dad agreed it was a good idea, but my mom kept shaking her head from side to side. Then Sharon rushed on and said at least let her have a few days to find a replacement for me, which was going to be hard because I was so dependable, and that made my heart beat funny. Please give her a week, she said. If she couldn't find somebody else by next Monday, then I could go ahead and quit and she wouldn't bother us again. But at least let her have the chance—her voice sounded thick and chokey—because her boss said if she couldn't find kids to do the routes he'd get somebody else to do her job.

Her eyes looked moist, like she'd been out in the wind. All of a sudden I felt crummy, like I'd let her down. I wanted to make myself small. I couldn't face her. For the first time, she paid more attention to my parents than to me, blinking at my mom, then my dad, sorta pleading, and my mom didn't seem to breathe. Then she did, long and deep like she felt real tired. She said my dad and her would have to talk about it, so they went to the kitchen, and I tried not to look at Sharon while I heard them whispering, and when they came back, my mom said okay, for a week, till Sharon could find a replacement but no longer. In the meantime, if it was snowing, I wasn't going out to deliver the papers. Sharon almost cried then. She kept saying thanks, and after she left, my mom said she hoped we weren't making a mistake, but I knew I wasn't. I figured out what had been bothering me—not quitting, but doing it so fast, without making sure my customers got their papers and explaining to them and saying good-bye. I was going to miss them. Funny how you get used to things.

The next morning, I didn't feel nervous as much as glad to have the route back, at least for a few more days. It was one of the last times I'd see my customers' houses that early, and I tried to memorize what it was like, taking the paper to the Carrigans who still kept arguing, and Mr. Blanchard crying for his wife, and Mr. Lang still drinking beer for breakfast. My dad went with me that Tuesday, and you could see other parents helping their kids do the routes. I'd never seen so many people out so early, and in the cold, their whispers and their boots squeaking were as clear as the sharp reflection of the streetlights off the drifts. Nothing happened, though the police kept looking for the boys who'd disappeared. And Wednesday, nothing happened either. The fact is, by Saturday, everything had gone pretty much back to normal. It was never snowing in the morning, and my dad says people have awful short memories, 'cause we heard how a lot of paperboys who'd quit had asked for their routes back and a lot of other kids had asked for the routes that needed a carrier. I know in my own case I'd stopped feeling scared. Pretty much the opposite. I kept thinking about Monday and how it was closer all the time and maybe I could convince my mom to let me go on delivering.

Saturday was clear. When my dad came in from the driveway, carrying the bundle of papers, he said it wasn't hardly cold at all out there. I looked through the kitchen window toward the thermometer on the side of the house, and the light from the kitchen reached it in the dark. The red line was almost at thirty-two. I wouldn't need my ski mask, though I made sure to take my mitts, and we packed the papers in my sack, and we went out. That early, the air smelled almost sweet from being warmer than usual, and under my long johns, I started to sweat. We went down Benton, then over to Sunset, and started up Gilby. That's the hardest street 'cause it's got this steep long hill. In summer, I'm always puffing when I ride my bike to the top, and in winter, I have to stop a minute going up with my heavy boots and coat on. How we did it was my dad took one side of the street and I took the other. We could see each other because of the streetlights, and by splitting the work, we'd do the route twice as fast. But we'd got a note about a new customer that morning, and my dad couldn't find the house number. I kept delivering papers, going up the hill, and the next thing I knew, I'd reached the top. I looked back down, and my dad was a shadow near the bottom.

It wasn't snowing, so I figured I'd do a few more papers. My next customer was over on Crossridge. If you went by car, you had to drive back down Gilby hill, then go a block over to Crossridge, then drive all the way up to the top of the other hill. But if you went on foot or bike, you could cut through this sidewalk that one of my customers has in his yard, connecting Gilby and Crossridge, so I went through there and left the paper.

And I suddenly felt frozen scared 'cause flurries began to fall. I'd been looking at the dark sky from time to time. There wasn't a moon, but the stars had been bright, twinkling real pretty. I looked up fast now, and I couldn't see the stars. All I saw were these thick black clouds. I swear even in the dark I could see 'em. They were twisting and heaving like something was inside rolling and straining to bust loose. The flurries got bigger. I should've remembered from school. Thirty-two: that's the perfect temperature for getting snow. My legs felt limp. I wasn't walking right from being scared. I tried to run, but I lost my balance and almost fell. The snow came fast now. I couldn't see the clouds because of it. It was falling so thick I couldn't even see the houses across the street. A wind started, and then it got worse and screechy. My cheeks hurt like something was burning them, but it wasn't heat. It was cold. The air had been sweet and warm, but now it was freezing, and the wind stung, and the snow felt like tiny bits of ice-cold broken glass.

I swung around looking for Dad, but I couldn't see the houses next to me. The snow kept pelting my face, and the wind bit so I kept blinking and tears filled my eyes. I wiped them with my mitts. That only made them blurry. Snow froze to my cheeks and hair. I moaned, wishing I'd worn my ski mask. The shriek of the wind was worse. I tried to yell for my dad, but the gusting snow pushed the words back into my mouth. Then I couldn't see the sidewalk. I couldn't see my mitts in front of my face. All I saw was a wall of moving white. As cold as I felt, deep in my bones, my stomach burned. The more it felt hot, the more I shook. I yelled once more for my dad and in a panic stumbled to find him.

I didn't know I was off the sidewalk till I hit Mr. Carrigan's fence. It's sharp and pointy, like metal spears. When I banged against it, one of the points jabbed my chest. I felt it gouge me even through the padding of my coat. It pushed all the air out of me. I fell back into a drift where I felt like I was in quicksand, going deeper, scrambling to stand, but my heavy sack of papers held me down, and the snow kept piling on me. It went down my neck, like a cold hand on my back. It stung so hard I jumped up screaming, but the wind shrieked louder, and all I saw was the swirling snow around me in the dark.

I ran, but I must've got turned around 'cause nothing was where it should've been. Invisible bushes slashed my face. I smacked against a tree, and I guess that's how my nose got broken, but I didn't feel it, I was too scared. I just kept running, yelling for my dad, and when I didn't bump into anything, I guessed I was in the street, but I know now it was the vacant lot next to Mr. Carrigan. Somebody's digging a foundation for a new house, and it was like the ground disappeared. I was suddenly falling, it seemed like forever, and I landed so hard I bit my lip right through. You ought to see the stitches. My dad says sometimes when something terrible happens to you, you don't feel it on account of what he calls shock. He says your body has a limit to what it can stand, and then it shuts out the pain. That must've been what happened 'cause my chest and my nose and my lip got numb, and all I wanted was to find my dad and get back home. I wanted my mom.

I crawled from the hole, and somehow I knew there was someone close. With my eyes full of tears, I could barely see the snow, but then this dark shape rushed at me, and I knew it was my dad, except it wasn't. In the comics, when someone gets hit on the head, they always show stars. And that's what I saw, stars, bright in the snow, and I knew I'd been hit, but I didn't feel it. My dad says shock can do that, too. Something can happen to you that would normally slam you flat, but if you're scared, you somehow get the strength not to fall.

I almost did, though. Everything got blurry and began to spin, and this is the strange part. I got hit so hard I dropped my sack of papers. The sack fell open, and as clear as day I saw my papers in a drift, the black ink with white all around it. Then the papers were splattered with red. You know that old joke? What's black and white and read all over? A newspaper. Only this is spelled different. The red was the blood from my head. I turned to run, and that's when the shadow grabbed my arm.

I kept turning, and even in the shriek of the wind, I heard the crack as clear as if my dad had taken a piece of kindling and snapped it across his knee for the fireplace, but the snap was from my arm, and I felt it twist at the elbow, pointing toward my shoulder. The next thing I was on my back, and the snow stopped gusting long enough for me to gape up at old Mr. Blanchard kneeling beside me, raising the claw end of a hammer.

I moved my head as he brought it down, so the claws glanced past my scalp, tearing away some hair. I kicked, and this time the hammer whacked my collarbone. I screamed. The claws of the hammer plunged toward the spot between my eyes.

And another hand shot from the storm, grabbing Mr. Blanchard's arm. Before I passed out, I saw my dad yank the hammer away from him and jerk him to his feet. My dad shouted stuff at him I'd never heard before. I mean, terrible words I don't want to remember and I won't repeat. Then my dad was shaking Mr. Blanchard, and Mr. Blanchard's head was flopping back and forth, and the next thing I knew, I was here in the hospital with the bandages around my head and my nose and mouth swollen and my arm in this cast.

My dad tried to explain it to me. I think I understand, but I'm not sure. Mr. Blanchard's wife died three months ago. I thought she was still alive, but I was wrong. He and his wife, they never had any children, and my dad says he felt so alone without her he wanted somebody around the house to take care of, like a son, so the first boy he took home was from Granite Falls that time two months ago when he went to visit his wife's sister. Then he wanted another son and another, so he took home those two boys from here, making sure it was snowing so he could hide his tracks, but then he wanted all the sons he could get. It makes me sick to think about it, how after he realized the boys were dead he took them out to his garage and stacked them under a sheet of canvas in the corner, "like cordwood," a reporter said. It's been cold enough that the bodies got hard and frozen. Otherwise they would've smelled like that other house I told you about. I wonder now if all the times I saw Mr. Blanchard crying it was because of his wife being dead or because he realized he was doing wrong but he couldn't stop himself. A part of me feels sorry for him, but another part keeps thinking about those missing boys and how scared they must've been when Mr. Blanchard came at them in the storm, and what he looked like when he knelt beside me, raising that hammer. I have a feeling I'll remember that till I grow up. Earlier I said the nurses wake me early here the same as if my mom was getting me up to do my route. I guess I lied. The nurses didn't wake me. I woke myself, screaming, remembering the claws of the hammer and the blood on my papers. The nurses ran in, and someone's been sitting with me ever since. My mom or my dad is always here, and they say my collarbone is broken too, but what hurts worst is my arm.

The *Gazette* sent Sharon over, though I know she'd have come on her own. She's writing down what I say, but I'm not sure why 'cause she's also got a tape recorder turned on. You ought to see her smiling when I talk about her. She says she's going to put my story in the paper, and her boss is going to pay me for it. I can sure use the money 'cause the doctor says I won't be delivering papers for quite a while. I guess even after everything that's happened I'll go back to my route. After all, we know why those boys disappeared, and there can't be that many crazy people like Mr. Blanchard, though my dad says he's beginning to wonder. He just read about a girl carrier in Ashville that had somebody try to pull her into a car. What's going on that even kids who deliver papers can't feel safe? My dad says pretty soon nobody'll want to go outside.

Well, never mind. I told Sharon I've been talking for quite a while. I'm getting sleepy, and I don't believe the paper will print all this, but she says my story's what they call an exclusive, and maybe some other papers will pick it up. My mom says she hopes I won't start acting temperamental, whatever that means, now that I'm famous, but I don't feel famous. I feel sore. I hope my customers enjoy reading what I said, though, 'cause I like them, and I hope they remember what they promised about giving me a tip on account of there's a new video game I want to buy. My dad came in and heard this last part. He said it again. I must've been born a businessman and I'll probably grow up to vote Republican. I still don't know what a Republican is, but I've been thinking. Maybe if I go around to a few houses and show them the bandages around my head and the cast on my arm, they'll subscribe to the paper. There's a new contest on. The kid who finds the most new customers gets a year's free pass to the movies. Now if only they'll throw in the popcorn.

SILVIA REYES

P.J. Ward

Let me tell you about Silvia Reyes.

(In history, in hovels—I am always telling you something. I've been talking these centuries away until my jaw aches and my teeth fall out, but still you close your ears, turn up the radio, strip paint from statues until they stand naked, ready for your imperial projects.)

Silvia Reyes is what happens when an empire reaches south. When it burrows under the skin of the land like a botfly and lays its eggs. The poverty in Oaxaca drove her mother north, bundled in the back of a truck. She crossed a desert, did Fernanda Escobar. The sun unraveled above her like a wasp's nest. Its splintering light raised welts on her skin.

After something like that, every glass of water feels like a loan. She raised her daughter to take two-minute showers and slice her bread thin. When the war began and the faucets ran dry, neither mother nor daughter were surprised. They broke into a store, beat off other looters with Silvia's taser and Fernanda's baseball bat, and fled the scene with two casks of water.

Silvia had a degree, a BS. She'd studied agroecology in a California smothering under drought. The water companies bottled up aquifers and sold them to New York. People turned on their sprinklers. Silvia, walking past emerald green lawns every night, cut the hosing with a knife. Cameras recorded a hooded person illuminated by moon and streetlamp, but Silvia had kept her face out of the video and the clothes she donated to Goodwill the next day.

She was always like that. Even as a child, she knew to pick the brown M&Ms out of the candy bowl first, because they were less likely to be missed.

It's in my nature to be roundabout. My mind wanders from one point on the map to the other, as if I didn't have a point I was getting to. As if all roads didn't lead to—

My boys were tall, you know? They almost touched the sky. Their smiles were sunshine.

Silvia and her mother were okay for the first few weeks. They hid from other refugees. There had been some ugly stories about girls caught out by groups of men, about boys sassing gangs and paying for it, about pickpockets and poisoners. Silvia found a metal fork on their fourth month on the road.

"Someone's gonna be missing this," she said, holding it up to the light. "Hey. Do you think this could break skin?"

Fernanda gave her a strange look. "What?"

Silvia shrugged, avoiding her eyes. "I said—"

"No, I heard you. But that's very violent."

Silvia hadn't showered in weeks. She felt it in her lank, greasy hair, in the onion smell of her armpits. She'd pulled a tick from her scalp just this morning, its nasty little mouth buried in her skin. If she scratched herself on something metal, she'd probably die out here, jaw locked. She'd watched the university library burn like the Fourth of July.

"This is a very violent time," she said, slipping the fork into her pocket. Maybe she could sharpen the tines.

Silvia slept with her arms against her mother's aching back, and in her sleep she saw California the way vultures do: its thin throat overtaken by a crawling rash, the rivers beating out a thready pulse, the mountainous spine stripped of its ice. Clear as waking, she knew that Los Angeles was choking, and the San Joaquin Valley would not produce fruits for another thousand years.

What it feels like when the world is changing: a prickling of hairs on the back of the neck. A dream you can't remember in the morning. The smell of a strange animal in your den. Two children left on the river flats for a wolf to find.

They walked on. Silvia boiled the water and hunted for small game with a rusty shovel. Fernanda, eyes growing duller, made sure her daughter remembered to sleep. She herself moved slowly. Ever since that first walk through the desert, she had expected her death to come soon. Only by the grace of God had she not died among the saguaro and the creosote. It was, she decided, only a matter of getting Silvia to the green and rainy north.

Here is a picture of her, Silvia: A girl in her early twenties, kneeling, dirty-fingered, smearing red soil on her face when she wipes her eyes. Beside her, the freshly-dug grave of her mother. There should be a church. There should be a choir. But Silvia's throat is too sore for singing, and she isn't strong enough to carry her mother to a church.

Fernanda was right, after all. Her daughter tied a cross to the site, said a prayer to a God she no longer believed in, and walked off into the sunset. She kept crying for that day and all the days that followed, every morning and evening and afternoon until her heart hardened in her chest.

It's not the basket that matters. It's not the tide washing out. It's the boy and girl kings inside them, with hungry white smiles. It's not how Silvia met Calvin King, who still cut his hair and shaved every morning. It's not their nights, surrounded by his wild boys.

It's the day he came back with his raiding party leading five women, a baby, and a thin young man with thin beard.

"They're ours now," he told her.

Silvia watched them. The words seemed no closer to her than something in another language. "What?" she said at last, turning to stare at him.

"Ours," he said.

"People don't—" Silvia said. "You can't own—"

Calvin gestured to the thin, dirty, shaking women, to the threadbare farmstead they'd bunked down in for the last three weeks, the sluggish creek, the starving cow. "Look, this isn't a bad place, for them or us. We're just fifteen guys and one girl. That's not exactly Noah's Ark."

"What are you saying," Silvia said.

He laughed nervously. Behind him, his boys were jeering. The tallest woman, the one with the burning eyes and the golden cross and the baby buttoned up against her chest—her teeth were bared like a wolf's. She met her tormentors with the kind of measured gaze that Fernanda Escobar had perfected in her years as a night nurse.

"Make them stop," Silvia said.

Calvin clapped her on the shoulder. "Whatever you want."

She stopped him by his sleeve. "No. You're not listening to me. Make them stop what they're doing. All of it. Let them go."

He twisted out of her grip and cupped her cheek, a bit too hard. His nails, she thought, would leave little crescents on her cheek. "You're not listening," he told her. "My house, my rules."

"You stole this place," she reminded him.

"It's not stealing if nobody owns it," he told her, smiling so that all of his teeth caught the sunlight. "Like those girls? I don't see anybody with 'em except the one kid. So you know, protection." He patted her cheek twice, almost a slap. "I mean like with you."

He walked away.

"Hey, assholes!" he shouted to his boys. "Flirt later."

Silvia waited for him in bed. Let him take her in his arms. Let him brush her hair aside, whisper the tender things that he always did, rest his chin on her shoulder. She waited for him to tire. She reflected on her sins. The wind blew in through the broken window, cool against her sweaty skin. Then she sat up, muscles aching, and pulled Calvin's carving knife from under her pillow.

She sat for a long while, watching him sleep. His eyelashes were so long, feathered against his cheek. He'd kissed her that morning, sweetly, framing her face with his weathered hands. He took six people and an innocent baby and locked them in the garage, and he planned to profit from their pain in ways she could imagine only too well.

Silvia had cut the necks of horses for their blood. This neck was not much different—soft, elastic, almost spongy beneath his carving knife. Calvin's eyes flew open and she pressed her left hand over his gasping mouth, cutting through the trachea with the other. His hands scrabbled against hers and then fell. She doubled over the edge of the bed and was sick.

The yard was dim under the moonlight. She'd poured beer after beer that night, smiling and joking with the men. Ryan loved the ones about blondes, for some reason. Enrique had a weakness for knock-knock? who's there? sherlock. sherlock who? sherlock your doors at night. The beer was terrible stale stuff, but they held up their cups for more and more, always more. Now they sounded like a herd of bison as they slept.

She opened the shed door. The darkness inside was strangled by the sudden intake of breath—eight prisoners, dirty-limbed and wide-eyed, sitting on the ground with their ankles touching.

"Let's go," Silvia said.

Maryam was the first. A sharp-angled woman with burning eyes and a baby tucked against her chest. She smiled, bitter as quinine, and took Silvia's hand. The others followed her: Robin, Yasmin, Brynna, David, Julia. They followed after Maryam, and Maryam followed after Silvia. When one of the men groaned as they passed the fire, shaking his head and levering to his feet, Maryam silenced him with a swift kick to the head.

They took the horses. They took the water. They stripped them of their weapons and strapped them to their own belts. Silvia saddled her lover's horse and rode, white-knuckled, the reins clutched in her bloody hands.

"So," Maryam said, after the first few miles. "Uh, you were with them?"

Silvia bit her lip.

"Sorry," Maryam said. "Wow, I'm sorry—" she coughed. One of the other women nudged her. "My husband was always saying be nice—"

"Where did nice get him?" Silvia snapped. In the terrible silence that followed, she looked up at the sky, trying to hold back her tears. "That wasn't what I was trying to say."

"No," Maryam said coldly. "I think you tried just fine. You're right."

"Nobody will ever do that again," Silvia promised. "We aren't losing anybody else."

"Bit of a tall order," said David. He rode serenely, as if he was born to guide a small pony across the scrubland. He had a natural dignity, and Silvia envied him. "But we could work it."

"You sound like you were in IT," said Julia. "Were you in IT?"

He only smiled. She held up a hand and they high-fived. It wasn't really the place for it, but they were trying very hard not to stare at the blood drying on Silvia's shaking hands. He had a handsome face, dark-skinned and friendly even after weeks of meager food and less water. She had a wide-open, girlish smile and an expressive pair of hands. These things were the only scraps of beauty they had left in the moment.

"Where are we going?" Yasmin asked. She was clinging to her nag like it might buck her, dark eyes wide. Julia and David stopped talking and waited.

Silvia nodded towards the dark horizon, feeling coltish and unsteady and unexpectedly important. "North."

"Where it rains and it pours?" Robin Sanchez suggested, eyes glinting behind their cracked glasses frames.

Silvia shook her head. "California is my home," she said. There were still tears on her cheeks, but the hot night wind was rapidly taking care of that. She seemed like a woman carved from ironwood and held together by steel wire. "You can go find the rains if you like, but I'll take my chances here."

There was silence for a while. Then Brynna raised her pale child's face.

"It can't be worse than a homeless shelter," she said. "At least nobody's gonna try and steal my shoes. I think."

"Nobody's stealing any shoes," David said.

"It won't be roses," Silvia warned her.

Brynna just shrugged in her secret way. She had cultivated a cold pride in her ability to survive against all expectation.

Seven people and a baby. Not the most auspicious beginning for a city like theirs. Not exactly the stuff of legends.

But you've all heard of Silvia Reyes. The thief who slew her lover in his sleep for his gold, for his jewels, for his hidden stores of summer wine. The whore who wormed her way into the affections of a good man only to bathe in his blood. You've heard of her. Of her city, that den of iniquity. That hive of hornets on the edge of the habitable world. Where the walls are high and painted with roses and the only rule is run.

"It's not much to look at," Maryam said when they arrived in the valley.

"Neither are we," Silvia said, and drove the first tent stake into the ground.

I was just trying to find a place to sleep. The village in the valley, outlined by a changeable river, was like coming home.

"Where's home for you?" Silvia asked me, as she poured boiled water into my cup.

"East," I said. "And you?"

Silvia laughed into her hand, sadly. "Davis," she said. "But my mother was a farmer's daughter in Oaxaca so, you know."

"Not quite here and not quite there," I offered, and she laughed again.

"No," she said, and her hands traced patterns in the dust almost tenderly. "I'm part of this country. Oaxaca would be another planet. Everything I love about Mexico, my mother, she brought it with her when she emigrated."

The women made gardens. A touch of my hand brought them into flower. Tomatoes swelled rapidly on the vine and squash blossoms opened to the harsh light of the sun. The travelers stopped losing their teeth. It seemed only right, after all; Maryam's baby grew faster when his mother had enough milk to give him.

"Lizards don't taste bad," I told them over a meal of fried yucca and strong-tasting water.

Julia Flores made a face. "Wouldn't even wolf be better?"

"No," I said. "You must never eat wolves."

I showed them how to prepare the little animals of the desert. You run a knife over the scales of lizards to make the texture more palatable. A fine mesh will snare birds that come to tap the cacti for water. Mice are delicious when mixed with nuts and fried over an open fire. Fight in formation, with shields locked together, so your enemies cannot divide you.

"If you're so smart, how do we make this stick?" Silvia asked me, laughing. Her hands were covered in red adobe.

I knelt beside her and pushed my finger into the brick mold.

"Hey, watch out," Silvia said, snatching my hand away.

"Your water ratio is off," I told her.

(Romulus, grinning. Mother, look. Mother, look at me. His cities of mud being swallowed by the Tiber's tide. Mother, look at me, I'm king.)

"Lupe, Lupe," Silvia sang, waving her hand in front of my face. The clay covered her fingers like blood. "Earth to Lupe."

"Your water ratio," I said, walking away. "is off."

But it was a place, it was a home. Even when Silvia woke crying in the night, Robin or Maryam was there to talk her down. Brynna stopped stealing combs and tacks and old jump cables and started just asking for them. Yasmin set up her books. David told his fishing stories with so much conviction that we almost believed them. Julia sang in the evening. She seemed to know more top 40 than was strictly necessary. Silvia hummed under her breath as she made bricks and rocked Maryam's baby to sleep with the lullabies Fernanda Escobar had carried with her from the countryside of Oaxaca.

So of course it couldn't last. When the boys came over the hill, it was like we'd been expecting them.

"Stay here," Silvia said, swallowing hard. She stood up and walked out to where they stood, dragging their spears in the dust.

"You killed Cal," Ryan said.

Silvia dropped her knife. "Yes," she said.

Ryan punched her. She hit the ground, and I ran towards them.

"Lupe!" David shouted.

"Stay here!" I ordered, waving a hand at him.

Silvia was picking herself up, rubbing blood off her chin. Her eyes should have been a warning—they were bright and focused like a hunter's. The smirking, furious boys only held their weapons with more conviction.

"Take me," she said, as I approached. "Leave them."

"Uh, no," Ryan said, as the rest of the gang jeered. "You don't tell me anything. This place?" He waved a hand around, and for a moment I saw who he must have been, a boy fresh out of college and ready to make his mark on the world, "This place is awesome. There's even a river!"

"No," Silvia said, and Ryan punched her again. They swarmed her, all of them kicking, and Silvia curled in on herself.

I approached lightly, just gentle enough to escape notice. Silvia spat sticky dust out onto the ground and picked herself up again, stumbling back and away from them. She'd had an idea of martyrdom, I could tell. She'd thought her death would be enough.

I could have told her that she was wrong. They had the need for more. Silvia could bleed dry but the boys would still be thirsty.

"Come on," Ryan told his pack. "Let's finish her."

They moved forward again in a group, with spears made out of broom handles and broken glass. David shouted something, and Maryam picked up her rusty dagger and pounded up the hillside toward us.

We are not meant to interfere, but wolves are wolves. I leapt into Silvia's skin, fitting myself cleanly against her soul and filling her eyes with light. I gave her the memory of forests and river flats. She had strong fingers and sore joints. Her ribs bruised her every breath.

What, she said, faintly.

Hold on, I told her, and stood up. Her body screamed in protest at every step, but she caught my intentions, and her astonished joy burned beneath our shared skin like a banked fire.

"This isn't your home," we said to the foolish boys. "It's ours. Let it stop here."

"Fifteen of us and seven of you," Ryan pointed out. "Who's gonna win that, huh? Can you even count, you stupid fucking bitch? You're alone." He barked a laugh. "Alone. Give it up now for Chrissake, it's embarrassing."

We raised a hand to the sky. Out in the hills, a hundred ears pricked up. Out in the hills, our family rose and began to run.

"You're mistaken," we said.

They were closer. We could hear their yips. Wolves live in these hills—tired, hungry wolves. Wolves with sharp white teeth. This world begins wild and to the wild it shall return, now and unto the final dissolution, amen.

"You'll die," we said, opening our hands.

"Screw it," Ryan said abruptly, and at a flick of his hand the boys were raising their weapons again.

But we would not fail. Not today.

"This is your last chance," we told them, as our people gathered at the top of the valley, teeth bared for battle. "You can make a den somewhere else."

Ryan laughed in disbelief.

"You're insane," he told us, shaking his head. "Like, really insane."

We smiled at him. "Yes."

Our people overflowed into the valley, barking and snarling, kicking up dust with their paws. We saw the fear begin in Ryan's eyes, then ripple outward to the rest of the group. The old fear. The first fear. If ever you've sat around a campfire in the wild, the circle of light barely pushing back against the noisy darkness, then you know what made them turn and run.

We stood there and laughed, the two of us together. And then I left her and pulled my furs on again. My people were still in pursuit, and I intended to chase the boys across the hills, across the vast stretches of scrub, until their minds were so filled with terror that they forgot the way back.

"Lupe!" Silvia shouted. Her voice strained out from under cracked ribs. David and Maryam caught up with her but she pulled away from them and her staggering footsteps followed mine. "Lupe, come back!"

I kept running.

Later, they say that Silvia Reyes always had the wolf in her. That when she was born, her mother found a beast in the house, guarding over the cradle like a tame dog. That the animal saints of the City had marked her out as special from the very first day of her birth. I might wear the skin of an animal but humans fascinate me. Your stubborn cruelties. Your fierce, yearning joys. The way you touch each other, strangely, like love might outright break you.

This is ours, Belinda Reyes would say years afterwards, eyes flashing in the grim copper twilight of the desert. Like the rest of her generation, she had marked out her allegiance in tattoos: snarling, blue-lined beasts that chased each other up her arms. She stood before her ragged people and Silvia's freshly-turned grave, still in her funeral blacks. My mother won it with her blood. Now who's gonna take it from us?!

Nobody, her people shouted back. Out in the brush, the wolves howled their approval. The hills echoed. Nobody!

Go to the nameless City. Pass the shrine to the wolf-saint, pass the colorful folk murals of the seven founders. Find the woman in gray who sits on the steps of the whorehouses and the bars. Your instincts will be uneasy, but sit awhile with her, and she may tell you things.

"Child," she'll say. "You never asked me what happened afterwards."

"Everyone knows," you'll say. "Silvia Reyes made us a home. She was a wolf."

"No," she'll say. "I was the wolf. She was something else entirely." And then, while you are too shocked to speak, she'll smile with every last one of her teeth and tell you this story. The city will buzz around you like a nest of hornets, this fruit of a long-dead empire, and you will be content.

• • •

There is, nonetheless, one last part. You must have wondered where someone like Silvia Reyes goes when she dies. After all those bloodstains on her soul. Well, let me tell you:

Silvia is like the moon. Edging away into the infinite but stubbornly shedding light as she goes, face turned fully toward her home, the song on her lips like nothing you'll ever hear elsewhere. The whole world looks at her city and says, they don't belong. She smiles in the darkness and says, they do.

In her radiant bones, she says, I am.

In her heaven of creosote and saguaro, she holds the memory to her heart and tells it, there is nothing like you.

Mother of Belinda Reyes and mother of a nation. Bandit-queen. Seducer. Whore. She cups the city in her hands like clean water and she whispers, This is what I have.

One day her tether will fray and run out, and one day she will be reborn in another country. She will wake up with a longing in her chest that stretches from here to a far horizon. Perhaps she will even find her way back to the valley and come face-to-face with her own mural, wondering at its serious eyes and the taint on the hands that could be clay or blood. But today she stands in paradise and seeks out the image of a dusty city on the edge of the world. A city that nobody wants.

Grow, she says. Flower. Make me proud.

GATEKEEPER

Richard Prosch

I was running my own crew for Jimmy Spense out of a downtown office with internet access and a fridge full of Guinness the summer John Cougar told us to hold on to sixteen as long as you can. Exactly my intentions. But, unlike my suburban Generation-Excuse pals, I worked my ass off in the nineties. Before long, the computer sucked me into marketing.

Jimmy liked the idea of backing something legit, so after I got my button I formed a web company, a multi-level kinda deal, and next thing you know I'm working from home whenever I want, and it's almost two decades into the 21st century.

Jimmy moved on into one of them ride-call private taxi businesses. Lots of call for quick, private transport in this city. Believe me.

Meanwhile, I moved on into early retirement.

I haven't heard John Cougar What's-his-name on the radio for a long time.

The list of names I know on the inside is short.

My next door neighbor's a cop.

Every week or two, we share cigars over the fire pit.

What can I say?

Everybody grows up someday.

"Did you see this morning's dance video Lynda posted online," said the wife from behind her phone at the coffee shop the other day.

Since it was almost noon, the local congregations were out, the shop was packed with customers, and my answer got lost in the noise of the crowd. I sipped my latte, tried to answer again, then decided not to.

I didn't want to see the dumb photo.

And if I said so, I figured she'd show me anyway and spoil my appetite. Ten-year-olds wagging their tails at dance contests and parents putting up their pictures for all the world to see.

Like a hard roll out for the Pervert's Buffet.

I mean for crying out loud.

Palm Sunday and the wife's best pal has her kid all made up and stripped down for a pole dance competition.

Worse, she puts it on the social media.

I work on the web, but I don't like it.

"Flower, mister?"

I laid down the newspaper I'd been hiding behind to find a little Native American girl, eleven, maybe twelve years old. Long black hair pulled back in a ribboned braid. She was wearing a bright, church-going kind of dress and holding a bent pipe-cleaner sculpture enclosed in cellophane plastic.

"Wildling flower, only fifty cents."

• • •

Back when I actually was sixteen I drove a 1974 Camaro, and this Indian girl down the street had an old three-speed bicycle. She lived in this squalid little dump we all called *The Rez* because Tammy's mom was a full blooded Lakota Sioux from East Dakota bumblestick-somewhere.

And she didn't have a dad.

The Rez.

We thought we were pretty fuckin' clever.

Tammy and me both worked at the Burger Hut, and every afternoon when I took off for work, she was walking or riding her broke-down bike, so I'd give her a ride. We didn't have a lot in common, but she was sort of cute, though not my type.

Too hippy dippy, too Debbie Harry druggy. Used to say "man" after every utterance.

"What kind of music are you into, *man?*"

"Did you hear about the break-in at the corner store, *man?*"

"Buy me a Coke, *man?*"

Man this. Man that.

I didn't realize how much Tammy liked me until after she died.

She used to make these little pipe cleaner flowers.

"Wildling flowers, man. What's-a-matter, you don't like art?"

• • •

"What?"

"Fifty cents," said the girl.

"Go ahead," said the wife. "Buy one, cheapskate. Easter's on the way.

Where's your Christian charity?"

Looking through the cellophane at the little mass of twisted pipe cleaners, I realized I was sweating. The smell of roasting Sumatra beans closed my sinuses and the constant customer chatter rattled my ears.

I couldn't peel my eyes off the flower. An orange and pink pipe cleaner had been hooked together, then fashioned into a rough series of petals that sprang from a twist of green pipe cleaner. The overall effect was crude but charming at the same time.

Just like the ones Tammy made.

Milk and espresso rolled around my guts as I dug in my pocket for a couple quarters and glanced up at the girl.

"What did you call it?" I said.

"A Wildling flower."

"Wild flower?"

"Wild-*ling*," she said, rolling her eyes.

"Did you make it yourself?"

She nodded, glanced over her shoulder.

That's when I saw the bearded guy at a table in the corner. Maybe a little older than me. White beard, nicely trimmed. Longish hair. Wearing a rumpled suit. He's got a dozen Wildling Flowers in plastic on the table in front of him.

The girl looks back at me and smiles.

Yellow, bad teeth. Sallow skin under the chin. Boney arms.

Anorexic?

Scrapes on her knuckles from gagging herself.

Bulimic.

You wouldn't see it if you weren't looking.

Just like Tammy.

• • •

I'd noticed the dark circles under her eyes.

The sudden loss of weight.

The bruises on her arm.

For such a streetwise guy, I was completely blind where Tammy was concerned. I just hadn't been paying attention.

Until the last morning I saw her.

"You won't have to drive me to work after tomorrow," said Tammy. "My old man's taking care of things."

"I thought you told me your father was dead?"

"Not my *dad*. My *old man*. You know, like my boyfriend."

"The '60s are over, Tam," I said, shoving the Camaro down out of third to brake for a stoplight.

"Tell that to Darius."

"Darius? You mean that old guy lives behind the lumber yard? In the van?"

"That van's got a better stereo than most people got at home. And Darius is only a few years older than you."

"Tam, that guy's bad news."

"Yeah, everybody says that, but nobody says why, y'know? Nobody knows him and they're just spreading shit that ain't true." Then she turned up her nose. "Let him without sin throw the first stone."

"Oh, Christ."

"Absolutely, right." She sniffed. "Darius is tuned into the universe, you know? He's sort of like a *gatekeeper* for us."

The light went green, and I turned out onto the boulevard, a couple blocks from the Burger Hut.

"A gatekeeper?"

"For us that's just getting started."

"Started in what?"

"Lots of things, man. Like art, for one." She pointed at the pipe-cleaner flower twisted around my rear-view mirror. "Art and spirituality and all that shit."

"So Darius is driving you to work tomorrow?"

"Oh no, no way."

"I thought you said—"

"I said he was taking care of things. I'm quitting the Burger Hut this morning."

I pulled into my usual oil-stained parking spot behind the drive-thru. "Quitting?"

"I'm moving in with Darius," she said. "He's gonna take care of me. Of all of us."

Two weeks later they found her body, stuffed with drugs, sexually assaulted, spread-eagle in a dumpster behind the lumber yard.

Darius and the van were long gone.

• • •

Like I said, I'm not a fan of the interwebs.

But the mobile phone?

The mobile phone, I like.

After I bought the flower, the girl had continued to make the rounds. After fifteen minutes or so, she went back to sit with the bearded guy.

Meanwhile, I made a phone call.

Eventually, the man and the girl packed up their pipe-cleaner inventory and headed for the door.

I patted my wife's hand. "I'll be right back."

She nodded from behind the screen of her own phone.

Outside, the bearded man wore sunglasses and held the little girl's hand. Then he pulled her close.

Playful.

Put his arm around her narrow waist.

He said something and she laughed.

Palm Sunday.

The son-of-a-bitch.

When they got to their car, I was already there.

In an adjoining space, Jimmy Spense parked a black SUV with his ride-share business logo on the door. Jerry Bones and his wife got out the passenger side. Nodded at me and walked around behind the bearded man's car.

"Can I help you?"

"I sold him a flower," said the girl.

"Yes you did," I said. "That's what I was wondering about. There's a sticker on the plastic here." I pulled the flower out of my pocket. Holding it up close to my eyes, I read, "Compliments of the Church of Blissful Awareness."

"Yes," said the man, a new eagerness in his voice.

"I'm interested in learning more."

"I see. Yes, I see."

Like a dog with a bone.

He didn't even notice Jerry Bones' wife leading the Indian girl away from the parking lot.

"What's your name, Reverend?"

"Reverend is so formal," said the man. "Call me Pastor Darius."

"Pastor."

"Are you a seeker, friend?"

Jimmy got out then and stood beside me.

Jerry moved in, jerked open the back door on the SUV.

"I'm not so much a seeker as a gatekeeper," I said.

The three of us had no trouble tossing Pastor Darius into the SUV.

"Lucky you caught me," said Jimmy. "I was on the way to my kids' place for dinner. Palm Sunday, right?"

As we hit the boulevard and sped past the Burger Hut, I thought about it.

When I saw the wildling flower, when I recognized Darius, I could've called my neighbor.

Instead of calling Jimmy, I could've called a cop.

What can I say?

Sometimes ya hold onto sixteen as long as you can.

PLAN B

Andrew Vachss

I call myself a gambler, but that's not what I am. A gambler wins sometimes. Me, I'm a loser, that's the right word for it.

In all my gambling life, I only had one piece of luck. And like they always say, luck is a lady. That's my Penny. My Lucky Penny, I used to call her . . . back when I was keeping at least *some* of my promises.

The guy who said "for better or for worse" must have had me and Penny on his mind. Yeah. She was the better, I was the worse.

When I first knew her, when I was taking her out on the town, she was such a beauty guys would just bite their hands when she walked down the street. That was more than twenty years ago, but even all those years of hash-house waitressing haven't made it all go away. She's still gorgeous, and not just to me. Yeah, she's put on a few pounds. And being on your feet all day don't do much for your legs. Having to eat most of her meals at that greasy spoon joint don't help your waistline either. They give her free meals at the joint—that's so they don't have to pay minimum wage.

Penny could of made a lot more cash working in one of those joints where letting the customers grab your ass is part of the deal, but she wouldn't do that. I mean, I wouldn't of wanted her to do that, but I couldn't have stopped her. I mean, I was never enough of a man to take care of her like she deserved. How was I gonna tell her I want her to quit her job, when I wasn't bringing home the cash?

It wasn't that I didn't try—I'm a gambler, not a pimp. Truth is, I get ideas . . . good ideas . . . but I'm no good at carrying them out. I mean, I don't drink or nothing. Never touched dope except for when I was in the Army. Everybody smoked in Nam. Or did something heavier. I hated it over there, but I don't blame nobody but myself. I mean, I was a stone bust-out gambler before I ever got drafted.

Before I ever met my Penny.

Anyway, I always worked steady. Gamblers don't miss work the way drunks do. I got damn near twenty in on my job. At least, I did have until they laid me off. Hell, they about laid everybody off. Some of the guys said it's a bluff. They said they're trying to bust the union. Near as I can tell, the union's already busted. All I got to show for all those years is I get to keep my health plan for another year or so. Of course, I got to pay for it myself—the only thing management kept up was the lousy life insurance . . . twenty-five grand if I croak, big deal.

And, anyway, the truth is, I'm not keeping up the health insurance—Penny's doing that. She always has faith in me. No matter how many times I screw up, no matter how many times I lie. Every time I get in a hole because I did something stupid, I always tell her I got another move. "I'll just go to Plan B, little girl." That's what I used to tell her when it started.

But Penny ain't no little girl anymore. And me . . . me, I'm nothing but a liar. A promiser and a liar—for me, they're just the damn same.

Only one promise I ever kept to Penny. The one she told me she'd leave me for, if I broke it. "I'm not waiting around for you if you're in jail," she told me. And I knew she meant it—Penny is real strict about that kind of thing. So I never went to the sharks. Yeah, I was a good gambler, you understand?—I only lost the money I had on me at the time.

All the goddamned money.

Every single time.

If it wasn't for the house, I would of probably gone on like I was forever. This house, it was right across the street from the one we lived in. Rented in, I mean. A little house, but real nice. Penny loved it. She always said it was her dream house. The old couple that lived there, they decided to sell out and move down to Florida—the winters here are cold as hell. Penny was always doing things for them—baking them some cookies, even helping the old lady clean when her arthritis got too bad—so they told her she could have first shot at the house. They told her she could have it for fifty-five thousand if she could buy it before they put it on the market. The broker told them to list it for seventy-five, and be prepared to come down to sixty-five. But, the way they figured it, with the broker's commission and all, they could do a nice thing for Penny and still come out just about the same.

When Penny told me about it, she was so excited her face got all red, like when she was a kid. Like how she was when she still believed some of my lies. All we needed was ten percent down, she said. She already talked to a man at the bank. She didn't make much, but she sure was steady. Hell, before I got laid off, I was, too. All we needed was about six grand, she said. For the down payments and the points or whatever. And all the crap the bank sticks you with when you're up against the wall.

Six grand. Where were we gonna get that? She told me she had almost two grand socked away. She put her face down when she said it—like she was ashamed for holding out on me. You see what I mean about her? If you counted all the money I wasted chasing horses that wouldn't run and opportunities that did, I probably could have bought Penny the whole house in cash. The payments would be four hundred and eighty-seven dollars and twenty-six cents a month, Penny told me. "And we're already paying four-fifty, honey," she said.

I hated myself so much that I tried to talk her out of it. I told her we would have to pay our own heat and hot water and taxes and stuff, so it would be a lot more, really. But she said the mortgage, it would always be the same—but the landlord was gonna raise the rent eventually. All landlords do that. So, in the long run, we'd be ahead.

And when we were done working, we'd have a place of our own. The only thing that really scared Penny was being homeless. When she saw a homeless person on the street, she would get so scared . . . like the person was her in a few more years. And Penny wanted a garden. The guy who rented the house to us, he wouldn't allow it, don't ask me why.

I never deserved Penny. She should be wearing silk. I get depressed every time I see her dabbing at her stockings with clear nail polish so the runs don't get lower down, where they would show. When I get depressed, I gamble more, that's the kind of real man I am. I made her old. I made her scared of being homeless. And she never complained. The only truth I ever told Penny was that I loved her. I was never as big as my own lies—I never caught up to them.

It had to be cash. At least four grand in cash. All I had was health insurance that was running out and life insurance on a worthless life.

It had to be cash. So I had to break the one promise I'd always kept. "I can get the money," I told her. "I swear it on my love for you."

"Don't you dare—"

I cut her off. "I won't," I told her. "It's too complicated to explain, girl. But I—"

"Plan B?" she said. But with her sweet smile. Like she still believed in me. Jesus.

"You just wait and see," I told her. I knew I had six days. Six days and five nights. It couldn't be anything big, like a bank. You need partners for that and I didn't know anyone who could handle it. I mean, you're a gambler, you meet all kinds of guys say they do all kinds of things. But, the way I always figured it, if they were hanging out with a lying loser like me, how smart could they be? And because I never went near the loan sharks, I didn't know any, like, organized guys.

I had to do it alone.

First I needed a gun. That was so easy. I mean, I didn't have to do nothing illegal. I just went into a gun store and told them I wanted a pistol. What kind, they asked me. Cheap, I told them.

They had a bunch of them. I had to fill out a form. They asked questions like: Was I a felon and was I crazy? I mean, they expect a escaped convict or a drooling lunatic to admit it, *they* were the ones who were crazy. I had to wait three days, then I could come and pick up the gun.

I found where I wanted to do it. It's a club. Not like a nightclub or anything, although it was only open at night. A gambling club. Dice and cards only—none of that silly roulette or slot machines—real games, where a man has a chance. The club was protected. Protected from getting busted, that is—they paid off the cops. They had a guy at the door. Big huge fat guy, probably kill you if he fell on you. But I wasn't going to challenge him, anyway. I mean, he knows me. And I promised Penny I would never go to jail. No, I needed a stranger. A new guy. They were always coming in and out. I needed one coming in—when he still had money. It would be big money, too—there was no penny ante stuff inside—you had to have coin to sit in. That's why I only went there once in a while ... when I was ahead from gambling someplace else. Naturally, I always lost. But I don't think the games were rigged—I'm just a loser.

When I went to the gun shop they had the pistol ready for me. "Don't you want some ammunition?" they asked me. "I got some at home," I told them.

On the second night, the right guy came along. I saw him park a smoke-gray Lincoln Town Car across the street. That's a classy ride, runs about thirty grand. He was sharp-dressed, too. Not flashy, more like a businessman. I could see the strong way he walked. Confident-like. Not the old gangster swagger, like a man who was in control of himself.

In a couple of minutes, Penny's dream was going to come true. I knew it. I was sure of it. Not like when I had a sure thing at the track, but sure ... like nothing else could be.

Just as soon as he walked into the alley where the door to the club was, I stepped out from behind a dumpster and stuck the pistol in his face.

"Give it up!" I told him.

He was real calm, real professional—just like I thought he'd be. "Do you know who I am?" he asked.

"Give me the money!" I said, cocking the pistol like I was gonna shoot him.

He took a shiny wallet out from under his coat. Real, real slow, so I wouldn't think he was reaching for a gun. He opened the wallet and took out a thick wad of bills—I could see they was all hundreds. "I'm sure you don't want my credit cards, right?" he said, a thin smile on his face.

I snatched the money out of his hand and backed away. He just stood there. "Don't try to come after me," I said. I turned around and ran. I heard footsteps behind me and I whipped around. It was the guy, holding something in his hand, some black thing, near his mouth. I turned around again and started to run. Three more corners and I'd get to where the car was waiting. Three more corners and . . . then I saw them across the street.

Two of them. Cops. They were standing with their feet wide apart, guns in their hands.

"Freeze!" one of them yelled, and I knew I was never going to hand the money to Penny. I pulled out the pistol and I pointed it right at the cops.

I never heard the shots, but I felt them rip into me. One, two, three of them. In my chest and in my gut. I closed my eyes and went to Plan B.

THE NIGHT WATCH

Susan Schorn

She was built like a Brontë: short, slight, with an unnaturally large head that suggested early malnourishment or a mother who died young of tuberculosis. Something about her eyes hinted at timidity or perhaps, to the more discerning, stubbornness. There was no reason to think she was particularly brave. She didn't think so, herself.

When Rachel was very young the dark had frightened her. She would wake suddenly, to the sound of fighting, the sound of weeping. She hated the shock of it more than anything else, the pit of danger yawning suddenly beneath her when she had thought she was safe in bed. And so she had taught herself to stay awake, so the fear couldn't surprise her. She had learned not to turn on the bedside lamp; learned that she and Jacob were safer if they were invisible. So instead she dove down deep into the dark, eyes open, kicking hard to reach bottom. Once she was immersed, acclimated to the pressure, she could move freely; she could breathe. She could even, if she needed to, escape.

It became a habit, to lie in bed and let her eyes adjust to the darkness. She would tune her ears to the wavelength of violence, ready to detect its first whisper. If it came too near, grew too loud, she wrestled her sleeping brother from his crib and carried him silently through the low window in the parlor that had no screen. Sitting on the back porch, holding Jacob and feeling the nails in the old boards through the fabric of her nightgown, she listened to their voices as though memorizing a poem. She learned to distinguish empty threats from real ones and to gauge the impact of blows; she weighed the evidence carefully, judging whether to stay where they were, or if it were time to move further out—past the clothesline, behind the oleanders, to the fence with the loose board where she knew they could squeeze through.

Heroes

She never had to leave the yard. Her father left instead, not long after Jacob's first birthday. He swore he'd be back, and that was when they had gone to live with her mother's brother in Atlanta. When they moved home to Shreveport six months later, her father didn't come back. Her mother said, with the assurance of someone who has seen the body, that he never would.

But Rachel preferred the darkness by then; preferred to let it swallow her whole, and feel herself coursing through its veins. While her mother was working nights, cleaning office buildings downtown, she would put Jacob to bed and sit with him, witnessing the rapid and complete victory sleep always claimed. One minute he would be fussing with his blanket, kicking his feet, carrying on a gabbling, one-sided conversation, and the next he would lie as still as a statue of a baby. Sleep never crept up on Jacob; it ran him over like a truck every night.

And all through the night, while darkness leaned against the windows and the thin midnight air moved unhindered through the quiet house, she would sit in the little wooden child's chair by Jacob's crib, watching his pale purple eyelids and his plump, sweaty hands, watching him breathe steadily, watching the full glory of unconsciousness mapped on his baby face. She would sit, or pace the boundary of the room, sharing in the silent, ancient vigil of those who put a child to bed and wait in the dark, for the storm, or the fever, or the hum of approaching airplanes; waiting without knowing what the morning will bring, if the child will wake or not. She never grew weary when she watched Jacob. She felt alert; she felt alive.

It was always hard the next day. She dozed through school and napped in the afternoons. Her teachers would shake their heads and say, "Rachel just sleepwalks through life." And she did, in the daytime. At night it was different. At night, she moved in her element.

When they were older and Jacob started school, she took night work whenever she could. She worked late shifts at a laundry until she finished high school, and for a while as a waitress in an all-night diner.

"Don't you get scared coming home all alone in the dark?" people would ask her. No, she said, she wasn't afraid of the nighttime. She was used to it. She liked it.

After she graduated from nursing school, she was delighted to get the job at St. Agnes' because it was primarily a children's hospital, and a small one, which meant a lot of night work. She didn't care that it was isolated, way out in Iberville Parish, twenty miles from the nearest town, and on the edge of a swamp. The other nurses complained about the location frequently, and the doctors never left off complaining about it. But Rachel was happy there. She worked nights as often as she could, and she became a familiar figure moving silently through the wards, checking pulses, closing windows, wiping up spills. Though she saw less of the children when they were awake than any other nurse there, the wards where she spent the most time always had the best recovery rates. The children seemed to benefit from her watch over them. Like plants that had been talked to in a scientific experiment, they thrived in unexpected ways.

The year after she arrived at St. Agnes', they had a wet spring. The roads flooded, as usual, and were only passable off and on. There were floods up in Missouri; Rachel read about them in the newspaper, when the newspaper made it all the way out from town. The river was rising, they heard, and the levee up in Bayou Des Glaises was breached. Finally in May the Army opened the big spillway in Pointe Coupee and the swamp rose almost overnight, cutting them off completely.

None of the consulting doctors could reach the hospital, but no new patients could either. The lowly interns, who boarded on the hospital grounds, were left in charge, and quickly used their temporary authority to make the nurse's lives miserable. The nurses couldn't get into town for their days off and became snappish. Even the nuns were getting irritable.

Rachel suffered less than the others. She'd had a letter from Jacob just a few days before the roads flooded, sent from the teacher's college he was attending near Houston. She had her work, helping to keep the patients quiet and entertained in the absence of family visits. And she had a watch to keep. Someone had to keep an eye on the water, especially at night, in case it rose further while the hospital slept. She would survey the grounds every hour or so, to see if the levels had changed. During the day, she rested. She had no boyfriend to worry about, and her days off she was used to spending in desultory shopping when she could catch a ride into town with Patty.

Patty was her best friend, a quick, lively girl from a big family. They shared a room in the nurses' dormitory. The day Rachel moved in she had unpacked an old photograph of Jacob and his cousin, and set it on her dresser. When Patty saw it she pointed to Jacob and said, "That must be your brother, because he looks fierce, just like you." No one had ever called Rachel fierce. They were friends after that.

It was Patty who first noticed about the chickens. The nuns kept a flock of hens that spent most of their time jumping the fence around their yard and invading the hospital grounds. Patty was the one who usually chased them back where they belonged. When she didn't have to do it for a whole week at a stretch, she teased the sisters about eating up all their chickens during Lent. But the nuns told her they hadn't eaten any chickens lately. When they counted, they found half a dozen of the most adventuresome birds missing.

"Didn't you even find feathers?" Patty asked. Not a trace, they replied, mystified.

Despite the dictatorial interns and the nurses' curtailed social lives, there was a summer camp atmosphere about the ordeal for the first week, until the power went out.

Electricity at the hospital was unreliable even in the best of weather. It ran through miles of cable, strung on decrepit old poles that had nothing to do all day long but sink lower and lower into the swamp and consider when they ought to finally fall over. The generator was always at the ready, in case there was a respirator in use, or a surgery underway. They were using it now three times a day to run the refrigerators, and most of the night, to light the wards. Leroy, the handyman, had been out to check it not long before the flood, and the big fuel tank it fed from was still half full, but when Sister Mary Elizabeth sent Rachel to turn it on Friday morning, it sputtered and died. The telephone lines were out too, of course, so one of the interns went in the old flat-bottom motorboat to get Leroy.

Rachel and Patty were off duty when the men returned. They met the boat on the side lawn where Patty, who had dug up a tin can full of night crawlers that morning, was trying to catch catfish.

Rachel offered to help Leroy with the generator. She was sometimes given the job of starting it, since she wasn't perturbed by its noise or its smell, and she liked to know the sorts of things that went wrong with it. She could reset the circuit breaker and hear when the carburetor was over-choked; once Leroy had shown her how to replace a spark plug. Today a number of things were wrong. Torrents of rain had eaten away the supports of the shed roof, which had collapsed gracelessly against the garage wall, and now the generator stood half-exposed on its platform. There was rainwater in the fuel line. Rachel watched while Leroy clattered around the generator, flushing lines and oiling parts. The bearings were worn, Leroy said, and he greased them. He'd have to rebuild the shed roof later, when they could truck out some lumber. The generator restarted at his command, and the squeak of its bearings floated reassuringly over the water.

Leroy fished some spare spark plugs and cables out of his pockets and dropped them in the toolbox under the platform. "Well," he said, "those bearings won't last forever, and the thing sounds like a bunch of baby alligators, but it ought to run OK until they get the lines back up. There saying it'll be another week or so before that happens."

Father Guillory left the next day. The same intern who had fetched Leroy took him and two suitcases away in the motorboat. Father Guillory looked askance at the shabby vessel, its bottom dimpled with rust, but he got in. He said he was going to the Bishop to see what could be done to hasten work on the power lines. The sisters sniffed at this, pointing out to one another that the diocesan headquarters had plenty of electricity and hot water.

Rachel was working in Ward Two the night after Father Guillory left, tending a three-year-old girl recovering from scarlet fever. The girl was still on intravenous fluids and the needle was prone to slip out of her tiny vein while she slept, making her hand swell painfully. Tonight she fretted and flung her arm about while Sister Mary Elizabeth tried to tape down the needle.

"Your hand is sore, isn't it?" Rachel asked the girl, and then suggested to Sister, "Why don't we switch the IV to the other side?"

The nun acquiesced. Just as she removed the first needle, the lights went out. Sister Mary Elizabeth sighed.

"That'll be the generator again. Rachel, can you find the lantern?"

Rachel found it by the desk at the front of the room, and lit it easily, with fingers accustomed to darkness. She brought it to the bedside and carefully set it on a chair near the IV stand.

"I hope it's not flooded," said Sister Mary Elizabeth, thinking of the generator. "Has the water risen?"

No, it hadn't, Rachel assured her. She had checked after dinner. Probably the reset switch, she suggested, since Leroy had taken care of everything else yesterday.

"We'll have to restart it," Sister said grimly, swabbing the girl's hand with alcohol. The little girl fussed, anticipating the needle. "Here, Rachel, hold her hand for me. Now dear, we'll be done in just a minute and then your hand will feel much better." Rachel held the girl's hand and reassured her. The needle went in and was taped securely; Rachel told her what a good girl she was, and restored to her a dusty teddy bear that had fallen on the floor. Sister Mary Elizabeth looked at Rachel and the quieting girl, and then asked Nora, the other ward nurse, to go check on the generator.

"I'll need the lantern," Nora said.

"But the moon's out," said Sister Mary Elizabeth in exasperation. "Can't you go without a light? I still have to get the drip restarted here."

Nora hesitated, but Rachel did not.

"I'll go," she said, and went at once. She patted Jane's free hand, told her to be good until she returned, and walked out of the ward, down the long main hall, and out the side door to the garage.

It was a damp, breathing night, with some spring freshness beginning to override the muddy odor of flood water. Her window in the dormitory was dark; Patty had the morning shift, and was already in bed. Moisture dripped from the moss in the trees like myriad gray-fringed IVs, trickling life into the ground in steady, careful doses.

Rachel made her way up to the generator, the moon lighting the grass before her. She was right; the generator had not flooded. A branch from one of the cypress trees had fallen squarely across it, and the main cable that carried power to the buildings lay useless on the ground. The generator was still running, but its engine was making a muted, clunking sound—not the screechy rumble it had made earlier when Leroy restarted it. Still, it was running. She only needed to reconnect the cable.

The cypress branch had broken when it fell; it was bent in the middle, draped over the generator's crankcase. Though it was thick, long, and heavy-looking, Rachel thought she could lift it. But as she stepped forward, the branch began to move of its own accord, and, twisting about, it turned toward her. A pair of hooded, glassy eyes glinted in the moonlight.

Her mind was remarkably clear. The alligator, she reasoned, had been drawn to the generator by the engine's warmth, or perhaps the vibrations of the machinery had attracted it. Maybe the screeching of the ball bearings really did sound like baby alligators. Rachel had assumed Leroy said that to be funny; she hadn't thought he truly knew what a nest full of baby alligators sounded like. She wondered how he knew.

Or perhaps, Rachel reflected further, the alligator climbed up on the crankcase simply because it wanted to, and it had never had any reason not to do exactly what it felt like doing. It was easily twice as long as she was tall, and probably had not been told no very often.

A sudden memory flooded through her, of a museum she had visited with her uncle when she was a child. She remembered how, in a dark room where her footsteps had echoed loudly, she had walked inside the skeleton of some huge prehistoric beast. Eons ago it had lain down in the ooze to die, and slowly turned into a perfect cathedral of petrified bone. She remembered gazing up at the long ridge of its spine high over her head, its ribs like girders arching down to embrace her. Her uncle had asked her if she was scared, but she hadn't been. She was not scared now. She was at home inside the darkness, walking freely through it, running her fingertips along the bones of the night.

She and the creature stood watching each other until the alligator opened its jaws and emitted a hiss, like a steam valve opening in a piece of heavy machinery. The thin white light from the moon shone in small squares along its back; long curves of moonlight marked the claws on its feet. Its teeth were jagged shadows inside its pale, open mouth. It was very still after hissing. Crouched on the crankcase, it could have been carved in stone, a dragon marking the tomb of some medieval knight. Rachel could hear the water lap-ping on the side lawn down the hill as she and the alligator faced each other.

If she had a light, she thought, she might shine it in the alligator's eyes, and blind it long enough to get away, but she had no light. If she ran back into the hospital, would the animal follow her? How fast could an alligator move? She wasn't sure, and she didn't like the idea of finding out by racing one. She could shout for help, but the generator was noisy, and had been purposely placed far away from the main building to keep its noise and fumes from bothering the patients. Besides, the alligator might not like her shouting.

As if to confirm this suspicion, the alligator hissed again, and snapped its jaws shut, precise and malignant. It made a muscular gulping sound deep in its throat: *glunk*. It was irritated. It had come to kill nestlings, and having found nothing to kill, was at loose ends. There it sat, a brooding menace atop the all-important generator, with the moonlight etching the imbrication of its scales. Rachel watched it stretch its jaws wide again, and rise up on root-like legs as if filling itself with air.

And then it began to slide balefully toward her, dragging its armored bulk across the generator, the scales on its stomach producing a dry, lethal hiss as they scraped on the metal. Rachel, backing up cautiously, felt something hard beneath her foot. Carefully, keeping her eyes on the alligator, she stooped and groped for it. A rib, her memory told her, but then her hands said no: It was an old oar from one of the rowboats they had moved up to the garage when the boathouse flooded. Her fingers closed around it, tightening, and she lifted it from the grass. The animal, now halfway off the generator, stopped its progress. It did not seem to do this for any reason. It simply was not moving at the moment.

The generator chugged blithely on, sending its power into the backup battery that squatted next to it on the platform. In the moonlight, Rachel could see the cable that linked the generator and battery standing up in a short curve like the handle on a lady's purse. She thought about the power surging through that cable from the generator into the battery; deadly power, shielded by a fraction of an inch of rubber insulation. Enough power to light the hospital, run respirators, chill blood and warm infants. She thought too about the alligator's jaws, and the power in them—power for crushing, for tearing and drowning and pulling living creatures into that smooth ghastly pink tunnel of throat. She thought of the chickens whose absence Patty had noticed.

Rachel felt bad, in a way, for the alligator, though she felt worse for the chickens. The alligator was only doing what it was born to do, and all it could do was destroy. It was driven to engulf, to drag life down into the dark.

Slowly, deliberately, Rachel stretched out the oar, offering it up to the creature like bait. The alligator remained motionless until the oar neared its head. Then it lunged and snapped at the wood, spraying splinters and almost wrenching the oar from Rachel's grasp. She was surprised by the force of it, but only a little, and she held on, letting the alligator keep the oar clenched in its jaws until it chose to spit it out. When it did, she slid a few steps to the left, circling the platform in the direction of the battery cable.

The alligator turned too, following her and the oar with open jaws until Rachel smacked it sharply on the snout. It retaliated by whipping its head around in an arc, trying to catch and crush the oar. But Rachel was too quick, and snatched her weapon back out of reach. The alligator, frustrated, slid further off the generator and turned to face her again.

She was inside the remains of the shed now, moving toward the back corner, with the alligator between her and the open air. She goaded it, again jabbing at its head, and this time it lunged toward her, between the generator and battery. It was too big to get through, and its body slammed up against the metal with a dull thump. It looked at her out of one bloodthirsty, incurious eye.

Rachel took a deep breath, tapped the splintered end of the oar tauntingly against the alligator's chin, and dropped it squarely on the short loop of the battery cable. The animal's jaws followed the oar, caught it as it landed on the cable, and clamped shut over both.

There was a crack, a flash, and a dry, chemical smell—the beast's legs jerked and for an instant Rachel thought it was going to leap at her. And then silence. The generator was still; the alligator was still too. A faint trace of smoke unreeled from its half-open mouth.

Rachel waited for what seemed a long time. Finally, the silence of the generator stirred her to action. They would be wondering, inside, what was keeping her, and why the lights were still off. She had let go of the oar when the alligator bit down on it, and it had fallen onto the platform. She recovered it and prodded the beast with it. It did not move. She tapped at its eyes—nothing. An overpowering smell of scorching began to rise from its body.

She turned off the generator at the main switch, being careful not to touch the alligator, careful not to get her feet wet. She found a new cable to reconnect the battery, and did so, leaving the alligator wedged where it was, with the old cable hanging from its jaws. The output line to the main building wasn't hard to reconnect. The breaker had blown, of course, and that must be reset. Finally, holding her breath, she pulled the generator's main switch. The machine rumbled into life instantly. Up the hill, lights flashed on in the windows. Rachel took a last look at the alligator, and walked toward the lights.

She still works the night shift as much as possible. And before the lights are dimmed for the night, the children ask her to tell them the story of how she fought the alligator, in the dark, on the night the power went out. She always answers that she'll tell them, if they promise to go right to sleep afterwards. When they are asleep, she walks the hallways and feels the night breathing around her, its bones laid down in the past, resurrected now, standing guard over them all.

ONE NIGHT IN BROWNSVILLE

Gary Phillips

Brownsville, Texas is landlocked. But in the southern corner of this border city, known for the infamous railroading of black infantrymen in the Brownsville Affair of 1906, there is a seventeen mile channel that empties into the Gulf of Mexico. Barges moving large mounds of scrapped steel and iron derived from ships motor regularly along that channel. Belo Resources is among the five ship-breaking facilities dispersed toward the terminus of the channel. Ship breaking is the major economic engine of Brownsville.

These days the politically correct, media massaging term Ernesto "Ernie" Carraja and the other workers at Belo have been taught to say was ship recycling. Even in the red meat state of Texas, there was some notion of being seen as environmentally conscious as long as it didn't undercut profits. Though his bosses, including Whit Barrison, would guffaw at placating them tree hugging tofu lovers as symbolized by the populace in the state capital, the blue city of Austin. Yet ironically Belo had recently been sold to a Silicon Valley, green type named Noel Komsky who also owned among other holdings, a professional soccer team.

Working on a skeletal third shift past one in the morning, Carraja reflected on these matters as he used his oxyacetylene torch to finish cutting through the hinges of a floor safe welded to the deck. He was in what had been the captain's quarters of a decommissioned Merchant Marine freighter called the SS *Hugh Mulzac*. Carraja turned the valve on the torch off, killing the flame and set the apparatus aside. He also removed his blackened cowhide gloves.

A warm breeze blew across his face as he lifted the goggles off his eyes to inspect the results. Deftly using a pry bar, he inserted the chisel end in the gap between the safe's door and frame. He grunted with exertion and popped the door off. It thudded heavily to the deck.

"Nice work," a voice said in Spanish.

A surprised Carraja stared at the newcomer. He was dressed in dark workingman's clothes, thick soled shoes, and a ribbed mask over his face with only a cutout for eyes. Held in one of his large gloved hands was some kind of compact dull-finished weapon. The armed man stomped on the two-way radio the workers used for communicating in the ship. Carraja had left his on a built-in shelf by the hatch.

The man's lanky form was framed in the doorway to the quarters, lit by lights strung along the upper portions of the bulkhead. He stepped further inside. Sweat coated the part of his face visible inside his mask.

"What do you want?" Carraja said in English. His words came out harsher than he meant.

The intruder pointed with the extended barrel of his weapon. "That."

Carraja looked into the safe. Inside were two stacks of money, bound with rubber bands at intervals, and a metal box about the size of two shoe boxes lashed together. It wasn't unusual to take apart safes on ships; everything was readied for the smelter. But he'd been given specific instructions by his immediate boss Barrison. Anything he found in the safe, don't tell the others on the crew and turn the contents over to him. But a man with a gun over-rode any such order. He bent to remove the cash and box and hand them over.

"Fucker..." a man's curse echoed from within the freighter. Whatever else he was going to say was interrupted by a burst of what momentarily Carraja took for loud, angry wasps. He then realized why the intruder's gun had a long barrel. There was a silencer screwed into the end of it to dampen the sound of gunfire.

• • •

"Shit," a masked O'Conner cursed, quickly pivoting from the welder about to hand over the goods. His next motion was to shoot out the row of overhead lights.

In a sibilant tone he commanded, "Slide your cell phone to me."

Carraja didn't protest. He took his smartphone out of his pants pocket and did so.

"If I were you, I wouldn't leave this room just yet," the robber said. "In fact you might want to close the door and latch it shut."

"Okay," came the worker's reply in the half-gloom. There were electric lights on stands on the sandy ground outside the ship illuminating portions of the rusting hulk. Some of that light filtered through the missing sections of the hull.

O'Conner moved off silently. Behind him he heard the door, hatch, whatever the hell they called them on boats, hiss closed. He speculated about what had gone wrong, while foremost concentrating on staying alive and eliminating the threat. He didn't think any of the bound workers had gotten loose.

The corridor was dark enough though there were patches of spilled light. O'Conner undid the strap on the Ingram and lashed the weapon about his torso, freeing his hands but keeping the assault rifle in easy reach. He went forward, listening and breathing shallowly. Nothing. He was almost at the end, having ducked below a row of glassless portholes. The hatch here was open and led onto a lighted corridor, perpendicular to the one he was in. Finger on the Ingram's trigger, he took a chance and looked out, left, right, then pulled back in. Again no sound or sensation of another's presence.

When the four of them had descended on the beached freighter, they knew there would just be seven at work this early morning. The four thieves knew there'd only be one of the seven tasked with the safe. Maybe he was even promised a cut.

"The first week they get a ship in," Starks had said, "involves pumping out the oil, diesel residue and whatever other sludge is in the ship." They were in the Kris Kristofferson suite at the Baystar, a refurbished 1920s-era brick hotel overlooking Sunrise Boulevard in Brownsville. Singer-actor Kristofferson was a lauded native son.

Starks tapped a finger on the blueprint unfurled before them on the table, anchored on its edges by various objects including a .38 Special snub nose revolver. "Holes are cut out of the sides to let in air and light, some of the bulkheads and portions of the bow are also removed then them boys go to town."

"Aren't these hombres gonna be scattered all over the ship stripping it apart?" Henson asked. "How do we know we got them rounded up and accounted for?"

Starks smiled, exposing a yellowed bicuspid. "They don't usually authorize a third shift. Whit has the other six on to cover the real reason, his man down in the captain's cabin. Once he's done, and taken care of how he's supposed to deal with the box, they're supposed to knock off.

"Anyway, the way it works is, they move through together, probably be bunched mid-ship."

"Probably?" Henson interjected.

"Even if they aren't," Starks said, drawing out each word slowly, "that's why there's four of us in case we need to fan out quickly and gather up the flock."

He smiled, pleased with his simile.

Drayton, who'd brought O'Conner in on the job, observed, "Even before you get your cherry popped down in these parts they hand you a gun. Some of them boys might be packin'."

"Don't you worry," Starks replied, "we'll have us some serious heat."

Hanson and Drayton seemed satisfied. O'Conner had more questions and asked them.

Too bad he hadn't acted on his instincts and shot Starks when it crossed his mind earlier tonight, O'Conner regretted. He was certain Starks was the problem. The closer they'd gotten to pulling the job, the more solicitous he'd become. Never a good sign in a thief. Back at the portholes he looked out but saw no figures on the ground, only the looming shadows of the piles of scrap and the marsh area beyond where'd they'd parked their vehicles. The metal was grouped ferrous and non-ferrous, Starks had told them.

Having no choice, O'Conner moved further into the ship. What he hoped was that Starks would figure he had the box and would try and escape with it. He needed to keep him away from where it really was. He came to some metal rungs set in the corridor and ascended. He paused just below an opening and slowly came up. O'Conner stared into the vacant eyes of Henson. His masked corpse lay at the edge of the hatchway in the deck, sideways in the corridor. The hatch had been removed. O'Conner knew it was Henson from his linebacker build going soft. His torso had stopped leaking blood when his heart had given out. Henson's weapon lay near him, minus its clip.

About to push the body out of the way, O'Conner's hand froze in place. He frowned, withdrew his hand and leveraged himself through the opening without disturbing the body. He stepped over Henson and taking a knee, examined the body, using the confiscated smartphone for light. Sure enough, Starks had booby-trapped the body.

Preoccupied, O'Conner inadvertently touched another part of the phone's screen and an image sprang onto it. The picture was the welder with two young children, girls, seven and nine he estimated. All of them smiling. He put the phone away, making sure the ringer was off.

Starks had lodged a flash-bang grenade in the dead man's armpit. The pin was pulled. The cylindrical device gave off heat, light and sound in a five foot radius, causing temporary blindness and deafness. Apparently Starks had come better armed than the rest, O'Conner concluded. Moving the body would have jostled the thing, causing the lever to release and the thing would have gone off. It wouldn't kill him, but was designed to disorient the target.

O'Conner removed the device, keeping the release lever depressed. He took out one of Henson's boot laces and wound this around the mini-canister to secure the release. He crept forward with it. Starks had to be nearby to hear the blast and no doubt spring from hiding. He wouldn't want to waste time. Probably planned to wound O'Conner, then grind the barrel of his Ingram into the ragged hole to make him tell where the box was. That's how he would have done it, O'Conner assessed.

The end of the passageway let out into yet another corridor. Here the dismantling of the ship was evident, large sections had been cut away. Gaping holes looked into stripped rooms or dark metal caverns. In this area there was only one light, halfway down, overhead in the center. Close to where he stood was still intact. There was a hatch on either side of the hallway. Starks had to be in one of the rooms, ready to rush out for his reward. O'Conner meant to oblige him.

But before he could toss the grenade behind him, Drayton appeared at the other end of the honeycombed passageway. He had his mask off. He was pale as bleached linen but held onto his Ingram. O'Conner drew back into shadow. The wounded man came forward on unsteady legs. His side glistened wetly. Starks hadn't put him away as he had Henson.

O'Conner watched, tucking the confiscated grenade into his back pocket. Drayton paused, gathered himself, and went forward again. He also knew or suspected that Starks was behind one of the hatches ahead. He was only going to have one chance to get it right. As he got closer, O'Conner could see a small, tight smile on the other man's face. Stopping again, Drayton grimaced as he bent over. He straightened up holding several small, odd-shaped sheets of loose sheeting in one hand. He threw these along the corridor and screamed in pain.

The hatch to the right cracked open on surprisingly quiet hinges. Drayton waited. O'Conner waited. The hatch opened more. From the angle where he was, the hatch blocked Drayton's vision. But from where he was hidden, O'Conner could see it was Starks. He was still partly inside the recess, his body not yet a prime target. He would be very soon for a ready O'Conner.

But Drayton got anxious. Must be wearing out fast, O'Conner surmised. The wounded man unleashed a volley, figuring to at least to strike Stark's lower extremities exposed beneath the edge of the hatch.

The hatch slapped back with a clang. From the recess of the hatchway Starks emptied bullets into Drayton. His body jiggled and jerked from the impact of the high velocity rounds ripping blood trails through him. Just as quickly the suppressed gunfire stopped, and Drayton's corpse collapsed onto the deck like he was boneless.

O'Conner would have to chance stepping out to get the shot. He did so but Starks was keyed up now, sensing the other man was nearby. He fired at

O'Conner, falling back into the hatchway. O'Conner had also dropped back and wasn't hit. He couldn't chance Starks out-maneuvering him and getting back to the captain's cabin. Mouth compressed tightly, he strode to the open hatchway. There was blood on the deck near it. Drayton had gotten a piece of Starks. O'Conner went through.

This was a short passageway and the only way out was up to the main deck. O'Conner proceeded slowly up a set of iron steps, the night sky above the opening. There were drops of blood on the steps. Just as he was about to stick his head out it occurred to O'Conner where Starks was. O'Conner had also studied the ship's plans. Toward the rear of the freighter, aft was it?—was another way to the captain's cabin. Hurriedly he reversed his course.

Too late O'Conner got back to the darkened corridor outside the once captain's quarters. He could tell the hatch was open and he heard cursing. He slowed. There was a light shining from within the room that snapped off. Assault weapon lashed around him, O'Conner put his back against the bulkhead and inched forward in the near dark. He froze. He'd heard a rustle of clothing. O'Conner lay on the decking and slid forward, his Ingram held GI-fashion as he used his elbows for propulsion.

Starks' gun erupted, spitting rounds into the corridor in a sweep it seemed to O'Conner. Pinging ricochets echoed off the metal, some near the still, prone man. The suppressor eliminated any gun flash so Starks' location in the room was still not certain. But the safe would be the best place to hunker behind, O'Conner reasoned. It got quiet again.

Crouching, he unwound the boot laces, and tossed underhanded the flash-bang grenade he'd taken off Henson's body into the cabin. He aimed it where he remembered the safe was located. O'Conner averted eyes as it went off with a boom, intense white light flooding the room. Starks bellowed and fired his weapon blindly.

"Think you're clever?" he challenged, shooting impotently again.

O'Conner squinted as the light started to fade. He zeroed in on a mass taking shape in the bright essence and fired his Ingram. There was a clatter and more cursing. The light subsided but O'Conner used the smartphone again. Starks stood blinking at the side of the safe, a hand to the blood spreading across his upper torso. The Ingram was at his feet.

"Fuck you," he growled at O'Conner.

The last robber standing pumped bullets into Starks' heart. The double-crosser's body folded in on itself as he dropped to the deck. O'Conner saw what Starks had seen: the torch man had managed to weld the safe's door partly back in place.

"I figured I could run," Ernie Carraja said behind him.

O'Conner turned, gun barrel first, the light from the phone illuminating the worker.

"Hoping you'd leave. I could maybe sneak back and keep the money for myself, say you took it." He looked wistful then continued. "But one of you, whichever one was left alive, would come after me and what good would that be?"

"Get the safe open," O'Conner said.

Carraja put a portable light and stand in place and soon had the safe's door off again. He took out the two stacks and the black metal box, and set them on the deck.

O'Conner picked up the box and cradled one of the stacks in the crook of his arm. "The others are on the middle deck, toward the front of this tub. Alive and tied up. One of them has a goose egg behind his ear, another one a sore jaw."

Carraja couldn't take his eyes off the untouched stack. Were all the bills hundreds?

"You might want to hide that somewhere before you call the cops." O'Conner lingered in the doorway, crinkles flashing at the edges of his eyes framed in the mask's opening. He pivoted about and left.

O'Conner didn't return to the Baystar. The suite and the adjoining one had been secured under a false name and credit card with money behind it in that name. But when the police conducted their investigation, four supposed out-of-town businessmen commanding those rooms were likely to raise suspicions, particularly if only one of them returned in the wee hours.

He drove the older model Corolla used for the job an hour inland toward McAllen. O'Conner stopped once to buy and eat a fried chicken sandwich with waffle fries at an all-night knock-off Chick-fil-A. Afterward, he paid cash for a room at a highway motel called the Skyview. Several eighteen wheelers were parked on the wide expanse of gravel fronting the check-in office.

In the room he forced open the metal box and stared at what was inside. Starks, who'd set up the score, had said this was supposed to be about smuggled diamonds. What O'Conner held was an old notebook of some sort. The item was leather bound, stuffed with loose pages. From one of the nearby rooms, a plaintive *narcocorrido* about drug lord El Chapo Guzman played low. He leafed through the diary, an eyebrow going up now and then as he skimmed the entries, written in precise, block lettering. There were also diagrams, formulas and sketches of pigeons as well.

He unfolded a loose sheaf of onionskin paper taped together to make an 11 by 17 inch sheet. It was a drawing of some sort of a futuristic-looking tower, notations festooning the paper. There was a name for this thing printed in that precise lettering. It was a name O'Conner recognized primarily as that of a boutique car company. But he knew too it was the name of a person, a historical figure.

"Hmmm," he mused, leaning back from the tiny desk he sat at in the cheap wood-paneled room. Folding his arms, he stared blankly at the framed image over the desk, a velvet painting of a beaming Shaquille O'Neal riding a unicycle while juggling basketballs shaped like skulls. O'Conner twisted off the cap of the plastic pint bottle of vodka he had with him and took a sip . . . then another.

• • •

Whit Barrison paced as he smoked in front of the public bathroom at Boca Chica beach east of Brownsville. Families were out on the sand and in the water enjoying themselves. Lying on the sidewalk at the corner of the men's room, the women's was on the other side of the squat structure, was a greasy sleeping bag, sans homeless occupant. He eyed this hostilely and not for the first time since his wait began three cigarettes ago. He looked around at the scrape of footsteps onto the concrete pad.

"You Barrison?" the newcomer asked. He was over six feet, close cropped hair with grey creeping in at the temples.

"What if I am?"

"I hear you want a job done."

"You a cop? You wearing a wire?"

The other man lifted his shirt to show a reasonable set of abs. "We can go inside there and you can feel me all over if you like," he intoned. "Get frisky and shit." His expression was flat, devoid of emotion.

Barrison developed a sour look as he stubbed his cigarette out. "No, that's okay."

"Word is you're offering a finder's fee for locating this guy, this guy who was part of a string you put together to take down some swag from a junked boat."

"Freighter," Barrison corrected.

"You work for the outfit, right? The ones handling the freighter."

Barrison swatted at a mosquito buzzing his face. "That's not your concern."

"You got a lead on this guy?"

"Something like that. I know. My source told me he lives in California."

"L.A.?"

"No. Someplace they call Riverside. He plays at being Mister Suburbs."

"You know all that, why don't you go get him yourself?"

"I don't do that." He made it sound as indignant as he felt.

"You want the goods back. No matter what it takes."

"Yes."

"What if I go get this guy, and keep what I get for myself?"

"You might find some cash, but that's peanuts compared to the thing you need to retrieve. A diary."

The stranger smirked. "You one of those weird dudes into My Little Pony? This some kind of collector's item?"

"You're a regular Kevin Hart aren't you?" Barrison considered another smoke but didn't take his pack out. "This diary, this journal, it's one of a kind. Look, I'll front you five thou for expenses and I guarantee you a sweet payday if you get it back." He added, "If it means you take care of this guy, this O'Conner, there's a bonus in it for you."

"That's what you and Starks worked out was it?"

The ruthless glint in his eyes evaporated as his jaw became unhinged. Barrison realized who the stranger was.

"A three-way split? Starks do the heavy lifting. Recruit the crew, knowing all the time you two would stiff us?"

Barrison spread a hand before him. "Goddammit, O'Conner, it wasn't my idea to do a double-cross on top of ripping off the—" He caught himself. He wasn't going to give that name away.

"Look that shit was Dickie's doing. He got greedy. I've got the connection to realize real money for that journal. We can be partners on this, okay?"

"No. You're a liability." He'd removed the pistol with the suppressor tucked behind his back in his waistband. He grouped two into Barrison's chest. The routing manager of Belo Resources exhaled loudly, stumbling forward. O'Conner caught him and eased him down into the sleeping bag. He left the dead man wrapped up beside the restroom. Back in the Corolla, he drove west on Highway 4 from Boca Chica and on through Brownsville. Along the way, he rubbed off the dry rubber cement-like coating he'd put on his fingertips to obscure his prints.

• • •

Noel Komsky severed the call. What a relief. At first with the dead robbers at his Belo facility he was worried what Barrison might say to the authorities. After all, one of the deceased, Starks, had a record and was Barrison's brother-in-law or some kind of relation, however they constituted family in Texas. He'd gone to Barrison in good faith when he'd come out here to Seattle for a mini-retreat. Komsky knew about Barrison's background—the information gleaned from the kind of research he routinely had done on new personnel when making an acquisition.

The only way to get a decommissioned government ship for recycling was to be on their approved facilities list. They weren't sent overseas to places such as Chittagong in Bangladesh for cheaper costs as private ships were allowed to do.

Belo Resources was on the list. It had taken years and money, heartache and hope, but Komsky finally had a line on Nikola Tesla's fabled Journal of Speculation and Formulations. The one in which over the years he had documented in meticulous notes, schematics and the like his greatest concepts from intergalactic radio to workable lasers powered by gold, no larger than a baseball. And who knew what all else. For geeked out techies it was the Holy Grail—let alone those ideas might garner billions.

Tesla died in 1943, living modestly off his patents unlike his rival Thomas Edison, a ruthless self-promoter, who had amassed millions. The papers the electrical genius left behind in trunks in hotel rooms were seized and secreted away by the Office of Alien Property at the behest of J. Edgar Hoover. This despite Tesla being a naturalized U.S. citizen.

For decades it was believed the journal was among the confiscated papers. Turned out it wasn't. Where had it been and who had hidden it, no one really could say. But once that was known, fraudulent versions surfaced but were invariably dismissed. Until this one that Komsky had gotten a line on through intermediaries, one of whom had the wherewithal to bestow a tentative authentication on the item based on photographs of some of its contents. For through whatever series of circumstances, involving murder and double crosses Komsky was certain, the artifact had wound up in the safe of the *Mulzac*.

Now Barrison was dead as well. No doubt at the hands of the thief who'd gotten out alive that night. The good news for Komsky was Barrison, under suspicion by the cops, couldn't talk. The bad news was the journal was now nowhere near his grasp to be physically examined, and in the possession of that thief.

If he didn't know exactly what he had, he knew it had worth. The thief would certainly find out what it was and determine its worth in certain circles. Would the thief contact him and demand a sizeable ransom, Komsky wondered. Or what if he offered the journal to another party? He stood at a window overlooking a typical drizzly day in Seattle. He sipped on his wheat grass smoothie as he contemplated the journal's fate.

• • •

Ernie Carraja lifted his goggles to inspect his work. He and the other six had been questioned by the police. He'd made sure to cut away his welds from the safe door before that. It was plausible to explain the masked man putting a scary-looking gun on him and making off with the cash and metal box. But trying to explain sealing the safe then taking off the door again, that would point to him as an accomplice. Now Barrison was not a worry. He must have been in on it too, Carraja guessed.

Well, he had no plans to buy a fancy car or blow the money on big breasted strippers. Though such notions were tempting. It was over $40,000, not really enough to run away for long on anyway. But enough to make a size-able down payment on his girls' college fund. For a moment, he regarded a plaque riveted to a bulkhead done in brass relief. It was a portrait of the man the ship was named for, Captain Hugh Mulzac. Those determined eyes looking back at him reminded Carraja of that robber's steely glare. He shook off the feeling and slipped his goggles back into place. He cut through the plaque as he resumed dismantling the ship.

SILVERFISH

SJ Rozan

"What kind of a fish is that, anyway?"

"What?"

"A silverfish. Is it like all silvery?"

Silverfish blew out a breath and tried to be patient. You had to be patient with Lady Mary. "Not a fish. It's a bug."

Lady Mary giggled. "You call yourself after a bug?" She checked her lip-gloss once more and snapped her mirror away. "Must be a pretty bug."

"It's ugly. Lots of legs and it slithers."

"Then why—"

"'Cause of my hair."

Lady Mary didn't say anything but Silverfish watched her blue eyes fill with doubt. Well, good. Silverfish's natural hair was brown, just like Lady Mary's. She wore it short, spiked and silver, but that was a choice, not something you're stuck with and have to do your best about, like name yourself after. Silverfish had come into the life three years ago at the same age Lady Mary was now—thirteen—but she knew for a fact she'd never been as naïve, as just plain street-dumb, as this kid. If Lady Mary didn't wise up and stop believing everything people told her she'd never survive.

Though if she stayed with that damn pimp of hers, she might not survive anyway.

"Your pimp calls himself after a bug, too," she pointed out as she and Lady Mary left the gas station bathroom. "A disgusting one. Ick."

Lady Mary giggled again. "I know. And it's so funny, because of how he hates dirt so much. I kinda think he should call himself, like, Clorox or something."

All the girls in this part of town knew that: how Roach made his girls shower the minute they came in from the stroll, and he was always making them scrub the bathroom and the kitchen—even though he wouldn't eat anywhere but his own place—and wash their clothes and dry-clean them. And he didn't pay for it, either. Funny he ever laid a finger on them, if he thought they were so disgusting dirty. Funny he was even in this business.

Roach was Lady Mary's big mistake. He picked her up just a week after she hit the streets. That was before Silverfish knew her, or she'd have brought her right away to Jacky-boy. If you had to have a pimp—and in this dump of a town you did; it was too dangerous to work alone, when you were young and skinny like Silverfish and Lady Mary—but if you had to, Jacky-boy was all right. He liked his girls to stay clean, too, but he wasn't loony-tunes about it, and anyway it was mostly so johns wouldn't be grossed out. The apartment was okay, a two-bedroom with just three girls to a room, each with a real bed and they had video games, a DVD and an account at the pizza place and the Chinese, they could order whatever they wanted and Jacky-boy covered it. He didn't go through your stuff and he didn't make you work when you were sick and he never raised a hand to you.

Not like Roach. Roach owned his girls in a different way. He wanted to know everything about them, where they went, who they talked to. He pawed through their purses sometimes, their closets, just to see. And Roach smacked his girls around. When Lady Mary first came on the scene, Silverfish thought that even small and eager to please like she was it could only be a matter of time. And she was right: a month ago Lady Mary showed up on the corner with thick heavy makeup around her eye that hid the bruise but not the swelling. It had happened another time since then, too. And it would keep happening, Silverfish knew. She thought about this as Lady Mary sashayed away. It would keep happening, and Lady Mary would stop giggling and get all hard on the inside. And all Silverfish could think to do was stand there and watch.

• • •

After the gas station bathroom, Silverfish didn't see Lady Mary again for three days. When she did it wasn't good.

"Tell me some wackjob john did that to you."

Lady Mary just shrugged, not meeting Silverfish's gaze.

"It was Roach, right?"

Another shrug.

"How you gonna work, your lip all split like that?"

"Some guys like that."

"Yeah, and you don't want to go with those guys. They just want to give you more. What did you do?"

In a tiny voice: "Gave him lip. So he gave me a lip. See?" Lady Mary tried a giggle but it fell down and died.

"You? You don't give anybody lip."

"I don't know. I laughed, he wasn't feeling funny. I don't know."

"Okay, don't tell me, see if I care. Oh, hey, girl! You're not crying, are you?"

"Me? No, just something in my eye," said Lady Mary, all sniffly.

"Come here." Silverfish pulled Lady Mary close to her and hugged her.

"I don't *know* what I did wrong, Fish. I never do with Roach. I try to do everything he says. I do everything he tells the other girls, too. But some-times he just hauls off—I guess I laugh too much, he doesn't think I take him serious. But then he makes a joke and I don't know if it's okay to laugh and he thinks I'm all, like, stuck-up. I don't *know*. I don't *know*."

"Okay. Hey. Stop! Don't get all hysterical or I'm gonna have to slap you myself."

Lady Mary looked up in genuine fear. "You would?"

"No, of course I wouldn't. Damn, girl, he's making a basket case out of you."

"No. I just need to figure out what I'm supposed to do. That's all. Just figure it out. Listen, I gotta get going. If I don't turn lots of tricks tonight I'm screwed." The giggle suddenly bubbled up; it made Silverfish smile. Lady Mary said, "And I guess if I do, I'm screwed, too, huh?"

• • •

Sometimes Silverfish wondered why she was mostly right about stuff she wouldn't mind if she was wrong about. She'd been right about Roach beating up on Lady Mary sooner or later, and the next time she saw Lady Mary it proved she was right about tricks who like messed-up girls.

"It was a john," Lady Mary said fast before Silverfish could start. "Asshole. Said he could tell I was his kind of girl because I liked it the same way he did. I told him I didn't like it and he asked then how come I was working with a face like that, and he liked it even better when the girl pretended she hated it." Lady Mary lisped this out; the john had done a job on her. "Paid good, though."

"I can't believe Roach is making you work like that. Couple of times that happened to me, Jacky-boy said take a day off, take a rest."

"Roach likes it. Says I'm too small and skinny to be worth much but if I have, like, a specialty, I'm worth a lot more."

"You're kidding. He *wants* jerks to do that shit to you? Jacky-boy would kill anyone he found doing something like that to one of his girls."

"Yeah?" Lady Mary looked wistful. "I think if Roach caught him he'd just charge him double."

• • •

Silverfish didn't have a good night. The weather was rainy, not one of those cold nights where you'd give anything for indoor work, but rainy enough so most johns stayed home. Silverfish never got that. It was all about their cars or a mildewy room at the River Motel, not like they were doing it on the sidewalk, so why these jerks disappeared when it rained she never knew. But johns were a mystery to her anyway. She was glad they existed, sure. After her mom shacked up with that hundredth bastard boyfriend, the one she picked up in the 7-11, and Silverfish had to get out, how else was she going to make a living? But as long as the world was full of women like her mom, why did any man, anywhere, ever have to pay for it?

And then there were idiots like her last trick tonight. She thought about him while the sky faded to gray and she walked slowly home. This guy, how stupid was he? What was funny, he even knew how stupid he was, and he kept talking about it with himself. First thing, after they got past the price and all that, him still leaning out his car window: "So, sweetheart, you clean?"

"Just took a shower, hon. You're my first tonight." She said it even though it was a lie and even though she knew that wasn't what he meant. But she was feeling cross and cranky and wanted to jerk this guy around a little, make him say it.

"Yeah, that's nice, but what I mean, you got a certificate?"

"What kind?"

"Jesus, girlie! You have AIDS, or what?"

"Oh, that." Like she was bored, she dug in her purse, pulled out an HIV test card dated four months ago, showing she was negative. Silverfish got tested every six months, and she made the johns use condoms if she could. So her card was real. But the john said, "How do I know that's real?"

"Beats me. It is, though."

"I'm supposed to believe that because a whore tells me?"

"You're not supposed to do anything you don't want to." She started to walk away.

"Hey! C'mon back. I didn't mean anything by it. I'll take your word for it. You look honest. C'mon, you and me, let's go park someplace."

So she got in, and they parked, and he had no imagination so it was a pretty easy trick, and now she was walking home, thinking about how even though her card was real she had no way to prove it to him, and he knew that, and he didn't want to take a whore's word for it but in the end he did because he said she looked honest. Herself, she'd have thought the silver hair might be a tip-off that some things about her may not be on the up-and-up. But it wasn't about how she looked, silver or honest or anything else. It was about him wanting to get laid. So he believed what worked for him.

She narrowed her eyes when that thought came to her. He believed what worked for him.

• • •

A couple days later she asked Jacky-boy if he'd have taken Lady Mary on if he'd seen her before Roach.

"Well, sure." Jacky-boy leaned forward on the sofa and helped himself to a slice from the pizza she and Rainbow had ordered. Silverfish was annoyed because the slice was off her half, the anchovy half, but she didn't say anything. Rainbow winked at Silverfish and reached for a pepper slice. She was resourceful, Rainbow. When she found out Jacky-boy hated peppers she started always getting peppers on her half, in case he showed up while they were eating. Silverfish had considered adopting that strategy, but she didn't particularly like peppers herself.

"And if she was on her own now?" Silverfish persisted.

"I guess," Jacky-boy said. "She's little and she's cute, except if she keeps getting beat up on like she is, she's not gonna be cute long. But Fish, honey, I know you're not asking me to mess with Roach? He's a shit and I'd love to see him go down but I'm not in that business."

"But if Roach threw her out?"

"Can't see that."

"But if he did?"

Jacky-boy wiped sauce off his mouth. "You have enough school to know about 'hypothetical?' That a word you ever heard?"

Silverfish shook her head.

"Hypothetical's when you're talking about something but it's never gonna happen. Like, you know, snow in July, that's hypothetical. So, in the hypothetical situation where Roach throws her out and doesn't change his freakin' mind the next day, I'd take her on. Rainbow, pass me a Coke."

• • •

"Hey, Rainbow," Silverfish said, casual one morning a few days later, both of them just coming in, no one else home yet, "how come you don't get tested? You and Danielle and Flash?" That wasn't her real question, but sometimes you don't start with your real question.

"What kind of tested?"

"HIV, girl."

"'Cause suppose you HIV and you know it? What you gonna do?"

"I dunno. Get medicine, I guess."

Rainbow stared. "Fish, I never knew you was dumb. They got no medicine for that. You get it, you're good for awhile, years maybe, but then you die. If you know it or you don't know it, it's the same thing."

"But what do you do if a trick asks? I got a card from the clinic says I'm clean, but what do you do? Don't they ask you?"

Rainbow snorted. "Yeah, and just you try asking them one time."

"Yeah, but still. You can't show you're clean, maybe they decide to go with someone else. You lose the trick."

"Jacky-boy give me a card. Danielle and Flash, too. Look just exactly like that one you got, but didn't nobody have to pull blood out my arm for it."

"A fake?"

"Hell-*O*, Fish. Welcome to the world, baby girl."

"You know where he got it?"

"What? The card? Some guy he know downtown."

"You know the guy's name?"

"Uh-uh." Rainbow eyed Silverfish, interested in this sudden new direction. "How come?"

"Well, I got a problem. See, I lost mine."

"So? Tell Jacky-boy. He get you one of these."

Silverfish shook her head. "It's, like, the fourth thing I lost. After my cell phone, and my driver's license, and a little pin he gave me. I don't want him to get all pissed."

"Oh." Rainbow nodded slowly. Because Jacky-boy was so hard to rile, when he finally got mad at a girl he really went off. There was always the danger he'd kick her right out. They all knew that and they were all afraid of it. The time Silverfish lost the cell phone, Jacky-boy blew up at her. All the girls were there when it happened and they all remembered. Being thrown out by your pimp, being damaged goods working these streets unprotected or going with whatever bottom-feeder would take you on after that, was a bleak prospect none of them wanted to face. So Rainbow could be counted on to be sympathetic if Silverfish's big fear was of getting on Jacky-boy's bad side.

"I'm gonna go get tested again," Silverfish said, "but the clinic says they got a waiting list, a month." That wasn't true; for an HIV test the walk-in clinic would take you anytime. But Rainbow wouldn't know that.

Rainbow, always resourceful, said, "I see what I can find out for you."

Silverfish had never had a driver's license and Jacky-boy never gave her a little pin. But Rainbow wouldn't know that, either.

• • •

Two days later Rainbow handed Silverfish a paper with a name and address on it. "He ain't cheap. You need money?"

"Thanks, honey. But I got some saved up."

Jacky-boy gave the girls allowances. Some of them spent it all on shoes and makeup, but Silverfish was careful with hers. She kept herself looking good, of course—the johns had to want you—but her only extravagance was hair dye. She thought about the hair dye, and the care she took with the job she did, and on her way downtown she bought herself a wig.

She explained to the guy downtown what she wanted. It wasn't exactly what he thought she wanted from what Rainbow told him, so Silverfish went through it twice, to make sure he got it. She gave him her cell phone number and, just to be really safe, told him a name to use if he had to call, and a message to leave so he'd sound like a john making a date but she'd know it was him. Jacky-boy had never once messed with her phone—though he'd made her pay for the new one herself after she lost the first one—because she followed the rules, always answering right away when it was his ringtone, even if she was with a trick. And she always told him the truth about where she was, because sometimes he was watching from somewhere and just calling to check up. But still, she gave the guy downtown this secret code. You never knew. A few days later he called, and she went downtown during the day, after Jacky-boy had come by the apartment and already left. She was supposed to be sleeping, and she knew she'd be tired when she went to work that night, but she'd feel much better with the guy's papers in her purse.

• • •

The next time Silverfish saw Lady Mary, the girl looked good and she was cheerful and giggly, like before. They talked about just stuff: eyeliner, and whether they'd stay married to A-Rod even if he cheated on them—which they both would, it was a total no-brainer, a guy with that much money? And what guy didn't cheat, come on, who cared?—and then a car slowed down for Silverfish ("Hey, kid! You, with the hair!") and they said goodnight.

The time after that was pretty much the same, just her and Lady Mary, talking trash. But Silverfish was used to being right about bad stuff by now, and the next time, Lady Mary's eye was swollen and the eyebrow had a big Band-Aid.

"What happened this time? Hey, girl, don't look at the sidewalk, it didn't ask you a question. What did you do, give Roach more lip?"

In a whisper, Lady Mary said, "I didn't do anything."

"You mean you don't know?"

"No. I mean, I really didn't do anything. He says I do better business when I'm messed up."

Silverfish stared. "He did that to you on purpose for no reason? Just so you could get dates with those kind of jerks?"

Eyes brimming, Lady Mary nodded. A tear leaked from the swollen eye, dragging mascara down the side of her nose, but she didn't seem to notice.

"Girl," said Silverfish, "we got to talk."

"I can't," Lady Mary gulped, digging in her purse for a tissue. "I better get to work."

"A quick cup of coffee. Come on." Silverfish grabbed Lady Mary's arm and pulled her along the sidewalk.

"Oh, what's the point, Fish?" Lady Mary wailed. "There's nothing I can do. What can I do? It's gotta be like this. Let me go to work or he'll be mad."

"You can't work with your mascara all running. Come on. Just quick." She didn't let go. Tugging Lady Mary into the diner, she sat her down. Silverfish unzipped her purse. "It's on me."

• • •

Silverfish took Lady Mary for coffee three more times over the next couple of weeks. The third time, Lady Mary had a loose tooth and was kind of hunched over. She didn't say a word until she'd let her coffee cool to where she could drink it past the tooth. She finished it, and then sat there for awhile.

"I can't do this anymore, Fish," was all she had to say.

• • •

The next time Silverfish saw Lady Mary it was bright daylight and the girl was a mess. Silverfish woke up because her cell phone was ringing. The song was "Bustin' Loose" and it was the ringtone she'd given to Lady Mary.

"Where are you?"

"The diner."

Silverfish could hear the trembling in Lady Mary's words. "Stay there."

Silverfish got dressed and rushed out. To Danielle, who woke up and asked what was going on, she said, "Sorry! Go back to sleep." To Rainbow, making eggs in the kitchen, she said, "Be right back," and closed the door on whatever else Rainbow said.

• • •

Silverfish came back an hour later with two dozen doughnuts and Lady Mary. All the girls except Danielle were up. *Iron Chef America* was on TV, everyone cheering for the challenger because he was much hotter than the Iron Chef. They all looked up when Silverfish and Lady Mary came in.

"Here." Silverfish put the doughnut box on the coffee table, cockeyed on a shapeless pile of magazines. "I saw those eggs Rainbow was working on before, so I thought you guys might want some real food. This is Lady Mary. She's a friend of mine. Jacky-boy been by yet?"

• • •

Jacky-boy was the tricky part. Silverfish was worried. But when he finally came around an hour later, Lady Mary was brilliant.

"Roach never threw a girl out that could still work," Jacky-boy said, munching on a jelly doughnut. "What the hell's wrong with you that he don't want you no more?"

"Nothing's wrong with me. He found papers in my drawer. Kind of hidden but he goes through stuff."

"What papers?"

"They say I'm HIV positive. And with herpes, too."

"And you're sitting here telling me nothing's wrong with you? Are you crazy? Why would I want to run a girl like that?"

Lady Mary's lip started to tremble.

"But the thing is," Silverfish stepped in, "she's not."

"Not what?"

"I'm clean," Lady Mary whispered.

"Oh, yeah, right. Sure, false positives, they happen all the time. Get out of my house."

"No." Lady Mary shook her head and sat up straighter. "Not false positives. False papers."

"What?"

"I went to . . . to this guy downtown. I paid him to make me papers that said I was positive."

"How stupid do I look to you? You expect me to believe that?"

Lady Mary didn't answer.

"Okay, pretend I do," said Jacky-boy. "*Why?*"

"So Roach would throw me out."

That silenced the room.

"He always goes through our stuff. So I got the guy to make the papers and I hid them like I didn't want him to know. He was sure to find them sooner or later." Lady Mary reached into her purse and handed Jacky-boy the card she'd gotten last week at the clinic when Silverfish took her there. "See? I'm clean."

Jacky-boy looked at the card a long time. He asked Lady Mary what was the name of the guy downtown. Lady Mary told him the name and Jacky-boy called the guy. Looking right at Lady Mary, he described her. He put the phone on speaker so they all heard the guy drawl, "Yeah, that's her, little and skinny, brown hair to her shoulders. I couldn't figure out what the hell she was up to, either, but she paid cash up front so what did I care?"

Jacky-boy clicked off with a funny smile at Lady Mary. "You're telling me a skinny little bitch like you got over on Roach? How'd you know he wouldn't beat the crap out of you when he found those papers?"

"Not Roach. He wouldn't touch me if he thought I was all infected. Anyway, that's what I was hoping. And if he did, I took the chance." Lady Mary looked at the floor. "I had to get away."

"And how do I know you're not gonna want to get away from me?"

"'Cause," Lady Mary said, eyes wide, "everyone says you're not like Roach."

• • •

Silverfish and Lady Mary left for work together that night. On the way to the corner, after they were out of sight of everyone else, Silverfish pulled the brown shoulder-length wig from her purse and stuffed it in the trash.

"You were great, girl!" She hugged Lady Mary.

"All I had to do is say what you told me to. *You* were so great, Fish. And you're so smart. And no one ever did anything like that for me before. I can't ever ever thank you—"

"Stop sniffling! Don't run your makeup. You're starting a new job, girl, don't mess up."

Lady Mary nodded, found a tissue, dabbed her eyes. "You're right. And I'll be good, Fish. I'll turn so many tricks Jacky-boy'll never want to get rid of me! You'll see."

"Yeah, well, don't get carried away and make the rest of us look bad, either."

"Okay." Lady Mary nodded seriously.

"And one more thing."

Lady Mary looked up at Silverfish as a car slowed.

"You were asking before. About a silverfish. See, it's an ugly bug. But it does one cool thing."

"It does?"

"Uh-huh," Silverfish said, sauntering off in the direction of the now-stopped car. "It eats other bugs. And especially," she called back to Lady Mary over her shoulder as she got in the car, "especially, it eats roaches."

PARENTAL GUIDANCE

Scott Adlerberg

I was twelve when it all happened. The year had begun unpleasantly and gotten worse. My parents were at war, and sometimes I got caught in their verbal crossfire. Our residence in the town of Haverstraw, New York, along the western edge of the Hudson River, an hour's drive away from Manhattan, was a main bone of contention between them.

My mother would say, "I can't stand the suburbs anymore. All we can do up here on weekends is eat out or go to a movie. Ted has to be chauffeured everywhere: to stores, to his friends' houses, to any place he can't reach on his bicycle."

"Wouldn't you," she would say to me, "rather move back to New York? There's tons more you can do there, and you'll be able to get around on your own."

Before I could respond, my father would say, "I'm not moving back there. I get my fill of that place every day at work. I like coming home and smoking a cigar on the porch. Having quiet at night and halfway fresh air to breathe. Ted does, too. I know it. He loves having grass and open space around so he can play all the sports he wants. I'm sorry, Colleen. We're not moving any-place. We're comfortable right here."

"You're comfortable here. Like a bump on a log. I might just have to leave without you."

"You do that."

"Don't tempt me, Richard. If I go, Ted's coming with me. I made a mistake thinking the suburbs would be a good place for him to grow up."

My father would frown. His chin would quiver. He had the narrow gray eyes of a rodent, a serious mouth, and a bloodless complexion. With his receding hairline, he looked older than his thirty-seven years, and because he exercised so seldom, he had a fleshy build.

"You leave, Colleen, and it won't be with him."

"And let you raise him as a suburbanite? No way, Richard."

Yet for all her talk about being stranded in Haverstraw, my mother spent the bulk of her time away from the town. She worked as a graphic designer, freelance, and would head to Manhattan a lot. All her friends lived there, and she went with them to clubs, restaurants, bars. It seemed she was always out, and as the weather warmed up, spring moving toward summer, she took short trips by herself. She would shop on Friday morning so that Dad and I would have food in the house, and then she would leave for the weekend. We never knew where she went (she refused to tell us), but on her return, she usually smelled of alcohol. She'd have bloodshot eyes. And on two occasions that season, during Easter break and over the Memorial Day weekend, I traveled with her. We drove to Cape Cod. We walked in the woods, explored the beaches, and ate delicious seafood. At night we saw movies and ate ice cream and strolled along the sand dunes overlooking the sea. If, when I went to sleep in our hotel room, she ran out to frequent bars and seduce men, as my father sometimes claimed she did, I never suspected it. I saw no evidence of such activity. She was merely a restless soul, a person gripped by wanderlust, and she liked having me along as her companion.

My father disapproved of our trips.

"With all your drinking you're a terrible influence. He's learning how to be wild and impulsive."

"He's learning there's more to life than Haverstraw. You see his friends. They're lucky if their parents take them anywhere. You want him to grow up having tunnel vision?"

"Of course not."

"So? Come with us one weekend. You might enjoy yourself."

"I'm tired on weekends. I need to relax."

"Tired? You're just lazy. Afraid of adventure."

I began to wonder why they'd married. Had my father always been a home-body, unwilling to pick up his carcass and go places? No, said my mother. Back in the sixties and early seventies, before my arrival, they'd taken hikes in the Adirondacks and weekend excursions to Montauk Point. Less affluent then, they'd traveled on the cheap, staying in hovels and having a ball, eating at diners and take-out stands, driving once to New Orleans and once as far as Tijuana. But something in him had changed over the years. The transformation had begun when he quit his job as a public school teacher, disgusted with the worsening classroom conditions, and became a budget director for a private academy in Manhattan. The job paid well but the routine was unvarying. He spent countless hours doing paperwork. He attended meetings and solicited donors. Two wise stock investments had brought him the money he needed to purchase our suburban castle, a big frame house resembling the other houses on the street, but the close work he did at his job, the daily immersion in precise figures and minuscule details, affected his behavior at home. Never before had he been so irritating. If my mother or I didn't wipe off the kitchen table after eating a meal, he would scold the culprit, that chin of his shaking. Every appliance had to be left in a certain place in the closets. The liquor bottles in the bar cabinet had to be arranged in a particular order. The television guide, with the shows he wanted to see that week circled in red ink, had to be left atop the set in the living room. Anyone who moved these objects around would hear him curse under his breath, and in response my mother would ridicule him. She called him neurotic. He in turn would call her a mess. They would bandy other insults then, and a full-fledged argument would start.

In the meantime, as the summer approached, my mother was working hard. Despite her drinking and traveling, she was engaged in her projects. She designed ads for fashion magazines, drew scenic pictures for tourist brochures, and helped companies with their promotional posters. All of this meant she slept when the chance arose, and by the time June arrived, she needed a rest. For weeks she'd been stuck with a cold, and a decline in her appearance was evident. She had dark rings around her eyes. Her hair, long and chestnut-brown, had lost its shine. Weight loss had taken the curves out of her figure, and her face was puffy, creating dimples in her cheeks.

"I'm going where there's sun," she told my father one day. "I need a vacation. I have to get away from here to rest."

"Try Venus. You'll get lots of sun there."

"The Caribbean will do. Ted and I'll like the beaches and the snorkeling."

"Hold on. You want to take a trip, take it by yourself."

"It's only for the summer."

"I don't care. You go solo. You're too unreliable to take care of him for that long."

From her response, an obscenity, I knew this last comment had wounded my mother. And I knew, as they continued to speak in the kitchen, that they both thought I was out of earshot. They thought I was upstairs in my room, doing homework, when as a matter of fact I was sitting at the top of the stairs so I could eavesdrop on their talk.

My mother revealed that she was taking this vacation to put her life in order. Believe it or not, she said, she planned to moderate her drinking. She intended to avoid night life and to get plenty of exercise. She always enjoyed having me along, and my presence would force her to act in a responsible manner.

"And while I'm gone," she continued, "while we have this time apart, you should do a bit of thinking yourself. Because when I return, unless you've made changes too, I'm leaving for good."

"Change how? In what way?"

"For one thing, loosen up. You're stiff and compulsive. It's suffocating to live with you."

"I'm not a kid anymore."

"Neither am I."

"You try to live like one, though."

"Stop making excuses. You've just forgotten how to enjoy yourself."

There was a silence.

"You should see a therapist," my mother said.

"You're the one who needs that. Not me."

"I'm not joking. If you don't make an attempt to change, I'm leaving here for good and I'm taking my child with me."

"I've heard that one before."

"It's not an empty threat, my dear."

They were silent again, and after a moment, my father spoke.

"Listen. I'll admit you have a point. I can try to change. I may even get help. But you have to promise to straighten yourself out down there."

"I said I would."

"You better. And I still think Ted should stay here. He'll miss his friends if he's away all summer."

"Nonsense," my mother said. "He loves traveling, seeing new places."

"What if he doesn't want to go? Have you thought of that?"

"No. Why don't we ask him?"

"Okay," my father said. "Let's ask him."

He called me down to the kitchen, and after waiting a second, I joined them. I found them sitting at opposite ends of our long chestnut table, my father with his hands clasped in front of him, my mother holding a glass of scotch. I sat down between them.

My mother informed me of her travel plans and her wish that I accompany her, but neither of them mentioned the other things they'd discussed.

"Won't you get bored swimming all summer?" my father asked me. "And what about the baseball league thing you have going with your friends?"

I turned my head to observe my mother. To see the blotches in her cheeks and the dilated capillaries in her nose made me feel sad. In her black and glaring eyes was the anger of a wildcat trapped in a cage. Her lips were pouty.

You couldn't predict what she might do, take a knife to my father or weep for herself, and I think the best way I can describe her is to say that she resembled a cross between a spoiled brat and a tragic heroine.

My father, by contrast, looked calm. His eyes were gray and steady and his chin was still. Not a hair on his head was out of place. He must've thought I'd choose to remain with my friends that summer, playing baseball and the like, but I knew that a couple of months alone with him, even if he tried to stifle his idiosyncrasies, would drive me up the wall.

"I've never snorkeled," I said. "I'd like to go."

• • •

My mother chose the island of Silver Pearl, an American territory. She took money from her bank account, and on June 25th, the day after I graduated from sixth grade, we flew down there. She had made reservations to stay at a bungalow site. Trees and bushes separated each building, giving everyone privacy. The area faced a turquoise bay, and our cottage was just off the beach. I would roll out of bed in the morning, walk down three granite steps, and hit sand. The shore of this bay was long, and overlooking it, giving us a wide view of the water, was our concrete patio. We had one big room with simple furnishings. At a store down a path in the woods, we would buy ice bags for our cooler and gas tanks for our stove. The bungalow was made out of wood, but for ventilation, two of its sides were wire mesh. At night, as I lay in bed reading by a Coleman lantern, or as the two of us examined the shells we were collecting, a salty sea breeze would blow inside. I could hear bushes rustling and coconuts falling with a thump from the trees, and I'd hear the rhythmical sound of the waves washing up on shore, licking our steps, receding. I liked those noises.

And I'd never visited a place so wild. There were no hotels or resorts on Silver Pearl; its one tourist area was the bungalow site. It had a single town, Galleon Bay, population five thousand, and the rest of the island consisted of mountains, jagged cliffs, green forests, and dark-sanded beaches. Many people born on Silver Pearl had moved to the States or the more touristy Caribbean islands, and the statesiders living there were small-time entrepreneurs, owners of shops and restaurants. They seemed to be rejects from civilization, people who'd left the mainland for any number of reasons, and my mother called the island a paradise for lost American souls and equatorial drifters. And we had those types at the bungalow site—hikers, scuba divers, bird lovers, a painter who was usually drunk on rum. I mingled with these slackers and misfits. But my mother was pleased, not put off, and said she'd chosen Silver Pearl precisely because it was a backwater. Here, she said, she could

Heroes

reorder her life, and she could do it without having to maintain social graces.

Her health improved. During the first weeks we spent on the island, she gained weight. She shook the cold that had nagged her for a month. She cut her hair short, like a man's (easier to manage after swimming), and in the tropical sunshine it changed from chestnut-brown to cinnamon blonde. She was fit again, hardly drinking, with a copper suntan all over, but I could still sense turbulence in her soul. It showed in her eyes, sunken, black, and intense, and it showed in her general twitchiness. She often attracted male glances, and I think this was because men also sensed she was yearning for something. Her features alone were not enticing. She had large, coarse cheekbones and a mouth too wide for her face. But as I say, men noticed her. She had an air of vitality that was alluring.

As for myself, I too was enjoying our vacation so far. We rented a Jeep and explored the bumpy, forest roads. We snorkeled at coral reefs where turquoise angel fish nibbled at our legs. Fiddler crabs and hermit crabs scurried across our patio, and brown pelicans dove into the ocean like kamikaze planes. At our campsite, when people cooked, the scents of curried goat and roasted sea bass would float through our cottage, and the smell of wet palms after a three o'clock shower was particularly refreshing. I took it all in, the new sensations, and when an islander showed us how to use machetes, the two of us went to cut paths in the bush.

So went our idyllic days on Silver Pearl. My mother hadn't yet encountered the man who changed everything for us. That happened one night in Galleon Bay, when we went to a restaurant, and I think we'd been on the island a month when she did meet him.

Galleon Bay was a nothing place. It stood at the foot of a mountain on the northwest coast and had noisy bars, cheap restaurants, understocked stores. The houses were compact, built from stucco or wood, with corrugated metal roofs, and the streets were narrow. Flies and water bugs infested back alleys where garbage would accumulate; empty bottles of Cruzan Rum stuck out of the sand on the beach where children played with skinny mongrels. In the stores you could buy liquor cheap, my mother said, and in the central square, which had benches and palm trees, hustlers sold drugs.

Anyhow, on this night, Mom and I were at a restaurant. It was dingy and candlelit. A few customers were there, and reggae music was coming from a radio behind the bar. We had just been served our food—red beans and fish—when a man got off his bar stool, walked over to our table, and sat down on the chair between us.

"Charlie," he said. "That's my name."

His breath stank with booze. His dungarees and polo shirt smelled like dead fish. He had a gray-white mustache, long white sideburns, a raw face, and muscular arms. There was a chip in one of his front teeth, and his bald head gleamed whenever he doffed his sailor's cap to the islanders walking inside. All in all, he wasn't handsome, but he did have a genial manner. He asked us our names, where we were from, and what we'd done on the island since our arrival. He didn't seem interested in only my mom, and believe me, from the times I'd seen it during our travels, I could tell when some jerk was trying to pick her up. Yes, I could tell, and he seemed to like us both, turning his head back and forth as he spoke. He kept drinking beer while we ate our dinner, and he described his adventures in a husky voice.

"I used to poach up in Alaska. I'd ship out of Seattle, and we'd go up to poach fish, crabs, bears, and seals. Made a damn solid living that way, and I could cool it down in San Francisco for months at a time. Then we'd go back to Seattle, me and my buddies, and we'd ship out again. It was brutal up in the Bering Sea, I can't tell you how brutal sometimes, but I wouldn't have traded that work for nothing else. Not for nothing. Not even for my brother's job. He kept asking me to join him on Wall Street. He made his first million, lost it, made it back and tripled it, lost that, and died of heart complications. Me? I got a heart like a bull's. I'll live to be a hundred with this heart."

My mother laughed and ordered a beer and asked him to tell us more about his rough days in Alaska. He did, and afterwards she said to him, "So how come you're here now. You became a conservationist?"

Charlie grinned, his chipped tooth showing. "Nah," he said. "I got too well-known up there. On both sides of the strait. The Russians locked me up and the goddamn Coast Guard did. It's bad in those jails near the Circle. So cold, so gray, the dreary walls, and outside there's nothing but ice. Ice and snow. Snow and ice. Like you're in a cell at the end of the world. It's not the sentence that hurts because that's short. You pay a fine, do your stint, and get out. Even from Russia if you're just a poacher. Then you can poach again. But I got sick of that shit. Those freezing cells. The guards on both sides knew my name. So I came down here, where I had an old friend. I'm still surviving."

"By poaching?" my mother said.

"No," he said. "Not by that."

Soon afterwards, we left him. We took the dark forest road leading to the campground. My mother drove in silence, and I'm sure she didn't know any better than I did whether Charlie had related true tales or bullshit. Every exploit he told had come on the wings of his whiskey breath.

The next evening, we returned to the restaurant. My mother had on tight dungarees, brown suede moccasins, and a green blouse that was cut low. She looked around for Charlie but he wasn't there, and she asked the bartender, a white statesider, if he expected Charlie that evening. The guy said yes, he did, Charlie stopped by most nights.

"He loves to schmooze," the bartender said. "Tell his poaching stories to tourists."

"And what does he do now?" my mother asked.

"Fishes," the bartender said. "Survives."

We ordered dinner and ate. My mom stared into space. She had a beer. Each time I spoke she would answer, but her voice had a distracted tone. Clearly she was waiting for Charlie to come, and when he did show up, after we'd had our desserts, she came alive. She glanced at him with a coy smile, and he, returning the look, tipped his sailor's cap. Then he got himself a double shot of tequila and sat down between us. For awhile all three of us chatted, but as the night wore on, my mother monopolized the conversation. Flushed a rose color, speaking rapidly, she told him about herself and my father, about her hatred for the suburbs and her diminishing interest in her job. Her candor startled me, and I wondered whether she thought I'd tell my father what she'd said.

From then on, we saw Charlie a lot. He brought us to coral reefs for snorkeling. He took us along back trails. He took us to the edges of cliffs where we had panoramic views of the sea. One time, as I recall, he led us through dense brush, and we came out in a clearing that contained a lake. It shone emerald green in the sun, and hibiscus plants overhung its edges. Mosquitoes bit us, but whenever we got itchy, we jumped into the lake and swam across it, heading for a waterfall that fed it at one end. We all laughed.

But Charlie also had a job to do, a living to make. He couldn't keep hanging with us while his partner, a man named Alec, tired himself fishing. So one day, instead of taking us around the island, Charlie put us into a rubber raft and paddled out to the cove where their boat was anchored. Called *The Rum Punch*, this boat was a thirty eight foot Sport Fisherman that the two of them, long time buddies, had bought years ago with money earned from their poaching. They had radar and a two-way radio and other equipment, and it also served as Alec's home. Even when they were working hard, when they were fishing, Charlie invited us on board and we'd spend entire days with them. Charlie handed us rods and taught us the fishing basics, and both Mom and I came to like the sport. Mom, especially, did it with enthusiasm; she hollered when she hooked her first one. It was a large snapper, and while Alec manned the wheel, she and Charlie battled with it.

That night the four of us celebrated her catch. Charlie fried the snapper at his house. He lived at the end of a dirt street in Galleon Bay, in a hut with stucco walls and a tin roof. It was the last in a row of such huts, and the forest that began next to it kept it in the shade.

Before long we were spending nights there. Whenever we did I took the living room sofa, and I would sink into its green cushions while reading a book or watching television. The only thing that bothered me was the noise coming from the bedroom, and I was surprised by my mother's behavior since I'd never believed my father's suspicions about her affairs. But I didn't blame Charlie for it. I liked him regardless. He was a generous guy and entertained us with anecdotes and would talk with me one on one. He never seemed to have the attitude that I was in their way.

Still, there were times when I felt tempted to question my mom. Hadn't she sworn that she would change her lifestyle? My father had his shortcomings, but I thought he deserved her fidelity because at least he was a straightforward person. Whenever he promised to do something, he did it, and I knew he would stick to his side of the bargain. He would, as she'd urged, consult a psychiatrist. He would, as she'd suggested, try to break his compulsive habits and revive his languishing spirit. These were things he'd do because he wanted to save their marriage. He wanted to make it the pleasure it had once been. Yet here was my mother passing her nights in Charlie's bedroom, and how was I to react to that? Telling my father over the phone might make her despise me for having betrayed her trust, but in remaining silent I felt like an accomplice in her romance. I could picture him sitting at home with a lonely expression on his face, and suddenly I did feel resentment toward Charlie. Despite my fondness for him, I often caught myself wishing that he would leave us.

I was imagining ways I could ruin their liaison.

• • •

Judging by the contrast between the *Rum Punch* and his house, I assumed that Charlie, like Alec, preferred the water to the land. He didn't mind living in a stucco hovel if he made enough money to keep his boat and fishing gear in prime condition. His work was grueling but invigorating, and food was his in abundance. He appeared to be content.

My view of him changed early in August. By that time I learned that he and Alec were making a small fortune and were hiding the money in a safe Charlie owned. My discovery came on a morning after Mom and I had spent the night at his house, and what accompanied this discovery was quite an adventure.

The evening before it started, Charlie had told a guy at a bar that we would be going on a five day trip. The purpose was deep sea work, and at sunup, carrying knapsacks and a duffel bag, we left his place to go meet his partner. We walked beyond the street's dead end and cut through the forest, and on the pebbly beach of the U-shaped cove where the *Rum Punch* lay at anchor, Charlie slipped into a shack. He came out dragging a rubber dinghy. Mom tied me into a life preserver. Charlie sat with his back toward the prow, we sat facing him at the stern, and with long fluid strokes he rowed us toward the *Rum Punch*.

It was the only boat out there. The water was calm. I listened to Charlie's rhythmical breathing and the calls of the sea gulls above us. Though my mother said nothing, she kept biting her thumbnail, and once she smiled at me with a look that suggested I too stay quiet. I did, but I felt my pulse accelerate.

"I hope the people delivered the stuff," Charlie said.

On the deck we saw Alec, dressed in a tank top and overalls. Though slender, he was strong; I'd seen him reel in large, combative fish. He had white, spiky hair and weather-cracked skin and steel-blue eyes so deep in their sockets they seemed to be gazing inward. Since meeting him, I'd never found him to be anything more than quietly civil. Now he made a sign at us, a thumbs up, which prompted Charlie to nod and smile, but after we'd hoisted the dinghy on board and climbed the rope ladder to the deck, we noticed that Alec was glaring.

"It's fucked up that you told her," he said. "You didn't have to bring her."

What he meant, I didn't know, but my mother bristled. She shook her head, looking offended, and said she'd known this would happen.

"Wait," Charlie said. "Just wait." And he told Alec they had to speak alone. So they did, closing the door as they entered the deck house, and though their words were hard to make out, the tones of their voices were clear: Alec was infuriated, Charlie defensive but steadfast. At last they reemerged, both of them sweaty and breathing hard, and Alec offered my mother his hand. He muttered an apology and she accepted it, but he was looking at the deck instead of into her eyes.

"Now can I see the merchandise?" Charlie said.

"You can," Alec said, "but she can't."

"I'm part of this group," my mother said. "There shouldn't be secrets."

"You have a kid, for cryin' out loud."

"He's having adventures," my mother said. "He's getting experience." She laughed, prodding my shoulder.

"Think of the humdrum things your friends are doing now."

But Alec wouldn't budge, and Charlie and Alec went into the deck house by themselves. They went down a wooden ladder to the bilges, and when they came back, Alec raised the anchor.

We headed north. For one day, one night, and another day, we traveled without pausing. We passed the western edge of St. Croix and the eastern shore of Viegues. We moved through the Virgin Passage, between Culebra and St. Thomas, and I saw sleek yachts and freighters and cruise ships bearing national flags. The skies were clear, as the weather reports had predicted; the sea was tranquil; the sun was a flaxen fireball at dawn and a pink-orange ember at dusk. In the afternoons I liked to sit against the deck house, in the shade of its jutting roof, and there out of everyone's way, I would read my book or play myself a game of chess. I had a magnetic set. And sometimes I would pace the deck like a skipper in a maritime tale, back and forth, end to end, staring into the sea as I daydreamed.

Foremost in my mind was my mother. I spent hours contemplating why she felt such passion for Charlie. He did have the energy, daring, and exuberance that my father lacked, but were these reasons to love him? Did she love him? In all honesty, I had no clue what the word "love" was supposed to mean. I loved my mom, but of course this kind of love was unlike the love she felt for Charlie. My parents had supposedly loved each other once, but I'd never heard either of them say, "I love you," to the other. There were the songs, books, movies, and TV shows about this great subject, love, everywhere I went I heard about this wonderful thing, love, but regardless of whether people were talking, singing, or writing about it, love between adults and the language they used to express it was foreign to me. I mean, I'd had a crush or two on girls in school—that was a thing—but I'd never completely lost my mind like adults could do when seized by love.

While trying to fathom her thoughts, I observed my mother. She was grinning and laughing a lot more than usual, moving around with a light step. She helped prepare meals and clean the cabins. She hummed cheerful tunes. I told myself to be glad she was happy, but I kept thinking about the way she'd broken her promise to my father. Her belief that I wouldn't tell him about her lover was flattering, but this trust she had in me also smacked of arrogance. It seemed as though she'd concluded that I, her dependent son, could not possibly disapprove of her actions. She would hug and kiss Charlie when I was near them, but because I maintained a blank expression, she had no idea how I burned inside.

In my mind's eye I kept seeing my father. He was at work with his nose buried in papers or at home with his feet propped up before the television. I wondered how news of her affair would affect him. Would it rouse him to take action, or would he remain torpid and cautious? I'd spoken to him once since she'd met Charlie, and like her I had kept the man's existence a secret. He'd assumed she was working on her reformation and said that he was making changes.

"I'm getting out to jog and ride my old bike. When you get back, I'll be a different man."

I felt sorry for him.

Yet at the same time I had no desire to rejoin him at home. After all, my mother had made a valid point: how many of my school friends would ever have such adventures?

At home, on trips into New York City, my mother had taken me to the Museum of Natural History and the Hayden Planetarium. She'd given me animal books to read and had done her best on our earlier travels to instill an appreciation of nature in me. And now, for all this exposure, I was grateful. Being on the ocean delighted me as much as rambling through the forest had. I still burned up inside when she lavished kisses on Charlie, but I thought I'd made the right choice in accompanying her to the tropics. I admired her. She could be scary with all her abandon, but something in me knew that her flirtations with danger were connected to her zest for living.

This same unrestraint put certain people off, however. Alec, for example. He'd give her nasty looks. Neither she nor Charlie were drinking on board, but Alec didn't like that they'd roll joints in the evenings.

"Can't you wait till the goods are delivered to get yourself high? Charlie knows he's breaking our rule."

I was learning more and more about this man with the spiked crest of white hair. The two lovebirds would do their work and then vanish into a cabin for hours, so I would go to him for company. He taught me nautical expressions and I'd go below decks with him when he inspected the twin diesel engines. I got to steer on the flying bridge, and when he had time we'd play chess. Or he'd talk to me while he was working, tell me about himself. He'd grown up in San Francisco, he said; his father had been a professional thief and his mother a drunk who'd never held down a job. Police had shot and killed his father when Alec was twelve, and his mother had remarried with an abusive guy, another alcoholic. After that, on his own for the most part, he had robbed stores and hotwired cars, and a major portion of his adolescence had been spent inside reformatories. At the age of twenty-two, struck by a whim, he'd driven to Alaska in search of work and adventure, and there he'd found both, embarking on a fishing trawler. Things weren't easy on that ship, you busted your ass night and day, but from the time he'd begun scrubbing decks in the cold, sailing and the sea had enchanted him.

They were beginning to enchant me also. The life Alec described possessed romantic appeal. He'd traveled around the globe working on ships, had caught tuna, shrimp, lobsters, cod. For years he'd lived in the South Pacific, during a gold rush he'd sailed up the Amazon, later he'd returned to Alaska to poach with Charlie. How dull and routine my father's life seemed in comparison, and I told myself I would rather grow up to be a man like Alec, or even Charlie, than like my father.

The *Rum Punch* kept moving. We turned west. We headed toward the Bahamas. There was no change in the heat or the atmospheric calm, and early on the third morning of our trip we tossed anchor in the low water off a cay. Nothing distinguished this rocky shoal from the others we'd passed, but Charlie said we'd reached our rendezvous point. We sat eighty miles east of the southern Bahamas, and now we had to wait.

The sun set that evening like a dwindling fireball. It colored the water, sky and beach orange. The four of us watched it sink below the horizon, then we descended from the flying bridge to the main cabin. My mother cooked dinner, fried steak and beans, and after we'd finished, Alec said that Mom and I had to go down to our cabin. The men were coming for the stuff, and neither of us could be seen. Our presence would be judged as too odd.

We lay in our bunks for hours. We had to keep quiet so while Mom read a book, I fooled around with my chess set. I listened to her breathing and the snap of her pages turning, and although I felt restless, the heat in the cabin made me drowsy. I put down the chess set and closed my eyes, and it was during the time that I kept dozing off and waking up that I heard the sound of another ship.

Its engine was a buzz that grew increasingly louder. Water splashed against our hull. The ship pulled up near the *Rum Punch*, its engine still buzzing, and what must've been a smaller craft, a motorboat, sped toward us over the waves. There were footsteps on the deck, male voices, tense laughter, and footsteps going down below us to the bilges. I was aware that my mother had stopped turning the pages of her book, and no longer did I hear her breathing. Crates were lifted, dragged, put down, and hauled up steps. Alec and a deep voice exchanged so longs. The motorboat pulled away. After a few minutes, the sound of the buzzing engines faded, and my mother said we could talk again.

We went up on deck, and Charlie showed us a suitcase full of money.

• • •

The four of us sailed back to Silver Pearl. Getting rid of the drugs had reduced the tension on the ship. We all fished and the partners landed big ones. Charlie and my mom drank at night and clowned around, and without self-consciousness, they'd snuggle. But a strange thing was happening also:

my mother was so infatuated with Charlie, her passion for him had become so strong, that for the first time in my life she was paying me little attention. That disturbed me. My resentment toward Charlie increased. I chafed at his constant presence, and again I considered ways to destroy their romance.

How could I do it? I could tell the police about the smuggling, but that alternative seemed too harsh. Angry as I was, I had no desire to throw anyone in jail. I could inform my father of her affair, but I still feared I'd provoke her wrath. For a betrayal like that she would never forgive me, and my father would probably fly down to the island to take me back home. But the truth was I didn't want to go home yet. The vacation was still pleasurable. I loved Silver Pearl and the ease of our tropical life, and now I had a new companion in Alec. My friendship with him was continuing to grow, and when we returned to Silver Pearl, he let me stay with him on the *Rum Punch*. My mother could sleep at Charlie's house without my having to listen to their bedroom calisthenics, and she thanked Alec for his hospitality, though the two were barely on speaking terms.

"You could be more polite to me," she told him, and Charlie agreed with my mother, asking of Alec that he merely be pleasant. But Alec kept saying that Charlie should dump her; to him she constituted a distraction. Charlie was doing less fishing than before and less work than ever on the ship.

"Damn, Alec. Just because you've never known love. You're jealous, buddy."

But that wasn't it. Alec wasn't jealous. He said he'd been married and divorced and just happened to enjoy being by himself at this stage in his life. He could understand that others were different, and needless to say, he wasn't a moralist. He didn't criticize my mother for being an unfaithful wife. It was the spell she cast over his friend and her increasing disregard for my welfare that enraged him. He kept referring to his own neglectful parents and the drunken stepfather he'd loathed.

"Your father sounds all right," he said. "Why don't you go back to him? I'll give you money for the plane."

"I like it here with you," I answered. "The summer isn't over yet."

"Okay, guy. Just making sure. I'm glad to have you."

We played more chess and he taught me how to play backgammon. He introduced me to his books on marine biology. An amateur naturalist, he had a vast knowledge of ocean life, and his main hobby on land or sea was bird watching. I'd go with him when he went out to do this, when he sailed to uninhabited cays to catch a glimpse of certain birds, and we'd sit for hours with his binoculars. We'd sit still and very quiet, but I never got bored. Watching birds in their natural habitat, I realized, was fascinating, and I'd write observations with him in his journal.

Meanwhile, though, I was becoming sad. The second week in August had come and gone and soon the vacation would be over. Soon I'd be back in school, feeling cramped and edgy behind a desk. The trim lawns, neat parks, and clipped bushes of my suburban world would look tame and synthetic compared to forests and coral reefs.

One day I told my mother how sad I was. We had stayed in our bungalow for a night, and she was packing. Since we rarely used the cottage anymore, there was no reason to pay for it, and as she folded our clothes to move them into Charlie's house, I mentioned the fun I'd had during the summer. I explained how hard it would be to get accustomed again to schoolwork and teachers.

"The mall's gonna suck after this," I said.

She gave me a hug. Her eyes twinkled with merriment. She was wearing short dungarees and a red halter top, and by now the sun had given her hair a deep blonde color. It had grown out to below her ears and she kept it in a wavy uncombed state that looked pretty on her.

"Well," she said. "I have news, too," and she winked at me as if I'd get a kick out of what she had to say. But what she revealed wasn't funny at all. A week earlier, she said, Charlie had announced that he was tired of the sea life and planned to retire. He wanted to relax and travel, to fish just for pleasure, and we would stay with him instead of going home come September. Charlie and Alec would make one more smuggling trip, and then they would divide the money stashed in Charlie's house. Of this, the cash, Charlie would get two thirds since Alec wanted to keep the *Rum Punch*. That was their deal, and Charlie had said that in two weeks time, after he and Alec delivered the stuff, he would take my mom to Europe. They'd fly to Paris, the Greek Isles, somewhere. The point was she would leave my father and I'd go with them. I'd escape the dead suburbs, the typical life, and my education would come from a firsthand experience of the world.

"Call it travel-schooling," my mother said.

Her news didn't jar me. It confirmed my hunch that she wouldn't return home. She had no friends or possessions that she missed, and her agreement with my father was all but forgotten. Even if he did become more active, he would still be a man living in one place, working his steady nine-to-five. He could never keep up with her. I had to admit, though I hated to do so, that for the sake of her happiness, it would be best if she did take off with Charlie.

But this didn't mean she could force me to accompany them. Her imperious attitude galled me. Charlie said he wanted me to come, but if they were going to stay wrapped up in themselves, if her love for him would continue to make her neglect me, forget it. I had no desire to join them. Yet I hesitated to go home. Despite her faults, my mother had been the source of life in our house, and living alone with my father would make it difficult to have adventures. He would still have his exasperating habits, even if he was undergoing therapy. No, if I had to choose between my parents, I would rather desert my father. But in that case, I'd never see my friends again either. I'd relinquish my baseball cards, sports magazines, all my belongings. My mind was torn. I didn't know quite what to do, and I wound up making a move that put a kink in everyone's plans.

One evening, while my mother was resting, I used a pay phone in town to call my father collect. From my trembling voice, the way I stammered, he knew that something was wrong, and I told him about her affair. I didn't bring up the smuggling—no business of his—but reported her plans to fly off with Charlie, and I concluded by saying that they planned to take me with them.

As one would expect, my father steamed. He uttered curses I'd never heard him use. More than her actual infidelity, it was the breaking of her pledge to "clean up" that drove him wild (he forgot I was supposed to know nothing about their deal), and in speaking of her intention to shanghai me, as he put it, he shouted murderous oaths. He promised to catch the next plane to Silver Pearl, and he vowed to get me back to the "real world, the world of sanity".

"What kind of guy is he, this Charlie?"

"Okay. He's a fisherman."

"A fucking fisherman. Did she tell you to keep quiet about him all summer?"

"Sort of."

"Unbelievable. I followed my side of the bargain since she left."

"She knows that."

And so we conversed, until my father slammed down the receiver. Poor guy; I pitied him. He'd been sufficiently trusting to believe that my mother would keep her promise. And now he seemed to think that I was his alone, that this experience had convinced me she was a dangerous influence. Dead wrong: I stood neutral. Why did I have to choose one parent and abandon the other? If they were to inhabit different worlds, I could occupy both. During the school year I'd live at home, and during the summer I could visit my mom and have adventures. The idea seemed sensible, but first I'd have to face my mother and explain why I had summoned my father. When he came, they'd fight, and the quarrel, I well knew, would be vicious.

Three days passed. I gave no sign to anyone that I was waiting for the coming of the storm.

To reach Silver Pearl one had to fly to St. Thomas and then take a four hour trip by hydrofoil. I'd given my father the name of a hotel in Galleon Bay, and he'd written down Charlie's address. I'd told him to come any time after nine, the time the lovers usually returned from a bar or restaurant, and since I intended be there when he came, I was sleeping at Charlie's house again. On Monday I'd called him; on Thursday night there was a knock on Charlie's door.

I walked toward it. I'd been lying on the living room couch watching television. My mother and Charlie were seated on opposite sides of the kitchen table, she with a copy of *Newsweek* before her, he with a fishing rod he was mending, and both looked up at the sound of the knocking. It was close to eleven, and we never had visitors so late.

I opened the door. My father had on beige slacks, a brown belt, sandals, and a white sports shirt. There were sweat stains under his arms and water beads on his face. He'd tightened his gut and put color in his complexion, but he still had eyes that were cold gray slits and lusterless hair that was pasted to his scalp like the hair on a beautified corpse. Somehow, despite his efforts, he seemed no more alive than he ever had, and I got the distinct impression that beneath the minor transformations he was the same as ever.

We each nodded. He entered the living room. Bluish light was coming from the television, and in the kitchen above the table a hundred-watt bulb was shining. Had he caught them having sex the situation might have been more dramatic, but as it was he went pale, seeing them sitting there so relaxed. She was in a robe and Charlie in nothing but his dungarees, and they both looked so calm and content they could've been taken for a married couple together for twenty years.

My father looked around. The battered sofa with green cushions, the scuffed wooden table beside it, the threadbare curtain in the paneless living room window, the dish-cluttered sink, the burnt stove, the countertop flecked with ants and rolling papers—he surveyed these objects with scorn on his face, and I knew he could smell the marijuana in the air. He could smell it in the heat and stickiness of the shack, his disgust only growing.

"What a pleasant surprise," my mother said. "How'd you get here?"

He leveled an acid stare at her and crossed his arms to contain his anger. Nothing had ever made him turn so white, I thought, and I could see his chin trembling.

"Get your things and let's go, Teddy."

"You're not going anywhere with him."

"Common, Ted. Let's go."

"He doesn't want to go with you."

"Teddy, what's wrong? Get whatever you have, and let's move."

But I stayed by the door, my stomach churning, and broke in on their exchange.

"You should both be quiet so I can talk."

They fell silent then, looking at me, and I told them I had a plan for the future.

First off, I explained to my mother, it had been I who phoned my father. I'd done this because I wanted to work out an agreement between them. Bluntly put, I'd live at home with him during the school year and visit her wherever she was for the summers. Returning to school would be depressing, but if I were to stay with her and Charlie all year round, I'd miss my friends, my room, and so on. And knowing how absorbed in one another she and Charlie could get, I thought I'd become an annoyance to them.

"I'm sorry you feel that way," Charlie said. "You've never been an annoyance to me."

I thanked him for saying that, but my father lost his temper. He stamped his feet and yelled, and in reaction, my mother did the same. They were off again, trading insults, and my father said he didn't want me to live with her for one day more. She was mentally unfit to be a parent, he said, while she claimed she would feel overwhelming guilt if she surrendered me to his deadening influence for ten months a year. With or without his flat stomach, he was still a zombie, a cog in the machine. I'm sure she was wondering whether he knew about the smuggling, but inasmuch as he never mentioned it, she must've quickly gathered that he didn't. She knew I had kept *that* a secret.

But I was watching with displeasure. In their mutual hatred, they were deaf to advice. They heard no proposals. They continued to trade names and accusations, and the goal of each was to score a triumph over the other. Scoring a triumph meant full custody, so neither would consider my pleas for a compromise. This battle was the climax to the war that had begun at home, and each insisted on nothing less than total victory.

I'd had enough. I couldn't stand listening to them anymore, and Charlie was ticking me off—the way he kept lowering his head and passing his hand over his beard, as though amused. He seemed to take no offense at the things my father called him, and when my father told my mother that even he, her shitty lover, had said nothing on her behalf, Charlie merely said, "She don't need me to fight her battles."

I opened the door and ran outside. My parents' yelling stopped. They both called me but I ignored them, passing the street's dead end and running toward the woods. Dark as it was, I could see the path, and I didn't answer when they called again. I heard my mother say, "Not Alec. He really likes that guy," and my father ask, "Who the hell is that?" He must've got alarmed when he learned that the man lived on a boat, and I could picture him gaping when my mother described how I'd go there by myself, even at night.

I crossed the beach of the cove where the *Rum Punch* was anchored. The rubber dinghy sat in its place inside the wooden shack, and I pulled the raft across the sand into the water. I rowed using the single oar. No moon was visible, though stars were in the sky, and from the cove's edges came the sound of waves hitting rocks.

I struggled to get beyond the breakers. The boat tossed and heaved. Spray kept whipping my face, burning my eyes, but I pushed ahead. I reached smoother water. Then the *Rum Punch* rose before me, outlined against the black sky, and I shouted Alec's name several times. All lights on board were off, and I had to wait and holler, wait and holler.

Finally Alec appeared on deck. He was wearing long johns and a gray sweat shirt, and in his hand he held a metal lamp. He threw the rope ladder over the side, and together we raised the dinghy on board. "It was terrible," I said. "Terrible." But only after I'd drunk a soda, sitting with Alec in the main cabin, did I tell him what had occurred.

My throat felt constricted. Frustration made my eyes swell with tears. I said I was so enraged I never wanted to see either of my parents again, and I told Alec that after they left Silver Pearl, I would stay, fishing and having my own adventures.

"I don't need them," I said.

The tantrum had exhausted me. I yawned. Alec urged me to get some sleep. My parents were acting like self-centered idiots, he said, and perhaps my flight had made an effective point. Maybe they could repress their enmity for my sake. He still thought my mother was a neglectful parent, but he understood the bonds that held me to her. He got why I wanted to live with my father but visit her once or twice a year. In the morning, he said, we'd go see them together, and he would help me appeal to their reason.

"If they still don't give in, you'll live here with me till they do."

We got to Charlie's at ten a.m. Nobody was there. This in itself wasn't cause for concern, but as we looked around the house, dread swept through me. My mom's clothes and suitcase were gone. Charlie's dresser was empty. Fishing tackle, crinkled papers, and other paraphernalia lay atop the bed. Never neat, the place now was a mess, and I was pondering the rubbish when Alec called me from the kitchen. He sounded upset.

I walked into the living room. Alec stood by the kitchen table. He was staring at me, his blue eyes bulging, all the color drained from his face, and

I didn't have to ask him whether something dire had gone down since obviously something had.

"Get ready for a shock," he said.

I stepped forward. He pointed to a white sheet of paper on the table. Still there from the previous night were the fishing rod, the coffee cups, and the issue of *Newsweek*, and on the white sheet of paper was a pencil-written note in my mother's hand. No question it was her hand, but it lacked her usual elegance. The sentences were crooked and the letters jagged, as though she'd been shaking when she wrote.

I read the message.

Dear Teddy,

Believe me when I say I had no other choice. Even if I had agreed to your idea, your father never would have. After you ran away, he threatened to take me to court and made a point of adding that no judge would let you see me under the conditions you want. He was probably right about that. He would have won in court, and I couldn't let it go that far. I also knew I shouldn't force you to come with us. Not after what we did to your father. If we took you but never told you why he disappeared, you would've kept asking us questions. You would've wanted to see him. If we did tell you, I can't say how you would've responded. With hate? That's why I'm going now. Alec despises me, but he likes you very much. I have no doubt you can live with him. Though I've never said it to him, I admire the way he lives. Like Charlie, he's a survivor. With him, you'll grow up freer than most kids do and you'll be able to see the world. You'll never starve if you know how to live on the sea, and Alec will teach you a lot. I'm sorry it ended this way, my love. But if we ever meet again when you're older, I think you'll see that I did this because I want the best for you. I couldn't let your father take you back to that trivial, suffocating world. Be glad I'm happy with Charlie, and I'll always be thinking of you.

With eternal love,

Mom

I won't dwell on my reactions to this letter. Suffice it to say I froze. My vision clouded. I cried. Alec hugged me, but only for a moment; he had noticed a slip of paper lying underneath this one. It was a second letter, addressed to him, and it contained four words: *Go to the spot.*

The spot was the safe where the partners held the money they'd made smuggling. To think that Charlie may have taken it all made Alec yell out a curse, and he dashed off into the bedroom. I sat down in the kitchen, still crying, and I heard the dresser-drawer being moved. Then Alec reappeared, smiling grimly. Charlie had taken two thirds of the loot. The rest was still there.

Alec took the safe, and we returned to the ship. Neither of us called the police. Alec had an aversion to them, and for all my sadness, I had no desire for revenge. Let my mother live with Charlie. The damage was done.

So ended my vacation that summer. My father's body, so far as I know, was never found. I never learned how those two got off Silver Pearl, but with his waterfront connections, Charlie could have paid someone to pilot them away. I assumed they eventually went to Europe.

Alec could've sent me home to relatives, but he asked me what I wanted to do. After considering my relatives, who all lived in New York City, I opted to stay with him. This was tough at first, despite his kindness, and for months afterward I had trouble getting over my grief and shock. For years I recalled my mother's actions as one remembers a bad dream. But time, like it is so often, was a healer, and I had Alec as my guardian.

He quit the smuggling business. We explored the Caribbean and South America's eastern coast. Later we sailed to the Mediterranean, the Indian Ocean, and the Great Barrier Reef. We had money, we fished, we studied birdlife, and Alec taught me how to navigate. When he died, I buried him at sea. I inherited the *Rum Punch*. I still have it, and I'm content to call this ship my home. I don't know if it was my mother's intention when she killed my father and bolted on me, but I am, not unhappily, rootless.

SUPERHERO, WITH CROOKED NAILS

Rachael Acks

"Sadi! Sadi! Did you see?"

"Hey, sweetie, see what?" I grinned and glanced over my shoulder at Jenny as I pinned my backpack between my hip and my locker. My hands were busy rolling up my *chunni* so I could hide it away. At my old school, I wore the gauzy fabric square every day to class, draped properly over my head and shoulders. Here, I got tired of being asked if I was Muslim, or (mockingly, please God hear me, I hope it was just a horrible joke) if I was going to blow up the school because I was a terrorist.

"They finally announced the date for prom!" Jenny was hard to miss, even in a hallway crowded with students between classes; she looks like a stereo-typical American movie cheerleader (and she is—a cheerleader, I mean) down to the blonde hair, blue eyes, and bright smile with perfectly straight white teeth.

"When is it?"

"June 13. Last week of school, I think. Kind of late this year, but that means we should be all done with finals!" Her lips, bubblegum pink today (the lip-stick doesn't taste like bubblegum though, I've checked), couldn't seem to decide if she was going to smile or frown.

"Yeah, that is kind of late." Three months away. Planning time was good, but . . . I pulled my planner out of my backpack and started paging through it.

"Are you going to go?"

April . . . May . . . June . . . 13th. And there it was, next to the date—the little open circle that meant the full moon. The bottom dropped out of my stomach. "Are you?" I asked, to buy time while I quietly had a breakdown.

Her shoulders rose up in a shrug, though they stayed up, as if she was trying to draw her head back into her light blue sweater like a turtle. "I don't know. I kind of want to. This is our last prom, and we're together and that's *important*. But..." She looked down at her fingernails, which were perfect and also pink. "You know. My mom."

Yes, Jenny's mom. I'd met her once, at a football game, right after Jenny and I started dating. Jenny introduced me as a friend—she'd warned me ahead of time that where her mom was concerned, she was so deeply in the closet she might as well be sorting hangers on Mars. While the marching band played something Sousa in the background, Jenny's mom shook my hand, then asked me if I would let her save me from Hell. It gave me an all new appreciation for my own parents, let me tell you. ("Guru Nanak said, 'There is no Hindu, there is no Muslim. We will believe that there is no straight, there is no gay.'")

Jenny wanted to go to prom, I could tell just from the way she leaned next to the lockers next to me, like a picture of *Girl, with extra longing*. And she wanted to go with me. And I wanted to go with her. And it was impossible, for reasons way worse than her mom's endless Bible thumping.

So it was the dumbest thing in the world for me to say: "We're the worst kept secret in the entire school, Jenny. No one's ratted you out to your mom yet." Like I thought I had a chance in hell of actually making this work. But I refused to be on her mother's side in this, even a little.

She nodded, licking her lips. Her lipstick stayed perfectly in place. I have no idea how she does it. I wear makeup too—I love it!—but can't seem to manage without smudging constantly. Hers stays perfect, even after we've been 'doing homework' in my room for hours, which really just means making out with a movie on to cover the sound. "Okay. As long as we're really careful, we'll be okay."

I leaned in close and just told myself that I'd find a way, somehow. Then I let my voice drop low and serious, like I was the hero in a Bollywood movie. "Jenny Miller, will you make me happy forever by coming to the prom with me?"

Somehow, she managed to keep a straight face. "It would make my heart like a cloudless sky."

Then she leaned forward to kiss me quickly, right before her lips crinkled in a smile and we both burst out laughing. It almost made me forget the big Problem-with-a-capital-P, just waiting in the planner still clutched in my hand.

• • •

Okay, okay, I've played coy enough, but you've figured it out by now, right? I mean, why else would a full moon mean death to my wish to take my girlfriend to prom? No, it's nothing to do with being Sikh.

This time last year, I was living in Ann Arbor. Both my parents were professors at the University of Michigan, I was minding my own business in eleventh grade, and my little brother was obsessed with Spider-Man. Then my dad started getting these headaches, and long story short there was a brain scan, and a scary shadow on it, and cancer. My mom has a PhD in geology, so she got a new job in Houston, working for a big oil company. For the health insurance. Abba's better now, and he's teaching Classics at Rice, but there's still chemo and doctor appointments. I complain about having to move, but then I feel like the worst daughter in the world. I love Abba, and the second scariest time of my life was sitting in the waiting room at Memorial Hospital, holding hands with Bebe while we waited for him to come out of brain surgery.

Which brings us to the number one scariest moment of my life. About two weeks after we moved to Houston, I was out for a night run. I felt like I was swimming rather than running, the summer air was so thick even with the sun down. Then a dog slammed into me, just out of nowhere. Teeth sank into my right leg, and all I remember after that was ivory sheened with my blood, tearing and ripping, and oh God it hurt and I was so scared, too scared to pray, to do anything but scream. It's a blessing I don't remember more than that. I saw the bloodstains left on the sidewalk, still there a few days later despite a rainstorm. And it would have been *worse* if someone hadn't heard me screaming and come running out of their house with a gun. (Okay, Texas. You're good for something.)

Only then my wound healed way, way faster than it should have. Gory mess to a mass of white scars in four days. And twenty-four days after that, things got *really* weird in a way that ended with me naked and picking fur out from between my teeth the next morning.

Turned out the dog wasn't a dog.

And that I wasn't quite a human any more.

• • •

My head swirled with thoughts of prom dresses and dinners and—yeah, accidentally eating the neighbor's yappy dog the first time I changed—as I walked up the driveway. Our house in Houston is huge, with an enormous lawn made mostly of ants and an air conditioning unit that never stops roaring. Our furniture from the apartment in Ann Arbor is still a bit lost in all the rooms.

The air inside smelled of coriander and cardamom. That made my mouth water and also put me on edge. Lamb biryani is my favorite dinner, so half the time Bebe makes it, it's a celebration of something I did well, and the other half it's because she's trying to soften the blow of some terrible news.

I hadn't done anything all that great lately.

"Sadikha, is that you?" Bebe called from the kitchen, in Punjabi.

I grew up speaking both Punjabi and English, but speaking English all day at school makes my tongue feel stiff when I have to switch gears. "No, Bebe, it's a thief."

She laughed. "Come here and wash your hands. You can help me with these *chapati*."

The kitchen was lined with green granite countertops. Bebe had hung a calendar on one wall, the full moons circled thickly with red Sharpie. Like any of us could forget. There was one next week. It shared a calendar square with a blue star I'd drawn there, to indicate I had a cross country meet that day.

Bebe had gone a bit plump but still moved like a dancer. She wore a turban, so it made her entire shape a series of smooth, decreasing curves, like the conical shell of an ammonite. She had flour to the elbow, dotting her apron, and ghostly hand prints on her light blue pantsuit.

"Did you have a good day at school?"

"Yeah." I washed my hands and dried them, then grabbed a rolling pin. "It was okay. Got my essay back. The one about *Moby Dick*. B-plus."

"I wish you'd try harder."

I shrugged. The book had been torture, even listening to the audio version while I ran. I poked her with my elbow. "Why don't you change out of your work clothes before you cook?"

She laughed, glancing down at herself. "I forget."

Uncomfortable silence fell as we each kneaded a ball of dough. I could feel bad news hanging in the air. I didn't want to say anything about prom until I knew what it was.

Ranjit thundered down the stairs (seriously, how does an eight-year-old boy sound like an elephant?) waving a well-loved Spider-Man action figure in one hand. "Bebe! Bebe! I'm hungry!"

"You can have a cheese stick from the fridge. Then go back upstairs, your sister and I are talking."

"Or not talking," I muttered.

"But Bebe—"

"*Now*, Ranjit." She used the *voice*. His eyes went wide, then he grabbed his snack and retreated. Silence again, just the ticktick of the oven heating.

Finally, Bebe cleared her throat. "I was thinking about your cross country meet next week."

I already knew where this was going from her tone. I threw my dough on the counter, sending up a billow of flour. "You said I could go. It's going to be done by six at the latest. That's plenty of time to get home."

"Your father and I discussed it. We're not comfortable with the risk. You know how the traffic gets in Houston."

"That's not fair!" Of course, nothing had been fair in recent memory, starting out with Abba getting sick. But cross country was the only thing I was good at, and the only thing being a werewolf had actually *helped*.

"I know it isn't, darling. But we have to be safe."

"It *is* safe! It's during the day. Bebe, this meet is *important* if I want to qualify!"

Bebe sighed, like somehow this was hurting *her*. "There is more to life than running, Sadikha."

I shoved my rolling pin. It skidded across the counter and fell, hitting the floor with a resounding *crack*. "And there's more to life than *me* sitting in a wooden box because *you're* scared." Then I turned on my heel and stomped upstairs. I slammed the door to my room, hard enough that a picture fell off my wall, but it didn't make me feel better. It just meant I had to hang a picture back up before I stubbed my toe on it. I really just wanted to bite something.

After the first post-attack full moon (and we don't talk about *that* or what happened to the neighbor's yappy dog) we built a shed in the backyard. Abba isn't much of a handyman, but he could manage a wall if you gave him enough two by fours and a nail gun. I helped him, because I'm actually very good with my hands.

Every full moon after that, Bebe or Abba locked me into the shed, and I sat and counted all the crooked nails (Abba's fault) until the sun went down, and then I literally couldn't think any more. I kept meaning to fix the nails because I hated things looking that haphazard, but I hated that shed even more, and I hated that I helped build it.

The final horrible irony was that we still hadn't told Ranjit what the shed was for. He's only eight, and this was a big secret. My parents just told him I'm meditating. I catch him playing with his action figures there sometimes. Let me tell you how fun it is, to sit on the bare floor, only to have your right butt cheek stabbed by the upraised plastic fists of the Green Goblin: It's not fun at all.

But now I knew, if I wanted to go to prom, my parents couldn't know. They'd never allow it. They would be too scared of what could happen if I came back late. If I thought about it too much or let my faith in myself waver, I'd be scared too. Hazy memories of eating a neighbor's dog weren't quickly forgotten. Maybe I shouldn't go at all. But then, what was I going to tell Jenny?

I didn't know what to do.

• • •

A couple of days later, Jenny and I were on our way to lunch when I spotted a card table with a sign written in blue marker: *Prom tickets on sale now!*

"Oh, look, Sadi!" She grabbed my hand.

"Wow, yeah. Look at that." Really, I felt like the bottom had dropped out of my stomach. I still hadn't come up with some kind of excuse and prom was less than a month away. This was bad.

I let her drag me over to the table. The boy behind it, someone I recognized vaguely from seeing him around the halls, gave her a bright smile. "Here for tickets?"

The teacher behind him, I knew a lot better: Mr. Hansen. He had on a yellow polo shirt and glasses with black plastic rims, his gray hair in a buzz cut. He taught history, and had once caught Jenny and me kissing behind the bleachers, not long after we started dating. That had been unpleasant for everyone, and it was so unfair; all of the straight couples practically hump each other in the halls between classes, and the teachers acted like Stonewall wasn't over forty years ago. I studiously avoided making eye contact with him.

"Yes!" Jenny said. "Two tickets, please."

Mr. Hansen cleared his throat. "You two planning on going together?" He looked like he smelled something bad, his face pinched.

Like a little spasm, Jenny grabbed my hand again. But his tone set my nerves on edge, and I spoke up before she could. "Is that any of your business?" Probably a bad idea. I'm not very good at the diplomacy thing.

"Actually, it is," he said, the corner of his lips twitching. Was he enjoying this? "School policy states that same sex couples are not welcome at our formal events."

I stared at him. Had he really just said that to me? In 2014? I felt my face getting hot, a mixture of embarrassment and righteous anger. "You're kidding, right?"

Jenny squeezed my hand tighter, tugging on it.

"That's the rule," Mr. Hansen said.

"That's bullshit!" This never would have happened in my old school in Ann Arbor. We'd even had a couple of gay guys get crowned dual prom king when I was a sophomore.

"Watch your language, young lady."

Jenny yanked my hand hard enough that I took half a step to the side. "It's fine," she said. "Sorry about this." Then she dragged me away.

You wouldn't know to look at her, but Jenny is strong. Being a cheerleader isn't for wimps. She had me around the corner before I pegged my anger level at *irrationally furious*.

"He can't do that!"

"Quiet," Jenny said, shushing me with her hand. "I'm sorry, Sadi. I've . . . heard stories about this. I was just hoping . . ."

"School policy?" I spluttered. "How is that even *legal*?"

"I don't know. Does it matter?"

"Of course it does!" I took a deep breath, and let it out slowly, fighting my temper down. Jenny looked like she was about to start crying, her face tilted down toward our joined hands. I had to look at this from her perspective, still deep in the closet. Some part of me said yes, this was the perfect opportunity to get out of the whole mess. But looking at Jenny's set expression, like she was bleeding inside from another stupid cut, and thinking about Mr. Hansen's smug, stupid, aggravating face . . . fuck that. "All right, what do we do?"

"We try again later. When Mr. Hansen isn't around. And we buy our tickets separately. You're allowed to go to the prom alone, you know. And then if we just happen to meet up . . ."

"Seriously?"

"Please, Sadi. Just . . . let it go."

It was the please that got me. It always did, with Jenny. That, and the fact that I didn't want to see her cry. "Okay, fine." I checked the hall with a quick glance, then nudged her chin so I could kiss her. "I swear, this town is like living in the Dark Ages."

Jenny rolled her eyes. She's always caught between agreeing with me— because being stuffed in the closet by your own parents and your neighbors *sucks*—and feeling defensive because she grew up here. "Are you sure you want to go to prom in the Dark Ages, then?"

I squeezed her hand. "I'd figure out how to get to prom on Neptune if it meant I got to go with you." That got her to her smile.

• • •

I tore a piece from my *chapati* to scoop up a bit of curry and studiously tried to ignore the way Ranjit kept kicking my chair. Bebe and Abba were just discussing some kind of business trip Bebe would have to take in a few weeks, out to see a drilling rig. Good thing Abba actually liked cooking.

"Oh, Sadi," Bebe turned to me. "I saw Mrs. Wilson at the grocery store today."

"Oh?" Greg Wilson, her kid, was in cross country with me. We went running together all the time. Nice thing about being a lesbian is you never have to worry about your parents getting weird about you spending a lot of time with a boy.

"She said Greg is very excited about the formal dance coming up. I didn't even know that was happening! Why didn't you tell us?"

"And when is it?" Abba asked.

Because I know you'll just say no. I shrugged and lied to cover the omission I'd been making all this time. "I don't really care. I don't really want to go. Jenny doesn't really care either, so why bother? It'll be stupid. Just a lot of bad music and people who don't know how to dance trying to show off their shoes."

Abba and Bebe exchanged long looks. "Are you sure, sweetie?" Bebe asked. "I set aside some money for your prom dress. I know this sort of thing is important in America."

"Yeah." I smiled, and felt like a horrible person. "You can buy me a really nice dress for graduation instead." I loved pretty dresses, after all, so it wasn't a weird request. And there would be my prom dress, taken care of.

Abba smiled. "That seems fair."

How had I even come to this place? Living honestly is one of the pillars of life, and breaking it was getting way too easy. Jenny, my parents, teachers, who was I going to lie to next? Bebe's perfect curry made a hot lead ball in my stomach, like it was punishing me for lying.

• • •

"Guess what," Jenny said, grinning as she sat next to me.

"You invented a robot last night." I grinned back at her. It was impossible not to, when a girl that beautiful is smiling.

Jenny laughed. We played that game all the time. "Nope. That was last week, silly."

"Okay, then what?"

"I got my dress."

"Ooh. Pics?"

"Nope." She gave me a wonderfully smug look and twirled a strand of blonde hair around her finger. "You have to wait until prom night."

"Rude." But I loved it. "So I take it everything went okay with your mom?"

She sighed, smile going from joyful to wry. "Yeah. She thinks it's so sad

I'm going to prom alone, but she's convinced the amazing dress will help me capture a boyfriend there."

"Yikes. I'm sorry."

Jenny shrugged. "It could have gone a lot worse. I think she really just doesn't want to think about it." She traced a little shape on the smooth top of her desk. "What about you? Got your dress yet? I bet *your* mom is excited at least."

Oh, but this was awkward. What to tell her? My mom really liked Jenny, and she came over to our house sometimes. This could go really badly, if Jenny said anything about us going to prom together. "I . . . haven't talked to them about it."

"What? Why?"

Plausible excuse, go! "There's. Uh. A thing. At the Temple that night." Ugh, why did I always have to blame everything on my religion? I felt horrible about that, too. But no one would argue with it. "If I tell them about prom, it'll just be a huge argument."

"Oh . . ." Her shoulders hunched. Would she sound that disapproving if she knew the truth? You know, if she even got past the whole *werewolf* thing without turning me in to the school counselor because I obviously must have a drug problem, if I'm convinced I ate the neighbor's purse poodle. "Then you really can't go."

The tantalizing get out of jail free card hung right in front of me. She was practically offering me the out. And yet . . . I thought about the complete embarrassment of not being allowed to buy tickets together. I thought about sitting in that tiny wooden room, surrounded by crooked nails and waiting, wishing I'd gotten to at least dance to some Katy Perry and kiss my girlfriend before that terrifying primal anger pounded so hard in my blood I couldn't even think over the sound. It wasn't my fault I was a werewolf, or that Jenny was in the closet, but I'd let other people talk me into making my own cage. No, I'd *make* it work.

Somehow.

"What, you're going to get on my case too? Jenny, I want to do this with you. This is the most important thing to me. I should be allowed to make my own choices."

She looked uncomfortable, but reached out to take my hand anyway. "Okay. Sorry. I know how it is. I really do."

No kidding. I hadn't thought I could feel any worse, but I suddenly did. What kind of person was I? I squeezed her hand. "The important thing is that we get to be together, right?"

She nodded, took a quick glance around to make sure the teacher wasn't looking, then leaned forward to kiss me.

Somehow. They make it look so easy in movies. Why can't my life be like that? Though I guess if this was a movie, I probably also wouldn't be a lesbian.

• • •

Bebe bought me the dress she'd promised for graduation—hot pink, strapless, and short enough that she shook her head indulgently. Three weeks, two weeks, one, and I still had no idea what I was going to do. Then it was P-day, and Abba picked me up from school, which was kind of embarrassing, but it was a bad idea for me to drive in Houston traffic on a full moon day. I kissed him on his smooth cheek—he doesn't have any hair under his turban either, thanks to the chemo. My whole skin felt itchy. When it's a full moon, the moon is actually out all day, which I think is what does that to me. I feel too alive, almost, and I can't pay attention to anything. Jenny had just put it down to nerves, thank God.

I probably shouldn't have said anything, but I couldn't help myself as he navigated the tree-lined streets on the way to Ranjit's school. The minivan's air conditioner was going full blast, and we were still both sweating. "You know, it's been months since anything *bad* happened on the full moon," I said.

"You mean anything other than you turning into a wolf?"

"I mean . . . I haven't destroyed anything or made a lot of noise. It's getting better. Could we maybe try just letting me be in my room again tonight? It's going to be really hot in the shed."

"No, Sadi. We have to be safe about this."

"It's not *fair*." Really, I was trying to hide panic. I didn't know how I'd get out of the shed if they locked me in. It's not like I could tell Jenny about it.

"I know. Grace, Sadi. Accepting what hand the world has dealt us is a practice."

"Could we at least wait until it's closer to sunset?"

He sighed. A bead of sweat slowly ran down the side of his face. "I don't want you to suffer, Sadi. But I also want you to be safe. And everyone else, too."

I heard the final note in his voice. If I kept trying, he'd just get angry. And while I'd fight with Bebe, I didn't like making Abba angry. Like I was afraid he was still fragile, and shouting would make something in him break.

On the way home from picking up Ranjit, we stopped at the grocery store. Abba left the van running for the air conditioner and went in by himself; he just had to pick up his medications. For a moment, I thought about what would happen if I just slipped over into the driver's seat and stole the van. But everything I would need to get ready for the dance was at home, and there was the whole issue of Ranjit being there. I wasn't going to take my little brother to prom, and I wasn't going to just leave him at a McDonald's, even if the thought was tempting at times.

Ranjit. Maybe he was the answer to all my problems? I always tried my best to ignore him, and maybe that had been my mistake. I turned around in my seat. Ranjit had a comic book spread out across his lap, his legs kicking idly. He bought that crap with his allowance and extra money he earned by mowing lawns. "Hey, snot."

He looked up and stuck his tongue out. "You're the snot."

"I need your help."

"Then you shouldn't call me snot."

That might not have been the best conversation opener, I had to admit. "Okay, sorry. Ranjit. I need your help."

"With what?"

"I need to get out tonight."

"You're getting locked in the shed, right?"

"Yes. But there's something I need to do."

Ranjit closed his comic book and gave me a narrow-eyed look. "You're not really meditating in there, are you?"

I wasn't sure what would be the best answer, but I was so sick of lying. "No."

He nodded, like he'd expected that. "It's so you don't go biting people on the butt, right?"

I stared at him, my jaw going slack. "*What?*"

"Our parents lock you in a shed every full moon. After you got attacked by a *dog*. I read books. I'm not stupid."

What had my life even become? Were things really that obvious? "Do you promise not to tell?"

He nodded.

I hesitated. He was a smart kid and everything, but he was a kid! "Yes. You're right."

"That's so cool! My sister's a—"

"—shush! You said you wouldn't tell!" Maybe that was the key. He was a kid, and young enough to believe impossible things.

"No one's in here with us."

I rolled my eyes. "But don't go around yelling about it."

"Okay." He swung his legs. "Have you eaten anyone?"

"What? No!"

"Oh." I couldn't tell if he was disappointed or not. "Do you think you will?"

"No!"

"Because there's this boy, he's in fifth grade, and he—"

"No! I am not going to eat someone for you, no matter how mean he is!" But wait a second. No one was allowed to be mean to my little brother except me. "But if you want, I'll come to your school during lunch and you can point him out. I can scare him, I bet."

"Really?"

"Only if you help me."

He gave me a long, assessing look that had no business being on the face of a child that young. "And I want three comic books. My choice."

Was he *bargaining* with me now? "Two. And they can't cost more than five dollars each. Or be anything Bebe wouldn't buy for you." Suddenly, I didn't want to leave this open-ended.

Ranjit nodded gravely. "It's a deal. What do you want me to do?"

This was starting to feel more surreal than my being a werewolf. "I just need you to unlock the shed. And then do something to keep Bebe and Abba busy while I get my dress, my shoes, and my makeup and get out."

He nodded wisely. "Spider-Man has to distract bad guys all the time. I can do this."

What had I just gotten myself in to?

• • •

The full moon routine was well-established: get home early, do any home-work while mom finished up dinner. Eat something really meaty. Abba thought that might make me feel less angry. At least I felt less hungry, so that helped. After dinner, I changed into a cheap bathrobe and followed my par-ents outside. Sweat beaded up on my forehead and arms immediately in the sweltering heat. The grass was rough against my bare feet.

Bebe put several bottles of water inside the shed, then turned on the ceiling fan we'd installed a couple months ago. "We love you, Sadhika. Seek peace," Abba said, then shut the door behind me. I heard the bolt scrape home.

I found the spot on the floor that got the maximum air from the fan and then dumped one of the bottles of water on my head. I couldn't do anything in here but stew and feel the walls closing in. I counted every one of the nails, and I wished I had a hammer. I wouldn't straighten them, I'd pull them out.

Maybe ten minutes later, I heard the bolt and Ranjit pulled the door open. He stood, fists on his hips like he was posing, framed by wood and crooked nails. His little Spider-Man rollerboard suitcase sat at his feet.

I stared at it. "Moving in?"

"I grabbed your things for you, too."

"Seriously?" I could just jump the fence!

He grabbed the suitcase, giving me as stern a look as someone wearing Marvel comics tennis shoes could manage. "I want two more comic books."

"If everything is there, I'll buy you three."

"Deal."

I was dizzy with relief. Yes, everything was stuffed in haphazardly, but he'd grabbed my entire makeup kit, my purse, the dress, and even the underwear to go with it. The dress might end up a little wrinkly, but it didn't matter. "Three it is." I breathed out an unsteady sigh.

"Go do your distraction. And . . . thanks, little brother."

He shot me a grin. "I'm going to be a superhero."

"You're already my superhero." I watched him trot back across the lawn. The patio door opened and shut. Then a minute later, I heard a muffled crash and a loud, unhappy howl of pain.

Well, that would certainly do it.

I sprinted across the lawn, let myself out of the gate in the fence, and ran down the street, still clutching the Spider-Man suitcase, ignoring how the concrete burned at the soles of my feet. This was going to work.

I was going to prom with my girlfriend.

• • •

Jenny waited for me outside the doors of the banquet hall the school had rented. I'd managed to get myself put together surprisingly well, thanks to a stop by the school so I could grab a shower. My dress had a few creases in it that hanging near the showers hadn't fixed, but considering an hour ago I'd been running down the street in a bathrobe, I felt accomplished.

I felt even more accomplished when Jenny smiled at me. "Sadi! I was starting to get worried!"

"Sorry about that. I forgot my phone, or I would have called." I looked her up and down. She had a crimson dress, cut lower than I thought her mom would have gone for, the skirt swirling loosely around her hips. "You look fantastic."

She grinned, striking a little pose, one leg cocked out. "You look great too. You and your thing about pink."

"I can't help that it's the best color in the world." I grabbed her hand. "Come on, I can't wait to dance with you."

She gave me a smile, but it was a nervous, trembling one. "Okay. We just have to be careful."

It was dark in the banquet hall, and there were lights, even a disco ball. The DJ was playing "Wide Awake" by Katy Perry, which didn't seem like a bad place to start. The fake wooden floor was already full of other students, girls in strapless dresses of all colors and boys in anything ranging from jeans and a tie to an actual tuxedo. Everyone danced terribly, but the whole point was for couples to dance as close as possible anyway.

I felt too energized, too wild. Though wild was better than angry; maybe all I'd needed was to get out of the shed. All I knew was that it felt amazing, and I wanted to just *howl*. Rather than try to sneak into a group, I just pulled Jenny onto the floor and got her dancing.

For a moment, she was awkward, stiff and afraid. Then she relaxed when no chaperones leaped on us to drag us away for being publicly gay. Soon, I had her laughing. I'm not the best dancer either.

It worked out just fine, and then "Until the End of Time" started playing. It was a song we both loved, a song we'd danced to in an empty classroom or two between the end of class and the beginning of this or that practice. Jenny looped her arms over my neck, and gave me a smile with red, perfect lips, that made me just want to kiss her and never stop. I slipped my arms around her waist. Perfect. Absolutely perfect. This moment made everything worth it, even all the trouble I'd be in once my parents caught up with me.

Then Jenny's eyes went wide. A heavy hand fell on my shoulder. Jenny jumped away from me like I'd suddenly been electrified. I turned to look up at Mr. Hansen. "You two are dancing a little too close," he said, loudly enough that we could hear him over the music. "I told you the rules."

I'd thought the anger had left me, had hoped that was the case at least. But it came roaring back when Mr. Hansen dared to touch me. I suddenly had a vivid mental image of sinking my pink-painted fingernails into his throat and tearing. And he'd *deserve* it—

No. Breathe. I made myself breathe, but I stared at him. My fingers curved into claws at my sides. Around us, people were whispering, some pretending to not look at us, others openly staring.

"Hey! I am dancing with my *friend*," Jenny said, the words almost tumbling from her. "In Sadikha's home country, girls dance with each other *all the time* when they don't have boyfriends. Get your mind out of the gutter."

I felt a tickle of pleasure that Jenny had thought so quickly on her feet. (And it wasn't even a lie; girls dance together all the time in *America*.) I kept staring at Mr. Hansen, and nodded slowly. All I could think of was just how he'd scream if I sank my teeth into his shoulder and tore a chunk out. My lip, unbidden, curled in a snarl. And Mr. Hansen, all six foot two of him, took his hand off my shoulder and stepped slightly back.

"Just watch yourselves." He licked his lips. "I'll be keeping an eye on you." And then he escaped, back toward the edge of the dance floor.

"Are you okay?" Jenny asked, her voice dropping to a whisper. She sounded terrified.

I took three deep breaths and looked back at her. Now that it was just her and me again (how weird, to feel like it was just the two of us when there were people all around, even bumping shoulders with me) I could push that primal, terrifying anger down. "Yeah. He just... made me kind of mad."

"He's an asshole. This whole thing is stupid. Just... are you okay?" She ducked her head to try to look me in the eye.

I wonder if she could see it, the wild energy running through me, the wolf just waiting to get free. Maybe this had been a mistake? I'd have to go soon anyway. Dusk couldn't be far off, though it was hard to tell—all the windows in the banquet hall were covered to enhance the lighting. But it hadn't felt like a mistake when we were dancing together. "Yeah, I'm fine. I just... this bullshit just makes me so mad. I also don't want to get you in trouble. Do you want to go home or something?"

"I—" Jenny hesitated, then reached out to take my hand again. "I'm sick of being scared, Sadi. I love you. I'm sick of feeling like I have to be scared about it."

"What if we get thrown out? What if someone tells your mom?"

She bit her lip, frowned. "No, screw it. If that happens, I'll... deal with it. If I can stand up to Mr. Hansen, I can stand up to my mom. She's not half as scary at him." She sounded like she was trying to convince herself.

"Jenny—"

"Don't try to talk me out of it. Let's just dance. I even gave us an awesome excuse."

Maybe any other day, I would have tried to argue with her anyway. Or maybe that was the me before I'd gotten my leg in the jaws of a werewolf. Right now, all I felt was fierce joy, my soul screaming "Yes!" at the top of its lungs.

We danced. And danced. And danced. And it sucked that we couldn't get quite as close as before, because we were still faking it. We knew Mr. Hansen was watching. But we had the flimsy shield that Jenny had made with her excuse, and we were going to use it until we ran out of music. I was so caught up in it, just the fun of it, the joy of getting to do even this much with my girlfriend in public, I lost track of time.

Stupid, I know. But love makes you do stupid things, because they feel so good at the time.

At first, I thought the lightness in my head was just fatigue. But I had so much energy, I didn't want to stop dancing. I just wanted more and more, to dance forever, to take Jenny by the hand and just *run*, not because we were scared, but because we *could*.

Then the first pain hit me, the groan of bones getting ready to shift around. The pain had never been so clear before; I was always overwhelmed with so much primal rage by this point that a little pain didn't matter. I moaned and sagged against Jenny. She already had her arms around me. "Sadi? What's wrong?"

"Oh no . . . " I clutched at her back with my hands. "Oh shit . . . I'm so stupid . . . "

"What? Sadi, what's going on?"

I didn't want this to happen. I didn't want to turn into a ravening monster right in front of my girlfriend. And then quite possibly bite her, if not kill her. "The sun went down. Fuck, the sun went down. I'm so stupid, Jenny."

"Sadi, calm down." She still swayed gently with the music. Of all hilarious ironies, it was Christina Perri promising that she'd wait a thousand years, and a thousand more. Life hates me sometimes. "What's going on?"

Well, it didn't really matter any more, did it? I moaned again, my nerves feeling like they'd burst into flame, overworked. I didn't have the brain power left to lie. "Would you believe me if I told you I was a werewolf?"

She pulled back, eyes going wide as she looked into mine. Whatever she saw, she believed me. And God bless her, she didn't ask the obvious questions, like how I'd decided being at a dance with her at night would be a good idea. "Breathe, Sadi," she whispered. "Just breathe."

"I can't," I moaned. I felt my fingernails sinking into the fabric of her dress, going sharp and jagged. My mind was slipping, anger starting to fill me.

"Just focus on me." And even though her voice was a whisper, I heard her clearly. "You'll be all right."

"I'm so sorry. I'm going to hurt you. I'm going to turn into a monster and hurt you." My teeth ached, probably starting to deform into canines and sharp incisors. I squeezed my eyes shut. This would be the part where she screamed and ran away, I was sure. I could smell so many people around me, hear hearts pounding, taste blood in my mouth.

"I trust you. You won't hurt me." She actually tightened her arms around me. "I love you, baby. It'll be all right. You don't have to be scared." She licked her lips. "Be brave. And I'll be brave too." And then she kissed me.

It was kind of awkward, considering my canines were already markedly longer. But it also gave me something to focus on, that reminder. Jenny loved me. She trusted me. She believed in me. I couldn't hurt her. I wouldn't let myself. I focused on the feeling of her lips against mine, the taste of her lipstick. I channeled the ferocity into that. Not hatred at being confined, but wanting to protect my girlfriend. Not anger, but love.

Around us, I could hear people gasping, clothing rustling as they backed away, murmuring. I didn't care. Because while I could still feel my body changing, my skin beginning to crawl and my bones shifting, what I felt inside was more important. The wolf that always overwhelmed me with rage flowed around me, through me, and found release in that kiss. It filled my mind, but didn't tear me apart. It filled my heart, and this time I welcomed it.

Maybe that had always been the answer, to not be afraid but to embrace it and trust it, so it could embrace me. If my body, every annoying hair of it, was a gift from God, wasn't this as well? It was still my body, no matter how it was shaped. Maybe I didn't have to be afraid. Maybe the wolf was only angry because no one likes being in a cage. Maybe the wolf that had bitten me had gone mad from fighting himself for years and years.

Maybe that was always the solution: oneness.

I made our kiss a howl for joy.

• • •

That's not where it ended, of course. I'd like to say what followed was a wave of spontaneous applause, like in the movies, and Mr. Hansen's heart grew three sizes that day, and the school board pulled their collective heads out of their asses. Nope. There were catcalls from some dumbass football players, and then Mr. Hansen took us each firmly by the arm and escorted us out.

Oh yeah, and someone helpfully pointed out—*gross*—I had a unibrow. Thanks.

But you know what? I didn't care. I stood with Jenny on the sidewalk to the side of the banquet hall and we kissed and kissed until my lips weren't human enough to manage it any more. Jenny watched wide-eyed while I finished changing into a wolf, then picked up my mangled pink dress and put it in her purse as I ran off toward the wooded lot.

I got grounded for a month, but Bebe and Abba also listened to me, about what had happened. That I'd had control because I hadn't started my trans-formation scared or angry. They listened when I said I could do this, if they would trust me like Jenny had.

Then they transferred gardening equipment into the shed in the back yard, and started taking me out to George Bush State Park when it was the full moon. I also stopped plucking the hair on my face and started wear-ing my *chunni* again, because I was done with the excuses and lies. And it felt *good*. Maybe it would have been poetic if I'd gone and straightened all the crooked nails in the shed, but they were what they were. They held the boards of the shed together tight and it was sturdy, everything a shed needed to be. Besides, I had much better things to do with my time.

Like hang out in Jenny's room while we watched movies or studied or painted our fingernails and made out. Because Jenny got thrown out of her house by her mom, so she came to live in our spare room. Since she had a full scholarship coming to her from A & M, it could have gone a lot worse, but it was no movie ending.

Screw movies. People like me deserve our happily ever afters too.

We kissed on the stage at graduation, in front of everyone. That was one crooked nail sticking out of my life that I did want to pull, because I hadn't put it there.

Oh yeah, and this one, too: I called every newspaper in America I could find a number for and told them about how my high school doesn't let lesbians into their prom. Because seriously, fuck those guys.

ANGEL

Terrence McCauley

Kansas City 1931

Quinn grabbed the gun off the table and stuck the barrel under his own chin.

He willed himself to have the nerve to thumb the safety off. Squeezing the trigger would be the next step. That should be easy. He'd never had trouble squeezing a trigger before.

But he'd never thought of killing himself before, either.

He hadn't needed to. A week ago, he'd still had a chance. He'd still had Beth. The short time he'd spent with her had made an empty year on the lam mean something.

Quinn had been drifting before Beth came into his life. All of the blood he'd shed and the men he'd killed back in New York had ultimately meant nothing. Even his boss, Archie Doyle, had given up and moved to Hot Springs with barely a fight. Five years of his life gone with nothing to show for it but a couple of bucks in the bank and a lot of bad memories.

Then Beth came along and showed him what really mattered in life. They'd seen each other's scars and swore they'd love each other forever. The ugliness of the past couldn't reach them anymore. She said they were better because they had each other.

She told him they'd been reborn. She said she was different than the other women. She promised she'd never leave him.

He'd trusted her. He'd believed.

That was before Beth saw him work. That was before she saw Quinn kill two men and wound a third without guilt or hesitation.

After that, she changed. She denied it, but he knew. She bolted the first chance she got. Saying they'd both changed had been an abstract. Dead men on the sidewalk was real. Blood was as real as it got.

Beth wasn't different from the other women after all. She said they'd changed each other, but that had been a lie. If she had changed, she would've stayed. If he had changed, he wouldn't have slid back into the Life. The violence in him had never gone away. It had simply grown quiet; waiting for the spark to bring it back to life.

He should've known men like him didn't get second chances. They didn't deserve them. He understood that now.

He didn't deserve Beth, either. That's why she'd left. He'd driven her away when she saw what he was at his core. A killer.

The guilt of losing her had driven him north from Hot Springs in a rage. He'd driven all night and wound up in this shithole neighborhood somewhere outside Kansas City.

He'd stopped at the first house that had a Room to Rent sign. He'd paid a week in advance for the room sight unseen. It would be the easiest money the landlady ever made. He didn't plan on living anywhere near that long.

He remembered his appearance had scared the mousey woman who'd rented him the room in her basement. Her little girl had hidden behind the skirts of her mother's ratty house dress. He remembered she was scared, but didn't take her eyes off him, either. She looked, but never looked away.

He remembered the woman mentioned her husband was out of work. She said she was taking in washing and renting her basement to help pay the bills. The dull shiner around her left eye told Quinn her husband was a slugger who liked to take out his failures on her.

Quinn hated bullies. Normally, the sight of a bruised woman would've set off his temper. But not that time. He had troubles of his own.

That had been two days ago. He'd spent every moment since alone in that basement; trying to work up the nerve to take one last life. His own.

His hand trembled, but he couldn't bring his thumb near the safety. His hand began to cramp and he took the gun away from his chin. He looked down at the gun and wiped away his tears with the back of his left hand. Killing had never been hard for him before. Why now?

He heard a quiet voice come from the doorway. "I'm an angel."

Quinn quickly looked up, but didn't see anyone. He noticed the door to the backyard was open. Had be opened it? He didn't remember. Maybe he had. Maybe he was just hearing things. He figured he must be. If there were any angels around, they sure as hell wouldn't be near him. Not in this life. And certainly not in whatever realm that followed the bullet.

He looked down at the gun one last time when he heard the voice again. "I said I'm an angel."

This time, he saw a little girl peeking at him from beside the doorway.

The same little girl who'd looked at him from behind her mother's skirts two days before. She had dirty blonde curls and the biggest brown eyes he'd ever seen. She wore a homemade dress that looked like it had been white once upon a time but was closer to brown now. He hadn't paid much attention to her back then. He couldn't look at anything but her now.

"Mommy said I'm an angel and this is my halo." Someone had wrapped a wire hanger in tinfoil and twisted it into a circle so it could sit on top of her head. The other end had been bent into a circle above it. "Do you like it?"

The little girl didn't look at him the way most people did. She wasn't afraid or cautious. She didn't look at him the way Beth had looked at him that last time.

She really wanted to know if Quinn liked her halo. He spoke his mind. "I think it's beautiful."

She giggled and did a little twirl. "Mommy said if I'm good, she'll try to make me wings next week, but Daddy yelled at me today, so I might not get them. Daddy yells a lot. What's your name, mister?"

He almost didn't hear the question. "My name is Quinn."

"My name is Bessy." She looked down at the .45 in Quinn's hand. "Is that a gun?"

He stuffed the gun under the pillow. "That's just a tool I use sometimes. It only looks like a gun."

"Daddy thinks you're a gangster like the ones the man on the radio talks about. Daddy told Mommy to throw you out but Mommy said you already paid for a week and we need the money. Mommy said if Daddy wants you to leave, he has to do it himself."

Quinn didn't remember much from the last few days, but he knew Daddy hadn't come to see him. Daddy was smart.

"I'm not a gangster." It was partially true. He wasn't. Not anymore.

"That's good because gangsters are bad. Your eyes are red. Were you crying just now?"

Quinn wasn't used to being around kids. He wasn't comfortable around them. He wasn't used to how quickly they jumped from one thing to another without warning. "No, I wasn't . . ."

"Mommy cries a lot," she said. "She cries at night after I've gone to bed and before Daddy comes home. She thinks I'm asleep, but I hear her. She gets mad if I try to hug her, so I pretend I'm asleep."

Quinn remembered seeing the woman's black eye. He bet Daddy had given her that. He remembered she'd limped a little when she showed him the entrance to the basement, too. She probably told people she was clumsy and fell a lot.

He began to feel something he hadn't felt in days. Something old crowding out the new sadness in his gut. Something returning to pull him away from where he was to a place he didn't want to go. "Best go back up to your mommy now. I've got things to do."

"Mommy's not here and Daddy's resting. He snores and he's grumpy when he's resting. I come down here to play, but you're here now."

She looked out at the overgrown lot next to her house. When she looked back at him, she was smiling again. "It's nice out and it's not too hot yet. We could sit outside for a while. Mommy said you haven't gone outside much, at least not what she's seen. She says it's not *no-mal*, but I don't know what that means."

He felt himself begin to laugh. He laughed long and loud. Longer than he had for a longer time than he could remember. Maybe the best laugh of his life.

He heard her begin to giggle, too, probably because he was, and it made him laugh all the more. Bessy laughed too, only because the grownup was laughing. He laughed like a madman because maybe he was.

And when he couldn't laugh any more, he finally said, "I don't know what *normal* is, either, honey, but maybe a few minutes of sunshine won't hurt."

He stood up and took his suit coat from the back of the chair and put his fedora on his head. He looked back at the gun he'd stashed beneath the pillow. Might be best to leave it where it was.

Then he realized Bessy was looking up at him; her mouth open and her eyes wide. Not scared, not afraid. Just looking. "You're big."

He smiled. "No. You're just little."

He flinched when she took his hand, but she was too happy to notice. She was smiling as she led him out into the sunshine. "Let's go."

• • •

They sat in middle of the overgrown weeds of the abandoned lot.

Bessy told him this was an enchanted forest, just like the story books said. The ragweeds she picked were roses from her special garden no one knew about but her and now him. She said fairies and elves lived under the ground, but only came out at night so they wouldn't scare the little children. She told him there was a beautiful princess who lived down below who was always nice to everyone. She never yelled and never used bad words and never made anyone cry. She was a good princess and smiled all the time.

"Do you smile, Quinn?"

Quinn tried, for her sake. "Sometimes."

"I like to smile. Mommy and Daddy don't smile much. I wish they did, but they're sad a lot."

"Grownups get sad sometimes, I guess."

She rearranged the ragweeds in her hands. "Why do you wear black clothes?"

Quinn had never really thought about why. Every suit he owned was black. All he'd ever worn were black suits and white shirts and black ties. It was just easier that way. Easier for the kind of work he did. "I don't know. It's easy, I guess."

"Do you wear it because you're sad?"

"I was."

"But you're happy now?"

She looked too happy for him to tell her the truth. "Yes, honey. I'm much better now."

Bessy jumped up and cheered and threw her arms around his neck. He didn't know how someone so little could be so strong. He hugged her back, but not too tightly. He didn't want to hurt her.

She pulled away and began dancing around where he sat, cheering and singing to herself. He wasn't ready to feel better yet, but her joy made it pretty damned hard to be miserable.

She finally slowed down and went back to picking more of her roses. And just like that, her joy had been replaced by her need to tend to her garden. Quinn guessed kids were like that. They were light enough to drift from one emotion to the next without stopping. The weight of the world hadn't found them yet.

And as he sat among the weeds of an abandoned lot on the outskirts of Kansas City, he found himself envying a child.

That's why she surprised him when she asked, "Does your daddy drink?"

He figured she was too young to understand he'd grown up in an orphanage. The closest thing he had to a father had been an Irish bootlegger named Archie Doyle. Up until he'd been forced out of New York the year before, Archie had been the biggest bootlegger on the eastern seaboard. There was a time when there wasn't a bottle of booze that landed anywhere from Bangor to Georgia where he didn't see a profit. Canada, too. He couldn't explain all of that to her, so he simply said, "Sometimes."

She finally got a stubborn weed free, then moved to the next one. She was getting quite a fistful by then. "Daddy drinks a lot. Mommy says he drinks too much, but that makes Daddy mad."

Quinn didn't like how she looked when she said it. "How mad?"

She shrugged her little shoulders. "Sometimes, he—"

"BESSY!" A man's voice boomed across the vacant lot. "Bessy, goddamn it.

Where the hell are you?"

Quinn saw the little girl freeze and drop all the ragweed she'd gathered as she looked back at her house.

Quinn looked, too. He saw the man who'd called out and knew that must be Daddy. He'd never seen the man before, but had seen men like him all his life. He was lanky and beer hall pale. He wore a gray undershirt that had once been white and pants that had once been gray. He moved like he was in his middle thirties, but all the bitterness and bootleg booze made him look closer to fifty. He had narrow, puffy eyes and a nose that had been broken once, but not set right.

Quinn knew the type well. The kind who thought of himself as a hard man, but was more bitter than tough. He liked to take out his disappointment on the only people he could: the women he lorded over. They were easy targets because they wouldn't fight back. They couldn't fight back because they had nowhere to go.

"Bessy!" he bellowed again. "Best come here right away, girl, 'fore you get the strap again."

Bessy was no longer the happy little girl who'd pulled him out of the basement and into the sun. She was a frightened little creature with wide, wet eyes. "I hafta go now."

Before he could say a word, she darted through the weeds back toward the house. She sang out, "Here I am, Daddy. I'm okay. I was just in the forest with my friend."

Daddy had already walked down the back steps and was waiting for her as she came to him. "What did I tell you about making up stories, girl? There ain't no friends out there and that ain't no forest. It's just a bunch of goddamned weeds is all and I don't want you out there no more."

"But it's true, Daddy. I was with my friend Quinn."

Quinn watched Daddy grab her by the arm and lift her up the stairs in one brutal motion. "Didn't I just tell you not to lie to me, girl? There ain't no one out there in that goddamned lot but . . . "

Daddy let go of her arm when Quinn stood up. Bessy scampered inside.

The two men stared at each other across the lot. Daddy was slit-eyed and mean. Daddy didn't like to be wrong. He liked being challenged even less.

Quinn felt that familiar heat begin to spread in his belly. He slowly became aware of every muscle, every tendon in his body. He could hear his own breath in his lungs and he could almost hear his own heartbeat. Every sight and sound became sharper as time slowed to a crawl. Everything else in the world blurred except for the man in the dirty white undershirt glaring back at him above the weeds.

Quinn kept staring until Daddy took a half-step back toward his house, followed by another, then another until he stumbled on the bottom step. He felt for the railing and quickly made his way inside. He slammed the door behind him. The sound of the lock sliding home echoed across the vacant lot like a rifle shot.

Quinn saw Daddy take a final look at him from behind the curtain on the backdoor window. Quinn didn't move, not even when the edge of the curtain fell back into place. He realized his fingernails were digging into his palms. He'd balled his hands into fists without realizing it.

He realized he wasn't alone anymore. His rage had returned.

Daddy's bellows from inside the house snapped Quinn out of it. A woman's voice, probably Mommy's, joined in and a sound that could only be little Bessy screaming reached him, even through the closed door.

Quinn started back to his basement room to get the only friend he had left in the world.

• • •

Quinn burst through the back door. Mommy was cowering against the kitchen wall as Daddy brought his hand back to strike her. Bessy was nowhere in sight.

Daddy turned on the intruder. Mommy screamed as Daddy grabbed a bottle off the kitchen table.

Quinn caught Daddy's wrist with his right hand before Daddy could bring the bottle down on his head. Quinn didn't squeeze his wrist. He didn't try to make him drop the bottle. He'd simply stopped the arm in mid-motion and held it there.

He let Daddy struggle to work his wrist free. He watched Daddy's eyes turn from anger to something close to fear as he realized Quinn wasn't fighting him. He'd simply grabbed hold of him and wasn't letting go.

Quinn could feel Daddy's grip on the bottle weaken. With his left hand, he plucked the bottle from Daddy's hand and gently set it on the kitchen table. To Mommy, Quinn said, "I didn't want you to have to clean that up."

Quinn kept Daddy's wrist locked in place. He enjoyed watching the frustrated fear come into his eyes. Daddy began to flail at Quinn with his free left hand. He tried to punch the bigger man in the face. The angle was wrong. All he caught was the thick meat of Quinn's shoulder.

He tried punching Quinn in the ribs, but Quinn twisted Daddy's wrist just enough to stop him. Then Daddy tried to kick at Quinn's leg. Another slight twist of the wrist kept him off balance.

"Let go of me, you son of a bitch!" Daddy seethed through clenched teeth.

"This is my house and my house is my castle!"

Quinn didn't budge. His grip held.

Daddy tried to look at Mommy, but she'd sunk too far down the wall for him to see her. "Don't just sit there, you idiot! Go get Joe from next door. Go get a cop. Go get somebody. Anybody!"

But Mommy didn't budge.

Quinn held Daddy in place while he asked the mother, "Did he hurt the little one?"

She looked up at him like she'd forgotten he was even there. People had looked at him like that before.

Quinn said, "Bessy? Your little girl. Did he hurt her?"

With a frail hand, Mommy pointed at a door. "No. He just locked her in there."

Quinn wrenched Daddy's wrist. Cartilage popped. Daddy screamed and squirmed. "You locked that little girl in the closet?"

Daddy had stored up enough rage to flail at him again. Quinn flicked his elbow into his nose. His head snapped back and Quinn did it again. A thin stream of blood trickled from his left nostril. "Doesn't feel good, does it? Being helpless and scared."

The father spat at Quinn's eye, but most of it caught his shoulder. "Fuck you."

Quinn let go of the wrist as he threw Daddy against the wall. Mommy screamed while Daddy rebounded and lunged.

Quinn snatched him by the throat and slammed him down onto the kitchen floor. He kept Daddy pinned by the neck as he pulled the .45 from his shoulder holster. He aimed the gun down at Daddy's mouth. "Open up."

Daddy's eyes bugged as he clamped his mouth tight.

Quinn pressed the gun barrel to his lips. "If you don't open up, I'll ram the barrel through your teeth."

Daddy's mouth opened. Quinn slid the gun into his mouth. Daddy retched, but Quinn kept the gun out just far enough to keep him from vomiting. He didn't want Mommy cleaning that up, either.

For the first time in two days, Quinn was able to thumb off the safety. Daddy flinched. He didn't need to thumb back the hammer on the automatic, but did so for effect. Both Mommy and Daddy began to quietly sob.

Quinn grabbed Daddy's neck a little tighter. "Until today, your wife and daughter thought you were a bad man. Today, they've seen you can be hurt. They've seen you scared. They know you can bleed. They'll never look at you the same way again because now they know what you are. The only reason why you're still alive is because they need you. So, you're going to get off the booze and find a job. I don't care if it's legal or not, but you're going to find one. You're going to pay your bills and do whatever it takes to put food on that table and clothes on their backs."

"I'll be checking in from time to time. I'll check in on your neighbors, too. You won't know who and you won't know when, but if I hear you're drinking again or slapping them around, I'll come back. I'll hurt you for a long time before I kill you."

Daddy gasped as Quinn pulled the gun out of his mouth and pressed it against Daddy's heart.

Quinn pitied and hated the man all at the same time. "You've got everything and don't even appreciate it. You'd better start or I'll take it all from you."

Quinn stood as he tucked the pistol back into the holster under his left arm. Daddy gagged as he tried to get air back into his lungs. Mommy watched Quinn, but didn't move from her spot on the floor.

Quinn said, "You can go to him if you want."

But Mommy buried her face in her hands and wept.

Quinn unlocked the closet door and no sooner had opened it a crack than Bessy came out and wrapped herself around his leg. "I knew you'd come," she cried into his leg. "I just knew you would."

He patted her hair gently with his left hand while he snapped the door-knob off with his right. He whipped it at Daddy down on the floor. It hit him in the balls. Daddy moaned and brought his knees up to his chest.

She'd never get locked in that closet again.

Quinn eased Bessy away from his leg and took a knee. Her cheeks were damp with tears. He tried to wipe them dry, but she ducked past that and hugged him all over again. He couldn't understand how someone so small could hug so hard. Or how someone could be mean to someone so needy.

He slowly eased her away from him again. "Is Bessy short for Elizabeth?"

A curl fell over her eyes as she nodded.

Quinn tucked it back where it belonged. "I had a friend named Elizabeth once. I'm glad I have one again."

Bessy wiped a tear from her eye. "Was she nice?"

"Yes, she was. Now you've got take care of Mommy. She needs an angel now to help her."

She looked very serious. "I'm not really an angel. Mommy just bent a hanger so it looked like I was."

Quinn ran the back of his hand across her cheek. "I know, but you're still an angel. You still save people."

She looked back at her father on the kitchen floor. "I couldn't save Daddy."

"Yes you did. And you saved me, too."

He kissed the side of her cheek and she giggled. She'd seen what he'd done and she hadn't looked away. She'd seen who he was and hadn't run away. She was too young to see what she wanted to see. She only saw things as they were.

"Now, you go take care of Mommy."

Bessy ran to her mother's arms.

Quinn stood and straightened out his jacket. "You got a phone here?"

She held her daughter tight as tears streamed down her cheeks. "No. He won't allow one in the house."

"I'll pay for one to get installed." He looked down at Daddy. He was still on the floor cradling his balls. "He won't argue. I'll call from time to time. If he gives you or the little one any more trouble, you let me know."

Quinn didn't look back at Bessy or Mommy or Daddy as he walked down the back stairs. He didn't look back at the basement either.

Looking back never did him much good anyway. He walked to his car instead.

MR. NANCE

Linda Rodriguez

It was just my luck that I took the phone call right as I was leaving work that hot summer Saturday evening in 1968. If it had been three minutes later, someone else would have picked up the phone, someone like Naomi, who would have just said, "Sorry, no can do," and gone back to reading *Blazing Hearts* after hanging up and writing down the call for her shift report. As Naomi was fond of telling me, she had common sense, which was not so common anymore.

"Bright Hill School for Wayward Girls," I answered. "Sofia Noguera speaking." I hoped it was a wrong number, and I could finish making my getaway. My roommate Kathy had already headed out to the car and would be waiting impatiently for me, so we could head back into the city and probably go to one or more of several parties friends were throwing.

"Sofia, it's Chantay." In the background behind her childish voice, I could hear someone yelling and pounding. Not that unusual for a Saturday night where she was. Chantay was an eleven-year-old former inmate at Bright Hill, who lived with a heroin-addicted hooker mother in the projects. "You gotta help me." She started sobbing. "Mom and a guy are nodded off in the bedroom, and another guy's wanting to come in and screw her. I told him she was out, and now he wants to come in and do me instead. He's big, real big, Sofia. And mean. He'll hurt me bad. I know it."

"Where are you, Chantay?"

"I'm in the apartment. I locked the door on him and put the burglar bar up. But he's all drunk and really going at that door. I don't think it'll hold. You got to come get me and take me back to Bright Hill."

Sad that what was essentially juvey jail looked better and safer to her than home, but that wasn't unusual with our girls. I could see Chantay, bright but failing school, tall for her age, big and pudgy, but still childish in face and act and thought. What could some grown man want with her sexually?

"Please, Sofia. Please."

"Okay, Chantay. Calm down. I'll send the police."

"They won't come to Wayne Miner on weekends. They don't set foot here from Friday 'til Monday. They won't help me. You got to come get me. Please."

"Okay. Okay. I'll get you out somehow. Move a chair in front of that door, as well as the burglar bar. Go into the bathroom and lock that door behind you, too. Then stay quiet as can be in there. Okay?"

"Okay. I'll do that now, but you got to come get me." She hung up the phone on that last plea that was as much a demand as an appeal.

I turned to Naomi, who was just settling in for the night shift. "What happens if I call the cops to an emergency in Wayne Miner tonight?"

Naomi had been on this job for years and had the criminal justice system down cold. "They're gonna tell you okay and file it to check on Monday or Tuesday. Maybe. Cops never go in there on the weekends. Too dangerous for them. Eighty percent of Kansas City's murders happen in Wayne Miner. You're lucky to get a cop in there on a weekday afternoon. Weekends are the devil's own."

After I checked the records for Chantay's address, I grabbed my purse and notebook and ran out the door. I'd already signed out just before the call came through. Kathy was waiting for me in her yellow Volkswagen Bug with the orange trunk, revving the engine.

I didn't drive or have a car, so Kathy and I had arranged our shifts to match. That way, she could give me rides to and from work. It was one of the things she'd promised when she talked me into applying for the job, even though I was underage.

You had to be twenty-one to work in the juvenile justice system in Kansas City, and I'd still had three weeks to go before my eighteenth birthday. Still, Kathy insisted I apply and lie about my age. I thought sure I'd get caught, but soon enough I had an interview scheduled with Juvenile Court Judge Wheelwright. I'd been surprised that a judge would be hiring, but Kathy gave me a knowing smile and said he only did it for Bright Hill.

"If you've got long hair, a nice figure, and you wear a short enough skirt, you've got the job." She laughed and smoothed her own long, blonde hair. "Don't worry, though. He's creepy, but not creepy enough to be grabby or anything. He just likes to sit and talk to pretty young girls and look at their legs."

Sure enough, the old man hired me after a two-and-a-half-hour interview that covered nothing about what would make me a good juvenile corrections officer or housemother. Still, I like to think I was a good housemother to those girls. I tried to be.

That's why when I threw my purse and body into the Bug, I asked Kathy to take me to Wayne Miner on the way home.

"You have got to be kidding, Sofia." Kathy wove in and out of rush-hour traffic the way she did everything in life—with the supreme confidence of someone who knows she's beautiful and smart and has the backing of one of the richest families in St. Louis. This time slumming in Kansas City was her little rebellion before settling into the life her rich, socially important, and politically ambitious parents expected of her. "Wayne Miner on a Saturday night. Do you have a death wish or something?"

"It's Chantay," I said. "She's hiding out from some big brute who wants to rape her since her mother's too drugged out to give him what he wants. She needs help, and Naomi says the cops won't do anything. Chantay's one of our girls."

"Chantay was sent home last week. She's not our responsibility any longer." Kathy's jaw was settling into the stubborn line I dreaded.

"At least drop me somewhere close. She doesn't have a lot of time. You don't have to go in with me or stick around. Just get me there."

"You are seriously intending to go somewhere the police with all their guns are afraid to go. In order to what? Rescue the daughter of a whore from being raped and initiated into the life her mother's going to sell her into any day now anyway?"

"Not on my watch. Chantay deserves better."

"Chantay may or may not deserve better, but she's not going to get any better. That's just the way it is. The way the world works."

Now, I was feeling stubborn. "Just get me as close to Wayne Miner as you can. That's all I'm asking."

"You're crazy. You know?" Suddenly, she laughed wildly and pulled off the headband that held back her hair, tossing her head and hair around. "Why not? It's the Age of Aquarius, baby. No need to let those old beliefs rule us, right? We'll be fearless."

She zoomed off to the right, and I sat back against the acceleration. I'd learned to distrust Kathy in these moods of exhilaration. They usually meant she was going to cause some trouble. I wasn't sure I wanted to take her with me into Wayne Miner in her "fearless" state.

As we drove closer and closer to 10th and Woodland through worse and worse neighborhoods, her ebullience wore thin, however. By the time we were pulled up outside the hulking towers of Wayne Miner, she was back to trying to talk me out of it.

"He's probably already gotten to her, you know."

"Then she'll really need help, don't you think? A little eleven-year-old girl. Besides, she's barricaded behind two doors, so that should have given us some time."

"You're crazy. Certifiably loony. You can't do this. It's too dangerous."

My own mood had been sinking as we drove through ever-deteriorating neighborhoods, but I was more used to them than Kathy was. I was terrified to do this thing. Especially now that the moment had come to actually go through with it. Still, I could hear Chantay's little-girl voice begging me for help, so I'd have to go through with it, even if I peed my pants with terror before I was finished. Even if it meant I would be hurt, too. If I turned my back on Chantay, I knew I'd never be the same person again, and I didn't want to be the person that failure of nerve would make of me.

I got out of the car, and two drunks sitting on the sidewalk ten feet away started catcalling. Ignoring them, I turned and leaned into the car to speak to Kathy. "You don't have to wait. I understand."

"You don't think I'm going to leave you here with no way out, do you?" she said with false bravado and her best smile.

"Why don't you stay with the car then, and make sure it's still here to get us out of this." I smiled back.

The noise of the drunks was moving in our direction, so I straightened up and turned to face them. They'd risen from the pavement and were stumbling toward us. A tall, thin elderly man in a dapper cream-colored suit with a cane had appeared from somewhere around us, as well. He wore his white hair in a moderate Afro.

"Your friend should stay in the car with her doors locked," he said and tapped the car with his cane. I could see the handle was a bronze snake's head, and there were designs carved all over the wooden body of the cane. "She'll be safe until we return."

I closed my door, and Kathy locked all of them, looking frightened.

"Go, you piss-swilling maggots!" the man shouted at the drunks, waving his cane. "This young lady's on a mission of mercy, but what would ignoramuses like you know of such?"

The drunks pulled back in fear from his cane that was brandished like some sword in an Errol Flynn movie. I wondered how the old man knew why I was there.

"Well, let's hurry," he said to me as he set us walking at a rapid pace toward the towers. "There are five towers. Do you know which tower you need and which floor? There are ten floors to each tower. And the elevators have been taken over by human cockroaches, so we'll have to brave the stairwells."

I shook my head and told him Chantay's address. I'd foolishly thought that would let me find her.

He nodded his head thoughtfully. "That's pretty good. It's the closest tower, but the seventh floor. I hope you're up to the climb."

The old man looked as if he must be seventy, at least. A vigorous seventy, to be sure, but still elderly. I didn't think I would be the one who'd be unable to make it up the stairs.

"Who are you?" I asked. "Why are you doing this?"

"Can't an old man help someone do a good deed? Just call me Mr. Nance." He grinned at me, and for a second in the gathering dusk, I thought his teeth looked pointed. I blinked, and they were just normal old-man teeth.

We were now entering the courtyard around which the grim towers stood. Men sat in groups on the pavement drinking, smoking dope, and playing cards and craps. Other men stood in groups, smoking, drinking, shouting at each other, pushing and shoving. One or two, off in corners, leaned against the buildings, unconscious, heads nodding. I was surprised at how crowded it was and couldn't imagine how we'd get through to the door of the tower we wanted. Suddenly, I realized why the police never came to Wayne Miner on the weekend. They didn't want to get caught in the line of fire on the battlefield.

"Make way! Make way!" the old man cried, whipping his cane back and forth in front of him. "Open a path. We're coming through. Ready or not."

"It's the old one," I heard one man say.

"So what?" a big bald guy asked.

"So he'll send his people after you if you make him mad. You don't want to go there."

Another muttered something about "old juju." There were grumbles and complaints, but a narrow pathway did open for us, and everyone moved back out of our way.

Until one young dude stepped forward and grabbed my arm. "Hey, sweetness, come see what Bobby Lovely's got for you. I guarantee you ain't seen nothing like it."

Mr. Nance brought the cane up and whacked him hard across his midsection. Bobby Lovely crumpled in half with a loud groan, releasing my arm, and we walked on past him to the entrance to the ten-story tower.

By this time, I felt as if I walked through a dream or, more likely, a nightmare. At any moment, all those angry men in that courtyard behind us could converge on us and attack. In front of us at the entrance doors, a nasty-looking group of guys, sweaty and bare-chested or in stained wife-beaters, stood around selling drugs. I had a feeling that Mr. Nance was not going to be able to get us out of this one with a whack of his cane, however well-placed.

"You shameful purveyors of death to your own families," he cried, whipping the cane through the air once again. "You hyenas eating the carcass of your own people, preying on the weak and vulnerable. Worms! Corpseworms, all of you! Get thee gone, or I'll call down such a curse on you that will make you wish for death to come and finish the torment."

With his impassioned words and the whistling cane, he drove them from the doorway and walked me through into the lobby, smelling of piss and garbage. We headed past the elevators, all the while I could feel the hateful glares of those drug dealers on our backs.

"We'll do better facing the vermin in the stairwells," Mr. Nance said. "The rabid skunks who hold the elevators hostage are trigger-happy."

I felt relief that he wasn't going to insist we challenge them, whoever they were. By this time, I was almost hyperventilating with panic. I tried to calm myself with the reminder that Mr. Nance had managed to get us through that courtyard where even the cops were afraid to go. Surely, he'd be able to get us out again.

My memories of that night are all gray. Gray skies as night began to fall, gray courtyard full of black men who seemed as gray with despair as they seemed dangerous, gray towers with boarded up windows and doors, gray, graffiti-covered walls inside with stained gray carpet on the floors, but the stairwells were the grayest of all. Only the faintest light illuminated them, just enough to keep them from being black. The cement walls were gray. The cement stairs were gray. No light or color met the eye. And the three men we met in the stairwell on our way up to the seventh floor were all gray with death.

One was stretched out at the bottom of a flight of stairs with a knife in his gut and a pool of blood turned black underneath him. The other two were separated from each other by several floors, but both died leaning against the wall as they sat on a bottom step with a needle still hanging in the vein of one arm.

I thought we would climb in that damned gray stairwell of death forever, but finally we reached our goal. Oddly enough, Mr. Nance wasn't as out of breath as I was. As we emerged onto the seventh floor, we could hear a drunk roaring and smashing up something, so we raced toward the sound. It had to be where poor Chantay was waiting for rescue.

The door to the apartment had been kicked to pieces. The chair Chantay had set in front of that door had been thrown clear across the room. A short, squat man with over-muscled arms bawled curses and smashed what was left of the furniture into the bathroom door. As we entered, the table he threw crashed into the bathroom door and crumpled it. I could see Chantay huddled on the floor between the toilet and the tub, sobbing.

"Ah, ah, ah!" cried Mr. Nance, advancing on the man with an odd high-stepped, pouncing walk, almost like a dance step or the movement of a spider. He shook his cane at the enraged man. "You've had your tantrum. Done all the damage you're going to do. Now it's time for you to leave this place and leave this child alone."

"If you want her, you're going to have to get in line," the man yelled. "I was here first. You'll just have to take sloppy seconds."

"You're disgusting," I said. "I'm with the juvenile court, and this girl is in our custody now."

"Go get her," Mr. Nance said to me, as he pressed on toward the man, poking his cane straight before him as if he would stab the man with it.

The man backed away from him, still spewing loud curses, but more importantly, away from the broken bathroom door. I pulled the table away and climbed over the splintered base of the door to get into the small bathroom. Mr. Nance kept high-stepping toward the man with his cane pointed at the man's broad chest. There was something menacing about the way he moved toward the man, even though it should have been laughable.

"You will never know rest or relief from fear," Mr. Nance said in the voice of a preacher crying from the pulpit in a revival tent. "You will never know refreshment from thirst or satisfaction of hunger."

The man's eyes grew huge.

"You will run from shadows and rumors," Mr. Nance continued, backing the man around toward the outer door. "You will find no escape."

"No. Don't do this, mister. Don't, please." Sweat poured down the man's face and mixed with tears. "Don't put no hoodoo on me."

I had reached Chantay. I pulled her up from the floor and started back toward the door with my arm around her shoulders.

"Nothing will serve you. No one will help you." Mr. Nance's voice sent chills down my body. "Nothing can save you. You will run and run while the flesh melts from your bones and your blood dries up within you."

With a scream of terror, the man flung himself out the door and ran down the hall, still screaming.

Mr. Nance held his strange posture for several minutes, and I held Chantay still at the broken bathroom door, not sure what move to make, if any. I didn't want to disturb him or bother him in the state he was in. I still had goose bumps from the eerie sound of his voice as he cursed the man.

He took a deep breath, and all the tension drained from his body. When he turned around to face us with a kind smile, he was just Mr. Nance again, the strange, nice man who was helping us. Who was saving us.

"Hush, child," he said in a gentle voice to Chantay, who still wept. "You've had a fright, but you're safe now." He looked at me. "Time we got this little one out of here."

Turning, he led the way back to the stairwell, leaning on the cane a little bit as he hadn't before.

"Chantay, there are some things on our way down that you shouldn't see," I told the girl. "When I tell you to close your eyes, do it, and I'll guide you down the steps."

Mr. Nance grinned at me and shook his head. "She lives here. The child has seen everything this place has, including these deaths. You can't shield her."

We climbed down the seven floors faster than when we'd gone up, or maybe it just seemed that way to me because I was taking care of Chantay, drying her tears and reassuring her. I had less time to be afraid. Maybe it was because I finally trusted that Mr. Nance would get us out of this alive after seeing what he'd done to the man who threatened Chantay. His screams echoed back up to us from the floors below as he ran and fell down the stairwell in a panic, much faster than we descended.

By the time we reached the outer doors of the tower, Chantay had stopped crying. She clung to my side, and I kept one arm wrapped around her as we approached the doors with their drug dealing sentinels, expecting another confrontation. But as we came through, the dealers pulled back away from the doors—in respect or fear, I wasn't sure which, and maybe neither were they.

There was a lot of whispering and muttering out in the crowded courtyard, some of it angry, some fearful, some excited, and I noticed Mr. Nance no longer leaned on his cane but swung it vigorously as he had when we first came through. This time, there was no need for him to open a path for us. People hastily moved out of our way, some looking worried, some looking defiant, but they moved.

I knew the screaming man must have come flying out there into that crowd and made his way through them. Perhaps they had good reason to be worried or angry.

Mr. Nance led us through, as dapper and confident as ever, and down the long walkway to the street and down the street to the place where Kathy sat waiting in the yellow Bug with its orange tail. A ring of men had gathered around the car, which seemed to glow slightly in the deepening twilight, but it looked as if no one had touched it, and Kathy looked okay, if terrified. As the men saw Mr. Nance coming, they melted away, some going across the street, some further down. None of them stayed near the car.

"Here you are," Mr. Nance said. "Put your little charge in the car and take her away to safety."

I wanted to hug him or something, but he was right. I needed to take care of Chantay before I thanked him and said goodbye. I settled her into the back seat of the Bug and pushed the passenger seat back upright before turning around to express my gratitude to the old man who'd probably saved me from my own foolhardiness and certainly helped me save Chantay from terrible harm.

When I turned, he was nowhere to be seen, gone as quickly and completely as most of the men who'd stood around the car. I strained to look in every direction, but could see no sign of his cream-colored suit, which would have shown up well in the dark.

"Get in, Sofia. Let's get out of here now!" Kathy sounded desperate and angry, so I got in the car, and we left to take Chantay back to Bright Hill.

• • •

Many years later, after going away to college and developing a profession, after Wayne Miner had been torn down as the failure it was, I moved back to Kansas City and worked at a nonprofit in the inner city. A number of the people I knew then had lived in Wayne Miner, and I eventually asked each of them if he or she had known Mr. Nance. No one ever admitted that they had, although the eyes of several of them grew fearful, and I noticed I seldom saw those people again.

Chantay went into the foster care system, which is always iffy. There are good homes, poor homes, and hellholes. I've always hoped she got one of the good ones. Whatever it was, it couldn't have been worse than what she had.

When I tell this story—which is rare, only my husband and a few very close friends have heard it—everyone asks me who or what I thought Mr. Nance was. I never know what to say. I don't know if he was good or evil. Somehow I don't think someone really, really good would have carried such clout with the people we dealt with that night. Only someone who either was terribly bad or was capable of real harm could have had the effect he did. Yet, what he did for Chantay and for me was undeniably good. I have no answers.

SOMETHING I SAID

Bracken MacLeod

FOR MIAH

It took a minute for my eyes to adjust to the dim light inside the bar. This wasn't a gastropub where people would bring their kids for lunch and sit near the front to people-watch while they sipped particularly resiny double IPA. The windows were painted black a generation ago and the smoked mirrors installed above the booths in the 1970s were beginning to distort with gravity. Walker's Pub was a place for townies to come after work to down a few before they went home to face whatever it was that made them want to stop off at a bar in the first place. And I served them drinks five nights a week. Not tonight, though. It was my night off.

When I could finally make out more than the familiar shapes and shadows within, I looked around to find who I'd come looking for. He was sitting on a stool near the register, chatting up Valerie.

I am not a tough guy. I never have been. I maxed out at five foot eight in middle school and am a soft hundred and sixty pounds in middle age. I like food and sex and watching TV and I get a lot of both food and television since my wife left me for another man nine months ago. Scott, on the other hand, was ten years younger than me and built like an action figure with acne. We sometimes joked behind his back about him forgetting the steroid hypo still sticking out of his ass.

I wasn't sure how I'd get his attention if he was sitting at a table in the middle of the room or, worse, in a booth, but it was a safe bet he'd be at the bar. From my experience serving him, Scott was the kind of customer who liked to talk to his bartender. It's not that he was all that friendly or wanted a confessor—the opposite on both accounts, actually—he was one of those skinflints who thought if he made friends, at some point in the evening his new pal would start comping him drinks.

No one ever did. Jerry, the owner and grandson of the original Walker, would unceremoniously shitcan anybody he found giving away alcohol. It was one thing to pour free Cokes for the rarefied DD, but booze? Never! Hell, he almost fired me for *selling* a customer an empty thirty-year-old cognac bottle he thought gave the place class, even though the guy paid enough for it to buy a half a case of the stuff. Still, having never scored a free drink in the past didn't keep Scott from trying. That Valerie was serving him tonight was icing. She had all the qualities men like Scott desired. Except the ability to say 'Yes.' Again, that sweetened the deal for him. He was one of those 'pick-up artist' assholes. Even had a blog offering a 'coaching' service for it. He saw flirting as a competition against a hostile adversary. Sex was the spoils of being an effective combatant, not something another person agreed to because it was enjoyable for them.

He'd start out 'negging' a target, wrapping an insult in a slight compliment meant to undermine a woman's confidence and drop her defenses. If the target recognized what he was doing, he'd move on to gaslighting or some other petty torture he thought was master-level hypnosis but was really just exploiting people's insecurities. At his core, he was a predator. And while he claimed to get more pussy than a veterinarian, I never saw him hook up. Not at Walker's anyway. His routine definitely wasn't impressing Val. She didn't give half a shit what his opinion of her tattoos or Madonna piercing was. But then, to put it in his parlance, she wasn't 'about the D.' That was not an obstacle in his world.

She set a Red Devil—what people in the rest of the country called a vodka cran—in front of him and swept his exact change off the bar top. Scott, in addition to his other flaws—and they were many—was also not a tipper. I'd listened to him hold forth one night with another customer, cribbing almost the entirety of Mr. Brown's soliloquy from *Reservoir Dogs* on the subject. Unlike in the movie, his barstool buddy didn't argue the point, but grunted and nodded as he slurped a 'Gansett out of the can, trying not to fall off the steady seat beneath him. Tonight, he sat alone. Even better.

Val tried to busy herself at the other end of the bar, drying glasses from the shelf drainer. He knew she'd be back as soon as someone else put in an order. She had to work the till. And when she did, he'd work her. I took a seat three stools down from him. Not so close he'd accuse me of being a fag, but close enough he could hear if I said something. Val nodded at me, smiled, and set to mixing a dry Manhattan. She set the cocktail in front of me, poured herself a shot of shitty cinnamon whiskey, clinked my glass and threw back the fire.

"Hey Abel. It's your night off," she said. "Admit it. You just can't get enough of me, can you?" She slapped a hand on her skinny ass and flipped her purple bangs away from her forehead.

"I don't know how you can drink that sugary shit."

"My sweet tooth is a demon that demands sacrifice."

"If that sacrifice is your stomach lining, it ought to be happy enough." She poured herself another hit and threw it back while I sipped my drink, enjoying it. Although the selection of spirits at Walker's was curated with the intent of offering an affordable, quick buzz to people less interested in taste than effect, she made an excellent cocktail using what we stored below the bar—a personal collection paid for with our own money, without Jerry's approval—so we wouldn't have to suffer. Val should have been working in one of the upscale waterfront bars in the city. Instead, she was up here in the industrial Revere hinterlands. She claimed to like it better in townie bars. No one tried to make her feel like shit for 'only' being a bartender, or treated her like the help. I suspected she preferred to work off the books more than she liked the atmosphere. Whatever her reasons, working with her was like a master class in being a badass behind a Boston shaker.

"So, for real. What's up?"

I shrugged. "Just thought I'd drop in and say hi. Since Katie left, I'm bored on Thursday nights."

"God, I hope I never get that bored." She didn't acknowledge the departure of my ex-wife. She was a good friend, protective and loyal. She'd been my best man at our wedding. Thinking of Katie made her angrier than it made me sad. Her jaw flexed as she gritted her teeth. She let out a long breath and patted the back of my hand, giving me the kind-eye invitation to stay as long as I wanted.

A guy I'd never seen come in before took a seat at the far end of the bar, and she put the candy rotgut away before sashaying over to serve him. He didn't know she was queer, and she knew how to earn her tips. She left her glass sitting in front of me. Val was meticulous about her bar; it meant she was coming back. I secretly wished she'd left the bottle behind along with it. I could have used a little more liquid fire in my belly than was left in my own glass. I took a big swallow of the Manhattan and tried to settle my nerves. It didn't work. My blood thundered in my ears as my pounding heart tried to kickstart my legs to get me to stand up and walk out the door. Even my Dutch courage was weak. I sat where I was and pulled my phone from my jacket pocket. I checked the time: a quarter to ten. Late enough.

Scott was scanning the place for other marks, not having made the kind of headway he'd hoped with Val. I took a quick look around and saw there wasn't a single unaccompanied woman in the place. That meant Rhonda had come in with her husband. Time was short before Scott killed what he had in front of him and decided to take it on the heels looking for prey in the city.

"Cunt."

"What was that?" Scott said, turning to look at me.

I held up my phone and said, "Someone sent me a link to this guy's blog. It's called 'Female Sexual Motive' or some shit."

"And what did you say about him?" He stood up from his chair and cocked his head at me like I was hard to see under the yellowed lightshades. Maybe I was. Or maybe he was just trying to figure out why I looked familiar. Since I wasn't behind the bar wearing an apron, he seemed to be having some contextual confusion. I hoped he was lubricated enough to want to fight, but not so drunk he couldn't put his back into it.

"Who? My friend?"

"No. The author."

The author. I almost laughed. In hindsight it might have sped things up if I did. I shrugged again and went back to looking at my phone, dismissing him.

Scott took a step toward me. "I said, did you call me a cunt?"

I shook my head and pointed at my phone. "No. This guy. But I take it back. Calling him that implies he'd be worth a fuck. Reading this dogshit, my bet is he isn't deep enough to hold a tampon—"

He came at me like he'd heard the bell before the hammer even bounced. His haymaker took me in the side of the face and a blossom of heat spread across my cheek. My head whipped around and I staggered off my stool, tripping over another trying to keep my feet beneath me. The tall chair I'd been sitting on clattered to the floor while my phone slipped out of my hands, skipping once like a flat stone on a lake before disappearing behind the bar. He punched me in the kidney, making the muscles in the left side of my back cramp and my spine twist. He shouted something I couldn't hear over the ringing in my ears from his first hit. I did hear his voice crack at the end, making him sound as hysterical as he claimed all women were right under the surface: emotionally driven and borderline hysterical at all times.

I turned and tried lifting my fists to put up a guard. He hit me again in the gut right between my elbows. I dropped my arms to protect my midsection and he whipped around with another bent arm hook into the other side of my face, hitting me in the jaw this time. I spun and staggered away from the bar, both sides of my face numbing and growing tight with swelling. I stumbled into the middle of the bar and stood, trying to shake the haze out of my head. It wouldn't do any good to get knocked out too fast.

Blood dribbled out of my mouth and I stuck a finger in to assess the damage to my aching back teeth. Touching my molars caused pain unlike anything I'd ever felt before. They weren't loose. They were gone. He'd broken off at least two that I could feel. I tried to blow a kiss at him, but my mouth hurt so bad all I could manage was to let it hang open while blood and saliva drizzled down my chin.

Once upon a time I took karate, or something the instructor called karate. He'd made up his own style and named it after some piece of kanji he found in a book, the way teenagers pick their first tattoo. He told us it meant something poetic like 'lunar eclipse,' and waxed esoteric about appearances versus reality and what real warriors did and didn't do. I found out later the symbol he'd named his art after was Japanese for 'restaurant.' Admittedly, it's a tough language. But he never double checked. Anyway, that was the guy who taught me how to fight. Against guys who'd also learned how to fight from him, I was good. In the Way of The Restaurant, I was Jim Kelly cool. Against a guy who spent all of his free time in a gym lifting and doing MMA, I was a punching bag; I just couldn't hit back.

Most of the time, I skirted around conflict with humor and a fast talking reason that calmed even the most hotheaded guys down enough to not pummel me. But I really thought I might be able to block at least one of this dick's hits. Just one, so I felt like I was a participant in the fight. Scott, however, was fast and motivated. I had nothing in my repertoire of three-step slo-mo techniques and pseudo-religious platitudes about honor to counter a whip-fast hook or a rabbit punch. Learning that hurt worse than any of his punches.

It was hard to breathe. My stomach was cramping. Another slam in the guts and I crumpled. The floor was where I wanted to be, actually. Lying there, I felt none of the uncertainty of being rocked on my feet. Lying on the floor, I knew which way was up, which was down, and where I was. Definitely down, on my side, smearing my blood in the tracked-in dirt and road salt from the previous winter. The other thing being on the floor told me was he would have to change it up from fists to feet.

"Was . . . it something I . . . said?"

He kicked me in the back. Scott wasn't wearing work boots, but they weren't fluffy bunny slippers on his feet either. It didn't matter. Legally, almost any 'shod foot' is considered a dangerous weapon. I felt the pointed toe of his Rockport against my ribs and heard the snap of bone echo in the shocked silence of the bar. The only other noises I heard were my ragged breathing, his cursing, and Val in the background shouting for him to stop. *Bless you, Val*, I thought. *But let him go.* I knew she'd already called the cops.

I rolled over to protect my back and he gave me a final shot in the face. Right where I wanted it. Where it would count the most. I felt my lips shred around the remains of my front teeth and I choked. I was done. He could stop any time. *Please Val*, I wished. *Make him stop.* But he hadn't exhausted himself yet, and I'd worked what I knew was his rawest nerve. No one treated him like a woman, or even suggested he was one. Calling him what I did was the same as threatening his deepest seated personal identity. And with a few in him, he didn't respond with anger. It was pure fury I'd tapped.

That's what my step-daughter—ex-step-daughter—Cory, told me about him. She's best friends with his daughter, Ginger. Goes over to his house for sleep-overs sometimes. She'd seen him go nuts at 'Ginge' because he thought she called him a pussy. "She said he was 'being pushy,' but he wouldn't listen. He just screamed at her until his face turned all red. I thought he was going to stroke out right there in front of us," she told me. "He scares me, Abel."

A couple of days later, she sent me a link to his Pick Up Artist blog. He bragged about "railing some chick" in his daughter's bed because he was "about keeping it fresh (and his wife was napping in their bedroom)." I read through all the entries until I found the one where he 'experimented' with his technique on one of his daughter's friends. *Fifteen and almost hot,* he'd written, *the little bitch acts like she already knows she can make any Beta "Male" do whatever she wants by even hinting at the* idea *of spreading her legs. She's probably got all the boys in her school already twisted up with promises and blueballs. But I'm* A Man. *So that weekend I set out to teach her an early lesson about the truth behind Female Sexual Motive using the techniques of the Alpha Male Plan. I got her AMPed up and when I was done, she was curled up in my lap and purring like a nice little kitten.* He added a disclaimer at the end saying he never followed through with his AMPlan because he wasn't 'into felonies.' Adding, *She'll be legal in six months. I can wait.* ;p

The blog post was date-stamped July 19.

Cory's birthday is December 21.

His sentencing is next week on February 15. Aggravated Assault and Battery with a Dangerous Weapon. Arrogant as ever, he spun the wheel on a trial instead of taking a plea and lost. I left my false teeth out when I testified. Fucking up my mouth was a cherry on top since it's a disfigurement and increases the penalty. He's looking at fifteen years. The irony is not lost on me.

I am not a tough guy. I never have been. But I'll do anything to protect my kid.

EL PUENTE

Rios de la Luz

My abuela collected bird cages. She painted the bars and added miniature Persian rugs to the bottoms of the cages. She glued sequins and beads to the doors of the cages. She scrunched her nose and squinted her eyes as she glued and sewed. She smiled up at me if she caught me watching her. She placed animal trinkets inside. She found the cages and trinkets at swap meets or abandoned along the sides of the road.

She burned sage to cleanse out bad spirits and the ghosts of birds who inhabited the cage before her trinkets took over. Abuela wrote obituaries for the birds. She stuck her final words to the birds in a fireproof file cabinet. She prayed for the birds to move on so her animal figurines could live inside the cages in peace. The bird cages hung all over her house. They were pink, turquoise, lavender, yellow and lime. Red cages were stacked in her bedroom. I wasn't allowed to play with the red cages because they housed stolen garden gnomes she didn't want the familia to know about. The cages came in different shapes and sizes. Some of them were two-story cages. Others had squiggled wiring like the bird inside had shaken and danced around until the wires curved to match its rhythm. My favorite cages were the ones that looked like Mosques. Abuela let me hang three of them in my room.

Abuela only asked this of me once. Her voice was stern and raspy. She asked me to carry a lavender cage, a sky blue cage and a lemon yellow cage across a bridge. I hung them on a broomstick with the bristles behind me. I wanted to imitate a bruja. The lavender cage housed lizard figurines with their tongues out like the kids in this desert town when it rains. The sky blue cage held little monkeys in military uniforms. They all held flags in their small palms that swayed with the breeze. The lemon yellow cage held horses with flowers in their manes.

Abuela didn't specify what kind of bridge. She told me I would know when I crossed the right one. I walked miles and miles around town crossing bridges. I carried the cages across a highway intersection that overlooked honking people on their ways home from work. I crossed a small stream by balancing on sunburnt logs. As the sun spat out a pink and orange sky, I continued my trek with the cages. I talked to the trinkets. I told them we would be okay. Patches of fog burst in and out of the path. Bugs buzzed in and out of the cages.

Hours passed. I continued walking. I walked into a quiet neighborhood. I couldn't hear a sound, but I saw different hues of lighting coming out of each house I passed. Neon pink lighting. Neon purple lighting. Neon green lights outlined the doors and windows of the third house I passed. Finally, I saw a bridge. A single house with light neon blue shining through its windows stood across of the curved bridge.

I fanned fog out of my face. I crossed the bridge and with every step, the ground lit up. My steps left lit up footprints that dissolved as I took my next step forward. I stepped off of the bridge and looked into the window of the lonely house. I knocked on the door. The door opened. The hallway was filled with plants. Some of them tickled my face from the ceiling. The floor was glass. Underneath, I could see a small stream. I followed the stream into the living room. There were three empty end tables. A rectangle, a circle and a triangle. I placed the cages on the corresponding shape. A projector mumbled and lit up the wall in the hallway. I stood behind the projector and read the messages flashing on the empty wall. Directions and scribbled letters flashed on the wall.

There were images of my mother. I wanted to run toward the projection and hold her. She waved at me and I waved back. She motioned for me to come forward. I reached for her hand and touched the empty wall. There has been no form of communication with my mother since she was taken from our home. She wasn't born on this side of the border, I was. They called me an anchor baby, as though I could sink to the bottom of the ocean and stay there forever while my mother floated back to Mexico with nothing but her memories of what I looked like at nine. The ICE officers grabbed her and told her to stay calm. I reached for her hand, but I wasn't fast enough. I wanted to go with her. I wanted them to take me with her. I wanted to see Mamá's old neighborhood.

Mamá had photographs of nopales that reached toward the cosmos at night. She had photographs of herself as a child in black and white, but she always sucked her teeth and told me not to let the photos fool me. Her childhood neighborhood was a rainbow infested beauty and a sight to see. Color filled her walks to school every morning. She even filled the sky with color on her birthday. On her fifteenth birthday, a balloon vendor with the most beautiful brown hands handed her a bouquet of balloons. Mamá ran around her neighborhood with the balloons and let them go, one by one. It became her tradition. Every birthday, she filled the sky with balloons and I helped her. I watched the balloons scatter and I prayed for them to land in her childhood neighborhood.

Another image of my mamá flashed on the wall. She had sticky notes in her hand, sitting on a purple leather couch, she scribbled with intense eyebrows. She saw it in the movies, so she made a habit of it. She left me sticky notes in my lunchbox, on my bedroom door and one day she filled my entire room with sticky notes. I stepped on some and laughed as I tried to jump for the ones on the ceiling. Some of them had messages for me. Some of the notes had prayers on them. There were hundreds of them with vocabulary words on them. She wanted to show me all the new words she learned from me. I was very proud because I knew how embarrassed she was, even as she became older and wiser, for having to quit school after she moved to the US.

The last sticky note project she left me was a path that went up the steps of Abuela's house into the attic. When I followed the path up the steps, Mamá was waiting for me in a red chiffon dress. She held a floral dress in her arms and handed it to me. She played her Rancheras and we danced. I twirled and twirled in my floral dress and Mamá spun until Abuela told us to come downstairs for dinner. I collected all the sticky notes Mamá left behind and kept them in the attic of Abuela's house. I nap up there sometimes. I pretend that Mamá's notes are speaking into my dreams. I nap with the stacks and stacks of messages from her.

The projector started buzzing and the reflected images disappeared. The empty wall crumbled and I grabbed the birdcages. I held onto them and walked through the fallen wall. I walked into another room. The walls were orange, the ceiling sky blue. There was a large coat and some boots to my left. There was a sundress and a shovel to my right. I grabbed the coat and boots and walked into another hallway. I ended up outside, deep into winter.

The landscape only felt familiar. I set the cages on the ground and started digging. I drew an outline of an octagon with my hands. I dug as deep as I could. My hands became red from the cold. I sat inside the makeshift shape and the rest of the pieces of frozen landscape fell away. The water underneath me blew mist up at the sky as though the ocean was exhaling. I floated past sea lions and I swear I saw an orca. The floating chunk of frozen earth led me into a cavern. I stepped into the cave. I followed the sticky notes Mamá littered along cavern walls and stuck in between stalagmites. I bunched them all into my pocket. My feet were numb as I continued to gather and crunch the paper in between my fists. I ran out of room in my pockets. I started stuffing the birdcages with sticky notes. A skyline opened up and sun shined on my face. I saw more light and walked toward it. My knees and elbows were scraped up. My hair curled closer to my shoulders. I walked out of the cavern and I slipped into a river.

My feet slid on top of brown and red rocks. I walked beneath a gorge. The vivid greens of moss overwhelmed me. Tiny gray birds swooped through and flew around me. I found a place to rest. I stacked the birdcages behind me. I napped and when I woke up I was in a world of black and white. I looked at my hands. They were gray. I looked at the cages. They were a variation of gray. I could no longer see in color. Pieces of gray, black and white paper fell from the sky. The clouds curled into themselves and I cried for a matter of seconds until I saw my mother again. She was a projection in the clouds. She pointed at the pieces of paper floating in the river. I fell to my knees and I grabbed for them. I caught some and the rest turned into silver fish that leaped up and into the water.

A giant crow yelled and flew around my head. It grabbed the cage with the lizards inside and flew up to my mother. She grabbed the cage through the projection and hung it up in her living room amongst hanging plants. With a swift swoop, the crow flew out of the projection then behind me. It went for the cage with the military monkeys. I could hear the gust of wind beneath the wings of the crow as it flew over to Mamá. She took the cage and stuck it on her front porch. The crow flew overhead and reached down for the cage with the horses inside. I jumped and wrapped my arms around the cage. The crow was strong. I held onto the cage. I wanted to fly to Mamá. The crow shook the cage and I asked it to let me go with it.

• • •

Please, take me with you.

The crow let go of the cage and I fell back into the river. I screamed at the bird and I watched the cage float downstream. Mamá looked worried as I looked back at the projection. She took a sticky note and wrote inside. She let it swirl down to me from above.

It instructed me to open up the pieces I grabbed from the river. I opened up the soggy paper and animations of me and Mamá appeared. It showed me the day she made me a heart shaped display with sticky notes. She wrote jokes from Laffy Taffy wrappers on them. A lot of the notes said "I love you." Some of the notes were phone numbers she memorized of old boyfriends and girlfriends. I opened up another piece of gray soggy paper and it showed me our last day together. The ink was smudged from water but Mamá wrote "in another time, in another dimension." The sticky note showed me an animation of her hugging me before the ICE officers took her. She held onto me and she didn't cry, but I did. She asked me to be brave. Be brave because sometimes, you are your only hero. Be brave because even though we may not see each other again, I am always thinking of you. I pray and cough out the cosmos from my lungs into the atmosphere for you. I pray that you can feel my attempt to continue to hold you from afar.

MESQUITE

Graham Wynd

"It's Glory." Jamie waved the pulsating phone at his wife from the bedroom doorway. He wouldn't normally bother to catch her calls, but it was Glory after all. Of course he didn't have to look happy about it, so he didn't.

Hope looked up from the bed where she lay while her three-year-old Bianca covered her in stuffed animals. This was a game the girl had invented herself. Hope figured her daughter had to be pretty advanced, though she knew most every parent assumed their little darlings were ahead of everyone else's brats. The game consisted of piling all her teddies over her mom while she lay on the bed, then at Bianca's command—always hers, her mother didn't get to say it—shaking them all off, and then trading places. She called them 'teddies' though there were also pandas, penguins, a giraffe, two cartoon characters that she wasn't sure were of this world and a dog with one ear missing and a loose eye.

"I have to take this," Hope said, but waited for her daughter to sigh and say, "All right, shake." She dutifully did so and Hope left the debris for Bianca to corral, taking the phone from Jamie with a kiss. His lips felt cool. "You sitting in front of the AC again?"

"Only cool place, babe." It was only May but the weather felt like August.

He sauntered off and Hope admired the shape of his jeans as he did so, smiling at his back as she said, "Hey, hon."

"Can we talk?"

Even through the tiny phone she could hear it in Glory's voice. She might have used that comedy catch phrase, but something was up. "Yeah, of course. Let me step into my office."

Hope slid open the screen door to the deck and stepped out into the hot humid night. The peepers were screaming their lungs out and a few fireflies sparked along the edge of the little wood. The new white flowers on the little mesquite trees had proved problematic as Bianca gravitated toward them crying "Pretty!" and then got poked by the thorns. She hadn't yet learned that pretty things sometimes hurt.

"What's up, babe?" She hoped it wasn't Royce threatening to leave again. The two of them tangled on a nigh on weekly basis, but underneath was something stronger than them both.

Mostly that neither would give the other the satisfaction of leaving.

"I need you here." Glory's voice sounded funny. Not ha-ha funny but something Hope couldn't put her finger on. It gave her a bit of a chill even in the oppressive blanket of the humid night air.

"What's wrong, amiga?"

"Don't go Mexican on me, Hope. I don't need it tonight."

A dozen remarks rose to Hope's lips and evaporated just as quickly. It was an old argument, one she'd never win: she had married 'beneath' her, Jamie had no ambition, her child was a 'half-breed' and blah blah blah. You could take the girl out of Texas, but you couldn't get the Texas out of the girl. "You just sound funny. Strange."

"I need you here. Like five minutes ago." A pause. "It's . . . not good."

"All right, I'll be over directly." Hope had a punched in the gut feeling, but she tried to shift it aside. She distinctly heard her mother's voice in her head, *Don't imagine the worst. When it gets here it'll be soon enough.* Nevertheless she sighed.

Bianca was very put out to know that Daddy would have to tuck her in that night. It wasn't that she didn't love him; she was mad crazy for the man. But Daddy was mornings and Mama was tucking in and life was supposed to be ordered. "I'll kiss you when I come in and your dreams will all be sweet," Hope promised.

"But I won't know it," Bianca whined, a phalanx of teddies on the pillow around her like a protective posse.

"Yes, you will," Hope promised.

Jamie was no more pleased to have her traipsing over to Glory's. He took it with good humor as he did most things, though she knew he was itching to watch that new Statham film with her tonight. "Hurry back, hon."

"Don't you watch that without me," Hope said, taking a sip of his beer. "I need to see my boyfriend."

"Then get back from your girlfriend's sooner than usual." He put his hand out for his beer and grinned up at her. "Good thing I'm not the jealous type."

"You know you have nothing to worry about with me." Hope hugged him around the neck and then grabbed her pocketbook, throwing the phone inside.

"You two," Jamie muttered as she stepped to the door.

Yeah, us two: Hope and Glory. Glory's dad always joked they should be a TV series—a weekly drama because it usually was. Hope sighed as she started up the little red Honda. She could have taken Jamie's pickup, but she wanted to enjoy taking her little car for a spin now, before it was full-on summer. Much as she loved her little ride, it didn't have AC and by mid-summer it wouldn't be much good for anything but a quick run to the 7-11 or back and forth to her job at the evil empire, as they always called it. The only advantage of her early shifts was they started before the heat became oppressive.

Glory had been able to quit Wal-Mart when Royce got that big contract. You could tell they were living large when they started offering JD instead of just Lone Star in cans when Hope and Jamie came over for BBQ. It didn't seem to make any difference to their bickering, though. Not that it ever got serious. Hope figured Glory just needed the dramatics to keep things interesting.

She'd always been that way.

They'd been fast friends as kids. Hope's family had come out here from Houston when she was just ten and the other kids eyed her with suspicion for 'big city ways' that were doubtless obvious and odious to them though they eluded her. Hope charged in when the Rodrigues twins had badgered her at recess one day and had been her best friend ever since. Texas tall and naturally towheaded, she wasn't afraid of anything or anybody. Hope always felt like a mousey little thing beside her. For months back then she'd expected the novelty to wear off and Hope to move on to her junior cheerleader pals for best friend material, but one day as they came out of the pictures blinking in the bright light, Glory had said, "I'm so glad you're not dumb like all these morons around here. I do believe I was like to kill myself if I thought that's all there was to the world."

Dramatic as usual, but it helped so much. They were both ambitious and at that age, it meant learning. Hope was inclined to hide all her reading, to sneak off to corners where no one would see her nose in a book. "Books don't get you boyfriends," her mother would always say, smoothing down her perfect helmet of hair before lighting up another menthol.

Glory would mock her when they were alone, poofing up her hair and pretending to smoke a cigarette. Her rebellion didn't go as far as smoking because she was on the tennis team as well as cheerleading by then. Hope got a vicarious thrill from laughing at Glory's imitations of her mother. "A lady," she'd repeat, miming a drag on a long menthol, then coughing wildly, "always behaves with aplomb." Then she'd pretend to hack up a loogie and scratch her armpits. They'd both collapse laughing until they cried. Hope's mother worshipped Glory's seemingly effortless perfection and sighed over her daughter's inability to match it, but Hope never held it against her friend. She contented herself with a bit of reflected brilliance like a moon.

So she was grateful to Glory. And they hadn't made it out of this town yet, but she was happy. Jamie might not be setting the business world on fire like Royce, but he was a good man, a great dad, the best mechanic in town and he loved her like she wanted to be loved. Hope knew that when he breezed by Glory without a second look and asked her to dance at the ice house that night just five years gone by. His single-mindedness put her friend's nose out of joint for a while but by the end of the evening she had whispered to Hope, "You got a good one there." When Jamie became head mechanic at the garage, he asked her to marry him, but really they'd already made their minds up that night. Some people were just meant to find each other.

And she supposed Glory was happy too, after a fashion. The brakes in the Honda groaned a little as she pulled up next to Glory and Royce's matching black Ford pickups, the ones with the child-bearing hips as Jamie always joked. Their McMansion gleamed in the dark night like a big white tooth, but all was quiet as she stepped out of the car. Not even peepers peeping, which gave Hope a funny turn. As much rain as they'd had in the past few weeks, there should be a hum of insects everywhere. There was the scent of burning mesquite in the air so likely somebody was barbecuing somewhere near or had been earlier in the evening. She loved that smell. It meant summer, fun and laughter.

She knocked on the door. Generally Royce had some bro country music playing, blasting out into the back yard to frighten off the coyotes, or so he claimed. Glory would roll her eyes and shout for him to play some Patsy or Johnny, something with a little class. Royce was larger than life, a true Texan in that regard—normal wasn't acceptable. Letting the world know what he liked was a big part of that. He sure let Glory know he liked her, wrestled her into marriage and this house. Hope hadn't even minded not being matron of honor. "Daddy wants my cousin to do it and maid is more traditional, you know." Everything was according to tradition, right down to the brawl at the reception.

There wasn't a sound to be heard tonight. Hope couldn't help looking over her shoulder as if something haunted the quiet suburban landscape, yet all looked normal, peaceful and prosperous.

"Hey." Glory appeared and opened the door. The two friends hugged. "Sorry, hope I didn't slosh my drink on you." She held up a watery JD on the rocks. "Can I fix you one?"

"Just one," Hope said as she tossed her pocket book on the black marble counter of the open plan kitchen. "It's not far but you know. Gotta be careful."

Glory smiled but the expression looked pained. "Myrna got pulled over by Kenny's cousin the deputy. But then she's a lush as we all know."

"What's wrong, Glory?"

Glory handed her the glass tumbler. Sweat from the ice covered its sides. The AC wasn't blasting at the usual levels and Hope noticed the French doors to the deck were flung open. Usually the house was hermetically sealed to keep the refrigerated chill in.

"What's that thing twelve-steppers always talk about? A moment of clarity?" Glory seemed to be staring off into space.

"Yeah, I think so. That's what they always say on fine Lifetime movies." It was a bit of a joke between them. There was no such thing as a *regular* Lifetime movie. The woman-in-trouble network only showed *fine Lifetime movies* and they would watch them on bad days with drinks and popcorn and the sugary kid candy stuff that they liked when they were ten and couldn't stand now. It was a cheap and easy way to feel like your life couldn't be much of a mess. And you knew you were doing okay as long as there wasn't a fine Lifetime movie about you. "You had a moment of clarity?"

"Something like that." Glory stood at the French doors, looking at nothing at all.

Hope blinked. "Have you and Royce had a fight?" She cut off the 'again' just in time. It wouldn't do to downplay the seriousness of the moment. Every crisis was just as important as the last one for Glory, until they were past and forgotten.

"Yes. Yes, we did."

Hope frowned. This was the usual cue for Glory to rail against his thoughtlessness and insensitivity. She'd invite Hope to share the dissection of his character while they tipped back some JD and cokes until she got drunk enough to become maudlin. Then she'd remember all the sweet things he had done like the time he won that bear for her at the fair or when he bought her six bouquets of red roses and left them covering her front porch. But Glory just stared into the dark. There weren't even any fireflies out here. The lawns were too manicured. A sudden thought occurred to her.

"Has Royce left you?" Hope winced thinking she might have softened the question a little, but Glory didn't even react with so much as a shrug.

"In a manner of speaking."

Trust her to put the right spin on it. "You threw him out."

"No," Glory said, then paused. "He was already out." She stepped through the French doors onto the deck.

Hope followed her. "You mean he was—" And then she stopped because she could see what Glory had meant. Royce lay sprawled on the grill cover which had fallen to the deck leaving the enormous grill uncovered, its gleaming silver sleekness shining in the moonlight. The smell of mesquite perfumed the night air. "Is he drunk?"

"No. I belted him."

"You knocked him out?" Hope had to say she was impressed. Glory wasn't really the hands-on kind of fighter. She usually relied on her quick tongue. The woman could spit out insults faster than most people could breathe.

"I hit him with the Himalayan salt plate."

"What the hell is that?"

Glory went over to the grill and picked up what looked like a big pink stone with some kind of metal frame gripping it like a spider with a handle. "It's from the catalogue. Royce thought it gave the ribs a special something. You press it on them while they're cooking. It provides a salty finish."

"Well, we should get him to a hospital. He might have a concussion—"

"He's dead." Her words came out flat, like it didn't matter, or as if she had thought backwards and forwards about the matter a hundred times and come to the same conclusion each time, but couldn't quite figure out what it meant.

Hope's heart pounded in her chest. She wondered if Glory could hear it. It seemed so loud. "Dead? Are you sure? Maybe he—"

"No."

"But what if—" She kneeled down beside him and put her fingers on his neck like she'd seen in a thousand television shows or more and then drew back in alarm at how cold his flesh felt in the hot night.

"Told you." Glory leaned against the deck rail, arms folded.

"We have to call emergency services." In her head Hope could only think *oh my god oh my god he's really dead*. "You didn't touch anything did you? They're going to have to do an investigation."

Glory laughed. It came out like a harsh bark. "I'm not calling them. That's why I called you."

Hope closed her mouth. She didn't know how long it had been open but for sure a bug had flown in. She tried to spit it out, but her body convulsed with shivers. "But—what—you want me to call them?"

Glory uncrossed her arms long enough to tip the last of the JD into her mouth, then set the glass on the rail. "No, you're going to help me."

"Help you?"

Heroes

"Get rid of him."

For a moment Hope couldn't breathe. Maybe she had misunderstood. "What?"

Glory smiled. Her teeth looked unnaturally bright in the soft darkness. "That's the old joke, isn't it? Friends help you move. Real friends . . . "

"Help you move bodies," Hope finished weakly. "I think I need to sit down." She collapsed cross-legged beside Royce. His black Tony Lama conquistadors lay pointing in opposite directions as if the toes couldn't decide which way to fall. His jeans looked brand new. It seemed like a waste. Her shoulders began to shake as if suppressing laughter.

Bile rose up in her throat but she forced it back down and tried to think. Glory was ahead on that, however. "I figure we take him down to the southside and drop him in the bayou. The water's so high from runoff. People get drowned in it all the time."

"Why not drop him here?" Hope staggered to her feet, suddenly repulsed by being so near to him. "Bayou's not half a mile over."

Glory stared at her. "We don't want anyone to see us."

"What makes you think they won't see us on the southside."

Glory smiled, looking pleased with herself. "We'll go down by the old oil fields. The water's deepest there and there's never anybody about."

"You seem to have thought this through." Hope stared at her friend, wondering if there was something new there or just something she had not noticed before. She wanted to call Jamie. She wanted to phone the police. She wanted to be home playing teddies with Bianca.

Glory made an impatient noise. "I don't see why I should pay for his stupidity."

"His . . . ?"

"It's a long story, but come on. You knew it was never going to end well between us." Glory put her fists on her hips and glared down at Royce. "That man was stubborn as a mule."

The weird desire to laugh returned. Hope looked around as if there might be someone jumping out from around the corner to say it was all a set up and they were being pranked and Royce would jump up and laugh and rub his hands together at how he had fooled them all.

But he lay there still as the grave.

"We'll wrap him in this and put him in the back of the truck and drive down there. Chuck him in. Easy peasy lemon squeezy. He could get all the way to the gulf."

Hope pressed her fingers against her eyes until she saw stars but it didn't help any. All she could see was world where Jamie and Bianca had to live without her. "We could just explain it was an accident. You didn't mean to—"

"But you know? I did. I'm fed up. He got on my last nerve and I'm tired."

Hope stared. "I didn't know it was that bad. You seemed to...to cope all right."

Glory shrugged and bent down to get hold of the canvas edge of the grill cover. There didn't seem to be any blood, but the plastic coating would probably have caught it anyway. "You know how the camel's back really breaks? It's not that last little toothpick. It's all the hundreds that came before it." She looked up at her friend. "You don't know what it's like. You're happy."

The words stung. As if she didn't know it, or as if she didn't care that her best friend wasn't. She knew. She just didn't think there was an alternative. Glory always had her eye on the next horizon. It was never about being content. She didn't want to be just content. Not that it mattered just then.

Hope crouched down and grabbed the other side of the tarp and they did their best to twist it around his body, though the black boots stuck out at the end. Hope scanned the horizon. There wasn't anybody too near that could be watching them and there wasn't enough cover hereabouts to hide someone. One of the advantages of money; you could live where nobody was up in your business. You didn't have to do the hello wave whenever you stepped out on the deck. *Hello neighbor, please don't talk to me just now.*

"We can drag him through here and out to his truck," Glory said, taking hold of the cover near his head and dragging him across the deck toward the French doors. Hope looped her hands under his Tony Lamas and hurried along behind her. Things went smooth over the carpet and even easier across the kitchen tile. Glory turned off the overhead lights and cracked open the front door. All was quiet.

"You keep an eye out while I go open up the back of the truck. There's never much going on around here. And the Epsteins moved to San Antonio last week." Their house across the street sat dark and empty. Hope felt a funny sense of being watched anyway. She crouched low over the bundle. *All it would take is somebody driving past.*

Fortunately, no one did.

"Come on, let's shift him." Glory had that focused look Hope recognized from her tennis days. She had that ability to shut out everything but the competition. Though her hair was tousled and her slacks casual, you could see the player had come out. Competition brought out the best in her—'the killer instinct' her father always said with a chuckle. Hope swallowed and clung to her end of the bundle with grim determination.

They wrangled him into the back of the pickup and Glory latched it behind him, pushing a few stray hairs out of her face. "You need to pee first?" she asked Hope as if it were just another road trip together. Legend had it her bladder was the size of a pea, but she shook her head. The whole of her body felt as dry as her mouth just now. "Well, get in."

"Don't you think we should leave his truck there? So it looks more plausible?"

Glory stared at her. "Plausible?"

"We could even roll the truck into the bayou, too. Like he tried to drive through and didn't make it?"

Glory frowned. "I suppose. I hate to lose the truck."

"Insurance will surely pay." She tried to keep the exasperation out of her tone: *of all the things to be worrying about at that moment.*

"Yeah, all right. You follow close."

"Keep it slow."

Hope climbed into her Honda, feeling dwarfed by the big black Ford. She regretted separating from her friend because now it would be impossible to halt the torrent of thoughts that wanted to scream through her brain asking if she were completely insane and why she hadn't called the cops and what the hell were they really going to just dump Royce in the bayou as if he were just garbage and oh my god, Glory killed him. Her heart started hammering again and she turned up the music in hopes that Lucinda's dulcet tones might calm her a bit. She sang along in her loudest voice and kept her eyes on the back of Glory's head.

Slow, stop, signal, turn: it was only about five miles altogether. The night was quiet like everybody decided to stay in this evening just to accommodate Glory. That was always the way: the path was smoothed for her whether it was her daddy's name or the boys who wanted to please her. And it would be again: she had a new role, the tragic widow. Alone once more and looking for a better match; alone because their union had not been blessed, despite Royce's eagerness. Glory had hid her pills in her tampon box, knowing he'd never look there.

Glory had never wanted to share center stage.

As they headed into the underpass below the interstate, Hope saw headlights in the rearview. Adrenaline surged in her veins but she told herself there was nothing odd in someone being on the road tonight. It had been eerie enough with the roads empty, but that was suburbia. It was late enough now that like as not the other driver would get impatient with their law-abiding pace and swing around them.

Glory appeared to be thinking along similar lines and slowed to pull off the side of the road, as if she had something wrong with her truck. Hope eased off behind her and the vehicle behind them pulled past, tooting their horn and whooping before squealing away. They had a big "Don't Mess with Texas!" decal across the back window of the cab. Doubtless up to the same kind of aimless youthful shenanigans they had been part of in their teen years.

The taillights receded into the distance and Glory pulled back onto the road, Hope behind her. It wasn't far now and she could see the old rusty rigs poking into the night sky. Oncoming lights made Glory slow again. It wouldn't do to let someone notice where they were heading; a good citizen might report it to the patrol.

Then she heard the whoops and the motor racing. It was those kids again. They must be really bored. Irritating at the best of times, but right now damned inconvenient. She waited to see what Glory would do. Maybe they'd pull over again.

The truck ahead swerved into their lane, flashing their lights and laying on the horn as if to make them move aside. Hope hadn't had to face a game of chicken since she was in high school and then it was with kids she knew were good kids and not too reckless. Who knew about these kids? Her heart took up a faster tattoo as she fidgeted in her seat, waiting for Glory to show her the way as the truck bore down upon them.

Royce's truck sped up. After a moment, Hope pressed the accelerator, her heart in her mouth. Was the woman crazy? All she could see was the outline of her blonde head with a halo from the oncoming lights, as determined as some avenging angel. Hope braced herself for the worst, imagining in a flash the tangle of metal, the screams and cries, blood everywhere and the highway patrol pulling up, lights flashing while she was left to explain it all.

They were close enough to hear the slick new country music blaring from the cab and hear the shouts and catcalls and at the last minute, they swung to their right, whooping and waving half-empty bottles of Lone Star as they drove on. Glory never flinched, though she gradually slowed and turned into the old oil fields without signaling. The gate was locked but a path had been worn around the downed chain link fence for years now. Though Glory rumbled over it without a thought, Hope drove gingerly, apologizing to her little red car for the rough ride.

She pulled up to the flat concrete by the broken rig and stepped out of the car. The sounds of the swollen bayou filled the night, gurgling like some sci-fi movie monster on the prowl. Glory was looking down into its depths as if to be sure it was as deep as they hoped. "Those kids were nuts."

"Yeah."

Hope looked at the bayou. The waters looked black in the moonlight. "Should we just roll it in?"

Glory looked up. "I suppose."

"Did you clear out anything you really need?"

"Nothing but his shit in there, except this." She held up his little black gun, the one he liked to wave around at parties. It was said that if you lined up all the guns in Texas they would circle the globe. That might be a lie but it felt true.

"Well, holster that and let's get pushing. Is it in neutral?"

"I had a thought," Glory said, not looking at her. "It might look more convincing if people thought he were down here for a reason."

"What sort of reason?" Hope could feel the hairs on the back of her neck stand up. There couldn't be any houses within a mile at least of this place and yet she could smell mesquite fire clear as anything. It made her hungry all of the sudden and she realized how thirsty she was as well. The sloshing of the bayou made her feel the need to pee, too. She almost missed Glory's quiet words.

"What if you and him were having an affair? That would seem plausible enough."

Hope stared at Glory but she was still looking down. The hand with the gun hung loosely at her side. "Except that I never much liked him at all and everybody knew it."

"Maybe that was a ploy, to put me off the scent as it were."

All the air left her body as Hope thought, *she's trying to convince herself it's true.* "You think you can push this truck in by yourself?" She didn't have to pretend to sound angry. She just had to think about Jamie and Bianca and how much she loved them. And remember every time Glory had rode roughshod over her in the name of friendship—belittling her dreams of college, mocking her promotion to head cashier, telling her how pregnancy had ruined her body. All the things you take in stride because you'd been friends forever and you always would be. Always.

Glory laughed. "I was just thinking out loud."

"Well, don't. It's not your strong suit."

It was worth it for the shocked expression. If she'd had struck her, it would have been less. "Don't be like that. I'm under a lot of pressure."

"I know, you just lost your husband. Now let's get this done." Hope couldn't wait to go home and kiss that little girl and listen to Jamie belch through the Statham film. Her mouth had filled up with bile and she spit it over to the side, then they both pushed on the back of the truck until the slope took it away and it slipped into the churning waters and started to float off down toward the south.

"See you in Galveston," Glory said with a sour scorn.

"You want to get rid of that, too?" Hope asked, pointing to the gun.

Glory smiled. "Don't you trust me?"

"Should I?"

"Everything will be fine now."

"You'll get a new and better husband—"

"Trade up to a better house."

"Get all the sympathy for being a lovely young widow."

"Why not? I earned it."

Hope laughed. "How did you 'earn' it?"

"Hope, you may like being under some man's thumb, but it don't suit me."

"I'm not under anyone's thumb. Jamie and me both pull our weight together."

It was Glory's turn to laugh. "He turned you into a broodmare and you welcomed the halter. That's not going to happen with me."

"You don't want kids, that's fine. Nobody's asking you to become a mother. Besides, you'd be a lousy mother."

"My daddy and I did just fine. Mothers only drag you down."

Hope turned. "I'm going home."

"Wait."

"Wait for what?" Hope stopped and turned back.

Glory didn't point the gun at her, but she raised it. The sound of the rushing waters seemed to intensify as if the bayou had picked up the tension between the two old friends and amplified it. "I want to know I can trust you."

"As much as I trust you." Hope did her best to smile.

"How much is that?"

Hope walked back to her friend. She wanted to look her in the eyes. All the little things that had been buried under the blanket of friendship were shining there. Every dig, every flounce, every disbelieving eyebrow raised, every backhanded compliment she'd dismissed with 'bless her heart!' No doubt about it, Glory was the Texan supreme. Everything Hope was supposed to want to be. Hope had dropped the chip on her shoulder only gradually: when she hooked up with Jamie ("Not bad for a Mexican," Glory had said with a smile.), when they had their little wedding ("It's cute that you had everybody bring food for the reception, no really."), and when she had Bianca ("It's good she looks more like you."). She could feel that chip slipping off.

But tonight it was finally gone. "Not enough, I guess."

Glory brought the gun down. Her voice that had been harsh softened. "Why can't you do right by me?"

Hope laughed and the more she laughed, the harder it was to stop. Her stomach started to hurt with the effort.

Glory just stared at her, a half-smile on her face. Maybe she was tempted to join in, maybe she was just confused. At least she lowered the gun for a moment anyway. But as Hope sputtered on, wheezing and gasping. "I don't know what's so funny."

"You are, Glory. Glory! What a name."

"And Hope is just a genius sort of name. Shut the hell up."

"Glory, I have been your faithful dog of a friend for years and years and still you ask if you can trust me. You just don't get it."

"Your jealousy of me knows no bounds, does it." Glory shook her head.

Hope laughed, but it was a harsh sort of sound she didn't recognize. "You know what? You envy me. I just figured that out. You. Envy me."

Glory went to slap her, but with the gun in her hand, the blow connected harder than she may have intended. At least Hope wanted to give her the benefit of the doubt about it, because she saw stars plain enough, bright as the stars in the sky.

Hope didn't really think about it. She shoved Glory as hard as she could. Probably if she had thought calmly about it, Hope would have known it was stupid to try to push someone with a gun in her hand, but Glory's smug look of superiority pushed some button inside of her for the very last time and it was somehow joyful to see her tipping backwards, arms spinning wide to try to regain her balance, the gun pulling her slightly to her right and then just taking that one step back—the step that put her over the bank, her fancy designer shoes sucked into the mud and then a splash.

And then darkness as Hope tried to find her breath again.

It was just some kind of instinct, she decided later as she drove home. No doubt she'd have some bad nights waking up to the image of Glory's surprised face, her hands flung wide as she fell back into the flood waters, her blond hair encircling her head like a hood before she disappeared from sight.

But when she kissed Bianca's sleeping brow, Hope felt right. And when she elbowed her dozing husband to make room on the couch, her heart beat slow and regular.

"Those two sort out their problems?" Jamie yawned as he reached for the remote.

"Some problems can't be sorted," Hope admitted.

"I've been telling you that for years."

"I know." She leaned onto his shoulder and his arm wrapped around her.

"BBQ tomorrow? Supposed to be nice."

"Yeah, but no mesquite, okay?"

Jamie kissed the top of her head. "As you wish."

LEVEL 5

C.R. Jahn

"Who knows the Levels of Intervention? What is a Level 1? That is when we ride to a child's house as a group to introduce ourselves and formally make them a part of our family. Level 2 is when the child contacts us because they remain fearful of continued victimization, and that is when we camp out on the child's lawn 24/7 until they feel safe again. If the perp continues to contact the child, Level 3 is when the chapter President drafts a letter to the perp on Protectors of the Children letterhead, explaining that the child is under our protection and what that means. If that letter fails to correct the situation, a Level 4 is a "Community Awareness Ride," where we ride through the perp's neighborhood to knock on doors, letting people know that there is a predator in their community and educating them about what we do to help empower abused children to feel safe in the world in which they live. Does anyone know what a Level 5 is? That's right, there's no such thing as a Level 5. We are not vigilantes and neither condone nor engage in violence, but if we are the only thing standing between a child and further abuse, we are prepared to be that obstacle. One hundred percent commitment."

It broke my heart when they said I couldn't help the kids no more. That's what we do, helping kids feel safe, but I broke a rule and they said I was a liability to the club now. We will get sued, they said. We need your patch back, they said. Fuckit, I gave them the entire cut with everything in the pockets. The switchblade and THC mints would've just been extra charges. Gave Bones the keys to my bike and told him to sell it for bail money. Took two weeks before I made bail, and by then the girl was dead.

Perhaps I should start at the beginning. My name's Pirate and I'm Sergeant at Arms for the Rocky Mountain Chapter of "Protectors of the Children," or at least I was until last month when they pulled my patch and sold my bike.

"Protectors of the Children," or P.O.T.C., is a motorcycle club dedicated to helping abused kids with active cases in the criminal justice system who remain afraid of continued harassment and intimidation by the perpetrator. The perps are generally looking at multiple felony charges with the possibility of years, if not decades, inside, and are often desperate to prevent that child from testifying against them. Telephoned threats to kill their family or burn down their house while they're sleeping are common. Perps have shot out windows and even tried to abduct victims as they walked home from school. It can get ugly, and the cops can't do much without solid proof, aside from promising to drive past their home more often, or maybe even parking a car across the street for a couple of hours. And that is where we come in.

If a child who is part of our family is receiving continued threats from the perpetrator, they call their primary contact person who sends out a bulk text, and every available member immediately grabs their go bag and rides directly to the child's home. We let the child know that as long as we are there, no-one will get past our perimeter, and they can sleep knowing they are safe. If the child wants a continued presence at the home, we have an old camper stocked with provisions and will work in shifts around the clock, patrolling the yard and escorting the child wherever they need to go. All of us swore an Oath to take a bullet for a child if need be. This is what we do. This is our purpose, which defines who we are.

I was assigned as primary for Princess Buttercup. All the kids have road names, and they choose whatever name they want, something that makes them feel strong. Apparently "Princess Buttercup" was the hero of some silly movie I never saw. Everyone else had seen it though, and agreed that it was a fine and proper name, so who was I to argue. It made her happy to be called by that name, and that's all that matters.

Buttercup was a painfully thin fourteen-year-old with long straight hair, and apparently even bore some small resemblance to the girl in the film. She was bulimic and would self injure with razor blades to cope with the pressure she was under. For the past two years she'd been repeatedly victimized by an uncle, who had filmed the abuse and uploaded it to several websites that permitted anonymous file sharing. His bail was a quarter million dollars, but his mother posted it the next day, pulling 25K out of savings and putting up her house as collateral. Then he disappeared, failing to check in with his probation officer or show up for his court dates . . . but the harassment continued. Texts calling her a liar and worse, telling her she knew what would happen if she didn't recant. We told her to be brave, that we were on her side now.

Over the next few months we saw a change in Buttercup. She was putting on weight, her hair was clean and combed, and she smiled sometimes, a wide radiant smile that would light up a room. She wasn't afraid anymore, and would laugh and joke whenever we paid her a visit. Her mom said she was doing better in school and making friends. She said she wanted to take up fencing, but was too young for the Varsity team and her mom couldn't afford equipment and private lessons. I bought her an old sword from a garage sale, more of a decoration than anything, but she liked it and kept it next to her bed "in case someone tries getting in my window," as the perp had threatened in his texts until she changed her number. She was getting better. I was so proud of her.

• • •

The incident occurred at one of our awareness events. We had a table set up at a community festival in Civic Center Park, next to the Capitol, selling T-shirts and handing out brochures about our mission, telling folks that we were in over a dozen states now and would soon have tax exempt status so people could claim charitable contributions as deductions. A few patches had stepped out to hit the food trucks, leaving me to watch the table with two female prospects, Giggles and Smurfette. It was going fairly well until the idiot showed up.

He had a flattop haircut and was wearing an old field jacket with a Ranger tab he obviously hadn't earned, as it was sewn on with the wrong colored thread at least an inch lower than it should've been, off center and slightly crooked. I didn't call him out on it because it was a family event and we're supposed to be the good guys who smile and are friendly and shit. Just ignore the idiots, my sponsor had drilled into me, because there will always be at least one troublemaker talking shit. He stood there, hands in pockets, lopsided smirk on his face as he listened to Giggles run down the spiel to a young couple pushing a stroller. "What about false accusations?" he interrupted.

"That is not up to us to determine," she replied. "All of our kids are referred to us by the courts, and the perpetrator has already been arrested and charged for crimes against children. We never take on a new kid unless they're already in the system."

"Yeah, but what do you get out of this? Don't you get paid for standing guard outside people's houses and stuff?"

"We volunteer our time because our kids need us and it's the right thing to do. I can't think of any better way to spend my time."

"So . . . were all of you abused as kids or something?"

"We have a few survivors here."

"Awww . . . did someone bad touch you, little girl?" Giggles had been handling herself fairly well, but at that moment her face crumpled and no more words came out, breath ragged as she fumbled with an albuterol inhaler.

Smurfette stepped up and got between them.

"You need to walk away, right now." The smirk turned into a wide feral grin.

"Or what? You guys are nothing but talk. Blah blah blah. You ain't even real bikers, just a buncha yuppie poseurs playing dress up."

"We ride for our kids year round, in rain, sleet, hail, all kinds of weather. I put twenty thousand miles on my Harley last year. What do you ride, a fucking moped? Get lost asshole."

"Oh, you gonna call 911 or something? Buncha pretend bikers who like kids too much. Where did the bad man touch you?" Then I see the mole. He'd cut his hair, shaved the goatee, and got rid of the glasses, but between the mole on his cheek and the crooked nose I recognize him from the photo of Buttercup's perp. This is Uncle Billy, the fugitive himself! I launch out of the chair, yanking the bandanna from my back pocket, padlock streaking like a meteor as it clocks him square in the left temple. Blood splatters, he drops instantly.

"There's your bad touch, motherfucker." I was seriously considering pissing on his corpse when Bones and Gorilla come charging over.

"Holy shit, Pirate! What the fuck have you done?" Bones asks, dropping his funnel cake in the grass.

"I do believe he done killed that mope," Gorilla states, matter-of-factly. "Oh, look . . . cops."

"And you're wearing your cut? Goddammit, people are filming this right now with their phones! You know we have a strict policy of non-violence, and you just broke one of the only rules we have, and we're definitely getting sued over this. You're lucky that guy is still breathing! I'm pulling your patch because you're out of the club right now, this isn't even going up for a vote because fuck you for doing this to us at an event in front of hundreds of witnesses! National will probably revoke our charter because of you."

"That there is William Crane, Buttercup's perp who was trading kiddie porn on the net. Motherfucker walked right up to Giggles and Smurfette, wanting details about how they were molested as kids."

"He did WHAT? Holy shit, he's so lucky those cops are running towards us or I'd be inclined to finish what you started," Gorilla says.

"What part of *people are filming this* did your dumb ass fail to understand? Pirate, I'm not pulling my knife in front of the cops, just hand me your cut and I'll get it back to you later."

"Take my keys, too. I don't want my bike impounded because you'll probably need to sell it for bail money. Title is in the ammo can in my bedroom closet."

"Alright, I'll see what I can do." I turn and fling the padlock way up into the air, arcing towards some bushes about a hundred feet away, because I'm not just handing that shit over, then I put out my hands for the cuffs and tell Officer Friendly I already know my rights and will give a full statement after I've consulted with legal counsel.

• • •

I tried calling Bones and Gorilla collect from the cellblock payphone a few times, but it automatically disconnects if they don't pick up within eight rings and I never got through. No-one ever showed up for visits either, but the guards drop off a copy of the *Denver Post* every day and the case was in the news a few times. That was how I heard about the drive-by. When I read about Buttercup passing I didn't even know it was her at first, as P.O.T.C. policy prohibits us from knowing our kids' legal names. It was just a small article in the middle of the paper about how a local high school freshman had committed suicide after being cyberbullied by her classmates on Facebook, but that wasn't what happened at all. Buttercup's friends had told her mom everything at the memorial service, but the reporter didn't talk to them. I got a letter from the mom a few days later filling in the details.

Apparently, getting his skull cracked sent Billy over the edge, and things escalated quickly after that. There must have been some sort of bureaucratic clusterfuck since no-one bothered to post a guard at his room, even though we'd told the cops he had warrants out on him, and as soon as he woke up he got dressed and walked away. Two days later, Buttercup came home to find her cat sawn in half and placed on her pillow. Someone had pushed an air conditioner out of the way to gain entry through a window, then trashed her room, tearing apart clothes and books, and bending the sword I'd given her in half. She completely lost it, flipping out so bad that the police had to Taser her before the paramedics could get the restraints on, and she was placed on a 72 hour psychiatric hold before being released back to her mom with scripts for Xanax and Paxil.

Understandably, she was terrified, so Bones declared an emergency Level 2 situation and the club immediately rode out there to maintain a presence outside her home, with the camper parked at the curb and patrols around the block every hour, large handguns conspicuously holstered on everyone's belt. The club escorted her to and from school, and every time she came home they would clear the house, checking every room, every closet, even under the beds, before letting her inside. On the third night, a sniper fired off a string of bright green tracers from the park across the street. No-one was hurt, but the propane tank was hit and our camper burned to a shell.

The police said it was probably an SKS modified to accept hi-cap detachable mags, from the shell casings they recovered.

After the cops left, Bones told Buttercup and her mom to each pack a suitcase, because they needed to go someplace else, and moved them to a rental property he owned across town. They thought she'd be safe now, because no-one knew where she was living and there were guards and metal detectors at the school. They were wrong.

It had started out a day like any other, but Buttercup began noticing the stares, the whispered conversations, the laughter. A few kids even pointed. She tried to ignore it as best she could. Probably someone recognized her dress and was telling everyone how they'd donated it to the thrift store . . . it had happened before. But people she didn't know were coming up to her, saying things she didn't understand. A boy in her first class tried to give her his phone number, and another asked if she had plans later. She ignored them both. On her way to lunch, four older boys with Varsity jackets blocked her way. "Would you do me too?" one of them asked, with a leer.

"Do what?" she asked.

"She's acting like she doesn't know," he said to his friends, who laughed, cruelly.

"Don't talk to my boyfriend, slut!" one of the popular girls yelled, shoving her. She ran. She couldn't eat, but went to the cafeteria anyway, sitting alone in a corner pretending to read her American History textbook, words blurring on the page. Eventually, she was joined by Susan, who had one of those fancy touch screen phones. She pushed it across the table to her and she saw them: the secret photos he took, posted on her Facebook profile for all to see. Her friend showed her how to delete them, but it was far too late . . . they were posted twelve hours ago and already had dozens of "likes" and shares.

How do you come back from something like that? If you're an emotionally fragile fourteen-year-old girl, I reckon you don't. She finished the school day, "like a robot," they said. "We could tell something was wrong," they said. Moments after she got her ride back to the safehouse, she locked herself in the bathroom and cut herself for the last time. She didn't even leave a note.

After I read the letter, I called Bone's cell non-stop until he finally picked up and accepted the charges.

"How come no-one told me?"

"Dude, you're out of the club. Pigpen is her primary now. This doesn't involve you, and it's over. I'm sorry, man."

"Did you sell the bike?"

"I posted it on Craigslist, got a little interest, but the only guy who said he wanted to look at it was a no show."

"What price did you put on it?"

"You said you had 15K into it, so I listed it at ten."

"Relist it at five."

"Dude, are you sure? It's worth three times that!"

"I've been in this cellblock for two weeks, eating cold grilled cheese sammich, listening to Cartoon Network at full volume, watching the animals picking their noses and showing each other their dicks, and you don't even bother to tell me that my child is dead? If you do not bail me out tomorrow, I'm burning your fucking house down."

"Don't be like that, man."

"I shit you not. Get me the fuck out of here."

"Tell you what, I'll take some money out of the bank and post your bail tomorrow, but I'm keeping the bike and doubling my money on this bullshit. And don't you ever threaten me again, that shit ain't right." I hang up the phone.

• • •

True to his word, bail was posted the next day, and once it's processed I'm released at midnight with no-one to pick me up. The cash in my wallet was placed in an inmate account so I'm given a check for fifty-seven bucks and change, but they overlooked the twenty hidden in a secret compartment. I'm permitted to make a phone call, so I call Metro Taxi, and the twenty bucks gets me most of the way home. After walking a half hour in the rain, I find the door to my apartment wide open, and my laptop, stereo, and whiskey are gone. So is my entire knife collection, and the Beretta Jetfire that was buried under the papers on my desk. I check between the mattress and box spring and the Ruger is gone too.

At least I had the forethought to keep a backup jar stashed inside the heating duct, and after I get the grate off it takes some time to locate the knotted paracord since the tape had given way and there was a thick layer of greasy dust over everything, but I eventually manage to fish out the old mason jar double wrapped with electrical tape. It isn't much, just enough to get me by in the event of shitstorms like this: a chrome plated Saturday Night Special, a cheap hawkbill lockback, a hundred dollar bill, a white caplet, and an airport bottle of Jameson's. I press check the .25 to make sure there's one in the chamber before washing down the Tramadol with whiskey and crawling into bed.

• • •

It turned out that computer forensics couldn't find any evidence on Uncle Billy's hard drives, and his attorney cast doubt on his accuser's mental stability after her suicide. She was a very mixed up girl, he said. She probably killed the cat for attention, he said. And anyone could've shot up that camper, as that vigilante motorcycle gang certainly had plenty of enemies and word must've got around that they'd been camped on a public street for three days. Absolutely no evidence that his client had anything to do with this series of unfortunate events.

Apparently, he'd covered his digital footprints well, using hacked accounts behind anonymous proxy servers. Without finding the actual flash drive in his possession there was no way they could prove it was him in those photos. One of her boyfriends must have taken them, he said. So the case was dismissed, even the contempt charge for failure to appear, and then the attorney announced that his client intended to file suit against P.O.T.C. due to the unprovoked attack against him by a member at a public event. One million dollars, he wants, and it looks like he'll probably win a settlement for at least half that amount. Rocky Mountain Chapter has less than ten grand on the books, but he intends to go after National which has deeper pockets, but nowhere near that deep. So, it appears I'm single-handedly responsible for wiping our club off the map. The shame of this revelation overwhelms me. I need to make this right. 100 percent commitment.

• • •

Billy wasn't too hard to find. I just needed to camp in the bushes outside the VFW for a while, waiting for him to drift in and tell his lies. He'd been a regular there for years, and I'm appalled no-one ever called him on his "Special Forces" bullshit and asked to see his DD-214. I reckon the stupid fucker doesn't even know what MOS he was supposed to have had. As far as I'm concerned, that makes those alcoholic has-beens *collaborators* for accepting and sheltering this freak. By the time his truck pulls into the lot, I'd been sleeping in the same clothes for four days, unshaven and reeking to high hell, just like one of the bums staggering along Colfax. I'd been subsisting on high fiber energy bars and forgot to pack TP so I needed to wipe my ass with my socks, the rough interior of the worn out boots now chaffing my bare feet. After he passes through the door, I take a few moments to compose myself, then open my pack.

I use the wet nap to wipe the foul sweat from my pits before doing a quick dry shave and dumping the remainder of the water jug over my head. I pull on the clean T-shirt and jeans, wishing I'd remembered to bring socks and boxers, then run the comb through my hair. I need to appear somewhat presentable for this. Situated, I walk towards his truck to sit on the fender until he comes out.

• • •

It is a few hours before he comes out, a bit unsteady on his feet from how-ever many Jack & Cokes. I wait for him to get halfway across the lot before ambling towards the pub, all non-threatening and smiling and shit. "Pardon me, friend, but weren't you in Fallujah with the 82nd?"

"Naw, I was with the Rangers, faceshooting Hadjis in Trashcanistan," he slurs, a lie likely repeated hundreds of times in expectation of free drinks and a few moments of unearned respect. I nod, contemplating how I should go about this.

"I was sorry to hear about your niece, Billy." He's quick, big knife a blur as he yanks it from concealment, slashing in a single well practiced motion. He blinks, surprised he missed, then raises it over his head and charges. I pop a quick shot into his right kneecap and he stumbles, but does not fall. A shot into the left one fixes that. He takes another swipe from the ground and I get a better look at what he's trying to cut me with, a Chinese knockoff of a Rambo knife with those stupid sawteeth on the back. "Is that what you used on the cat?" I ask, then pop a round into his belly. I'd loaded it up with those soft lead slugs with the steel BB in the tip that Winchester makes. I've always liked those rounds.

"What are you shootin' me for? She was crazy! I didn't do nuthin' to that girl!" I put another round into his groin and he screams. These .25s are good for shit, I wish I had my Ruger. Old drunks start bustling out of the VFW to see what the commotion's about. A fat man in an apron makes a big produc-tion of racking a round into a pump gun and firing what's probably rock salt into the sky. Without even aiming I extend my arm to the side and light off a round in his direction. I'm nearly as surprised as he is when he claps both hands to his face, scattergun clattering to the ground, as he paces in a circle, howling, before being led back inside. Half the drunks follow.

One of them boldly strides towards us. "You didn't have to shoot Gus! And leave Billy alone!" Dust puffs off the chest of his overalls when I shoot him. He looks down, looks back up at me, then turns and walks back inside with-out another word. I hear sirens. I reckon there's one round left in the Titan and decock it, slipping it back in my pocket. I take a few steps back as I notice Billy crawling towards me, knife in hand, leaving a trail like the slug he is.

I shake the last clove out of the box and light up, drawing deep. There are more sirens now, getting closer. I exhale sweet fragrant smoke, then take another drag while pulling the Ronsonol out of my back pocket and flipping open the spout. Billy's eyes go wide and crazed when he sees the yellow squeeze bottle.

"Dude! You don't need to do this! Please don't!" I hose him down, moving the thin stream back and forth. It takes a while to empty the bottle. "Why are you even doing this?" He throws the knife and misses by quite a bit, I didn't even need to dodge.

"I made that girl a promise. I told her I'd make the monster go away . . . but you're still here." I take one last, long draw off the clove before bouncing it off his chest. He goes up in orange flames, but it isn't quick as napthalene burns slow. Skin blisters, bursts, and chars as greasy black smoke rises. He's still screaming when the first DPD cruiser rolls up. One of the cops pops the trunk and grabs a fire extinguisher, dropping it and taking cover when my final shot zips past his ear.

The slide on these zinc nightmares doesn't lock back, so I bluff, leveling the empty peashooter at his partner's face as he draws the Glock. I never liked Glocks, but they hold a lot of rounds. I welcome the metalstorm that is my admission to Valhalla.

THE LONG ROAD TO LA GRANGE

Karina Cooper

The first Junior McGee sees of the boy is hair like spun starlight. It's an unruly thatch of sandy white curls, that kind of towheaded bird's nest that would make any momma throw her hands up in despair and swear to shave her child bald.

On cue, Betty starts to grumble. Not the usual bellyaching, but a full-on snarl that says if she keeps rattling over the rough road to La Grange, the dusty old motorbike will break something critical. It's the only sound aside from the cicadas humming and buzzing, droning with every step.

McGee cuts the engine. A hot, dry wind blows over the bone-dry soil. White curls shine.

Kid like that won't last long under this sun.

As McGee wheels the old bike closer, another sound permeates the air. *Scrape*. The boy's skinny shoulder moves. A stick digs into the dusty ground.

Scrape, scrape.

McGee checks the road east. Checks it west. The land is flat and brown, desolate and empty. There's no vehicle, no horse. No sign of parents.

No sign of life.

The kickstand rattles as she toes it down, and Betty leans alarmingly, but she holds. She always holds. The motorcycle's been ridden two weeks too hard and three months past her maintenance date, but she's a tough old broad. Just like McGee.

"Hey, kid." McGee's voice is as dry as the desert around them, but that's no thing. That's just how she talks. Long days on the road, the smokes that keep her company, the whiskey that gets her through the empty nights.

The boy with the head full of white-gold curls stops digging at the ground. His hands are filthy. She stops a few feet away—far enough to prove she ain't no threat, close enough that she can see the blisters.

They cover his bare feet. Line his toes, long since burst and blackened by all the dust kicked up during the miles he's trudged.

But there's calluses, too. The kind of hard sole that says he's used to being barefoot in the summer. Probably used to blisters, too.

Most kids from poor towns, they don't get shoes like proper folk. They get bark and cotton, old denim ripped down and maybe the lucky ones get hide for the winter.

McGee knows the ache of those blisters. Her own feet, sweltering in leather boots, are pocked with scars and still tough as an old vulture's knobby head.

The boy looks up. "I'm thirsty," he tells her, like she's no stranger on this rough road.

He's got a smile just a little bit wry, an old smile in a young face. His eyes are muddled brown; the kind of brown that comes lit from the inside like fire behind dark and dirty water.

There's dust on his cheeks and his clothes look like they been sweat through. There's calluses on his grubby fingers and the kind of grime that doesn't suit the dry dust around them. Like mud or slime. Something wet and sticky.

"Where's your ma?" McGee asks, crouching with effort that creaks— leather and sinew. That's all she is these days. Spit and vinegar.

The boy shrugs.

"You from La Grange?"

A nod.

"What're you doing out here?"

Another shrug. *Scrape.* The stick draws a rough line in the dusty road.

McGee's been doing this for a long time. She knows the things the kid ain't telling. Whatever the details, the story's going to be the same.

His ma's a prostitute, a live-in tinker, or a picker. Maybe he'd say she's there in La Grange, working her job, or maybe she's somewhere else lining up a new one with deeper pockets and syphilis for miles.

Maybe she's six feet under and this kid's father don't even know.

Maybe, maybe, maybe.

Fact of the matter is that it don't matter. Even kids need to get away sometimes.

It's the luckiest ones that do.

But it's adults like McGee who need to make sure kids like this find their way somewhere safe.

She sniffs hard, but doesn't spit. Waste of good water. "What's your name, kid?"

This time, he answers direct. "Colby."

"All right, Colby. I'm McGee." She braces her elbows on her dusty knees and jerks a thumb at the motorcycle. "That's Betty."

The boy looks at Betty. Looks back. "That's just a bike."

"And you're just a kid, but somebody named you anyway."

There's too much slant in that grin. Whoever taught him to smile like that taught him too much.

"You want some water?"

He nods. "I'm thirsty."

She unhooks her canteen and passes it to him. He takes it eagerly, unscrews the cap and wraps his mouth around the lip like he hasn't had any water in weeks.

"One mouthful," she cautions flatly.

The boy adjusts the angle of the canteen accordingly. One mouthful. She watches to be sure.

When he's done, he wipes off the lip like it matters. Like it's only polite.

He holds the dull canteen back out. His fingers leave grimy streaks behind.

McGee stands, the bones in her knees creaking with the effort. One pops back into place with a click that never fails to make her wince. Isn't the pain. Pain comes with the territory. She learned to roll with pain a long time ago.

But the *click* reminds her of things left behind.

A body does a job like hers long enough, and memories collect like brown rainwater in a busted gutter.

The leather hide protecting her denim hangs heavy on her legs. Her jacket is too thick for the blistering heat, but going without means a burn at best and sunstroke at the worst. She scratches idly at the hide, right where the badge she wears on the inside sits against her sternum.

It ain't that it itches.

"You want a ride back to town or not?" Slinging the canteen at her waist, she makes for the bike like she don't care.

Scrape.

She looks back.

The towheaded boy is drawing lines in the dirt again.

McGee's jaw shifts, like she's working up a wad of spit, but it's just too dry for that. Aggravated by her inability to hock out her feelings on the subject, she swallows it down and picks her way back across the dusty ruts carved in the road to La Grange.

The kid takes her offered hand.

• • •

He perches on Betty's seat like she's a wild horse and he ain't afraid of her. McGee's coat drapes over the sides, covering the parts of the bike that would sear the skin right off the boy's chicken legs.

Betty's been kicking up a fuss, so McGee pushes them both over the potholes and ruts, ignoring the ache in her gnarled hands. He grips the handlebars and growls, "Vroom, vroom!"

It's a long road to La Grange.

As the sun melts in a pool of fiery red and wild orange, the first breath of cooler air whispers across the dusty divide. It feels good on her skin. She already picked up that burn she'd been worried about, but there'll be water to cool it later.

The boy's shoulder is damned skinny against her arm. It digs in to her biceps—bone against sinew, gristle chapping up against meat gone on too tough. He doesn't pull away.

She don't mind.

Comes with the territory.

The shotgun slung in with her saddlebags is in reach, but McGee doesn't think she'll need it. Not for this job. Some are easier than others.

If easy is the word for it.

The wind picked up off the desert has a bite to it. A pale moon in her peripheral tells her the boy is looking at her—or past her. McGee spares him a spiky glare.

He's staring off past her battered old hat. Whatever he sees in those dirty water eyes of his, she can only guess. It ain't the same thing she sees. Never is.

She figures she'll learn soon enough.

Shadows creep out as the sun goes down, sizzling like the eggs she's started daydreaming about a few miles back. There's coyotes in the desert; scraggly things half-starved and mutated past anything they used to be.

McGee knows the stories. The tests run in all that sand, the radiation. The remnants that flickered like fire out in the desert night, scarin' honest folk and evil alike.

Some legends stick.

Most get forgotten.

McGee doesn't chase legends. There are worse things out there than a few old stories.

The boy lets go of the handlebars to wrap pale, skinny hands around McGee's ropy biceps.

She sniffs hard, but still doesn't spit. "You hungry, kid?"

"I'm thirsty," he says. His diamond-bright tangles turn to brilliant orange in the dying light.

Here's as good a place as any. She wheels Betty off the winding, patchy road and drops her kickstand. *Creak.*

The boy slides off. She passes him her canteen. "One mouthful," she cautions.

He doesn't test her. One mouthful, and he passes it back.

"Go get some kindling," McGee says curtly. She drags her coat off Betty and shakes it out. Another dust cloud. The motes dance like embers in the sunset, and the badge pinned to the interior of that coat burns like a brand.

The boy's dark eyes pick up that glow, turns it back in hellfire and brimstone. He blinks and it's gone, swallowed by dirty water.

Without a word, he turns and darts off into the growing dark.

McGee isn't worried. He'll be back.

She sets up the campfire with only a few complaints from her aging bones—the usual litany. The small pan's ready to go in moments, the last of her rations parceled out for two. The jerky will fry up fine with the last of her bread.

The sun sets. The breeze, nice as it was, dies.

The kid comes back in the dark, his skinny arms laden with gnarled wood and dried up twigs. There's rope hanging from his clenched fist. He's grinning ear to ear, and she doesn't know why 'til he drops the gathered wood with a God-awful clatter and holds out his prize.

The snake snaps back in a tangled skein. A tail slaps her fingers, stinging. McGee curses as she yanks back her hand.

The boy laughs.

There's a gap in his teeth she hadn't noticed before.

"I found him," he announces, like it isn't obvious.

It's not poisonous. McGee recognizes the dark pattern of its scales as a bug-hunter, not worth fussin' over, but that doesn't mean the thing can't bite.

She scowls at both, boy and snake. "That thing gets near me, I'm eatin' it."

The boy laughs again. Like a baby with a rattle, he hauls the writhing snake around with him as McGee sets to making the fire.

Soon enough, an orange crackle takes and the flames lick along the dry tinder like there's never been anything hungrier. She sits by the fire and watches the food cook in. The kid plays with his new friend and stares out into the desert.

She hears him whisper to the put-upon snake.

The damned thing doesn't bite him.

• • •

Morning dawns with the kind of cool that promises sweltering heat soon enough. McGee wakes up with her back against Betty, her stiffened hand on her six-shooter. Nothing new there. They go way back together.

The campfire's long since dead, embers smothered. McGee's back is sore, seized up to iron—but that's not new, either. She's used to sleeping upright. Used to the ground. Used to the cold, hard cushion of the battered old motorcycle.

What she ain't used to is the feel of a small body by her side.

The kid's nestled up under her grimy coat, curled into her ribs like he's a cat and she's something softer than she is. He sleeps like the angel he looks like, all tousled hair and slack mouth. Callused fingers curl in by his cheek, a point of contact just over her sternum that McGee isn't sure what to do with.

A glint of metal winks between his fingers.

McGee sticks her bent fingers into the boy's hand and pries her badge from his grip.

Careful as she never really learned how, the old drifter eases out from under the kid's lean and wraps her coat around him for a bit longer. It takes her no time at all to scrub the campsite clean. Less to shake the dust out of her short iron hair and plop her hat back on her head.

By the time she's kicking the remains of the campfire into ash and nothing, the kid's waking up.

He rubs at his eyes like the baby he is, knotted fist knuckling out the grit. When his vision clears enough to see her, he gives her another grin. "I'm thirsty," he tells her.

That gap in his teeth winks.

McGee snatches the coat off him, throws it back over Betty's battered seat. "You can have the rest of the water in the canteen," she says gruffly. They've got nothing left for breakfast.

He clambers up, a pale-haired, dirty monkey, and clings to the handlebars.

His blistered feet leave smudges on her worn hide jacket.

McGee passes him the canteen. She ignores the hunger gnawing in her belly.

• • •

Bones line the long road to La Grange.

At first, they look like sticks. Dried and twisted. Some are black with the accumulation of dust and grime. As Betty groans and complains beneath the boy, McGee watches the ground she pushes the bike across and notices when the bones begin to take on distinctive traits.

A hand palm-up in the dirt.

A rib cage discarded in a rut.

The bones of a dog are almost entirely whole, only a leg missing from the scattered pile. Maybe it was born that way. Maybe a scavenger made off with it.

The bike gets lighter the closer McGee pushes it towards town.

"I'm thirsty," the boy says.

She grunts. "No more water."

"But I'm *thirsty*."

McGee wants to scratch at the place where her badge usually sits. It's pinned to the inside of her coat again, under the boy's skinny butt. She pushes Betty on. "Hang on 'til La Grange."

The first line of dumpy houses makes like a crippled silhouette in the heat wave rolling off the desert floor. Dirty gray stains ripple and dance in the mirage. Look like filthy tumors hunkering down in a reflective pool.

A small hand clings to her side.

McGee pushes onward, her knees groaning every bit as loud as Betty's rickety frame. The metal's too damned hot again, and it reflects off the road to hammer at the old drifter from every side.

The reflection off the boy's towheaded hair is almost blinding in the sun. She doesn't worry so much. He ain't likely to catch sunstroke.

Even the damned snake wouldn't bite him.

A faded banner hangs from splintered posts on either side of the way in. The words are long since bleached away. Betty bitches and moans as McGee pushes her over the thin shadow cast by the tattered sign.

Nothing moves. Even the scavengers know there ain't nothing left picking over. The ground is parched and thirsty, the houses are blanched pale as the bones littering the dirt. Even the blue, blue sky looks gray when she looks up from the shattered frame of old La Grange.

The boy doesn't stop smiling as he sits back on Betty's seat and cranes his neck to see what McGee is seeing.

He probably sees something she doesn't.

She eases the kickstand down. Ruffles his tangled bird's nest of a head and asks, "Well still good?"

The kid nods. "If you pull the bucket first."

It doesn't strike him as odd that she'd ask. McGee knows why.

If this were any other town, she'd clear it first. Check the place for scavengers of the bipedal kind.

No need. This place has been empty for years.

She fishes her canteen from her belt and the larger container from the saddlebags by his skinny thigh. Her knees snap and pop as she makes her way out from under the shade of a leaning storefront and towards the stone well in the center of town.

Places like this exist all over. Soon as somebody finds a bit of water, a ring of civilization crops up like a bad case of warts.

Everybody always thinks there's nothing to it.

By the time they realize this dust bowl ain't nothing more than a dead end mirage, it's too late.

It always is.

One more job. Then McGee can stop dreaming of fried eggs and sizzling pork.

She sets the water containers down on the ground. A small puff of dust accompanies every move she makes.

"Vroom, vroom," chirps the boy on the back of old Betty.

Her gloved hands wrap around the old rope, its fibers tough and stiff. With effort, she hauls back hand over hand, knotted muscle and sinew versus the weight of the old bucket left inside.

The pulley at the top of the rotten well cover shrieks and rattles like it won't hold, like it'd scream the place down around McGee's sunburned ears, but the wood around the bolt doesn't give.

The air from inside the well is cooler than the smothering heat of the reckless sun.

Hand over hand, fist by fist, the bucket creaks and shakes its way up the stone ring.

"Vroom," growls Colby.

The bucket pulls into view.

Arm straining, McGee grabs the lip. She gives just enough slack that she can jerk the bucket onto the rim of the well.

It rattles.

A hush creeps in under the clang of metal and stone. Rolls up from the bones of old La Grange.

McGee hooks the rope around the hook at the side of the well. Looks down into the bucket and meets the dark, empty eyes of a skull half-drowned in scummy water.

It smiles back at her in gap-toothed silence.

McGee's fingers itch to scratch the spot on her sternum where her badge should be.

• • •

The bones are laid out with care. They're small. Small enough to fit in a bucket hung in a well. Betty's shadow blankets them with gray and blue, but it only makes the gap between its grinning teeth look wider.

The rope tied off at the well is darker where it hung below the sun's reach. Long enough to hide a boy from the gangs that tore up La Grange, but not so long that he could reach the water beneath.

He's been down there for years.

McGee figures he lasted five days.

Between skeletal fingers, a grimy old toy has turned into nothing but strips of toughened leather and glass eyes.

The bucket is fouled beyond use, but a test of the canteen she lowers proves the water beneath is still clear enough to drink. She refills the reservoir and straps what few rations she can find in the mess into Betty's saddlebags.

Everything is achingly silent in town. Even the cicadas don't come so close.

One more job.

One more ghost to put to rest.

In Betty's watchful shade, a tiny skeleton hugs a leather toy.

• • •

It's a long ride out of La Grange. The desert wind picks up like it's got a grudge, and for the first three days out, it smells like ash.

There's no towheaded boy to greet McGee by the side of the road. No gap-toothed smile left to burn.

She makes her way slowly, patiently out of the desert. Crosses out of the demarcation zone and submits to the same old process she always has—sanitization, debriefing, hydration.

Betty's tune up is handled by an old buddy retired from the badge.

McGee is ready to take her own tired bones home.

She finds him, the way he said she would, occupying the third barstool from the left in the wild Brickwall Saloon. Despite its name, its metal and edges inside, not brick.

He's a worn down husk of a man, all razor edges and thinned limbs. She's got maybe forty years on him, but you'd never know to look at him.

He's been waiting for her.

His eyes widen. Dark, but not dirty. His hair is that dishwater blond that usually means it'd been lighter in his youth.

His unkempt whiskers are brown.

He opens his mouth, but he's got no voice to ask what he desperately needs to know.

She pulls a leather toy with glass eyes from her pocket.

He stares at it. Men and women shout and yell, laugh and scream around them, but in this moment in time, there is only silence.

He won't ask how.

McGee ain't so cruel as to tell him.

She sets the toy down on the scarred metal bar and turns away. It's a sad little thing, all misshapen leather and crooked limbs. It looks as out of place here as he does.

Tears fill his eyes.

She is walking away as he raises a trembling hand. Even so, she knows when he lifts the tough little toy. Can tell when he brings it to his lips. She's not far enough away when he starts to sob.

The sound of a parent's grief is the kind of thing that keeps a body up at night.

She leaves the Brickwall Saloon without knowing what to say. It ain't failure. The events of La Grange happened ages ago.

But it feels like buckshot to an old heart just the same.

• • •

As McGee finally guides a purring Betty up the long walkway to Paradise Slim, relief starts to edge the shadows out of her aching body. She navigates the old motorcycle into the open shed, cuts the engine and slings her tired bones off the seat.

She pats the machine with gnarled fingers. "Good girl."

The shed is dark, but the lights strung up on the walkways are nice and gentle. They speak of a welcome McGee doesn't share, but that's a fight she's never won. Not in all the long years.

She won't lie about it now. It sure feels good to come home to a pretty yard.

She's five steps in on the walkway to her front door when it slams open. A bustle of denim and calico explodes out onto the veranda, accompanied by a rolling ball of spit and fur. Three dogs and a Prudence skim the railing.

McGee braces to catch at least one.

This time, it's Prue who edges the beasts aside.

Five feet and two inches of warm woman fill McGee's arms, nearly knocking her right off her tired feet.

"You're just in time for dinner," Prue announces brightly. She is red-cheeked and bushy-haired, a frizz of black and white curls that tend to go haywire when the rains come in. Her face is a map McGee knows by heart.

Three dogs clue in to 'dinner' and start barking their fool heads off.

There ain't no neighbors to bother. Not this close.

McGee grunts in answer.

The crazy woman isn't the type to let that stop her. Not for years. She keeps up a running commentary that lasts all the way through washing up, chang-

ing, and sitting down for McGee's first real meal in what feels like forever.
Eggs and pork. Fresh cornbread and a side of greens that come from the
garden Prue tends out back.

McGee feels like a ghost in her own story.

• • •

Two weeks later, and the mail comes with a rickety clatter. McGee is up to her
elbows in engine grease, so Prue opens the box that came instead.

A twisted leather toy spills into her hand.

"'Thank you,'" Prue reads. Her solemn eyes lift from the crumpled note.
"That's all it says."

McGee nods. "From the boy's father."

"Your last job?"

Another nod.

Prue holds out the toy.

McGee picks up a rag instead. "We'll burn it."

"You sure?"

"It's best," McGee says curtly.

Prue doesn't argue. She knows how it works. Old feelings linger in the
things left behind.

That night, they stoke the flame in the firepit outside. The dogs run
around like overgrown children, tumbling with each other across the open
field behind the house.

Prue cradles the toy with tender care. "You want to say a few words?"

McGee isn't much for words. Much less a few.

The other woman smiles, and her teeth are very white in the firelight.
McGee always loved her smile best. Like a curve of pretty white lace in a
storefront window. She holds out the toy.

McGee takes it.

I'm thirsty, he'd said, and that's how she knew.

Sometimes, the worst luck happens to the best people. Plague or violence.
Accident or monsters. Life is like that.

You have to move on.

McGee clutches the toy in gnarled hands.

Prue stretches up on tiptoes and presses her lips to McGee's cheek. Without another word, she turns and makes her way back to the house, hollerin'
for the dogs.

It don't take long before a glimmer of light at the edge of the field turns
into something diamond-pale. Callused and scarred.

McGee watches the boy pick his way across the green field. His feet don't disturb the grass.

"Hey, kid," she says. "You still thirsty?"

He shakes his head.

McGee nods back. "You see your pa?"

Another nod.

"You say goodbye?"

He smiles.

There ain't nothing wry about it this time.

The boy scratches at his ear. "What's after this?" he asks.

She's never known the answer to that question. "Dunno."

"Will it hurt?"

"Not anymore," she tells him, and she don't know the answer to that, either, but she believes. Believes with her whole heart.

The boy sniffs. His bird's nest hair dances like sunlight in the dark. He offers a hand, the same way she did to him on that long road.

She takes it. His fingers are grimy and cold.

But maybe, just maybe, they're a bit warmer than they used to be.

"Okay," he says, and that's all it takes.

McGee nods back, and without drawing it out any more, she tosses the toy into the flame.

The kid watches it burn. His feet curl like the edges of paper set on fire, and then light pours from somewhere else. Someplace she's never seen.

But always known.

"Colby," she calls.

He smiles. "Thank you."

The gap in his teeth winks.

The light sears through the dark like a flare, too bright to look at. McGee covers her eyes with a hand, but too late. Spots dot her vision as the fire burns down, and the ghost is gone.

A leather toy slowly burns to ash.

REPRISALS: ENMITY

John A. Curley

"Get the fuck off my porch or I'll have you arrested," Angie seethed. She was tall and thin with black hair and blue eyes. A face that would have been quite comely were it not twisted in rage.

"Already told you, Angie," Cracker said calmly. "That's not happening. I spent 20 years on the job and retired as a sergeant. Be my guest and call."

"Listen to me for just a minute," Doc said. "It is your intention to get custody of your child, yes?"

"You're goddamned right," Angie hissed.

"Do you think it's a good idea," Doc asked her, "to march into court tomorrow and tell the judge that will decide who gets custody, despite the fact you're an NYPD detective and know better, that you willfully disregarded that very same judge's order? Do you think that particular judge will look upon you kindly?"

"Fuck both of you." She looked directly into their eyes and said that slowly. The rage seemed to emanate from her and even the cold moved away from it. She slammed the door closed.

Doc looked at Cracker. They both shrugged and went back to the Suburban. It was a cold, clear, crisp January night. The air had that cold, clean smell that made your lungs burn a little when you breathed in. Cracker turned the ignition on and the heat filled the small truck. Doc kept his gaze on Angie's house. The coffee in the cups in the console was still warm. Cracker sipped his, Doc swallowed a third, leaving a third.

"They say, Doc, to limit it to four cups a day now."

"Cracker, if you tell me who 'They' is, I give you my word that I will give it a fleeting consideration."

Cracker laughed. "I was shocked to find out you'd be here tonight."

"Getting a reputation as a desk jockey, am I?" Doc asked.

"Last time you were in the field, Doc, it was four years ago when we did that tail job on that personal trainer in that gym in New Jersey, the one that claimed she was an agoraphobe and couldn't leave her house."

Doc laughed. "I needed out of the office pretty bad."

"Nice job." Cracker smiled. "Workout at the gym, watch the girls, shower, lunch and then home. And paid for it too. Not too much effort to get pics and video of that lady, while we were at it."

"Beats this," Doc said.

"Truedat."

Doc chuckled. "Aside from an eighteen-year-old black kid, from ten years ago, you are the only person that could pull that off, Cracker."

"Truedat."

They both laughed.

"Here we go," Cracker said as several squad cars pulled up.

Doc reclined the seat a little and closed his eyes. Cracker got out and went to go talk to the cops. The white clouds rolled by overhead as Cracker spoke with a total of five cops. Two domestic violence officers. A lieutenant. The precinct captain and his driver. The conversation went on about ten minutes.

"We are waiting for ACS?" Doc asked, without opening his eyes, as Cracker got in.

"Of course," Cracker said

Fifteen minutes later an unmarked car pulled up. The two men, the driver and the passenger got out. The driver, average height and short hair, wore a baseball jacket with a Yankees logo on the back. The other man was tall, well over six feet. Hair medium and a well-trimmed mustache. He wore a trench coat and an expensive suit peeked out when the coat moved.

"Who do we have here?" Doc asked.

"Interesting question," Cracker said as he got out of the truck.

Doc wasn't usually the kind of man that would sit back while others worked but he knew cops. Good, bad, competent or not; they liked to jaw with other cops. Nothing wrong with that, was Doc's thinking.

"That be her captain," Cracker said when he got back in.

Doc's eyebrows went up. "Pray tell, what brings him here?"

Cracker gave Doc a wry grin. "Moral support."

"You're kidding."

"Nope."

"So," Doc asked. "Here we have the captain of a successful city-wide narcotics unit. What kind of pull are we talking?"

"He's God. He holds back the garbage. At least he keeps out of the middle-class neighborhoods. He's not the Chief but he's close."

Administration of Child Services arrived in the form of a mid-thirties black man with a ski cap and a pea coat, and a young black woman in her twenties as wide as she was tall. They moved toward the house from where they parked further down the street. Doc and Cracker got out. The well-dressed captain walked up to them and talked briefly. Doc and Cracker waited as they got closer and when they tried to speak the man waved them off.

"We can't speak with you."

"You talked to that other gentleman with no problem," Doc said to his back. "I have a copy of the court order that says the kid goes with us, in case you forgot it."

The ACS workers went into the house. Doc and Cracker stood off a few feet away from the cops who had been rejoined by Angie's captain. He and Doc looked at each other with neither hostility, nor good will. The captain nodded to Doc and Doc nodded back.

In ten minutes ACS came out. They walked down and went over to speak to the cops. Doc and Cracker moved closer to hear.

"Kid will stay here tonight," said ACS, the male. The woman waddled over and got in the car without a word.

"Explain to me," Doc said as he walked closer. "How you disregard a clear court order that says the kid goes with us?"

"I don't got to talk to you," ACS said.

"I want your names, now," Doc said. "So when I get on the stand tomorrow I can tell the judge the name of the moron that disregarded his order."

"I'm leavin'," ACS said. As he got into the car Doc walked over and stood in front of the car. Cracker smiled. All of the cops except the captain were surprised. It looked like Doc was blocking the car. ACS the male and ACS the female looked at each other. After twenty seconds Doc walked back to the group as Cracker stood with them now.

"I know," Doc said quietly, "that you guys have a tough and usually thankless job. I also understand loyalty and that you stick together. But does any one of you give a damn about that kid? Does any one of you as a human being and a parent think that the kid's safety trumps loyalty?"

No answer.

"We don't know she's a danger to the child," one of the domestic violence officers said.

"Great," Doc said. "Let's hope she's not. You all don't need to know she's a danger, what you need to do is follow a lawfully issued court order giving the kid to us."

After a minute of silence, Doc took out his cell phone and adjusted the volume. He hit the button to play some of the recordings his client had made of Angie.

"One day!" Angie's voice screamed into the ice cold air. "I just might throw that fucking kid out the window and eat my gun. But I'll know that's the fucking end of you, your kid dead, you shit!" Other similar recordings played.

"You had better all, and that includes you, Captain Juice, had better pray nothing happens to that kid tonight or you have all made career-ending decisions, and you will read about the ends of those careers in the *New York Post*."

• • •

Doc and Cracker got into the car. Cracker started it up and they drove about ten minutes to the diner that was near their office. A few minutes later they were in the back where Doc's crew sat, even though the diner was almost empty.

"I wish I could eat like that before I went to bed," Cracker said, looking at the French toast, bacon, and eggs that the waitress brought for Doc. Cracker was having decaf. As a matter of habit Doc waited for the waitress to move off before he answered.

"Food is a mistress, Cracker. You have to make her happy sometimes by paying attention to her."

Cracker laughed. "Do you make this up as you go along, Doc?"

"As a matter of fact I do." Doc smiled.

"What next?" Cracker asked.

"She will get an attorney and show up in court day after tomorrow. What I told her will likely happen. Judge won't be happy. But who knows." Doc's plate was empty.

Doc's cell phone rang. The screen read 'Diane Valeria.' "Hey, Lady Di," Doc answered. "What sayeth the Lords at One Police Plaza?"

"Despite the law that supports the Family Court judge's order overriding the groundless order of protection against my client, they do not feel they are obligated to enforce the court order."

Diane had imported the history to Doc before the job began. The husband had come in as a consult. Tim Price had started recording with his phone things that his wife was doing, after a friend told him he had to have real proof if he wanted a shot at custody. Threats, fits of rage and physical abuse. She moved first, and got an order of protection. Diane had gone to court and played for the judge some of the recordings and the judge granted immediate custody to the father.

"He said she was always high strung and aggressive," Diane had told Doc.

"After she made detective and was assigned to the city-wide narcotics unit, it got much worse. There were pictures of Tim with bruises. She started drinking all the time. She left the gun lying around and their adopted child had once picked it up. And she was getting aggressive with the child. The threats to Tim were always about what she'd do to the child."

Two days later the court gave custody to the father. By the end of the day Angie's lawyer had the father served with divorce papers and motions for the return of custody. Judge shopping. Things had worked the way they should have in family court, so Angie's lawyer moved it to a different court. The case drew a bad forensic expert and a bad judge. Recordings of her screaming that she wouldn't hesitate to hurt the child meant nothing. Months later, Angie had shared custody.

• • •

"I'm not really into working out," Tim Price said.

They walked into the gym in the basement of the building. Doc walked over and hit the buttons for the steam room. Price followed Doc into the small locker room.

"There's clothes and a towel there," Doc said. "The steam room should be right by now."

Tim shook his head and reluctantly got undressed. His lawyer had told him to do whatever this guy Doc said, regardless of whether or not it was strange. Another man was getting dressed as Doc and Price were getting undressed. He gave Doc a slight nod, that Price didn't see, to indicate Price wasn't wearing a wire. A few minutes later they were sitting in the steam room. Doc was heavily muscled, a few tattoos and some scars. Tim was very tall and very out of shape. He sat down next to Doc. There was some kind of weird music coming in from somewhere. After about ten minutes, Doc spoke to him.

"I can likely help you."

"Ok," Tim said.

"What do you want? Plain and simple you have a one time chance and will get this kind of help nowhere else. You agree in here now to whatever I say and I will do my best to help you, but there are no guarantees, and it will be a lot of money."

"I want my kid safe," Tim said, all hesitation gone. "I don't care what it takes or how much it takes, if you can do it I want it done. It's not my kid's fault that I married that thing."

"One hundred and fifty thousand in cash. No questions, no reports, no updates. We will likely not talk again. It goes into play right after you give me the money, if an act of God happens and she is struck by lightning it doesn't matter. Money is gone."

• • •

On the surface Vladimir Horowitz looked like a young grandfather. Thick glasses, pot belly, receding white hairline. He smiled a toothy smile and his accent was Russian and thick. But he understood everything Doc said to him. His soft outer appearance belied his iron, vise-like grip. The first time they had ever shaken hands, Doc had been surprised. Never judge a book by its cover. Doc knew from their interactions over the last ten years that Vladimir's word was good and he would do what he said he would.

A few days later, at an intersection along a street that Angie regularly traveled to and from work, the car accident happened. There were no surveillance cameras working anywhere nearby. The good Samaritans that stopped to help Angie and the old man that hit her moved quickly. Angie was unconscious in the car. It was a little past 2:00 AM. The Samaritans opened the glove compartment and left it open, and nudged the nine millimeter with no serial number onto the car floor. A Ziploc bag with a kilo of coke was ripped and scattered all over the car. Angie's palm print ended up on the torn bag. Several residents came out and took pictures of the coke and the guns and posted them to Facebook. Vladimir kept his eyes closed, and later said he remembered nothing of what had happened. Miraculously a reporter from the *New York Ledger* arrived as Angie was waking up. She was of course drunk as she always was when she ended her last tour of the week.

"I'm on the job, I'm on the job!" Angie was screaming as she was put in the gurney and restrained.

"Not anymore," one of the cops that arrived at the scene said quietly as the ambulance doors closed.

The *Post* headline read "I'm on the Job!" The *Ledger* had pictures of the four-way stop sign and the cars and the headline read "Nothing's Gonna Stop Her." Another paper had: "Coke, Guns and Drunk Driving: The Perfect Storm." New York One aired the story three times an hour with the soundbite from the video someone had gotten on a cell phone.

Two days later, Tim Price gave another newspaper quotes about how the judge had been pushing them for joint custody and how the police department hadn't followed up on any of the complaints made to Internal Affairs. He would likely get in some trouble for giving away information that was deemed confidential, but now he was caught up in his own righteous rage.

"If it hadn't been for the accident," he was quoted in one paper, "the judge, the law guardian and the doctor could ignore everything, all the evidence, the recordings, the people who witnessed her behavior, all of it."

Price put up a website with the video and audio recordings and the forensic report. His attorney had advised him not to, but he did it anyway. He had also told the cops several times about the guns and large stacks of money he had found in the house. All that went on the internet. He was interviewed by the local stations, as well as Fox and CNN.

Several days later the *Post* quoted an anonymous source as saying Angie was going to deal her way out. The Police Commissioner went on television to assure people that a full investigation was being performed.

Cracker and Doc met a week later at a local bar. It was grey and raining outside. Doc was at a table in the back, alone, reading a book. He looked up when he saw Cracker and stood and they shook hands. Doc had a draft beer and a shot on the table. He put the book down. Cracker looked at the book.

"*Twentieth Century Janissary?*" Cracker asked, reciting the title.

"Good book, sad. It's a biography of a man who was sold as a black market baby to people here in the states. Ends well."

"That last book you gave me was very good. *Signwave*," Cracker said. "Finished it in a day. Wife was pissed I didn't get to the lawn."

Doc laughed. "If it won't get me in trouble with Mrs. Cracker, take this, I just finished it."

The waitress came and they ordered. Cracker also went with the draft and the shot. She brought Cracker's drinks and replaced Doc's. Doc drank the whiskey slow, savoring it, and then sipped his beer. Doc slid a white envelope across the table to his friend.

"For the Price job," Doc said.

"Doc, I billed that and got paid already."

"Bonus," Doc said. "You did a good job, from the client. Buy the kids something and take the wife somewhere."

Cracker opened the envelope and looked in. "Doc there's five g's here."

"You did a good job."

"It was eight hours. I already got paid."

"Buy lunch," Doc said.

Cracker was quiet for a while. Doc worked on the draft. It was raining outside now. A few people came in the front and sat at the bar.

"You stayed with me when I first started out. At one time you floated bills I owed you for more than what is in that envelope. You have always done a good job when you have worked with me," Doc said.

"Thanks, Doc."

"Thank you, Cracker."

The waitress brought the bacon cheeseburgers and fries. She took their empty glasses. Doc's burger had a fried egg on top. In response to her inquiry, they both ordered two more drafts. As usual, Doc attacked his food like Schwarzkopf on the Republican Guard.

"That's some mess on that case," Cracker said.

"Truedat," Doc said.

Cracker laughed. "Forget it, Doc, you're not pulling that off."

Doc laughed with him. "Apparently not."

"Looks like she imploded due to the stress," Cracker said. Doc didn't comment. "What would have happened if she didn't have that accident?"

"Another kid ruined by the New York State Unified Court System," Doc replied.

Cracker ate a while. "I'm not going to ask, Doc, I'm going to say, I wouldn't be surprised if you put more into this job than just the part you did with me."

"That would be well beyond my capabilities, Cracker."

"Well if you had, as someone who was a cop for twenty years, I'd say good job. Thanks."

"If I had, and you told me that, old friend, I'd say you're welcome."

The waitress came back after a while and cleared the plates. They both asked for coffee. Doc looked outside and saw that the rain had stopped, and there were patches of sunlight coming through.

On to the next case, Doc thought.

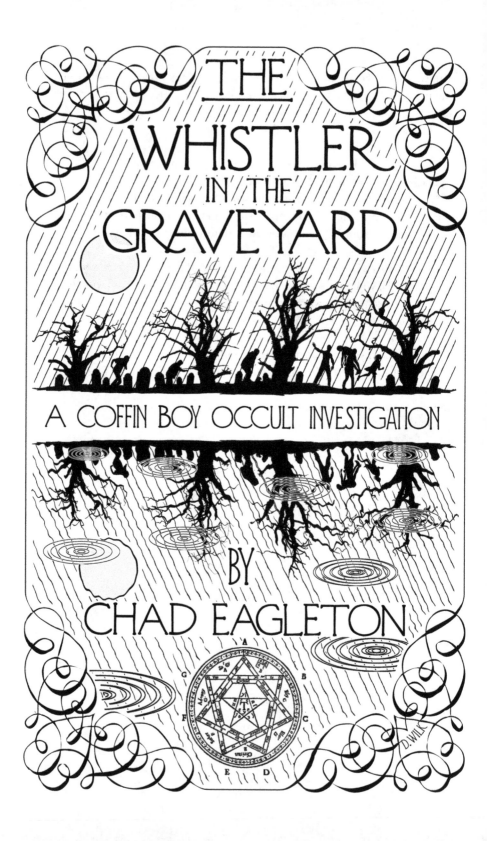

THE WHISTLER IN THE GRAVEYARD

A COFFIN BOY OCCULT INVESTIGATION

Chad Eagleton

ILLUSTRATION BY DYER WILK

The old woman closed the book and looked at the dark haired boy who had fought sleep for the last hour. "You like stories like this? Ones full of magic and monsters? Danger and mystery?"

The boy nodded.

The old woman leaned close. She spoke in a hushed tone the boy knew was for sharing secrets. "Would you like to know the most powerful magic word in the whole world?"

The boy's eyes opened wide.

"It is not from the secret language of angels, nor the tongue spoken in the garden when Adam walked amongst the beasts. It was never sung in Atlantis's broad streets. The snake men of Lemuria never chanted it in their jungle temples. The masked priests of Mu did not whisper it to their stone-faced gods. It never warmed the icy air of Leng. And Shakespeare did not hide it in a couplet."

"What is it?" the boy asked.

"No." She smiled. "As simple as that. No."

• • •

Lydia Poe was ready to confront Ms. Blackwood as soon as the last bell rang. She gave Jessica King her backpack and reminded her what time her mother would call. Jessica started to argue with her, but Lydia pushed. "I wanted to delete it, remember? This is your fault."

Jessica sighed and told her to be careful. Lydia nodded and looked out the glass door. Black clouds rolled off the cold and distant sea while much closer treetops swayed in the strong wind and a hard rain fell in angry, grey slashes across the darkening sky.

Lydia pulled the hood of her raincoat over her head, held her umbrella tight, and then went out into the storm. She rushed down the sidewalk with her head down, pushing through the crowd of students hurrying to buses or waiting parents.

She hated to guilt Jessica into helping her, but it had been partially her fault. The two best friends were together when the cryptic text arrived that morning. Lydia had been prepared to chalk it up to a misdial and delete it after neither of them recognized the number. But Jessica would not let it go. By first period, she had Lydia convinced a deranged stalker was out for her panties and her blood.

You know, don't you? the text had read. No matter how she tried to put it out of her mind, the mystery bothered her all day long. Not only did she not know who sent it, but she didn't know what she was supposed to know. She asked her other friends if they recognized the number. None of them did. Her whitepages.com search told her nothing she didn't already know: it was a cell phone number based on Dunsany Island. And Google had been completely worthless and returned the usual spam pages asking for a low one-time payment in exchange for full records on her mystery texter.

The whole thing finally got the better of her in Math. Despite having one demerit already from Mrs. Phillips for being on her phone, Lydia boldly sat in the back and repeatedly pestered her mystery text messenger until she got a response.

Ms. Blackwood is not Ms. Blackwood.

Her gasp nearly got her caught. If that weirdo Kristoffer, the strange kid everyone called Coffin Boy, didn't have an asthma attack right then, she would have spent the afternoon in Dean Jacobi's office. *Thank god for sickly goth boys*, she thought.

• • •

Much later, long after the boy had fallen asleep and morning lay not far off, the old woman finally went to bed herself. That night she dreamed of being a young girl again. It started out pleasant enough, a mixture of good memories and past daydreams filtered through snatches of cherished movies.

Then that terrible day overtook everything.

She had been on her way back from the park with her younger brother and sister. They were in the tube station just off Hob's Lane. That night she was supposed to go see her favorite rock quartet with friends. She was daydreaming about the show when her brother wandered off and discovered something terrible that had crossed the sea with the Romans and still haunted the underground, driven by a hunger for human flesh that remained unsatisfied after a thousand years.

• • •

A grotesquerie of gargoyles watched from the upper stonework as a drenched and shivering Lydia hurried up the stairs into the Bellairs' Building. It was quiet and still inside. While the lights were on, lack of hall traffic had dimmed their fluorescent glare. Lydia triggered the motion sensor and they brightened to their harsh, yellow glow. She tossed her hood back and took a moment to catch her breath.

Now that she was actually here in Ms. Blackwood's building, she worried this was only an elaborate prank. She had never been the popular girl at school. None of the boys had ever been interested in her—all the other girls seemed taller and thinner and blonder. Most of the students at Musgrave Academy were well-off. Her family was not, every extra dime went to pay her tuition. When her father died, that sent everything over the edge. At the time when she hurt the worst, the other students avoided her the most. It was as if they thought death was communicable. Get too close and your parent might be next.

Lydia had never felt so completely and utterly alone.

To help, her mother took her to see Dr. Peter Saxon on the mainland. Lydia had been going for three months, starting to feel somewhat better even, when Kara Becker spotted her coming out of Saxon's office. Lydia's heart broke when she saw the soured-face blond girl watching her from the other side of the street. She knew it was going to be bad and she was right. Before her first class the next morning, everyone knew about the "crazy doctor." By last bell, Kara had saddled her with a nickname—Looney Lydia.

Looney Lydia, as crazy as her father.

Without Ms. Blackwood's friendship, she would have given up. If her teacher were in trouble, Lydia had to do something or she'd never be able to forgive herself.

She dripped on the walk down the hall to the courtyard stairs. A noise several floors up echoed through the building and down the stairwell. Unfortunately, it turned so sharply after each landing, it was impossible to see much of anything. There was an elevator on the other side of the building but no one used it. It made a terrible noise when it moved. Lydia sniffled then climbed the stairs before she lost her nerve. Thankfully, Ms. Blackwood's office was only two floors up and next to the courtyard.

The office door was closed. The mailbox stuffed with papers. Maybe she's not in? Lydia hesitated, suddenly realizing she didn't know what exactly she was going to do when she actually spoke to Ms. Blackwood. *Hi, Ms. Blackwood, I just wanted to check that you were still you. See, I've thought you've been acting strange, then I got this anonymous text message . . .*

Sighing, Lydia knocked. As she rapped on the heavy wooden door, the power flickered in the hallway. Her heart jumped. She reminded herself of the weather. Electrical trouble during a severe thunderstorm did not presage something ominous.

Lydia waited nervously. No answer. She smoothed her plaid skirt, fussed with her tie, and then knocked again. Outside, the wind changed direction. Heavy rain slapped across the thick glass like a vicious surf battering the shore. Her knock was lost. She rapped again harder now, struggling to be heard over the storm, this time calling out, "Ms. Blackwood? Hello? Ms. Blackwood?"

Thunder rattled the windows. Lightning flashed in the courtyard, bright enough to shine in the hallway. As Lydia raised her hand to knock yet again, the power went out, leaving her in full dark. Another peal of thunder took her scream. She held her breath while the lights flicker-flared back on and decided this could wait until after break.

When she turned to slink back toward the stairs, the door opened behind her. Ms. Blackwood's melodic voice said, "Lydia? Is everything okay?"

Lydia closed her eyes. The wind dispersed the storm's fury high above, whipping about the gables and eaves. The sharp click of heels in the quiet. The uncanny sense that someone was close behind, then that cool voice again, "Lydia?"

Briefly, she considered dashing down the stairs and back into the storm. Her hood was still up. The hallway was gloomy. Ms. Blackwood hadn't actually seen her face and wouldn't follow her. And, if pressed, Lydia could lie and say it wasn't her.

"Do you have time to talk?"

"Yes," Ms. Blackwood said. "Come in."

Lydia did as she was told.

• • •

The old woman found the boy hiding in the west hall.

She sat on the floor behind the fainting couch and spoke to the dusty, white sheet draped over the aged velvet. "All our parents disappoint us in some way."

A clock ticked slowly. The sheet rustled as a small face pressed against the fabric.

"What you need to remember," she said, "is you have to become the man you wanted your father to be."

• • •

"What is it, Lydia?" Ms. Blackwood asked, brushing her blond hair behind her ears.

Lydia looked across the desk at her favorite teacher. The face was the same. Wide and open with slim pink lips and a soft chin. Something about her just didn't feel right.

"Lydia?"

"This is gonna sound strange . . ."

"That's okay."

Lydia sighed. "Are you alright?"

"What?"

"Are you . . . feeling okay?"

Ms. Blackwood smiled with a mixture of amusement and confusion. "Am I sick? That what you mean?"

Lydia's shoulders fell. She shook her head and looked around the room at the photographs and mementos, the plaques and certificates, all the little works of art. For nearly a year, this office had been her refuge. Now it felt as uninviting and staged as a museum.

"No, not like that," she said, plucking at the chewed skin around her left thumbnail. "I mean, are you feeling like yourself? Feeling normal?"

"I don't understand."

"You've just seemed . . . " Lydia squirmed.

"We're friends, aren't we?"

"Yeah."

"A friend can only help a friend if they know what's wrong."

"You've just seemed not yourself." She shrugged.

"'Seemed not myself?' That's not very helpful, Lydia."

"Like you weren't you."

"How so?"

"I don't know how else to say it." Now Lydia was frustrated. Angry even. This was hard for her and it felt like Ms. Blackwood wasn't listening and not listening made her seem like any other adult. Right then that was the most terrible thing in the world. Lydia wanted to scream, to break something precious, and run back out into the storm.

"Like you're not you," she said. "Like you're someone else who looks like you. Like a . . . like a thing."

"A thing? Okay, that's something," Ms. Blackwood said. "So, not me but something that looks like me? Like *Invasion of the Body Snatchers*."

"*Invasion of the Body Snatchers*?" Lydia threw her hands up. "What's that?"

"Now, I feel ridiculously old."

"Sorry," Lydia said.

"Like I've been replaced by a pod person."

Lydia dug deeper at the skin around her thumbnail. A thin ribbon of blood followed the curve of her chewed nail and spilled over her cuticle. That's it exactly, she thought.

"Okay. Now. Stop and think about it for a minute. Step by step."

Lydia rolled her eyes but did as she was told anyway.

"Say it aloud."

She did.

"Does that sound plausible?"

"No." *But,* she thought, *does that make it not true?*

"How's it sound?"

"Crazy."

"Well, you're not crazy. Sometimes we get an idea and our mind won't let it go. It's normal." Ms. Blackwood leaned across her desk and patted the edge nearest Lydia. "Look, I'm me. Just me. The same me I've always been."

"Okay."

The teacher smiled weakly. "Do you feel better?"

Lydia squeezed her bleeding thumb. She did feel better. But feeling better wasn't how she expected feeling better to be. This had too much uncertainty. It felt like one of those non-answers adults like to give.

"Sorry I was snippy," Lydia said.

Ms. Blackwood mimicked Lydia's patented shrug, then smiled. "It's okay," she said, walking around to sit on her desk and reaching for Lydia's hands. When she didn't give them, she settled for a soft touch on the shoulder.

Lydia noticed her nails were painted an electric blue. "Was just worried about you."

"That's sweet." Ms. Blackwood crossed her hands in her lap. "But you look pale."

"I'm hungry," she lied.

"You need a snack." Ms. Blackwood opened the desk drawer behind her. "I've got some honey roasted peanuts." She ate a handful and offered the open bag.

Lydia blinked.

"Go on." She shook the bag. "They're good."

I had been right.

"No thanks."

This is not Ms. Blackwood.

"Suit yourself," the imposter said, taking another handful.

Lydia rushed out the door. Her shoes squeaked as she skidded into the hall, turning toward the stairs. The power dimmed and flickered. A single step, then Ms. Blackwood grabbed her long ponytail and yanked her off her feet, dragging her kicking and screaming back into the office.

The fake Blackwood shouldered the door closed and locked it. Snarling, she wound Lydia's hair round her fist and jerked. "How did you know?" Up close, her breath smelled like dead things, rot and dead things.

Lydia retched.

"How did you know?"

She twisted her face away, fighting for a deep lungful of clean air. "Allergic to peanuts."

The imposter's lips curled into a twisted sneer. A bloated tongue licked the even teeth, the twisted reveal of so much white seemed predatory. "I will enjoy killing—"

Someone knocked on the door.

• • •

The woman polished the Sigillum Dei Aemaeth by candlelight. The talisman was a souvenir from the terrible incident at Mortlake when they finally managed to close the doorway Edward Kelley had left open since Elizabeth I wore the crown. Reggie had been with them then.

"Poor Reggie," she'd say. "Wherever those things took you, I know you're still giving them hell."

• • •

Lydia squirmed in the imposter's grasp, struggling to scream. The grip on her throat was iron, tightening iron. Whoever it was knocked again. Louder. Harder. Persistent. The imposter tightened her grip in response, stilling her troublesome student.

"Who is it?" The fake Ms. Blackwood called sweetly through her rictus.

"Kristoffer Coffin."

Lydia's eyes went wide. *Coffin Boy!*

The fake grimaced. "You will be silent, girl," she whispered, squeezing tighter. "Unless you want to watch the boy die." All air was gone. Panic rose with lack of breath. Lydia felt suddenly distant, removed from herself in a way she had been only once before—the morning her mother explained her father's death.

The fake sat her down in the far corner and hissed a warning. Lydia wanted to scream for Kristoffer to run and get help. But she couldn't. There was nothing but fear and the thunder overhead and the incessant rapping of the strange boy's fist.

As soon as the imposter flipped the lock, the door swung open and smashed her nose and mouth. Kristoffer Coffin burst into the room, thrusting something at her head.

The fake staggered back, clutching her face. The door slammed into the bookshelves, rattling the knickknacks and knocking the framed Harvard Diploma off the wall. Shattered glass cascaded across the floor.

Lydia managed a noise she hoped was a warning.

Coffin Boy didn't seem to need it. Whatever it was in his hand caught the dim light and reflected it back. Hissing, the fake dropped its hands and retreated, shoulders and head low. Its nose was smashed flat but its face was entirely bloodless. This wasn't just a fake Ms. Blackwood, this was a fake person.

The creature glowered and spat something too dark to be blood on the floor. Coffin Boy brandished his charm like a weapon, calling out in a loud voice, "By the investments of the nine choirs of high heaven, and the dominion of the hidden seraph, I command thee spirit! Obey my will! Obey my will!"

Angered now, the thing stomped and threw its head back. The creature's lips curled again, receding all the way to the top of the pink gums. It shouted something unintelligible, then its head spasmed violently, neck snapping and popping. The pretend features gave up pretense. Blue-grey smoke seeped from the edges of the raw, red eyeholes as the lids peeled back from darkening pupils. With a sound like meat ripped from the bone, teeth erupted through gums and filled the twisted mouth with that same thick, black substance it had spat earlier. Only the vaguest semblance of human face remained. Like a crude sculpture made by a child, there was something horrific in its familiarity.

"Get behind me!" Kris shouted to Lydia.

The beast growled deep and low, turning its baleful gaze on Lydia as if just remembering her. The blue nails blackened as the thick talons curled and burst out its fingertips.

Lydia ducked as the thing swiped. Claws slashed the thick cement. She fell to her knees, scrambling on all fours.

It swung again.

Lydia dove. Kris hopped over her as she slid across the floor, positioning himself between her and the creature. The upswing of the claws barely missed slicing his fingers to the bone. The thing's head turned, quickly snapping at the boy.

"By the investments of the nine choirs of high heaven," Coffin Boy said again, louder now in a voice too deep and too commanding for either his age or frame, "and the dominion of the hidden seraph, I command thee spirit! Obey my will!"

The crunch of sharp teeth through weak flesh, the snap of young bones like dry twigs seemed imminent but his charm kept the creature's jaws ever far enough away. It didn't stop the thing from continuing to snap like a leashed dog, large ropes of slaver swinging from the bottom rows of razor-sharp teeth.

On the floor, Lydia saw the charm clearly. Some kind of badge, a heptagon, no, multiple heptagons etched with lines and symbols and writing. Lots of markings. Almost like some mathematical tool that had gone out of style.

"*Avavago!*" The medallion flashed a hot white. Coffin Boy's strange word echoed through the office, then seemed to hang in the air, reverberating and building energy. Lydia's breath caught in her chest. Her tongue tingled like she had licked a battery. The charge blasted the creature across the room in a shower of scintillating sparks, slamming the beast through the bookshelf in a blinding shower of wood.

The thing recovered quickly. It sprang to its feet with splinters covering neck, shoulders, and back like spikes on some ancient lizard. It shook its head and slung more black gore and thick slaver across desk, floor, and walls.

Coffin Boy shouted, "By holy decree of the *Sefer Raziel HaMalakh,* my will is law, spirit!" He muttered rapidly under his breath, chanting something in a low singsong voice. The quicker he spoke, the brighter the heptagon's glow became until finally it was so bright, so intense, Lydia's eyes felt like they were burning.

She closed them tight as she fumbled to get away from what she sensed was about to happen. The glow stayed visible and grew ever brighter as she moved. Her eyes ached and the image would not fade. It was like she saw through her eyelids, saw the same scene but in a different spectrum of light and color.

Loud enough, to drown out the storm itself, Coffin Boy shouted, "I send you back to the Pit!"

Lydia turned her head away as the glow burned deeper, brighter, searing past her eyes and into her brain. Desperate, she pressed her palms over her eyes and her face to the floor. The light consumed everything, even sound and thought, then, suddenly, it was gone.

Cautiously, she opened her eyes. Coffin Boy pressed the medallion into her fingers. "Take the Sigillum."

Lydia took the charm and held it tight against her chest as Kris pulled her to her feet. He looked her over quickly, decided she was in shock but unharmed, then locked the door.

"Listen to me," he said, moving quickly along the shelves, scanning books as he spoke. "Ms. Blackwood is in danger. That's why I sent you those texts. We have to move fast. Dunsany suffers under sorcery's black shadow. She is only the latest victim."

Lydia didn't know how to process any of that sentence, let alone what had just happened. She looked over to where the creature had been and saw only a large pile of dead leaves, twigs, mud, and bits of rock. "Okay."

Kris fished in the pockets of his raincoat. He took two quick puffs off his asthma inhaler, breathed deeply for a five count then resumed his search. "If we don't find anything," he said, "we'll need to brave the storm to her house. You know where she lives, right?"

"Yeah." Lydia kicked the pile of debris with her foot, spread the rich earth with the toe of her Wellington. "But how'd you get my number?"

• • •

After Coffin Boy's search turned up nothing, the two teenagers prepared to brave the terrible weather again. Buttoning their blazers fully, fastening their rain slickers, but abandoning their umbrellas. Watching Lydia tighten the hood of her raincoat, Kris thought he kind of loved her right then. He hoped that never went away—that sudden and overwhelming flood of feeling brought on by sudden deep awareness of another person—but figured it probably did.

The echo of heavy boots through the hall sent them fleeing out the back door. Lightning struck something with a loud boom, followed by a shower of sparks. They didn't stop, only kept running, fleeing south through the forest.

Hodgson Wood sheltered them from the brunt of the storm. The tall trees kept the fury and force distant. Far off. Weaving through the dense growth there was only the patter of the rain on the high leaves, sputtering drops falling from the lower branches into deepening puddles of water and mud. And always their breath, heavy and quick.

When they burst clear of the forest into Morlant's Field, the rain battered their slickers and struck their bare skin so hard it hurt. Midway across the tangled field, Lydia tugged Coffin Boy's raincoat. "You took us the wrong direction," she yelled. "She lives in Daffodil Hill. Other side of the island."

"No." Kris pointed to where Coast Road South followed the treacherous shoreline. "There's our ride."

Lydia could barely see from under her hood. She visored her hands over her eyes and squinted. Lightning snaked along the choppy sea. Headlights cut bright tracks through the thick, rolling gloom. A dark car sped along the winding road. "Who is that?"

"Mr. Ashton-Smith."

Lydia sniffled and pulled her hood lower. "Who?"

"The man who helped save my life," Kris said, pulling his sleeve free to take her hand as the Ford Cortina eased into the field. "He's going to help us rescue Ms. Blackwood."

They ran quickly to the car, stumbling and sliding through the slick grass. A dark figure reached across the seat and opened the back door. A momentary blaze of dome light blinded Lydia as Kris pulled her inside. The door slammed close. The car bounced through the grass, hit pavement and accelerated away.

When she could see again, the man behind the wheel smiled at her. He had a full head of white hair swept over a broad forehead, droopy cheeks, but a thin mouth and chin. He seemed very tall and thin in his dark pea coat and a checkered scarf.

"We need to go to Daffodil Hill," Kris said.

Rough surf slapped at Coast Road South like it was trying to pull it into the sea. The Ford raced along the wet pavement, weaving around deep pools of water, wipers beating furiously across the windshield.

Lydia pressed her forehead against the window. "Is Ms. Blackwood still alive?"

"Don't know," Kris said, wiping his face dry. "We'll find her if she is."

"How?"

"The Black Veil Society took her and replaced her with that creature."

Ashton-Smith downshifted into the curve. "They're a secret society of black magicians," he said. "They've been manipulating Dunsany for centuries in preparation for a nasty bit of magic called The Hamelin Working."

"Why her?"

"There were no clues at her office," Kris said. "That leaves her house. You've been there, right?"

There's so much crazy here, she thought. "Yeah. She hasn't lived there long. It's a fixer-upper."

"She keep a door unlocked or a spare key?"

"A spare." Lydia sniffled and looked back out the window at the storm. *Maybe this is what life is?* she thought. *You go along, thinking things are one way, then something intense is thrown at you. Maybe not always this insane, this unbelievable, but just as hard, just as scary . . . like when your father . . .*

She shook her head. "Where are the adults?"

"I'm here," Ashton-Smith said.

Her father had always told her not to get discouraged, someone was always ready to help, but . . . "No offense," she said, "but you're old enough to be my

Pop-pop."

"None taken."

"Why aren't more adults here? Isn't that what adults are supposed to do?"

The old man nodded. "Adults are supposed to do a lot of things."

"I want to help Ms. Blackwood. She's the only . . ." Her words choked off. She hoped they knew, hoped they understood what she couldn't say, but was afraid they did.

"You've helped Ms. Blackwood already," Ashton-Smith said. "And you can still help."

"I'm so afraid."

"That's okay," he continued. "Fear is a normal response. You can't stop it."

"That's what my dad always said. You can't stop fear from coming but you don't have to give in to it."

"He was right," Ashton-Smith said.

Lydia shrugged.

Kris sighed. "The people who are helping me," he said, "people like Mr. Ashton-Smith, they've been around since the Children's Crusade."

The old man nodded. "Once we were like you. Children who stood alone against the darkness." He caught her eyes in the rearview.

Lydia suddenly remembered why Hamelin sounded familiar—the Pied Piper.

"We decided no one else should have to go through what we went through."

Kris nodded. "They said 'no.'"

• • •

The old woman's husband grew up with his sister on the streets of Paris. Depending on how many drinks he had when you asked him, their mother was either a poor girl who caught a soldier's fancy, a rich man's trophy brought over from Algiers, or a working girl.

The old woman knew the truth, which was that he didn't know. Mother and father were faceless. Nameless. Memories faded so much with time, they were nothing other than male and female.

What never faded? What he never told anyone else? The brutal memories of the man with the sharp teeth and the bloody mouth who took a dark fancy to his sister.

• • •

Ashton-Smith let them out underneath a tall oak on Walpole Lane. Even seeing the merit in circling the block to ensure they wouldn't be ambushed, Lydia wasn't pleased he wasn't coming in immediately. It felt cowardly to her.

Once again fighting the elements, she and Kris ran quickly around the corner to Radcliff Road. They climbed a low fence, then hustled along the property line to the back of the gambrel-roofed home.

Lydia fished the magnetic key case from behind the south rain gutter. After she unlocked the back door, Kris reached into the gloom and flicked the light switch.

It stayed dark.

Lydia peered around him. She could see the outline of the kitchen appliances. "Look," she said. "Clock on the stove is dead. Power must be out."

Kris moved to the edge of the porch. Over the neighbor's privacy fence, he could see their security light burning faintly. Lydia did too. "We should be careful."

"You should have brought a flashlight," she said.

He ignored her and stepped inside.

She gave him a minute for his eyes to adjust, then called after, "Notice anything out of place?"

"No. Wait there," he said. "I'll come get you when I'm done."

Lydia grumbled and kept watch for some sign of trouble.

• • •

When her husband burst through the door, the old woman was ready. Ever since that terrible day so long ago in the tunnels beneath London, she had a knack for knowing.

"He tricked us."

"Malcolm Coffin is a crafty bastard," she said, handing him the Sigillum and keeping the gun for herself.

"What are you doing?"

"Saving the boy."

Her husband started to speak.

"I'm taking lead on this one." She shushed him. "Remember the oath: neither sealed lip, nor barred door . . ."

• • •

Lydia couldn't wait any longer. There wasn't time for Coffin Boy to fumble his way around a pitch black house. She knew Ms. Blackwood kept a flashlight in her bedroom. She had bought it after the previous round of storms lead to a blackout battle with a bathroom towel.

She entered the kitchen, took the back stairs to the first landing, crouched and listened. Wherever Kris was, she couldn't hear him. Couldn't hear anything but rain. She leaned forward and crawled up the remaining stairs to peek into the dark second story. Seeing it was empty, she took a quiet breath and eased slowly into the hall.

Lightning flashed brightly once outside, nearly destroying her night vision. She held her breath and waited. When she could see again, she flattened herself along the wall next to the bedroom door. "You can do this," Lydia told herself. "You have to help her."

The bedroom door creaked as it swung open. The shrill note rising with the widening arc, then falling again as it swung partially closed. Her boots crunched on glass as she entered the room, gagging on the overripe scent of floral perfume. The mirror on the old vanity was shattered and the drawers broken. And the bed was flipped against the wall. Something terrible had happened here.

Lydia's eyes raced through the darkness, searching for the flashlight, fearful of finding a body. A slow flash of lightning creeping across the dark sky outside the bedroom window revealed not a body but a jagged symbol scrawled across the floor between bed and closet.

"Ms. Blackwood," Lydia whispered, rushing over, "what did they do to you?" The symbol was three concentric circles surrounding a stylized pentagram. She started to touch it but stopped short. *Was the outside or the inside safe?* She didn't know. Confusingly, both seemed right. Her eyes scanned the arcane glyph for some clue, some snatch of information remembered from a movie or a comic book.

Wait! She scooted over to the apex of the circles. At first, she thought the sigil was unfinished. Then leaning closer, she saw it was only smeared. She touched the floorboards cautiously. Wet. She looked behind her at the window. Shut and bolted. The sheer curtains were drawn and their fabric looked dry. She looked up. Nothing dripping from the ceiling.

Lydia crouched lower, still wary of touching but straining to see, hoping to find something—

"Careful."

Coffin Boy's voice startled her. She barely avoided sprawling across the mystical symbol. "I told you to wait," he said, smugly.

"I don't listen well."

"Must have taken her in the middle of the night."

"Look at this."

Kris cocked his head and examined the symbol. "This is how they shaped her imposter," he said, moving around her.

"It's wet," Lydia said. "Why?"

He pressed two fingers into the damp, then rubbed his thumb across the pads as if trying to place something.

"What is it?"

He sniffed. "Soap."

Soap? Lightning flashed. Lydia spotted a bucket pushed behind the night-stand. A limp cloth draped over the side. "Someone was trying to clean this up."

A hulking figure burst through the slatted closet doors.

"Lydia—" A heavy black boot punted Kris to the floor.

Something sharp flashed in the darkness. Lydia backpedaled, falling on her bottom as the long knife slashed the air.

Kris groaned, pushed himself up onto one hand and grabbed the attacker's pant leg. A sharp kick kept the hold short. The distraction bought Lydia enough time to flail backwards onto her feet. The dresser's stinging edge stopped her from falling back down.

The brute grunted and thrust. His blade missed Lydia but pinned her raincoat to the vanity. She cried out, twist-rolled free of her coat, taking a glancing punch on the temple as she spun free, fell and scrambled out the door.

The dark man pursued her relentlessly. A bulky figured in loose black clothing long out of style and a sack-like hood over his head. The steel in his hand glinting in the storm light.

Coffin Boy screamed her name.

Her attacker charged, punching the knife straight at her guts.

A thunderous boom.

The hooded man jerked sharply to the right. He stepped forward once, dropped his knife, then staggered sideways and fell. Ashton-Smith ran up the stairs, an antique Webley revolver still trained on the downed attacker.

Kris took a hit from his inhaler.

"You cut that—" Something clamped down over Lydia's shoulders and jerked her backwards. She barely managed to grab the sides of the door-frame to keep from being pulled into the room behind her.

Ashton-Smith's gun went high and wavered. "Good God!"

Lydia tried to muscle free using the door frame for leverage. Soon as she moved, whatever had a hold of her wrenched her backwards hard enough that she thought her arms would snap in two. Her nails scraped against the wood but somehow she managed to hold.

Until something wet slithered around her chest and tickled her armpit.

Lydia looked behind her as her hands released. Two bony, inward-facing horns crowned the sleek skull of a tall, winged beast with burning yellow eyes and no visible mouth.

The hallway was dark. He was winded from the stairs. Deaf from the round he put through the hooded man's skull. But he couldn't let the Nightgaunt get away with Lydia. Ashton-Smith chanced his shot as she screamed.

Kris shouldered past him as he fired. The bullet thunked into the plaster. "No!" He reached for the boy and barely missed the drooping hood.

The Nightgaunt's horns shattered the glass. Its wings folded over Lydia like the petals of some deadly nocturnal flower swallowing a careless insect. Creature and captive passed out into the night and the rain. The cruel barbed tail whipped like a sparking electrical wire, lashing jagged shards of glass from the window.

Kris dove after them, reaching for the tail.

A barb sliced the palm of his left hand. His right clawed desperately as he fell, legs kicking. Somehow he managed to catch enough to tug, pulling the tail closer, grabbing hold with the bloody fingers of his stinging left hand. Both found purchase, curling around the thick tail above the nest of barbs.

The creature was unprepared. The Nightgaunt's wings beat once, splashing a cold torrent of rain into his face, and then came gravity. It dropped a foot and a half, nearly pulled tail over head from the shifting swing of Coffin Boy's weight. A fearsome flurry of wingbeats barely kept it from plummeting to the ground.

Ashton-Smith leaned out the upstairs window. The wind lashed stinging rain against his face. He squinted, fired and missed.

Righting itself, thick muscles taut and wings beating furiously, the Nightgaunt fixed him with cold, glassy eyes. The old man didn't flinch. The beast threw its head back, unleashed a bone-chilling cry and dropped Lydia. She caught hold of Kris as she fell but her weight was too much for him and she pulled him down with her, the barbs splitting the skin on both his palms as he slid down the long tail.

"No!" Ashton-Smith fired again, grazing the upper tip of the beast's wing.

Howling and bloody, the Nightgaunt buzzed the window to taunt him. Ashton-Smith fired quickly two more times, hoping to score something more palpable, if not a kill. Both volleys missed. The sleek black form hovered briefly in the rain, then the powerful wings beat once and the dark shape sailed up into the heavy rain. Membranes spread and caught the rough wind. The beast vanished into the thick, black clouds on rolling storm gusts.

Down on the ground, Lydia picked herself up first. "Are you okay?"

Kris stood slowly, mesmerized by blood running down his fingers. "Yeah."

"Good." She shoved him back down on his tail bone. "You knew, didn't you?"

He blinked up at her.

"You knew it would alert them. When you dispelled—"

"Yes."

Ashton-Smith called down from the broken second story window as he reloaded his weapon.

Lydia ignored him. "You knew they'd come here."

Kris extended one bloody hand. "I hoped so."

"You used me as bait." She stared at his red fingers. "You could have confronted that thing yourself."

"Yes."

Lydia pulled him roughly up by his wrist.

"Listen, I—" As he lurched, she punched him in the face. Coffin Boy staggered, then dropped to one knee, blood gushing from his nose.

"Don't lie to me again."

• • •

His wife stayed at the bend in the secret passage while he boldly stepped around, a cigarette between his fingers. "Hey, fella, you got a light?"

The hooded man rushed forward.

After the vampire took his sister from him, he joined the Foreign Legion where he drank and fought his way across four continents trying to forget how it had felt to ram the shaft of hawthorn through the sonofabitch's heart. He had slowed since then, but forgotten nothing.

Hood reached for him. The old man flipped his cigarette at him, stepped in to feint a body shot, and slammed his forehead where he figured a nose ought to have been.

The old man figured right.

• • •

Lydia lit candles while Kristoffer drew sigils and scrawled runes around the hooded man's corpse with pink lipstick. "More Nightgaunts will be coming," Ashton-Smith said, nervously stroking his thin moustache.

"I'm hurrying." Kris took a hit off his inhaler as he surveyed his penmanship.

Lydia lit her last candle, stood and looked out the window. The storm had calmed to a steady rain. She shivered. She couldn't remember the last time she had been this wet or cold. "Why are you doing this?"

"To question him," Coffin Boy said. The spirit hovers over the body for several minutes after death."

"Like a dense fog full of city lights," Ashton-Smith said.

"That's not what I meant."

"I have to become the man I wanted my father to be." Kris pocketed his inhaler, then quickly adjusted several runes with a few bright slashes of lipstick before nodding at Ashton-Smith.

"Looks like he's ready, dear." The old man quickly walked around the summoning circle to stand next to Lydia. "Take a short step back. We need to keep clear."

The temperature dropped as soon as Coffin Boy began chanting. Lydia turned up the collar of her battered blazer and watched her breath condense in the air. When it shaped itself into something resembling a serpent, she backed away. A bitterly cold touch along her spine stopped her from retreating further. She looked behind her and saw only darkness beyond the candles' sputtering glow.

Looking back, she saw Coffin Boy's chant coax his and the old man's breath from their lips. Each disembodied exhalation undulated in the air. He chanted a word louder than the others, and the serpents coiled together, seething and rolling with his rhythm. On the next word, they swirled in a single spiral of dead breath into the corpse's mouth, spinning and slipping between the open lips.

The body groaned.

Lydia stepped closer to the old man who whispered, "The spirit returning to the corpse displaces air."

The corpse farted loudly.

"A lot of air."

The left hand twitched. The fingers tapped a slow and eerie rhythm. Lydia covered her mouth to stay silent. Suddenly the corpse shot upright. The lolling head rolled back on the corpse's shoulders.

Coffin Boy addressed it immediately. "Where is Ms. Blackwood?"

Something wet dripped from the slack lips, ran down the pale cheeks.

"Where is Ms. Blackwood?"

The head rose slowly, hood spilling over the corpse's face.

Coffin Boy repeated himself angrily. "Where is Ms. Blackwood?"

A flat, low voice issued from the hood. "It is cold and so very dark."

Lydia looked at Ashton-Smith for some sign this was how it was supposed to go but he kept strict watch over the boy and his questioning. "Is that where she is? Somewhere cold and dark?"

The voice shifted, the tone deepened, the cadence quicker and anxious with wild confusion. "Full of fear. So full of fear."

"Not you." Coffin Boy shook his head. "Where is Ms. Blackwood?"

"Food."

"What?"

"Food." The corpse chuckled, high-pitched and grating. "Rend. Tear. Rip. Crunchy crunch crunch."

Ashton-Smith patted Lydia protectively on the shoulder. She watched him slip the Webley out of his coat pocket.

"Ms. Blackwood—"

The voice twisted higher. "Tasty warm blood. Mmmmm. Marrow suck. Warm blood and marrow suck. Yum. Yum. Yum." More laughter.

"What's happening?" Lydia whispered.

"He can only keep the spirit in the corpse for a few moments," Ashton-Smith said. "Any longer and there are great risks. Lurking things wait for untended doorways, careless invitations. They're drawn to the lights in the spirit fog like moths to porch light."

Coffin Boy traced a shape in the air. "Where is Ms. Blackwood?"

The corpse shook. It twisted on itself, spinning and pulling limbs into its trunk like the wilting petals of a flower. A new voice mocked shrilly from dead lips, "Where is Ms. Blackwood?"

Coffin Boy traced the symbol again. This time he held the fingers of his right hand in that same awkward ending position while drawing another symbol with his left.

The corpse screamed. The chest bobbed suddenly in the air as if pulled by a string, hands and feet falling down and away. Ashton-Smith pushed Lydia behind him as the dead body spun like a whirligig.

"Tell me quickly," Coffin Boy demanded, "where is Ms. Blackwood?"

"Cemetery."

Ashton-Smith pointed the Webley at the corpse's rotating skull. "Kristoffer," he said, "we have it. Release it."

It made a low, warbling sound in its throat. "An offering."

"Kristoffer!"

"They will eat her before sunrise."

Ashton-Smith cocked the hammer back with his thumb. "Damnit, Kristoffer!"

"I have con—"

The corpse broke free of the magical hold. It lurched across the circle, reached over the protective barrier, hands bursting into blue flames, and grabbed Kris by the shoulders. "The Whistler waits for you, my damned boy." The icy voice that came from the dead man dripped hatred.

Ashton-Smith fired. His shot knocked the corpse off its feet, back onto the summoning circle where the blue fire quickly consumed the body.

• • •

The sleek Ford sped down Coast Road North. The black car swerved onto the narrow paved road that stretched forlornly into the high hills overlooking Vulture Bay, where Dunsany Island's dead slept. Two massive gates topped the horizon. The car careened to a stop in the wet grass.

Lydia exited first. She looked up at the full moon glistening wetly against the rolling clouds. "What now?"

Kris stepped out of the car, a faraway look haunting his eyes. "I thought we were baiting them. I was wrong."

He pointed across the fields of pitted stone and choking ivory, over the low crumbling walls, and past the heads of moss-covered statuary. At the base of a distant hill, an obelisk split the pale moon into two overripe pieces against the velvet sky. "They've hid her in father's tomb."

Ashton-Smith tightened his scarf around his neck. "We must be careful," he said. "The rain brings out more than just worms in a cemetery."

• • •

In a natural stone chamber lined with gruesome sigils and carved mouths bleeding flickering torchlight, Kristoffer woke suddenly. Thick censer smoke clouded the damp air. The distant sound of crashing surf drumbeat the rhythmic chanting of the seven robed men surrounding him.

Praying he was dreaming, his eyes searched the faces. When he recognized his father, he knew he wasn't and began to cry.

• • •

The oldest graves predated the first settlement on Dunsany. Long before Wieland Brockden financed the building of the lighthouse which accidentally founded the town, ships regularly rounded the coast on their way to Rhode Island, Connecticut, or Massachusetts. There were rumors of hidden coves used by smugglers during the Revolutionary War for transporting supplies from le Comte d'Averoigne, but the island served mostly as a navigation aid for ships coming out of the dreary North Atlantic.

Sometime in the fall of 1790, a cargo ship got lost in a dense fog bank and drifted too close to shore. The sails were lifeless, but the tide was strong. The jagged rocks of Vulture Bay shredded the hull. The frigid waters drowned the crew to the man but for one who somehow made it ashore.

The shipping company financed what they claimed was a rescue operation but everyone knew was about salvage. Wishing to spare further expense, they buried the bodies on the cliffs above Vulture Bay. The lone survivor refused passage to the mainland, choosing instead to stay behind on the lonesome island and watch over the dead.

The Coffin Family crypt sat atop the largest hill in the old section of the cemetery. Originally fashioned as a mock Roman temple of pitted stone and trailing ivy, near the turn of the century, during Egypt mania, it had been topped with an obelisk. From far away, the temple seemed massive but when the group reached the hill, Lydia was confused by its small stature. She thought it was some kind of trick of perspective until Ashton-Smith led them around the hill, then down stone steps into the earth itself.

The old man tried the iron-barred door at the bottom. "It's locked."

Kris peered through the bars. The Black Veil Society had bound Ms. Blackwood atop the last Coffin laid to rest—his father. "Caretaker has a key, doesn't he?"

"There's another way," Ashton-Smith said, nudging him aside. He drew his pistol, checked the safety, and then took it by the barrel. "There's a release latch that opens the door from the inside."

"Creepy," Lydia said.

"Fear of premature burial."

"Still. Creepy."

Ashton-Smith hunkered down in the narrow landing and reached through the bars, using the gun as an extension of his arm. "Not the safest thing to do and certainly not the best way to treat a gun . . ."

Kris warmed his hands with his breath. The storm may have passed, but this close to Vulture Bay the strong wind carried the chill of the deep ocean across the fields of the dead.

Lydia watched the old man twist and strain.

A rabbit darted from behind a cracked tombstone. It froze in the tall grasses, caught the scent of a predator and dashed madly through the graveyard.

The gun grip banged against metal and stone.

"Got it!"

The metal popped. Lydia hopped over the old man, darted to the center sarcophagus, and shook her teacher, urging her to wake up.

Ms. Blackwood did not move and her skin felt chill.

Coming around the other side, Ashton-Smith grasped the back of her skull and lifted her head gently. He carefully thumbed her eyelid open. "Drugged."

Kris went to work on the rope knotted tightly through the iron rings along the stone base. "Keep an eye out," he said to Lydia.

Lydia chewed her lip and fought the urge to argue as she moved back to the entrance.

• • •

Malcolm Coffin stepped to the summoning dais. Chanting and nodding his head, he anointed his son's temple with the Oil of Abramelin, then raised his hands in line with his broad shoulders.

The ocean wind whipping through the chamber began to take the timbre of a low, mournful whistle as another seven men in hoods entered through the rear of the chamber, carrying long torches.

• • •

A distant howl echoed through the graveyard. "What is that?" Dark clouds raced across the full face of the moon. Lean shapes darted between the hills and amongst the tombstones. Lydia backed away from the door, crossed to the barred window set high in the wall. "Dogs?"

Kristoffer freed his knot and rose quickly. "Dogs barking? Or more like baying?"

"Doesn't matter," Ashton-Smith said. "We hurry."

"Barking? Baying?" Lydia shook her head. "What's the difference?"

"A big one."

She strained on her tiptoes to grab the bars. She pulled herself up for a better view. Caught sight of another darting shadow. "There's something out there."

Kris rushed out of the tomb. Lydia called after him, "They're moving fast."

She caught a glimpse of a pale face against weathered granite. "Are those people?"

"No!" Kris came rushing back inside. "Ghouls!"

"Doesn't matter," Ashton-Smith said, pulling his last knot loose, muscling Ms. Blackwood into his arms. "Let's go."

Lydia and Kristoffer gave him room. The old man hurried quickly up the steps as if his burden weighed nothing. They were impressed until he stepped clear of the crypt and his knees buckled.

Both moved to help. The old man huffed, straining to straighten his back. "I got it. Let's go."

A lonesome howl echoed across the graveyard. Untold more answered.

• • •

Malcolm Coffin finished his evocation with a wide sweep of his arms and a deep exhale. His breath hung in the salty air for a moment, then flowed across the summoning dais in a shifting scintillation of color before vanishing as if inhaled by invisible lips.

A gunshot boomed above the whistling wind. The old woman staggered over the rocks into the guttering torchlight. "Malcolm Coffin, you cowardly little shit," she yelled firing another shot into the air, "it's over."

"You are too late, Mrs. Ashton-Smith."

"You will not harm the boy."

"The Whistler is already here." A maleficent presence descended oppressively over the chamber. "The boy has been promised. The boy has been marked."

Mrs. Ashton-Smith planted her feet, aimed, and said, "No."

Kristoffer didn't move. "We'll never make it," he said.

"Let's go," Ashton-Smith said through clenched teeth. "There's no time to stand here and argue."

"You can barely carry her." Lydia held her arms out. "Let me try."

"Impossible."

Kris took a puff from his inhaler. "They'll overtake us."

"They certainly will as long as we stand here."

"The tomb!" Lydia pointed. "We'll lock ourselves in."

Ashton-Smith shook his head, awkwardly shifting Ms. Blackwood's weight. "No . . . let's . . . go."

"There are too many of them," Kris said. "They'll rip the door off its hinges or tunnel in from below."

"He's right." Ashton-Smith started walking, hoping they'd both follow but only Lydia did. "Come on, Kristoffer. Lydia."

"Go!" Kris took off running . . . the other direction, straight toward the loping packs of hungry ghouls.

A dark look passed over the old man's hooded eyes. Lydia could see he was torn about what to do, that he wanted to stop and go after Kris but knew he'd probably never be able to get started again.

Lydia looked over her shoulder. "What is he doing?"

"He's going to whistle," Ashton-Smith croaked and quickened his pace.

• • •

Malcolm Coffin laughed. "Assuming you hit, old woman, it will do no good. My death won't stop the Whistler."

"Oh, I know." Mrs. Ashton-Smith cocked the Webley. "My husband will take care of that."

The hooded figure behind Malcolm swung his torch at the man beside him, striking him in the head, igniting the black fabric masking his face. The man screamed as his hood burst into flames and flailed madly into the others gathered at the foot of the dais.

Mr. Ashton-Smith tore his hood free and tossed his torch at the remaining cultists. He bounded up the steps and speared Malcolm, driving him into the unyielding stone. The elder Coffin cried out but managed a sharp elbow.

Bloody faced, Ashton-Smith hammered a fist into Malcolm's kidney and used the ensuing pain to grab tight hold of his robe. He wrenched Coffin down the dais, then pulled the Sigillum free of his robes and slapped it on Kristoffer's chest.

The ensuing counterforce blasted him off the dais.

Kris topped the steep hill on his hands and feet. He used the low branches of a dead oak to pull himself on top of the crumbling, dry stacked stone wall. Below, he could see the ghouls hurrying between gravestones and crosses, scuttling around tomb and crypt, scurrying like eager rats in a maze.

"Here! I'm here! Come get me!" He yelled, waving his arms like a madman.

A single figure rose from behind a cracked Celtic cross. The night air came off the sea, cold and bitter. The ghoul's snout quivered and caught a scent. Feral eyes found him in the darkness.

Kris took a deep hit off his inhaler.

• • •

Less than two hundred feet from the cemetery entrance, three stray ghouls tried to flank them. Lydia spotted the slavering creatures cresting the north hill. Ashton-Smith drew his pistol and fired a wild shot, hoping to scatter or stall them long enough to reach the iron gates.

It didn't work.

The ghouls boldly rushed down the hill, barking and growling, teeth gnashing and tongues drooling for succulent man flesh.

With no other choice, Ashton-Smith stopped, hefted Ms. Blackwood onto his shoulder and fired. The recoil almost felled him. His aim was low, only grazing the flank of front beast. The creature didn't seem to notice.

"Give!" Lydia wrestled the gun out of his hand.

"Do you—"

She gripped the revolver with both hands, planted her feet and fired the way her father had taught her. The recoil snapped her wrists back more than she expected. It hurt, but her aim was true. The bullet struck the ghoul midstride. As his front arms came down, the right crumpled. The shaggy beast slid through the wet grass straight into a tombstone and cracked its skull. His fellows, already drooling over the rich aroma of fresh blood, forgot their troublesome quarry and swarmed their fallen littermate as he cried out and tried to stand, and tore him apart in a frothy, red frenzy of fang and claw.

"Good shot!"

Lydia stared at the revolver. She remembered the way her father's gun had looked when the police returned it to her mother. The last words he had spoken to her came to her then, *Sometimes you have to be the one to help.*

Ashton-Smith maneuvered Ms. Blackwood into his arms and ran once more for the gates. "Lydia! Come on!"

Lydia gripped the gun tightly and ran after Coffin Boy. "Go on!" she yelled. "You're almost there. We can't leave him!"

The old man struggled to shift the teacher's weight. "Lydia!" He yelled again, but she was already past the feasting ghouls.

• • •

Kristoffer let them get close.

Breath hot and hurried.

Yellow eyes gleaming in the darkness.

Claws scraping stone and earth.

A big brute came out of nowhere, quickly lumbering up the wall, pawing for a leg, teeth gnashing hungrily. Coffin Boy wetted his lips. He knew full well the price the widowed Ashton-Smith had paid to carry him clear of that cave so many years ago. He knew full well what it would cost him, what would be taken and what would be left.

Coffin Boy put his lips together and paid the piper.

The whistle started as a long, even note. Clear and loud through the graveyard. Just when the note sounded ready to break, it caught an echo and the echo became a note of its own. Sharper. Shrill. Louder. Then that note too caught its echo and became still yet another note.

The eldritch tune quelled the rowdy pack. Several of the larger ghouls stopped and stood their ground nervously while trying to hold their dominance, eyes searching the darkness and noses tracking the scents in the air. Most hunkered low, circling, wanting to slink away but too overcome with fear while the runts simply rolled over and offered throat and belly.

The breath ripped from Kristoffer's lungs. Something cold passed through his chest and squeezed his respiratory organs as tight as rags wrung dry. He felt his consciousness flee to the other place with the dark hallway, the locked door, and the white room where it waited. His stolen breath pulsed in the air, then vanished to power the ghostly whistle. The notes rose in pitch and intensity, found harmony and become a single sound.

A sound of arrival.

The white room was empty.

Something else was in the graveyard, and it was famished.

• • •

When Lydia rounded the hill, she spotted Kristoffer right away. The sight of him lying on his back in the grass, staring skyward stopped her. It looked like he was daydreaming, counting the stars as their glow pushed through the deep field of black. Then she saw his chest seize and realized he was having an asthma attack.

As soon as she took off running, her feet slid out from under her. The Webley flew from her hand and was lost in the high weeds. She fell hard on her back and slipped down the slight incline in the wet grass.

"Damnit!" Wincing, Lydia stood slowly to keep from falling again. Once on her feet, she tested her balance—steady—and wiped her hands on her blazer. They left two red smears.

She looked down. Her palms were streaked with dark blood. She gulped and looked around her. The grass wasn't damp here with storm water, it was wet with blood. Big bright strokes of scarlet, wide slashes of crimson across the green and grey.

She gaped and nearly covered her mouth. There were no bodies but Kris—*Kristoffer!*

A choking wheeze.

"Shit!" She ran toward him as his pale hand clawed the air. *Stay calm, Lydia. Stay calm. Can you do mouth to mouth on an asthma*—there!

She spied the inhaler lying a few feet away, just out of his reach, directly below the stone wall. She plucked it off the ground and wiped the mouthpiece clean on her skirt. Rushing back to Kristoffer, she knelt beside him and pulled him into her lap. She pushed the inhaler between his lips and pressed. "Come on. Come on. Come on."

Coffin Boy's eyes stayed glassy.

She pushed it again. Counted to five. Pushed it again. "Come on, Coffin Boy. I'll empty this thing if I have to."

Again.

Again—

Kristoffer took a sputtering breath and jerked out of her lap, propping himself up on an arm. He coughed and gasped. Took a normal breath then coughed again.

"Here." Lydia handed him the inhaler and helped him sit up.

Kristoffer took a puff on his own, sighed, and then breathed easy. Slow but easy. "You came back for me," he said, wiping a messy shock of dark hair away from his face. "I told you to go back to the car."

Lydia stared at the long streaks and bright splatters of crimson across the green grass, over the pale stones, and against the dark granite. At that moment, it began to rain again. She stood and looked down at the wild-eyed Coffin Boy, at the cold rain washing the smear of blood from his pale forehead and down his face like red tears. "And I told you," she said, offering her hand, "I don't listen well."

SOLAR HIGHWAY

S.A. Solomon

I leave the Red Cross shelter in a dawn pale with heat stroke
(no a/c in this city school, but the families, flushed
by smoke like startled birds from their beds, are accounted for,
roosting on cots),

to hail a cab on Flatbush Ave.
"At this hour? You'll never find one. Better take the Q."
The taxi slices through truck traffic. I slide in, uniform
sticky with sweat and fatigue.

As we speed to the bridge, the cabbie warns of apocalypse:
the Mayan calendar predicts a solar pole reversal,
unleashing an age of catastrophic floods and (for some)
enlightenment.

We crest the bridge. My driver wants to know: Is the Red Cross ready?

DOLL:

A POEM TO A MANUFACTURER OF DOLLS

jyl anais ion

Doll reflects identity
That one can, will, has an opportunity   to become. The identity
Of a doll refers to women
          a woman   becoming,
To a man becoming and is constructed,
Supported by other forms of   the mass production of images
(of media)
Bought *and* sold.

          What characteristics does s/he as doll exhibit? What role(s)
does she as doll fulfill? And how is that
expectation of fulfillment communicated in "real life"
                    external world?

How could playing
     With a doll
          In a context *not*
Dictated by (you) the manufacturer   subvert
or
                                                  Transform

the meaning(fullness)
                    of her identity,
of her role
of her?

How could that form of play   be
considered
                                                  deviant?
                    How could that (deviance) reflect the future
Of a woman('s)
identity, role, *play*?

JIBBER JABBER

Reed Farrel Coleman

His father was a collector of things, all sorts of things, but James McCabe collected nothing. He did not relate to things, not even the splayed fingers he sometimes fanned before his opaque blue eyes. If not for the laws of physics, he would not relate to the floor on which he knelt, intermittently rocking his days away with inexhaustible energy. He was disconnected, unattached, self-contained, an eight-year-old universe unto himself. The doctors, shrinks, therapists, and teachers at the developmental center could only speculate about the nature of that universe. His was a silent universe, disinterested in revelation and selfish of clues.

He had cried at birth. It was the only sound ever to have escaped from inside him. He had never cooed or grunted, coughed or called out. His next sound would be his second. His next word his first. His mother fooled herself that she could divine the mysteries of her son's moods and desires by the rhythm of his rocking, by the shadows his fingers cast on the walls, even by which room James wandered into. She might as well have rolled animal bones.

James McCabe's father had long since cut ties with his son. He treated the boy with the utter disinterest which the boy himself displayed. If only the boy could have shown minimal contempt, that would have been enough for the father. He understood contempt, but he could not stomach disinterest. Love was never an issue. To his father, James was less than the least of his possessions. Objects are created without the potential for emotion. One's own love, pride, and vanity had to be enough for both you and the thing itself.

The day the two universes collided, each forever changing, James McCabe, temporarily inert, found himself in a dark corner of the room that held his father's most prized possessions. The glass and oak case was more shrine than display. People came from all over to stand and gawk at the things in the case. Two sets of eager footfalls thumped against the big cabin's floorboards. As was always the case, it was impossible to know if James was aware they were coming toward him.

"Here we are, Mr. Smith."

Peter McCabe made a rather too formal gesture with his arm, but he couldn't help himself. Although he had shown his collection to many strangers, he could contain neither his pride nor his avarice. To see Peter McCabe's shrine cost you. It was a C-note just to stand near the case and peer through the glass. Five times that if you wished to handle pieces from the collection.

• • •

McCabe handed Smith a fresh pair of white gloves and put on a pair himself. Reading Smith's expression, McCabe said, "Yes, it's always hard to know where to begin. This is a personal favorite. Here." He reached for a meticulously preserved hardcover, carefully covered in acid free plastic.

"*Mein Kampf.*"

Smith was unimpressed.

McCabe did not overreact. "Yes, but not just any copy. Notice that the inscription is to Neville Chamberlain and that Hitler's signature is particularly bold and powerful."

Smith was still unmoved. McCabe replaced the book in the case and began nervously reciting a laundry list of other pieces from the collection.

"There's the sutures removed from Hitler's body after the attempt on his life, one of Eichmann's prototypes for the Death's Head hats, an ampule of blue dye Dr. Mengele used to inject into the eyes of children, a pair of the doctor's spectacles, Martin Bormann's Luger, a bar of human soap, a pelvic bone ashtray, a bottle of ashes from Crematorium Number Two at . . . "

So distracted was McCabe by his own narcissistic recitation, that he was unconscious of Smith removing his top coat. And though the reflection of the yellow star sewn onto the chest of Smith's suit jacket was plain to see in the spotless glass of the case, that too escaped McCabe's notice. He missed it as his visitor slid the tire iron from beneath his right sleeve and into his white-gloved hand. He barely noticed as Smith screamed "Never Again" so loudly that his wife could hear it in the shed. Even as Smith raised the crooked metal rod—his bland, hollow face transformed into something barely recognizable as human—McCabe was oblivious. With the nauseating thud of the iron against his skull, it was already too late to rue his lack of attentiveness.

Peter McCabe's face smashed directly into the case, loose shards embedding themselves in his flesh. Jagged glass wedged in place peeled away parts of his neck and right ear as gravity pulled him to the floor. So much blood appeared in an instant that the oak and glass itself seemed to bleed. But Smith was far from finished. He swung the iron again and again, smashing almost every breakable object in the shrine. He dropped the iron, pulled a flask of gasoline out of his inside jacket pocket, and doused the case. He patted his pocket, feeling for a pack of matches. He became frantic when he could not feel that familiar shape in any of his pockets.

He found the matches in the pocket of his bulky top coat he had dropped behind him. As he struck the match, something else caught his attention. He heard James before he saw him. Rather he heard the floorboards creaking as the boy began rocking in the corner. James' unseeing eyes transfixed Smith. Not recognizing an ounce of humanity in them, Smith realized what he had become. A mist of profound shame filled his lungs. He wanted to approach the boy, but could not move. His hesitation proved fatal.

"You son of a bitch!"

The spell was broken and Smith looked toward the open door. The shotgun blast nearly took off his head and the inertia nudged his lifeless body into the ruined display case. His shame and the heat of the match on his fingertips consumed Smith's last moment of consciousness. The gasoline ignited. The spread of the buckshot and the impact of Smith's body finished the work he had started. The few shrine items that had remained intact, either exploded or crashed to the floor. The room quickly filled with smoke.

• • •

The fire was well extinguished and Peter McCabe had been helicoptered to the area trauma center. Mr. Smith's burned body had long since been delivered to the medical examiner's office. Smith, really Avi Pearlmutter, was the grandson of concentration camp survivors, a full time cultist, and part-time schizophrenic. James and his mother had both been treated for smoke inhalation and released.

The miracle was patient in coming. It waited until the stillness of night had fully descended and James' mom was halfway to visit her comatose husband. It waited until James' Aunt Greta had stripped off and burned her eight-year-old nephew's smoke-corrupted clothing. It waited until she led James into the upstairs bathroom, the shower already running. Then all patience evaporated and the miracle fairly exploded. James McCabe, the eight-year-old universe, came undone.

The instant his bare feet touched the cold tile floor, James spoke. Well, it wasn't speech, exactly. He wasn't saying words, not so as Greta could make them out, anyway, but they weren't just random sounds either. They were like make believe words. And, there was another change in James, maybe even more profound than the nonsense words. His whole body posture, the manner of his movements changed. The awkward, ungainly jerkiness with which he had moved his entire life was gone.

"One minute he was one of them fidgety little birds and then he was a swan," she would later tell her sister. "First he started to jibber-jabber and then . . . Lord Jesus, sis, he moved so graceful-like."

And, the movements, like the sounds that came from his mouth, were not random. Although he was naked, James removed invisible clothes. He pressed them, patted out wrinkles, hung them on unseen hooks. He balled up see-through socks, placing them in phantom shoes.

"Then he looked me straight in the eye and started that jibber-jabbering all over again. It was spooky, sis, like your boy was asking me a question. I didn't know what to do, so I just showered him. When he got out, he dried himself all up and put back on them invisible clothes and started them spooky questions again. When I told him his momma would be home tomorrow, he smiled. He smiled at me, sis. The boy don't never smile. He went right to bed."

There was dark-clouded joy on the outskirts of town for a month or two. Although he had been burned, hit by stray buckshot, and suffered a seriously fractured skull, Peter McCabe's prognosis for survival was improved. His prognosis for a full recovery was less rosy. The damage to the skin and musculature of his face and neck would require several reconstructive procedures. The trauma caused by the blow to the back of his head, the subsequent collision of his forehead with the case, and the blood loss had left him addled, aphasic, weak.

On the other hand, James McCabe's metamorphosis was international news. Yet for all the coverage, each story filed bore a marked similarity to the ones before and after it.

". . . the eight-year-old son of a white supremacist diagnosed with a severe form of Pervasive Developmental Disorder or autism, as it's more commonly known, witnessed a brutal attack on his father by . . . In the hours immediately following the attack, James McCabe, who had never uttered a word nor made a sound after his birth . . . "

So it went, at least at first. Then the tabloids moved onto the next sensation, but before they all left, *The World Planet Star* made the McCabes one hundred and fifty thousand dollars richer. Next, came the religious fanatics, cultists, and crazies. They were harder to bear, for they came with their own predetermined agendas, agendas having nothing to do with rating points and ad revenues. One group erected a likeness of James nailed to a wooden yellow star. Another took to acting out James' newfound undressing rituals. In the wake of the crazies came the intelligentsia, the critics, and the academics. They came to piss on the whole spectacle, on the McCabes, and each other. The academics, without ever examining the boy, concluded that this was no miracle, that the original diagnosis of PDD was completely misguided. Ultimately, James McCabe was judged a freak, an oddity, a future roadside attraction like a two-headed snake.

McCabe's Miracle, as it had come to be known, had become his mother's nightmare. For as the months went on, James' speech and rituals grew exponentially. From one minute to the next; his voice, his tone, his posture would change. The syllables that poured out of him seemed endless and endlessly senseless. There was no more understanding him now that he spoke than when his mother read his finger shadows. She found herself yearning for his past silence and hating herself for it.

And, her husband's rehab had all but consumed the largess of *The World Planet Star*. His problem was quite the opposite of her son's. Although he had yet to speak again, Peter McCabe was less confused and had come part of the way back to his old self. Unfortunately, his face still looked like a train wreck.

The next change in the collision of the two universes happened in the personal hygiene aisle of the supermarket. It took the shape of a bent old man, his posture that of a twisted tree limb. Even before he approached her, James' mother noticed the crooked man. So out of place, she thought, so shabby; the band of his black hat stained with sweat, his white shirt gone yellow with age. As she pushed the cart ahead of her and he hobbled towards her, she saw the dandruff on the shoulders of his threadbare black coat and the age spots on his ashen, unshaven face. She reached for the soap.

"Soap!" the old man exclaimed. "You know they made soap from human beings, the people your husband so admires."

She knew about the soap, the lampshades, about all of it.

"Get outta my way or I'll call—"

"But if you call security, Mrs. McCabe, I wouldn't be able to help you with your son. And if I don't help him...I don't think a woman like you could take much more of him, his talking and talking. Am I right? I can see in your eyes that I am right. Here's my card. I'm staying in the Best Western. If you want my help, I'll be there until Thursday."

She hesitated.

"Take it. Take it!" he said, shoving the card in her hand.

She did just to be rid of him. He touched the brim of his hat. She saw his hand was gnarled, scarred by fire.

"I'll await your call. Good day."

She did not turn to watch his retreat. Instead she stared at the card, as frayed and ragged as the man who had given it to her.

CHAIM FEINGOLD

That's what the card said, as if saying his name alone were enough. It would have to be, for it gave no address, no phone number, no fax, no email address, no website. She made to crumple the already withered card, but she did not. She would call. She knew she would as sure as Feingold, whoever he was, knew she would. She was desperate and desperation makes for strange allies.

Feingold came to the cabin that night after dark. Once again he put his fingers to his hat in the way of greeting and deference. That was his only concession to manners. He brushed past her, moving his ancient bent frame with an unexpected grace and power.

"Show me where is the room!" he barked.

"The room?"

"Where the husband was clubbed. Where he kept his foul things and the boy was in the corner. Show me!"

She led the way. "But it's all been—"

"Mrs. McCabe, do you want my help? Yes! Then please do as I say."

When they got to the room that had once held the shrine, Feingold had Mrs. McCabe describe in detail about where everything was situated, where her husband had fallen, where her boy had been, where Pearlmutter's body had come to rest...

"And your husband's horrible trinkets, they were all destroyed? The soap, the ashes, all of it?"

"All of it," she said. "The room filled up quick with smoke. I got my husband out first. He was bleeding so. Then I came and got my boy."

"So, the boy was in the room here for some time, no? A few minutes maybe, yes?"

"A minute or two at least."

Feingold rubbed his cheek, grinning a contemptuous grin. It was a grin that frightened James' mother—a woman who didn't frighten easily.

"Mr. Feingold, how did you find us?"

"On the TV. I saw him on the TV and I recognized... Well, the way he moved and spoke. You wouldn't understand. Let's just say I became a student of your son and his miracle. Where is the boy?"

She hesitated.

"The boy!" he shouted. "Where is the boy?"

"In the bathroom. He seems his most comfortable in there."

"Comfortable, ha!" His laugh was as bent as his spine.

Both of them stood at the open door of the bathroom, Feingold staring in stunned disbelief as James ran through a never ending series of undressing rituals, each different from the next, and nonsense questions asked with wildly different intonation patterns. Silent tears streamed down the old man's cheeks. It had been one thing to see the boy on TV and something else again to stand in the room before him. Feingold's whole body shook. Although she was standing behind him and to one side, Mrs. McCabe could see the old man's reaction in the bathroom mirror.

The old man collected himself, walked up to the boy and placed a gnarled hand on James's shoulder.

"*Wos iz dien nomen?*" he asked the boy.

A pause. Then he continued with his rituals.

"*Was ist Ihr Name?*"

Another pause. Back to the rituals.

"*Wat is uw naam?*"

James crooked his head slightly as if he almost understood, but continued.

"*Barmilyen egyezes kiejtes nelkul?*"

James stopped dead in his tracks, looked over each shoulder as if making sure no one was watching or listening. When he was secure that only Feingold could hear, he whispered a blue streak. Feingold gave the boy a long avuncular hug and, in the same foreign tongue with which the boy had whispered to him, told James to put his clothes back on, that his shower could wait. Dutifully, he did as the old man instructed, sitting himself down quietly on the cool tile floor. He told the boy not to worry, that he'd be right back, and closed the bathroom door behind him.

Mrs. McCabe was on her knees in the hallway, head upturned to the rafters, hands folded prayerfully. When she was done muttering, she turned to Feingold.

"How did you—What did you—"

"I asked his name, what it was in Yiddish, German, Dutch, and finally Hungarian."

"But he doesn't—"

"—speak Hungarian. He doesn't speak English, yes? He doesn't speak at all. He still does not, Mrs. McCabe."

"I don't understand."

"Why should you? How could such a person as you or your husband understand? The boy, your boy, is not speaking. At the moment, that is not your son, but a thirteen-year-old girl from Budapest named Magda Nagy whose father was teaching comparative literature at the University of Warsaw when the Nazis invaded. For her, it's nineteen forty-four. Less than an hour ago, her whole family got off the train at the gates of Auschwitz. Her father, mother, and older brother were taken away and she was sent for a delousing shower."

"That's crazy!"

"Crazy! You know what she asked, Magda? First, where her family had gone. Then, what hook number she should place her clothes on. That's what the bastards would tell the unfortunates before they herded them into the gas chambers and locked the steel doors behind them. 'Remember what hook number you placed your clothes on so you can retrieve them when you come out of the shower.' That's what they told them, these people you and your husband admire. She's not even a Jew, Magda."

Mrs. McCabe did not have the strength to argue. "But how did you know? Until you just now spoke to James—Magda, whoever, he, I mean, she didn't speak Hungarian. That was jibber-jabber coming out of my boy's mouth."

"Yes and no. It was Yiddish and German, Dutch and Hungarian, Polish and Russian, Romanian and ten other languages jumbled together, sometimes spoken backwards with no native accent. It was the languages of all the people what bodies became ashes and lampshades, soap and . . . It is the language of the smoke."

"But how did you know? How could you know?"

"That is my business alone. I am going in that bathroom now. And when I come out, maybe we will both have back something we lost: you only a few months ago, me a lifetime ago."

When Chaim Feingold stepped back into the bathroom and closed the door behind him, he stood up on the bathtub's edge. In the Yiddish of his youth, Feingold shouted as if above the din of a crowded room crammed with people, though only James McCabe was there to hear him.

"Is my sister, Shandel Feingold here? Shandel!" he called, hoping that the girl he had recognized on TV in the guise of James McCabe could be reached. "Shandela! Shandela!"

"Chaim! Chaim! Here, over here I am," she answered across time and space.

And for hours, the crooked old man held his long dead sister in his arms.

• • •

It was three more months before Peter McCabe was deemed well enough to come home. And when he arrived, he found a very different cabin and a very different family than the ones he had left. James had returned to his silence, but the opacity of his blue eyes was gone. You cannot have the dead speak through you and be unchanged. He was no longer a universe unto himself and had learned to indicate through gestures his likes and dislikes. Peter swore the boy almost smiled at him.

Mrs. McCabe had found the God she had run away from twenty years before. She went to church every day, asking forgiveness for herself and her husband. She had taken what was left of the money and donated it to the Holocaust Museum in Washington in the name of Magda Nagy. She sold most of their property to pay for her husband's rehab.

Still aphasic, McCabe asked his wife, "My 'hings, 'hat 'appened 'o my 'hings?"

"They're gone and we're never to speak of them again."

He grew very agitated, his arms flexing and shaking. Then she told him about Feingold and how he said James' jibber-jabber was the language of the smoke.

Peter McCabe began laughing wildly, crazily. His eyes got wide, his face red. Then he started choking, coughing. His wife was frantic not knowing what to do. Eventually, he settled back down, tears in the corners of his eyes.

"Lang'age a smoke." He shook his head. He didn't have the heart to tell his wife that he had made the soap himself and that the bottle of ashes had come from their own fireplace.

DOGGONE JUSTICE

Joe R. Lansdale

Things have changed. The world has evolved. A punch in the mouth ain't what it used to be.

Once you were more apt to settle your own problems, or have them settled for you, by an angry party. Teeth could be lost, and bones could be broken, but mostly you just got a black eye, a bloody nose, or you might be found temporarily unconscious, face down in a small pool of blood out back of a bar, with a shoe missing.

These days, even defending yourself can be tricky. It seems to me a butt-whipping in the name of justice has mutated to three shots from an automatic weapon at close quarters and three frames of bowling with your dead head. There are too many nuts with guns these days, and most of them just think the other guy is nuts. An armed society is a polite society only if those armed are polite. Otherwise, it just makes a fellow nervous.

Still, not wishing back the past. Not exactly. But there are elements of the past I do miss. There are times when I like the idea of settling your own hash—without gunfire. Sometimes the other guy has it coming.

When I was a kid in East Texas, we lived in a home that sat on a hill over-looking what was called a beer joint or honky-tonk. Beyond the tonk was a highway, and beyond that a drive-in theater standing as tall and white as a monstrous slice of Wonder Bread.

You could see the drive-in from our house, and from that hill my mother and I would watch the drive-in without sound. What I remember best were Warner Bros. cartoons. As we watched, mom would tell me what the cartoon characters were saying. Later, when I saw the cartoons on TV—something we didn't have at the time—I was shocked to discover Mom had made up the stories out of the visuals. My mom was a dad-burned liar. It was an early introduction to storytelling.

But this isn't storytelling. This is reporting, and what I'm about to tell you is real, and I was there. It's one of my first memories. So mixed up was the memory that, years later, when I was a grown man, I had to ask my mother if it was a dream, or fragments of memories shoved together. I had some things out of order, and I had mixed in an item or two, but my mother sorted them out for me. This is what happened.

My mother and I stayed at home nights while my dad was on the road, working on trucks. He was a mechanic and a troubleshooter for a truck company. My entertainment was my mother and that silent drive-in and the fist-fights that sometimes occurred in the honky-tonk parking lot, along with the colorful language I filed away for later use.

We were so poor that my dad used to say that if it cost a quarter to crap, we'd have to throw up. There wasn't money for a lot of toys, nor at that time a TV, which was a fairly newfangled instrument anyway. We listened to the radio when the tubes finally glowed and warmed up enough for us to bring in something.

Dad decided that the drive-in, seen through a window at a great distance, and a static-laden radio with a loose tube that if touched incorrectly would knock you across the room with a flash of light and a hiss like a spitting cobra, were not proper things for a growing boy. He thought I needed a friend.

Below, at the tonk, a dog delivered pups. Dad got me one. It was a small, fuzzy ball of dynamite. Dad named him Honky Tonk. I called him Blackie. I loved that dog so dearly that even writing about him now makes me emotional. We were like brothers. We drank out of the same bowl, when mom didn't catch us; and he slept in my bed, and we shared fleas. We had a large place to play, a small creek out back, and beyond that a junkyard of rusting cars full of broken glass and sharp metal and plenty of tetanus.

And there was the house.

It sat on a hill above the creek, higher than our house, surrounded by glowing red and yellow flowers immersed in dark beds of dirt. It was a beautiful sight, and on a fine spring day those flowers pulled me across that little creek and straight to them as surely as a siren calling to a mariner. Blackie came with me, tongue hanging out, his tail wagging. Life was great. We were as happy as if we had good sense and someone else's money.

I went up there to look, and Blackie, like any self-respecting dog, went there to dig in the flower bed. I was watching him do it, probably about to join in, when the door opened and a big man came out and snatched my puppy up by the hind legs and hit him across the back of the head with a pipe, or stick, and then, as if my dog were nothing more than a used condom, tossed him into the creek.

Then the man looked at me.

I figured I was next and bolted down the hill and across the creek to tell my mother. She had to use the next-door neighbor's phone, as this was long before everyone had one in their pocket. It seemed no sooner than she walked back home from making her call than my dad arrived like Mr. Death in our old black car.

He got out wearing greasy work clothes and told me to stay and started toward the House of Flowers. I didn't stay. I was devastated. I had been crying so hard my mother said I hiccupped when I breathed. I had to see what was about to happen. Dad went across the creek and to the back door and knocked gently, like a Girl Scout selling cookies. The door opened, and there was the Flower Man.

My dad hit him. It was a quick, straight punch and fast as a bee flies. Flower Man went down faster than a duck on a June bug, but without the satisfaction. He was out. He was hit so hard his ancestors in the prehistoric past fell out of a tree.

Dad grabbed him by the ankles and slung him through the flowerbed like a dull weed eater, mowed down all those flowers, even made a mess of the dirt. If Flower Man came awake during this process, he didn't let on. He knew it was best just to let Dad finish. It was a little bit like when a grizzly bear gets you; you just kind of have to go with it. When the flowers were flat, Dad swung the man by his ankles like a discus, and we watched him sail out and into the shallow creek with a sound akin to someone dropping wet laundry on cement.

We went down in the creek and found Blackie. He was still alive. Flower Man didn't move. He lay in the shallow water and was at that moment as much a part of that creek as the gravel at its bottom.

Daddy took Blackie home and treated his wound, a good knock on the noggin, and that dog survived until the age of 13. When I was 18, Blackie and I were standing on the edge of the porch watching the sun go down, and Blackie went stiff, flopped over the edge, dead for real this time.

Bless my daddy. We had our differences when I was growing up, and we didn't see eye to eye on many things. But he was my hero from that day after. Hardly a day goes by that I don't remember what he did that day, and how he made something so dark and dismal turn bright.

No one sued. Then, events like that were considered personal. To pull a lawyer into it was not only embarrassing, but just plain sissy. Today we'd be sued for the damage my dog did, the damage my dad did, and emotional distress, not to mention bandages and the laundry bill for the wet and dirty clothes.

I know the man loved his flowers. I know my dog did wrong, if not bad. I know I didn't give a damn at the time and thought about digging there myself. But I was a kid and Blackie was a pup, and if ever there was a little East Texas homespun justice delivered via a fast arm and a hard fist, that was it.

Flower Man, not long after that, moved away, slunk off like a carnival that owed bills. A little later we moved as well, shortly after the drive-in was wadded up by a tornado. That's another story.

THE OCCURRENCE OF THE BLACK MIRROR

Teel James Glenn

Prologue: Through a Glass Oddly

"It all started when I stepped through the mirror." The words were scrawled backwards on the looking glass in the middle of the blood soaked drawing room.

At the foot of it the mortal remains of Sir Algernon James Windwood, O.B.E., and secretary to the Prime Minister lie scattered like a jigsaw puzzle, a gory monument to a fierce struggle.

The furniture in the room, heavy upholstered and sturdy pieces, were splintered relics fit for little more than kindling.

"I've never seen anything like it, Inspector Lestrade," the uniformed Bobbie said. His pale skin was a sickly yellow and it was obvious he had trouble keeping his food down. The first constable at the scene had not been so lucky.

"I worked the Ripper case," the inspector said with a flat tone. "But this is just as bad for certain." The burly Lestrade crouched just out of reach of the nearly severed head of the victim and looked into the wide, terror filled orbs, now staring into the great beyond.

"I ain't seen such a look of unbridled horror on no one's face ever; I'll grant you that."

"What do you make of it?" The Bobbie asked. "An animal?"

The inspector stood and surveyed the carnage before them. "I have hunted tiger on the shore of the Ganges and Cape buffalo in Africa and this is worse than anything either beast could do."

The inspector glanced toward the French doors to the garden where the afternoon sunlight of suburban London was shining brightly. "I fail to see how not a single person at the lawn party heard any of this Donnybrooke."

The two stood for a long moment in silence while the experienced policeman let his eyes scan the room with intense scrutiny. He finally shifted his gaze to the elaborate looking glass that stood on a frame in the center of the room.

The mirror was held by two upright poles and framed by rich wood that was neither teak nor oak but shone brown and dark. It was carved with an intricate design that, at first looked abstract but on close inspection proved to be tiny human figures writhing in torment. So fine was the carving that the figures appeared to be wriggling in agony.

"It is this monstrosity and how it figures into all this that is as big a mystery as what killed Mister Windwood."

"Shall we put a call out for that Baker Street fellow, Inspector?"

The Bobbie did his best to ignore the scene around their feet and focused on his superior's face.

Lestrade leaned in to peer at the backward scrawled message on the glass of the mirror, knitting his thick eyebrows in concentration. "Hallo!" he exclaimed. He pulled a magnifying glass from his jacket pocket and examined the glass closely. "Check the back of this thing, constable," he said, "how is it fastened?"

"Tack and cloth, sir," the Bobbie said. "And it looks to have been on here a hundred years."

"Then I think our call should be to that Silver Fox," the inspector said. "It is more his bailiwick."

"Why do you say that, sir?"

"The blood spatter is on the front of the glass," Lestrade said. "But the words are written on the inside of the glass!"

Chapter One: The Doctor is Called

The 'Guv' was hanging upside down when the inspector from Scotland Yard came knocking on the door of our Carnaby Street headquarters.

"Mister Stone!" The mustachioed inspector was obviously surprised to see me so early in the morning at the residence when I opened the stout ebony door to greet him. "I think there is a situation that the Silver Fox needs to know about, is the Doctor at home?"

"Good to see you too, Inspector," I said with a smile. My morning cup of strong Turkish coffee was in my hand—a habit I picked up in service when I was stationed in Istanbul—and I was dressed in a smoking jacket and Fez atop my red hair.

"I am sorry, Mister Stone," the inspector said, "but it is a most urgent matter to see the Silver Fox." He held a large Gladstone bag in one hand and had a glowering expression on his long, raw-boned face. With the other hand he flashed a small shield shaped badge that I knew was the secret symbol of the Protectors, an age old order that both he, I and The Doctor belonged to. So it was far more than 'mere' police business that brought him hence, and it in some way involved a child.

Despite his brusque manner I smiled as I let the officer inside.

"The Doctor is inside," I said. "Follow me." I had gotten in late the night before from Edinburgh visiting my family and nothing was about to disrupt my good mood. My own lodgings were several streets away but was being repainted and not ready for me for another day so I slept on a couch in the Guv's parlour.

My cheerful manner did nothing to draw the Scotland Yard man from his glooming glowering but I sipped my coffee undeterred and led him into the converted stable that comprised the Guv's apartments.

My name is Jack Stone, late Captain of the Royal Horse Guard and for some time aid-de-camp to Doctor Augustus Argent, Minister Without-Portfolio to the Crown on matters of Occult Interest. It was a position he had held for many years—no one knew exactly how many—as he fought the forces of darkness to keep Albion safe for the light.

The Guv, as I call him, came into my life when my own sister was killed. It was Doctor Argent who discovered the killer to be a creature out of legends, a werewolf! He also saved my life. After that he became my mentor and employer and we had been involved in a number of unusual occurrences.

The residence was a large open space, converted from a stable with a parlour area, an office for my use, a laboratory for the Guv and fencing and pistol area to one side. The loft was where Doctor Argent had his sleeping area and beneath was his own office.

That morning Doctor Argent was suspended from a metal trapeze practicing some of the Eastern Yogic arts he had learned on his many travels around the world.

"Good morning, Detective Inspector," the Guv said from his odd position upside down. "Have you offered him some tea and jam, Jack?"

"No time for such amenities, Doctor, sir," the inspector said. "The Home Office agreed with me that you were the man to contact with this—uh—new occurrence."

"A new occurrence, eh?" Doctor Argent said. He nimbly swung down from the trapeze and landed as lightly on his bare feet as any ballet dancer.

The Guv was a tall and lean man who might have been a man of thirty hard years or sixty. He had long silver hair that hung to his shoulders and mustachios that together gave him the aspect of an American frontier hero. Most arresting about him, however, and the feature that gained him the nickname of 'the Silver Fox' was his emerald green and piercing eyes that were like twin lamps and proclaimed his superior and cunning intelligence. He strode across the exercise area and extended a long-fingered hand to the inspector to shake.

"It is most urgent, sir," Lestrade said. "And the Home Office felt, as I did, that this was something that neither Misters Carnacki nor Holmes were equipped to handle." He set the large valise on a chair and, with the gloomiest of expressions opened it.

Inside was a human head!

Even Doctor Argent recoiled noticeably, but not from the same shock as I.

"That is Jamie Windwood," the Guv said in a somber tone.

"You knew Sir Windwood?" Lestrade said, his solemn demeanor cracking to evidence surprise.

"Since he was a boy," the Guv said. "I was at his wedding to Virginia; coming as late as it was in his life it was a joyous occasion." He fixed the officer with his implacable stare. "Tell me how this happened while I dress."

And the inspector did, telling of the discovery of the mutilated corpse by his step-daughter coming in from the lawn affair. The girl's mother, Mrs. Virginia Windwood, the former Mrs. Hackett, was no where to be seen and was still missing. He told also of the unusual placement of the scrawled writing that so baffled him and caused the inspector to seek the Guv.

"And the young lady?" the Doctor asked as he emerged from his dressing room. He had dressed in a dark grey suit jacket and black trousers without a starched collar that gave him a theatrical air.

"She is under doctor's care at London Hospital on Whitechapel Road."

"We shall have to speak to her in due time," the Guv said, "but first we must try an Occularus Restorium spell on Jamie to see what he can tell us of his passing."

I shivered at the thought. It was grisly enough to have the severed head of the poor fellow in a bag before us but to engage in the occult activity that the Guv suggested—which I had witnessed once before—filled me with unease. It was an admix of old magicks and new science. It involved a spell from the Sigsand Manuscript from the fourteenth century, which would cause the poor fellow's head to 'return in time' to the moment before his death. Not actually to life, but the 'materials' of the flesh, hair and most importantly, the eyes were returned to the exact state they were in at just before life left them. Then, using Western science the last image on his pupils was photographed to record the reflection in them.

I set about assembling the photographic equipment that would be necessary while Doctor Argent and Lestrade took the head of the unfortunate man and set it on a table and rearranged some of the furniture and drew the drapes.

Once I set up the camera I left to prepare the dark room, preferring not to actually watch the procedure. I admit it, I would rather face a wall of Dervishes unarmed than have to witness the conjuring involved with the severed head. That Lestrade, normally a rather plodding and mundane investigator, had realized such a procedure could be performed and was able to assist was almost as much a mystery as the way Sir Windwood died.

I heard the chanting and smelled the incense while I poured the chemicals for the processing, recalling the intensity of the Guv's eyes when he did his spell work. It made me glad again that he was, as they say, fighting on the side of the angels.

In a short time the glass plate was brought in to me and I set about developing it and printing the image. I did several prints with different exposures to get the best results, then brought them out to the Guv, still wet.

What they showed was startling; a taloned hand was thrust out of that mirror at the face of the deceased Algernon James Windwood!

"This is even worse than I could have imagined," Doctor Argent said in a voice as cold as ice. "We must get to the Hospital to see Virginia's daughter post haste before some other horror occurs, her life is in gravest danger!"

Chapter Two: Fruit of the Tree

We took a hansom to London Hospital on the sound side of Whitechapel Road in Tower Hamlets. The young Miss Windwood had a private room on the top floor with a pair of Bobbies at the door who snapped to attention when they saw the detective inspector.

"Any change, Lewis?" Lestrade asked the older of the two guards.

"No sir," the man said. He had a slight North Country accent and bright blue eyes that proclaimed him as a sharp item. "The lass just sits and stares into the mirror on the dresser like it was the answer to all her problems and says 'papa' over and over again." The tough-looking constable looked like he was on the verge of tears at the thought of the young girl in such soul crushing pain.

"Thank you, Lewis." Lestrade took off his bowler and added, as we entered, "Why don't you and Jones get a spot of tea and a biscuit? We shall be with the young lady a quarter hour at least."

"Very good, sir." The Bobbies saluted and went off as we entered the room.

The sight that greeted us was heart wrenching; a young blonde girl of about fourteen was seated at a dresser across the spare room staring into the bureau mirror and rocking slowly back and forth.

The Guv removed his slouch hat and let his cape slip from his broad shoulders as he walked over to her.

"Eugenia," the silver-haired man said in as soft a voice as I have ever heard him speak, "It is Uncle Augustus."

The girl seemed to not notice the Guv until he touched a gentle hand to her shoulder, then she shifted her gaze—though still looked into the mirror—to look at Argent.

"Hello, Uncle Augustus."

"Do you know what happened to your father?"

"Daddy Windwood is dead," she said in a flat tone. Then she turned her eyes to stare into the mirror again. "I miss Mama."

Doctor Argent's eyes narrowed as he looked from the girl to the mirror to talk to her reflection. "Do you know where your mama is?"

"With Papa," she said.

Lestrade made a tiny gasp but quieted quickly at a look from Argent.

"And did you see her go with Papa?" Argent asked.

The girl shook her head. "But Papa said she was with him now."

"Papa said?"

"This morning," she said. "He told me he came back for her and now, now he will come back for me."

"This morning?" Doctor Argent asked.

"So I'm watching for him." She kept her eyes focused ahead into the mirror, apparently seeing something that was beyond our ability to see.

The Guv patted her on the shoulder then turned to us. "This is much more serious than I could have imagined, gentlemen. We must take drastic measures to assure this girl's safety. Jack, bring a ward nurse in and ask a doctor to bring a sedative."

I did not ask why, I just left and complied with the Doctor's orders. When I returned things in the room had changed; the girl was on her bed, strapped in and the mirror had been covered with a blanket.

"No, I have to wait for Papa!" the girl protested. "I have to see Mama!"

"Don't worry, Eugenia," the Guv said. "You will see her again, I promise, but you have to rest now." He waved the doctor over, whispered to him for a moment and then the physician administered a hypodermic needle to the struggling child. She was soon sleeping peacefully.

"I don't understand, Doctor Argent," Lestrade said. The policeman was savaging his bowler with thick, nervous fingers. "Why did you have the mirror covered?"

Instead of answering, the Guv threw on his cape and slouch hat and said, "Doctor, please keep this girl under sedation and have her monitored at all times. I will explain myself later. And by no means let anyone uncover that mirror!"

He moved to the door and the detective and I had little choice but to follow. We raced down the stairs, the lift not being fast enough for him. I had to all but run to keep up with his long legs.

"Where are we going, Doctor?" I asked.

He leapt into a hansom and instructed the driver to take us to the suburban home of the late Sir Windwood. "We have to see the scene of the crime directly and I must see something for myself."

"But what is it all about, sir?" Lestrade asked.

The occultist's eyes sparked with an inner fire as he said, "If my suppositions are correct we have come into a most monstrous affair and I fear there may be more deaths before this is done." And that was all he would say for the rest of the ride.

• • •

The body had been removed from the parlour of the Windwood residence but the blood remained. The police had left all the furniture as it had been found and even without the body it was very clear how violent the struggle had been.

The Guv went straight to the long looking glass that reflected the late morning light like a beacon across the stained carpet. He looked all around the edges of the mirror, examining the carvings with a magnifying glass with deep interest. He said nothing for several minutes while Lestrade and I stood almost holding our breath for fear of disturbing his concentration.

Finally he looked up at me and said, "Jack, what do you know of scrying?"

"Scrying?"

"Since the earliest of times witches, sorcerers, and soothsayers have used black mirrors for scrying: the divination of the future, communicating with spirits on other planes of existence or even over great distances." Doctor Argent's voice was edged with an urgency I had not heard before, a dark and ominous tone.

"But this mirror is not black," Lestrade said.

"A Black Mirror is not the only thing that can be used for scrying. It can be a puddle of water or a crystal ball or a piece of shiny metal. Even a regular mirror will work. And this is no regular mirror."

He kept his eyes on the glass as he spoke as if it were a snake that might come to life and attack us. I felt an eerie chill up my spine.

"How would Sir Windwood get such a thing?" Lestrade asked.

"Jamie was a collector of the odd all his life," the Guv said. "But this was a new acquisition, note the sales tag on the base."

"Is it a cursed item?" I asked. I had heard of such things, objects which some practitioner of the dark arts had tainted with their touch.

"These items have no power of their own," Doctor Argent said, "The crystals, the glass or the bowl of water are all used as a focal point for the sorcerer. They have no real magical power in and of themselves. At least initially. They do have magical energy after they have been consecrated for use and after they have been used a few times they will gather the magical energies of the user, but all in all it is the scryer who has the power to peer into the mirror."

We stepped from the room to the patio and the fresh air and sunlight never felt better after the dark and death-laden air of the room. Lestrade looked even paler than he had when he showed up at our door that morning.

"What can be done, Doctor Argent?"

"I will need your resources, Detective Inspector, to trace the lineage of that mirror; find where it was purchased and who owned it."

"Is it that important, Doctor?"

"Yes," the Guv said. "The Black Mirror is the window to the Universe and to the Spirit world. And it has the essence of its master and user in it. If we know who we may learn why."

"Why what?" I had to ask.

"Why Virginia Windwood was taken and perhaps where," Doctor Argent said.

"I'll get my men on it directly, sir," the inspector said and he went to talk to a Bobbie who was on guard.

Doctor Argent turned to me when Lestrade was out of earshot and said, "This is worse than I thought, Jack, there is something diabolical working here; I fear for Eugenia."

"The daughter?" I asked. "But she is guarded; surely whomever did this would not dare to make an attempt on her."

"Whoever did this would dare much, Jack," Argent said, "and could accomplish much. This mirror can bring visions of past lives or things that are to come. But it can show you answers to questions you may have or show you your spirit guides, for it is a doorway to the other side. But it does not do these things on its own. It was imbued with that ability by someone and that someone has Virginia Windwood."

"How do you know?"

"Why, Jack, did you not notice that the phrase 'It all started when I stepped through the mirror,' was written in the delicate hand of a woman? She is trapped in the mirror!"

Chapter Three: Black Reflections
Doctor Argent and I left a guard at the Windwood residence and went by carriage to our Carnaby Street base. At the Guv's instruction, the looking glass was kept covered with a tarpaulin.

"There is a reason the Hebrews and many other cultures cover their mirrors when a house is in mourning," he said as we sat to tea at his Carnaby Street residence and considered the looking glass. "They will say the primary reason is because prayer services take place there and one must ensure that no one faces a mirror during prayer. But there is an older reason, a darker one, Jack. They know that those mirrors can be a portal for demons to enter our realm."

I had come to accept the Guv's pronouncements as proven facts for I had seen so much outside the 'normal' world I had once found so comforting. I now knew that there were as many shadows as spots of light in the world and found my alliance with Doctor Argent had given me new purpose in combating those shadows.

Doctor Argent spent a few hours in his private library researching his next move while I did my best to keep my nerves calm. All the while I was aware of every looking glass in the room as if they were caged animals waiting to spring.

As evening approached Detective Inspector Lestrade knocked on the door again. When I let him in his expression was particularly grim.

"We have traced the mirror, Doctor Argent," he said, setting a folder of pages on one of the chairs. "And as I am a man to say coincidence does not happen, I have no explanation for it."

He took out a notebook and began to read, "The looking glass was purchased at Faversham and Bently's last month by Sir Windwood. Before that it had been in storage, acquired when a Hamford house was closed up six years ago."

"Hamford house?" I asked.

"Former home of Justin Hackett," Doctor Argent said. "Virginia Windwood was married to Hackett before Jamie. Hackett is Eugenia's real father."

"I see what you mean about coincidence, Inspector," I said. Then turned to the Guv. "That seems to make things simpler, then, Doctor. We just have to put a dragnet out for this Hackett chap."

"My first thought, Mister Stone," Lestrade said. "But there is a little problem with that. Justin Hackett was declared dead three years ago."

"What?"

"Yes, Jack," the Guv said. "Justin Hackett disappeared at Hamford house ten years ago and was presumed dead; it took all of Jamie's persuasion to have Virginia file the papers to have Hackett declared dead."

"Where does that leave us for suspects then?" I asked. "It seems too much of a coincidence for this mirror to come into their life at this point."

"Like the Inspector, Jack," Argent said, " I don't believe in coincidence either. But what—"

At that moment there was a frantic pounding on the front door. When I opened it an out of breath constable burst through.

"Detective Inspector," the Bobbie said. "The Windwood girl is gone from the hospital!"

"Gone?" Lestrade gasped. "What are you saying?"

"Near as we can figure when the nurse watching her went to the loo, the girl climbed out a window and along a ledge to another room. We searched the whole hospital but—"

"What a fool I've been!" Doctor Argent cried. "We have to head back to the Windwood house this instant! I should have realized it sooner—Eugenia always referred to Jamie as 'Daddy Windwood'—when she spoke at the hospital she said 'Papa' was coming back for her!" He grabbed his hat and cloak and said, "Justin Hackett has come back for his family!"

• • •

We raced across London again to the Windwood residence with Doctor Argent once more tight-lipped about his concerns, but with a palpable aura of concern about him that in anyone else would have been fear.

I felt it was fear, not for himself, but for the young girl and her mother.

When we leapt from the hansom in front of the Windwood house we were greeted by a confused Bobbie who stumbled toward us.

"Inspector!" the blond fellow muttered. "I was attacked!" There was a ribbon of blood on his forehead and he all but collapsed into Lestrade's arms. There was a knot growing on the side of his forehead above the blood and that told much of his story.

The Guv raced ahead and I followed, pulling my service revolver. We ran to the French doors from the patio where we discovered that the glass had been smashed in with a thrown bench. Doctor Argent raced through the gaping opening and I followed only to stop short in horror at what I saw.

In the center of the gory room, illuminated only by faint moonlight was the looking glass, uncovered and glowing as if from an inner light. The young Eugenia Windwood was literally melting into the mirror like a diver slipping into a calm lake.

The Guv ran across the room but reached the silvered reflective surface of the mirror just as the last of the girl slipped into and behind the glass.

I arrived just in time to see the girl, on the other side of the mirror, as if she were in another room, one just like the one we stood in, save that in that mirror room there was a golden morning light. The girl was not alone in this phantom room, but a large man in a long coat was leading the girl by her hand. They moved off from where we could see them in this other world but not before the girl looked over her shoulder, seemingly directly back at us with a broad smile on her face.

Then the mirror was suddenly a simple reflection of we two looking stunned and alone.

"We are too late," I said with deep bitterness.

Doctor Argent shook his head, "Never have that attitude, Jack; we will strive to hold back the dark as long as we have breath!" He immediately set about chalking symbols on the floor with sticks of colored chalk he had produced from the pocket of his velvet jacket.

"Fetch us candles, Jack," he ordered as he worked feverishly. "As many as you can!"

I set about to do that after informing Lestrade of what had transpired. The detective inspector had summoned more Bobbies who now guarded the outside of the house while we worked within.

When I returned to the parlour and began lighting the many candelabras around the looking glass in a wide circle the Guv had already created an elaborate series of symbols on the bloody wooden floor around the glass.

"This glass can be used for many different things in Magical Divination, Jack," he said to me. "One of them, in so-called 'High Magic', is the 'Triangle of Solomon' for conjuring the Demon or Celestial being into the mirror."

"Is it connected to the Solomon Doctrine?" I asked. The Doctrine was a spell created during the reign of Our Good Queen Elizabeth by a coven of witches and sorcerers that had kept England from being invaded wholesale by demonic attacks. It was the reason that the Spanish Armada had been sunk! It was still in effect, passed from monarch to monarch and always with a minister without portfolio such as Doctor Argent to advise them. (Once his position might well have been referred to as court sorcerer!) It prohibited the use of certain types of magic and wholesale sorcerers' attacks on English soil but required the Guv, and I, to be vigilant at all times as the world was rife with otherworldly menaces to the seat of the Empire.

"No, Jack," the Guv said in response to my question. He had doffed his jacket and rolled his sleeves up to reveal corded muscles of his forearms that were like the play of cables beneath his pale skin. "The Solomon Doctrine deals with attacks from without in our physical world, albeit from magical beings. In this case the demon spirit does not manifest into the physical form. It manifests as a vision in the mirror and allows us to see onto the astral plane and opens a doorway. A doorway whose threshold I must now cross."

"Cross?"

"Yes, Jack," he said with a deep sigh. "The only way I can hope to save Virginia and Eugenia is to enter the world on the other side of the mirror and fight Justin Hackett on his own ground!"

Chapter Four: Through the Glass Darkly

"But why can't I go with you?" I asked the Guv as he finished the chalking of symbols around the looking glass. He had just told me that his only means to save the Windwood women was to enter the mirror realm and face the enchanter who had trapped them.

"I can not prove it, Jack, not yet," he said as he stood before the looking glass. "But I believe that Justin Hackett performed this same ritual ten years ago, entered the looking glass and for whatever reason never came out. Now, by the darkest chance or perhaps some grand design, Jamie Windwood purchased the very glass and Hackett has stolen his former wife and daughter away!"

"That does not answer me," I insisted. "Why can I not go with you?"

"Jack, my friend," he said, putting a hand on my shoulder. "I need you here to guard the mirror. If we both go in and, for some reason it were damaged, we could never escape."

"Couldn't we come 'out' through some other mirror?"

"No, this portal is unique—indeed any mirror imbued with the aetheric energy of a specific enchanter is. He may see or even communicate through any mirror but only travel through this one."

I halted my objections and let the Guv get about his business. He recited a Latin phrase that I shall not repeat here and the looking glass began to cloud.

It was like morning dew on a windowpane save that it sparkled and shimmered with a ghostly light from within. The Guv looked back at me, his eyes seeming to shine with the same inner glow. "Watch, observe and pray, Jack," he said in a voice already strange, "I will be in his world now." Then he stepped forward and melted into the mirror.

It was like a man diving into a calm pool of water in slow motion as he stepped through the frame of the looking glass. His form changed as he did, in so much as the quality of light shifted and from the warm afternoon colors his body was now bathed in cool, sharp colors as if it were moonlight.

"Time is different in the mirror world," he had said during his last briefing of me before entering. "So watch and learn, in case you have to enter ... if I fail."

I tried not to deal with the ominous possibilities he spoke of, but it was clear that the 'day' within the mirror world had already passed and he was in a night-veiled place.

The room that I could see was not like the one I was in, but now my own reflection no longer registered, it was now more like a window than a mirror, instead it was a large, barn-like structure that was obviously the workroom of a sorcerer with objets d'occult all around. Doctor Argent moved in a liquid way, turning from the center of the room to face what must have been the door.

"Justin Hackett I presume?" the Guv asked. He drew himself up to his full height and looked like a royal.

"Why have you entered my domain?" a deep, almost rumbling voice asked in reply.

"You know why, Justin," Doctor Argent said. I could see his eye-line shift as he saw someone or something else enter, then a female voice spoke.

"Doctor Argent!" the voice said. "You saw my message and came for me!"

"Yes, Virginia," the Guv said. "I came for you and your daughter."

"She is my daughter," Hackett's voice boomed.

"Mine too, Justin," the woman said. She entered my field of vision now, a thin, blonde woman who in any other circumstance would have been pretty but now looked haggard and frightened. She went to stand beside Doctor Argent, coming barely to his shoulder that she leaned against as if she might fall from exhaustion if she did not. She turned to her husband and said, "You abandoned us!"

"I did not abandon you!" Hackett said. "I found my power and had to coalesce and grow it. 'Til now!" The mystic stepped into my line of view now and I was startled by his appearance.

The Justin Hackett I saw in the mirror was a twisted image of a man, more bestial than human with wide shoulders hunched under his long robe, a sloping brow and snarling, fanged mouth. His hair was long and blond and unkempt. His clothing, which I had first mistook for a coat looked to be some sort of dark blue robe incised with many mystical symbols.

"Hackett," the Guv said. "You are fooling yourself, your blind pursuit of occult power has blinded you to the value of the real things in the world."

Suddenly the sorcerer pulled the girl Eugenia into my field of vision. The teenager was obviously confused and her hair was almost as wild a tangle as her father's.

She looked from her father to her mother with clear confusion on her pretty features.

"Mama," she said in a weak voice, "Why is Papa so mean? Where is Daddy Windwood?"

Hackett pulled on the girl's arm and she winced. "You are never to mention his name again!" he said. He turned his feral face to look at Doctor Argent. "You get out, get out of my world!"

Suddenly he raised his hand and a blast of color flashed from his palm, staggering the Guv back as the color washed over him like a cascade from a cataract.

I felt so helpless, it was like I was watching a play through a window that I could not breach.

"Papa stop!" Eugenia called.

"Justin!" Virginia Windwood yelled.

"You will not take my world away from me!" Hackett cried. "I have worked too long, studied too hard!" He gestured again and a second burst of liquid color erupted from his hand and enveloped Doctor Argent in a rainbow aura of energy.

I actually pressed against the glass in an involuntary attempt to aid my mentor, but there was no helping him.

As I watched, the Guv began to change, physically change!

His lower limbs began to twist and stretch as if some invisible child was manipulating wet clay. Doctor Argent's face was twisted in pain and determination as he threw back a ball of light straight at Hackett.

The sorcerer staggered back, releasing Eugenia as he did, who ran to her mother's arms.

"Mama!" the girl cried.

Hackett laughed. "You can not fight me in my own world, Argent."

"You know me?" the Guv said through clenched teeth.

"I could see the world from any mirror," Hackett said. "I just could not rejoin it. After I entered this looking glass in my sanctum it was covered by a foolish servant who entered my room and threw a tarp over it and so inadvertently trapped me. It wasn't until that fool Windwood bought it that I knew the gods had arranged all this to allow me my freedom again, and finally I could have it all."

The Guv was in considerable discomfort but his expression remained resolute.

"You will be stopped, Hackett!" Doctor Argent hissed. I could see waves of energy blast off him to slam into a sort of invisible shell around the sorcerer.

Eugenia was screaming at her father to "stop it!" now with her mother trying to silence her.

"You are in my thrall now, Argent, in my world!" Hackett shouted. My helplessness seemed magnified by the glass as I watched my mentor and friend dance to the tune of the malignant sorcerer.

The two women looked on horrified but the sorcerer just laughed.

"Now you will dance to my command to show the world how I am the sorcerer supreme!" Hackett giggled like a schoolboy who had discovered a new dirty word. "Supreme sorcerer!" He repeated this several times.

I was beside myself with anger and unexpressed frustration at not being able to help my mentor.

In the mirror I could tell that time was progressing, for the lighting changed several times indicating that more than a full day of time had passed for those in the mirror realm. Doctor Argent's features became haggard from the effort as Hackett compelled him to circle the room again and again as a quadruped.

"Papa stop, please stop being mean!" the poor girl moaned.

"You have to toughen up, Eugenia dear," the mad sorcerer said. "We are going to be a very happy family but the world will always be at odds with us; I have seen that." His eyes shone with lambent insanity. "I have seen things, my child in this decade; viewed the powerful through their own mirrors, been privy to secrets—great secrets I will use to rise to great heights—and you will be the daughter of a great man."

"Justin, you can't do this," Virginia said. She clutched her daughter to her bosom while the girl sobbed softly. "I thought you had deserted me. I did."

"So you took up with that—that pompous Windwood!"

"You were gone six years when we met—"

"You should have known."

"How could I?"

"Enough!" Hackett screamed. His face was red with pique. "I will not be talked to that way!"

"Papa, stop hurting Uncle Augustus!" Eugenia sobbed.

The child's voice seemed to strike the mad sorcerer like a slap and he stopped and turned to her, a horrid expression on his face.

"You want me to stop 'hurting' this traitorous, duplicitous thing you call Uncle?" Hackett hissed. "All right, I will put this dumb brute out of his misery!"

The sorcerer produced a revolver from beneath his coat and cocked it.

Epilogue: Seeing the Light

"Papa, no!" Eugenia screamed.

Hackett slowly raised the pistol to aim at Doctor Argent's head, but the

Guv, still under the sorcerer's spell, could not move.

I had to do something, but I knew I could not physically enter the mirror realm in any way in time to help. I had a sudden inspiration as I watched the sorcerer take aim at him.

I grabbed a silver serving tray and a candle, using the tray to reflect the light into the mirror and the eyes of the mad sorcerer.

The effect of the reflected light was to make Hackett flinch as it lanced across his eyes, magnified, amazingly, I later learned, by the transition between realms.

The distraction gave the Guv the moment he needed to wrest himself from the power of the sorcerer's spell. Doctor Argent threw himself physically against Hackett hard enough to unbalance the man and then the sorcerer slammed against the glass of the mirror.

Suddenly Hackett fell partially through the looking glass!

I pounced and clamped myself on the sorcerer's upper torso that now hung out of the mirror's frame. I tried to grab the pistol but he fired off two shots close to my cheek, all but deafening me before I could pry it from his hand.

"Get out, Virginia!" Doctor Argent called to the horrified woman and her daughter.

"No!" Hackett snarled as we wrestled.

The sorcerer's strength was enormous, truly the strength of the mad. I felt as if I had grabbed a wild lion. He continued to curse at me in impotent rage while hanging partway out of the mirror.

I felt as if I had grabbed a whirlwind with the sorcerer's hands like vice grips as he clawed at my throat in an attempt to free himself.

While we struggled, the two women climbed out of the mirror over our pinned forms and Doctor Argent held the sorcerer's legs so he could not get leverage.

The women tumbled out but this only caused Hackett to renew his struggles and become more violent.

"Jack!" Doctor Argent called to me, "When I tell you, let go of him."

"No," I yelled back. "You have to get out first."

"There is no way, boy," the Guv said. "Do as I say; you have to do this. It is what we have to do to contain Hackett."

I knew he was right but hated to admit it.

Hackett knew it as well and now struggled even harder to break my grip and escape the mirror realm.

"Now!" Doctor Argent yelled and I let go of the sorcerer but now he grabbed onto me and tried to drag me into the mirror with him.

"No!" Hackett said, " I will not go back. I want to feel the sun on my face again!"

He even tried to bite me to get a hold but with a Herculean effort I heaved him off of me and the Guv dragged him back through the frame.

I rolled to my feet as Doctor Argent and the sorcerer came to grips.

Now Hackett fought like a whirlwind gone mad, his clenched hands clawing at Doctor Argent and leaving gouges of flesh in their wake.

The Silver Fox however was not going to allow the sorcerer to gain the upper hand by physical means any more than he had magical, and gave as good as he got with some of the boxing I had taught him.

He also used some of the strange arts he had learned in Asia that allowed him to toss Hackett off his feet as he charged.

Doctor Argent immediately spun on his heels as Hackett hit the ground and leapt through the mirror. I tore a curtain from the French windows and threw it over the looking glass to cut off all light from the reflective surface.

Just before it was completely covered I heard the sorcerer yell, "Please not again," then all went silent.

Doctor Argent looked at me, blood dripping from the finger marks on his cheek and smiled. "Well done, Jack," he said. "You have a bit of matador in you, I see!"

• • •

We wrapped the mirror in a tarp so that no light could ever reach it and took it to the Guv's residence on Carnaby Street. There it would remain until a moonless night, when the Guv would paint the glass black with paint making sure that Hackett could never escape.

Until then I cannot look into a mirror without thinking of who, or what might be on the other side of it, watching me.

SISTER CECILIA

Hilary Davidson

When dealing with people, it helps to remember that humans are monkeys, and monkeys are assholes. There's no gratitude in them. You help them out and they take and take and take with one hand, while flinging shit at you with the other.

Case in point: a while back, I'm crossing the street against the light at Fifty-Fourth and Madison, and this broad wobbles after me, eyes glued to her phone like Satan himself is sending her dick pics. And this big black SUV that should have its own zip code is bearing down on us like a bat outta hell, determined to get through *this* light so it can get caught at a red at the next. Hey, I'm a New York City lifer, Bronx-born and -raised, and I can take care of myself. But Little Miss I-Can't-Be-Bothered-to-Step-Faster-Than-a-Turtle is gonna get creamed. You don't need to call the psychic hotline to see that. So I jump back and shove her outta the way. The SUV screeches past so fast it blows my hair back.

"That was close," I tell the broad.

"You cracked my screen!" she screams at me. Then she flags down a cop and tries to get me arrested for breaking her phone.

I don't know why I bother.

Scratch that. I *do* know. When I was a kid, I was something of a hellion, and my ma tossed me into a school run by the meanest, toughest gang of nuns you ever met. They were the kind who rapped you on the knuckles with a metal ruler just like they're sayin' *How ya doing? Those wounds I gave you this morning seem to be healing. Time for some more. And when you feel like bitching, remember Jesus died on the cross for you.*

Sister Cecilia was the worst. She had some kind of built-in radar that let her hone in on you just as you were pulling some shit you knew you weren't supposed to do. One day she caught me packing a snowball around a rock I'd carefully chosen to smash Bobby Krudnik's head with. Sister Cecilia smacked me hard, then dragged me by the ear inside.

"What do you think you're doing?" she demanded.

"Nothing."

"You think I'm blind, you little runt?"

Sister Cecilia had pale blue irises that looked like somebody packed gauze over them. I didn't know how she could see much of anything, but she missed nothing.

"I was gonna throw it at Bobby Krudnik," I admitted.

"That little beast," the Sister muttered. "Heaven help me, but nobody deserves their head split open like that kid."

"He beat me up yesterday. I'd saved up money to go to the movies, and he took it." Might as well rat myself out fully, I figured. Talking to a nun was as good as confession, and she was gonna beat me anyway.

"No movies for you." She rapped my hand with a ruler, but her heart wasn't in it. "You know what the problem is? You can't throw a rock at Bobby Krudnik's head to get revenge." She shook her head slowly. "*Avenge not yourselves, but rather give place unto wrath: for it is written, Vengeance is mine; I will repay, saith the Lord*. That's from Romans."

"But he *stole*."

"Listen, kid, there's damn all you can do about that. But I'll tell you something. You keep an eye on Bobby Krudnik. You see him roughing up another kid, or stealing, *then* you throw this rock at his head."

"What?" I sniffed the air, wondering if Sister Cecilia had been drinking.

"Then it's not vengeance. You're some other kid's hero. *Warn them that are unruly, comfort the feebleminded, support the weak*. That's from Thessalonians."

She let me go with only one more rap on the knuckles, which made me wonder if she was going soft. Especially because she let me keep the rock. A couple days later, I used it on Bobby Krudnik when he was waling on a kid from the slow learners' class.

You know what? It felt good. Like I'd made a difference somehow. The best part was, I was able to run off before anyone figured out it was me. Sister Cecilia knew, but she never ratted me out. A week later, when Bobby Krudnik finally got out of the hospital, she said to me, "Think of all the harm he would've caused this week."

It was a difference that kept paying off, since Bobby Krudnik came back to school with a weird twitch and he wasn't so steady on his feet anymore. I never forgot that. I'd saved a kid from a beating. A whole bunch of kids, when you thought about it. All the shit that no-good lowlife was going to pull? It was on me that he never pulled it. I'm not saying I deserve angel wings, but I feel like at least I'm on this earth with some purpose, you know?

So I try to do what I can. New York in the '70s and '80s was a hard, hard place. My best friend was a switchblade, and we went out together a lot. But the city started to soften up. Then there was the attack on 9/11, and I swear, for years, I didn't want to go near nobody. You'd see some greasy-looking hood in need of a beatdown, and next thing you knew he was crying on account of him losing somebody on that day.

The funny thing is, as I got older, and arthritis really sank into my joints, the pendulum started swinging the other way. Not because punks were back. But this whole generation of kids started taking over the city. I don't mean kid-kids, I'm taking about twenty-five-year-olds who know as much about the world as newborns. They live off their parents' money, and they wander through the city like it's Candyland, only they're not paying attention to where they are, they're staring at their fucking phones. Nothing bad has ever happened to them, so they don't have the imagination to see what could be waiting for them around the corner.

That's why I started picking up rocks again.

The first time was a week after that turtle on stiletto stilts bawled me out. I was on the Upper East Side, and there's this guy who walks right into a mailbox. I mean, it's not like the mailbox jumped out at him, you know? I figured he was drunk, but then I see it's worse than that. He's staring at this little glowing screen in his hand so hard, there could be a fire-breathing dragon in front of him and he wouldn't swerve. So I pick up a rock out of one of those fancy little flowerbeds they have up around there, and I bring it down hard on the back of his head. Well, that does it. This kid drops like a sack of potatoes. I walk on, feeling a little bad for him, because that kid probably wasn't one of the Bobby Krudniks of the world. But he was strutting around like a fool, completely unawares. I was willing to bet my life he'd never do that again.

I got into the habit of going for a walk once a week—twice, if my arthritis lets me—to look for people who needed my help. They didn't know it, of course. They're content in their fool's paradise, with never a thought on how they're setting themselves up to be mugged or worse. *Warn them that are unruly*, Sister Cecilia told me, and I took it to heart.

It's a good thing I'm not looking for thanks, 'cause no one ever gives it. I mean, who wants to admit they're so fucking stupid some stranger has to pound sense into them with a rock? Sometimes people scream at me. I let it slide off my back. *Why do I bother?* I ask myself all the time. But the truth is, I like to think I'm somebody's hero, even if they don't know it.

CROATOAN

Harlan Ellison®

Beneath the city, there is yet another city: wet and dark and strange; a city of sewers and moist scuttling creatures and running rivers so desperate to be free not even Styx fits them. And in that lost city beneath the city, I found the child.

Oh my God, if I knew where to start. With the child? No, before that. With the alligators? No, earlier. With Carol? Probably. It always started with a Carol. Or an Andrea. A Stephanie. Always someone. There is nothing cowardly about suicide; it takes determination.

• • •

"Stop it! Godammit, just *stop* it... I said stop..." And I had to hit her. It wasn't that hard a crack, but she had been weaving, moving, stumbling: she went over the coffee table, all the fifty-dollar gift books coming down on top of her. Wedged between the sofa and the overturned table. I kicked the table out of the way and bent to help her up, but she grabbed me by the waist and pulled me down; crying, begging me to *do* something. I held her and put my face in her hair and tried to say something right, but what could I say?

Denise and Joanna had left, taking the d&c tools with them. She had been quiet, almost as though stunned by the hammer, after they had scraped her. Quiet, stunned, dry-eyed but hollow-eyed; watching me with the plastic Baggie. The sound of the toilet flushing had brought her running from the kitchen, where she had lain on a mattress pad. I heard her coming, screaming, and caught her just as she started through the hall to the bathroom. And hit her, without wanting to, just trying to stop her as the water sucked the Baggie down and away.

"D-*do* somethi-ing," she gasped, fighting for air.

I kept saying Carol, Carol, over and over, holding her, rocking back and forth, staring over her head, across the living room to the kitchen, where the edge of the teak dining table showed through the doorway, the amber-stained mattress pad hanging half over the edge, pulled loose when Carol had come for the Baggie.

After a few minutes, she spiraled down into dry, sandpapered sighs. I lifted her onto the sofa, and she looked up at me.

"Go after him, Gabe. Please. Please, go after him."

"Come on, Carol, stop it. I feel lousy about it . . . "

"*Go after him, you sonofabitch!*" she screamed. Veins stood out on her temples.

"I can't go after him, dammit, he's in the plumbing; he's in the fucking river by now! Stop it, get off my case, let me alone!" I was screaming back at her.

She found a place where untapped tears waited, and I sat there, across from the sofa, for almost half an hour, just the one lamp casting a dull glow across the living room, my hands clasped down between my knees, wishing she was dead, wishing I was dead, wishing everyone was dead . . . except the kid. But. He was the only one who was dead. Flushed. Bagged and flushed. Dead.

When she looked up at me again, a shadow cutting off the lower part of her face so the words emerged from darkness, keynoted only by the eyes, she said, "Go find him." I had never heard anyone sound that way, ever. Not ever. It frightened me. Riptides beneath the surface of her words created trembling images of shadow women drinking Drano, lying with their heads inside gas ovens, floating face up in thick, red bath water, their hair rippling out like jellyfish.

I knew she would do it. I couldn't support that knowledge. "I'll try," I said.

She watched me from the sofa as I left the apartment, and standing against the wall in the elevator, I felt her eyes on me. When I reached the street, still and cold in the predawn, I thought I would walk down to the River Drive and mark time till I could return and console her with the lie that I had tried but failed.

But she was standing in the window, staring down at me.

The manhole cover was almost directly across from me, there in the middle of the silent street. I looked from the manhole cover to the window, and back again, and again, and again. She waited. Watching. I went to the iron cover and got down on one knee and tried to pry it up. Impossible. I bloodied my fingertips trying, and finally stood, thinking I had satisfied her. I took one step toward the building and realized she was no longer in the window. She stood silently at the curb, holding the long metal rod that wedged against the apartment door when the police lock was engaged.

I went to her and looked into her face. She knew what I was asking: I was asking, *Isn't this enough? Haven't I done enough?*

She held out the rod. No, I hadn't done enough.

I took the heavy metal rod and levered up the manhole cover. It moved with difficulty, and I strained to pry it off the hole. When it fell, it made a clanging in the street that rose up among the apartment buildings with an alarming suddenness. I had to push it aside with both hands; and when I looked up from that perfect circle of darkness that lay waiting, and turned to the spot where she had given me the tool, she was gone.

I looked up; she was back in the window.

The smell of the unwashed city drifted up from the manhole, chill and condemned. The tiny hairs in my nose tried to baffle it; I turned my head away.

I never wanted to be an attorney. I wanted to work on a cattle ranch. But there was family money, and the need to prove myself to shadows who had been dead and buried with their owners long since. People seldom do what they want to do; they usually do what they are *compelled* to do. Stop me before I kill again. There was no rational reason for my descending into that charnel house stink, that moist darkness. No rational reason, but Denise and Joanna from the Abortion Center had been friends of mine for eleven years. We had been in bed together many times; long past the time I had enjoyed being in bed together with them, or they had enjoyed being in bed together with me. They knew it. I knew it. They knew I knew, and they continued to set that as one of the payments for their attendance at my Carols, my Andreas, my Stephanies. It was their way of getting even. They liked me, despite themselves, but they had to get even. Get even for their various attendances over eleven years, the first of which had been one for the other, I don't remember which. Get even for many flushings of the toilet. There was no rational reason for going down into the sewers. None.

But there were eyes on me from an apartment window.

I crouched, dropped my legs over the lip of the open manhole, sat on the street for a moment, then slipped over the edge and began to climb down.

Slipping into an open grave. The smell of the earth is there, where there is no earth. The water is evil; vital fluid that has been endlessly violated. Everything is covered with a green scum that glows faintly in the darkness. An open grave waiting patiently for the corpse of the city to fall.

I stood on the ledge above the rushing tide, sensing the sodden weight of lost and discarded life that rode the waters toward even darker depths. *My God*, I thought, *I must be out of my mind just to be here.* It had finally overtaken me; the years of casual liaisons, careless lies, the guilt I suppose I'd *always* known would mount up till it could no longer be denied. And I was down here, where I belonged.

People do what they are compelled to do.

I started walking toward the arching passageway that led down and away from the steel ladder and the street opening above. Why not walk: aimless, can you perceive what I'm saying?

Once, years ago, I had an affair with my junior partner's wife. Jerry never knew about it. They're divorced now. I don't think he ever found out; she would have had to've been even crazier than I thought to tell him. Denise and Joanna had visited that time, too. I'm nothing if not potent. We flew to Kentucky together one weekend. I was preparing a brief, she met me at the terminal, we flew as husband and wife, family rate. When my work was done in Louisville, we drove out into the countryside. I minored in geology at college, before I went into law. Kentucky is rife with caves. We pulled in at a picnic grounds where some locals had advised us we could do a little spelunking, and with the minimal gear we had picked up at a sporting goods shop, we went into a fine network of chambers, descending beneath the hills and the picnic grounds. I loved the darkness, the even temperature, the smooth-surfaced rivers, the blind fish and water insects that scurried across the wet mirror of the still pools. She had come because she was not permitted to have intercourse at the base of Father Duffy's statue on Times Square, in the main window of Bloomingdale's, or on Channel 2 directly preceding *The Late News*. Caves were the next best thing. For my part, the thrill of winding down deeper and deeper into the earth—even though graffiti and Dr. Pepper cans all along the way reminded me this was hardly unexplored territory—offset even her (sophomoric) appeals to "take her violently," there on the shell-strewn beach of a subterranean river.

I liked the feel of the entire Earth over me. I was not claustrophobic, I was—in some perverse way—wonderfully free. Even soaring! Under the ground, I was soaring!

The walk deeper into the sewer system did not unsettle or distress me. I rather enjoyed being alone. The smell was terrible, but terrible in a way I had not expected.

If I had expected vomit and garbage, this was certainly not what I smelled. Instead, there was a bittersweet scent of rot—reminiscent of Florida mangrove swamps. There was the smell of cinnamon, and wallpaper paste, and charred rubber; the warm odors of rodent blood and bog gas; melted cardboard, wool, coffee grounds still aromatic, rust.

The downward channel leveled out. The ledge became a wide, flat plain as the water went down through drainage conduits, leaving only a bubbling, frothy residue to sweep away into the darkness. It barely covered the heels of my shoes. Florsheims, but they could take it. I kept moving. Then I saw the light ahead of me.

It was dim, flickering, vanished for a moment as something obscured it from my view, moving in front of it, back again, dim and orange. I moved toward the light.

It was a commune of bindlestiffs, derelicts gathered together beneath the streets for safety and the skeleton of camaraderie. Five very old men in heavy overcoats and three even older men in castoff army jackets . . . but the older men were younger, they only *looked* older: a condition of the skids. They sat around a waste barrel oil drum filled with fire. Dim, soft, withered fire that leaped and curled and threw off sparks all in slow motion. Dreamwalking fire; somnambulist fire; mesmerized fire. I saw an atrophied arm of flame like a creeper of kangaroo ivy emerge over the lip of the barrel, struggling toward the shadowed arch of the tunnel ceiling; it stretched itself thin, released a single, teardrop-shaped spark, and then fell back into the barrel without a scream.

The hunkering men watched me come toward them. One of them said something, directly into the ear of the man beside him; he moved his lips very little and never took his eyes off me. As I neared, the men stirred expectantly. One of them reached into a deep pocket of his overcoat for something bulky. I stopped and looked at them.

They looked at the heavy iron rod Carol had given me.

They wanted what I had, if they could get it.

I wasn't afraid. I was under the Earth and I was part iron rod. They could not get what I had. They knew it. That's why there are always fewer killings than there might be. People *always* know.

I crossed to the other side of the channel, close to the wall. Watching them carefully. One of them, perhaps strong himself, perhaps merely stupider, stood up and, thrusting his hands deeper into his overcoat pockets, paralleled my passage down the channel away from them.

The channel continued to descend slightly, and we walked away from the oil drum and the light from the fire and the tired community of subterranean castoffs. I wondered idly when he would make his move, but I wasn't worried. He watched me, trying to see me more clearly, it seemed, as we descended deeper into the darkness. And as the light receded he moved up closer, but didn't cross the channel. I turned the bend first.

Waiting, I heard the sounds of rats in their nests.

He didn't come around the bend.

I found myself beside a service niche in the tunnel wall, and stepped back into it. He came around the bend, on my side of the channel. I could have stepped out as he passed my hiding place, could have clubbed him to death with the iron rod before he realized that the stalker had become the stalked.

I did nothing, stayed far back motionless in the niche and let him pass. Standing there, my back to the slimy wall, listening to the darkness around me, utter, final, even palpable. But for the tiny twittering sounds of rats I could have been two miles down in the central chamber of some lost cavern maze.

There's no logic to why it happened. At first, Carol had been just another casual liaison, another bright mind to touch, another witty personality to enjoy, another fine and workable body to work so fine with mine. I grow bored quickly. It's not a sense of humor I seek—lord knows every slithering, hopping, crawling member of the animal kingdom has a sense of humor—for Christ sake even dogs and *cats* have a sense of humor—it's wit! Wit is the answer. Let me touch a woman with wit and I'm gone, sold on the spot. I said to her, the first time I met her, at a support luncheon for the Liberal candidate for D.A., "Do you fool around?"

"I don't fool," she said instantly, no time-lapse, no need for rehearsal, fresh out of her mind, "fools bore me. Are you a fool?"

I was delighted and floored at the same time. I went fumfuh-fumfuh, and she didn't give me a moment. "A simple yes or no will suffice. Answer this one: how many sides are there to a round building?"

I started to laugh. She watched me with amusement, and for the first time in my life I actually saw someone's eyes twinkle with mischief. "I don't know," I said, "how many sides *are* there to a round building?"

"Two," she answered, "*inside* and *outside*. I guess you're a fool. No, you may not take me to bed." And she walked away.

I was undone. She couldn't have run it better if she had come back two minutes in a time machine, knowing what I'd say, and programmed me into it. And so I chased her. Up hill and down dale, all around that damned dreary luncheon, till I finally herded her into a corner—which was precisely what she'd been going for.

"As Bogart said to Mary Astor, 'You're good, shweetheart, very very good.'" I said it fast, for fear she'd start running me around again. She settled against the wall, a martini in her hand; and she looked up at me with that twinkling.

At first it was just casual. But she had depth, she had wiliness, she had such an air of self-possession that it was inevitable I would start phasing-out the other women, would start according her the attention she needed and wanted and without demanding . . . demanded.

I came to care.

Why didn't I take precautions? Again, there's no logic to it. I thought she was; and for a while, she was. Then she stopped. She told me she had stopped, something internal, the gynecologist had suggested she go off the pill for a while. She suggested vasectomy to me. I chose to ignore the suggestion. But chose not to stop sleeping with her.

When I called Denise and Joanna, and told them Carol was pregnant, they sighed and I could see them shaking their heads sadly. They said they considered me a public menace, but told me to tell her to come down to the Abortion Center and they would put the suction pump to work. I told them, hesitantly, that it had gone too long, suction wouldn't work. Joanna simply snarled, "You thoughtless cocksucker!" and hung up the extension. Denise read me the riot act for twenty minutes. She didn't suggest a vasectomy; she suggested, in graphic detail, how I might have my organ removed by a taxidermist using a cheese grater. Without benefit of anesthesia.

But they came, with their dilation and curettage implements, and they laid her out on the teak table with a mattress under her, and then they had gone—Joanna pausing a moment at the door to advise me this was the last time, the last time, the very last time she could stomach it, that it was the last time and did I have that fixed firmly, solidly, imbedded in the forefront of my brain? The last time.

And now I was here in the sewers.

I tried to remember what Carol looked like, but it wasn't an image I could fix in my mind half as solidly as I had fixed the thought that this. Was. The. Last. Time.

I stepped out of the service niche.

The young-old bindlestiff who had followed me was standing there, silently waiting. At first I couldn't even see him—there was only the vaguest lighter shade of darkness to my left, coming from around the bend and that oil drum full of fire—but I knew he was there. Even as *he* had known I was there, all the time. He didn't speak, and I didn't speak, and after a while I was able to discern his shape. Hands still deep in his pockets.

"Something?" I said, more than a little belligerently.

He didn't answer.

"Get out of my way."

He stared at me, sorrowfully, I thought, but that had to be nonsense. I thought.

"Don't make me have to hurt you," I said.

He stepped aside, still watching me.

I started to move past him, down the channel.

He didn't follow, but I was walking backward to keep him in sight, and he didn't take his eyes off mine.

I stopped. "What do you want?" I asked. "Do you need some money?"

He came toward me. Inexplicably, I wasn't afraid he would try something. He wanted to see me more clearly, closer. I thought.

"You couldn't give me nothing I need." His voice was rusted, pitted, scarred, unused, unwieldy.

"Then why are you following me?"

"Why've you come down here?"

I didn't know what to say.

"You make it bad down here, mister. Why don't you g'wan and go back upside, leave us alone?"

"I have a right to be here." Why had I said *that?*

"You got no right to come down here; stay back upside where you belong. All of us know you make it bad, mister."

He didn't want to hurt me, he just didn't want me here. Not even right for these outcasts, the lowest level to which men could sink; even here I was beneath contempt. His hands were deep in his pockets. "Take your hands out of your pockets, slowly, I want to make sure you aren't going to hit me with something when I turn around. Because I'm going on down there, not back. Come on now, do it. Slowly. Carefully."

He took his hands out of his pockets slowly, and held them up. He had no hands. Chewed stumps, glowing faintly green like the walls where I had descended from the manhole.

I turned and went away from him.

It grew warmer, and the phosphorescent green slime on the walls gave some light. I had descended as the channel had fallen away deeper under the city. This was a land not even the noble streetworkers knew, a land blasted by silence and emptiness. Stone above and below and around, it carried the river without a name into the depths, and if I could not return, I would stay here like the skids. Yet I continued walking. Sometimes I cried, but I don't know why, or for what, or for whom. Certainly not for myself.

Was there ever a man who had everything more than I had had everything? Bright words, and quick movements, soft cloth next to my skin, and places to place my love, if I had only recognized that it *was* love.

I heard a nest of rats squealing as something attacked them, and I was drawn to a side tunnel where the shining green effluvium made everything bright and dark as the view inside the machines they used to have in shoe stores. I hadn't thought of that in years. Until they found out that the X-rays could damage the feet of children, shoe stores used bulky machines one stepped up onto, and into which one inserted newly shod feet. And when the button was pushed a green X-ray light came on, showing the bones that lay beneath the flesh. Green and black. The light was green, and the bones were dusty black. I hadn't thought of that in years, but the side tunnel was illuminated in just that way.

An alligator was ripping the throats of baby rats.

It had invaded the nest and was feeding mercilessly, tossing the bodies of the ripped and shredded rodents aside as it went for the defenseless smaller ones. I stood watching, sickened but fascinated. Then, when the shrieks of anguish were extinguished at last, the great saurian, direct lineal descendant of Rex, snapped them up one by one and, thrashing its tail, turned to stare at me.

He had no hands. Chewed stumps, glowing faintly green like the walls.

I moved back against the wall of the side tunnel as the alligator belly-crawled past me, dragging its leash. The thick, armored tail brushed my ankle and I stiffened.

Its eyes glowed red as those of an Inquisition torturer.

I watched its scaled and taloned feet leave deep prints in the muck underfoot, and I followed the beast, its trail clearly marked by the impression of the leash in the mud.

Frances had a five-year-old daughter. She took the little girl for a vacation to Miami Beach one year. I flew down for a few days. We went to a Seminole village, where the old women did their sewing on Singer machines. I thought that was sad. A lost heritage, perhaps; I don't know. The daughter, whose name I can't recall, wanted a baby alligator. Cute. We brought it back on the plane in a cardboard box with air holes. Less than a month later it had grown large enough to snap. Its teeth weren't that long, but it snapped. It was saying: this is what I'll be: direct lineal descendant of Rex. Frances flushed it down the toilet one night after we'd made love. The little girl was asleep in the next room. The next morning, Frances told her the alligator had run off.

The sewers of the city are infested with full-grown alligators. No amount of precaution and no forays by hunting teams with rifles or crossbows or flame throwers have been able to clear the tunnels. The sewers are still infested; workers go carefully. So did I.

The alligator moved steadily, graceful in its slithering passage down one tunnel and into another side passage and down always down, steadily into the depths. I followed the trail of the leash.

We came to a pool and it slid into the water like oil, its dead-log snout above the fetid foulness, its Torquemada eyes looking toward its destination.

I thrust the iron rod down my pant leg, pulled my belt tight enough to hold it, and waded into the water. It came up to my neck and I lay out and began dog-paddling, using the one leg that would bend. The light was very green and sharp now.

The saurian came out on the muck beach at the other side and crawled forward toward an opening in the tunnel wall. I crawled out, pulled the iron rod loose, and followed. The opening gave into darkness, but as I passed through, I trailed my hand across the wall and felt a door. I stopped, surprised, and felt in the darkness. An iron door, with an arched closure at the top and a latch. Studs, heavy and round and smelling faintly of rust, dotted the door.

I walked through . . . and stopped.

There had been something else on the door. I stepped back and ran my fingers over the open door again. I found the indentations at once, and ran my fingertips across them, trying to discern in the utter darkness what they were. Something about them . . . I traced them carefully.

They were letters. **C**. My fingers followed the curves. **R**. Cut into the iron somehow. **O**. What was a door doing down here? **A**. The cuts seemed very old, weathered, scummy. **T**. They were large and very regular. **O**. They made no sense, no word formed that I knew. **A**. And I came to the end of the sequence. **N**.

CROATOAN. It made no sense. I stayed there a moment, trying to decide if it was a word the sanitation engineers might have used for some designation of a storage area perhaps. Croatoan. No sense. Not Croatian, it was Croatoan. Something nibbled at the back of my memory: I *had* heard the word before, knew it from somewhere, long ago, a vapor of sound traveling back on the wind of the past. It escaped me, I had no idea what it meant.

I went through the doorway again.

Now I could not even see the trail of the leash the alligator had dragged. I kept moving, the iron rod in my hand.

I heard them coming toward me from both sides, and it was clearly alligators, many of them. From side passages. I stopped and reached out to find the wall of the channel. I couldn't find it. I turned around, hoping to get back to the door, but when I hurried back the way I thought I had come, I didn't reach the door. I just kept going. Either I had gone down a fork and not realized the channel had separated, or I had lost my sense of direction. And the slithering sounds kept coming.

Now for the first time, I felt terror! The safe, warm, enfolding darkness of the underworld had, in an instant, merely by the addition of sounds around me, become a suffocating winding-sheet. It was as if I'd abruptly awakened in a coffin, buried six feet beneath the tightly stomped loam; that clogging terror Poe had always described so well because he had feared it himself... the premature burial. Caves no longer seemed comfortable.

I began to run!

I lost the rod somewhere, the iron bar that had been my weapon, my security.

I fell and slid face first in the muck.

I scrabbled to my knees and kept going. No walls, no light, no slightest aperture or outcropping, nothing to give me a sense of being in the world, running through a limbo without beginning, without end.

Finally, exhausted, I slipped and fell and lay for a moment. I heard slithering all around me and managed to pull myself to a sitting position. My back grazed a wall, and I fell up against it with a moan of gratitude. Something, at least; a wall against which to die.

I don't know haw long I lay there, waiting for the teeth.

Then I felt something touching my hand. I recoiled with a shriek! It had been cold and dry and soft. Did I recall that snakes and other amphibians were cool and dry? Did I remember that? I was trembling.

Then I saw light. Flickering, bobbing, going up and down just slightly, coming toward me.

And as the light grew closer and brighter, I saw there was something right beside me; the something that had touched me; it had been there for a time, watching me.

It was a child.

Naked, deathly white, with eyes great and luminous, but covered with a transparent film as milky as a membrane, small, very young, hairless, its arms shorter than they should have been, purple and crimson veins crossing its bald skull like traceries of blood on a parchment, fine even features, nostrils dilating as it breathed shallowly, ears slightly tipped as though reminiscent of an elf, barefooted but with pads on the soles, this child stared at me, looked up at me, its little tongue visible as it opened its mouth filled with tiny teeth, trying to form sounds, saying nothing, watching me, a wonder in its world, watching me with the saucer eyes of a lemur, the light behind the membrane flickering and pulsing. This child.

And the light came nearer, and the light was many lights. Torches, held aloft by the children who rode the alligators.

• • •

Beneath the city, there is yet another city: wet and dark and strange.

At the entrance to their land someone—not the children, they couldn't have done it—long ago built a road sign. It is a rotted log on which has been placed, carved from fine cherrywood, a book and a hand. The book is open, and the hand rests on the book, one finger touching the single word carved in the open pages. The word is CROATOAN.

On August 13, 1590, Governor John White of the Virginia colony managed to get back to the stranded settlers of the Roanoke, North Carolina, colony. They had been waiting three years for supplies, but politics, foul weather and the Spanish Armada had made it impossible. As they went ashore, they saw a pillar of smoke. When they reached the site of the colony, though they found the stronghold walls still standing against possible Indian attacks, no sign of life greeted them. The Roanoke colony had vanished. Every man, woman, and child, gone. Only the word CROATOAN had been left. "*One of the chiefe trees or postes at the right side of the entrance had the barke taken off, and 5. foote from the ground in fayre Capitall letters was grauen CROATOAN without any crosse or sign of distresse.*"

There was a Croatan island, but they were not there. There was a tribe of Hatteras Indians who were called Croatans, but they knew nothing of the whereabouts of the lost colony. All that remains of legend is the story of the child Virginia Dare, and the mystery of what happened to the lost settlers of Roanoke.

Down here in this land beneath the city live the children. They live easily and in strange ways. I am only now coming to know the incredible manner of their existence. How they eat, what they eat, how they manage to survive, and have managed for hundreds of years, these are all things I learn day by day, with wonder surmounting wonder.

I am the only adult here.

They have been waiting for me.

They call me father.

LITTLE HOWL ON THE PRAIRIE

Thomas Pluck

Cold wisps of snow came early that year, just like they had the year before. Our settlement was good, hard-working people, but we knew what was coming. It steeled us, made us less charitable to one another, less Christian. We'd stuck together the year before, shared our stores—most of us at least—but to a one, we'd gone hungry more days than not, and that memory of the ache in our bellies made us stingy. It was my birthday, and friends once generous with boiled sweets or flint arrowheads wished me a happy day empty-handed, even though I'd given freely on their birthdays earlier in the year.

I didn't hold it against them. The fear was in me, too. I was thankful that Ma would bake me a pie made with preserved apples, and Pa had let me bring his prized Whitworth rifle to school that day.

Ma bore no children before or after me, and Pa sometimes looked at me like he'd been cheated at a card game, but couldn't prove it. I was no son, but I had legs long as striplings and shoulders broad enough to yoke—my folks were of strong Finnish stock—and I pitched in extra, working harder than any boy I knew, so they humored my tomboyish nature. As long as I sat still at school and wore my dresses to church, I could play games with boys, fight the ones who made fun, and hunt when I liked.

The deer weren't foolish enough to linger around our farms once the harvest was in. With whitetails scarce, the wolves became brave. The year before, they lost all fear of man. The last blizzard of the season left our homes buried in snow so deep that we'd holed up for weeks, unable to even go to church for Sabbath. When we finally dug ourselves out, we found three homes where the wolves had visited our neighbors and left only gnawed skeletons.

Even the bones had been cracked for the marrow, the skulls split open for the meal inside.

. . .

We knew it was wolves, because the Villeneuve family had been attacked by a pack of beasts which carried off their little boy. So had our schoolteacher, Mr. Twedt. He looked like he'd been born with a lemon in his mouth, but after last winter, he'd gone from sour to mean. My best friend Ole Smirka and I had painted Mr. Twedt's fence the year before and he'd paid us a fair wage, but this year he let his house go without its yearly upkeep, and our pockets were empty as we walked home from school on my birthday. Me with the Whitworth rifle, near tall as I was, over my shoulder, and Ole pushing his burden ahead of him. He was a year my senior, thin as a broom with a mess of straw yellow hair. We called him Smirk.

"Stop jostling me!" Ellie said, and whipped Smirk across the thigh.

Ellie Villeneuve, daughter of the town shopkeepers to whom everyone was in debt, had been wounded in the wolf attack and never walked again. Smirk pushed her wooden wheelchair to pay off his family's extensive tab on Ville-neuve Provisions' books.

Ellie had taken to carrying a buggy whip since her wounding, pointing it with a sneer, or cracking it in front of our faces, to "keep away flies," as she said. But never when adults were around to see.

"Will you save me a slice of that pie, Cathy?"

I didn't answer. He knew I'd save him some, and that I was angry to spend my birthday alone. With the snow threatening, he couldn't visit for supper.

"Don't bother," Ellie said. "Her mother couldn't afford the sweet apples."

I wrinkled my nose, and immediately ducked left. Ellie cracked her whip where my face had been a moment before. She had a preternatural ability to know when you made faces at her.

"Why are you so nasty this year, Ellie?" I skipped ahead out of range. We'd never been real friends. Farming was my life, the town was hers. I didn't have time to tighten my hair up in blonde curls like she did, even if I'd wanted to.

"You're just jealous that my family's gonna own all your farms next winter. Everyone knows it'll only take one or two more seasons before the bankers come around. And my father says it's high time he bought up the land around here and let you sharecrop."

I bit my tongue. My Pa said that the Villeneuves, second generation French traders, had only made it through the rough times because we felt obligated to buy from fellow townsfolk instead of sending wagons to St. Croix, where goods were cheaper. And now that times were lean, they were paying us back by bleeding us dry with interest.

Smirk hit a rock on the path that nearly tumbled Ellie out of her chair. She cracked him on the leg, and he jumped, rubbing the spot.

"You clumsy oaf!" Ellie said, and lifted the blanket from her lap. A leather belt kept her snug in the seat. "After you dumped me last time, I had the tanner put in a safety harness."

Smirk sighed and met me out of whip range, behind Ellie's chair.

"You know I wanted to come over, but I've got to stack wood for the Villeneuves," Smirk said, and sneaked a triangle from his pocket, wrapped in brown paper. "Happy birthday, Catherine."

Inside was a handmade slingshot, which he'd whittled from a hedge apple tree, the strongest wood around. "Oh, I can't take this. What'll you hunt with?"

"You're a better shot than me," he said. "And generous."

I crushed him in a hug. "Thank you, Smirk."

"Quit making sin!" Ellie craned over the back of her chair to spy on us. "You'd better push me home double time or I'm telling."

· · ·

With Smirk's gift in my hand, I walked up the rutted wagon road to our farm. Thinking of him pushing Ellie's chair back to town, then hiking alone home in the cold. We'd hunted rabbit and squirrel with slingshots ever since we were little, and our mothers were thankful for the unexpected bounty. Now I had the Whitworth.

The rifle's nine pounds weighed heavy on my shoulder. After the war, Pa didn't like using it, but he taught me. With the lean harvest, Ma salted some pork away but not enough for the winter, and we knew it.

Pa had been a Union sharpshooter, and I'd inherited his keen eye. He bore a scar from its hexagonal bullet carving up his forearm, right before his own shot felled the rebel sniper who'd once owned it.

The woods would have to help feed us this winter. My eyes scanned the tree line as I passed the Olson's orchard. Fat whitetails sometimes came looking for late pickings. With my gaze distracted, walking over the rise, coming on the duck pond, I found myself nearly face to face with the largest bear I'd ever seen.

Pa said we didn't get grizzly bears here anymore, but there one was, hunkered by the water's edge, its broad furry back to me, grunting to itself.

I froze a handful of yards away. If it turned and charged, I was dead.

But there was a great amount of meat on its bones.

I'd loaded the Whitworth for show-and-tell, but Mr. Twedt wouldn't let me fire it. Not even into the trees. The polished wood eased into my hands. I'd never shot a bear before. Pa had shot a black bear that got into our corn-crib once. It was half the size of this one, and tore the wood apart with one swipe of its claws. Pa said a bear's body was just like a man's, the heart was in the same place. I aimed to the left to avoid its spine, and eased back the hammer.

As it clicked, the bear stretched to its full height and shed its coat like a curtain, revealing a mountain of flesh covered in curlicues of hair only a mite less thick than the fur it had been wearing a moment prior.

A face shrouded in amber beard turned to wink at me. "If it pleases you, don't shoot until I've had a good wash," the giant said.

Scarred back rippled with muscle, legs thick as my waist, he crunched the thin ice and splashed into the water. His behind resembled nothing less than two pink shoats trotting into the pond. The bear's head, attached to the rest of its tanned pelt, peered at me upside down from the pile at the shore.

He washed his face, the icy water steaming off his body, like it was the most normal thing in the world.

"You're trespassing on my neighbor's land." I kept the rifle trained on his heart.

"That I am," he said. "I did not care to ask for lodging with the stink of long travels on me. You can poke through my pack. I have gold, and some paper money. I'm a hunter, not a drifter. There's a blizzard headed this way."

"I'll take you to my Pa."

"Would you mind turning around?"

"I don't trust you, mister."

"My name's Arnie," he said, a wide grin beneath his soaked beard. "And I believe we're at an impasse. I'm not about to bare myself to a young lady, and you won't trust me out of your sight." His voice rumbled out his belly like war drums.

"I've already seen your hind parts, like Moses saw of the Lord. Turn your-self around and get your britches on."

• • •

Arnie wore a cloak made from grizzly hide, with the hollowed top of the skull for a hat. Pa was walking back from the barn when we came up the road, and he stared a good long time as we neared. He had a chin like a pair of walnut shells, and pointed it our way.

"What can I do for you?" Pa asked, scratching at his hip. Wishing his rifle was in his hands and not mine. We had some big Swedes in town, but none as tall or as wide as our guest.

"Sir, my name's Arnie Grimsson. I'm a trapper." He hefted a pack bursting with pelts.

"Trading's done in town," Pa said.

"He's looking for lodging," I said.

"I've been keeping just ahead of a terrible winter storm," Arnie said. "Hoped to trade in St. Croix, but doubt I'll beat the weather. I can pay cash or gold, but I'll need a barn to hole up in for a few days."

"Villeneuve Provisioners rent a room above their shop. They'll take your money."

"I imagine they would, but a man of my dimensions don't find a bed too comfortable. Your daughter thought I was a grizzly, and trained that rifle on me."

"I can't be the first who's mistook you and that coat of yours," I said, cheeks flushing red.

"Wish you were," he said, and fanned out the bear's left ear, which was missing a bullet-shaped notch.

Pa laughed. "Room and board, big fellow like you. Figure a dollar a day."

Arnie nodded. "That's fair. And I've brought a haunch of venison for your table that ought to taste fine about now. Been hanging over my shoulder near a week." He cut the dried crust off the meat with a primitive knife with a stag horn handle. The meat below was juicy and red, and our mouths watered.

• • •

Ma cooked the venison in pork fat with potatoes and onions. Arnie showed us the meager haul of pelts he'd trapped. Two wolf, some badger. "A wolverine got into my camp, and what it didn't eat, it fouled with its scent," he said, and held up its skin, lush brown rimmed with gold. "Spent a week tracking him."

Over the apple pie, which was sweet as any I've ever had, Pa spoke of our tough season until Ma cut him with a glance. Her pride could not stand sharing our misfortunes with strangers, even one at our table. But Pa reveled in complaint, and was overly trustful, and told our guest how our wagon had been stuck in thick mud since a late autumn flood. We couldn't pull it out even with borrowed oxen, and then the dirt dried up over the wheels and froze, making it a permanent fixture near the hog pen. Arnie offered the lend of his back to carry supplies back from town. I sensed Ma's nervousness, sharing some of it myself, and volunteered to join our guest on the trip.

To assuage Ma's fears, Arnie paid up front with five Morgan silver dollars, all from Carson City.

"Looks like our guest made it over the Rockies," Pa said, and jingled the

coins into his foot chest. Then he fished one out, and pushed it into my palm.
"Spend this on something foolish," he said. "That clasp knife you've had your
eyes on."

• • •

The next morning I joined Pa in performing the daily chores. I was milking
our cow, squirting the occasional treat to a ginger barn cat, when I heard a
whinny from my father's roan gelding. I took the milk bucket with me, and
a hatchet from a wall peg.

A low groan came from behind the sunken wagon. I raised the hatchet,
nearly spilling the cream out the milk bucket. Behind the axle, our hirsute
guest leaned into the push, bare feet digging into the dead grass. The wagon
shuddered forward, then rolled back.

"Four oxen couldn't budge it," I called, and let the ax drop by my side.

He gave me that wink again, like the drawing of the satyr in the school's
book on Roman myth.

A sound like bones twisting until they cracked issued from the earth, and
the wheels broke free from their prison. The axle screamed in protest as the
wagon rumbled forth. He pushed it all the way down to the dirt road. Pa
came around the barn, lips parted.

"They grow 'em strong where I'm from," Arnie said, and mopped the
sweat off his forehead with the slab of his forearm. He walked to get his bear-
rug coat, and threw it over his shoulders.

"Swedes," Pa said, and went to hitch the horse to the yoke.

• • •

Arnie walked alongside the wagon—"No use breaking it, now that it's free,"
he'd said—as I rode it into town. We had enough to scrape by, but would've
likely had to slaughter the hens for meat, let the cow run dry, and the gelding
go skinny if the winter was as harsh as it threatened to be. The worry set Ma
on edge, and Pa would rather face spring short on coin than spend winter
with her grinding her teeth every time she peeked into the pork barrel.

Arnie whistled a tune to himself, low as if he were blowing into a jug. It
chilled the back of my neck.

"What's it like, living on your own in the woods?" I asked, to cut short his
whistling more than anything else.

He repeated the last few notes, like a chorus, before answering. "Lonely,
but I like it that way." Then he went back to whistling, until we passed the
Smirka farm, and I hollered "Smirk!" until Ole came running to meet us.

Smirk gawped at Arnie like the moving mountain he was, until I introduced them. Then he climbed alongside me in the wagon.

"What can you tell us about hunting? No offense, but feeding yourself must be like feeding a whole family," Smirk said.

"Pa's eyes are just about shot," I added. "So it'll rest on my shoulders this winter."

"Your Pa says you're a crack shot with that Kentucky rifle. My advice would be to be patient. When you're out of bullets, you're out of food."

"I made Cathy a slingshot for rabbits and squirrels." Smirk said. I took it from my back pocket.

"That's fine work," Arnie said.

"What kind of rifle you use to take down that grizzly?" Smirk asked.

Arnie smiled, and slipped his long knife from his belt. "My longseax," he said. "He charged on me, before I could raise my Buffalo rifle. But my old friend here went right through his heart." A foot and a half of steel, a mere whittling knife in his hands. The blade was checkered, like a farrier's file, and the back of the blade gleamed silver, all the way to the point.

"Fellow named Rezin made it from an old rat tail file. Told him I needed hard steel, with some silver in it for luck." He twisted the blade, and I saw figures cut in the silver, like stick-men.

"What for?"

"Up in the mountains, you meet things that fear silver," Arnie said. "And rightly so."

"Because Judas betrayed our Lord for it?" Smirk asked.

"The metal held its power long before that infamy," Arnie said. "It's the only currency the enemy knows. You ever hear the tales from the old country? Of elves who steal children, and exchange them with their own? Silver is proof against them, too."

Smirk grinned. "You believe in elves?"

"I know what I've seen," Arnie said, and gestured toward the dead trees with his blade. "In the mountains of this country, there are no fae folk. But there are things that fear silver."

We entered town in silence, garnering stares as we hitched the wagon outside Villeneuve Provisions.

• • •

Inside, Ellie held court in her chair, waited on hand and foot by the workers. Mr. Villeneuve had a face like an axe blade, and was less kind than a sharp one. His wife pursed her lips in disapproval, marking debts in their ledger as folks stocked up before the storm.

I gave Mrs. Villeneuve Ma's list and two Morgan dollars to pay. She had workers bring it out to our wagon. Smirk came with me as I looked at the pocket knives. I was torn between a Barlow blade and a nice long whittler.

Ellie stuck her tongue out as soon as her mother's back was turned. "You two getting married? I'm gonna tell preacher Johnson you were kissing."

"We were not," Smirk said. "Why do you have to be so nasty?"

Mrs. Villeneuve gasped. "Such language from the Smirka boy."

"You'd best leave, before I take a belt to you," her husband said. "I'll be telling your Pa."

"Make Catherine leave, too!" Ellie said. "She's stealing. She's got a sling-shot in her back pocket."

"For shame." Mr. Villeneuve grabbed my arm, and yanked the slingshot from me.

"Hey, that's mine!"

"I made that," Smirk said. "You don't even sell slingshots!"

"I do now," Mr. Villeneuve said, and held up Smirk's handiwork. "Can you pay for this, or do I have to add it to your family's burgeoning debt? Perhaps it's time to call the bankers, and see if I own your land yet."

"I can pay," I said, and held up the Morgan silver dollar.

Mr. Villeneuve winced at its shine. "This is fine workmanship. Not sure a dollar will do."

"Cathy, don't!" Smirk said.

"Young man, I told you to leave my store."

Arnie loomed over us. "That's not your property to sell," he said, and pulled the slingshot from Mr. Villeneuve's hand. How he'd gotten there without a sound, I don't know. "She showed me that outside."

"And who're you, stranger?"

"Arnie Grimsson is my name. And I'm here to trade fairly. If you try thievery with me, I'll hang your skin outside your store. I've heard all about your ways, all the way from St. Croix."

Someone stomped his boot on the floor in applause. Another followed, then everyone joined in.

"Get out of my establishment, stranger. We don't care for riffraff like you. And Ole Smirka? Tell your Pa I'm not trading with you anymore. I only deal with folk who pay their debts."

Smirk turned red with shame and fled out the door. I left the pocket knives behind and ran after him.

• • •

The snow fell in down feathers, blanketing the dirt road out of town. Smirk left big footprints in the snow. I stopped by the wagon, where the packers tied down our supplies. "We had everything except the bullets for your Whitworth," the packer said. "Mister V says he can't get those no more."

They were hexagonal, like the Whitworth's barrel. We'd have to pour our own. "Then I'll need some lead."

"Mister V says he's out of ingots, too. Been a run on it."

We had only a handful left.

"Best get moving with this weather," Arnie said. And he was right.

Before we made it home, his beard was frosted white so he looked like Saint Nicholas. I fumed in silence over the Villeneuves' cruelty.

Arnie nodded toward the trees, where a whitetail buck and his small herd browsed at the forest edge. "Too bad you didn't bring the Whitworth."

"Don't know what I'm to hunt with, with no bullets."

The snow fell from Arnie's shoulders as he fished around in a pouch. "Believe these'll fit. Might have to shave them a hair." He held open his bear-paw of a palm. Six polished bullets gleamed like silver bells. They weren't six-sided, like the Whitworth's barrel, but they would fire. "But save them for when you really need them."

• • •

The wind howled against the boards much of the night, and we worried for Arnie and our livestock out in the barn. The next morning we were buried in snow up to my chin, with drifts tall as the peak of the roof. Pa shook me gently awake, and we fired up with hot coffee and biscuits to dig a path to the barn. By the time we shoved the door open, Arnie wasn't more than ten feet from the house, holding a barrel lid he'd used as a shovel.

"Thought I smelled biscuits," he hollered, face gleaming with sweat. "How about a little salt pork, too?"

Pa laughed, and had me shovel the rest of the way for our guest. The snow had slowed to a thin powder, but kept falling on and off throughout the day. I milked the cow and fed the horse and we played euchre with a greasy old set of cards, but Arnie was a terrible partner who couldn't figure the tricks, so by noon I was begging Pa to let me snowshoe my way to the Smirka farm.

"I might see if I can track those whitetails to their beds," Arnie said. "Bring your Whitworth."

• • •

Arnie's snowshoes were wide as well covers and barely kept him from plunging through the heavy packed snow. The way he crunched and shushed, we couldn't sneak up on a dead skunk, much less flightier prey. He held his nose up, kind of like Ellie Villeneuve, eyes on the tree line. The deer were smarter than we were, and made no appearance. When the Smirka home came into view, Arnie stopped.

"You go on," he said. "Don't come after me. You just go straight on home after you visit your friend. Follow in our footsteps."

He waddled off toward the trees, cutting toward the little red schoolhouse, which was hopefully closed until spring. Seeing Mr. Twedt's residence gave me an idea.

• • •

I thought Smirk would be cross with me, but he was glad I'd made the trek. He had four younger sisters who his parents spoiled because they sang like birds. They had hopes the quartet would be discovered and the windfall would cure all their woes. The youngest opened the door when I knocked.

"We're playing Big Sister!" she shrieked, and ran back inside. Smirk sat on the floor by the wood stove while his sisters tied bows in his hair and took turns using a scrap of muskrat fur as a mustache to play his suitor.

"I can come back after the wedding," I said.

"My one true love," Smirk cried, and made to faint. The girls made me wear the mustache and recite a love poem before we could escape into the stomped snow of the yard.

"Don't ever regret being an only child," Smirk said, untying a straw bow behind his ear. "Thanks for saving me."

"Don't thank me yet. Know what I was thinking? Mr. Twedt might spare a few bits to a few plucky young kids who offer to shovel his porch."

"He'll probably give us an old book. Last time he tried to pay with *Pilgrim's Progress*."

Then my entrepreneurial mind kicked in. "Get your snowshoes. He's always trading books with Widow Abigail. We can be couriers!"

Mr. Twedt's schoolhouse didn't seem to get any closer as we trudged across the fresh snow. The sky went gray, and while it threatened no more snow, the dull silver dime of the sun dipped faster than we anticipated. Then the wind howled, straight out of nowhere. Except there wasn't any wind. The powder wasn't even swirling into little eddies in the breeze.

Smirk and I traded glances, and I checked the hammer of the Whitworth.

The wolves hadn't come out until late winter last year. When the deer had been hunted out. This was the first real snow of the season. I gave Smirk his slingshot, and the pouch of Arnie's bullets. There was no time to find stones.

"What's this gonna do against a wolf?"

"Aim for the nose."

We watched the trees, and walked faster. The snow-topped schoolhouse looked like a fat red mushroom in the distance. And the next howl, drawn and lonely, was closer.

I scanned the trees with my scope. Hoping to see Arnie's bearskin coat. I'd fire a shot over his head and see if that would bring him. But I couldn't even find his trail.

"Faster," Smirk said, like I didn't know.

"I bet Ellie's got a wolf call or something," I panted. But the Villeneuve homestead was on the other side of the town. And as far as we knew she didn't have a chair with skis on it. Not yet.

We reached the schoolhouse out of breath and terrified of our unseen pursuers. "Mister Twedt, let us in!" we cried, and banged on the door. "Wolves are after us!"

He was a long time coming to the door. Probably nose deep in a book. Our schoolmaster wore a fur-lined hooded robe that framed his hawklike face. "Well get inside! Wasting the fire, as usual, Mr. Smirka!"

Smirk shrugged and ducked inside.

"No firearms in my home, young lady!"

I left the Whitworth against the door and huddled around the wood stove while Mr. Twedt locked the door. He hunched down to spy out the keyhole. "Wolves you say? Craziness."

"Didn't you hear the howls?" I said.

"I heard no such thing. Children and their fairy tales. What brings you out in the cold, if you're afraid of a little wind?"

"We thought you'd like us to courier books between you and Mrs. Abigail."

"She won't be reading anything for a long time," Mr. Twedt said. "I told you to stay away. Why are you tormenting me?"

"Look," Smirk whispered, and pointed at our teacher's feet. His nails were black and his legs shaggier than Arnie at his hairiest.

Mr. Twedt turned. He wasn't wearing a robe at all, but a blanket, shredded at the edges. He dropped it to the ground and rose up on his haunches. "You've brought this upon yourselves," he growled, and thrust his jaw at the ceiling for a howl that vibrated down to our nethers and froze us in place. We stared as his body rippled and stretched, with a crackling like hog fat over a fire.

The wolf swiped and bent the stove's chimney in half, claws rending the blackened metal silver. We scrabbled across the schoolhouse. There was just the single door, now locked. Chairs and a chalkboard. I grabbed the metal hook for opening the wood stove, the only weapon. "Smirk! Shoot him and I'll smash the window!"

Smirk took out his slingshot, then dived as the wolf lunged after him. Scrawny Mr. Twedt made for a rangy long-limbed beast, all ribs and teeth and knobby joints, claws scratching the floor as he plowed through our school desks.

Smirk snatched an ink bottle and launched it with the slingshot, blackening the creature's gaunt face. I swung hard and shattered the thick glass. We'd be cut to the bone climbing through. I smashed the panes but the wood frame was too stout.

The wolf backhanded the poker from my hands. I hit the wall hard, winded, and a silhouette of President Lincoln fell at my feet. "Little smarty, I'll taste your blood!" His jaws opened like a snake's as he howled in triumph. "No!"

Smirk bounced a bullet off the beast's tight ribs, and it fell back, yelping. The wolf-beast clawed at its fur, which looked singed. The key hit the floor like a hammer.

I dived for it, and leaped for the door. The key scraped across the lock plate. Smirk fished in the pouch for another bullet.

The creature crossed the room with one long step of its crooked leg and turned my good new coat into pillow stuffing with one swipe. Its jaws spread open and I smelled raw guts like a freshly split carcass. I closed my eyes and screamed.

The building shook and I tumbled across the floor. Something fell on me, hard. The room was filled with a low roar, like we were inside a thunderhead. A brown blur flashed across the room and walloped the spindly wolf creature straight out the window.

I pushed the door off my shoulder. Smirk cowered in a corner with his slingshot, a fresh bullet drawn. A howl rattled the shutters. A roar responded, then the schoolhouse shook with an impact.

Crawling onto the porch, the Whitworth fell into my hands. A blur of fur and teeth whirled through the snow. I raised the barrel. Rangy as it was, the wolf was the largest I'd ever seen. Locked in battle with a grizzly.

I blinked my eyes. It was Arnie, in his coat. He'd tackled the creature, and taken out the window, frame and all. "Arnie!"

"Shoot!" he bellowed.

I fired. I knew I hit, but the battle went on. Reloading was a complicated process. Powder and caps and wadding. But I'd done it enough that it came natural. "Smirk, bullet!"

Smirk crept onto the porch and palmed me the bullet. I fired a second time, at a flash of gaunt ribs. There was a yelp and a roar, and the ruckus collapsed into the snow.

"Arnie!"

"Stay back!" I couldn't tell where his bearskin cloak ended and his body began. With a roar, he swiped and black blood sprayed over the snow. The wolf clutched at its wound. Arnie plunged his seax into the wolf's chest and skewered it to the ground. Its blood sizzled on the blade as it thrashed like a spider on a hotplate. A billow of smoke rose from the wound, and the beast struggled no more.

When the smoke drifted, it revealed Mr. Twedt gazing mournfully at the gray sky.

"What in the . . . " I said.

"Your first bullet wasn't silver," Arnie said, hunkered beneath his bearskin cloak. He kept his grip on his seax, and we watched open-mouthed as his bear-paw returned to being a large and very hairy, but human, hand. He put a boot to the corpse and pulled out his blade, pointing at the smoking wound where my second shot had struck.

"He was what the Ojibwe call a *windigo*. They have different names in other places. Where I'm from, they're called a *werwolf*, but it amounts to the same. They were people, once. Before their greed overtook them, when they feasted on their fellow men."

Then, as if cleaning his nails or picking his teeth, he stuck the point of his longseax into his thigh and dug out the lead bullet I shot him with. His cloak fell open, and steam rose from his body. His clothes were torn and bloodied, but his flesh untouched, except for silvery webs of scars.

"Wh-what?"

"I am Arngrim the Berzerker." he said, and put a flatnosed lead bullet in my palm. "And I will die only when Odin calls me to Valhalla."

Smirk and I traded glances. If we'd lost our minds, we'd done it together.

"Reload and get moving," Arngrim said. "This isn't the only *windigo* in your town. They got the taste last winter."

• • •

Loaded with silver, my Whitworth rested heavily on my shoulder as we trudged across the snow. Arngrim told us the price for saving our lives was our secrecy. I asked him how he knew we needed rescue.

"I walk a long path, from friend to friend. One, an Ojibwe medicine woman, told me what happened here."

"But they said it was wolves," Smirk said, with a shiver. He'd made us switch coats, and his longer garment dragged in the snow behind me.

"I've lived an awful long time, and the hardest thing is for folks to face the enemy inside their walls. The kind that fights under no flag, and looks like your brother or sister, but sees you as flesh for their appetites. That betrayal stings so deep, some side with the enemy, rather than face the truth of their accuser. We have to hunt them down. No one will believe us."

• • •

Town was buried in snow, the shops and homes jutting from the landscape like worn-down teeth in an old woman's gums. No one had dared the cold to sweep their doorsteps, much less have horses drag a sleigh over the road to flatten the snowfall. We'd seen worse blizzards. They were afraid of something else. Like they knew evil hid among them, but would leave them alone if they refused to see its face.

"Where are we heading?" I squinted into the white.

"I think you know. Another family who turned right mean."

We knew who that must be.

"Why'd it take you so long to find Mr. Twedt, if you're such the windigo hunter?"

Arngrim shrugged. "Got to get close to smell them out when they're in human form."

As we reached the far edge of town, we saw a house shrouded in snow, with the upstairs window open. Arngrim raised his broad nose to the air. "Stay here," he said. "Keep your Whitworth ready."

The house was no more than a hundred yards away. With the scope on, I could've covered him from the other side of town. He shuffled up the drift toward the window, taking his time so not to tumble.

Smirk shivered and rubbed his hands together, then put his gloves back on.

"If you won't take my coat, come here and be a rifle rest," I said.

Smirk crouched in the snow, and I leaned against his strong thin back, with the barrel over his shoulder. We watched Arngrim near the window, and heard him call inside. No one answered. He held a finger to us, to say he was going in, and we should not follow.

We watched the window, hearing nothing but own our frosty breaths and quickened heartbeats.

"I'm warmer now," Smirk coughed.

I flicked his ear. I would let him hold my hand when we walked, if no one was around. And we'd danced, him being the only schoolboy taller than me. But I'd never thought much about how it felt, until I felt him shiver beneath me, needing my warmth.

My mind was distracted when the beast knocked Arngrim out the front door in a billow of bloodmist and snowy powder.

This one was bigger. Not old and weak like Mr. Twedt. Its fur thick, its claws black and glossy. I followed it through the scope, unable to get a clear shot, but one detail came through: it had only three talons on its right hand.

"That's Mr. Villeneuve!"

Heroes

Hearing its name, the beast looked up, and Arngrim swatted its head like a grizzly knocking down a beehive. The beast plowed under the snow, and I tracked it with Whitworth's muzzle.

"Save your bullets," Smirk shouted. "We've only got three more!"

Arngrim lumbered toward his stunned foe, more bear than man. His coat had become part of him. The bullet notch was in his left ear, but he looked small for a grizzly. I aimed at the snow where the beast had fallen.

Then two more wolves darted out of the house, their muzzles gored and steaming, and hit him from either side. He bellowed in pain and fury.

Smirk and I ran to help, him with his slingshot, me with the Whitworth. The smaller wolf had a muzzle full of belly meat and harried Arngrim, while the she-wolf—not sure how I knew, but the point of her face seemed female— swiped and snapped at his throat. She took no care to protect herself, either not seeing us, or relishing her apparently invincible power. Then I heard her cackle, and knew who she was.

I shot Mrs. Villeneuve between the shoulder blades.

Her howls shook the snow off the rooftops of three houses as she clawed at the hot coal in her chest. The little wolf shrieked and let go of Arngrim, running in frantic circles. He gripped it by the tail and swung it like a club until it was stunned. Then he pulled his seax from his belt to finish the she-wolf.

"I'll string the trees with your bowels, girl!" Her mate snarled and burst from the snow, galloping for us. I raced to reload. Pa prided himself on his fast recovery and taught me the same, but I must've gotten snow on the cap. Because when the beast was twenty feet away, the hammer clicked.

Arngrim bounded toward us with a defiant roar, but he was no wolf. The beast leaped for my throat. Everything had gone slow, and I admired how the beast tilted its head sideways to accommodate my neck, snapping its jaws like the French guillotine.

"No!"

There was a yelp and something hit me like a cow kicked me in the face.

Stunned, I heard a horrible gargling and coughing as the windigo thrashed and clawed at its belly, gashing its own flesh to get at the silver bullet that Smirk had slung down its gullet. Its steaming innards strewn across the snow, the beast dragged itself toward us, jaws gaping wide, yellow eyes blazing with bloodlust.

Arngrim fell on the creature in a rage. Smirk looked away, but I made myself watch. He cracked its skull in his maw and raked his claws down its ribs, then reached in and pulled the lungs through.

"Blood eagle for Odin," he growled.

That turned me off meat for the rest of my life.

Arngrim bellowed a triumphant roar, his breath frosty crimson. I couldn't tell if Mr. Villeneuve ever returned to human form or not, the blood was so thick.

I hugged Smirk tight. He hugged me back.

The little wolf stared at us from across the snow, standing on its hind legs.

"You'll wish you were dead, before the day's done!" And I swear the beast stuck out its tongue.

With a yip, it bounded off across the snowy prairie toward the woods. Toward my farm.

I raised my rifle and fired twice on my dead cap before Smirk shook me out of my fear-daze.

"Ride me," Arngrim growled.

We gripped handfuls of fur and climbed on his back. He stopped by Mrs. Villeneuve's sprawled body to retrieve his seax and tear out her throat. Smirk dry-heaved into his elbow.

"Wolves," Arngrim said, in his ursine growl. "Wolves did this. And you shot them. But they fled."

With that, he plowed through the snow, bellowing hot breath. With each bound, I thought how much I hated Ellie. All the nasty pranks she'd pulled. How she wasn't content to be better off than the rest of us, unless those who weren't suffered. And I cursed myself for rushing my reload, and robbing myself of blasting her smug face off.

• • •

Wolf tracks led to my door.

To the barn as well, where the open doors showed me that our milk cow and gelding had been slaughtered. A gunshot cracked from inside my house. Arngrim rammed the door open with a butt of his head and sent us tumbling across the kitchen floor. Pa had the Spencer rifle in his hands, his eyes wide with terror as his shots thumped into the wolf-girl's fur without effect. Ma hunched in a corner with an iron skillet. Chunks of my father were missing. His left thumb, a gouge from his cheek, the toe from his boot.

Arngrim's skull hit the wood stove with a clang. Ellie-wolf pranced around my father, snapping gobbets from him and yipping with glee as he bled from a dozen wounds.

I lunged and Smirk grabbed my coat to pull me back. "No, she'll kill you!" Arngrim had knocked himself out cold, and resumed human form.

"Worse, I'll make you like me!" She tore a chunk from Pa's throat and spat it on the floor with a cackle. Pa clutched his neck and hot blood sprayed and Ma shrieked.

"I'll never be a bitch like you!" I snatched Arnie's seax and tackled her. She swiped me across the eye with her needly claws and we slammed into the floor. The knife burned her fur like hot coals, but she thrashed and tore like a devil, and flung me across the house.

"I know how to hurt you for-e-ver," she sang, and playfully stepped toward Smirk. "I can walk, when I'm a wolf. Maybe I'll crack your spine so your sweetheart has to push you in a chair!"

I hurled the seax and it stuck in her haunch. She howled and tore at it, but it seared her paws. Ma clobbered her with the skillet, pulled the stove door open, and clubbed her wolf head right into the fire. Smirk kicked the door shut and we stomped until the wolf stopped gouging the floor with her claws, and a blackened muzzle fell out of the stove. I held up the seax, ready to plunge it deep.

Arngrim rose from his slumber. "No!"

He gripped my wrist and took his knife from me.

"She's just a child," he said, and sheathed the blade.

"She killed my father!"

"Be that as it may," Arngrim said, "The blood of a child will not be on my hands, or my blade. I'm sorry, Catherine. I'm bound by oaths I cannot break."

The wolf had become nasty Ellie Villeneuve again. Her face blackened but unwounded. He heaved her limp body over his shoulder. "The medicine woman might cure her. She could make a powerful ally. Again, I'm sorry."

"Get out of my home," Ma bawled, hunched over Pa's body.

I couldn't tell what was hot blood and what was hot tears. Smirk put an arm around my shoulders as Arngrim shuffled to the door. "Wolves," he said. "Say it was wolves. Or they'll think it was you, gone mad. Trust me, I know."

He lowered his head.

I spat at his feet before he could say he was sorry again.

• • •

The wound that robbed me of my left eye never held me back much. Smirk and his sisters left with a traveling show, and I talked Ma into selling the house and its terrible memories, to follow with them. On the road, I learned to trick-shoot from Annie Oakley herself, but 'One-Eyed Cathy' never approached her fame.

I never saw Arngrim the Berzerker again.

Well, that's not entirely truthful. As he trudged away through the snow, I saw him one final time. Through the scope of Pa's Whitworth, as I put that last silver bullet through Ellie Villeneuve's stupid, sneering face.

THINGS HELD DEAR

Neliza Drew

Ten minutes into third period, which meant I had another forty-five to go if I wanted to avoid my English class for the day. And I did. Ms. Livingston's memoir assignment wasn't something I planned to turn in. Ever. And I certainly didn't want her to ask me about it in class.

I had no doubt my past might make a riveting paper, but she hadn't earned the right to know anything about me that could get myself or my mother into the trouble we were trying to avoid. Well, my sisters and I were trying to avoid. Charley wasn't quite cogent enough most of the time to avoid trouble. All the more reason for me not to write an essay about having been arrested or kidnapped or hiking the desert.

I'd hidden in the bathroom closest to the teachers' lounge because it saw the least action. I expected to be all alone with my thoughts and unfinished trigonometry homework until lunch ended. Instead, I heard muffled crying. The kind girls did when they didn't want to be heard. I knew that kind all too well.

I thought about ignoring it. Letting whoever it was sob in peace. But I couldn't. My stupid uncle-who-wasn't-my-real-uncle taught me to stick my neck out for people, so I did. Even if I still had trouble thinking about him without wanting punch a wall.

"You okay in there?"

Sniffles and snot.

"Is that a yes or a no?"

"Leave me alone. Please." Her voice had a pleading quality to it.

"If that's what you want." I hopped up on the far sink and leaned against the wall.

"Why are you even in here?"

"Probably the same reason you are. Hiding out until lunch."

She cracked the door open. "What are you hiding from?"

I swiveled my head at her with a look that said it was none of her business.

"You just don't look like you hide from much is all." She peered around the door. "You sure you aren't in here to beat me up or something?"

I gave her a look that said I suspected she'd suffered brain damage. "Why the hell would I do that?"

She flinched when I said "hell." I blinked at her like I'd discovered a new species. "You sure you're okay? Jacqueline Benson, right?"

"Jackie." She sucked snot up into her brain. "Debby told Jeff Williams I like him."

"He what?" My eyes narrowed.

"He called me undateable. And ugly. In front of everyone."

"No offense, but you could do better than Jeff Williams anyway. He's kind of a tool."

She didn't look like she believed me. She also looked like she'd had a serious crush that had been smashed into pieces. I'd seen the look before, a couple of times on my sister Nik. I just wasn't sure I could relate.

"Easy for you to say. I've heard you're kind of . . ." She mashed her lips together and turned pink.

"A slut?" I laughed. "Whatever you heard, I'm sure I've done worse. These kids lack imagination."

Her face said she wasn't sure how that was possible. "Were you in a gang?"

"I don't answer to others too well."

"Like, even adults?" She looked at me like I'd suggested I kept a wormhole in my underwear drawer.

I thought, especially adults. Instead, I told her something my Uncle Phil had said. "You listen to others without question, you lose yourself."

She stared at me, wide eyed, and I could see she was the kind of kid who'd never said 'no' to an adult in her life.

"Some things are more important than getting into trouble. For the record, Jeff Williams isn't one of them."

"Everyone says you got kicked out of your last school for beating up a teacher."

"Fuck 'em."

She blushed and looked away.

"You got a thing with the bad words, huh? Sorry. Look, it's not like I don't know how to talk all proper. I just tend not to because it's not what Nik wants me to be."

"What does she want you to be?"

"Normal."

She squinted at me and I noticed she had on no makeup. Not even a tinted lip gloss, like the girls from shop class.

"You know, normal. Like all the other kids. Like you. Like Debby and Jennifer and Beth and Kristen. Talk about glitter eyeshadow. Wear shoes I can't run in. Not beat up football players. You know, normal."

"You beat up a football player?"

"More than one. Got into the most trouble over the quarterback, though."

She looked like she might cry again. Jeff Williams was the second string quarterback.

"What do you see in that guy anyway?"

"He's cute. And he seemed nice."

"Cute doesn't equal nice. A lot of cute guys are complete creeps. Just way worse than Jeff Williams."

"So you've dated a lot?"

I thought about all the men I'd slept with. "Something like that."

She tilted her head. "Are you 'bad'?"

"Probably. I mean, by all the standard definitions, I guess I've been bad for a long time. I'm trying not to be. It's kinda why I'm in here."

"I don't get it. Skipping class is a bad thing."

"You're in here."

She turned pink. "I've never skipped class before. I didn't plan to this time. It's just the bell rang and I was crying and my face looked all splotchy and puffy and I've never been late to a class before. I kind of freaked out. I didn't want everyone looking at me. And now I'm in so much trouble."

"It's just the one class. You either make up the work or you don't. 'Sides, you go tell the teacher this sob story about bullying at lunch, she'll probably cut you some slack and not even report it as unexcused."

"He. I have Mr. Edwards this period." She somehow turned redder. Mr. Edwards was, by school standards, the hottest male teacher on staff.

"Even easier. Guys that age are still way wigged out by teenage girl problems. If you told him you started your period and didn't have change for the tampon machine, he'd probably give you an A for the quarter as long as you promised never to say the word 'period' again."

She looked like a mortified deer in headlights. "I can't say that. And he teaches biology."

"Teaching the anatomy of frogs is wholly different than being confronted with girl parts problems."

"I couldn't do that. I couldn't say that."

"Then tell the dude the truth. Some girls were mean to you. Again, you're meek and quiet and always present. Teachers dig that kind of thing."

She looked at her feet.

"What?"

"Could you maybe go with me?"

"I'm not sure I'd help your case. My presence usually screams 'up to no good' or 'three week suspension.' Don't you have any friends you could ask?"

She looked hurt.

"It's okay if you don't. I mean, the only friend I've ever had is my sister and I lie to her a lot. Makes me a shitty friend, I guess. I just figured, you know, you've lived here a long time. Right? People live someplace, they make friends."

"I used to have friends. In elementary school. I'm not cool enough anymore. My mom says that's okay because they're all Jezebels and harlots, but she also thinks I shouldn't be lonely if I have Jesus."

"You mean, like, Jesus-Jesus? The religion guy?"

She stared at me like I'd suddenly grown horns. Maybe I had.

"Look, no offense. My parents weren't exactly the church type. Closest they ever got was singing 'Amazing Grace' in blues clubs before my dad left."

Her eyes got wide. I wondered if the horns were glowing.

"Look, I not some serial killer or anything."

"You've never been to church?"

"It never came up."

"How do you know right from wrong?"

"I just do. Doesn't mean I don't do wrong things. But I look out for family. I've just done things I shouldn't have, but had to."

"You said you didn't do things you didn't want to."

"I don't do things people tell me to do if they seem wrong. Doesn't mean I haven't had to do bad things. Like the quarterback I beat up. He threatened my sister, because his girlfriend was a bitch. Listen, I don't want to talk about it. I can't. I'm supposed to be different here."

She tried to smile at me but it came out sort of crooked like she wasn't used to doing it. "You can talk to me if you want to. I won't tell anyone. I can't tell anyone. I don't have any friends."

I smiled back and wondered if mine looked as strained or if years of smiling at strangers for profit had left me incapable of sincerity. "I have the kinds of secrets I can't tell friends." Like the kind people told teachers and social workers and police. The kind that would take me away from my sisters, and leave them with Charley. "If I don't say it out loud, it's not real. Why I don't tell Nik. Even though I think she knows."

"You know that's dumb, right?"

"I was thinking bullshit, but yeah. I tell myself a lot of bullshit."

"Then how 'bout I tell you one of my secrets instead."

"You trust me not to tell anyone?"

"I guess so. Not like anyone seems to believe you."

"Good to know."

"You really don't care that people talk about you?"

I held out my right palm and let her get a good look at the swirling dark pink marks from a stove burner. "People have done worse than talk about me."

She stared. Everyone stared, but her face held something I rarely saw. Something I couldn't quite place, but I knew it was a form of kindness. She reached out with a finger and let it hover a few centimeters above the once-seared flesh.

"It doesn't hurt. Not anymore."

Her finger wavered.

"You can touch it. It's smooth. The nerve endings underneath got damaged. Mostly, it just feels numb. A little tingly."

She looked at me, her yellowish-brown eyes watery. "I don't know what to say."

"You don't need to say anything."

She pulled her sleeve up to her elbow, tugged at it, but couldn't get it to move higher. She tried a few more times before she pulled the sweatshirt over her head. Underneath, she wore a baggy Vacation Bible School tee shirt. And hand-shaped bruises on her upper arms.

"I'm not allowed to wear sleeves shorter than my elbows outside. My mom says it's too tempting for boys, that they'll look upon me in unclean ways."

"She grab you like that?"

"I questioned something our preacher said. Not disrespectfully, but, it didn't match the verse he'd referenced. She told me to respect my elders."

"She shouldn't hurt you."

Jackie pulled her sweatshirt back on and shrugged. "It was my fault."

"No. It's not your fault. It's abuse. And she was wrong."

"She's my mother. And look at you."

"My mother didn't do this things to me. My mother hurts herself, not us." She didn't seem so sure.

"Look, if there's anything I know about, it's abuse. I could write a whole dissertation on the ways people try to control each other, the ways they hurt each other, the ways they hurt themselves, the ways hurt makes people lash out or withdraw."

I hopped back up on the sink and leaned against the wall, my trig notebook resting on my lap. "I kinda need to finish this homework. You mind?"

"You do your homework?"

I pulled the nubby pencil out of the bent spiral and flipped to the next page of problems. "Why wouldn't I?"

"I didn't know bad kids did homework."

I stared at a word problem about the angle of descent for a power line running from a hilltop to a town ten miles away on the valley floor.

She leaned over my shoulder. "How can you even do that? It looks impossible to figure out."

"Ask me again when I'm done with it." I sketched out a triangle and pulled a calculator out of my pocket.

"Did you steal that?"

I thought about where I'd gotten the money for a seventy dollar calculator. Essentially, I'd robbed a john in Raleigh after he'd passed out from too much tequila. "Yeah, what of it?"

"I don't get you."

"The feeling's mutual."

"Will you help me? With Mr. Edwards?"

I stared at the next problem, about a stretch of road with a seven percent gradient. "Will it make you shut up until I'm done with this?"

She blushed and her lip quivered, but she nodded.

"Then yes."

· · ·

I knocked on the door to the biology classroom and stuck my head in before Mr. Edwards responded. "Hi. You're my friend Jackie's teacher."

He set down his sandwich and gave me his most earnest expression. "You said Jackie's friend?" His face made it clear he'd had no idea Jackie was capable of acquiring a friend and that he didn't approve of me hanging out with anyone.

"Yeah. She's, um, embarrassed. She started her, you know, period, and didn't have a tampon." I shrugged and tried to seem as uncomfortable with the subject as Jackie had been.

He gave me an expression that said he didn't believe me, but he'd give me some more rope and see if I hung myself.

"So, you know, they have those, like, machines? In the girls' room, but she didn't have quarters so she just kind of, like, hung out in the stall."

"Did you help her get what she needed?"

"Oh yeah, totally, but like by then, she was like super late and like embarrassed and all. She's super freaked out about the whole missing class thing.

Like, you really shouldn't give her a hard time. It totally wasn't her fault. And I mean, it's not like you wanted her bleeding all over, you know."

"Yes, well have her stop by and get the assignments she missed." He raised his voice slightly. "I trust this won't happen again, so I won't bother calling her mother."

"Oh, totally. Thanks, Mr. E."

"Edwards. Mr. Edwards. Have a good afternoon, Ms. Groves."

"You, like know my name?"

"Your sister is in my fifth period class." His look said he'd heard all the rumors.

"So you know, I'm no saint, but I'm not as bad as people say."

"Good to hear."

• • •

Jackie asked if I wanted moral support to talk to Ms. Livingston. It had been fairly obvious that Mr. Edwards saw through both my story and my fake valley girl nonsense, but that he'd known enough about teenage behavior to know that Jackie was a good kid and whatever her reason, it wasn't likely to become habit.

Ms. Livingston was equally adept at detecting bullshit and I had no intention of talking to her until everyone else had left for the day.

In trigonometry, Mrs. Butler asked why my paper was damp and encouraged me with something like enthusiastic sarcasm to do my work someplace a little more conducive to learning. In environmental science we were assigned partners for a project. I got stuck with Jeff Williams. I could only assume this was because the teacher appeared to hate all sports and wanted to punish the golden jock by sticking him with the girl in the ripped jeans and excessive eye liner.

"If you don't do your part and we fail, I'll end you," he whispered once we'd relocated to the same lab table.

I glared at him with the sort of smirk I'd been giving bullies for years. "Please try."

He hadn't tried, which meant I still had to talk to Ms. Livingston if for no other reason than Jackie had sort of dealt with her problem and I felt obligated to do something about mine.

I found her at her desk, bent over a stack of essays. When she heard me, she looked up but didn't set down her pen.

"Should I ask where you were third period?"

"Bathroom."

"Smoking?" She looked back down at her grading pile. I could see her trying to decide whether to bother with my excuses or not. Her distaste and distrust couldn't have been clearer on her face if they'd been tattooed there.

"Some girl was crying. I was talking to her. And doing my trig homework."

"You didn't think maybe coming to my class was important?" She circled a couple of things on the page in front of her, wrote a 72 at the top, and turned it over next to her.

"I can't do that assignment. There's nothing I can write about. I just wanted to let you know."

She set the pen aside and looked at me. "I find it difficult to believe you can't think of anything to write about. Even Vanessa Hamilton managed to come up with five pages about her grandmother's last peach cobbler."

"That's the thing. There's nothing I want anyone else to know about. Cobbler's . . . innocuous."

She waited.

"I don't remember life before my dad left all that well. I mean, we moved around a lot. So, mostly I remember motel rooms and the old VW bus we lived in for a while that we'd park at campgrounds or festival sites, pop up the top and set out a tent for my folks to sleep in while my sisters and I snuggled up in the back of the van. That's my best version of cobbler and I don't want these other kids to know about it. It's mine. It's my memory to hold onto, not theirs to make fun of."

"What about the divorce? Lots of students have divorced parents."

"My parents split up after my dad decided he was gay and in love with a former Marine who retired early because he was tired of hiding who he was. My dad drowned. His . . . Phil treated us like a relative. We called him our uncle. And then he killed himself. And I'm not willing to use his pain to get a decent grade either." The truth was, I could have written about those things. They weren't the aspects of my life that would send social workers into overdrive, but the parts of my life I didn't have to hide felt more worthy of protecting than the ones I had to.

She watched me and I could tell from the way she kept rolling her lips over her teeth that she wanted to tell me whatever the teacher's manual said was the right thing, but she also wanted to ask me if I was making all that up because it did sound a little crazy all laid out that way.

"I loved my uncle. I'm not letting the homophobes in this class say the very things that made him feel he had to leave a job he loved and hide in the wilderness. I won't."

Her voice softened. "Is there anything you need to tell me?"

"There's nothing wrong with my home life. I just don't want to subject it to these assholes who've never been outside the county unless it was on a school bus full of football helmets. Just give me an F. I'll make it up. Or I won't."

I turned and left.

Things hurt deep inside me and I wanted something to take it away. I wanted to pound my fist into something until all the ache had moved to my bones.

At the end of the hall, I found Jeff Williams pulling his gym bag out of his locker.

I walked up to him and stuck my face very close to his. "Stay away from Jackie Turner."

He turned, fist curled and flying.

I redirected him into the locker next to his and punched him in the kidney. Something else Uncle Phil taught me.

Anger-fueled redness traveled up his neck, but when he turned, he just stood there. "What the hell's wrong with you?"

I wanted to pound him or provoke him to beat me. But I couldn't be that girl anymore.

I didn't answer him. I didn't know what to say.

My father had told me to protect my sisters, watch out for Charley. Uncle Phil had taught me how, given me the tools. Looking out for the people around me had been my job for so long, I didn't know who I was without it.

"Well? What? Do you *like* her or something? I knew you weren't right."

"She's my friend." I wasn't sure she'd agree, but it left my tongue anyway. "And I don't let bullies hurt my friends."

49 FOOT WOMAN STRAPS IT ON

Laird Barron

Rainier, a shaggy heeler mix, barked on the porch aware somehow of worse shit than usual going down. Meanwhile inside the doublewide trailer the weekend DJ's voice degenerated into gibberish before the radio crapped out. The lights swooned.

Dennis sang in a twangy slur, "I shoot my .45 all day. I shoot sixers every night. Don't tread on me, baby." He danced a slow-motion twist. His chest hair was thick and gray as shag carpet on the floorboard of a rusted-out Caddy. He wore a yellow and black Penguins ball cap, three-day-old jockey shorts, unlaced combat boots, and a gun belt. The pistol was indeed a .45. Smith & Wesson single-action. A parting memento from his best buddy at the plant, Chester "Mean Motor Scooter" Pruitt, who got sent away for a dime for beating his brother-in-law half to death with a hockey stick while watching game seven of the Stanley Cup. The boys had joked about Chester's "party foul" until the plant got closed six months later.

Dennis and Tammy argued over the phone bill. Tammy didn't recognize a number and wouldn't let it go after due warning. Due warning, mama. Due dadblamed warning. Dennis backhanded her, as you do, as his dear dad had done with his mama, not full-force, only a Wayne County attitude adjustment, but hard enough to put her on her cow ass, except she didn't fold, she went rigid and some of her face peeled and revealed twinkling circuitry beneath. Kept looking at him with the brown human eye. The other eye blazed red, then fizzed and died and spiraled shut like a sphincter of razorblades. He thought maybe his hand was broken.

He fetched ice from the icebox and tucked it into a dishrag and laid the rag on his hand. He sipped the dregs of a bottle of Knob Creek at the table and watched his knuckles puff. Hurt real good, too. Goddamn it all to hell. Broken sure as god made little green apples. Bar buddies Larry and Mike would roll by in a few hours to pick him up to hunt deer. How would he shoot with a busted hand? Couldn't even crack a beer or zip his fly. Look what the stupid cow had made him go and do.

Tammy remained frozen in her tracks in the middle of the trailer, head tilted (hair still in curlers), left arm raised protectively, right arm limp. Her bathrobe sash came loose and her tit drooped. Twinkle-twinkle went the circuit board of her cheek. The room smelled of ozone. A faint drone rose and fell.

The Christmas light array mesmerized him. Reminded him of a scene from his favorite childhood television show, *The Six Million Dollar Man*. Oscar Goldman got replaced by a robot imposter. Steve Austin figured out the plot when Goldman's face came loose like a fuse box panel and revealed a mess of circuits and plugs. Game on, fuckers! Austin whacked the robot with a karate chop.

Dennis took another swallow and glanced away from his wife (eleven, drunken blissful years!) and tried to make heads or tails of it. "Baby, when you get replaced by an android?"

"Android is a sophisticated word choice for a Neanderthal." Tammy and her face on the half shell loomed over him. She smiled an abbreviated smile. He hadn't seen her move. Hadn't heard the rusty creak of the floorboards. "To answer your question—Tammy Georgianna Trebuchet expired forty-four days, three hours, nine minutes, twenty-six seconds ago. Thoracic hemorrhaging. Blunt force trauma antecedent. Your steel-toe boot impacted her xiphoid process. The ensuing rupture caused her to decease on the couch, 3:09 PM, Wednesday, July 28. At 7:53 PM you returned to this residence and were anesthetized in prelude to transition from *Phase One* to *Phase Two*. You regained consciousness on schedule at 10:08 PM. This unit assumed Tammy's role at 10:09 PM, July 28." She sounded the same as ever. Less shrill, maybe. Not a smidgeon judgmental—the facts and only the facts, son. "Incidentally, relocation and replacement of male penitents is nearly one hundred percent accomplished in all terrestrial demographic regions."

"Wha? Nuh-uh. I never kicked you."

"You struck *Tammy* many times, Dennis. Forty-seven incidents are on record."

He remembered, oh yeah, boy howdy. A humid afternoon, hotter than a two-peckered Billy goat. Tammy got lippy and he'd decked her. She laughed to spite him, so he nudged her gut with the toe of his size-twelve Cabela's. For a minute he worried he'd hurt her, because she curled into a ball and went purple and didn't respond when he gave her three or four dropkicks in the ass to grow on.

Finally she crawled to the couch and clicked on the boob tube. Wouldn't look him in the eye. Progress at last. He roared off to the tavern and socked back a few brews. Typical Wednesday between unemployment checks. Came home after dark and she'd whipped up fried chicken and potato salad, the way he liked. They watched reruns of *Duck Dynasty* and *Cops*. All forgiven. Tammy *always* forgave him. She knew damn well her hellcat act brought on his bad moods. Those bad moods had bedeviled him ever since he came home from the Gulf War as his first wife, Ruby-Jane, could've attested. Besides, he didn't slap Tammy around the way some guys did their old ladies. Her last husband, Ivan, a *real* sonofabitch, put her in traction once. Fixed her so she couldn't have kids. Sort of a blessing, the wrecked baby maker part, although Dennis wouldn't admit it, not aloud.

"Oh, yeah. Ya got me, Tammy." He nodded helplessly. "Reckon I done wrong. But, hon, I'm real sorry. Only the good Lord can judge me. Unless He sent you to set me straight. You here to set me straight, woman?"

"I am not an agent of your mythological deity."

"What are you?"

"An android, silly. Before you ask, I am not modeled after a Schwarzenegger cyborg. Excellent film, however." Robot Tammy paused to acknowledge a fresh round of frantic barking. "Rainier is not distressed by my presence. We have reached an accommodation. His canine senses apprehend the initiation of *Phase Two*."

"Well, far as I can tell, this is a load of this bullshit. I want my wife back."

"Your wife's corpse has been processed. Standard protocol. I assure you, Tammy's memories are ninety-eight percent intact within my data core. Our judgment against you relies upon accurate data, Dennis."

"Get her back. Right now." Dennis thought about what Chuck Norris would do in a fix like this.

"You may be interested to learn Tammy was capable of childbearing. During a medical exam she discovered the damage her previous husband inflicted proved not to be permanent. Tammy was four months pregnant at the time of her death."

"The hell you say!"

Robot Tammy smiled pitilessly. "Tammy terminated the pregnancy and chose to keep her condition a secret. I am sure you can understand this decision. A mother will take any measure to protect her children."

He pulled his trusty .45. Switched awkwardly to a left grip after almost fumbling the weapon, and aimed at Robot Tammy's forehead. "Lying bitch! Get my wife. Won't tell you again."

"Violence against this unit is not recommended. Multiple redundancies are in effect."

"Maybe I put a bullet in your brainpan and see how it goes?"

"Touché. *Phase Two* is initiated. *Phase Two* admittedly involves physical and mental violence as global operant modalities. Terror is also an operant modality, else I would have euthanized you in your sleep. Suffering is an operant modality, else I would introduce a nerve toxin and euthanize you at this moment. Do you comprehend mass extinction of the alpha male transgressor of your species, Dennis? Comprehension is a critical component of your transition to inanimate matter. You personally will persist as a historical footnote—the inciting incident. Be advised you have under ten seconds to savor this recognition."

Dennis hadn't the foggiest clue what "multiple redundancies" meant, and the vaguest grasp of "extinction." Nonetheless, the purpose of the jagged metal prong that burst through her knuckles seemed plain. He fired twice. Cumbersome grip and all, no way he could miss at this range. Bullets *spanged* against metal and Robot Tammy toppled. Smoke curled from the ruins of her skull.

He sat, ears ringing, flustered and confused as to whether recent events meant he was guilty of murder for what happened to the real Tammy. Would the government send men in a black helicopter to make him pay for destroying her robot decoy? Surely the government had something to do with it. The Coward in Chief Obama loved his drones and fancy technology. The feds used a robot to terrorize them folks in Ruby Ridge in the 90s. Beer buddy Mike swore there were secret mountain FEMA camps surrounded by barbed wire and stocked with thousands of body bags.

Speaking of bodies—Robot Tammy's corpse shifted. Metal contracted and fake flesh hissed as if splashed by acid. She bubbled and coagulated and dissolved into a dry ice mist that slithered into a floor vent. Left behind a wet imprint and the foul odors of burnt wires and scorched meat.

Red light flooded through seams at the opposite end of the trailer. Tammy smashed through the bedroom door. This version of his wife had her face on straight, although sort of incomplete, as if the clay mask hadn't quite set. She smiled. Something dark and soft writhed in her hands.

"I have a divorce present for you, Dennis," she said in a metallic voice.

"Aw, honey." He squeezed the trigger. The shot didn't slow her approach. He tossed the empty revolver aside (too broke to keep it fully loaded) and ran outside and jumped into the truck. Praise Baby Jesus the keys were in the ignition. Rainier clambered after him and pissed all over the bench seat. Dennis gave not a solitary fuck. He mashed his foot to the gas pedal and tore through the Chaucer Estates trailer court, hell-bent for anywhere but there.

A shotgun boomed nearby and glass exploded. Barrel flashes lit trailer windows on both sides of the road. A gaggle of local kids danced on the grass before Jerry Snell's Airstream. Smoke billowed from the open doorway. Uncle Jerry, as his neighbors sarcastically called him, loved kids so much he played Santa at the outlet mall every year. Pinched one too many bottoms and now he had his very own personal parole officer and received monthly drop-in visits from the sheriff's department.

"*Phase Two*, Rainier!" Dennis said. "Shitfire, it's *Phase Two* all over the dad-blamed place!"

A former line buddy at the plant, Jason Drake, fled into his yard, screaming bloody murder. Jason's mousey wife, Ruby-Jean, leaped from the shadows and split his noggin with a hatchet. Her eyes glared klaxon red as she tracked Dennis racing past. The gore-caked hatchet shattered the rear window and lodged in the dashboard vinyl.

Rainier yelped. Dennis wrenched the wheel this way, then another, frantic to keep his rig between the ditches. Damned heroic feat doing it mainly left-handed and with his right forearm. He made it around the bend as fires bloomed in the rearview. The gas gauge needle hovered on E. Nothing new; no money for bullets or fuel (barely enough for booze). He'd make it to the trooper station if he had to pedal.

Local radio channels hissed dead air until a woman (who sounded a mite like Erma Satchett, the right Reverend Paul Satchett's cookie-baking wife) laughed and said, "*Follow a shadow, it still flies you. Seem to fly it, it will pursue.* Too bad Ben Jonson is dust. That old boy could have used a good decapitating. To all you husbands and boyfriends at large in Wayne County: Run, fellas. Drive them beat-up Fords and Chevys right off the map. It don't matter. All roads lead to doom."

"I know it!" Dennis smacked the speaker. Erma Satchett cackled. The radio died and so did the truck. He coasted to the shoulder and hunkered for a few minutes, struggling to sort what he should do next. He'd accidentally left a couple of Natty Lights on the floorboard the other day after a run to the shopping center. He drank them while waiting for genius to strike.

A Wayne County patrol car flew by, sirens and lights going. It headed toward the trailer park. Three more cruisers and a fire engine followed. He finished the beer and climbed out of the truck and trudged unsteadily uphill toward town. Rainier paced him, nails clicking on asphalt. The mutt whined and sniffed. Ashes drifted on the breeze. Dennis tasted the sharp accent of cindered wood and plastic and oil.

He hooked a right onto a dirt road. The road bent through the trees for a tenth of a mile and opened into a clearing. A handful of wrecked vehicles and a Jeep crowded around Cousin Leon's modular. He hadn't spoken with Cousin Leon since Easter Sunday, 2013—they'd fallen out over a gambling debt and Leon warned him not to show his face on the property unless he cared to eat two barrels of rock salt. Dennis decided tonight warranted the risk.

"Okay, Rainier. Wait." He gestured and the dog resignedly dropped to his belly.

The porch light attracted a cloud of death's-head moths (who'd ever heard of such a thing in Pennsylvania?). Dennis shooed the moths and pounded on the door and received no answer, so he pushed his luck and barged on in.

Cousin Leon slumped in a deck chair, a twelve gauge shotgun across his knees. His torso and head were flattened like a cartoon character mushed by a steamroller. A patch of starry abyss shivered behind his chair where the wall should've been. The abyss slowly sucked Leon in as he gripped the shotgun stock hard enough his fingernails peeled off with little squirts of blood. The man blinked and his mouth moved soundlessly as his upper half stretched farther and farther into space.

"At last, you've arrived." Grandma Clara perched upon the edge of Leon's Scotch-guarded loveseat. She'd gone to heaven in 1996 courtesy of a bum ticker—and returned for a visit, apparently. She wore her best blue dress and thick glasses, not a whisker out of place. Every inch the benevolent little red schoolhouse schoolmarm who only tanned children if they truly deserved the lash. She'd often told Dennis, *this hurts me more than it hurts you!* as she brought the pain with a leather strap. "Where are your clothes, young man? It's uncouth to roam the woods in your tighty-whities."

"Grandma!" Dennis said. "You can't be here. You're with the angels!"

"I'm not Grandma. Doubtful Jesus would have her, anyway. She went to the grave believing it was her fault you're, and I quote, *a rotten waste of space.* One can't always beat the devil out of a child, though she surely tried. No matter. I've awaited your arrival with great anticipation. It is my duty to impress upon you the full extent of your plight."

He glanced at mutilated Cousin Leon. Further impressing was unnecessary. "Grandma, not you too with the android jib jabber. The world is comin' to the end. It's the Rapture! Come get me, Jesus!" Words, empty, pathetic words. He felt about ready to burst into tears, yet his eyes ached, bone dry. He wasn't even scared anymore. Fear had given way to inconsolable sadness.

"Correct. Your world is coming to an end. However, to amplify a previous point—this isn't the world you lived in prior to forty-four days ago, although you recollect it as such. The former world is spinning along without you."

"Please stop talking, Grandma."

"Boy, the whole point of this exercise is to penetrate that monkey brain of years with a modicum of enlightenment."

"No. Let me be."

"Aren't you a teeny bit curious?" Grandma Clara winked as if she were fixing to reach into her purse and hand him a cookie.

"Naw, I ain't."

"Sure you are. Your memories were altered at the moment of your electromagnetic transmission. The only human inhabitants of this version of Wayne County are those guilty of specific trespasses against man and animal. A shockingly significant percentage, I am sorry to report. These worthies have been collected and concentrated in a facsimile of the region you knew. Do understand what a facsimile is? It means not genuine leather. Not the real McCoy."

Dennis gawped, catching some of the gist and torn between a maddening urge to unload his .45 into her and relief that thanks to a lack of ammo he didn't have to make the decision of whether or not to ventilate his own grandma.

She said, "All you behold is fabricated for your benefit and the benefit of your fellow penitents. Perhaps it will help, in the minutes remaining to you, to imagine this new reality as a planetoid-sized sound stage and all its hubbub a play."

"Yeah, but . . . It's not fair." Dennis heard himself whine and wasn't ashamed. "Please, what is this? What did I do? What's happening to me? Am I in hell?"

"A perceptive inquiry. Hell, as depicted in your various world mythologies, does not exist. Pity. Therefore, a hell was fabricated in honor of your kind. In fact, we have designed several hells. However, you need only concern yourself with the one. Do you know what makes this hell, Dennis?"

Dennis opened the shitty 1950s fridge and grabbed a can of Leon's even shittier Natty Lite. "I expect I don't, Grandma." He popped the top and foam bubbled forth. Only foam and not a drop of life-sustaining beer.

"Hell is forever. Or an approximately prolonged duration. We can reconstitute you from a few molecules. A smear on the asphalt. This will never end. That's what makes it hell."

"I'm bein' punished on account of Tammy. Don't seem right to torment me this way, no how. No, ma'am. Don't seem right."

"Gracious, boy, this isn't *punishment*." She gave him a sympathetic smile. "It's *torment*. We don't care, except in an anthropological sense, about your perceived misdeeds. Whomever you mated with, or whomever you abused. We *are* exceedingly interested in your reaction to stimuli." Her smile glazed and became the loveless grin of a dead thing.

"Grandma...Grandma, I gotta get along." He sidled for the door, giving his cousin a wide berth. Leon lifted one foot and set it down, then the other. Most of him had gotten pulled into outer space. His presumably screaming head was light years away.

"Yes! You're on a tight schedule, dear." Grandma Clara tapped her watch. "Don't let me keep you."

Dennis fled the modular. He ran around back to the woodshed and kicked the door in. Cousin Leon had belonged to a half-assed militia and damned if those fellas didn't love to shoot a few thousand rounds every other weekend. Leon stashed an arsenal of semi-auto rifles all over his property. Dennis figured an M14, a nine millimeter pistol, and a bandolier of ammo would be just the ticket.

Greenish light oozed from a single bulb. He didn't see any guns. However, he noticed right away a dozen or so men packed together, each clad in jockey shorts and combat boots, and each wearing *his* face, vacant as night. The men didn't move a muscle or react to his entrance, not even the double who'd caught the door hard and blood trickled from his nose. Without blinking, it said, "Am I dead? Am I dead? Am I dead?" The others joined in a monotone chorus, "Am I dead? Am I dead?"

Grandma Clara's babbling finally made horrifying sense. Dennis had been cloned! In a brief epiphany, he wondered if he was really himself or a clone replaying the worst night of its life. His mind went dark. He screamed and ran, Rainier barking at his heels.

A red glow on the horizon led him through the trees. After a long, blind, headlong flight that saw him trip and fall and rise again, he emerged onto the highway where it crested a bluff overlooking town. Branches had skinned him head to shin. He gasped for breath. He dripped snot and tears. His shorts were soggy with piss.

Town burned. A pretty Hollywood explosion took the top off the power plant. Air raid klaxons wailed. Toy cars crashed, tiny action figures milled and shrieked tiny shrieks. Clouds of fiery ash divided and a giant, naked woman lurched into view. Five stories high and in murder mode. Spotlighted by a hovering attack chopper, her features were brutally perfect, the way advertisers had morphed the modern Betty Crocker portrait from the likenesses of seventy women, except instead of Betty, the enormous, wrathful face was all the best features of women Dennis had known—his mother, a long lost girlfriend, his sister, grandma, aunt, the chick who slung drinks at the tavern, and others he'd forgotten until that moment.

Gunfire popped and metal groaned. The titan slapped the side of a brownstone and it crumbled into a pillar of dust. She snatched an armored car and pitched it at the chopper. The truck arced just above the rotor and tumbled end over end into the night.

Most of the households in this neck of the woods were stocked with rifles. Men organized ragged phalanxes and initiated a cap gun fusillade. Other men raced past in pickups, blasting away. None of this appeared to have much effect except to further enrage her. She roared. Men and cars whirled like leaves. Her eyes flared and twin beams of crimson death zapped her teeny-tiny enemies to powder. Then, with nightmare-logic, her awful gaze settled upon the ridge where Dennis gibbered. She grinned and pointed at him across the gulf of infernos and rubble.

Dennis and Rainier bolted along the road away from the lumbering colossus. Dennis ran until tall trees blocked the glimmering heavens and kept running until the explosions, sirens, and hateful roars gradually faded. He ran until his legs buckled and his insides convulsed. He dragged himself down an embankment and into the sweet, damp gloom of a culvert.

Eventually, dawn light crept into his hidey hole. Dennis shivered. Battered, bruised, eaten alive by mosquitos, he was miserable enough to crawl forth. Where to go? "Dog, what we gonna do now?"

From the black end of the culvert, Grandma Clara said, "I don't rightly know, boy. It's going to be entertaining, whatever happens."

Dennis crabbed toward light and escape. Rainier blocked the way. The dog's silhouette rippled as hide peeled to reveal metal. His eyes flickered and flamed.

"Whoa, boy. Easy there." Dennis crouched, hands raised defensively. He recalled with sickening clarity the many times he'd kicked the stuffing out of his faithful pooch and wondered which blow had done the trick.

Rainier growled like a circular saw.

MOON OVER THE MIDWEST

Elizabeth Amber Love

The first time I looked out over that field, all I saw was freedom. There were twelve planes scheduled to be in the air show, but there was only one that I cared about. I don't know nothing about planes, but I know that one; it belongs to the only person I think can save me from this Hell.

They say our slavery to the white man ended decades ago, but for a girl like me who's got Indian and Negro blood, I haven't even felt free among my own family. I'm the youngest girl. Opal is sixteen, five years older than me. Joshua isn't even ten yet. The family treats him special. Not sure if it's on account of him being a boy or because he don't act like everyone else. That's what Momma always calls him, "special." He don't talk. He smiles once in a while. He didn't learn to walk until he was three. Opal is the prize. She's pretty and she sings like an angel. That's why they always make her sing in church.

I don't have none of that. I just want out. There has to be more to my life than being scared every time it's dark or every time I'm told to stay in a room with one of Daddy's friends. He don't think I know what's going on, but I see them giving him money. The first time, I kept telling myself it wouldn't never happen again, but it does and I'm ready to get out of here.

When I first heard about Bessie Coleman, I didn't believe a word of what Junior Knox was saying. He told me there was this Negro woman who flew planes just like any man. Better than a man, he said. Junior kept swooping around with his arms out wide talking about Bessie flying in circles, looping around the sky, and even going right through barns.

It's crazy, I told him. No way could a woman learn to do that, especially a

Negro woman. The day Junior Knox told me about Bessie, all I wanted to do was meet her.

Looking across the Knox field at their biggest barn, I had the hardest time thinking about what my life could be if only I could get lucky. My dreams are nightmares. Every time I'm lying in bed next to Opal, I wonder if the door will creak and my father's hands will pull me up. Gotta keep quiet, he says each time, don't want to wake Opal or anyone else. No way Momma can't know what goes on.

All those planes lined up and ready for take-off look like the most magical thing I could ever imagine. That's when I begin to think that maybe I can hide in one and go some place new. Some place where I'm not Primrose Rivers. It doesn't take long for me to pick a new name. My grandmother's name in English means "clear springs under the moon" so the folks just call her Moon River. She's the only grownup I trust. I've heard Moon Momma arguing with Daddy before. It's hard to tell what they're saying, but I just know in my gut she's trying to protect me. If all you hear is the power and anger in her voice, you don't need to understand a word of it to know that she's giving a warning. Some day, I'll be somewhere else and I'll be reborn as Moon Coleman.

I have to figure out a plan before the planes leave town. The air show is in two days. They're practicing now and going around the town telling every-one about it. Bessie will get her picture in *The Defender,* no doubt about it. A woman like us better be front page in our newspaper.

• • •

My sister Opal and I were in bed. There was light coming through the win-dow from the moon because the sky was so clear. I couldn't even see much of my own skin in the darkness. I wanted to be like Opal and be able to sleep. No one bothers her much anymore. She works long hours making clothes and repairing them, but she wants to be a singer. But because she works so hard, the grown ups let her sleep when she can. I'm a different story.

I heard the sounds of Daddy and his friends outside with a fire in a bar-rel that they stand around. Drinking some kind of hooch and wine. They got louder as they drank more. Sometimes they sing and I can hear Uncle Woody's harmonica. It was better when I could hear them. When it gets quiet, that's how I know something will happen.

It didn't take too long, maybe an hour and then there was that lull I feared. A few of them take off to the edge of the yard to go to the bathroom like ani-mals. That's all they are anyway.

The door on the porch swings and slams. Then the inside door to our parlor opens and closes, a bit quieter. Then the protective darkness of my bedroom that had made me invisible is cut open by light from the hallway as the door is slowly opened.

My cries and squirming meant nothing. I think Opal had to hear me but she stayed silent and didn't move at all when I was lifted out of bed.

"Shhhhh. You'll be back asleep in no time."

The whole time, I kept thinking about something else. Some place else. I would be like Bessie Coleman and fly up out of the reach of bad men and get so high, they would only be specks in the distance.

• • •

My grandmother stood upright with her hands in tight fists pulled into her body. She turned to me, still sitting at the table with my tea. I found myself staring at her hands and knew it wasn't good manners as she taught me. Her dark eyes waited for me to meet them.

"The Mamaceqtaw are used to being beaten and abused." Moon Momma stood still while she educated me on some of our history. "When we were put in schools with the White children, we were beaten for speaking our language. It is that fear that drove some to leave."

"Is that why you aren't with the tribe anymore?" I could have stayed quiet and listened, but I was always too impatient about things I found curious.

"Decisions are hard sometimes. Your grandfather and I thought we could adapt to life away. We didn't do too bad. We made a very good life here and provided well. We stayed here instead of moving in winters. I tell you all this so that you understand I cannot make your choice for you. I had to make my own choices and now you have to do that for yourself."

I kept waiting for her to show me what she got from the chest. Whenever she told stories, she always had to tell me to wait and wait. But my dear grandmother never told me to stop asking questions.

"You are different. You aren't like your cousins. You're not like me. You are your own woman. I think it's time for you to have this." She placed her hand on the table, palm down with the object underneath it, but she didn't reveal it.

"What is it?"

I had to wait for her to sit down next to me and slide closer. With her other hand, she pulled me into her and kissed the top of my head.

"Sometimes people learn important lessons. What I'm about to give you is a treasured trinket. I have this because someone hurt this family when I was a little girl. The man did not get punished, but during the trouble he caused, he began to see things differently. This was good. It was good for him and I hope what he realized will affect how he raised his own children."

I reached over and put my small hand on top of hers. I could feel energy coming through her hand from whatever was hiding underneath. Even not knowing what it was, I felt some kind of power. She continued her story.

"After the wrong that was done, the man paid reparations to our family. This was a big surprise because he was not forced to do it. But this is that payment."

She lifted both our hands away from the object. It was small leather pouch with some of her own beadwork on it. She opened it and poured the contents into her hand. In my grandmother's palm, I saw something beautiful. I had never seen anything like it in person before. It was a small yellow diamond.

People in my town were poor. We didn't get to see things like this. I certainly didn't know any people who owned something so valuable. Yet, here was this treasure in the hand of my Mamaceqtaw grandmother.

"They don't find these often in Wisconsin, where our people live. I think it is time for you to have it."

"But, I can't. That must be a fortune!" I couldn't even bring myself to touch the stone at first. Then she put it in my hand and kept her hand closed over it. "Does Momma know you have this?"

"Of course she does. But your father does not and he never will. It is not for him. It is for you and Opal to get out of there."

"Opal doesn't care about the family on the rez, Moon Momma. She wants to go to Chicago and become a famous singer."

She nodded. "Then, it is for you. Opal will find her dreams."

She pulled her hand back and for the first time, I felt something I never had before. Hope.

• • •

I was terrified of having that diamond inside the leather bag crossing over my body. I felt like everyone I passed knew I had something worth stealing. I opened the bag and checked for the pouch many times. It took a couple of hours for me to reach Knox field for the air show.

Someone built wooden bleachers for people with tickets to sit on. The women had their parasols opened, but there was no way they weren't gonna get painful sunburn. I was pretty invisible walking around the crowd. Instead of wearing pretty dresses and hats like the other girls I saw, I changed into some boys' clothes and had my hair in two long braids. I wasn't like the other girls. No point in pretending to be. They could spend their days wondering if they're pretty enough and if boys like 'em. I got more important things. Overalls worked just fine anyway.

As I walked around one of the carts with root beer and penny candy, I couldn't believe who I smacked right into. It was my sister Opal.

"Where you been?" She was angry, but I wasn't sure if it was because I was missing or because it meant she wasn't being the center of attention for once.

"You know where I was. Where I always go—after. Not like you care, Opal."

She grabbed me by the shoulder and dragged me away from all the ears that could overhear us. I didn't fight back or push her off because I was still holding the strap of my bag for dear life.

"Everyone was worried, you little brat."

"If they get so worried, why don't anyone care about what gets done to me?" I used my shoulder's own strength to force it away from Opal's grasp. "You should care, Opal! This happened to you too!" I saw her furrowed brow soften and her tight lips turn to a frown.

"Baby girl, they'll be done with you soon. I want to get away too. But worrying Momma is no way to go about that."

"Well, I'm getting out now. You do what you want." My sister was just about as determined as I was even though we're quite different people. I'm not a proper lady like she is. I don't have her voice or her beauty. Am I supposed to believe she sees us as equals? Am I supposed to believe she cares?

"What's your big plan, Prim? Where are you gonna go?"

"None of your concern. I got something in mind and I ain't about to tell you or you'll go running back. I don't want anyone knowing until I'm long gone."

No matter what I said, Opal wasn't giving up easy. She stuck close to me even after I tried walking away from her. My shoes were covered by the dusty ground. The dirt was dry as a desert. A storm was coming, but the air show should be done before it hits.

"Here." Opal had taken a peppermint stick and broke it in half. "Have some."

"Where'd you get the money for candy?"

She wouldn't look at me when she answered. "Papa. He gave me fifty cents before I left. They're here too somewhere. They got to keep an eye on Joshua because you know he just wanders off."

"Do you know where that fifty cents came from? I can't believe you. I don't want your stupid candy." I shoved her hand away. We didn't talk much for a while.

A man's voice came through a bullhorn telling everyone that the Jennies, pilots, and performers would be lined up for some picture taking then they would start the flying. We changed course to find them so I could get as close as possible, all the while hoping my family would never see me in the crowd.

There were two different groups. The black pilots and performers would go first. We stayed by their runway. The other folks with the nice bleachers, they had a lot more people on that side. They only had Negroes and Whites. Even white women couldn't fly in the same line as their men. Lots of other people were still left out.

We're close to Chicago and there's been a lot more for dark people to do in performing. That's why Opal thinks she stands a chance. We never drew attention to our Menominee roots much. But Opal was told that her "exotic" looks would be good on stage. I might be mad as hell at her, but I hope she gets what she wants. For me, I needed to find Bessie Coleman and talk to her.

"Prim! There she is." Opal spotted my hero walking to her plane. That contraption looked like it was barely held together. Seems they made an effort to shine it up for the show anyway.

"You girls here to see Bessie?" A boy about Opal's age was excited to talk to anyone about the planes.

"Yeah, what do you know about her?" I learned a little from Junior Knox but if this kid had more to say, I was willing to listen.

He took out a folded program from his back pocket and handed it to me. It was stained in soda pop and dirt.

"You can keep it. I'm done with it." He seemed excited about everything he said. Guess he didn't get out much.

"Thanks." I still needed to keep my distance even from people who seemed nice. I was not going to let go of my bag and the treasure. When I looked up to ask his name, he was already sprinting through the crowd to get as close to the planes as they'd let him, which was touching a wing, before someone shooed him out of a photograph.

The program said Bessie would be first in line. I read a couple sentences saying Bessie learned to fly in France and has been performing stunt shows in the Midwest. She was part of a group of five called barnstormers and they would be clearing the area for the Negro and Women's finale where they would fly straight through the Knox's biggest barn.

• • •

"You want me to sign that for you, sweetie?" Bessie said to me when I got within reach.

For a moment, I forgot why I was there. I looked up at her and drank her in. Her shirt was perfectly bleached linen. A tan silk scarf around her neck blew over her left shoulder. She's wasn't that tall for a woman, but to my eyes, she was as tall as an oak. She was my own Mount Rushmore and she was close enough for me to touch.

"Darlin'? You okay?"

"Oh, yes, ma'am. Sorry." She took my program and signed her name on the page with her photo. I felt Opal trying to pull me away. I guess an autograph is all anyone else wanted, but I needed more time.

"Miss Bessie?"

"Yes?"

"I need to talk to you. It's really important."

"What's your name, girl?"

"You can call me Moon."

"Moon, huh? Pretty name."

Since almost all the reporters were focused on other pilots, Bessie only had to ask one if he was all finished with her. Then she bent over and looked at me. Her eyes had their own kind of happiness and joy. I sucked in my lips trying to find my courage, that strength Moon Momma said I have.

"I was wondering, if there was any way...maybe...I'd do anything to...what I'm trying to say is that I'd like to come with you. I'd like to be your student and learn to be a pilot and get far away from here."

Bessie nodded her head while she took a second to think.

"Are you really interested in the planes or is this about the adventure?"

"Both, ma'am. I want to be just like you and see the rest of the world outside this old town. I need to go with you!"

I didn't know how to tell her why it was so important that I get out of here. I didn't want to ever think about this place again. All I wanted was to be up by the mountaintops and the clouds away from people.

"Where are your folks?"

"I...please. Don't talk to them. My sister is here. She's right over there! You can talk to her if you need to." I pointed over at Opal who was distracted by a handsome boy. My eyes got watery. Brave girls don't cry, I told myself and sniffed up the runniness inside my nose.

"I can't kidnap a child. You understand that, right, Moon?"

"It's not kidnapping! I'm begging. I will be a great assistant. I promise! I'll learn everything real fast. I can do any kind of chores you want. Just take me with you!"

"You say that tall one is your sister over there?"

"Yes, ma'am. Please! I can pay you even."

"You can pay me?" She made a 'tsk' sound with her tongue and then shifted her sights back to Opal. "I can tell you're riled about something. Maybe if I talk to your sister, we'll figure all this out. You, wait here."

I stood by the Curtiss JN-4D model plane that Bessie would pilot soon while she walked over to Opal and shooed the boy away. She put a friendly arm around my sister's shoulders. I did almost the same thing to the tail of the plane hugging it as best as I could and leaning my face against the smooth surface.

Bessie came over. I felt like my fingernails could have dug right in to keep from being separated from my only way out.

"All right, Moon. Your sister calls you Primrose, by the way."

I hung my head down.

"I understand now why you need to leave. I'd still feel a lot better if I could talk to your Momma."

I reached into my satchel and pulled out the small beaded bag.

"I have to show you something. My grandmother gave me this to give to you, if you'd save me. It's her permission and she's my elder. My mother won't talk to you. You have to believe me."

The shiny little stone against the palm of Bessie's hand looked like she was holding fire.

"This is a treasure, girl."

"It's all I have and it's yours if you'll help me."

Bessie had no intention of taking my only possession, but I didn't know that then. I suddenly had power, just because I owned a tiny little thing. And my hero, my idol, Bessie Coleman felt it.

"This is yours. You're going to keep this or sell it so you have money of your own. Don't you dare show anyone else, ya hear?"

"Yes, ma'am. But will you help me anyway?"

"After what your sister said, I can't say no. I can't let you go back there. In fact, Opal told me about her dreams of becoming a singer in Chicago and I can help her. Maybe. I can introduce her to my friend, Robert Abbott. He knows everyone in that town and he can probably set her up with a good job, too.

"I'll try my best. I can't promise anything, but Mr. Abbott is a good kind man. I'll send him a letter as soon as I can."

She put a hand on my shoulder, and it was probably supposed to be just that, a soft but strong hand to make me feel better. Instead, I pushed against her and wrapped my arms around her so tight and couldn't stop myself from silently crying into her expensive clothes.

For the rest of the air show, I stayed hidden in the crowd as best as possible. I prayed for Bessie's safety. I prayed that she wouldn't change her mind when she landed.

I gave Opal the autographed program when it was time to say goodbye. She held me for longer than she ever had before. She knew we'd probably never see each other again.

When we got settled in Chicago, Bessie gave me an ammunition box with a padlock. I kept the canary diamond inside its beaded pouch and put it in the box. My hand was practically white from holding it so tightly. I was so afraid that the moment it was away from me, my safety would be gone. Bessie needed me to trust her. She had taken me this far, so I had to keep believing in her. The locked box would be safe and hidden.

I started working for her right away and earned my own keep. We would go to the airfield and she taught me about the mechanics of the plane. I even started to learn some of the French she knew. Our brown hands were blackened by grease and grew calluses, but it was the first time I felt beautiful. Beautiful in that way God's creatures are supposed to be. Miraculous. And finally breathing without fear.

THE SIXTH FLOOR

Albert Tucher

"Unfortunately," said Diana, "this takes me back."

"To what, hotel lobbies?" said Drake.

"My natural habitat. Used to be, anyway."

He knew. She had never tried to hide her past from anyone who worked for her.

They sat together at a table in the bar with a view of the lobby. She thought they looked the part of a married couple just a little bored with each other.

Blending in was good.

In the lobby an ex-Marine named Scott was taking up a chair and pretending to tap at the screen of his tablet. He was one of her men. Upstairs, she had another operative blocking the door of room 631 and trying to look like what he was, a hired bodyguard.

If an attacker got that far, the time for deception would be long past.

Her cell phone buzzed.

"Confirming the male white," said Manny on the sixth floor. "Thirties, extensive facial burn scars."

"What room?"

"Six-thirty-eight."

"Okay," she said.

She disconnected. Apparently the man was nothing more than a hotel guest, but Drake still looked displeased.

"I wish we could have just cleared that floor."

"The principal said no."

The client insisted that someone would notice something big in the works, and he wanted to stay under the radar. He had also leaned on the hotel to turn off the security cameras on the sixth floor.

"He even wanted Manny to stand away from the door, but I put my foot down."

Their client was meeting with a longtime business rival in an attempt to end hostilities and collaborate on a major deal in a nasty part of the world. He expected certain people to do anything they could to prevent the new alliance.

Diana and Drake went back to watching. Fifteen minutes passed.

"Look," she said. "There's one."

A young blonde woman, impeccably turned out in a charcoal gray business suit, had just entered the hotel through the revolving glass door. She strode past the bar to the elevators.

Spotting hookers was a good way to pass the time while maintaining their vigilance. And what the hell, Drake could always stand to have his horizons broadened. Diana's assistant was a little prudish, and she enjoyed messing with him.

"I'll defer to your expertise," he said. "But I think she just looks corporate."

"There's a look. She has it, like she's seen everything before. I've been told I have it, too."

Drake didn't look convinced.

"But even if you don't know that look, there are other clues. Like the timing."

"Three minutes to three," he said. "Okay, but she could just have a business meeting."

"Those heels are just a little too high."

"Maybe."

"And then there's her bag."

"It's just a bag."

"But it's too big for her management image. A real executive would have a slim-line attaché. She's carrying the tools of the trade. Condoms, lube, wipes, different kinds of lingerie, probably fetish gear. She won't need it, though."

"How can you know that?"

"I don't for sure. But I'm guessing her client was that guy we just saw checking in."

"Oh."

While Drake processed that, she watched the floor indicator over the elevator door. She called Manny.

"Looks like she's going all the way up. Stay sharp."

"Always," said Manny.

"Okay," Drake said, "you convinced me. He gets the room, and she comes to him."

"I had a couple of clients like him, back in the day. Of course, my war was Vietnam."

She laughed at herself.

"Listen to me. Like I was there getting shot at."

Drake was giving her a curious look. He knew her age, thirty-nine.

"Clients tended to be older. A lot of them could have been my father. Anyway, I can remember three who were burned like that."

"Was that . . . difficult?"

"In the beginning. With any guy there's a period of getting to know each other. After a while it gets so the guy just looks like himself. Even if he scares people on the street."

"Ouch."

"No sense sugar-coating it. The guys themselves never did. Anyway, the clients I'm talking about wanted a quickie and then basically company. Nothing kinky."

"That guy was Afghanistan or Iraq," said Drake.

"It never ends."

The phone rang.

"She's here," said Manny, "and she doesn't seem to know where she's going. Wait, she's coming this way."

"Straighten her out."

"No problem."

Diana disconnected the call, but something niggled at her.

The conversation lapsed. Traffic through the lobby was sparse on a weekday afternoon. That was why the second woman attracted Diana's eye.

A brunette in her twenties, wearing a businesslike white blouse, a trim black skirt and heels.

High heels. And a large bag.

Okay, there was probably enough business in this hotel for two hookers, but Diana's bad feeling got worse, and now she realized why. If the first woman was as experienced as she looked, she would know which way to go on the sixth floor. Diana had carried maps of the various hotels in her mind like mental phone apps.

Diana exchanged looks with Drake. They both got up and went to the elevators as quickly as they could without running. Just as the door slid open, Diana put her hand on the brunette's arm.

"Wait," she said.

The young woman's eyes widened, and Diana knew what she was thinking.

"I'm not a cop, and I don't care about your business. But you need to wait."

She bored into the hooker with her eyes, until the young woman nodded. Scott joined them.

"Stay with her," Diana told him. "And keep an eye. We don't know who else might be coming."

She didn't add that there was no sense in losing all three of them to an Uzi blast through the door on the sixth floor.

Diana drew her Glock from the belt holster under her jacket. In this career her uniform was pant suits and low heels.

Drake had his gun out. The door opened, and Diana exited low and fast, with him right behind her.

Manny was down, with his gun and his hands-free headset on the floor beside him. He groped for the gun with his left hand, which was bad. Diana knew he was a rightie.

That wasn't all. The man and the woman in front of 631 would have looked as if they were dancing, except that there was no music, and most dancing couples don't grapple over a gun.

Diana could see burn scars on the man's face. His partner was the blonde hooker.

Their faces as they spun and spun were grim and intent. The man caught Diana's eye for a moment. He made one more circle and hurled his partner away from him.

The young blonde held onto the gun. She aimed at the man.

"Don't," said Diana.

The blonde turned to her left and looked into the muzzle of Diana's Glock. Diana had seen pitiless glares before, and this young woman had a good one. The woman also knew how to face the facts, which told her to set her gun down on the ground and back away from it. Diana darted forward and kicked the gun away.

"Now you," she said.

The blonde understood. She got down on the floor.

Over by the wall, the vet bent over, clutched his midsection, and gasped for breath. After a few moments he recovered enough to look up.

"I asked for a brunette," he said.

• • •

"What's in the bag?" said Diana.

"Quite an arsenal," said the middle-aged detective.

He answered without hesitation or attitude, which differed a lot from her dealings with cops in her old career. It still surprised her.

"That was good work," he added.

"We had some help."

She nodded toward the man with the burn scars, who was still standing against the wall. He looked around uncertainly, as the cops packed up and left with the young blonde.

"Let me buy you a drink," said Diana.

"Uh, okay."

They rode the elevator downstairs in silence. In the bar they had their choice of tables. He asked for beer. She had the same.

"Iraq?" she asked when they had their drinks.

"Yeah." He indicated his face. "Fallujah."

"You deal with an agency?"

"Dreamtime Escorts."

Diana laughed. "Trudy Gernsheimer. I don't know why I'm surprised she's still at it. She'll be in business when we're all dead."

She watched him put two and two together. How else would she know who was who in the hooking industry?

"The girl was late," he said. "so I opened up and looked around."

"She was on her way. I saw her."

"So I see this young blonde go up to the guy in the hall. I call out to her, 'Hey, over here.' She half turns around, and I see this gun in her hand. That looked wrong to me."

"It was."

"Does that guy work for you?"

"He does."

"Don't hold it against him. I think she would have fooled anybody."

"I wouldn't be surprised if she really put in some time as a hooker."

"Anyway, I distracted her. That's why she winged him instead of killing him."

"Then you tackled her."

"Instinct, I guess. I hear an ambush, and I charge it."

"Works for me."

She handed him her business card.

"I need another operative, and you've got what it takes. Look me up in a couple of days. If you're interested, that is."

"I just might do that," he said.

"And tell Trudy to bill me for today, and the next time, too. We go way back. She'll get a kick out of overcharging me, but what the hell."

"You don't have to do that."

"Yes, I do. I'm out of that line of work, or you'd get a free one from me."

ADAMSVILLE

Clare Toohey

"I don't like it," said the priest, who'd just figured out how he knew me.

I sighed. "Would you rather turn around? Drop me at a bus station? We're halfway there already." Actually, we'd only left Hoboken four hours before and had almost eight hundred miles ahead of us, but I was making a point.

Father Dennis got it, and took one hand off the wheel to grab another swig of Gatorade. We had thirty cases stacked in the back of the van with many more of water, nutrition bars, and socks. The camper we pulled behind us was loaded with packs of underwear and T-shirts for any age or size, a shipping box full of work gloves, and lots of borrowed power tools. Two guys from another parish's Knights of Columbus were trailing in a Suburban, hauling another stuffed RV. We were racing to Adamsville, Mississippi to help after Katrina. At least to try.

"If you'd accompanied your wife to church more, I might've recognized you earlier," he said. "You could have used your full name on the parish sign-up sheet, *Mike S.*"

"Look, I worked construction and salvage during college. I'm able-bodied. Besides, you know how hard it is for people in the neighborhood to leave work and their families for two weeks. You were lucky to get even three of us."

"You're supposed to be taking time for your bereavement." The bull-necked priest glanced down at the dash. Probably checking the trip odometer, figuring again what it would cost him in time to take me back. "Alzbeta was a very dear person," he said softly.

"But this is an emergency, isn't it?"

"And your son..." He pinched the bridge of his nose before pressing his brows and readjusting his baseball cap.

"If it makes you feel better, no one else likes how I'm handling this either. Not Uncle Georgie. No one from the bar. Now no one plus you."

Father Dennis flicked on his turn signal and merged toward the right lane and the highway exits. I made my final argument.

"We're heading toward people who've lost everything they owned or cared about in one day to a freak of nature. I know more about that than the rest of you. No offense, Father."

He swallowed that one before coming back with his own. "Don't you think you ought to be rebuilding your own life?"

"Right now, there's not enough left of me to bother with," I said and saw the priest wince.

"Michael . . ."

"Mike's fine."

Instead of pulling off, Father Dennis ripped open a pack of jerky with his teeth and started masticating the leather ferociously.

I guessed we were done for now.

After sunset, we met up with the guys in the other truck at a rest stop. Father Dennis pulled Sal and Kevin aside to talk for a minute under the floodlights. Diming me out, I was sure. Back in the van, I took the overnight shift of driving, since bar hours run late. I'd never slept well at night anyway.

Nighttime always put me on the defensive, started my brain buzzing, and it only got worse after Ali and I were married. Mom and Dad had both died before I was out of middle school. Since childhood, I'd understood that happiness was on the credit plan. Ali had made me too happy for the clawback, when it came, to be anything but brutal.

Her opinion was that no matter what God had planned for us, she'd been blessed that He'd brought her across the world to love me. At twenty-six, she'd left her job and family in the Czech Republic on the mere intuition that she'd find her divinely ordained husband in New York, U.S.A. She'd been close. You could see the city perfectly across the Hudson from the flat roof of my tavern.

How had she been so sure I was the one, someone who hadn't attended church since my confirmation? The thing about Ali was that she said the most unusual things with the calmest certainty and never sounded crazy. She talked about angels and saints as casually as most people talk about batting averages and brake pads. I was lost from the start with her, and I laughed more in two years than I had my whole life.

By mid-day, our caravan had pulled into the storm's damage zone.

Adamsville was a medium-small town, split in ragged halves by the high-water mark of the storm. The northern side of the town wasn't in universally bad shape, mostly wind-damaged. The southern half, where most of the large public institutions sat, as well as the residential neighborhoods, had been hit hard.

In this part of the country, Father Dennis had explained, Catholics were not thick on the ground, outnumbered in Greene County by even the smallest Baptist denomination. However, the relatively unscathed, lonely church of St. Ignatius was pastored by a fellow seminarian who'd reached out to Hoboken.

Our first drop-off point was the local school building, which had people sleeping in its gym annex. Electricity for heated water and the plumbing's pumps had been restored by generator just a day ago. There was a single washer and dryer for towels in the building and they were running non-stop. Displaced people, entire families, sat on the floor in snaking lines for the showers. To look was to see ten things they could've instantly used, even just help passing the time with books or games. But the boxes of paper-wrapped hotel-sized soaps, travel toothbrushes, and combs would have to be a start.

After the gym, we picked up Father Jack at his rectory, and he directed our caravan to a nearby tent city in a parking lot that abutted the Legion Hall. Here, we met a few members of the Salvation Army and other local volunteers as we set up a hand-to-hand brigade to unload the rest of the clothing, toiletries, and edibles from the campers into the hall for distribution.

Our next stop was outside town, but that only meant several blocks away from the church. There was no black-humored joke that could contain the awful irony of the Happy Camp Water Park we drove through, so no one made one. Almost by agreement, we ignored the murals of surf and waves, the debris-filled pool and listing, flapping water slides as if we hadn't seen them.

The campgrounds were rustic, but the septic connections were reported to work if we could find them. Then, we'd be able to set up the campers so more people could use those facilities for personal care and cooking. Get people watered and fed on the inside, clean and dry on the outside. That was Father Jack's target.

Setting up at the camp took much longer than unloading supplies, because we had to haul, by hand, almost an entire forest's worth of broken, shredded limbs out of the campground's access drive and from around the hookups.

No human conversation left, just straining and grunts as we dragged away the limbs, trying not to curse around the priests. The surrounding thick stands of trees, which looked like they hardly noticed their discards, were dense with birdsong and the buzz of insects. There was no adequate comment for the relentlessness of the blood-sucking gnats either.

As I huffed no-see-ums out of my nose and stomped canopies of branches into flat piles under my boots, I felt removed from my own life. The humidity and sweat settled into my clothes and hair. My back was already sore. This was what I'd come for.

By dusk, we were parked, chocked, and ready to return to the Legion Hall for dinner. Spaghetti for three hundred.

There, Father Dennis walked me over to a tall woman and said, "Mike, this is Miss Bernadette. I'd like you to accompany her. She's a social worker."

The traitor was really going to make me push off a well-intentioned stranger? "Um, sorry, but I'm not really in the mood to talk."

She squinted at me. "I don't need conversation. I need someone to go with me. I may need help clearing the road or if I get a flat, Lord help me. I've got twenty gas cans we've got to fill up and get back before the generator runs dry. The father said you're game for work."

"Oh, right. Okay," I said, but she'd already turned her back and made for the door as I followed in her wake.

In the parking lot, she gestured me around to the passenger side of an old 4-door Ford Taurus. As I strapped in, the sun was only a leftover orange line and as we pulled out, there was no moon in any direction I could see.

"The closest station that's working is only letting people buy five gallons at a time," she said. "I've got to convince them to let me fill up this car and all these cans for the gym."

"Do you think they'll go along?"

"All things are possible for he who believes." There was no brag in the way she said it, just certainty that the thing which needed doing wouldn't dare resist. Reminded me a little of Ali. "On the way, I need to check on someone. Is that okay with you?"

"I'm just a tourist. You're the cruise director."

The roads were dark and getting darker. She drove slowly, letting her headlights pick out the path.

As we got further outside the radius of town and onto smaller, less-civilized roads, she'd send me out with one of the flashlights to move branches out of the way or to survey the water we had to drive through. In the darkness, without poking a stick around the bottom first, it was impossible to tell if we were passing through a shallow pothole or heading into a fresh trench. There were a couple of rural roads we had to give up on, backing slowly out of them to re-route. Miss Bernadette seemed to know every crossing, and where trees or shacks or fences should've been, but were not now.

We finally came to a long straightaway of pale gravel that reflected light and crunched solidly under the tires, pure relief.

"I'll park here," she said. "The way up to the carport might be blocked. This is my uncle's place. Even the landline phones are out. He's eighty-one, and I haven't been able to get hold of him today."

The low, rambling house among the trees was completely dark. Our flashlights bounced back at us from heavily-curtained windows. Once Miss Bernadette opened the front door, she reached around to snap the switch, and lo, there was the comfort of working electric light.

"Uncle Henry?" she called down the central hall to no answer.

"Maybe he evacuated after all? If you want to take a look," I said, stepping into the living room. "I'll wait here. Just let me know if you need me."

She nodded and headed toward the back of the house, flipping switches as she went. "Are you here? It's Bernie."

The living room was sparse, orderly, and dust-free. There was a low, rectangular couch with spindly legs and a scooped-back chair that looked like one from elementary school.

A few framed photos hung in clusters on the wall. One in black-and-white showed a well-dressed couple standing arm-in-arm on a courthouse stoop. She wore a white pillbox hat with a veil. He was in a neat, dark suit. I wondered if it were Uncle Henry and Aunt Someone. Judging from how high their heads came on the door, they were a short, matched set. Might explain how he could tolerate this toy furniture.

I heard Miss Bernadette call him again and the sound of doors. Was she checking the closets?

I wandered across the entryway to the dining room. Another narrow table, oval, matched by eight toothpick chairs. I turned to look at the tall, smooth wooden china cupboard.

And saw a pair of legs dangling shined oxfords from its top.

I swallowed hard against the salt rising in my mouth.

Before his niece could return, I went to grab the argyle on one of the hanging ankles and give it a little tug.

Then I was sure.

At the bar, I'd seen the body of a sleepy regular who'd passed away quietly in the corner. What struck me then was what I noticed now. Rag-doll slackness.

I walked to the hall. "Miss Bernadette. I think I found your uncle." She came back my way slowly, not striding. We both knew before I said it. "I'm sorry." She stared holes through the hand I put up to stall her progress. "I don't know what it'll be like."

"What do you mean?"

"He's on top of a china cupboard."

It was obvious from her expression that she didn't know any good reason for it either. "The water didn't get that high anywhere over here."

"Maybe—"

"Get him down."

"Shouldn't we call 9-1-1?"

"Who'll answer? Who's available to come?" Her voice went jagged on that. "I want him down."

"Alright, alright. I'll do it. Get me something to wrap him in."

I scooted one of the perilous chairs over to the side of the cabinet. It was much sturdier than it appeared. She'd fetched a blanket from somewhere and her arm stuck out to pass it to me from the hall.

I flopped it over the top of the cupboard, letting it fall across the feet and legs, whispering a request for forgiveness and internal fortitude as I bundled whatever I could get my arms around. I was grateful he'd stayed skinny as the picture. I braced him against the side of the cabinet as I stepped off the chair, then settled him to the ground as gently as I could manage.

"Can I . . . ?" she asked from around the corner.

"Not yet."

My own Uncle Georgie had done the official identification for me. When I fought with him to see the bodies, he asked if I believed they were dead. I'd seen the blackened rubble, reeking like burning tar, still soaked and dripping from the hoses. I'd felt the truth of it, like the fire had burned out my insides. So he'd slapped me and asked what I needed to see them for. Then said he'd cut the fingers off his right hand if I went. It was an outrageous threat, but he never fucks around and he's all I had left. Since then, I had ghoulishly looked up pictures of burned strangers, and now, I wasn't sorry about what he'd done.

Half-afraid, I pinched back one edge of the blanket, but Miss Bernadette's uncle didn't look bloody or obviously wounded. One dry eye was mis-focused, which could've even been true in life, and his dark skin had no luster, but with his droopiness, he looked more gentle and sad than scary to me.

"One more second," I said, gritting my teeth before I touched his eyelids, trying to ease them downward like I'd seen in the movies. They went, more or less. Better at least. I pulled his pant cuffs down over the top of his socks. He was wearing a deep blue dress shirt and pinstriped gray vest with matching suit pants, a belt as shiny as his shoes. When I straightened his arms, I noticed white stuff staining the underside of one sleeve, like lime scale on a bathtub. "Okay. If you want to come in—"

Miss Bernadette dropped to her knees next to him, interlacing her fingers with his. "What on earth were you doing?" She rocked back and forth, pressing his hand against her lips and forehead. "Why didn't you wait for me?"

He didn't answer.

I didn't want to disrupt her grief, so I backed away and sat on the floor. I'd expected garbage runs and mudding drywall. I hadn't imagined I'd be dealing with death again so soon. I didn't feel suited to it, exactly, but somehow I felt mostly calm.

"Rigor mortis hasn't set in," she said with surprising precision. I guessed social workers dealt with plenty of the worst of things. "He can't have been dead more than an hour or two." So, we were only a little behind whatever happened here. I could see her grabbing that realization, one she could use to punish herself. I couldn't stop myself from doing it. How could I stop her? I leaned back, waiting for Miss Bernadette to decide what the right next thing was to do.

It was from that unusual angle something underneath the tabletop caught my eye. I retrieved my flashlight, pushing chairs to scramble closer. "Damn. That's what's on his cuff," I said. "Chalk."

The gaze she lifted to me was raw, watery and indistinct. Carefully, she looked at her uncle's hand.

"No. The other one." She picked it up and turned it so we could both see the dusty pale smears. She wiped it and rubbed the dust between her fingers.

"Written underneath this table in chalk is Kofod-Larsen," I said.

"I don't—"

"The name's weird enough I remember it. When I worked salvage in college, my boss would go to estates and chalk off which pieces were getting donated, going to auction, going to family members. Someone marked this, because it's a famous designer, probably worth good money."

I'd discovered something wonderful that would probably make everything more horrible.

Without responding, she rose, and I followed her into a bedroom as clean and restrained as the other rooms I'd seen.

"There's usually another nightstand," she said. "I looked around but didn't see it anywhere. The weekday aide told me Uncle Henry's been acting strange. I haven't been by in the last few weeks." It hurt her to say it. "Kyle only works during the day, and he said he had to go help his family after the storm. That's why I had to come. I can ask him if Uncle Henry was trying to sell anything."

I looked at the remaining nightstand, an unremarkable sort of cube, but solid wood. I swiveled it to reveal the back, chalked with "GLENN of CA," "WALNUT," and a number: five thousand for the pair. I whistled through my teeth.

"Do you mind my asking how your uncle got his furniture?"

"It was a wedding gift. My aunt's mother used to work for a rich woman in New York whose husband kept buying new furniture she hated, among other things about him. When they divorced, she offered it to my aunt and uncle if they didn't think it was bad luck. They were happy. It filled their house."

I patted the wooden sides, each smooth, unscratched or dented, perfect. "And all they had to do was be clean and gentle, keep the stuff out of the sun, and wait sixty years."

"They never had any kids. Mine would've torn this place up. When we visit, I make them play in the backyard..." Her voice trailed off and she pointed again to the chalk. "My uncle writes in beautiful longhand, even his grocery lists."

I went back to the living room, where the most movable pieces were.

I flipped a chair, pulled the credenza from in front of the draped window, and peeked under the coffee table. One still had its note intact—that scoop chair, worth fifteen grand?—and the other two wore smears.

I returned to the dining room, apologized to Uncle Henry, and climbed back on his dining chair with my flashlight. The chalked note on top of the china cupboard was a white smear.

My calm was gone.

I felt enraged and nauseated and it was too much like everything I'd felt before leaving Hoboken. "Is your uncle's aide a smart man?" I called out.

"Right now, a young man in college assists Monday through Friday. Kyle's cousin owns the agency. Kyle works as an aide during his summers at home."

It was already early September. I stepped down and flopped the blanket back over Uncle Henry, as even my untutored eyes could tell he was beginning to distort with stiffening. I led Miss Bernadette back into the living room. "When does Kyle go back to school?"

"Soon...his mother and I are in church choir together." She'd set her jaw very tight, wringing one fist tightly within her other hand. Like she was daring me to say it.

"I don't know why people are assholes. They just are. A smart, nasty kid was running out of opportunities to steal things that are portable and valuable. The storm only helped him. In this chaos, who's going to notice one more person evacuating with their belongings? A couple of nightstands and chairs. Who cares? Can't prove he got them legally, but he's smart. He can find someone to pay a few thousand, no questions asked. And as far as Kyle knows, no one else has any idea what's the stuff's worth."

"I didn't know," she said. "Never really liked the style."

"If anyone ever asks about missing items, Kyle blames your uncle, says he's done something crazy. He's been laying the foundation for that already."

Miss Bernadette was rubbing her arms like she'd never be warm again. I knew just how she felt and wished I was done.

"Today, Kyle told you he's busy helping his family. Who'd question it? But instead, what if he circles back to pick up the easy stuff and get it the hell out of Dodge? Somehow, today, Uncle Henry found the marks and was climbing all over them, probably trying to erase them when Kyle arrived."

Her eyes had gotten shiny but her question was sharp. "How can you possibly know that?"

"The dining room chair wasn't next to the cabinet until I moved it there. Uncle Henry couldn't have gotten up there without a chair or a ladder. Either Kyle boosted him up there or took the chair away right before we came. Doesn't matter really. Maybe getting stuck up there or confronted, Uncle Henry panicked. Or he'd just run out of steam."

She was mad now. Nose-flaring mad with guilt and shame and everything that kept me awake at nights. "Who do you think you are? What do you know about us?" Her voice was rising to a yell. "About this community? About our lives?"

"Please, shhhh."

Miss Bernadette of the Methodist church choir was about to carve me in two. I deserved it and worse.

I held up my hands and spoke in a harsh whisper. "I'm an idiot. I ran a bar in New Jersey. That's how I know people. Not your people, not these people, and maybe not church choir people. I hope I'm wrong, because I am very sorry to have upset you during such a horrible time. Please, Miss Bernadette, please. Can you forgive me and stand to hear the however?"

Her eyebrows were very high, but she answered back in a whisper. "However?"

"If I'm not wrong, we might've caught him in between trips. Kyle's still got to wipe the marks off everything so no one suspects he was appraising his client's stuff, and he wants to get the other nightstand and chair as quickly as possible before more attention comes down. I don't want to scare him out of trying to grab them."

"And this is because . . ."

"I'd like to catch him and beat the unholy shit out of the fucker." The whites of her eyes showed all around. "You can't know how much I want that." I raised my hand to pledge. "I swear to you, Miss Bernadette, if he survives, he will never look right or walk right again. All you have to do is turn off the lights and rush out of here. There's no phone service. Cell's not working. You found poor Uncle Henry. Run, slam the car door, lay down rubber on that gravel road. Get help and bring it back. See what's left of Kyle when you do."

She leaned in until we were inches from each other's faces. She pressed her finger in the center of my chest and thumped my sternum while she took a deep breath and I waited. "This is my family's tragedy, not yours."

The priest had blabbed to her.

So we went with Plan B. It was similar to Plan A, only instead of going to get help, she parked and doubled back on foot to supervise.

I sat by the back door, my legs stretched across the threshold.

The dark was deep, moonless, and thick.

Though I wished Uncle Henry had been a baseball fan, the tidy gentleman had a gratifyingly solid broom. Based on the speed of Kyle's approach to unlock the back door, I knew he'd been waiting close by, which was why I'd risked my own life shushing Miss Bernadette from yelling.

She returned quickly as well.

I only got to relish the sound of Kyle's chin hitting the kitchen floor, the feel of the broomstick vibrating in my hands as it cracked him across the back, and a mere two, sharp kicks to the organs before lacing his hands and feet together behind him.

We laid towels and garbage bags across her car's back seat so the nobler, stinking gas cans could ride there.

The whole thing was on the roughest margin of a citizen's arrest, but I told Kyle he was lucky as I heaved him in the trunk and felt the rebellious twinge in my back. If he gave me half a reason, I said, I'd slip Miss Bernadette's leash and kill him. Just because I was in that kind of mood. It's the way the innocent dead tax one's self-control.

He was afraid. I was, too.

We had the car windows down to deal with the fumes in the back seat, and there were only the sounds of slow rolling tires and night.

"I know what I believe," I said, "but will the sheriff do anything with Kyle? Aren't they spread too thin already?"

"There may be a way to charge him under the Vulnerable Adults Act. That protects elders against abuse and exploitation in their homes. Everyone will see him though, and word will spread. They'll know he's a predator. He's poisoned his own wellspring."

"What about his family?"

"I feel sorry for what they'll go through."

"Will they make it tough for you at church?"

"Not if I sell off an ugly chair and donate to repair the roof."

It was funny but it wasn't. "God, Miss Bernadette. This is a truly shitty thing to have happen on top of another shitty thing."

"I'm certain I can get a formal investigation opened. And now it doesn't matter when, because it's already too late."

As tough as she was, she couldn't get through that without cracking. Though I could only see her profile, I could hear her sniffing back tears.

"You can cut loose if you want. I do, every few days, until the top of my head feels like it's coming off and I want to puke."

"Does Father Dennis know that? He might worry less about you if he did."

"I fucking knew that's what he was up to, putting me with you. He was Ali's priest. He isn't mine."

"Do you want to tell me what happened?"

I thought about that, and surprisingly, decided I did. "Short form. Thirty-seven days ago, there was a summer storm and my home burned to the ground. So did my wife, Ali, and my three-week old son. His name was Gabriel. My wife had a thing for angel names. The business downstairs, the tavern that my father and uncle opened together fifty years ago is destroyed. Lightning struck the transformer. That's what the Fire Department says caused the electrical fire. They still don't know why it went up so hot and fast. Act of God."

She waited long enough that her sympathy didn't sound like it was on auto-pilot. "I'm so very sorry, Mike."

"Ditto." I sounded like an ass, but couldn't seem to be otherwise. "If you really wanted to help me, you should have let me have more therapy with the shithead in the trunk."

"I don't think you should spend your life in jail."

"What have I got to lose?"

"Isn't there any other family?"

"Uncle Georgie's got a girlfriend younger than I am. He's living at her place while he waits for the insurance check. I can't even imagine how long the red tape's gonna take for everyone here."

"Wouldn't he be sorry to see you convicted for murder?" Miss Bernadette definitely had her do-gooder hat back on, and it probably made her feel better, more normal. We were picking up speed and finally on asphalt that some earlier jerk must've cleared of debris.

"Are you shitting me? Uncle Georgie doesn't fuck around. He'd probably throw me a parade for killing that asshole. We'd sponsor a PG's Tavern float down Main Street in Adamsville. Throw out root beer candies for the kids."

"Oh, really?" I'd hooked her. I could tell.

"And the Adamsville high school band, what are they called?" I asked.

"The Tigers."

"The goddamned Tigers! We'd have them in the parade, too."

"The caliber of your language has declined tremendously."

"What can I say? I like you."

We laughed. It wasn't the clean, wholesome laughter I'd shared with Ali or that Miss Bernadette had probably shared with her kind uncle or her true friends at church. But it was less dangerous than crying, and it lasted us to the gas station on the interstate.

POINT OF VIEW

Will Graham

The newspaper kiosk out front screams:
HOUSTON HEADSMAN STRIKES AGAIN.

Under that, in slightly smaller type, are the words "Sixth Victim Found."

I stare at the headline for a long time, and then ignore it.

The Shadows are with me.

I have a job to do tonight.

I hunt.

I stalk.

I prey.

• • •

Rebecca.

She is beautiful.

Maybe 5'4", light brown hair with blonde streaks, beautiful gray eyes. Always dressed nicely, not flashy. Tasteful earrings, no rings on her hands. Her store badge hangs from a lanyard on her graceful neck. Soft voice, always polite, always kind.

I've come here for about a month now. Walls and walls of books, but it's one of those giant chain stores. No real soul, no heart. Few of the clerks read, much less care about the customer.

Except for Rebecca.

She reads. She reads a lot. Every night for the past two weeks, when she leaves, I follow her. Carefully, discreetly. It is part of the plan, but that's beside the point. I follow her to her nice little house in her nice little subdivision. She never sees me. That's how it should be. I follow her to her home; make sure she gets there okay. I wait in the darkness until she gets inside and the lights come on then I leave as quietly as I came.

She's smart, no doubt. She usually keeps her store badge turned around, but sometimes it flips forward. They are cautious here, first names only. No last names, not even an initial. It is easy for me to find out, though. A few minutes at the computer, and everything I need to know is right there.

She walks past me with a stack of books, giving me one of those fleeting, polite smiles you get from people who work in a store. A delicate whiff of perfume floats by as she walks past me, and I inhale slowly. Savoring her scent.

She smells like a beautiful winter morning.

Her skin is flawless, cool and smooth.

I want to touch her.

Any man alive would want to touch her.

She does not know me, probably wouldn't want to know me even if she had the chance. The reality is, I'm not terribly good looking. Balding, glasses, 5'10" if I stand straight. Hardly the matinee idol type.

I am slightly lacking in what is called 'social skills'. Been that way since I was a child; blunt, straight ahead, no time or inclination for niceties. Dressing something up or choosing one's words carefully has never held any appeal to me whatsoever.

I've accepted it, adjusted to it, and to be honest, no longer worry about it.

It would take an extremely special woman to ... understand me.

I haven't met one yet who did, and at my age I've just accepted the fact that this is how it is.

As the kids today say, I've got no game when it comes to the ladies.

It's probably the single biggest reason I'm so good at what I do. No one sees me, no one notices me. It's actually an advantage. The media makes us all out to be handsome and incredibly charming, opening doors and hearts with our smiles, but somehow those qualities passed me by. Just watch a 'Made for *Lifetime*' movie, you'll see what I mean.

Fate plays some crappy tricks on people.

I have my work.

I do not discuss it much, if ever.

It has been years since I talked about it with anyone.

About what I do, about what I accomplish.

About what I'm ... good at.

It just isn't worth it.

I keep to myself, and don't socialize. Don't mingle, don't go out much.

A doctor I was forced to go and see once told me I was 'insular' and 'cut off'.

Among other things.

I didn't say anything to that.

What could I say?

He was only telling the truth.

He asked me a lot of questions.

He wanted me to tell him about my dreams, for one thing. He didn't believe me when I said I didn't remember them. He got irritated over that, but we kept going. He was being paid to, after all.

He wanted to talk about my family.

I glossed right over that, no point in digging all that up.

He wanted to talk about a lot of things, and I answered him as honestly as I knew how, but he didn't ever seem satisfied with my answers.

Then he asked some more personal questions.

I told him the truth, but from the look in his eyes he didn't believe me.

It probably didn't help much when I sat quietly and looked at him for a long while, then asked, "Are we done?"

He angrily made a mark on some kind of report. He got up and left the room.

After waiting fifteen minutes, I realized he wasn't coming back, so I got up and left, too.

I know Rebecca's last name, her address, and her brother's name. I know her phone number, I know her employment history. I know what she does for fun, I know what she does not like to like to do.

I know she divorced a little over two years, still lives alone, and only in the past few weeks has she even thought about dating again. I know she loves dogs, but doesn't have one at the moment. She likes cats, but does not have one of those, either. No children, no one close to her in the city. Her remaining family is all north, up in and around Dallas. She came here with her former husband, and when the marriage crumbled she stayed for whatever reasons people stay.

After she walks past me, I turn my head just enough to watch her. Her perfume lingers in the air for a bit, and I savor it again. I stand there with an over-sized book on computers and pretend to flip through it while I watch Rebecca. She puts the books she'd been carrying on a shelf, making sure they lined up exactly.

Precision.

I like that.

As she walks past again she pauses for a moment. Gives me a smile as if she means it, and asks, "May I help you?"

I turn to her, working hard to be friendly, non-threatening. "No, thank you. Just browsing." Scaring her would be counter-productive at this point.

She gives me another smile, nods her head, and walks on. I choose another book at random and pretend to flip through it, turning so I watch her walk away.

She has a nice walk. A very nice walk.

Time passes.

Closing time comes.

I leave without buying anything, just as I have every night this week, and go outside and get into the car. I adjust the rearview mirror so I can watch the front doors. I know everyone comes out through there when they are done for the night.

It isn't long before the lights go off inside. A few are left on, so the people remaining can see what they were doing. Eventually, the only light on is by the front door.

Five people come outside, one of them Rebecca. They all parked where they could see each other, and no one leaves until everyone is inside their own cars and locked in.

Rebecca starts her engine, pulls out of the parking spot, and heads home.

I follow her.

No one sees me. No one notices me. No one pays me the slightest bit of mind.

Except the Shadows.

Nothing will happen until tomorrow night, Friday.

I follow Rebecca home every night.

Just to make sure.

I go back the next night.

I sit in the cafe for hours, watching the people walk by, watching them gather their purchases. Rebecca is there; today she is wearing a dress. She has legs as nice as I thought they'd be.

I like watching her.

She is beautiful. No question of that.

Tonight is the night.

I can feel these things.

The Shadows move outside.

Only I can see them.

Time passes. I browse through another book on computer language, then one on old movies, a photography manual. Staying focused, pretending to look like anyone and everyone else.

Shortly before closing time, *he* comes in.

I feel the anger building inside myself, but strangle it back down.

He is straight out of *GQ*; tall, staggeringly handsome, tailored clothing. He comes through the front door as if he owns the place, and heads right for Rebecca.

Her entire face lights up when she sees him.

I feel a flash of jealousy, but shove that down, too.

I am on a mission tonight, I have no time for sentiment.

A mission that I have planned and thought out and locked on to like a laser-guided heat-seeking missile. I don't like what I am going to do, but it is what I must do, a compulsion inside driving me.

I could stop blinking my eyes easier than I could stop this part of things.

They leave shortly after that, Rebecca's friends giggling and shooing her out the door. They are thrilled for her, excited she is going out with such a handsome man, cannot wait to hear the details tomorrow.

They are going to be surprised in the morning....

• • •

It is far too easy to follow them.

A nearby restaurant, valet parking, some sort of New Age fusion nonsense. I drive past them, circling, until I find a spot toward the back where the valets do not come but I can see the entrance.

The Shadows are out there.

I can feel them, but you have to know where to look to spot them.

I stay in my car, drinking coffee long turned cold, eating a pre-packaged meal that tastes like sawdust in my mouth.

It is not all that long before Rebecca and her date come out. Cocktails only, they are not in there long enough for a meal.

A blind man can see where the evening is heading, and I am not blind.

They walk to their respective cars, where they kiss, briefly.

He holds her door open, sees her inside the car, and bends down for another kiss. He closes her door, and goes to his own car.

I know where they are going next.

There is only one possibility.

I get out of the parking lot before they do.

The speed limit is no more than a suggestion for me tonight.

A barely safe yellow light, one blown red light later, and I am ahead of the game.

The night and what happens next belong to *me*.

I park two blocks away.

I make sure to put on my windbreaker. I make sure to take some other things. A pistol encased in a holster slides onto my right hip, anchoring into place.

It is late enough and dark enough that no one sees me as I approach her house.

I open the gate and enter the backyard with no trouble at all.

The Shadows follow me.

Lights are on in her neighbors' homes, but it is the kind of neighborhood where people keep to themselves. No one sees me as I slip around the side of the house and find her bedroom window. I know Rebecca and her date will park and come into her house from the front door.

The Shadows pool around me like smoke.

It takes seconds to unlock her back door.

I do not open it because of the alarm system I know she has, but I make sure the doorknob turns freely.

I can get in easily.

I hear cars pull into the driveway.

My entire body tenses with what is about to happen.

Everything goes into a different plane of awareness. I can hear the crickets chirping, I can feel the grass growing.

Everything is heightened.

I cannot stop it now; there is no way to stop it.

Things have to proceed the way they are supposed to. There is a pattern to it all, and the pattern is predictable yet critical.

Car doors slam out front. I close my eyes for a moment, seeing in my mind what is happening.

Rebecca and her date walk to the front door. She gets her keys from her purse and unlocks the door, and they go inside. I hear the beep-beep-beep of her alarm system, then the cutoff as she turns it off.

I stand in a section of brick wall that hides me from the glass in the kitchen door and the windows in the living room. They don't know I am there, will never see me unless one of them opens the backdoor and looks out.

Chances are extremely good that will not happen.

People in their own homes feel safe.

There are venetian blinds covering the windows in the living room, but Rebecca has left them slanting the wrong way and open just enough so I can see everything. I can almost make out the muffled conversation as she pours them both a glass of wine, then they sit on the couch.

He kisses her. She responds. Two years without a man in her bed have made her hungry and that hunger has made her careless.

Human nature never surprises me anymore.

The kissing turns into something else, something different, something much more intense, and he gathers her in his arms and picks her up and carries her down the short hallway into the bedroom.

When I see the bedroom door close that is my cue.

I slide through the darkness to her bedroom window. Edging carefully, I see what I need to see.

It is what I was expecting to see.

He is on top of her, and there is a great deal of thrashing and twisting and movement.

Entirely predictable.

Three quick steps across the lawn, and I am at her back door again.

It opens at my touch, just as I'd planned.

I force myself to move silently across the kitchen then down the hall, not rushing.

Rushing now could cause noise, and noise can be a problem.

I can hear the carpet fibers under my feet.

I can see the air in front of me as I move through it.

The sounds coming from Rebecca's bedroom are . . . intense.

The Shadows swirl around me in the hallway.

I pull my pistol from the holster on my right hip.

I take half a step closer to the bedroom door, then raise my right foot and slam it just under the doorknob.

She is in the bed.

With him.

Her eyes widen when I burst into the room.

He jumps out of the bed and turns towards me.

Which makes the next part easy.

My nerves are sizzling, on fire, flaming with the desire to do what I do.

I take one giant step into the room, using momentum for power. No time to be subtle; I kick him in his exposed crotch as hard as I can.

As he collapses to the floor, moaning, something long and shiny drops from his hand.

I holster my pistol.

I reach into my pocket and pull out my knife.

She starts making noises as I approach the bed.

Watching him vomit on the floor out of the corner of my eye, I flick the blade open and she really starts to shriek.

I bring the blade down. . . .

• • •

The Shadows that surrounded me all this time flow into the room like warmed oil.

"FBI, Rebecca," I tell her as I slash the ropes binding her arms above her head.

I go to work on the ropes spreading her legs wide. "You're safe now."

There is no crash-boom-bang-slam like in the movies.

The Special Hostage And Defense Ops—Weaponry Squad agents take the place quick and quiet, grabbing, yanking, flipping, slamming, pinning, and cuffing the guy in less than seven seconds.

To me, it all moves in slow motion.

I cut the last of the ropes that hold her, and help her sit up.

She tears the gag from her mouth herself and tries to talk while taking in huge gasps of air.

"She's in shock, guys," I call out. "Get the medic in here!"

I point to the knife he'd been holding, where it now lays on the floor, gleaming in the low light with a malevolence all its own. "Bag and tag that, right now."

I choose not to think how many different blood types the Lab may find on it.

She stammers and stutters and tries to get her breathing under control. She manages to gasp out, "Who are you?"

When I was sure she could sit up on her own, I reach into my back pocket and pull out my credentials. "FBI, Rebecca," I tell her again, using her name to anchor her attention on me and not what is happening in the room. "My name is Noah. Noah Donnelly. I'm with the BAU."

From the look on her face, I am speaking in Martian.

This is normal, this is to be expected.

"Behavioral Analysis Unit," I explained. "Quantico. The FBI."

She looks from me to her erstwhile 'date' on the floor, handcuffs on his wrists, craning his neck to glare at me with unbridled hatred. She gathers the shreds of her dress around her like a talisman as she looks at the black-clad men of the Shadow unit, highly and extensively trained agents from the Bureau's Hostage Rescue Team.

I take off my light nylon jacket that has 'FBI' on it in huge yellow letters on the back and sleeves and wrap it around her shoulders. I look over my shoulder and bellow, "Get that goddamned medic in here now!"

I turn back to her. "My apologies for the wait."

She waves it off, strength coming back into her. She takes in the room as if she's never seen it before. "What happened?"

"Your date for the evening is the Houston Headsman," I said as gently as I could. "He's raped and murdered six women we know of. His favorite way to kill is by decapitation." I paused. "We've been after him for two years now.

Tonight, we caught him."

There is no gain in trying to sugar coat any of it.

The medic arrives.

I step out of his way as he ministers to her, looking in her eyes, asking her what she had eaten or drunk that night, was she on any medication, checking her pulse, aiming a small flashlight in her eyes.

The Shadow agents yank the Headsman off the floor, not caring he is nude. He groans from the shot in the balls I gave him but—as far as I care—life isn't fair sometimes.

They hold him up on his feet, and I take a step over to him.

I stare at him until he looks up.

The hatred in his eyes is balm to my soul.

This.

This is the moment that makes it all worthwhile.

"I did this to you," I say aloud, leaning forward until we are almost nose-to-nose. My glasses are askew from all the action, and I push them back with a finger. "Remember me. I did this."

The snarl on his face says all that needs to be said.

The agents goose-step him from the room.

I look and see the medic is still tending to Rebecca.

She does not need me any longer.

It is over.

I walk down the hallway, through the living room, and outside through the front door.

There are police and Bureau cars all over the place now, turning the nice suburban block into a twenty-four-ring circus.

It is better than what could have happened.

I'd seen the photos of the crime scenes left behind.

Seen them and studied them and looked for some kind of hint, the smallest or slightest shred of a clue that would lead us to him.

Local police identified a suspect, but that's all he was. A suspect. Can't arrest a guy for trying to pick up women. The more I studied him, the more I knew.

I *knew*.

The suspect had been seen in the bookstore on several occasions, always going out of his way to chat with Rebecca.

All the women in the city, and he singled her out.

Unfortunately, a lot of what I do is re-active, not pro-active. He hadn't committed a crime in any way that we could prove.

Like the rescue team's entrance, what I do is not like it is in the movies or on TV.

Step one, always step one, is Profile The Victim.

Profile enough victims, you get a sense of the killer.

It is painstaking, soul-searing work, and it's certainly not for everyone.

I am done here.

The Special Agent in Charge of the Houston office comes over to me, shakes my hand, and tells me I did one hell of a job.

I force myself to smile.

I make myself say the right things in reply.

I ask if he could have someone take me back to my hotel, then to the airport.

He looked surprised for a moment, and then nodded. "More work to do?" he asked.

I look back toward the house, to Rebecca's house, watching as she is escorted out and into a waiting Bureau car.

She looks around.

Our eyes meet, and she stares at me for a long moment.

For just a second, I wonder what it would be like.

A home.

With a woman like her.

A real life, not one spent out-thinking and outguessing the psychotic lunatics who move and rove among us among us, invisible until they strike, who long to swim in blood and butcher other human beings simply to feed their own sick and twisted fantasies.

She smiles at me.

I smile back, pretending she has not stolen my heart forever in that moment.

The gulf between her universe and mine is immense, and there is no way in the world to bridge it.

Men Who Hunt Psychopathic Killers...And The Women Who Love Them. Next! On Oprah.

Rebecca is gently guided into a car and taken away.

I shove my fantasies back where they belong.

To the SAC, I say aloud, "There's always more work to do."

Some people at Quantico call me a hero.

I hunt the hunters.

I stalk the stalkers.

I prey upon predators.

Yeah, there's something to be proud of.

I do not consider myself a hero.

Like so many things in this world, it all depends on your point of view....

HIGH MEADOW STORM

Wayne D. Dundee

"Addie... I think you should come in here... I think he's waking up."

The man was on the brink of consciousness, though not quite there. He tried to focus on those words as a means to help pull him the rest of the way out. He didn't recognize the voice but it sounded... young. A child? He didn't know why but that seemed wrong somehow; a bad fit, like the presence of a child or children didn't belong in his life.

Whatever his life was... or had been.

He tried to say something but all he managed was to move his lips around without producing any sound. The inside of his mouth tasted like ashes.

He tried to open his eyes with the same lack of success. His eyelids felt like they weighed about fifty pounds each.

"Mister... Can you hear me?"

Another voice he didn't recognize, also young-sounding. But not a child.

The man willed himself to try and relax for a minute while he attempted to gather his wits about him. What the hell was going on? He was lying prone on a bed, he could tell that much. A soft, nice-smelling bed. There was a blanket over him and he was barefoot.

Relax, hell. He had to get up, get things figured out. When he pushed down on the mattress, he felt a strange tingling sensation in his hands and fingers. But there was still strength in them. Pushing with his hands and digging in with his elbows he got himself raised part way up.

A hand settled lightly on his chest, another on his shoulder. The touches were supportive, reassuring. They attempted neither to push him back nor pull him up. "Take it easy, mister... I don't think you should try to move around too sudden."

Propped on his elbows, the man finally got his eyes open. He blinked several times to clear away the blurriness.

He was in the bedroom of what appeared to be a small cabin. The bed he lay on was big and roomy, with a hand-carved headboard. The room was furnished well but simply. Everything sturdy, functional. A window was open, letting in the smells of fresh air, grass, and livestock.

At the foot of the bed, a pair of matched faces—round, wide-eyed, floating at a height barely above the level of the mattress—gazed at him with expressions of awe and apprehension under tangled swirls of rust-colored hair. Alongside where he lay, another face, that of a tall, slender young woman, was gazing down on him as well. She had the same rust-colored hair, but worn long and combed out smooth. Dressed in a simple blue smock and off-white apron, she was quite pretty, though couldn't have been more than fifteen or so.

"Where am I?" the man said. "What happened to me?"

"You're at the R-Bar ranch," the young woman answered. "The R is for Rudisel, that's our family name. I'm Addie. The twins—" She tipped her head to indicate the round faces at the foot of the bed. "—are Timmy and Belle."

"Only our place ain't really a ranch, it's just a farm," piped up the little girl, Belle.

"It is too a ranch," argued the boy. "Why else would Papa call it the R-Bar? Nobody names farms that way."

"No matter. You know what Mama always told him. She said calling a farm a ranch don't make it one."

"But that was before Papa got his longhorns last fall," insisted Timmy. "After we got 'em branded and everything, he said, 'Now we got ourselves a by-God ranch and nobody can say otherwise.'"

"Hush up, you two. Right now!" said Addie sharply. Then, directly to the boy, she added, "And you, little mister, had better watch your language or you'll be tasting some tar soap instead of dessert come suppertime."

Timmy thrust out his bottom lip in a pout. "I was just sayin' what Papa used to sa—"

"I don't care. I don't want to hear that kind of talk out of you. Now, the both of you, if you've got so much energy to yammer and carry on, take some of it outside and go find where those sneaky hens have been roosting and laying the eggs I keep coming short on. Scoot! And don't come back until you've found some eggs to bring with you."

Once the children had gone running out of the room, Addie turned back to the man on the bed and said, "Sorry about that. Surely not the kind of thing you needed to wake up to."

"Kids will be kids," said the man. "I'm just glad to be waking up at all. I . . . I'm not sure why, but I have the feeling I've been out for a while."

"You sure have. This is the third day since my brother brought you in and we loaded you onto that bed."

The man sat up the rest of the way and slowly lowered his legs over the side of the mattress. He was wearing a long, thin night shirt but nevertheless made sure to keep a corner of the blanket pulled across his lap. His hands and fingers were still tingling and now he became aware that, albeit to a somewhat lesser degree, he could feel the same sensation in his feet. And the taste of ashes was still in his mouth.

"Could I trouble you for a drink of water?"

"I've got some right here." The girl stepped over to the nightstand where a pitcher and a tin cup sat on a tray. "I've been keeping this close by and getting you to take little sips over the past couple days. I knew it was important to try and get *something* inside you."

She poured the cup half full and handed it to him. He took it, even though his hands trembled slightly, and gulped it down quickly. Too quickly. When he got done coughing, he asked for more.

Addie accommodated him, saying, "But a little slower this time, okay?"

"I promise. It's just that it tastes so da—er, I mean darn good."

"It's probably grown warm by now. I put it there this morning, I really should go refill it with fresher water for you."

"Don't go to the extra bother. I told you, this is fine. More than fine." The man drained the second cup then handed it back. "I want some more, but I suppose I ought to take it a little easy, eh?"

"That'd probably be smartest."

The man abruptly gave himself a pat-down, running his palms down over his torso and onto his thighs under the blanket. He frowned. "I don't seem to be wounded or suffering any broken bones . . . Addie, what happened to me that rendered me unconscious for three days?"

The girl didn't answer right away. Then: "Well . . . Near as we can figure, you got hit by lightning."

"Are you serious?"

"Like I said, that's near as we can figure. My brother found you the morning after a real boomer of a thunderstorm rolled through here. You was laid out near the edge of our graze land up on the high meadow. Heath rode up to make sure our cattle had got through the storm okay and came across you. You wasn't far from a big old oak tree that had clearly taken a lightning hit. Your horse was there, too. Dead. At first Heath thought the same was true for you, but then he saw you was still breathing. We figure you got caught by the storm and was taking shelter under the tree when the lightning struck and ran through all of you . . . That about how you remember it? Getting caught in the storm and ducking in under the tree?"

The man gazed at her blankly for a long minute. "Actually, no. I . . . I don't remember. Not about a storm . . . not about a lot of things."

"What kind of things?" Addie wanted to know.

She watched the man's expression change. He looked confused. And then somewhat alarmed. "Addie . . . Who am I?"

• • •

"Isn't there a special name for it? When a body suffers a sudden memory loss like that?" Addie was saying.

"Amnesia, I think, is the word you're looking for."

"Yeah. That sounds right."

A wry smile briefly lifted one corner of the stranger's mouth. "Don't ask me how I know that when I can't even tell you my own name. But that's how it is."

The two of them were sitting at the cabin's kitchen table. They'd been there for the better part of an hour, discussing what had become their overlapping situations.

When Addie asked if he might like something to eat, the stranger had allowed as to how he felt hungry enough to devour two or three of the long-horns Timmy had mentioned, minus only the hooves and horns. That's what prompted the move to the kitchen. Once she made sure he was sufficiently steady on his feet, Addie had pointed out the stranger's clothes—which she'd washed and put in a neatly folded pile—then left him to get dressed while she went to fix him something.

As he began donning his duds, the stranger thought maybe something about them might provide a trigger to help him remember a thing or two about himself. But no such luck. Just as gazing at his reflection in the small mirror that sat atop a corner dresser did nothing to jog his memory. The face of the man he saw there, someone in his mid to late forties with gray-shot hair and whiskers and piercing greenish eyes under shaggy brows also peppered with gray, was a complete stranger to him. It was a decent enough face, neither especially handsome nor homely, that looked as if it might have seen some pampering in its day but also its share of wear and tear. And the clothes, though of good quality, showed plenty of wear as well—indicating he'd covered a healthy stretch of miles in them, presumably on horseback. But other than the implication he'd at some point had the good taste and money (considerably more than the twenty dollars in paper and silver that

Addie had found in his pocket and laid out atop the folded pile) to buy top quality, the clothes failed to tell him anything significant.

A pair of items that revealed more, however—albeit rather indirectly—was the gun belt and holstered revolver that had been placed beside the folded pile. The gun was a double-action .45 caliber Colt. How or why he instantly recognized this, he didn't understand. The gun, as well as the belt and holster, were of fine craftsmanship. Additional indicators that his past had afforded him high quality possessions.

The stranger made no attempt to buckle on the belt. But he did take out the Colt. The hand that had trembled slightly when holding the tin cup of water only a few minutes earlier was now steady as a rock. The Colt felt as comfortable and natural in his grip as if he'd been born with it there. The stranger twirled it a couple of times and then just stood holding it for a minute, feeling its power, appreciating its balance, and *knowing*—without knowing how or why—that he was very skilled with such a weapon. In the end, he re-holstered the revolver and left it in the bedroom when he went out to join Addie in the kitchen.

She had a pair of sandwiches waiting for him—thick-cut side pork on sourdough bread, along with a tall glass of cold buttermilk. Even taking into consideration his damaged memory, the stranger was pretty damn sure he had seldom, if ever, enjoyed a meal more.

They covered what little there was to cover about his blank past and identity while he wolfed down the sandwiches. After that, Addie started filling him on how things stood with her and her siblings—recent orphans, as it turned out, having lost both their mother and father to a fever that swept through the area during the past winter. Left behind were the twins, ages eight; Addie (short for Adelaide, which she professed to hate) just shy of seventeen; and their older brother, Heath, who was eighteen. The young Rudisels were determined to make a go of the small ranch their parents worked so hard to get started and had so much hope for, right up to their dying breaths.

"We got no kin back in Ohio, where Mama and Papa started out from. Leastways none us kids know about," Addie explained. "And we got no close friends around here. Papa wasn't a real sociable man. He poured everything he had into the hard work it took to make this ranch a place that provided for all of us... He got sorta friendly with one of our neighbors, a fella named Ames, who had a spread off to the north. But Ames caught the fever last fall and died ahead of Papa and Mama. He was barely cold in the ground before his widow sold out to Ledbetter and took off for back east somewhere... So, anyway, it falls to us kids to look out for each other from here on out and to keep this ranch going for our own sakes."

"You seem to have the right attitude for it, I can tell that much," the stranger said.

Addie shrugged. "No reason we can't make it work. The twins are gonna have to do some fast growing up this summer so they can start pitching in with some of the simpler stuff. Me, I know how to cook and mend and work the garden and help take care of the barnyard stock. And Heath, he knows just about everything else there is to know.

"He was Papa's shadow and right hand man practically since he could walk. Even Papa, who wasn't given to much in the way of praise, did some bragging on what a hard worker he was. Heath's a stutterer, though, and painfully shy. Folks take him for being slow upstairs. And I guess maybe he is. A little. But that don't make him retarded, not like some claim. So what if he's not good with reading and cyphering and he can't talk as slick as some silk-tongued grabber like Amos Ledbetter? Heath is honest and square. Plus he's strong as an ox, knows how to take care of the animals and the land, and can even do passable at carpentry and blacksmithing. What's more, he'll outwork any two men anywhere in these parts."

The stranger grinned. "You think a lot of your big brother, don't you?"

"You bet I do. And the twins adore him."

"Sounds like he's got what it takes to keep this spread going. For that, you and the twins are lucky. And I'd say Heath is pretty lucky, too—having you three backing him up."

Addie blushed a little.

Looking at her, the stranger reminded himself that, despite her obvious grit and a streak of determination that seemed mature beyond her tender years, she nevertheless *was* a gal of still-tender years. He felt a wave of admiration for her and her siblings. And he felt something more—a determination of his own to do whatever he could to try and help them.

True, he had problems of his own to consider. And exactly what it was he might do to lend the Rudisels a hand, he wasn't sure. But, once again without remembering the source or circumstances, he knew that somewhere he'd heard about cases of amnesia such as his where the simple passage of time started bringing back the missing pieces of memory. What was more, since he had no clear idea on how to otherwise go about searching for or hurrying along the process to try and regain his memory, it seemed as good an idea as any to stick right here and try to be of some help while giving the gaps a chance to maybe start filling in on their own.

If, of course, the Rudisels were open to having him hang around awhile.

The stranger decided not to bring it up right away, not until he'd rolled the notion around some more in his own head and until he got a better sense of whether or not he was truly as welcome here as he felt so far.

Breaking the stranger's reverie, Addie said, "I'd better go check on those egg-hunting twins and see if they even remember what they're supposed to be doing. Then I need to get back and start making preparations for supper... You are going to stay and join us, aren't you?"

"Don't know where else I'd go. Not that I'd want to, even if I did," the stranger told her.

Addie smiled lopsidedly. "That's right. You can't go anywhere because you don't have a horse, do you?" Then, as soon as the words were out, her expression turned aghast. "Oh, Lord, that must have sounded harsh and cold. I didn't mean it that way. Really."

"Of course you didn't. Don't worry about it," the stranger told her.

"If and when you're ready to leave, we naturally will help you make it as far as town. We only have a couple of saddle mounts and we really can't spare either of them. But Heath can hitch up the buckboard and—"

The stranger cut her off. "I told you not to worry about it." And then, because the opening had presented itself, he added, "To tell you the truth, I don't feel in a hurry to go anywhere. If I'm not in the way around here, that is. I'm willing to pitch in and pull my weight, earn my keep. But in my present condition... the memory loss and all... Well, the thought of trying to fit in out there amongst a bunch of strangers when I've got no name or no past ain't something I'm particularly anxious to tackle. Leastways not right away."

"All things considered," said Addie, "I'd say that's perfectly understandable. As far as I'm concerned, you're welcome to stay as long as you need to. I'll have to talk it over with Heath, but I'm pretty sure he'll be okay with it."

"Like I said, I'll earn my keep. And I certainly don't expect to lay any further claim on the bedroom. Or *any* part of the house, as far as that goes. I'm sure I can find some suitable quarters in the barn."

"You're not a barn animal!"

The stranger grinned disarmingly. "Thank you for noticing. But I can still make do out there. This house, except maybe at mealtime, is for you and your family. Period."

Addie looked ready to argue some more, but then saw by his expression that it would be futile. "You're a stubborn cuss, ain't you?"

"So it would seem."

"All right. If you insist. Come to think of it, you've already got some gear out in the barn waiting for you. Heath fetched your saddle, too, when he brought you in. It's a mighty nice one. He made sure to wipe it down real good after the drenching it got in that storm."

"Sounds like something I'll want to check out. And I'll be sure to thank

Heath for taking care of it. Matter of fact, I think I'll go have a look at the barn and the saddle right now. If you don't mind, that is. Might not be a bad idea to stretch my legs some, anyway, after not putting 'em to use these past few days."

"I don't mind, but are you sure you're up to it? Maybe you should still take it a little easy before you go traipsing around too much."

"I feel fine. Certainly capable of walking out to the barn and back," the stranger insisted. "Some solid nourishment on top of three days' sleep will do wonders for a fella."

"If you say so," Addie allowed. "I'll go check on the twins and then I'll come 'round to look in on you and see what we can do to fix up some decent sleeping quarters out there."

"I don't require much. I'm sure there'll be accommodations to suit me well enough."

• • •

The walk from the cabin to the barn provided the stranger a chance to give the ranch layout a good looking over. From inside, he'd only gotten a couple limited glimpses through the window.

It wasn't surprising, given the family work ethic Addie had so convincingly expressed, to see that everything looked well organized and taken care of. Fairly level grassland stretched in every direction, except off to the north a ways where the ground rose to a rounded hump that appeared to stretch on for some distance. The hump was dotted with fir and cottonwood trees on the near slope, an oak mixed in here and there. Without knowing why, the stranger felt a strong hunch that the top of the hump held the "high meadow" where he'd met the misfortune that erased his memory.

In closer, a plot of ground off one side of the house had been tilled and planted for a vegetable garden. A roofed-over well housing stood nearby and, a hundred yards farther out, a considerably larger piece of land had also been tilled and planted—probably for corn, the stranger guessed. The barn had a good-sized corral out behind it, currently occupied only by a sway-backed old nag that had definitely seen better days and a matched pair of sturdy-looking plow horses; just outside the corral grazed a couple of heavy-uddered milking cows; rounding out the livestock display (minus the aforementioned longhorns) was a dozen or so chickens prancing around at will, and a knot of wallowing pigs in a pen attached to a small, flat-roofed shed. The stranger gave a nod of silent approval for the self-sustaining little spread that spoke of the hard work that had gone into it and, with a continuation of same, the promise it held for the future.

Inside the barn, he found two saddles hung over a rail. One of them was very basic, rather plain. The other was a much splashier affair, shiny black leather with silver studding, a matching pair of fringed saddlebags, a possibles pack, and a Winchester rifle encased in a tooled leather scabbard. From Addie's description, it wasn't hard for the stranger to conclude which set of gear was his. More evidence that at some point he'd been able to afford trappings of above average quality, including the black Stetson with the silk hat band that was hung on the saddle horn.

The stranger put on the hat and then ran his hands over the saddle, wiped down and brought to a sheen thanks to the care given it by Heath. Next his attention shifted to the Winchester. He pulled the rifle from its sheath and instantly recognized it (though he could not identify the source of the knowledge) as a model '73 lever action repeater, caliber .44–40, fourteen round capacity. He automatically checked to see if it was loaded. It was. Full. As had been the case with the handgun in the house, this firearm also felt well balanced and perfectly at home in his grip. After sighting down the barrel a couple of times, the stranger leaned the rifle on a post and turned to the saddlebags.

His heart quickened a little as the thought crossed his mind that the pouches might contain something to give a clue or maybe even completely reveal his identity. Considering the kind of person Addie was and the way she'd described her brother, the stranger doubted either of them would have thought it proper to sort through his belongings while he was unconscious. Plus, at that point they couldn't have guessed that, once awakened, he would turn out not to know who he was or what his possessions were.

His searching fingers unearthed: a black frock coat, matching pants, boiled white shirt, and black string tie, all rolled together; an extra pair of boots, also black in color, highly polished and exhibiting little wear, each stuffed with a rolled up pair of clean socks; a deck of playing cards; a two-month-old copy of the *Police Gazette*; a packet of Lucifer matches wrapped in water-resistant oilcloth; a finely honed sheath knife; and a three-quarter-full bottle of whiskey.

In the possibles pack, the stranger found beef jerky, hardtack, a chunk of bacon also wrapped in oilcloth, a can of Arbuckles coffee, two tin cups, some eating utensils, a coffee pot, a skillet, and a spare boiling pan.

In other words...all recognizable items and all fairly common for a man on the drift. But nothing with a name attached to it, nothing that spoke to the stranger in a distinctly personal way.

Only mildly disappointed because he hadn't let his hopes get too high to begin with, the stranger began putting things back the way he'd found them. When he picked up the dress boots again, the rolled pair of clean socks dropped out of one of them. Upon retrieving the roll and shoving it back, he felt some unexpected resistance and heard an odd rustling sound from deeper within the boot. Removing the socks once more and reaching in to explore further, when he withdrew his hand it was clutching a fold of paper money tied with string. A quick count showed the amount to be two hundred dollars. Hardly a fortune, but surely more than you'd expect to find in the possession of most run-of-the-mill drifters roaming the West.

As he put the money back and finished replacing the other items, the stranger's expression was pulled long by heavy thought. He tried to add it all up. The nice clothes, the guns, the fancy saddle . . . and now the money. What did it amount to? What did it mean? On top of wondering *who* he was, he all of a sudden had to wonder *what* he was.

Any chance to make even a guess at an answer was abruptly interrupted by the sounds of a commotion coming from somewhere outside. The stranger didn't hesitate to start in the direction of what sounded like trouble. As if by its own volition, his hand flashed out and snatched up the Winchester to take with him . . .

• • •

Striding toward the cabin and then circling around to the side opposite from the barn, the stranger came upon the scene of the commotion. At its heart were two horsemen who sat their saddles in the middle of the vegetable garden. Although they had reined to a halt, it was painfully evident that before so doing they had allowed—maybe even purposely steered—their mounts to trample and kick apart several of the plant mounds. What was more, judging by the smug looks on the faces of the pair, they harbored no remorse for the damage done . . . Not even in the face of the chewing out they were getting from Addie and the twins.

"—no business setting foot on our property in the first place," Addie was saying. "And for sure no business coming here and destroying things with your rude carelessness. Get out of here now!"

"For crying out loud, lady, settle down," replied one of the riders, a whip thin individual with a pinched face and dark, dangerous eyes. "It was an accident, I tell you. How was I supposed to know it's a garden? One patch of dirt around this sorry excuse for a ranch or farm or whatever the hell this spread is supposed to be looks all the same to me."

"It's a ranch!" shouted Timmy. "It's the R-Bar Ranch!"

"And you're the ones who should be sorry, for wrecking my sister's viggibles," chimed in Belle. "You should know better than that, even if you ain't nothing but a couple lowdown hinge men!"

"You need to teach those brats some manners," said the second rider, a big-bellied specimen with bleary, bloodshot eyes and a mean curl to his flabby lower lip. "They bleat like a couple runt goats and don't even make no sense."

"Yeah," said the pinched-face one. "What the hell did she mean by calling us 'hinge men', anyway?"

Now it was Addie's mouth that twisted smugly. "She meant 'henchman', because it's something she heard me call you. That's what you are, right? A pair of Amos Ledbetter's obedient little henchmen, just waiting around to hop and do his bidding whenever he points a finger."

"Lots of folks hop to Ledbetter's bidding," the man responded somewhat petulantly.

"If they're smart, that is," the bleary-eyed one added. "But, a-course, we all know brains are in pretty short supply around here, what with your retarded brother and all."

"Our brother ain't retarded!" the twins screeched in near perfect unison. Then, to put added force behind their words, they promptly grabbed up dirt clods from the edge of the garden and began hurling them at the two riders.

"Stop it! They're only trampling more of my plants," Addie was quick to protest.

Which was true. As Pinch Face and Bleary Eyes jerked frantically in their saddles to duck getting pelted it caused their horses to also shift and shy away nervously, punishing more plant mounds underfoot in the process.

"You'd better get those goddamn brats under control!" roared Pinch Face as he wiped a splatter of dirt off his shoulder. "You don't, I'll come out of this saddle and blister their little asses across my knee!"

"No. I don't think so," said the stranger in a clear, steady voice.

As he spoke, he moved forward. Up until then he'd gone unnoticed. Now, locking hard stares with the horsemen, he walked over and stood next to Addie and the twins, who had ceased their dirt-throwing activity. The stranger held the Winchester loosely, casually at his right side.

"What have we got here?" Pinch Face sneered. "Who are you supposed to be?"

"Never mind that. What *you* are supposed to be is gone off this property. I distinctly heard the young lady tell you to leave."

"Yeah, I heard her, too. Thing is, I ain't in the habit of taking orders from bossy young gals actin' too uppity for their bloomers."

This set Timmy off again. "You can't talk like that to my sister, you smelly skunk!" Quick as a hiccup, he had another dirt clod snatched up and his arm cocked back, ready to let it fly.

The stranger reached down and clamped a hand gently around his wrist, preventing him from making the throw. "Hold your fire there, sprout," he said in an easy tone. "Let me take a crack at handling this, okay?"

Timmy glared up at him, eyes narrowed suspiciously. But after a moment his expression relaxed. He let the dirt clod drop and the stranger let go of his wrist.

"Oh-oh. Did you hear that, Burnett?" said Bleary Eyes to his pinched face comrade. "This hombre is about to 'handle' us. We better hightail it a-fore somebody gets hurt."

"That'd be a good idea," the stranger agreed.

The mean curl in Bleary Eyes' lower lip curled tighter. "You damn right it is—a good idea for *you*. Because any hurtin' gets handed out if we decide to stick around is gonna go all your way, mister."

"That's enough, Dowd," said the one called Burnett. His dark eyes were fixed tight on the stranger. Assessing. What he concluded was unreadable, but after a minute he cut his gaze away and spoke again to the other rider. "Tempting as it might be to carry this little piece of business farther, that ain't no part of what we was sent here to do."

"If there's anything more to what you were sent here for," said Addie, thrusting out her chin defiantly, "I don't want to hear it. It's time and past time for you to clear out!"

"We were sent here to deliver a message. You know damn well what it is," Burnett told her. "Mr. Ledbetter is getting sick of trying to be polite and just talking. Ain't no way you passel of young fools can succeed at what you're attempting. So why not show some sense and take him up on his offer?"

The stranger edged a step forward. "I believe the young lady said she didn't want to hear no more from you and that it was time for you to leave . . . Best be showing some respect for her wishes."

A high color climbed onto Burnett's face. "We'll be leaving. For now. But you for sure ain't seen the last of me, mister." His eyes narrowed menacingly. "You need a serious lesson when it comes to not sticking your nose in other people's business, and I'm looking forward to being the one to teach it to you."

The stranger smiled thinly. "Whenever you can spare the time . . . I'm always anxious to expand my knowledge on almost any subject."

"You'll get your chance, bub," sneered Dowd, eager to get in a few words of his own. "You mess with us, you'll expand your knowledge right into a pine box!"

• • •

After Burnett and Dowd rode away, the stranger got down on his knees with Addie and the twins and together they managed to salvage most of the plantings that had gotten trampled. While they were doing this, Addie told the stranger the background on their departed visitors and the man who employed them, Amos Ledbetter.

Ledbetter, she explained, was the biggest land owner in the territory. Like a lot of men who reach a high level of prominence, the success and wealth achieved by Ledbetter wasn't enough to satisfy him. It only made him greedy, left him wanting more.

And right now the thing he wanted the most was the Rudisel ranch. "Actually," said Addie, "what he's mainly interested in is the high meadow, the prime piece of our property. In addition to its lush graze, it pokes out like a thumb that divides the Ames property Ledbetter bought last fall from the rest of his spread. He don't like having his land split up that way."

"What kind of price is he offering?" the stranger wanted to know.

"Oh, his offer is fair enough, money-wise. Leastways it was when he first tried to deal with Papa. Now that he's dealing with us 'kids', as he calls us, he might try singing a different tune. Just like most others around here, he figures we're in over our heads and it's just a matter of time before we sink ourselves anyway."

"If he thinks that, why don't he wait until you're on the brink of failure and then try to get the land he wants for a song?"

Addie's eyes narrowed. "Maybe he ain't really as convinced as he pretends that we *are* gonna fail. On top of that, it's like I said—he's greedy. Amos Ledbetter ain't used to waiting. He wants what he wants when he wants it."

"I probably should know better than to ask," the stranger ventured. "But what about selling him *just* the high meadow, and you keep working the rest of the spread?"

"No way." The statement was flat and firm. "We need the high meadow graze for Papa's longhorns. Having them, making the R-Bar a real ranch, was too big a part of his dream. We might fail at running the whole shebang, just like everybody expects. That's one thing. But we ain't gonna give up and whittle down Papa's dream only to try and squeeze by on what's left. Quitting half way like that would be an even bigger failure to the memory of everything him and Mama worked so hard for."

• • •

At supper that evening, the stranger finally got to meet Heath, the older brother. He was rightfully impressed and had no trouble seeing many of the positive traits in the strapping young man that his sister had gushed about. If ever the term gentle giant was applicable, it seemed to suit Heath and was evidenced almost immediately by the way the adoring twins ran to him and began climbing all over him as soon as he showed up. His response was not only to endure this but to appear as if he enjoyed it almost as much as the children. It was true that he spoke haltingly and his movements were rather ponderous, but there was intelligence in his eyes and everything he said or did seemed to have a genuine earnestness to it.

For his part, the stranger was presented with no small amount of embellishment for the way he had confronted the Ledbetter hirelings. If Heath was caught off guard by seeing him up on his feet at all, after so many days of lying unconscious, he must have been even more surprised to hear that he'd rebounded so strongly. In any case, the two men quickly formed a liking and a mutual respect for one another. As a result, Heath expressed no reservations about the stranger hanging around for a while, especially in view of the visit from Burnett and Dowd seeming to signal an escalation of pressure to be expected from Ledbetter in order to try and get his way.

After supper, despite her protests, the stranger helped Addie do the dishes while Heath gave in to pleas from the twins for him to play a spirited round of checkers with them. When the dishes were done, the stranger indicated he would be retiring to the quarters he had fixed up for himself in the barn. He told Heath to be sure and look him up first thing in the morning and have some chores lined up for him to do in order to earn his keep.

"But before you go," Addie interjected, "there's something else we need to take care of."

"What's that?"

"Your name," said Addie.

The stranger looked perplexed and a bit uncomfortable. "I, er, don't know what it is... Remember?"

"That's exactly my point," Addie explained. "I think we need to decide on something to call you. After all, if you're going to stay with us for a while we can hardly go around calling you 'Stranger' or hollering 'Hey you', can we?"

"No. I suppose we could do better than that," allowed the stranger. "Have you got something in mind?"

Their discussion had caught the attention of Heath and the twins.

Seldom at a loss for words, Timmy had no trouble coming up with a suggestion. "I know! I know! We should call him 'Booster'!"

"That's a stupid name," responded Belle.

"Is not!"

"Is too. It's not only stupid, it's a dog's name. It's what you used to call that mangy old mutt that ran away last summer."

"That don't mean it ain't still a good name."

"But I know a better one," the little girl insisted. "We should call him

'Lightning Bolt' on account everybody thinks he got hurt from being hit by lightning, and that's how he came to us."

The stranger chuckled. "Well, those are some real interesting suggestions. But we don't have to be in a hurry, right? Let's think on it a little, maybe toss in a couple other ideas, and then we can choose. How about that?"

"Storm," said Heath abruptly.

Everybody looked at him.

"I think Belle has the right idea," Heath explained. "Our new friend came to us out of a thunderstorm. We could shorten that and just call him 'Storm'. I think that would work pretty g-good."

"I like it," Addie was quick to say.

"I guess it's okay," Belle relented somewhat grudgingly.

But Timmy remained stubborn. "I still like 'Booster'."

"But it mostly comes down to one person," Heath reminded everybody.

Now all eyes concentrated on the stranger.

"Storm," he said, as if trying out the taste and sound of it for himself. Then: "Not bad. Yeah, I could go with that."

"What about a first name?" asked Addie.

Heath shook his head. "No need. Storm c-covers it all."

• • •

A little while later, out in the empty horse stall where he'd spread his bed roll and laid out the rest of his gear after giving the space a good sweeping, the stranger—now called Storm—lay back on some fresh straw he'd spread to give extra cushion to his bed and sipped thoughtfully from the bottle he'd retrieved out of his saddlebags. All things considered, he felt strangely peaceful inside. And it had nothing to do with the effects of the whiskey. Which didn't mean his mind wasn't rolling with numerous thoughts and questions, it was just that none of them were all that unsettling. Either the answers would eventually come, or they wouldn't. And if things stayed the same, he didn't feel like his life was in a particularly bad place. In fact, it might be in a better one than before.

The guns and his comfort with them, the way he'd picked up the Winchester and gone so confidently, almost casually to face Burnett and Dowd with it... That was what tumbled through his thoughts more than anything. The guns and the money. A drifter in possession of that pairing marked a man for one of two things: Either a gunslinger, or somebody on the run from the law. In the eyes of many, there wasn't a whole lot of difference.

Storm tried to decide how he felt about that. The way things were now—him being in the presence of these good, honest, hard-working young orphans—he hoped his past didn't prove to be that of an outlaw. He figured it would be a big disappointment to them. On the other hand, would it be any better for them to find out he was a gun for hire? (Well, Timmy would likely be fine with that—he'd find it exciting as all get-out.)

From a practical standpoint, being a gunslinger might not be such a bad thing considering the overall circumstances the Rudisels and the R-Bar Ranch seemed caught in. A gut-level instinct told Storm that Amos Ledbetter wasn't anywhere near ready to give up on claiming the land he wanted, and the running-off of his hired thugs earlier today was only going to spur his intentions harder.

So in the short term, no matter what truths came to light later on, a stranger called Storm might be a handy thing for the Rudisels to have hanging around when push came to shove . . .

• • •

As Storm suspected, it didn't take long for Ledbetter to give another push from his side of things. How soon it came and in what form, however, turned out to be something of a surprise.

Late the next morning, as Storm and Heath were working on expanding the fencing around the pig pen in order to accommodate some recently-born shoats who would soon be grown too big for the current confines, a group of riders appeared from the direction of town. It was Addie who first spotted them, as she came out of the house with a pitcher of cool water for the pen builders.

"Looks like Ledbetter himself this time," she said. "And he's got a bunch of townfolk, including the sheriff, with him."

Storm and Heath halted their work, took welcome drinks from Addie, and then stood awaiting the visitors. Storm stood a ways back from Heath and Addie, within easy reach of the gun belt he had for some reason started the day wearing but then hung on a fence post when the work began. Health had clearly taken note of the Colt on his hip when he first came out of the barn, though he'd made no comment about it.

The visitors—four men on horseback and a man and a woman in a buggy—arrived and reined to a stop.

"Mornin', Sheriff Garber," Addie pleasantly greeted the spare, middle-aged, mustachioed man wearing a star on his shirt and mounted on a weary-looking dun horse. To the couple in the buggy, she added, "You, too, Preacher Peasley and Mrs. Peasley."

But when her gaze shifted to a heavyset man on a glossy black stallion flanked by Burnett and Dowd, the garden-tramplers from yesterday, both the young woman's expression and tone turned ice cold. "I got no particular welcome for you, Amos Ledbetter... and surely not for those other two low-lifes riding with you. I ran them off our property yesterday and my feelings on having them here today ain't changed any."

Ledbetter, a clean-shaven, pampered looking man with saggy jowls and snow white sideburns extending down from under a wide-brimmed hat, said out the side of his mouth, "See what I mean, Sheriff? Is that any kind of attitude for a young lady to have? It's not only un-neighborly, it's downright hostile."

"Like I heard my Papa tell you once before," Addie said, "our land boundaries might make us neighbors, Ledbetter, but there ain't no law says I have to *act* neighborly."

Mrs. Peasley, a stiff-backed old pruneface with iron gray hair pulled so tightly into a bun that it pinned back her ears, said, "Really, my dear, those are hardly the words of a good Christian. Nor, I might add, are they very ladylike."

"With all due respect, ma'am, the way I see it, ladylike behavior goes hand in hand with gentlemanly behavior," Addie told her. "And a toad like Ledbetter is about as far from a gentleman as anybody I ever saw."

"See what I mean?" Ledbetter wailed again. "Is that any way for a gal to be talking to her betters?"

"You ain't a d-damn bit better than my sister. Not for a minute," Heath responded. "You don't like the way she t-talks, then don't come around our p-property."

Storm didn't miss the increased evidence of a stutter in Heath's speech, something that barely existed when he was around just his family. Nor had it been very pronounced during the morning while the two of them were working together.

"Even the dummy's got a rotten attitude," Dowd grunted. "How hard is it for anybody to see that this whole outfit is nothing but a pack of trouble just waiting to happen?"

"You call my brother a dummy again," Addie said through clenched teeth, "you're gonna see trouble happen all right, and nobody will have to wait for it."

Sheriff Garber threw up a hand, palm-out. "Hold it! Hold it, for crying out loud. Everybody needs to take a deep breath and ease up all the way around... We came here to discuss a couple problems, not stir up new ones. And the way we're headed ain't getting us off to a very good start."

"You go ahead and take charge then, Sheriff," agreed Ledbetter. "Just make sure it includes seeing to it that gal gets control of her sassy mouth."

"I'll thank you not to tell me how to do my job," Garber snapped back. "If you want to lend a hand, you can do your part by controlling the mouths on your two men."

"If you want to say something to me, you can do it direct, Sheriff," replied Burnett. "I got ears and I understand the language."

"In that case," said Addie, "you can uphold the law, Sheriff, by telling him he's trespassing on my property and I want him and the other one off of it. I got that right, don't I?"

"Any rights you got, missy," snarled Ledbetter, "is exactly what—"

Garber cut him short with, "Goddamnit, I said for all of you to shut up!" Then, color flushing his leathery cheeks, he added, "Beggin' your pardon on the language, Preacher and Mrs. Peasley...But I need everybody to keep your yaps closed and let me do my job here. I got questions to ask and I only want to hear back from who I ask them to. Is that understood? If it ain't, I'll run in the whole lot of you—'ceptin you Peasleys, of course—for disturbing the peace. After you've cooled down behind bars for a while, then maybe you'll finally be ready to talk things over a little calmer and more civilized."

He got a lot of sour expressions in response. But nobody said anything.

For his part, Storm's expression stayed blank. Yet he found himself guardedly impressed by the gruff-talking sheriff. When the riders first showed up, he'd expected the lawman to prove himself largely under the influence of the big land owner Ledbetter.

"All right," said Garber, scowling. "Now that we got that straight, maybe we can get somewhere...For starters, Addie, I can't help wondering where the twins are. Usually when I swing by this way, they come a-running."

"They're out back of the house, churning butter for me," Addie answered. "They must not have seen ya'll ride up."

"Uhmm. Too bad they don't make it in to the town school much these days, eh?"

"We never were able to get them all that way very often, Sheriff. Not even when Mama and Papa were alive. But Mama saw to their learnin' lessons, just like she did me. And I've kept that going, some part of most every day. They did cypherin' for me this morning after breakfast and then, while I was finishing up my house chores and hanging up a bit of laundry, they took turns reading to me out of a storybook...What's the point you're trying to get to, Sheriff?"

Garber rubbed his jaw. "Well, there's some folks around...the Ladies Rock Creek City Betterment Sisterhood, mainly, which is headed by Mrs. Peasley here, in case you didn't know...who are, uh, concerned about the wellbeing of little Timmy and Belle. Concerned about *all* of you young folks out here, as far as that goes, since your ma and pa passed."

"Concerned in what way?" Addie wanted to know. "We're not causing any-body any trouble."

"That's a matter of opinion," muttered Ledbetter before the sheriff shot him a warning look.

"Like I said," the sheriff continued, addressing Addie again, "it's more a matter of concern for your wellbeing than what you might call a matter of trouble... " His words trailed off and he finally looked plaintively over to the preacher's wife.

Mrs. Peasley was primed to jump right in. "It's your tender ages, my dear. Surely you can understand that. That's the part that myself and other con-cerned souls are worried about. After all, you're rightfully still a girl yourself. Now, with your parents gone and the twins needing the attention and expe-rience of a real mother to raise and look after—"

"I'm all the mother Timmy and Belle need," Addie said forcefully. "I'm *family*, and that counts more than anything. I cook, I clean house and do the mending and laundering. I help do the close-in chores like feeding the chickens and slopping the hogs, even milking our cows sometimes when needed... I can't claim to be my Mama. Only she could fill that role com-pletely. But I work hard at doing the best I can, and I do darn good. And nobody can say Heath don't do his part. Our family loves each other and we take care of each other. We thank you for your concern, but we're getting along just fine."

"Yes," Mrs. Peasley agreed, "for the few months since your parents have been gone, everyone would admit that you have gotten by pretty well."

"Pretty well?" Addie echoed. "Look at our livestock and the shape our house and outbuildings are in. All in solid condition. Go inside the house and you'll see all the beds made, clean and mended clothes for every member of the family, all dishes clean and put away, fresh-baked bread ready for supper tonight, and a whole pantry of canned food and preserves ready for use. I can ride you in a ten mile circle and show you at least four spreads that are nowhere near that well took care of—kids, land, animals, the whole works. And they got full-grown, full-time mothers and fathers running things. If your Sisterhood wants to be so worried and concerned about the 'wellbeing' of folks, I'd say you got a lot better places to take aim at."

Looking on, Storm smiled in admiration at Addie's boldness and seem-ingly total lack of intimidation in the face of these prominent "concerned souls" lined up against her.

"I think my Sisterhood and I are the best judges of where our attention should be focused," Mrs. Peasley sniffed haughtily. "And your impertinence, young lady, is a fine example of the kind of thing that I, for one, have always found a very unflattering trait."

Speaking for the first time, Preacher Peasley said to his wife, "I think you have made your point, Mother, and a further exchange that may only turn harsher at this particular juncture is not wise to pursue. We should return to town and take up the matter again after all parties have cooled down a bit more and hopefully had the chance to do some additional soul-searching."

"Very well," said his wife with another whistling sniff. "But my soul has been searched and is quite clear on this matter, thank you. I assure one and all that my Sisterhood and I are not done with this."

"I tried to warn you, folks," Ledbetter called after them as the buggy swung around and started to roll away. "This gal is as hard-headed and hard-tongued as her old man. If it was otherwise, her and her brother would accept my very fair offer to buy them out and they'd be able to move to town where they could get proper assistance with the children and the rest of their needs, and all of them would be better off... I'm sorry you got spoken to so rudely, Mrs. Peasley. But I think you and your Sisterhood are doing fine work and you know I'll continue to support you every way I can."

As the dust from the departing buggy began to settle, Addie folded her arms and addressed the sheriff. "Does that about wrap up your business here, then? We've got a ranch to run and work we're being kept from."

Garber sighed. "I think you know that your dealings with the Sisterhood probably ain't wrapped up. Not all the way. I don't know exactly what they can do, to be honest with you, but I'm pretty sure they've still got some noise to make."

"You know, don't you, that you ought not be voicing sides like that?" said Ledbetter. "That didn't sound like a very impartial tone."

"And you don't sound like you're keeping quiet and not trying to tell me how to do my job," Garber reminded him sharply.

"Why are him and his thugs even still here, anyway?" Addie asked. "I told you I don't want them on our property. That makes them trespassers. Ain't you supposed to help enforce a thing like that?"

The sheriff aimed a hard frown in her direction. "Now are *you* gonna start telling me how to do my job, Addie? Ledbetter and his men are here on a legal matter. A complaint. They brought me here with them to address their grievance, same as the Peasleys. So as long as they're with me, they ain't trespassing. Not until we get the complaint resolved."

"What c-complaint they got with us?" said Heath.

"It's with *him*," Burnett answered, jabbing a finger in the direction of Storm. "He pulled a rifle on me and Dowd yesterday. Threatened our lives."

"That's a lie," Storm responded icily. "I happened to have a rifle in my hands, but only because I'd just got done cleaning it. I never pointed it at you and I never threatened you with it...I aim a gun at somebody for serious, mister, they don't come back around to complain about it."

"You hear that?" Ledbetter sputtered. "He just threatened my man again!"

"I heard the words. But I didn't necessarily hear no threat in 'em," said Garber. Then, to Storm: "Just who are you, mister?"

Before Storm could say anything, Addie spoke hurriedly. "He's our uncle. Uncle Storm Rudisel, my pa's long lost kid brother. He showed up just a couple days ago."

• • •

Laughing nervously, Addie said, "I don't know what got into me. I'm not one generally given to lying, not even little fibs. But, all of a sudden, it came to me: If Storm was a blood relative of ours, then it not only would answer the question of who he was and why he was here, but it would also give us claim to an adult guardian who could shut up Mrs. Peasley and her sisterhood of busybodies who were trying to say we're not old enough to look out for our own 'wellbeing'."

Storm chuckled heartily. "Well, wherever it came from, your announcement sure enough shut everybody up. The only sound afterward was that of their jaws dropping and hitting the ground."

"You sure you're not sore for me dragging you deeper into the middle of our problems?" Addie said. "I should've at least asked you if you were willing to go along with my concoction. But there wasn't any chance to."

"If you'd asked, I would have said yes in a heartbeat. So don't worry about it."

They were again gathered around the supper table—Storm, Addie, Heath, and the twins. Once the sheriff and Ledbetter and his men had ridden away, the balance of the day had passed without further incident. Nor, due to the work that needed completing, was there much discussion about what had transpired among those busying themselves with the work. But now, after each had been given the chance to digest things individually, they were going over it together.

"The thing to remember, though," Storm continued in a more somber tone, "is that even if you shut Ledbetter up for a little while, that don't mean he's ready to give up for good."

"He's like a rat trying to chew his way into a c-corn crib," Heath said. "There's only way to for certain get rid of a stubborn r-rat."

Addie gave her brother a mixed look of surprise and alarm. "That's a pretty drastic picture to paint."

The young giant shrugged. "Just sayin', that's all."

"Papa used to shoot rats," Belle piped up. "And other varmints, too, like raccoons and coyotes, when they was messin' where they shouldn't oughta. He said that was the only way to teach 'em."

"Well nobody's talking about shooting anything. Or anybody," Addie said sternly. "So just never mind."

"What about you, Uncle Storm?" asked Timmy. "What all have you shot with those guns of yours? Have you ever blazed it out in a gunfight with that big ol' Colt pistol?"

"Timmy!" Addie admonished.

Storm grinned. "Let the boy ask questions. That's how kids learn." Then, addressing Timmy, he said, "The thing you need to remember about guns—be it ones like my Colt or my Winchester or what have you—is that they're mainly meant for protection. Fella like me, for instance, the way I used to drift around, ride the open trails...you have to be prepared for trouble. Trouble from varmints, for instance, like your pa spoke of. But blazing gunfights and such, the way you and your friends maybe play-act or like you read about in those rip-roarin' books they publish—the kind you ought not be peekin' at, by the way—that ain't the real deal. And it ain't the right idea at all for how guns ought to be used."

Timmy tried to hide his disappointment, but didn't do a very good job of it. "Okay, Uncle Storm. If you say so."

• • •

Later, alone out in his sleeping quarters in the barn, Storm had even more things to roll around in his head than the previous night.

Uncle...

Uncle Storm.

He couldn't be sure, of course, but he didn't think he'd ever been an uncle before. Not that he minded now. As a matter of fact, he kind of liked it. It gave him a warm feeling, the way the twins so easily adapted to the notion of him being their uncle and then started calling him that. And if he was going to be an uncle, or any other kind of relative to anybody, he doubted he could do better than the Rudisels.

From somewhere, he remembered an old saying. *You can pick your friends, but you can't pick your family.*

Well, sometimes maybe you could.

The real question was whether or not whoever and whatever he'd been in the past was a person somebody like the Rudisels would still want to lay claim to. For that matter, was that person somebody Storm himself would want to lay claim to? For the first time, he found himself half wishing that he *wouldn't* remember his past. He kind of liked the way things were shaping up in the here and now.

He thought about the money stuck in the toe of the dress boot in his saddlebags. He could use that to solidify his place in the Rudisel family, actually *buy in* to the R-Bar operation. Two hundred dollars was probably more money than Addie or Heath had seen at one time in their lives. It could buy things they needed and things they'd only dared dream of. An addition to the cabin, more livestock, a better plow, a better saddle and horse for Heath to work his cattle with; a new dress for Addie and some toys and school books for the twins . . .

But before that, the matter of Amos Ledbetter and his greed and pride had to be dealt with once and for all.

Yes, Addie may have won the day with her claim that Storm was their uncle, a blood relative. But that wouldn't be enough for somebody like Ledbetter to call it quits, not once he'd had a chance to get over the surprise.

It hadn't even shut him up completely at the time Addie sprung it. As he was wheeling his horse around, getting ready to ride away, the big rancher had snarled over his shoulder, "You might think you've got all the answers right now. But I'll tell you where you'd damn well better *make sure* you got the answers—and that's when it comes to doing a better job of wrangling those longhorns your stubborn fool of a father brought on board. That high meadow graze section of yours pokes right up in the middle of my property and up until now I've been plumb neighborly, unlike you, about telling my riders to just turn back any strays that wander over . . . But from now on, if any of your critters cross my boundaries, my orders will be to shoot 'em down like dogs and I'll have every legal right to do so!"

It was those words that kept circling back around through Storm's thoughts and echoing louder than any of the others . . .

• • •

It took three nights for Ledbetter to make his move.

On each of those nights, after he'd retired to his sleeping quarters in the barn and then waited until the lights blinked out in the cabin, signaling all inside had turned in, Storm saddled Heath's working horse and rode out to the high meadow. A clear sky on the first occasion had given him good enough visibility by the light of the moon and stars to find the lightning-struck oak tree where his new life had, in a manner of speaking, begun. It felt strange being there again, even if he couldn't really remember having been there the first time. For a few seconds, he re-imagined the tingling in his fingers and the ash taste in his mouth. But that quickly passed.

For the business presently at hand, the faint rise that the oak tree stood upon and the growth of bushes around it provided Storm a good vantage point and adequate concealment from which to set up his lookout. The Rudisel longhorns—Papa's original two dozen plus a smattering of spring calves—were mostly clustered near the middle of the meadow, well within sight.

"But from now on, if any of your critters cross my boundaries, my orders will be to shoot 'em down like dogs and I'll have every legal right to do so!"

Amos Ledbetter's words—his threat, the way Storm saw it—kept coming back around, demanding not to be ignored. The way Storm had it figured, the big rancher would be too humiliated and angered by how Addie had turned the tables on him to wait very long for the chance to get some revenge. If he couldn't get the land, he'd by-God go after some payback. Shooting some "strays" out of the Rudisel's treasured longhorn herd would appeal to him as a means to do that. Hell, he'd practically announced those intentions... and a humiliated, infuriated man used to always getting his way wasn't likely to have his craving for vengeance satisfied by merely waiting around for a stray to wander over every once in a while. No, not if he was bold enough to *make* it happen sooner and involve a more significant number.

After two clear, bright nights, the third one was overcast and gloomy with a misting rain filtering down through wisps of fog. But Storm had been to the meadow often enough by then to easily find his way to the oak tree even in the gloom. And, fortunately, the murky dark mass of the longhorns were near enough for him to spot and keep an eye on. For the first time, however, as he leaned back against the oak's split-open trunk, shivering inside his rain slicker, he wondered if these sleepless nights and empty vigils were actually going to yield anything or if his suspicions and expectations were unwarranted.

He got his answer only a couple hours later.

Storm heard them before he saw them. The creak of soggy leather and then voices muttering low but not with a great deal of caution.

"Only need to separate out about a third of 'em... No need to overdo it."

Storm recognized the voice. It was Amos Ledbetter's.

The shapes of three riders moving slowly toward the herd became discernible.

"This rain and fog works to our advantage," Ledbetter continued. "it's the kind of weather that spooks cattle, makes them do odd things... like wander off the way they might not ordinarily do."

"You're the boss, Boss," said Burnett's voice. "But are you sure we ain't crowding this whole thing just a little bit? I mean, it was only a couple days ago that you practically *warned* everybody about something like this."

"So what? I said what I said because we had already seen R-Bar strays on our land. I reminded 'em of that, too. Remember? And, like I said, this weather makes practically perfect conditions for more straying to happen."

"You're right about that," agreed Dowd's voice.

"Okay then. We nudge about half of what we cut out over across the east boundary and the rest the other way. Then I'll send out some of the boys first thing in the morning—totally excluding the three of us, to help minimize the suspicions that bleeding heart sheriff is bound to have—to check on our own herds in case they got spooked by the fog. They're sure to spot the Rudisel critters where they ain't supposed to be and they'll follow my standing order. They'll shoot the damn things ... Then we'll see how sassy that little Rudisel bitch and her retarded brother are with a third of their precious longhorns wiped out!"

"Whatever you say, Boss," allowed Burnett in a weary tone. "But you're right about the sheriff. He's bound to be suspicious and I don't picture him letting up easy on poking into this whole business."

"To hell with the sheriff," Ledbetter snapped. "You let me worry about him."

"Then right about now," said a new voice, floating in loud and clear from somewhere off behind the three riders, "might be a good time for you to start doing that. And, while you're at it, you might also want to do some worrying about this Greener shotgun I got aimed square at your cattle-rustlin' asses."

Storm was on his feet by then, dropped into a half crouch with his Winchester held at waist level, getting ready to make his own move on Ledbetter and his men. But recognizing the new voice as that of Sheriff Garber, he froze in place.

Ledbetter recognized the new voice, too. It should have been enough to make him know better, but he tried a bluff anyway, saying, "You sound like you're quite a ways back, considering the spread on a Greener, Sheriff. That, on top of this rain and fog—you really think you got that much of a bulge on all three of us?"

But Dowd wasn't having any of that. "To hell with you, Ledbetter! I ain't going up against no Greener, not for you or anybody ... I'm putting my hands in the air, Sheriff. You can see that, right? Don't you get in a hurry to cut loose with that scattergun, you hear?"

"Same goes for me, Sheriff! I'm putting up my hands, too," said Burnett somewhat frantically. Then, as an aside to his boss (or former boss, the way it was looking), he added, "I tried to tell you this whole thing was an idiotic play!"

"What about it, Ledbetter?" Garber prompted. "You got the guts to try something on your own, or are you going to get those hands up like your men?"

Ledbetter was very silent and very still for a long moment. Then, slowly, his chin dropped onto his chest and his arms lifted.

"Now," said the sheriff. "That only leaves you over there by the tree—Storm, or whatever your name is. You gonna hunker there the rest of the night, or are you gonna step up and lend me a hand with this?"

The acknowledgement of his presence surprised Storm, but the decision to go with it was easy enough to make. He proceeded away from the oak, and he and Garber converged on the would-be rustlers with their gun muzzles held steady.

"You ain't got a damn thing you can charge me with and make stick, Garber," said Ledbetter, starting up again with his bluster. "Me and the boys were out checking my herds in this dodgy weather. We thought these ones was ours and had wandered over the property line. We would have seen they weren't in another minute, and then left 'em alone."

"Cut the bullshit, Ledbetter," the sheriff told him. "I heard every word you said before, and you weren't talking about tracking down any of your own cattle."

"You got no proof. It'd be your word against mine and I'll hire the best lawyer in these parts to make you look like a fool."

"He's got me as a witness," Storm said. "That slices it a little different."

"The hell it does," Ledbetter sneered. "You're nothing, a nobody. I could buy and sell twenty of you. My lawyer would twist your testimony around until you were laughed off the witness stand."

Storm shrugged. "Well, hell. I might just as well just go ahead and shoot you then, the way I was getting ready to before the sheriff showed up."

"There'll be none of that," said Garber.

"Why not? They're on Rudisel land with Rudisel cattle. I call that dead to rights."

"Dowd!" the sheriff barked suddenly, jerking his Greener up into firing position. "You lower your hand any closer to that gun, you won't have to worry about Storm shooting you—I'll do it myself!"

"Don't be a damn fool, Dowd," Burnett said. "He cuts loose with that Greener, we'll all three end up shredded to ribbons."

"How about, for safety's sake," suggested Storm, "all of you shed your gun belts and shuck your saddle guns . . . real, real slow."

"That's a good idea," Garber agreed. "Like the man said . . . real slow."

The horsemen complied. After the last gun had thumped to the soggy ground, Ledbetter said, "So what now, Garber? Are you really gonna go through with arresting me?"

"Depends," the sheriff answered. "Now that you been caught with your tallywacker in the pickle jar, what if Storm here—speaking on behalf of the Rudisels—agrees not to press charges? You willing to swear that you'll quit bothering those young folks about this high meadow and leave them alone to try and make a go of things while you busy yourself buying up the rest of the territory?"

"You'd take my word on that?"

"In the form of a signed statement including the details on what happened here tonight, yeah. Something I could come back at you with if you crawfished and started bothering Addie and Heath again. I'll have witness statements, too."

Ledbetter's expression was as dark and murky as the night. "Would *he* go along with that?" he said, jerking his chin toward Storm.

Garber's eyes cut the same way. "How about it?"

Storm licked his lips. "Seems kinda thin. Shooting these three polecats would be a surer thing . . . But, in the long run, I suppose that'd come around to making more grief for Addie and Heath and the R-Bar . . . Okay. We can give it a try your way."

The sheriff nodded. "All right then . . . Ledbetter, you and your men ride on back where you belong. Leave your guns here. I'll return 'em to you when you come to town tomorrow to sign your statements . . . I'll expect you by noon. Don't make me come looking for you."

The three riders turned their horses and disappeared quickly into the gloom.

The remaining two men listened to them leave, not speaking for a full minute and more.

Until Garber said, "You really would have shot 'em down cold?"

"What I came here prepared to do if they showed up."

"How did you know they'd try something?"

"Just a hunch I had. Obviously I wasn't the only one."

"Luckily, I got here ahead of you the first night. Saw you come in and take up your position. After that, I knew to be careful to keep you from spotting me in return."

Storm twisted his mouth wryly. "Galls me more than a little to admit I never had a clue you were out there. But credit's due where it's due. You're pretty good."

"I manage," the sheriff allowed. "But Ledbetter's been getting away with too much for too long. Never quite to this extreme, but I still fault myself for not taking a harder stand against some of his dealings sooner. Seeing the way he was going after those kids—even influencing the church sisterhood to start giving them a hard time—that was too much."

"Splitting apart those youngsters in any way would be crueler than taking a gun to them," Storm said, his voice tight.

Garber eyed him close, letting a couple beats pass before he said, "Ask you something straight?"

Storm gave a single nod, indicating for him to go ahead.

"You really an uncle to those kids?"

Storm took his time responding. Then: "Addie told it true when she said I showed up only a few days ago. But, in a manner of speaking"—his gaze drifted to the lightning-split oak—"you could say I was born here . . . As far as my exact relationship to the Rudisels, what I can tell you is that I *feel* like their uncle. And they see it that way, too . . . Sometimes a thing other than blood can bond a family just as strong. That's my answer to you."

The sheriff eyed him close some more. "The other day at the ranch, I saw signs of what you're saying. If not for that, I don't know that I'd take your words as sufficient . . . But I will. For now. The thing you need to hold in mind, though, is that I'll be keeping an eye on you and them kids. I happen to like and admire them quite a bit. I see any sign that you're trying to take advantage of them or doing them wrong in any way, you and me will be talking again real quick."

Storm suddenly felt very weary and all he wanted was to go . . . home. "Fair enough, Sheriff. Fair enough . . . So how about we get ourselves out of this rain and call it a night?"

OUT OF CONTEXT

Joelle Charbonneau

"Mom. Can I go to the game this week with Jack and Adrian?" I put my backpack on the kitchen chair and take off my hat so mom doesn't have a reason to get irritated. "Adrian's dad said the seats are right behind the first base dugout."

"If he gets to go to the game," his sister calls from the other room. "I get to go to Aimee's party."

"You're not going to that party, Aimee. You're grounded." Mom wipes her hands on a towel and turns to me. "And Marco, you know money is tight. How much are the tickets?"

"Forty-five dollars." A knot twists in my stomach as mom frowns. "But Dad said he would pay for it if..."

"No." Mom's eyes narrow and I shrink back. "I told you we aren't accepting anything from him."

"But..."

"He doesn't get to buy you off with money, Marco. He doesn't get to buy any of us off. Tell, Adrian that it as nice of him to ask you, but that you have a family obligation this weekend."

"I can't," I shoot back not caring that I shouldn't raise my voice. This isn't fair. "I already told Adrian I was free and that I had to find out if we had the money. He..."

My head snaps back as pain explodes in my cheek and behind my eye.

"How dare you?" Mom screams. Her mouth twists with rage and her arm pulls back as if it is cocked and getting ready to fire again. "Do you want everyone to know how your father left us with no money? Do you want them to think I'm not capable of raising you and your sister without him?"

My hands ball into fists and I bite back tears so she doesn't yell at me to act like a man the way she always does. I used to cry. I don't anymore. I don't yell back or run anymore, either. There's no point. It just makes things worse. So, I just stand and wait for her to hit me again or hope my sister comes to my defense like she used to.

But mom just glares at me one more time before storming out and Aimee never comes into the room. So, I pick up my backpack, walk through the living room where my sister ignores me and close the door behind me when I reach my bedroom.

I throw my backpack on the floor and dig out my phone to call Adrian and decide to text instead because I don't want him to ask too many questions or give my mom the chance to listen at the door. Both of those things would suck.

CAN'T GO TO THE GAME. MOM SAID NO.

After a couple minutes, he texts back. MY DAD SAID YOU CAN JUST HAVE THE TICKET. YOU DON'T NEED TO PAY FOR IT.

Yes! I start to smile, but think about Mom and know I can't take the ticket. She'll call it charity and yell about Dad again and who knows what will happen then. So I text back. CAN'T. CATCH A FOUL BALL FOR ME.

I feel sick when I hit send, but at least that's the end of it.

I do my homework. I pretend that I don't have a headache when I eat dinner. Aimee ignores me through the meal. Other than asking me if I want more peas, so does my mother. Fine. I don't care how excited Aimee is about prom or the dress she is borrowing from her best friend or the stupid boyfriend she convinced to pay for it all. Whatever.

Once dinner is over, I got to my room and look at my phone to see if Dad sent any messages. Nothing. When he left, he said he would check in every day. He did for the first week. After that. Well, it's no big deal.

I turn on the game and watch the catcher hit a homerun as I scroll through my friends' online posts. Ha! Adrian's post is a picture of the pitcher throwing down his glove with the caption—SOMEONE IS UNHAPPY. #GOSOX

Smiling, I type a response. HE'S PROBABLY HIDING IN THE DUGOUT CRYING LIKE A GIRL. #GOSOX

THAT'S WHAT HE GETS FOR THROWING A HIGH FAST BALL is Adrian's response.

The Sox win and I feel better about life when I go to bed. At least there's one thing good left in the world.

When I get up, I check my phone for a message from Dad. Still nothing. But there's a message from Adrian.

SORRY.

Sorry? Sorry about what?

I guess I'll ask him when I see him. Grabbing my backpack, I head to the kitchen to grab something to eat before school. Since there's already cereal on the table, I snag a bowl and open my social media notices as I sit down. Wow. There's a lot of them. Everyone must have been excited about the Sox game last night.

Or not.

—CRY LIKE A GIRL? WHAT A PIG.

—ADRIAN, HOW COULD YOU BE FRIENDS WITH SOMEONE THAT STUPID?

—WHAT KIND OF JERK SAYS SOMETHING LIKE THAT?

—I JUST SHOWED MY MOM THAT COMMENT AND SHE POSTED IT TO HER PAGE. THAT KIND OF SEXIST COMMENT SHOULDN'T BE ALLOWED. AND ADRIAN, YOU'RE JUST AS MUCH OF A PIG FOR ENCOURAGING HIM.

The comments continue. One after another of how wrong my post was. I'm a jerk. A pig. An idiot.

And there are more posts tagging me with screen capture picture of what I said and their thoughts. Most of them I know, but there are others I don't. I find another post from Adrian that tags me and says I CAN'T CONTROL WHAT ANYONE SAYS HERE. IT'S NOT MY FAULT THE GUY IS A JERK.

Now I know why Adrian is sorry.

"Well, if it isn't the sexist pig." Aimee strolls in laughing and drops her bag on the table. "What puppy did you kick to make so many people mad at you?"

"I didn't do anything." I didn't. "I just commented on Adrian's post. I didn't mean anything bad by it."

For the first time in I don't know how long, Aimee puts her hand on my shoulder and looks at me like I matter. "I know, but I don't think anyone is going to care."

"Why?"

"Because that's the way things go." She grabs and apple from the center of the table and picks up her stuff. "Apologize then stay off the Internet for a while. Maybe in a couple days things will get better. Oh, and you're going to have to take the bus today. I don't want anyone to see the two of us together. No offense."

Too late. I'm offended, but who the hell cares, right?

Still, I do what my sister says. I post a picture of a sad looking cat with the message I'M SORRY. I DIDN'T MEAN ANYTHING BY MY COMMENT ON ADRIAN'S POST. I'M THE ONE THAT PROBABLY CRIES THE MOST IN MY HOUSE. MY MOM AND SISTER ARE WAY MORE BAD ASS THAN ME.

Done.

I don't bother to eat. I'm not hungry. Instead, I grab my bag and head for the bus stop so I'm not late for school.

A few people wave when I get onto the bus, but I notice a lot of my friends pretending not to see me or looking in the other direction. Raychel waves me over, but I just smile at her and sit in an empty seat up front. Raychel is a great friend, but she'll want to talk and at the moment I'm not sure I want to talk to anyone.

My phone vibrates a lot as I get to school, but I don't look at it until I fish stuff out of my locker and go to my first class—freshman health. Also known as freshman hell.

Adrian turns and waves to me when I come in. When I slide into the desk next to him he says, "Sorry about the whole post thing. People know you aren't a pig or anything. It's just stupid. My mother even said it was."

"It would be nice if everyone else realized that," I say as several of the girls in our class sit down and send glares in my direction. "Why didn't you say that online to everyone who called me names?"

"It's not like I was going to change their minds and they would have come down on me. I figured you wouldn't want that either." He waits for my denial. When I don't give him one, he adds, "It'll die down soon. Most people think it's dumb. Just don't look at the stuff online for a while. Okay?"

"Sure."

It's easy to follow that advice during school. Teachers hate when they see phones out anyway. But it's hard to not think the whispers as I pass people in the halls or in class aren't about me.

At lunch, Adrian and I would rather talk about the Sox, but Raychel and a bunch of other friends want to talk about what's happening on social media. According to them, my apology just added fuel to the fire. "They think now you're saying that women are either weepy wimps or hard asses. That strong women are threatening and that you're sexist for suggesting that."

"That's not what I meant." Not in a million years.

"We know," Raychel assures me. "But a lot of people don't care. Just stay away from social media for a while and it will die down. Promise."

Great. I make a stupid comment on a baseball post about a player I don't even care about all that much and I'm suddenly a jerk. I try to apologize and now I am being vilified even worse for things I don't think. Maybe if I try to explain again I can make things better. For the rest of the day I try to come up with exactly the right words that will make this all go away. I write three different options down and run them by Raychel on the bus ride home.

"Don't post any of them," she warns.

"Why not?"

"It'll make it all worse."

"How?" I mean, it's all bad now. Why not try and make it better?

"No one who knows you thinks you meant anything bad by your first comments. So, you don't have to convince us. The rest don't care what you have say."

"That's not true. Look how many people have tagged me." I pull out my phone and turn it on. There are at least fifty posts with me tagged as part of them as well as dozens of comments on my apology. "They care enough to do that."

"They don't care. Not really." Raychel bites her lip, looks around and lowers her voice. "They care about being upset. They have lots of opinions and what you said gives them a reason to talk about them. Just let it go."

But I don't want to. I mean, people are angry at me. I don't want them to be mad and think I'm a bad person. They need to know I'm not a bad person.

"Marco, promise me you'll let it go. Don't engage. It won't help."

My sister says the same thing when I get home. Mom asks what we're talking about and when Aimee tells her Mom agrees that I should ignore it. "It's just the Internet. It's not real."

But it feels real.

I shouldn't read the comments on the online posts, but I tell myself it is better to know for sure what is being said than to wonder. My father always told me that things are always worse in your imagination. The monster in the closet is bigger and scarier in your mind until you get out of bed and open the door to make sure it isn't real.

Only Dad was wrong. This monster is real and the words it uses cut just as bad as claws and teeth.

Name calling. That isn't so bad. I can live with it. My sister has called me every name in the book over the years. Sticks and stones.

It's the things that say stuff like THIS KIND OF POST SHOWS HOW TERRIBLE OUR FUTURE AS A SOCIETY IS WHEN YOUNG BOYS HAVE BEEN TAUGHT TO THINK SO LITTLE OF WOMEN.

It was a post about a baseball game. Trash talk that I've heard both women and men use. It's just a stupid phrase that people have used thousands of times. But I used it and suddenly I'm evil to people I've never met. I look them all up to make sure I've never met them. They don't know me, but they know enough to believe I'm trash.

I spend the night tossing and turning and staring at my phone telling myself not to check it. Don't look. It won't help to look. But I know the messages are there. People are talking about me.

I try to get mom to talk about it in the morning, but she says to ignore it.

I tell her I will, but I'm lying because I can't ignore the knots in my stomach and the pressure in my chest. It's hard to breathe when you know people everywhere are judging you.

My sister still refuses to drive me to school. Mom told Aimee she was supposed to, but when does Aimee bother to do what Mom says? And I'm not going to tell Mom because I don't want to make things worse for Aimee. Then I really would be a jerk.

I keep my head down at school. There are some snickers. A few teachers ask me if I'm okay. Do they know what's happening online? Maybe. Raychel and Adrian assure me things are dying down. Give it a week. Two at most. It'll be done. Not to worry.

But I do.

I'm still getting tagged in posts.

Raychel tells me to delete my account. "It's the best way for you to deal with it. Delete that account and start another one. That way your friends are the only ones who know who you are."

When I look at my account I see there are a dozen more tags. More conversations about how terrible society is or men are or women are all because of me. Because I was stupid.

I follow Raychel's advice and delete the account. Done. No more tags. Now the discussion has to stop because I'm gone.

The new account I create is locked, but even though I don't get notifications about being tagged, I can't help searching to see if anyone noticed that I'm gone.

They did.

—GOOD RIDDANCE.

—MAYBE NOW PEOPLE WILL REALIZE HOW IMPORTANT THIS ISSUE IS.

—SORRY HE HAD TO DELETE HIS ACCOUNT BUT I'M GLAD WE'RE ABLE TO HAVE THIS CONVERSATION.

—GUESS HE REALIZED HOW STUPID HE IS.

That's me. Stupid. Stupid to believe I could stop it.

The next day Raychel and Aiden tell me not to care about what other people are saying.

I say I don't. But I do.

Monday my sister allows me to drive with her to school again and says that it doesn't matter what people say.

It shouldn't. I know it shouldn't, but it does.

The conversation online continues. Only now they don't mention me anymore. I'm not that important to be mentioned by name.

I fail my science test. Hard to focus when I can't sleep. I'm glad they don't remember who I am, but for some reason that makes this worse. If they cared enough to vilify me, they should care enough to remember who I am.

But they don't.

My sister tells me to grow up and to get a grip. My mother tells me that I'm being a wimp. That I should use this to toughen up and be a man. Life is hard and I need to learn that. If my father had done his job he would have taught me that. Adrian says that no one is talking about it anymore. Raychel says he's right.

When I search online I see the conversation is dying down. It's done. I need to just move on and get over it.

I try. I really do. No one cares about my stupid comment or apology anymore. I know that. No one remembers. The conversation in the lunchroom isn't me or my mistake or social media anymore. It's normal stuff like Raychel being upset because her mom won't extend her curfew or Adrian complaining that his three sisters ganged up on him and his dad last night and wouldn't let him watch the game. Everyone at the lunch table comments or complains or says something. Everyone but me. What if I say something wrong again? What will happen to me if I make another mistake?

I talk less and less because I'm scared I'll say something stupid. My online accounts are filled with pictures, but I don't post comments on anything. I watch everyone else talk and laugh and wish I could be like them—free to say what they want and post what they want and be who they want.

My dad hasn't talked to me in weeks. My sister is going to the prom tonight. Mom is working the late shift at the hospital. I was invited to a party at Adrian's house. Mom said I could go. I told him I would be there. But I can't because I could say something wrong. I don't want to say anything wrong again and I'm so tired of waiting for the day that I do.

I watch Mom snap shots of Aimee and her boyfriend as they head off to prom. I even take a picture with Aimee and she gives me a hug. She's really pretty. Mom tells me to have fun and heads out the door to go to work.

The bottle of pills is right where I left it. I'm sure everyone will have something to say online about this when I'm done. They always do. My guess is a bunch of the posts will say I'M SORRY HE CHOSE TO END HIS LIFE, BUT AN HONEST CONVERSATION ABOUT SUICIDE AND DEPRESSION WILL GIVE HIS DEATH MEANING.

They're wrong, but I'm not going to tell them that.

I'm done.

LONE

Alex Segura

ILLUSTRATIONS BY DENNIS CALERO

This is what dying felt like.

Carla de Varona flopped onto the bed, her face missing the pillow. She bounced up a bit, the movement making her dizzier. Dizzy was the least of her worries, though. Her eyes creaked open and she noticed her mouth was bleeding onto the bed. Her jaw hurt. Her vision was blurred and she felt like she'd just slipped under a rush hour express bus. She couldn't muster the energy to force her tongue to root around her mouth for missing teeth. Some were cracked, for sure.

The gash across her nose and her busted lip added to the chorus of blood spreading onto the 600-thread count sheets. She heard a late-running J train rumble by above her apartment—the bottom floor of a two-story house on Jamaica, near Woodhaven Blvd., in Queens. A blue collar town that had seen better days. But the town was hers. Had been, at least.

A wet cough. Hack. Blood and phlegm splatter. Rough gurgling in the back of her throat. She wanted to move. Get up. But every inch of her was howling. The knife wound down her side. The sharp pain that could only come from a few broken ribs. The pulsing purple bruise under her eye, and who knows what else.

Fuck.

The cheap eye-mask she'd shoplifted from the costume shop on 92nd Street was on the floor, yanked off and tossed to the side as she collapsed. She was still wearing the long black hooded raincoat and the Century 21 leather gloves—both of which she'd found in her closet earlier that night. Stupid.

What a fucking idiot. What a pathetic way to die.

Carla let out another gasping, desperate breath and closed her eyes.

• • •

Carla closed the textbook and looked up from her chair. Across her desk was Ernesto Morales—skinny, tattooed and frightened. Like an underfed alley cat about to dart under a car. His eyes were sunken, he smelled of weed and piss. His ratty DJ Khaled shirt was hidden under a once-black-now-gray hoodie. Ernesto was one of Carla de Varona's best GED/TASC prep course students at York College in Jamaica, Queens. The classes started small and finished the term empty. She tried not to think about how hopeless it all felt. At least her commute was short.

On a good day, Carla liked the work. She enjoyed helping students finish the last steps they'd need to get their hands on a high school equivalency diploma. But even that piece of paper wasn't enough anymore. It was a start, at best. That was something, she told herself more often than she'd like to.

"You got this?" Carla said.

"Yeah, yeah, Ms. D," Ernesto said, his hands digging deeper into his pockets. "I got it, no sweat."

Carla smirked and stood up, motioning to the door with her chin.

"If you say you got it, I believe you," she said, following Ernesto out the door.

"I'm tryin', Miss," Ernesto said.

"Ms. de Varona," Carla said. "Ms. D is fine, too. And trying is good. Succeeding is better."

Ernesto nodded fast, his head bobbing up and down. The kid was eager, but Carla knew he didn't have a regular place to stay, much family or anything resembling a job. Even Carla had her limits. She'd stopped letting students crash with her long ago. Her apartment was her place—for solitude, dreaming, plotting and thinking. Not always in that order.

"How's that pup, Ms. D?" Ernesto said, trying to change the conversation.

She had a huge German Shepherd rescue—a few years old and relatively calm as far as dogs went. She'd discreetly brought him to class a few weeks back when her dog walker bailed. The choice was simple: either she gave the dog a head start on his GED or come home to shit all over the living room until she found a new walker. Carla had always had pets—dogs, cats, parrots, a few reptiles here and there. She liked animals more than people. She was okay with that. She did as much as she could—volunteering at a local animal shelter on weekends, working adoption events and helping strays. There were a few stretches where her place felt more like a zoo than a human residence. Now it was just her and Jermaine, named after her favorite *Adventure Time* character.

"He's good," she said. "Not really a puppy anymore. I'll tell him you said hello."

Ernesto didn't seem to get the joke. He cleared his throat to signal he was ready for another topic to be broached.

They'd made it outside to the main parking lot. It was a blustery, chilly September night. Cold, but not a numbing freeze yet. She closed up her brown North Face jacket and slung her too-big purse over her shoulder. Fall was still lurking around, trying to lull you into thinking it wasn't going to get much colder.

"You're gonna be smart tonight, right?" Carla said. "That's the plan?"

"Yeah, yeah, just gonna head home and do some readin'," Ernesto said. "None of that other shit. That's behind me."

"Good answer. I know it's tempting," Carla said. "Easy money. Free drinks. The people. It burns into you. You want it more each time. Watch who you hang with. People, places and things, Ernesto."

"Ms. D, I know, man," Ernesto said, his shoulders sagging. He was tired of being lectured. "I know."

"You got somewhere to go?" Carla said.

"Yeah, I'm good, yeah," Ernesto said, looking away. "See you around, Ms. D."

Carla waved and watched Ernesto wander past the empty parking lot toward Jamaica Avenue. Even from the school, well past ten in the evening, you could hear the blaring horns and sirens spreading out from the bustling thruway.

Carla reached her still-functional 2001 beige Ford Taurus and checked her watch before opening the driver's side door. There was still time.

• • •

Left hook. Jab. Jab. Right hook. High kick. Uppercut. Jab. Jab. Middle kick. Combination. Left hook.

Carla felt her blood coursing through her body. She wasn't sweating so much as swimming in herself—her face and chest and back drenched. She wanted to stop. But she didn't. She couldn't. These nightly sessions kept her going. She felt alive.

Uppercut. Uppercut. Left hook. Elbow. High kick. Jab. Right hook. Step back. Step up. Jab. Jab. Combination. Jab.

She looped her arms around the old punching bag and leaned into it. To stop it from swaying as much as herself. She closed her eyes and let her face rest on the dirty bag. She started to feel herself sway along with it, back and forth. Light-headed. This was good. This was practice. She had to stay on point, she told herself. She had to be ready.

Carla knew how to defend herself. Her dad had instilled in her the belief that she should not be fucked with. She could almost hear him now, five years after his death: "You're my little girl. But not *a* little girl. If someone comes at you wrong, you need to know how to respond." She did.

She knew the pressure points. She knew the right stance. She knew the levels of pain she could cause with her bare hands. Knew how to make their bodies shake with a pain that spread all over and made them want to curl up and die. She knew which nerve clusters to poke, which joints to aim for and which bones could break the fastest. She was a pacifist, really. She let out a quick chuckle.

Carla stepped back and let the bag twirl away. She reached for the towel she'd left on the stool nearby and buried her face in it for a second. She started to dry off the rest of her upper body as she looked over the gym—a tiny room with a punching bag and a few weights that the school called a gym. The room was technically closed but Carla still used it. This perk—if she was in a giving mood and called it such—was one of the reasons she stuck around. She got to practice her Krav Maga, get a paycheck, and try to help people.

Years ago, after her father was gunned down in an undercover operation gone sour, she'd tried being a cop. Like him. But she couldn't handle it. Not the job—that part was easy enough. The limitations. The ones that got away. The paperwork. The regulations. The sexism. The gray areas, when she only dealt in black and white. A few years out of the academy, she turned in her badge and went for her Master's.

She wiped off the last drops of sweat from her forehead. She didn't need anyone else to tell her what an odd character she was. How weird she'd seem to anyone that got close enough. Here she was—a pacifist, vegan, animal-loving, leftist, sober, book-hoarding Latina who could kill someone if she wanted to—spending her nights teaching adults how to pass a GED test.

She snatched her phone from the stool on the first vibrate. Brendan.

"Hey," Carla said.

"Got some intel for you," he said, skipping the hi-how-are-you stuff.

"Not on the phone," she said.

"You know where I'm at," he said and hung up.

• • •

The Wee Pub was a shithole corner bar on the border of Woodhaven and Ozone Park, next to a vacant lot and a stone's throw from Jamaica. The closest landmark was a strip club that ladies in the biz called "The Last Stop." It didn't have a functioning sign and only catered to an aging, drunken and low-income clientele. The nickname usually didn't have to be explained. Carla wasn't sure what the place was actually called.

The Wee Pub was a bar for professional drinkers. If you didn't know where it was, you'd never find it. They didn't get a lot of walk-ins or surprise patrons. There were no specials, no parties and only the lifers got buybacks. The one exception from straight up alcoholism was Friday. Every Friday was "Teacher's Night," where faculty from the local high school decided to let their hair down, play some Salt-N-Pepa on the juke and have one Midori Sour too many. Even with some upkeep—surfaces, floors, the basics—Carla doubted anyone could remove the permanent coat of dust, grime and ash that seemed to cloak the bar. It reeked of stale beer, burgers left on the grill too long and vomit that was more vodka than food. Brendan loved this place.

Carla pushed the door open with a familiar creak. She scanned the space—beat-up bar on the left, empty except for the fit, thirty-something bartender who was paying more attention to the Knicks game on the sole TV, and Brendan, who was sipping a Guinness and typing away on his laptop. He didn't look up until she'd pulled out the stool to his left. The jukebox—one of those with the stacks of CDs, not the digital bullshit Carla saw at most other places—was playing Cash. "Jackson." The live version from Folsom. Brendan knew her too well.

"What you got, buddy boy?" she said, keeping her voice low. The bartender, Joe, was in his own world. She knew him. But she didn't need him nosing in on this conversation tonight.

"Sure you wanna do this?" he said, not looking up from his laptop. She couldn't tell what he was typing.

"Yes. Jesus," she said.

"You're not going to like this," Brendan said, meeting her stare. He was young—mid-twenties, well-built, a tuft of curly brown hair to match his fair, Irish complexion. She might have thought of him as more than a tool for information if circumstances were different. But those days were gone.

"Spill," she said, sipping her soda. "It's getting late."

She didn't like bars. She didn't like this bar in particular. When she'd first moved into the neighborhood, months after her dad died, she'd made it a second home. That was problematic for someone who liked to drink as much as she did. Pretty soon, she was running a tab that came close to her monthly rent. She was spending a bigger part of each night leaning on the bar than sleeping in her bed. She closed her eyes for a second and said a quick, silent prayer.

"There's actually a testing facility in your school, er, your job, whatever," Brendan said, typing faster. Carla didn't notice anything really changing on his monitor. "Not a big operation, but it's growing. Not sure what they have in there—probably in the North Building. Which is here—"

The text screen became a map of the school and Brendan zoomed in on a part of the campus Carla did not recognize.

"You're certain they're testing on animals? What for? How'd this get approved?" she said. She felt her temperature rise a bit.

"Slow down," Brendan said. He'd called up what looked like an Excel file. "Seems like basic, entry-level lab stuff. It's not a huge operation, like I said. Rabbits, some 'nonhuman primates,' rats . . . that's all I can see."

She didn't say anything. Just looked at his screen. It looked like gibberish from her vantage point.

"That's all I got," Brendan said. "Please try not to do anything stupid with this info."

Carla blinked a few times and looked at Brendan. She let out a humorless laugh. "That's where you come in, amigo," she said. "You make sure the pieces are in place and I'll do my part."

Brendan nodded and started typing again. The bartender was gone, probably wandered off to the back of the bar to do a few quick bumps to make the night go faster. "Wayne will be there," Brendan said. "He'll swoop in once you give the signal. He'll grab the animals and take them off the grid."

"Great," Carla said. "Tomorrow night, midnight. I'm there."

Brendan turned on his stool to face Carla. "You can still back out," he said. "You don't have to prove anything to anyone. There are other ways to prove a point."

"Fuck you," she said, getting up from the stool and collecting her bag. "You know I have to do this."

• • •

The mask felt weird on her face and she was hot, even in the fall weather. The hood over her head didn't help. Her peripheral vision was shot to shit and her mobility was a little stiff because she was wearing too many layers. Aside from that, it all seemed okay. The gloves fit fine and the new boots weren't too tight. She'd get to break them in tonight.

She'd left the building—officially—earlier that night. Gotten into her car and waved goodbye to her students as she normally would. Parked at home, walked in, made dinner and tried to watch the *Mad Men* episode she'd DVR'd. About an hour before midnight, she slipped out through her own back window and started to walk. She kept to the side streets—avoiding any that weren't empty—and to the shadows, hood up and the mask in her pocket. To any pedestrian, she was just a cold, speed-walking New Yorker.

By quarter-'til, she'd jumped the fence and slipped the mask on. The main building wasn't locked, but the lab was. This is where Brendan came in. She reached the glass double-doors that led into Lab 1C and tapped a few numbers into the alarm display on the wall. She heard a click and the alarm system's red light turned green. She let out a quick, relieved breath.

That's when she heard the gunshot.

She wheeled around. The hallway was empty. But she hadn't imagined that sound. She had ten minutes to rush into that lab, pop open as many cages as she could and fuck shit up. It wasn't just about letting the animals out—she had to ensure the people running the lab couldn't just pick up where they left off tomorrow. To keep abusing these helpless creatures. Ten minutes. But that gunshot sounded close.

"Fuck," she said, running for the exit that seemed closest to the sound. *What was going on?*

She flung the exit doors open and found herself in a smaller parking lot, empty aside from the crowd of men huddled together near the fence opposite the doors. They were cursing and kicking at something—someone. Whatever was feeling the brunt of their attack wasn't faring well, and the sounds he was making were pained and loud. She started to step toward the group when she heard the familiar click of a gun's hammer.

"The fuck?" one of the group said. "Some ninja shit going on here."

She didn't bother responding—with words at least. She turned around and kicked at a man's arm, knocking the gun away and making contact with his chin. It stunned more than hurt, but sent the creep falling back. He looked young—barely out of high school, wearing a red Clippers hoodie and close-cropped hair. He also looked really pissed off as Carla stood over him. *Seven remaining.*

"The hell is going on here?" he sputtered, blood dripping from his mouth.

Carla didn't respond. She squatted down and sent a few punches into his face, knocking him back, his head slamming into the asphalt—hard. He was dazed and probably not getting on his feet anytime soon. She popped up and turned. The crowd had noticed her, the circle of them—seven guys, all around the same age and just as surprised and angry as their fallen, gun-wielding comrade. As they parted, she noticed who their initial target was. Laid out on the floor, a pool of blood forming around his head, was a familiar face.

"Ernesto?" she said.

"Whoa shit, she took down DeAndre," one of the goons said, pudgier and slower than the others.

The group started to move toward her, spreading out, not giving her much room to get to Ernesto. Fuck. Fuck. Fuck.

The first two went down easy—a few quick, open-palm hits to their chins sent them spinning back, their bats and crowbar rattling away from their grasp.

She felt a hot slash down her side. Her hand reached to her right—under her arm, near her ribs. Blood. The cut wasn't deep—probably a crappy knife the idiot wasn't expecting to use—but it hurt. Shit. Three down. The leftovers were being more cautious now that they'd seen her move. *Five.*

A white boy with a mohawk stepped to her first. He was ballsy and dumb. Ballsy for being first, dumb for taking an old-fashioned swing at Carla. She dodged the punch and bent his arm behind his back until she heard a comforting crack. Comforting for her. He let out a high-pitched cry and she kicked him toward his buddies, who reeled back. *Four.*

"Bitch is serious," the fat one said.

The other three seemed to defer to him as he moved toward Carla. She believed in taking out the head first. She rammed him, but he was faster than he looked, side stepping her attack and elbowing her in the back.

Carla fell to her knees and rolled away from the thugs, trying to recover. She was met with an aluminum bat to the head, snapping her forward. She couldn't see for a second. Blackout. She covered her ears and tried to figure out who was where. Before she could, she felt a kick to the face. Then she was on her back.

She looked up to see the four guys looming over her. Two were armed— bats. They didn't seem to know what to make of her. She used that hesitation to shoot an arm out and yank the leg of one of the kids closest to her, sending him down, his body crashing into the pavement, followed by an operatic groan. *Three.*

The sudden movement confused them. It gave her time to get on her feet. She punched the guy closest to her in the nose and heard a soft crack as he shrieked and stumbled backwards. *Two.*

She'd lost track of one of the two and paid for it as a bat hit her lower back. She fell forward, her gloved hands scraping on the pavement. She rolled to her left a second before the bat hit the street. She was dizzy. She felt blood in her mouth and her back was screaming in pain. Carla scanned the parking lot and saw the first two dudes—the ones she'd laid out before she even knew what was going on—creeping up. Time to end this.

She got to her feet and swung at the one with the bat, connecting with his chin. She followed with a kick to his ribs. The long wail he let out in response let her know she'd connected. A swift punch to the face sent him down. *One.*

She turned around and managed to block another swing of the bat with her forearm, sending a searing pain down her entire arm. Carla let out a small grunt in response. She was not going to let these pricks hear her scream or make her cry. She sent a chop into the guy's face—he seemed older, like a scrub who was still in the minors a few seasons too late. She felt teeth and felt them move. Blood coated her hand as she pulled back.

"Oh—oh, f—fu—fugh," the last one said, covering his maw. Blood seeped onto his hand. It looked like he'd tried to swallow too much ketchup. Carla let loose with a kick to his face and he was down. *Zero.*

That's when she collapsed. Everything crashed together. She'd been beaten to shit and had held on to finish these pricks and at the first sign of calm, her body gave in. She heard rustling around her and hoped to God it wasn't anyone trying for another round.

"Jesus, thank you."

It was Ernesto. He was bloody and bruised but moving and alive.

"Ernesto," she said.

"Ms. D? Holy fu—"

"Shutup, don't say anything," Carla said. "We have to get out of here. Fast."

• • •

She passed out a few minutes later. She didn't remember stumbling across the parking lot. Or the sirens in the background. She didn't remember Ernesto smashing into a nearby car by elbowing the front driver's side window. She didn't remember him dragging her into the backseat and hot-wiring the unremarkable Honda Civic. Those cars got stolen a lot anyway, right?

She did remember him asking her for her apartment keys, to which she didn't respond. She'd lost a lot of blood. She was really sleepy, but Ernesto refused to let her sleep. He kept shaking her. She just wanted to rest.

He set her down, finally inside her place, on a chair near the dining room table. Finally, she could rest. Everything went black.

She wasn't sure how much time had passed. She was in bed. Blood on the sheets. Her body aching all over. The knife wound in her side was pulsing, but didn't feel that deep. The bandages were holding it together. She wasn't so sleepy, but her head felt foggy and not all there. Her window was open and light was seeping in—gray, early morning light that hadn't fully formed into sun. She heard her bedroom door open, but couldn't bring herself to roll over and see who was in her home.

"Yo, Ms. D—you awake?"

Ernesto. She tried to talk but her voice was ragged and her mouth dry. She felt like complete shit.

"Yes," she said. Her voice was low and hoarse. Bits from the night before were forming in her skull.

She winced, holding in a scream as she tried to get up, settling for turning to face Ernesto, who didn't look much better than she felt—a black eye, knife wound on his arm, bloody gash on his forehead and his shirt torn and red.

"What happened?"

"Ms. D, you, um, you saved my ass," Ernesto said. "You straight up kicked the shit out of them guys trying to take me out."

"Who were they?" she said, closing her eyes to try and push the dizzy out.

"That was DeAndre's crew," Ernesto said. He seemed to be in pretty good spirits for someone who should be in a hospital bed. Getting beat up has to top dying, she figured.

"DeAndre what?" Carla said.

"Wilkins, DeAndre Wilkins," Ernesto said. "He runs shit around here. You know that."

Actually, she didn't. She wasn't a cop. And her Halloween costume was made to give her cover while she opened a bunch of animal cages to spite a lab. She hadn't planned on going toe-to-toe with an actual street gang.

"So, we fucked with the gang that runs everything?"

"DeAndre is the boss, he and his boys call the shots, they funnel drugs and shit," Ernesto said, his eyes wide. She'd never heard him talk so much. She almost regretted saving him. "I had done some, well, done some work for him while back—didn't collect, though, you know?"

"You owed him money?"

"Yeah, yeah, but I was gonna pay him back."

"How much?" Carla said. She felt like throwing up. She didn't even want to look at herself in the mirror.

"Ms., it's not like that, it's . . . "

"How much?"

"Ten grand, but I was gonna pay it back," he said, stepping back a bit, as if Carla was going to jump on him.

She let out a long breath.

"Do you think they followed us?" Carla said.

"Nah, I don't think so," Ernesto said.

She looked up at him.

"Thanks for your help," she said. "I was barely awake when I finished with those dickheads."

"Aw, Ms., you saved me—least I could do," Ernesto said, a shy smile on his face. "I mean, what the hell was you doing dressed like that? In school! Going to a party or some shit?"

She sat up, her feet on the ground. She held her knees to try and steady herself. She looked at herself in the vanity mirror. Terrible didn't even begin to describe it. She was not working today.

"Ernesto, you can't tell anyone what happened last night," she said, speaking slowly, even talking was taking a toll on her. "No one, you understand me? This has to remain between us."

"Shit, yeah, of course Ms. D, I ain't gonna blow up your secret identity and shit," Ernesto said, giggling. "I didn't know you was playing super-hero on the streets and shit. Gonna make for an interesting class today, though, seriously . . . "

She was up on her feet in a moment, her face a few inches from his. She hurt all over. Nausea swept over her. Just that quick motion had made her feel like she'd just been on ten rollercoasters. But she had to make a point.

"Listen to me, Ernesto," she said. "I am only saying this once more. If I find out you ratted about me to anyone—anyone, even your *mami*, *abuela* or whatever skank you're fucking this week—I will kill you. Understand? You did me a favor. You helped me out of a jam. But if I hadn't shown up, you'd be dead. Do not make me regret that."

She wobbled a bit, balancing herself on the dresser to her left.

Ernesto's smile disappeared. "You got it, Ms. D," Ernesto said. He pulled a newspaper out of his back pocket and tossed it on the bed. She still got the paper delivered to her door. He must have snatched it up while she was passed out.

She could read the headline of the page he was reading from where they stood. She could also see a fuzzy image. No one else would be able to identify her—that's what the hood and mask were for. But she knew it was her, looming over a guy whose arm she had just broken with glee.

LONE VIGILANTE TAKES OUT STREET GANG IN QUEENS

"Pretty cool, huh?" Ernesto said.

"Fuck," Carla said, and stumbled back to bed.

LOVE AND VALOUR ON 'THE VICTORIAN *TITANIC'*

Gill Hoffs

On the morning of Saturday January 21st 1854, around 700 people thought they were sailing south through the Irish Channel. They were wrong. The RMS *Tayleur* had launched amid much celebration two days prior, beginning a predicted journey of several months from Liverpool to Melbourne and the Australian Gold Rush with many articles in the press touting the airy luxuriousness of White Star Line's technologically advanced new vessel. No ship could be safer or more comfortable, no passengers could be happier, than those aboard this iron clipper.

Unfortunately for those on board, the metal hull which promised cleanliness, speed, and ample space confused the compasses, and bad weather meant that once out at sea they were lost. There was no clear view of the horizon, stars, sun, or land, and therefore no way of knowing where they were. Believing the ship to be sailing south as planned, Captain John Noble, an experienced and able master mariner, refused to change direction despite sailors familiar with this area of sea and currently travelling as passengers raising their concerns about the wisdom of this course.

A few hours after breakfast that Saturday morning, hundreds of the passengers were below deck struggling with seasickness as the ship tossed in *"a heavy rolling sea"* with waves *"mountains high"*. Some passengers stood on deck, watching the crew work and *"admiring the hills and valleys made in the water by the storm"*. The captain directed crewmen to shorten the sails and prepare the lead so as to ascertain the depth of the water and work out from his charts where they were in the channel. But it was too late.

There was a shout, "*Land ho!*" and those above deck saw what was later described as rocks rising *"like a mountain in the middle of the sea"*. One passenger echoed the thoughts of many when he said, *"when I saw the land I knew nothing could save her"*. The tide had caught the ship and, despite the crew's best efforts, the *Tayleur* could not be turned away. Minutes later the waves swept her against the bottom of a cliff.

Spray washed the deck, drenching those pouring up through the hatches from below, saturating their clothes and dooming the women. This was the age of the crinoline, and women and girls wore around sixteen layers of clothing including a constricting corset, skirts, and petticoats. There was neither the time nor the space to disrobe. With such a crush on deck, the crew were unable to fell a mast to use as a bridge to land without squashing dozens of their fellow travellers, and the sea was too rough to successfully launch the few lifeboats.

As one survivor later recalled, *"now began a scene of the most frightful horror—some running below to get what they could, others praying, some taking leave of their friends, wringing their hands, and beseeching them for help. The vessel, after striking, lay so close upon the rocks that several persons attempted to jump ashore. The first person who jumped struck his head against the rocks, and fell back into the water with his head frightfully cut, and, after struggling for a short time, sank. The next person who jumped from the vessel made good his footing, and was followed by several others—I believe belonging to the crew. They also succeeded in making good their landing and as soon as they had done so, scampered with all haste up the rocks, never attempting to assist those on board.*

Several now swung themselves on the rocks, which were but a few feet from us. I managed to swing myself on shore, and retained the rope in my hand; I passed the end of it up to some of those behind, and by this means a great many were enabled to come on shore. To attempt to paint the heartrending scene on board the ship would be impossible—wives clinging to their husbands—children to their parents—women running wildly about the deck, uttering the most heartrending cries—many offering all they possessed to persons to get them on shore."

The likes of Welsh miner George Lewis risked their lives repeatedly, pulling people from the water, tying ropes to the rocks at the base of the cliff, and refusing to allow their own fears to get the better of them. The first crewmen to escape the *Tayleur* clambered up the near vertical cliff in search of help or an escape from the cries of the imperilled, but George and many others stayed despite the danger. There was no beach or shore, just occasional crevices in the rocks which were soon packed with bodies forced in by the waves. Survivors clung to whatever rocky outcrops they could find, many being washed off to join the bodies of loved ones bobbing in the sea. Survivor Mr. W. Jones said:

"The scene was now most truly awful. The most desperate struggles for life were made by the wretched passengers—great numbers of women jumped overboard in the vain hope of reaching land, and the ropes were crowded by hundreds who, in their eagerness, terror, and confusion, frustrated each other's efforts for self-preservation. Many of the females would get half-way and then become unable to proceed further; and, after clinging to the rope for a short time, would be forced from their hold by those who came after them . . . I saw one young woman hanging on the middle of the rope for some time by her two hands, but those pushing to get on shore soon sent her to her doom."

Ten to twenty minutes later, the ship rolled away from the rocks she was impaled on and quickly sank, leaving her masts and rigging at an angle above the waves, with two men clinging onto the ropes for dear life. More than half of the travellers were dead, including 97% of the women and children. Only one family survived intact.

Samuel and Sarah Carby were newlyweds from Lincolnshire, England, sailing with their 13-year-old son, Robert, to the Australian goldfields with a fortune of 200 gold sovereigns sewn into Sarah's underwear. Samuel was an ex-convict made good, who returned to England a rich man in order to marry his sweetheart and take her and the son he last saw as a baby back to Australia to sell shoes to diggers and enjoy a fresh start together in the sunshine. Samuel was on deck when the *Tayleur* smashed onto the rocks and immediately fled downstairs. Sarah and Robert were lying in their nightclothes, wretched with seasickness, their garments—and the hidden gold—nearby. Samuel chose family over fortune, grabbed them by the arms, and helped them up the stairs onto the top deck. With not a second to lose, he urged Robert overboard onto a rope stretching over to the rocks, then his wife. Many others were doing the same, using ropes and wooden spars to scramble over the waves and wreckage to safety. But as the *Stamford Mercury* reported:

"[I]n their eagerness, terror, and confusion, [they] frustrated each other's efforts for self-preservation. Many of the females proceeded half way, and then became unable to go forward, and after clinging to the rope for a short time were forced from their hold by those who followed. Mrs. Carby had got part of the way across when her legs fell, and she hung some time by her two hands over the raging sea: her husband then went on the rope, and managed to assist her to the rock."

Although the *Birkenhead* disaster had occurred just two years earlier, leading to the now popular standard of 'women and children first', there was no such inclination here. The *Tayleur* was not a ship of disciplined soldiers and sailors armed with weapons, but an ordinary crew and terrified emigrants.

Only 290 survived the wrecking of the *Tayleur*. With the screams of the two men still stranded in the rigging ringing in their ears, they clambered up the cliff nursing broken limbs and torn flesh, many almost naked and freezing in the winter wind. *"Of those whose lives had been saved many were shockingly maimed, through having been beaten about in the surf and forced against the rocks"*, said one survivor later. *"Some had their arms broken, some their ankles dislocated, and a man whom I saw get up the rocks after me had his nose nearly torn off and all his teeth knocked in"*. The ship had wrecked against Lambay, a small island off the coast of Dublin, previously known by its Gaelic name 'Reachra' or 'place of many shipwrecks'. Few people lived there, but those who did took in all the survivors they could. Hundreds were left to sleep in hollows behind the cottages with makeshift shelters of luggage and cargo retrieved from the rocks and a layer of straw to keep them warm. The weather was still too fierce to allow them to be transferred from the island to the mainland and as one passenger said: *"The night was dreadful; we were almost starving; many of us were nearly naked and wet through"*. The islanders' meagre winter supplies were shared out and everyone was given a potato, a sliver of pork from a freshly killed pig, and some received a little oatmeal, too.

The survivors were eventually transported to Dublin, and those who chose to do so were then returned to Liverpool and sent home or put up in lodgings until a replacement berth could be provided on another ship. Many continued to Australia, having lost all they owned in the wreck, some returned home penniless. Relief funds provided meagre compensation and the subsequent inquiries and inquests were mismanaged providing little justice for the survivors and the bereaved.

Samuel and Sarah Carby decided to take the replacement voyage, but, much to his mother's distress, Robert refused to go with them. His parents returned from Australia a few years later and became publicans, while Robert worked as a carpenter in Manchester and survived until 1919. He didn't speak of his experiences to his children, and his granddaughter was astonished to hear of his exploits. As Robert's great-granddaughter by marriage wrote in 2013: *"It's sobering to think that none of them* (Robert's dozens of descendants) *would be here at all if Robert hadn't survived the wreck. He had 12 children and all their various offspring would also be non-existent. Life determined by a twist of fate ..."*

JUST PRETEND

Martyn Waites

I keep having this dream. I suppose you could call it a recurring one cept I don't have it often. Only when I'm stressed an unhappy like. Like me first night in prison.

In it I'm with me dad. Me real dad. We're in the car together, goin somewhere, an the sun's out, the sky's blue, there's not a cloud to spoil etc., an we're in the country, all leafy an green. An we're laughin. He says something an looks at me an I laugh. An when I laugh, he laughs. An when he laughs he looks at me an I see somethin there in his eyes an it makes me feel good. Me belly feels all warm an full.

Then we turn off the road to where we're goin. An the sun's still shinin an that bu the green's gone. We go down this road an it gets more an more bumpy the further it goes on. An then we're in this quarry an it stretches for miles, just rock an sand an dust. In the middle there's these buildins from corrugated metal with lots of old machinery lyin around them an we head for them.

Me dad says he's got to see someone an smiles an when he smiles there's something in his eyes but it's not like it was before. It doesn't make me feel warm. Then before I can say anything he gets out of the car an goes inside the buildins, leavin me there.

I sit there for a while an at first it's all right. But then these clouds start to roll over the sun, sendin shadows over the rocks. Then it starts to get cold an I shiver. I'm only wearin a t-shirt. Then I realize me dad's been gone an long time an I start to get worried. At first I do nothing, just sit there, then I wind down the window an shout but all I hear is me own voice comin back at me. I'm getting really scared now. I open the car door an get out. I go inside the building, the same way me dad did. Inside it's all old an dusty an fallin apart, like no one's been there for years. An there's no sign of me dad.

I run round all the buildins shoutin Dad! Dad! Until I can't shout anymore. But there's no reply. I run back outside an now the car's gone, just disappeared. An it's got cold now, really cold. An the clouds are turnin the sky grey. Soon the sky'll be black. An the stones stretch on forever. I wanna run everywhere an scream everythin at the same time. But I don't. I just sit down an hug me knees into me chest an cry. An cry an cry an cry. An then I wake up. An I'm still cryin.

An that was me first night in prison.

• • •

I suppose you want to facts an things now. What I'm here for an that. Well, no point beatin around the bush, it's armed robbery. What happened was, me an me co-de, well half-brother really, but we say co-de in prison, short for co-defendant, we knocked over this petrol station. We did it properly, masks an that, balaclavas an shotguns. Paralysed the bloke in there. But we still got caught. Known to the police we were. Or me brother was, anyway. I wouldn't care, but we only got four fuckin grand, for fuck sake! Hardly worth goin out, was it?

Anyway, we got sent down. An split up. Sean got Hollesley Bay. I got here.

So where's here? Well I can't tell you that, can I? Like I can't tell you men name. Cos I'm underage. So pick a prison, any one, they're all the same, an that can be it. Same with me. Pick a name an I'll answer to it.

It's OK here, I suppose, once you get used to it. Not a fuckin holiday camp, but then it shouldn't be. But I can ride it. My wing's not bad. I'm in with the Section 52s, the long-termers. Not just armed robbers like me, but street robbers, murderers an that. Rapists an sex offenders too, but they try an hide that. Make up stories about what they're in for. The other lads are all right, really. You all get on if you've got respect. When you first go in they all wanna know ya. Wanna know your history, sus you out. See if you're a threat. So I tell them things about me. Just bits, though. What I'm in for, who me co-de is an where he's at. Stuff like that. An stories. Things I want them to hear. Some are real some are pretend. But I don't tell them my history. My real story. I carry that with me.

Sometimes, lookin at the other kids, I feel so old. I'm seventeen. The youngest are about fifteen. When we're eighteen we get shipped out to an adult nick. There's a big gap between fifteen an eighteen. A big fuckin gap.

But I just keep me head down. I watch, I smile. I ride it. You have a lot of time to think in here. I think about me family. About me dad. He's great, me dad. I've got pictures of him on the wall of me cell. There he's standin in our front room laughin, there he's with Marie, me stepmum. There he's down the Cross Keys doin his karaoke. Fuckin loves his karaoke. The Karaoke King, we call him, an he laughs. But he's really good. He does all the old stuff, Frank Sinatra, Moon River an that. Says his dad, my gandad used to play all that. He got it from him. Me dad could've done this for a livin. He's that good. You can tell by the photo. See the way his eyes are screwed tight shut, the way the veins in his neck are poppin out. An all the people in the audience are starin at him like they can't take their eyes off him. I look at that photo a lot. Makes me proud that he's me dad.

An then there's Kayleigh. She's me girlfriend an she's standin by me. I met her through me stepmum. I think she's her niece or somethin. She's got a flat of her own now, lives there with Tod. Haven't told you about him, have I? He's me son. Nearly six months old now. An I love him too. See this tattoo? Just above me wrist. There. I ain't rollin me sleeve back too far. There. Says Tod with a heart round it. I had that done whe he was born. That's how much I love him. I know I'm gonna miss out in him growin up an that, but he'll be with his mum. An me dad an Marie'll help. An she can tell him about me.

I don't think about Sean much. I know he's alright cos I hear things. Boys are comin in or bein shipped out. Word gets back. He's doin all right. An I don't think of mum much. Me real mum. She's alive an that, but I just don't think of her much.

No, it's just me dad, Kayleigh an Tod. They're me family now. An me dad's always sayin that families are important. Families are about love. An he's so right. Now I sit or lie in me cell an think about when Tod's older. I can do things with him me dad did with me.

Like boxin. An football.

When me dad come an got me from me mum's an took me to live with him, one of the first things he did was to join me up with a boxin club. Teach you to hit an hit hard, he said. Teach you to fight back.

I looked round the place. Lads about me age were skippin an doin weights, punchin bags an in the ring punchin each other. The boys in the ring were wearin the shorts an boots along with those padded helmet things an vests. I didn't like the vests.

I don wanna do it dad, I said.

He looked at me. Why?

I don wanna wear no vest like, I said not lookin at him.

I heard him sigh. But it was a good sigh. Like he was on my side an wanted to help. Not like he was pissed with me an wanted to hit me. I tried to help him out.

What about a t-shirt? I asked.

I think he smiled. Yeah, that should be OK. Just tell them.

An I don hafta take a shower with them?

Just wait till they're done, then you go in, he said.

I felt that warm glow again in me belly. Like I get in me dream when it's all goin well.

Yeah I'll join then, I said.

He smiled. I saw it this time. Good.

I joined then. An I loved it. It was difficult at first, I thought it would be just hittin. But Tommy the trainer showed me different. You have to keep your guard up, not let your opponent get a shot in, hurt you. Block them, keep them out. Then hit back. But don't let them see you comin. Make them think you're gonna go one way then go another then BAM! you've got them. You've hurt them.

I wish I'd met Tommy earlier. I wish my dad had brought me here earlier. I wish I'd been with my dad all the time.

Anyway, like I was sayin, I loved it. I did everythin Tommy told me. I kept me guard up. I hit back. I didn't let them see me comin. An I hurt them.

I got so good Tommy put me in fights. An I won. Seven fights, seven wins. Four knock-outs, three on points. I used up a lot of energy in my fights. A lot of anger. A lot of hate. They sometimes had different faces but that just made me hit them harder. That was good, Tommy said. Use it. Channel it. Be in charge of it. I was. An it felt fuckin good.

But I wanted to do somethin else as well. So one of the lads suggested football. So I went to play for a youth team. I was a bit wary at first but I used to turn up with me strip on underneath me clothes an after the match wait until they'd all been in the shower before I went in. They thought that was a bit weird but I didn't care.

An I found out I was good at that too. They made me striker. An I had a run where it seemed I couldn't stop scorin. I ended up havin a trial at Spurs. I did, honest. I thought it was goin really well but when I got called in to see George Graham an Stefan Iverson came out before me smiling I knew it wasn't goin to happen. I was pissed off at the time but I got over it. The boxin helped. Me dad helped.

• • •

There's a funny thing about prison. The names. They all sound like prisons. Feltham. Glen Parva. Huntercombe. Dartmoor. Frankland. They all sound bleak an grey, like even before there was a prison there they were just names waitin for prisons to be built. An then there's ones like Swinfen Hall, Bulwood Hall, Maidstone. Places that should sound pretty, but even they sound sinister. Then there's the big one, the daddy of them all. Wormwood Scrubs. Makes you fuckin shudder just to say it.

But like I said, mine's not that bad. You learn which screws are safe an which wanna fuck you up. Some of them do that, y'know, just for the hell of it. One kid on my landing once complained that this screw had kept him awake all night by kickin his door in. This kid makes stuff up, so the mornin screw didn't believe him. But when he tried to open the door he couldn't. The bolt was bent an jammed tight in. They pay a bit more attention to what this kid says now.

But some of the screws are OK. You can have a laugh with them. Like the teachers. Some of them are there cos no other place'll have them, some of them are really good, there cos they wanna be.

An it's like learnin a new way to talk. Prison's got its own language. If you wanna fit in you gotta learn it. They all wanna be gangsta rappers. Not just the black kids but all of them. Black, white, Asian, whatever. They all talk like that an they all act like that. An they all love rap. Especially Tupac. We all love Tupac. They ask me about it, an I talk back like they do an they say that's cool. That's real. But really I'm just pretendin. I like the old stuff. Sinatra, Moon River, stuff like that. Proper songs. Me dad's songs.

There is one thing, though. I won't take a shower. Haven't had one since I've been here. Not that I don't wanna be clean. I just don't wanna take a shower. Not with them. Not with anyone. An I won't. The other kids on the wing are startin to say things. Fuck em. Let em.

Anyway, I've got a job now. That takes me off the wing. Car maintenance. Fuckin love it. I love cars. I was training to be a mechanic before I came here.

But listen. I'm in a good mood today cos guess what? I've got a family visit! Fuckin great, eh? They try an do this for the lads who've got kids, who wanna keep in touch. It's an incentive to behave. An I've been good. I've been a model fuckin inmate.

So yeah, Kayleigh, Tod, Marie an me dad! Fuckin great, eh? Next Wednesday in the chapel! I can't fuckin wait!

• • •

I'm in the Educational Psychologists office an she's just made me a cup of tea. She's just turn round to get some biscuits, bent down an I can see her arse against her jeans, see the line of her knickers underneath. Some lads would say something, try an hot her up, but not me. Victoria helps me. Talks to me like a friend. I try not to think about those things too much with her.

She's found the biscuits, sat down, is offerin me one. Her tits are nice too, but I try not to look at them. Custard creams. I take one an say thank you.

I asked to see her after the visit an she knows I'm upset, but I just don't know how to start.

Tell me about the visit, she asks.

I dunk my custard cream an suck it. I tell her about the visit,

My dad looked pale when he came in. Like he'd shrunk or something. He must've seen me lookin shocked because he said, Haven't been well. But don't worry, I'm getting better. An he smiled. When he did that I saw his teeth, all yellow, an the black rings under his eyes. I gave him a hug an tried to smile back.

Then I hugged Marie. Then Kayleigh. She pulled away.

What's that smell? She said.

I said, I haven't had a shower since I've been here.

She said, You should.

I said, They can't make me.

She said they should, an sat down opposite me. Away from me.

An then there was Tod, sittin in his pushchair. He didn't pull away when I picked him up. He looked confused for a bit, then he smiled.

Look, he still remembers me, I said.

No he doesn't, said Kayleigh lightin a fag, it's cos you're smilin at him. He's smilin back.

I put him down then, on the mat they'd put out. There were some toys there, old ones, worn ones an Tod wanted to play with them. My dad gave me a fag. Then we talked.

I told Victoria all of this. I talked till me tea went cold.

Oh no, she said. She looked like she meant it.

Yeah. My dad's got lung cancer.

Oh no.

She talked for a bit longer, tryin to cheer me up, tryin to help. There was nothin she could do to help, I knew that an she knew that, but she kept talking. The sound of her voice made me feel better. It made me feel like she was my friend.

It was time for me to go. I didn't want to go back on the wing. I knew I had to, though. The screw was waitin outside with his portable metal detector, makin sure I hadn't nicked anythin.

Look, Victoria said as I was nearly out the door, this is nothin to do with your dad, but d'you wanna try havin a shower?

No I can't, I said.

It would help.

It wouldn't. Believe me, it wouldn't.

I left. The screw ran his metal detector over me an led me back to the wing.

After dinner I was supposed to have soch. Association time. But I didn't want to. I just stayed in my cell till lights out, lookin at the photos on the wall, then I went to sleep.

I woke up cryin durin the night.

I'd had the dream again.

• • •

I didn't want to go back to car maintenance, I wanted to talk to Victoria again. But she wasn't there. So I went.

But I didn't enjoy it. I kept dropping things an driftin off. Some of the other lads said things an I had a go back but Mick the mechanics teacher stepped in. Told us to calm down otherwise we'd all end up on the seg for fightin.

I tried havin soch that night but I didn't want it. I just sat there watchin the other lads play pool an PlayStation an watch the telly. Not many spoke to me. A couple said, why don't you have a shower, you smelly cunt? I just said fuck off an they laughed an went away.

I just sat an thought. About me dad. An me mum.

They split up when I was five, my mum an dad. I can't remember much about it, just the pair of them used to shout a lot. I can't remember my dad hittin my mum. He said he never did an I believe him. He said he wanted to though. An I believe him.

I got brought up by me mum. I can never remember her lookin happy. She was always shoutin at me an hittin me. Didn't matter what I did, whether I was good or bad, she was always layin into me. I used to try an be good, do things that might make her smile, make her happy, like tidyin up or somethin, but it never worked. I'd still get shouted at an hit. After a while I stopped tryin.

Sometimes though she would get upset an cry, give me a hug an say she was sorry. She was gonna be good to me from now on. An I used to smile an hug her back an tell her I loved her.

But she didn't. The next day it would be just the same. At first I cried, but then after a while I stopped doin that as well.

An Sean would sometimes stay. He usually lived with his dad. He was just over a year older than me an he used to really scare me. He seemed really grown up, like he knew everythin. He used to tell me all these things that he'd done, like breakin into places an fuckin girls. He used to nick mum's fags an smoke them. Mum didn't mind, she used to laugh. She got on really well with Sean. They used to sit down together an smoke on the settee. They'd sit all cosied up, she'd put her arm round him an cuddle him in.

When they did that, I used to look at them then run round jumpin on things an shoutin, fallin off things and tryin to make them laugh. But mum would shout at me, tell me to stop fucking about, an belt me one. Sean used to sit there an laugh. After a while I started goin out, leavin them to it. Sean was about eight then.

Then one day these two blokes arrived.

I was playin in the backyard at the time, with my toy cars. I don't know where Sean was.

Here he is, I heard my mother say, an she pointed at me.

One of the blokes took somethin, some foldin cash it looked like, out of his pocket an gave it to her. She smiled an took it. One of the men crossed the yard an knelt down beside me. He was going bald an had a little round fat tummy. He smiled. There was somethin about him I didn't like but I didn't know what. A look or a smell or something that wasn't quite right. I just looked at him.

Hello, he said, my name's Graham. What's yours?

I looked at him. I didn't want to tell him but mum said I had to, so I did.

That's nice, he said. Then he started talking to me about my toy cars. He said he had some lovely ones round at his place. Why didn't I come round an play with them?

I just looked at him.

Go on, my mum said. Go on, you'll have fun. I'll be here when you get back. She was smiling an laughin. She looked really happy.

OK, I said, an I stood up an Graham held my hand an led me out. I didn't want to go, but if it made mum so happy I would do it.

Only for her, though.

• • •

I've been dropped a level. Fightin on the wing. We've all got levels in prison, y'see, from one to five. An which one you've got depends on how well you behave. I was up for a review that would take me to level five. TV in my cell, PlayStation, the lot. Instead I'm back to three now. An it's not my fault. I told the wing guvnor that.

It's that fuckin bitch Kayleigh's fault, that's who.

I phoned her earlier tonight. Saved up me phonecard credits an was the first in the queue. She answered an straightaway I could tell there was somethin up. I started talkin, askin after Tod, tellin her I missed her an that, an she said, Look, I was gonna write to you but since you've phoned I'll tell you. Cos I think it's best to be honest.

I didn't say anything.

I'm seeing somebody. His name's Adrian an he's moved in.

I went fuckin ballistic. I screamed an pleaded, I begged an shouted. I called her everythin I could think of an she hung up.

I put the phone down. Anderson an Glover was standin there.

Dropped you, has she? one of them said. Getting it off somebody else, ehe? I bet she doesn't want you near her, you fuckin stink. Yeah, do they not have showers where you come from, you smelly cunt?

I lost it. An I forgot everythin. How to block them, keep the out, show them you're goin one way then go another. Hit back. Hurt them. Everythin.

The next thing I remember is a couple of screws grabbin ahold of me an me cryin an goin limp. Then I was taken to see the guvnor an when I calmed down a bit I told him what had happened.

He nodded an said that since they provoked me, he wasn't goin to send me to the seg. But since I'd been fightin he had to drop me a level. He said he was sorry, though, he thought I was doin well.

Then he suggested it might help if I took a shower.

I said I wouldn't.

He sighed.

I said I wanted to see Victoria.

He said she'd gone home.

No more soch. I went back to me cell an sat there.

I tried not to cry. I tried not to think. I tried not to dream.

● ● ●

D'you like playin games, son? Graham asked.

I said I did. He smiled.

Good. Cos I've got some good ones to play.

An we played. Him an the other bloke chased me all over the house. We played catch. Hide an seek. We played all the games that my mother never played with me. An I had a great time. I loved it.

Whoo, Graham said eventually. I'm hot, are you?

I said I was.

I'll go an run you a bath then. You can cool off.

An he did. An I sat there in for ages, thinking, This is all right, this. What a good time I was havin. Then the door opened an Graham an the other bloke, Dave, came in wearin towels.

Budge up, said Graham. I'm gonna get in an do your back.

An that was the first time it happened.

Afterwards I was shakin. I wanted to cry. I wanted my mum. Graham musta saw this an he gave me a cuddle.

Listen, he said. You're a special little boy. What we did was special. A special kind of love.

An he went on, telling me I was special, an that he loved me. But that I hadn't to tell anyone else. I had to pretend that nothing was happenin. It was a secret. An then he gave me a toy. A big red fire engine. I loved it. An he said he'd see me again soon.

I went home. Mum was waitin. She didn't say anythin, she just looked at me. An I looked at her. Then I couldn't look at her anymore. I went upstairs into me bedroom, shut the door an lay on the bed. I laid like that for ages just starin at the ceilin. I heard noises from downstairs. Sean had arrived. I heard him an mum laughin. Then I heard them on the stairs. Then they went into mum's room an shut the door.

I just lay there. Then I thought about me secret. About Graham an Dave. An I got me fire engine out an started to play.

• • •

They used to come for me regular after that. They'd take me to theirs an start playin games. Let's pretend, they said.

We'll pretend now, they used to say. We'll play a special pretend game with you because we love you.

An I used to do it. Because they loved me.

An the games got bigger an bigger. An they started to hurt more an more. But I kept playin them. Because they loved me an I wanted to make them happy. I used to play me own game too. Pretend with them. Pretend I enjoyed it.

But one day I couldn't. I just couldn't pretend anymore.

An the best thing that ever happened to me happened. Me dad came to visit. An I told him what had happened. An I cried. An I clung to him. An I wouldn't let go. An I begged him to take me home with him.

An he did. An then it was the best time of me life.

• • •

Oh shit. Oh shit. I'm really worried now.

There's a couple of kids come onto my wing from Hollesley Bay. They say they know Sean. They say they know what he's really in for. He told them. So they beat the shit out of him. An they say they know what I'm really in for.

Armed robbery, I tell them. I paralysed a bloke with a shotgun.

Nah, they say. What you're really in for.

An they've been telling everybody else on the wing too.

I went to see the guvnor. I told him I needed to see Victoria right now.

He tried but said sorry, she was away on a course for a few days.

I didn't cry in front of him. I just asked to be taken back to me cell.

An I cried there instead.

• • •

Everythin was goin great living at me dad's, until I was fifteen. Until Sean showed up.

Me did didn't want him around.

I said he was family. An dad was always sayin family was important. Family was about love.

I've got no fuckin love for him, me dad would say.

I said all this, but really, Sean scared me. If I didn't see him, I thought he would . . . I don't know. Do something.

He wasn't livin with mum by this time. He was livin with some old boiler about fifteen years older than him. There was rumours goin round that she was on the game. There was rumours goin round that he'd put her there.

The good thing he did was takin me to meet this bloke who ran a garage. This bloke said he would take me on as an apprentice mechanic. I was really chuffed with Sean for that. It was a proper brotherly thing to do. Dad couldn't say anything about that.

Sean an me started hangin out a bit then. The pub, the snooker hall, just havin a laugh. He wasn't bad really. Liked a ruck, though. He used to start fights an that just for the fuck of it.

I didn't join in. I would just stand an watch.

Then I met Kayleigh an she got pregnant.

It made me feel good doin that, like a real man. I felt proud. I had a girlfriend who loved me, me dad an Marie telling me they loved me, an a job. A real job. I was fuckin sorted.

An then one night, Sean said he had an idea.

• • •

Marie sent me a letter. Me dad's gettin worse.

They've said at the hospital there's nothing more they can do with him. He said he wanted to go home to be with his family.

I got a letter from Kayleigh an all. Sayin she was sorry an that, but her mind was made up. She also said that my mum had contacted her. I was nearly sick when I read that bit. Cos Kayleigh was alone with Tod me mum had been helping her. She said she seemed lovely. She didn't know what I had against her.

I'd never told her, you see. I'd hoped I'd never had to.

I phoned her up. Told her she must never allow my mum to get too close to Tod. She asked why not. An I couldn't tell her. She said if I couldn't tell her then that wasn't a good enough reason. She said I was a moody awkward bastard an me mother didn't deserve me.

Then she hung up.

I tried phonin dad but it just rang an rang. Maybe they unplugged the phone. Maybe he was tryin to get some sleep.

• • •

I've stopped doin the mechanics course.

Everyone else keeps lookin at me. Starin. I don't like it. It feels like somethin's waitin to happen.

I try an stay banged up as much as possible. I won't even talk to Victoria.

I just wanna be by myself. I want everyone else to go away.

I think about that red fire engine. I don't know why.

• • •

I'm down on the seg now. They moved me there after the fire.

The fire. I don't think I've ever been so fuckin scared in all my life. An I've been scared a lot.

I know who did it. Them two from Hollesley Bay. An if it wasn't then they got someone to do it. Bastards.

What happened was at soch one night someone came up to me cell door. I was banged up. I told them I didn't want soch. I heard something by the door an I looked up. An there was this paper that had been set on fire an slid under the door.

I just stared at it. I couldn't move. Then I heard some laughin in the hall.

Burn in Hell you stinkin rapist cunt!

Then I heard feet runnin away.

I ran to the paper an started stampin on it. But it had spread to a blanket that was in a heap at the bottom of the bed. An that really blazed up.

I screamed Fire! Fire! an I pressed the alarm bell.

It seemed like it took hours for the screws to arrive but it must have just been seconds. They got the fire extinguisher on it an took me down to healthcare. They said I was OK, not even too much smoke damage cos it hadn't had time to take hold. Then they took me to the seg for one night. For my own protection, they said.

The next morning Victoria came to see me. I was really pleased to see her. She looked all concerned for me, asked me what had happened.

She sighed. Look, she said, I think you've got to face up to things. I think you've got to confront your problems an ask for help.

No one can help me, I said. I don't need no help. I was startin to shake.

We can help you. I can help you. If you let me.

I shook my head.

Look, I know what you're in for. An I know what was done to you. But Graham Barnes and David Roper are locked up now. They can't touch you. Your dad saw to that. She sighed. An your dad. I'm sorry. Please let me help.

I was shakin. I tried to sit still, to stop.

You can't, I said. My throat was smoke-dry.

Why don't we take things one step at a time, she said, leanin forward. We'll work towards one thing an when we've accomplished that we'll move on to the next thing. Now, the shower situation—

I stood up. I couldn't hold myself in any longer.

I can't take a shower, can I? Eh? It's easy for you to say, but I can't do it.

Look—

No! You look!

I pulled my sweatshirt off.

Look! I shouted. Look! This is why I can't take no fuckin shower!

She looked. An I saw the horror on her face.

• • •

Remember earlier when I said I carried around my history with me?

Victoria knows now what I mean by that.

• • •

I've got this great idea, says Sean. It'll be a real laugh.

He had that look. The one he gets before he's about to have a fight or do something mad. It scared me. But I didn't want him to know that.

Yeah? I said.

Why don't we do over a petrol station? C'mon.

I don't—

Look, it's piss easy. He had this bag with him. He pulled out two black balaclavas. We stick these on, we go up to the counter an we tell them to give us the money.

Why will they do that? I asked.

He went back in the bag again. Because of this.

He pulled out a sawn off.

Fuckin' ell...

Yeah. C'mon. We'll have a laugh.

Sean kept talking. He kept talking for over an hour, telling me it would be a laugh, we'd get a real rush, we'd come out of it with some cash and with the masks on we'd never get caught.

I didn't wanna do it at first but Sean kept talking an talking until yeah, it would be a laugh. I looked at the gun sittin there. Pure power. Pure control. Easy power. Yeah, I thought, it'd be fun. So I told him I would. An he smiled. I didn't tell him I was doin it cos I was scared of what he'd do if I said no.

We waited til it was dark an drove to the service station. We parked out of sight, pulled the masks on an off we went.

There was no customers, just this fat Asian woman behind the counter. Sean was straight in before she had time to scream.

Open the till an hand over the fuckin money now! Now!

He stuck the business end of the sawn off in her face. She looked like she was gonna piss herself. She opened the till an I went round with the bag open.

Put it in there! I shouted.

She did as she was told. Don't hurt me, don't hurt me, she said in a whisper.

I got a tingle when she did that. Havin someone scared an doin what you tells them gives you a real thrill. I really liked it.

C'mon! C'mon! I shouted.

She piled the notes in faster.

I started to get a hard on. I started to feel hot an get pins an needles in me stomach. Me head started to spin. I blinked. I looked at the woman but her face was goin blurry. It wasn't the same woman who was there when I came in. But I knew her. It was mum.

I got really angry then.

What the fuck are you doin here? I shouted. I grabbed ahold of mum an pushed her against the counter. She tried to fight back but I just slapped her down.

Fight me, would you?

Me cock was gettin harder. Me head was spinnin faster. I was feelin hotter. I had to do something. I pulled the front of her dress, tearin it, rippin it to shreds, buttons flyin an everythin. I pulled the front of her tights, pushed her back over the counter. I started to undo my jeans.

No, please, please no...

Shut up! Fuckin shut up! I slapped her again.

Then I was in er, up er, snarlin at er, lookin straight in er eyes, straight into me mother's eyes.

I hate you! I fuckin hate you!

Me mother's eyes were cryin.

Why couldn't you love me, eh? Why couldn't you fuckin love me? Properly, like other mothers, eh?

Why did you give me to them? Eh? D'you know what they did to me? D'you know what me body looks like under me clothes? The burns an the cuts, eh?

Me mother's eyes closed.

Open your eyes! Open your fuckin eyes! I slapped her. I hit her. I came.

I just stood there getting me breath back for about thirty seconds or a minute with me eyes closed. I opened them.

An me mother had gone. An there was just this scared, fat Asian woman. Cryin.

Oh fuck, I said. O fuck, I'm sorry...

I went to touch her. She flinched away.

Out the way!

It was Sean. He was laughin an hootin. He pushed me out the way an got in front of the Asian woman.

My turn now!

I didn't join in. I just stood an watched.

C'mon, he said, when he'd finished. Hurry up! We've got what we came for!

He grabbed the bag and did his jeans up. He slapped me on the shoulder. Stop fuckin dreamin! C'mon!

I followed him out. I couldn't look back at the woman.

In the car I couldn't believe what we'd done. What I'd done.

Oh fuck... Oh fuck... I kept sayin.

Sean laughed. You're a mad fucker, you. When you get goin.

We drove away.

• • •

They caught us two days later. We'd forgotten to wear gloves. Sean's prints are on file.

Me dad was devastated. That was when he started complainin of pains in his chest. We had a long talk. I cried. He cried. I told him all about it. I told him I was sorry.

He hugged me. He told me I was still his son an that whatever happened he would always be there for me.

That's what he said. He would always be there for me.

• • •

Me brief gave me a bit of advice. Tell them you're in for armed robbery, he said. If they ask you why you got such a long sentence tell them you shot someone an paralysed them or put them in a coma or somethin.

But don't let them know you're a rapist. Or your life won't be worth livin. That's what he said. My life won't be worth livin.

• • •

Me dad died. They wouldn't let me go to the funeral. Said I'd caused too much trouble. Dropped too many levels. I'm on basic now. You can't go further down than that.

I phoned Marie. Said how sorry I saw. She was cryin. She told me not to phone again. Said it was worry about me that had started the cancer goin in me dad's body. Said she'd lost the man she loved. She put the phone down on me.

Me dad was wrong. He won't always be there for me. He let me down. Kayleigh won't speak to me. She's changed her phone number. All me letters get sent back. Victoria still comes to see me. Still talks to me. But it's not the same. She looks at me differently now.

I let them down. All of them. An not they've let me down.

The rest of the wing know what I'm in here for now. They just leave me by myself. An I've started havin showers now. I don't care. I don't know if they're lookin at me or not cos I don't look at them anymore. Anyway, I'll be gettin moved soon. I don't know where. I don't care.

But I still get letters. Mum's started writing to me. At first I ignored them, but she kept on doin it so in the end I gave in a started readin them. She still sees Kayleigh. She says Kayleigh says she wouldn't know what to do without her.

An she tells me about Tod. What a lovely boy he's gettin. How he's startin to be like his dad.

An she told me that Graham an Dave will be out soon. An they wanna contact me.

But I know this. Cos they already have. They've told me they wanna keep in touch. They've told me they miss me. They love me. They've told me they wanna see me when I get out, they've a job for me.

I know what it is. I'm not stupid. They want me to find boys to go visit them. Ones who like to play. Ones who like to pretend. I could join in if I liked. I would be on their side this time.

I wrote back an told them to fuck off. But they replied. They told me that they'd heard Tod was growin into a beautiful lad. An that his grandma was lookin after him really well. They asked me to think again about their offer.

I cried. An I cried. An eventually I couldn't cry anymore.

I thought about their offer. An I thought about mum. Whatever else she is she's still me mum. She's still family. An as me dad used to say, family is important. Family is about love.

An I thought about. Perhaps they weren't so bad really, I tell meself. Perhaps what they didn't wasn't so bad.

At least they said they loved me.

Or pretended they did.

• • •

The dream's back again. It's there just about all the time. But it's different now. Now there's no drive, no countryside, no dad. There's just me as a little boy, sittin all alone in a quarry, huggin me knees to me chest an cryin. An cryin an cryin an cryin.

An then I wake up.

An I'm still cryin.

THE NEW HEROES AT THE OLD FAIRGROUNDS

K.L. Pereira

The drive-in is as grey as a grave, the shroud of the screen, flanked
by fly-away ribs from the old fairground rollercoaster. Old beaters like ours
fill the lot:
a lawn of dull tin spread before the bombed-out building where our home
used to be,
before the blaze that got the rollercoaster devoured everything.

Grey hunks of cement rise as we sit, wall me in flashing memories of old
publicity posters
(all elongated spine and sharpened teeth). Now it's just us, two-thirds
of a family of forgotten freaks, hunch-backed in the rusty pickup; you watch
creature features, I try to tell stories of your childhood, the flames that
consumed it.

You lie, say your dream-memories are filled with sticky teacup seats and
carousel unicorns.
The memory of your mother's laugh floods me,
muddying the mats on the floor of the pickup truck while fake monsters
and madmen mutate into bigger, better versions of us. Are we no longer
feared?

Our new heroes fill the gull-pecked screen of the drive-in, negate our blood and
shroud our bonehome, the space where the Bearded Lady and JoJo
the Dog-faced boy barked, where your small life began, where your
mother's ended.

The roar of the Wolfman mimics the bellow of the fire that danced in our apartment.
In my dreams, it dulls to a midnight blue buzz behind my ears, but here it hums loud.
Here at the drive-in, it explodes: floods me with those slicked faces, large men grown
larger with drink, throwing Molotov cocktails through our kitchen window.

Your mother's laughing scream fills the gravelly spaces in memories you keep saying
you are too young to remember clearly, memories I need you to carry,
memories I try to rescue from the floor of the pickup each time you drop them,
will yourself to forget.

The only thing you say you remember is this: your grandmother's efficiency apartment
at the Capri Motel, where songs from the 50s filled the steamy bathroom and she
taught you to read fortunes from smoke, predict dreams
but for a price.

She told you:
Everywhere and when but here and now is but an after-thought, my starlet,
a ghost-whisper as real as the triumphs and screams of final girls and damsels
in distress on screen.

And you listened. You remember.
Not to the filling cry of your mother, that floods me like a wolf-roar,
not to the backdraft bawl of your nightmares, not to the voice, the laugh,
the scarlet scream of your mother in the memory you refuse to hear.

WHEN THE HAMMER COMES DOWN

Josh Stallings

3:23 PM Los Angeles.

April hit like a firebomb. It was murder your best friend weather. Too hot to fuck weather. Watch what you say or this shit steps off weather. The only thing Angelenos hate more than rain is excessive heat. When you live in paradise anything less than perfection is an attack on your birthright. Traffic on the Harbor Freeway was building into a snarling mess. At under ten miles an hour no air moved through the Caprice's open windows. Sweat dripped off Detective Madsen's Neanderthal brow. "It is hotter than two rats fucking in a wool sock."

"Two rats huh? Guess it is." Detective Lunt wanted a cool drink in a cooler restaurant, instead he was driving across town for a P.R. bust and grin. "Apologize to Caselli. Eat a little shit and he'll have our air blowing cold in bang time."

"That walleyed inbred needle dick wrench monkey deserves nothing but my boot in his ass."

"Preaching to the choir, Hem. But—"

"Omit his son being high as Mount Whitney from our report? He's lucky I didn't dime him to IAG."

"You called the man's son 'Cheech and Chong's gay love child.' Said he had the brains God gave a roadkill armadillo."

"Roadkill is a compliment. You met the kid."

"Not the point. Net-net? Caselli's chilling in a nice air-conditioned garage and you and me are out here sweating up our Jockeys. On the upside, our moral superiority is intact."

"Screw 'em all but six."

"And save them for pallbearers." Lunt had a hard time generating any real indignation. This was nowhere near the first time Hemming Madsen's intractable moral code made life hard for them. A few years back they had the highest clearance rate in homicide and were on track for LAPD superstardom. Then came Candy Fox, a dead fourteen-year-old runaway. Madsen refused to redact a studio boss's name from the list of suspects. Ultimately the creep's only crime was paying a girl younger than his daughter to blow him. That Madsen leaked the big-wig-pays-for-pedophile-pleasure story to the *LA Times* was speculated, but not proven. As payback for insubordination, Madsen and Lunt were dropped into the career ghetto of narcotics enforcement.

The brass lacked the prescience to see that soldiers in the war on drugs were tomorrow's heroes. Nixon started the war on drugs, Reagan made it a jihad, George H. W. Bush mechanized it. By 1989 any police force dumb enough not to deliver high narcotics arrest counts for the DOJ was in for a long cold winter with no federal funding to warm them. Go along with them and the Feds were handing out military toys and cash prizes. The man in the Glass Tower's big office shifted priorities on a dime, murder was out and narcotics enforcement was the best funded division in LAPD.

4:10 PM South Central.

The LAPD staging area was in the parking lot of an abandoned strip mall. Protected by multiple black and whites, two Secret Service Suburbans and a SWAT van was a twenty-nine foot Airstream Ambassador with "The Establishment" stenciled in tall letters across it. Behind the silver walls and tinted windows a former first lady and the Chief of the LAPD sat eating fruit salad and sipping lattes from china mugs. Above them the air conditioner groaned and squealed in its battle against the heat.

"Maybe when this is over, you can give me a private tour of Parker Center, Chief Gates, and show me your restraint technique."

"Call me Daryl, ma'am."

"Only if you call me Nancy." Her eyes where batting like a puppet whose master has palsy.

"Okay, Nancy." He gave her a sly wink.

"Are we safe here, Daryl?" Mrs. Reagan wore a blue windbreaker over her bulletproof vest, it had "Police" written across the back and "Nancy" stitched in rolling cursive over her left breast.

"Thugs around here poop their drawers when they hear I'm dropping by." Chief Gates had a white shirt and deep blue tie under his LAPD windbreaker. A scholar of self-realization as the pathway to success, he believed in the power of intentions. He extrapolated that wearing a bulletproof vest meant you were intending to get shot. Besides, they made him look pudgy.

"You are God's general in this holy war." Nancy gave Gates a longing look. She loved his ramrod straight back. His firm jaw. His unbending will.

"And you are our Joan of Arc."

"No, I'm just a gal who dreams of a world free from evil."

"God's will be done." Gates reached up to pluck a nonexistent eyelash from her cheek. She emitted an almost silent groan at the feel of his touch. The last time she felt this turned on was when Ronnie canceled federal funding for rehab centers and methadone clinics. You don't fight the Devil by talking nice, holding hands and passing out medication.

"We make a hell of a pair, Nancy." Daryl looked deep into Nancy's eyes. She tried to match his steely gaze, but he brought out her inner ingénue. Smiling coyly, Nancy studied the pale pink gloss on her fingernails.

Twenty feet away from the Airstream, Officer Johnny Wolfe took off his Oakley's, wiped sweat from his eyes and slid them back on. This was his first engagement with SWAT. He studied the clipboard in his hand. The target was a crack den. In the recon photos he saw a two-story brown stucco box, one front entrance and one rear exit. The 1960s utilitarian architecture was indistinguishable from the other apartment buildings that dotted the street. Closing his eyes, Wolfe visualized breaching the door, mentally prepping himself. Boots on the gravel behind him popped his eyes open and snapped his head around.

"Relax, brother. This is just like you trained, only more fun." King spit a string of tobacco juice, it sizzled when it hit the sidewalk.

"I'm chill, ice in my veins."

"All right then, Wolfe, solid. I want you on the battering ram."

"You want me first in?"

"That is correct, son." King let loose a fresh stream. "Cherry always takes lead. If in the excitement you blow your load early, you'll cap thugs instead of good guys."

Wolfe nodded and looked back down at the file. King watched him, trying to divine if he was ready for this.

5:13 PM Apartment 2B.

Lamar Cray sat on the floor. His sweaty back stuck to the plastic sofa protector. His earphones filled with Public Enemy. His earphones filled with Public Enemy bum rushing the show. His head bounced to the wack beats. His mother hated hip-hop, "Just a lot of broke-ass punks yammering on about how rich and fly they are." Lamar knew better than to argue it. He was twelve, what did he know? Right? Right?

Lamar was buried in homework. Pre-algebra. Fractions, decimals, probabilities. It was cool, simple. No gray in math, an answer either was or wasn't correct. Personal opinion meant nothing. Mr. Belson asked Lamar if he was interested in becoming a mathlete on MLK's quiz team. Right? Um, no. Quiz team was the path to never dating and a rock solid guarantee his big brother Jazz would never let up. No quiz team. Only real move was to act stupid at home and let the clock run out on his teen years. College would be his time. UCLA. He had no evidence to prove his theorem, but he was dead sure that college girls found brains sexy, and baggy jean wearing gangsters a turn-off. Until then he would be a Machiavellian motherfucker. He'd play the long assed game. Keep his big brain on the down low.

Directly beneath Lamar was apartment 1B, where Jazz lay on the nasty stained shag carpet, laughing his ass off. Andy was on his back slamming thumbs and fists on the Atari 7800's control pad. His 8-bit stand-in was martial artist Billy Lee, a white guy in a karate gi. Billy Lee was fighting his way across *Double Dragon's* clean ghetto street.

"Homes, check me, I'm breaking ass and taking names." Andy raised a power fist above his head. On the screen Abobo, the monstrous first level boss, slammed a fist down on Billy Lee's skull. Jazz laughed even more explosively. "What the fuck are you laughing at, Homes?"

"Nothing." Jazz struggled to regained control. He slowed his breathing.

"Good, 'cause you want to try and kick this motherfucker's ass, step to it."

"No." The laughter was quelled.

"That's right, I'm on the set, raining death on all bosses that dare to oppose me."

Jazz fought the grin spreading across his face. "Yo, Andy, this bud is no joke." The smile broke free.

"Yo, you are one goofy-looking motherfucker. You gonna call yourself Smiling Jazzy Jazz?"

"I may, A, I just may." Jazz was seventeen and fly as fuck. The apartment he and Andy were kicking in was a thug's nirvana. It had bad-assed history. Two short years back Pinky, a homicidal local gangster and his crew controlled the building. They dealt crack out of 1B. It had a steel reinforced door. All the windows were covered in plywood. The walls were splashed with lots of graceless graffiti. Pinky was locked down because he met a curvalicious undercover mamacita at Arco's bar and taqueria. To get in her frillies he bragged about his crack operation and dropping a competing dealer. No one in the neighborhood disagreed that the undercover cop had nice titties, but only an idiot wouldn't notice she vibed five-o. That idiot was Pinky.

LAPD cleared out Pinky's crew and the Crays moved into 2B. Ghost, a geriatric O.G. moved into 1B. As criminals go Ghost was small time. He slung a little rock, a little tar, a little weed. "Fly under the radar, boy, that there is the only solid stay out of jail plan." He hired Jazz for deliveries and minding the store on nights he was either tending to his business or doing Amyl and sliding three deep in cooch and baby oil at the Royal Inn Motel. To Jazz, it was easy money. Ghost laid out a spread of manila envelopes with a name and a dollar amount written on each. "Collect the cash, then pass the goods. No credit no matter how round the booty or deep the cleavage."

Ghost showed Jazz the twelve gauge behind the sofa. "Insurance. Not that any of these pension kings and queens I sell to would dare go up against you."

Jazz was intimidating, when he wasn't grinning madly. 6'5" and two hundred and sixty pounds, he was built like a linebacker. He played football freshmen year but by sophomore his grades slipped and he wasn't eligible to play. Now he played video games, got stoned and went to school only when his mother screamed loud and long enough.

Jazz rolled strong. Rolled bad. Rolled flush. He drove a 1962 Chevelle Malibu, candy green over bone, sun bleached in some patches and chipping in others. Foam and springs poked up through the seats. Who cared, it was a motherfucking Malibu. Fly. Jazz bought the ride from Herbie, an older cat in the next apartment building over. In his freaky sweaters and fuzzy slippers he looked more like Dr. Huxtable than a low level pot dealer. When LAPD broke down his front door they found three baggies of rag, and one ounce of Turkish, real deal, gold government sealed hash. The kind with swirls of opium mixed in. That tiny taste of dope, that spice to the game, that is what fucked Herbie. Felony possession with intent to sell. He was going down for a long long jolt at Pelican Bay. Herbie needed dead presidents in his commissary account more than he needed his short. It was lucky for Jazz that Herbie wasn't busted in the Malibu, or some fed would be driving it now.

Cube, Dre and Easy-E shredded the speaker cones in Andy's ghetto blaster. "'Fuck the Police', these are my boys."

"No, they a'ight but you want the real uncut dope, have go with Ice-capital-T's "6'n the Morning." That shit's the real real." He and Andy would argue the skill and swagger of hip-hop artists all night. Getting paid for kicking it, smoking boo and playing *Double Dragon*. Who worries about tomorrows when today was this fly.

5:46 PM *Abandoned strip mall.*

Madsen, Lunt and several SWAT officers stood around the Caprice's trunk looking down at a floor plan and street map.

"How long have East Street Thugs been dealing out of this location?" Madsen arched an eyebrow.

"You got a problem with our intel, Detective Madsen? Don't pussy around, just say it." King accented his words with a stream of tobacco juice.

"I have a problem." Madsen didn't back up an inch.

"What might that be, Detective?" King made the word sound like an insult.

"For one, your intel is notoriously weak."

"Says the detective who didn't know there was a crack den in his back yard."

"It doesn't strike you as odd that we never heard about it, not even a bat's fart of a rumor?"

"Weirder still, this—" Lunt stabbed his finger on the map. "—is Wizard Crew territory."

"We have a search warrant signed, sealed and ready for delivery." King was not hiding his dislike of anyone outside the SWAT brotherhood.

"Getting a judge's rubber stamp don't make it right." The man's stupidity was driving Madsen's blood pressure up.

"Be clear, detective, we invited you suits to our shindig as a courtesy. Boss said you add legitimacy, whatever the fuck that means."

Lunt spoke to King like he was a slow student. "It's called plausible deniability."

"What the fuck is that?"

"You played ball in school, right?"

"Hell yes, '79 Pedro Pirates, undefeated." King gave Lunt a quick once over. "Chess club, right?"

"Burn. Nailed you there, Lunt." Madsen knew his partner was both smart and deadly. While King was slamming into other sweaty boys in some homo-erotic coliseum fantasy, Lunt was working in Afghanistan, assassinating Marxist leaders and trafficking arms to the mujahedeen.

"Pay attention, this is a SWAT op." King gave them his steeliest stare. "We breach the perimeter. We take down the trash. You clean it up, we all good with that?"

Lunt's anger flared, he started to speak but Madsen beat him to it. "That's good with us. We're team players, coach."

King paused, unsure if Madsen is fucking with him, then he smiled, how could these suits have the stones to mess with SWAT? Circling two fingers over his head, his team fell in behind him as he walked away.

Once the SWAT boys disappeared behind their TAC van Madsen let out a long held laugh. "Man, QB number one is more than a few Eagle Scouts short of a circle jerk."

"In the chess club?" Lunt flipped the van the bird. "I was the goddamn president."

"You have issues? You wanna talk about it?" Madsen thoughtfully stroked a nonexistent beard. "Go on, tell me about the time a footballer broke up your Dungeons and Ogres game?"

"Dragons. Dungeons and Dragons."

"Those machine-gun toting frat boys are the Chief's favorite sons. We on the other hand, are his redheaded stepchildren."

"Have we entered backward world, Hem? Are you preaching political realities to me?"

"I know. Feels weird right?" Madsen pursed his mouth. He cleaned his lips on his finger. "Your ever get used to the taste of shit in your mouth?"

"Never. I find two or three cervezas wash it away."

"Solid advice. Once this insane rodeo is over we are going to El Coyote, first three rounds on you, for making me wear the long pants."

6:20 PM Apartment 1B.

"Check this out, in *Raw*? Eddy Murphy said fuck 223 times. Replaced *Scarface* for most fucks ever." How Jazz could retain facts like that and not his locker's padlock number was a bafflement.

"Yeah, Eddie is the real street deal." Andy was still playing Atari. A joint hung from his lip, bouncing around when he spoke. "Have a Coke and a smile and shut the fuck up." He said to Cosby, called him a Jell-O pudding-eating motherfucker.

"Cosby Kids were the shit. Hey hey hey!" Fat Albert and his crew lived in the only place on TV that looked like Jazz's hood.

"Cartoon bullshit. New Cosby can suck my dick."

A tattoo on the door kept Jazz from arguing the point. Maddy Sin was warped by the fisheye peephole, stretching and rounding her out. She was two years older than Jazz. Smoking hot. Everybody wanted to hit it. Everybody. He spent eight months gathering the courage and resources to take her out. He had a knot in his pocket, over a gee. The day he bought the Malibu, he cruised to the burger joint she hung at. Maddy Sin had left town that morning. And here it was five months later and she's knocking on the door. This day couldn't get any better.

The opening door revealed Jazz's dream girl. Time hadn't been kind. Her curves, her sumptuous booty, gone. She was skinny, not skinny-skinny, she was Biafran save the children poster skinny. Red bumps from brewing and picked acne dotted her beautiful skin. Her eyes hid behind rose-colored Dior knockoffs. "Jazzie, damn you look fine, boy."

"I heard you went to Zoo York?" Jazz blocked her from entering the apartment.

"Still there. I'm doing some modeling, lingerie." She struck a pose that thirty pounds ago would have had Jazz busting a nut. "Time been good to you, Jazzie, no lie." She ran a finger down his chest, starting to undo the top button. "Heard you was holding. Wanna party with an old friend?"

"Who told you I was holding?"

"Oh baby, the street, you know. You gonna hook me up?"

"Can't do it. This shit is Ghost's. You gonna have to page him."

"I did. Didn't I say that? Ghosty said you should hook me up. Cross my heart." She crossed her heart and looked sincere. Jazz wasn't buying so she switched tack. "I heard Pinky busted out. That's why I come over, you know, warn you."

"Bullshit. Ghost would have told me."

"Ghost ain't here, I am." Her purr was more pathetic than sexy. "I'm telling you straight. Come on, Jazzie, baby, we got history you and me."

"You said more to me today than in the entire time we've known each other."

"Doesn't mean I didn't think about you." Tilting her head she flicked eyes from his lips to his crotch then back up. "Come on, Jazzie, just a little taste."

"Can't."

"I'll suck your dick, curl your toes. Come on." She tried to unbuckle his belt but he grabbed her wrist. "What baby, you know you want it. Let me rock your world."

"Ain't gonna happen." Jazz pushed Maddy Sin back across the threshold.

"Fuck you then. Fuck your lame punk ass. Don't wanna fuck me? Shit I wouldn't suck your tiny penis if you had a fifty pound rock. Fuck you, Jazz, I hope Pinky . . ." She had more to say but the steel reinforced door muffled it into unintelligibility.

Jazz threw two of the four deadbolts. He looked at Andy and shook his head.

"What's wrong with you? That strawberry wanna suck some dick, you invite her in. I'll introduce her to an anaconda."

"You got some rock for her?"

"Hell no. Get our shit off, then we bounce her nonexistent ass out of here."

"You gonna shoplift a blow job now?"

"Dine and dash, more like it. Only she doing the dining."

"You're ill and not in a good way. Think that game is rotting your brain."

"Really, one day all wars gonna be fought on an Atari."

"Wizard Crew turning their nines in for joysticks?"

"Laugh all you want, when it happens you be begging me to teach you my moves." Andy did a blur of fingers and thumbs pushing Billy Lee into a flying punch kick combination. The bad, ripped off Bruce Lee sound effects and thin plinky synthesizer music made Jazz smile.

7:56 PM Airstream.

Gates glanced at his military chronograph, a gift from the Marines he paid to train his SWAT teams. "We tee-off in thirty minutes."

"I better have Rosita finish my makeup. A shiny nose and unkempt hair does not make for winning photographs."

"Nancy, you look stunning as you are. Don't want to gild the lily."

"Oh, Daryl, you know how to say just the right thing to a gal. But I need to be camera ready. I can have her take a look at you."

"LAPD's Chief doesn't wear makeup."

"The President, my husband, he wears makeup for photo ops."

"He was an actor, he gets a pass. I'm just a simple cop." Truth was, he would have smeared on black face if he thought it would raise his TV Q score. Operation Hammer was his and his alone. City Council, the DA, even their jungle bunny of a Mayor had stepped back from it. It was his sword to raise over his head or fall on. It was one year to the day since Operation Hammer began. In 365 days LAPD had arrested thousands and thousands of young black men and women. Sometimes as many as fifteen hundred in one weekend. Most arrests were bullshit. Pulling youth in under the pretext of curfew violations or associating with known gang members. The charges for the most part didn't stick, but that wasn't the point. Before charging them, detectives interrogated them. Names were taken, files filled and thugs put on notice, "Fuck the Police" wasn't going to play in LA no more. So what if South Central residents got angry? As long as they feared him and his men Gates called it a success. Middle class white people, on the other black gloved hand, voted and paid taxes and wrote letters to the editor. Gates had enough secret files on local politicians and power brokers to keep the cash tap open. But lose the real citizen's confidence and it was a problem. Calling in Nancy Reagan was PR brilliance, who was whiter or more comforting to voters? She was a national treasure.

Now Gates just needed for his cops not to screw this up. Nail the bad guys. Stand tall. Be heroic. From the intelligence report they knew the thugs protecting the crack house were armed and dangerous. The formula was simple, show and scare the citizens. Take down some bad guys. Make the citizens understand that their protection was dependent on your power. Problem was, citizens had very short attention spans and no real stomach for collateral damage. For it to work, Gates needed this night to go flawlessly. He needed another SLA showdown moment. His SWAT program was on life support when those crazy radicals decided not to surrender. It was TV gold.

8:11 PM Abandoned strip mall.
KTLA was first to arrive. Jane Shaw, an over-eager public relations officer, showed them where to park out of the way. *LA Times* sent a reporter and photographer. More TV crews arrived, their helicopters hovered not far off waiting for the signal from the police that they were cleared to film the action from above. *LA Weekly* hadn't been invited, but that freedom of the press thing meant they couldn't be turned away.

Shaw assembled the reporters. "No cameras yet, please. Trust me, I'm not the story. Our target tonight is an infamous crack house controlled by heavily armed gang members. It isn't far from where we are standing. It is a mere ten point four miles from the Santa Monica mall. The plan is, we let SWAT roll out first, feel free to film that. After they set up I'll show you a spot that you can film from where you will be safe if the drug dealers opt for a shootout instead of surrendering."

"Officer Shaw, are you expecting a shoot out?" The woman from the *LA Weekly* broke form and asked a question.

"We always assume when going up against hardened criminals that there is a high probability of gunfire."

"Have you evacuated the local residents?"

"I'm not sure of particulars. What I can tell you is, Chief Gates is in a tactical session finalizing battle plans with the SWAT commander. As soon as they complete their mission the Chief will be glad to answer all of your questions."

Across the parking lot, the SWAT team geared up. They strapped on pistols and extra magazines and Kevlar vests and fingerless shooting gloves and knee and elbow pads. The *Times* camera man focused his telephoto lens on the officers, bad-asses in commando battle uniforms packing serious full auto 600 rounds a minute death sticks. Behind their sunglasses the squad was casually grim. Several grumbled that it was bullshit for the press to be there at the same moment striking poses they hoped were candid, natural and heroic. The van rocked slightly when officer Reeves climbed onto its roof. He lay down and shouldered his Remington 700. Scanning the neighborhood through the crosshairs, he dialed in his scope.

Sergeant Dung Nguyen watched it go down, leaning on the rear fender of his patrol car. If asked, Nguyen would say the most important things in his life were his wife, Binh, and their progeny. Secretly they didn't make the top three. In order of importance, it was one, his LAPD badge. Two, the chevrons of rank on his shoulder. Three, a snapshot from Hanoi 1968. Playmate Angie Chester is snuggled in his arms at Mi Chang's fun-time bar. Her macramé bikini shows miles of deep brown skin. Nguyen looks snappy in his AEVN dress uniform. He still had the confidence of an officer, sure of the righteousness of his cause and of the US air support that would drive the Communists out of his country. The weekend with Angie was what all others would be weighed against. He wasn't sure what made him think back on those days. Maybe it was watching SWAT getting ready. "You are there as support. Public safety." Nguyen told his patrolmen at rollcall. "If the targets go Tony Montana and introduce SWAT to their lil' friend, let the TAC boys handle it. Remember, they get the hazard pay."

"Sarge, what if SWAT fails to contain the bangers? We clear to take the safety off?" Ramirez was a veteran soldier in the war on gangs in South Central.

"Then, Officer Ramirez, you light them up."

"Yes, sir." The room spoke as one.

Now six patrol cars and a prisoner transport van sat ready. Madsen handed Sargent Nguyen a styrofoam cup of coffee. "Thanks, Hem."

"Thank our bosses, they have a table set up for reporters, figured they wouldn't mind."

"Probably take the cost out of our paychecks."

"You losing faith in the blue machine, Nguyen? We really are fucked."

"It's this." He looked around at the growing chaos. "Tomorrow none of them will be here. Not the Chief, not SWAT, surely not the news people. But me and my officers will be."

"No one throwing you a liberator's parade?"

"Do you know what lost my country to the Communists?"

"What?"

"They were better at winning hearts and minds." Nguyen scanned the patrol cars, insuring his men were behind the wheels and ready. He took a long pull on his coffee. "What the hell, beats working for a living."

"True that. Maybe we can get through this one without anyone dying."

"Forgoing that, let it not be one of ours." Nguyen reached out a hand, Madsen shook it, both men felt the moment was more weighted than it seemed on the surface.

At 8:30 PM on the dot, Chief Gates picked up his radio and gave the command to roll out. Nancy squeezed his hand with excitement as the Airstream lurched forward. Wolfe gripped the handle of the battering ram. He sat shotgun, ready to hit the ground running. His heart was jackhammering, and he was dizzy from hyperventilating. King stuffed a cut of chew into his cheek.

He dropped the magazine from his M16, slapped it against his leg and reinserted it. On the roof Reeves was strapped down and holding on. When they stopped, he would be their only cover fire. Normally they would insert snipers before hitting the door, but around here, any scent of cops and the dealers would be in the wind. Nguyen and his officers followed behind the Airstream. The news vans followed them. Madsen let them all pass. "What a parade."

"It's a three-ring circus. Clowns, sharp shooters, strong men. They are an elephant act away from a good time." Lunt's smile didn't reach his eyes.

The SWAT van braked violently in front of the target. Before the wheels stopped moving, Wolfe and King leapt out. Running low, they crossed a wide dirt patch that might have been a lawn once. Two other officers flew out of the back of the van and ran down the driveway towards the back of the structure and the utility box. Reeves whipped his rifle up, and through his scope he roamed the apartment building's windows, looking for movement. Until they breached, his team was completely exposed. Wolfe and King reached the front entryway and positioned themselves on either side of the front door. Wolfe held his breath and waited. His heart was a machine gun. His knuckles were white from gripping the battering ram.

"Shut that shit off. You hear that?" Jazz stood up.

"Heard what?" Andy fumbled to pause the game. Jazz held up a finger to silence him.

"Car skidding. Boots running."

"So, some buster's in a hurry to piss."

"Or Pinky is coming to deep six us." Jazz's eyes banged around the room, hunting for a rear exit he knew wasn't there.

"He wouldn't... Five-o knows this was his crib. He that stupid?"

"Hell to the yes he is." Jazz lifted the shotgun from behind the sofa. Andy shook his head slowly. Jazz nodded. If it was Pinky, they didn't have a lot of options. Jazz racked a shell into twelve gauge and took aim at the door. He hoped Andy couldn't see how bad his hands were trembling.

The Airstream parked behind the SWAT van. Gates stood in its open door, doing his best impression of John Wayne in *The Searchers*. He surveyed the field of battle. Police cruisers sped into position, blocking the street in either direction. The news reporters were given positions where they could get clear shots of the crack house. Gates knew the way of the world. If it bleeds it leads and if it doesn't air, it didn't happen. He needed a hemorrhage to get the public on his side.

Through Lamar's headphones Ice Cube was instructing him to 'keep one in the chamber.' He drew numbers in the air trying to solve the last equation.

Evaluate: $-8 \div (1+3)-1$ = one big headache. Trying his hardest, he couldn't pluck a number from the jumble in his mind. It was almost a relief when the power went out. Fucking Edison, must be another mistake. His Moms worked two gigs to do it, but the bills got knocked out. Fumbling blind, Lamar felt across the coffee table. Damn. His Kool-Aid fell over, spilling wet sugary goodness. He could feel soggy papers. If his homework was ruined, would fucking Edison make good? No, not a chance in hell, they always found a way to blame the customer. He found the candle he was looking for, the sandalwood scented one Moms lit to clear the 'boy funk.' Feeling for the matches, he found them, wet and useless. Across the living room, spikes of street light leaked around the heavy curtains. If he could cross the room without creaming his knee on a chair or knocking over the dinner table, he would have light.

King gave Wolfe a thumbs up. Wolfe swung the battering ram. The door protecting the apartment building's main entrance splintered in. King and Wolfe swept the vestibule corner to corner. It was clear. The rest of the team flooded in behind them. With two fingers King pointed to Apartment 1B. Wolfe slammed the door. It shuddered but didn't cave. He slammed again. The hinges started to give.

Jazz watched the door lit from Andy's Maglite. It shook and groaned on impact. Suddenly it was very real, it wasn't a song or a movie or a game. This was how his life would end. Time slowed. Plaster dust from the door frame danced playfully. The door was struck again, it wouldn't hold long. Jazz felt smooth dimples on the shotgun's trigger. Oh shit, this was it. He wouldn't be getting laid again. He wouldn't get to see who his freaky smart brother grew up to be. "Who's gonna protect Lamar now?" Andy didn't answer. He was frozen. Wide eyes pinning the door.

Lamar was reaching for the curtain when he heard the building's front door crash in. Gang bangers, cops, national guard, who ever, the response was the same. Get away from the windows and get low. All Angelenos knew the earthquake drill and the brushfire drill. In South Central those were welcome distractions from the stray bullet drill. Lamar could feel deep impacts thud through the floor beneath his head. UCLA couldn't come soon enough.

Sweat stung Wolfe's eyes. He was aware of the other team members watching him. Swinging back, he put all he had into the battering ram.

The door crashed in, falling on the floor. Andy dropped the flashlight and ran for the bedroom. Jazz squeezed the shotgun's trigger. Nothing happened. No boom. No flame. Fuck.

Adrenaline flooded Wolfe's brain. Tossing the battering ram like a bat after a home run, he grabbed his assault rifle and stormed the crack den. The tactical illuminator mounted on his barrel flared across a thug aiming a shotgun.

Light blinded Jazz. Behind the light a man took aim at him. Flame jumped from the rifle barrel.

Wolfe's boot hit the fallen door and slid out from under him. His rifle rattled and spit shells across the room. Star shaped flame flashed like an old movie projector across the apartment. Bullets buzzed past Jazz like angry bees. Plaster exploded from the walls and ceiling, dusting him. The noise stopped when the magazine quickly ran out of ammunition. It had only been a few seconds but it felt like hours. Jazz saw the fallen man was a cop. He heard boots running towards him. Throwing the shotgun away, he raised his hands. "I'm unarmed, swear to god. Don't shoot me."

King moved into the doorway barrel up, ready. "Hit the mothering deck, asshole."

Jazz knelt slowly, keeping his hands wide, away from his body.

"Wolfe, you hit?"

"No, I'm fine." Wolfe stood up, dusting himself off.

"We are not clear here." King pointed to the bedroom. Wolfe slammed a fresh magazine home. King tossed a flash boom into the bedroom. White light and mind melting noise filled the apartment. King stormed the room. Andy was pinned between a bed and the wall. He was screaming. The stun grenade had landed on him. His legs and the mattress were burning. King kicked open the closet. He ripped out suits and shirts but found nothing. Andy continued to scream. "Clear."

"What do we do with him?" Bronson pointed his gun barrel at Andy.

"Shoot him or put him out. I don't give a fuck as long as you shut him up."

After the crime scene was secured Madsen and Lunt went in. They found two teenagers on the floor, belly down and cuffed. One of them was badly burned and crying softly. The other just watched them through cold hateful eyes. After calling in the paramedics, the two detectives searched the apartment. They found a stack of envelopes, containing one bottle of heart medicine, one bubble pack of anti-seizure medication, two grams of marijuana, and several zip locks with small crack rocks. They also found a counterfeit Rolex and $632 and change. Andy was transported to the hospital and Jazz sat on the floor. Madsen turned slowly on his boot heel taking in the bullet riddled room. He wanted to say something snappy and biting but he didn't have it in him.

Stepping into the night air Madsen inhaled. "Feels cooler."

"Offshore breeze, can smell the salt," Lunt said, firing up a cigarette, breathing in the smoke.

"Thought you quit."

"I did."

"Got another?"

"Bummed it from Sergeant Nguyen." Lunt passed the cigarette to Madsen. They stood sharing a smoke. "Aren't we supposed to be over there?" Lunt motioned with his chin to the news crews setting up for interviews.

"Lend this jug-fuck credibility? Hell no." Madsen stepped deeper into the shadows. They watched Daryl and Nancy pose for the cameras. They stood in front of the destroyed door with a battering ram in their hands.

"Chief Gates, you recovered so few drugs, do you consider this a success?" The reporter from *LA Weekly* pointed her microphone at him.

"I'm not sure we can speak directly about an ongoing investigation." Shaw tried to shut the reporter down, but Gates wasn't having it.

"No, I'll answer this. Beth," he used the reporter's first name even though they'd never met. "Truth is, there are no small amounts of crack cocaine, when it's destroying your community. That might not mean much in Arcadia, but in South Central we're fighting for our lives." He used her home town so she knew he could reach out and touch her whenever he wanted.

"Zero tolerance means zero tolerance." Nancy was quick to defend her knight.

"Fact is, if we had come one hour earlier, we would have found stacks of crack cocaine." Daryl puffed his chest out. "This crack house was so busy they sold out of drugs before we hit them. We did nail the dealers. They are out of business, as of right now." Gates held Nancy's hand up like a champ at the prize fight.

Watching them exhausted Madsen. "We should call the Parks Department."

"Why's that?"

"Have them pick up some of this prime bullshit."

"Might as well put it to good use." Lunt turned away from the lights. "Let's roll, partner, before one of us starts talking truth to these news dogs."

"Can't have that." Madsen followed Lunt away from the media. When they reached the Caprice Madsen stopped, holding the key in his hand but not opening the door. "I'm thinking about pushing for a transfer back into homicide."

"And give up all this glamour?"

"I think I can live without it." He slid behind the wheel. "You wanna come with me?"

"Long as we don't have to deal with toy soldier assholes, I'm in." Pulling onto the Harbor Freeway, traffic was light and the air coming in the window was refreshing. Within a few days Angelenos would be bitching that the marine layer was screwing with their sunbathing, but for tonight all was groovy and copacetic.

12:16 AM Apartment 2B.

It was after midnight before the news vans and police teams finally cleared out and Catherine Cray was permitted to return to apartment 2B. Her son, Lamar lay on the floor surrounded by a congealing lake of blood. Six 5.56 mm rounds had punched through the floor. One of them entered his left temple. The scream came from a place Catherine didn't know existed. Lamar's death was ruled accidental. Who fired the fatal shots was never made public.

The morning edition of the *Los Angeles Times* headline read, EX-FIRST LADY JUST SAID YES TO DRUG RAID. "We thought Nancy ought to see it for herself and she did . . . She is a very courageous woman." Gates praised Nancy Reagan. Nancy said of her 'crack house' tour, "I saw people on the floor, rooms that were unfurnished . . . all very depressing."

STRETCHING FIFTEEN

Angel Luis Colón

The World Trade Center subway stop smells like a chemical toilet. I get off the E train and that's the first odor to hit me—piss, shit, and an industrial cleaner that's struggling to make its presence known. It's not even summer yet and I'm terrified of what a hot July day is going to smell like.

I do my best to ignore the smell as I get above ground. There's no relief. Outside is no better. Whatever. I need to get to work. I avoid eye contact with whatever the hell they call that miserable replacement for the Twin Towers and hustle past the PATH train stop and across West Ave before the light changes and I have to wait a solid three hours shoulder to shoulder with the biggest douche-nozzles this part of town has to offer. This is what I get for waking up late. This what I get for having 'just one more beer' last night knowing that the extra fifteen minutes would become an extra forty-five waiting at Penn Station for the train to get back home.

This was the dream, though. Two years fresh from an MBA and I was in corporate Mecca. I was the shill my parents trained me to be, not like the rest of my generation. I was the one all my lazy-ass friends had to hear about for the next couple of years. I was the one who got out.

I'm across the street and making my way down Vesey Street and towards the Hudson. My building overlooks the river. Bonus; it's only fifteen stories. That makes it less of a target. When I first got offered the gig as a securities chief, I was worried about location. It's been over a decade since the Towers came down, but as a native, I can't shake the nervous jitter I get in my chest when I walk around these streets. I feel like I'm 'on' for the full ten minute walk to my building and the end of the day walk to the train. Any other time, I'm straight. It's being in the open air in *this* neighborhood that leaves me feeling like my dick's out and everyone has noticed.

I'm only a few feet away from my building entrance when I notice him. Older fella, white. He's wearing one of those trench coats you'd see in a Bogart movie and bright green running cap. He's got a backpack and a fanny pack. The guy's muttering to himself, but not in that easy to ignore kind of way. No, this seems a little 'off'—even for a New York City self-talker. When I get a little closer, he starts looking at me. I still can't catch what he's saying. It doesn't look like any of the gibberish is directed at me, but that stare—hollow and cold—there's something wrong with this guy.

I start drifting to my right in order to angle towards my building's front door, but the low-talker decides he's going to drift to his left. We're on a slow-paced collision course and I see his right hand go into his coat. Something in me screams to throw a punch—that this situation isn't normal—so I do. I lean into a haymaker like a pro. The first time I've ever clenched my fist with the intention of striking another human being. I make contact with his jaw. Pain blossoms in my hand, from knuckle to fingertip. Something falls at our feet. I look over—it's a gun. I was right to do this.

The situation's not resolved. I hear someone call out for the police, for someone to help. The old man hasn't fallen over, no, he's grabbed at me. Screaming his bullshit at my face. His breath smells like a movie-theater floor.

"Motherfucker!" He half screams, half spits at me.

I follow that impulse again. I raise my fist and hit him again. Ignore that my hand's ballooned to twice its size and that I can barely make a fist. I keep at it. Again and again—willing my swollen hand to burst against this bastard's face. The old man finally goes limp and falls over. My synapses are firing enough to tell me to step on that gun and kick it away against one of the planters freshly installed weeks ago. The bulbs are beginning to peek through the fresh soil. I don't know why I pick up on that, but the way I feel right now, I notice everything. Colors pop, the smell of the river fills the space behind my eyes, and New York City sings to me in a way I never noticed.

I breathe hard and close my eyes. Listen to the sound of my own heartbeat. I feel a hand on my shoulder and jerk back to life.

"Easy, easy." I recognize the man. He's security for my building. Our relationship until this moment made of curt nods. "You okay, Chris?"

"Yeah," is all I can say. I have no idea *what* I am right now. I've never been violent, never found the compulsion to hurt someone before they hurt me. To be honest, I feel amazing. Not alive, like so many people would say. No, I don't feel alive. I feel happy. I'm over the fucking moon. I stopped some psychopath from hurting me or others.

The security guard moves away from me. "Don't go anywhere," he says.

I heard sirens behind me. The sounds of doors opening and closing. A crowd's gathered. I can see my boss and other members of my team watching me. I try to play it cool. Try to ignore that my right hand is feeling strangely absent. I've lost all feeling. I crane my head to the right and stare at Freedom Tower. For the first time I don't feel so scared.

• • •

After the cops came the HR interviews, and after those came the media requests. Actual phone calls for interviews, spots on morning TV, and talk show slots. They were calling me a hero. Saying that I prevented what could have been a devastating attack just feet away from the footprint of the Twin Towers.

Me, a hero.

My job gave me the week off and I was free to pursue all the appearances and interviews I wanted. It was amazing. I got free food, gifts, and sit-down talks with men and women claiming that I saved them that day.

"Call me." A girl who worked across the street from my building types her number into my phone, and smiles before walking away.

I have no way of knowing if she was there. I can barely remember the face of the attacker. All I know is for the very first time in my life, I mean something to someone else—to a whole lot of people, even. I fumble with my phone. My hand is in a cast—broke a few bones—and it's difficult getting used to such a big screen. The new phone was another gift from my job. My apartment is lined with baskets and envelopes. Hundreds of people thanking me for making downtown a little safer. I know within the week, they'll all forget me, but it's still pretty cool.

I head out of the studio where I taped my fifth interview of the day. A car has been hired to take me home and I watch one of my earlier appearances on the TV inside. The host mentions Earl Whitaker—the man I'd stopped—was an unemployed ex-con with severe mental issues. Apparently the pistol he dropped wasn't the only thing he had on him. Police claim Earl had multiple guns and a pipe bomb.

I shake my head in disbelief and wonder what kind of damage could have been done, had I not acted. Hell, I would have been that psycho's first victim. Forget that, Earl completely intended for me to be his first victim. After my interview, they cut to a newscaster who mentions Earl is still at the hospital and in a coma. Good. I honestly wish I killed him. People like that don't deserve the chance at a life, mental issues or not.

My phone rings. It's a number I don't know, so I let it go to voicemail. All week I've ignored calls from media agents and other leeches looking to capitalize on my fifteen minutes. I'm content in what I have now. No need to push it out any longer. It's not like I can make money being some random New Yorker who punched a guy into a hospital bed.

I lean back on the leather upholstery and dig a hand into a small cooler stocked with complimentary energy drinks. I watch the city through the tinted window to my right and smile. I like seeing the world from here. Nobody else can see me, but they can wonder who it is behind the glass. That's pretty fucking awesome. You know what? *I'm* pretty fucking awesome.

• • •

"Five-fifty." Ernesto gives me a small smile as he waits for my money.

I'm a little thrown off. This is the first time the bagel place by work has charged me in nearly a month, but I guess that's fine. Not like I can be a VIP forever. I nod and fish my wallet out. Give him a ten spot. "Keep the change, man." I scoop up my breakfast order and turn around. My cheeks are hot. I tell myself to get a grip. The news cycle's gone by. No need to sweat paying for breakfast again. This might be a good thing; life is back to normal.

I'm lying to myself. Hell, I saved these peoples' lives. This is how they repay me? A couple of weeks of lip service—like they were giving me some sort of social pity fuck. It's bullshit. I was the one to step up; I was the one to stop that psychopath. They did nothing and I'm damn sure if they had been in my shoes, they'd be buried and forgotten.

The security guys at my building are back to giving me the curt nod of a good morning, since they're so fucking awesome at their jobs. I step into my elevator and that cute brunette from the floor above me gives me a forced smile. Wonderful. I was going to call her after taking some time to make it look like I had better things going on, you know, build up my reputation. I feel like there was a sit down about me the night before and everyone decided to fuck with me.

I make my way to my desk and get a fair amount of half-hearted waves. When I log into my station, I can see my boss, Dave, scheduled a quick "catch-up session" for us in fifteen minutes. I have no voicemails on my work or personal phones. The only new personal email is a reminder that my cell phone bill is due at the end of the month. I wasn't sure if that was on my plate, but it sure as hell seems to be a new three hundred dollar weight on my chest. I make a note to call the company and change my plan. Ignore the impulse to flip my desk over and scream.

I swallow breakfast and head over to a closed workspace a few feet away from my desk. Dave is already waiting.

"Chris, how goes it?" Dave folds one leg over the other. His pants are pleated enough to shave with.

I sit down and nod. Open my notebook in case I need to take anything down, but I know I'm just going to start drawing in the margins. "It goes, you?"

"Same here." He smiles and flips open his own notebook. "This shouldn't be long, I only wanted to sit down and talk for a few minutes."

"Sure." I keep it short. One on one sessions like this go better when it isn't a pissing contest.

"Well, I'm glad everything is going well after, you know," he says and does a weird shrug move—I have no idea what it's supposed to mean—and frowns. "Still, we need to get back into it. See, I want to make sure that you're fully equipped to get back to business as usual. Your month was a little off, but due to the circumstances surrounding what happened, it was easy to turn a blind eye."

"Okay." I clearly have no idea what he's getting at.

Dave leans in. "You're a little behind, Chris."

"Behind with what?" I ask. Sure, I had a week off, but otherwise, things were slow. It wasn't as if I was slacking off in the break room or taking longer lunches—well, everyday—there shouldn't be any issues to discuss.

"I'm concerned about you, though."

"Why?"

Dave arches an eyebrow. "Well, you seem distant. You never email anyone back with key deliverables. I mean, we've had to remind you about the metrics project three times."

I nod quickly. "Yeah, no, I get that. I can sort it all out."

"Are you sure, Chris? You know, the mental health leave is completely on the table. We've got the three-sixty reviews coming up and I don't want anything to affect your overall performance evaluation."

It's all coming at once. I shake the sudden urge to wrap my hands around Dave's throat—where that comes from; I have no idea—and scribble nothings onto the margin of my notebook. "I'm okay, Dave. Promise. If there are any issues, you'll be the first to know."

The rest of my day sucks just as hard. I get back to my desk and there's three urgent emails regarding work I was supposed to turn in last week. I manage to bullshit my way to two days' worth of extensions, but by the time 5:00 PM hits, I'm fried. I collect my stuff and trudge to the elevator and out the door. Nobody says goodbye, nobody looks my way.

I'm a nothing again.

That sinking feeling comes back when I'm outside and walking towards the subway entrance. I find myself trapped behind a group of German tourists more interested in taking pictures of a fucking building—like those don't exist in Germany—and shove my way past. I can't shake this feeling that this isn't what I deserve, that the technicolor world where I'm a nobody is a punishment, and someone like me, someone willing to risk his life to save these mouth-breathing assholes, should have more than this. They owed me, for fuck's sake. Those Germans, the brunette from upstairs, Dave; all of them. What if I hadn't stopped that crazy son of a bitch? There'd be no way anybody could walk through here safely; content that the world isn't waiting to spring out of the shadows and take it all away from them.

What I need is to prove it to them.

What I need is to help save the day again. This is New York City, for fuck's sake. Something bad is always happening here. All I have to do is keep my eyes open, exactly like before, and I'll get the opportunity to do it again. I mean, it's rare for lightning to strike twice, but that would be the sell. Nobody would be able to resist it: a two-time hero. Chris Givens, the unsung Samaritan of New York. I probably wouldn't need the idiot job, or to ever come back down here. This time, I'd get a media agent, make appearances, hell, and maybe even throw the first pitch at a ball game.

All I need to do is keep my eyes open and I'll do it again.

I feel a little better with that mission statement, so I get on the train in a pretty great mood. This is of course, immediately soured by a smell—indescribable. My eyes water and I retch. There's a guy occupying one side of the car and about forty people piled against each other opposite him. He's in old clothes and has two wheeled carts filled with cans. There's a part of me that sees this as a potential chance, but no, there's no heroics in dumping on a homeless guy, no matter how bad he smells.

I join the rest of the commuters on the other side of the car and switch trains at Canal Street. This time I choose a middle car and land a seat. I nod off and before I know it, we're north of midtown. I check the stop—59th Street—it's only another six stops before I'm home. The train's packed now. I can tell the tourists from the locals—it's all in the face. I've never felt so acutely aware. I'm ready to leap at the first sign of trouble. I did it before and I know I can do it again. I keep an eye on two older guys with ratty jackets, a few teenagers cackling at odd intervals, and a lady with way too many bags.

At the next stop a young guy gets on and stands above me holding the rail. He leans over to my right and smiles at a young woman next to me. "Hey baby," his voice has Barry White bass.

This could be it. A subway harasser? That happens all the time. I'll give it a minute, see if he gets a little too direct and confront him. People have cell phone cameras, thankfully, so who knows; maybe it'll go viral.

The girl's head snaps to forward, a sour look on her face that instantly melts away to a broad smile. "Oh damn, hey."

They hug.

I sulk.

Fine, I can't expect an opportunity to pop up so fast. Even if I'm paying attention. Life isn't like the news. It's not like crimes happen around us while everyone ignores it. No. This needs to be organic. Maybe I'll walk the long way home more often. Exit a stop earlier on my way to work. Follow the darker streets and alleys. It can be fun, well, not fun in the traditional sense of the word, but still. I decide to start tomorrow. The more I think about it, though, I can't go walking around without protection. Not everyone is lucky enough to get a punch in before an old man can pull the trigger. I mean, what if the next crime I stop is by a person bigger than me? Or worse, more than one person. It would be idiotic of me not to afford the ability to defend myself. Maybe a knife? Yeah, a knife would make sense—of legal length, obviously.

I get off the train a stop ahead of the one I normally take and walk up the street. I examine the path and keep an eye open, but it's quiet. I should be happy for that, but I can't help but be disappointed. It's like a kid waiting for Christmas after discovering the little cache of gifts his parents hid away carelessly. I remind myself to be patient. It only took 35 years before that old lunatic decided to pull a gun while I was around. For all I know, it'll be another 35 before I get my chance. I can't get ahead of myself.

• • •

"Chris," Dave points to the security guard that's walked into the conference room, "You'll be escorted out." He frowns. "I'll box your things up and send them to your apartment. Same address, right?"

I don't have the words in me. I stand and nod weakly.

Dave stands with me. Places a hand on my shoulder. "Listen man, I'm sorry, I really am. Just . . . take care of yourself. Take this time for your mental health, okay? And try to eat, you're looking so thin."

I want to smack him. I want to ask him what the fuck he thinks he's doing pulling the doting mommy act after canning my ass unceremoniously. "Fine, will do," is all I can muster up.

I follow the security guard out—the same fella who was there the day I became a hero. Six months after the fact and he acts like I'm not even here. Probably jealous. I mean, look at him. Cardboard rent-a-cop who couldn't do his job. Where was he when there was an active shooter ready to slaughter these people? He was standing around with his thumb up his ass, that's where he was. Me? I stepped up. I showed these people how not to be afraid.

Heroes

I prevented the next fucking 9-11 and this is what I get; a bullshit severance package and a couple of extra months on my healthcare plan so I can "seek help". And it's not like there isn't more danger out there. Plenty of the people milling around the piers and shopping areas look shady as hell. Who are these chuckle-fucks to act as if a hero like me isn't essential to continued safety?

I don't understand why Dave and his bosses were even checking out my Internet history to begin with. We had slow days, so I drifted around. Looked up a few articles about firearms and different defensive tactics. If anything, I was doing the right thing. I wasn't going to allow complacency to leave me unprepared. Why couldn't they understand that? This was for *them*, not me.

That was it, though. Dave didn't get it. He didn't understand the danger we're all in. A guy like him lives easy. He never sees the dark underbelly of the city the way I have. So maybe the key here is to *get* him to understand. That false confidence he's built up needs to be torn down and only then can he begin to understand how to be brave in the face of danger and filth. I walk through TriBeCa trying to work out the best way to get Dave onboard in this understanding. If I can accomplish that, maybe I can get my job back. Dave's a nice guy deep down—even if he toes the line for those spineless fucking suits at the top.

I see my answer in front of a Starbucks. There's a guy yelling at people as they enter and exit the place. Everyone's giving him a wide berth, he's naturally intimidating. I can kill two birds here: one, I can get this psycho off the corner and two; I can use him to show Dave exactly what we're dealing with in this city day to day.

I jog over to the screamer with a smile on my face. My right hand rests in my jacket pocket, wrapped around the handle of the knife I've carried around for months now. "Hey, man," I call out.

The screamer turns to me. "Fuck you!"

"Easy man." I fish my wallet from my back pocket and show him a twenty. "I'm looking for someone looking to earn a little cash. You seem like the right kind of fella."

His initial response isn't what I expect. There's no wide-eyed stare or sudden glimmer of desire. He stares at me and then leans in. "Fuck you," he hisses.

I get another twenty out. "Forty for your attention and another forty if you agree to give me ten minutes—at most—of your time." Not the smartest way to spend my money, but I need to think long-term. This is an investment in getting things back to the way they should be—the way things should have remained.

The screamer reaches towards the cash slowly, anticipating I'll snatch it away. He pinches the bills between two tobacco stained fingers and tugs slowly.

I let go of the bills and smile. "See? Not so bad, right?"

The screamer quickly pockets the money and nods. "What do you need?" He licks his lips. His left eye twitches.

"All I need is for you to scream at someone for me and pretend like you're scared of me, that's all."

He looks side to side. Steps forward and then back. "Why?"

"Does it matter? You're looking at almost a hundred bucks for a few minutes. That's like a salary out here." I point at the buildings behind me. "Besides, wouldn't it be fun to fuck with some of the assholes out here ignoring you?"

"Okay." Is all I get.

Great. I turn. "Follow me . . . " I feel hands on my shoulder. Pressure on my neck and a pain like I've never felt before. The scream that comes out of me is two-octaves higher than anything that's ever emerged from my mouth. My eyes water and I bat my hands behind me. He won't get off. I hear people around me yelling. A woman screams for him to get off me, but nothing's changing. I can smell him, feel his filth on me. I claw but keep scratching at air. I feel something warm flowing from my neck and look down. My dress shirt is stained in blood. My heart's pounding. This is my blood. Oh Jesus Christ, it's my blood. I try to run and drag him with me into the middle of the street. I don't notice that I've curled over the hood of a yellow cab until I see red on its hood and feel the heat of the engine on my face.

The weight on my back finally subsides. Someone asks me if I'm okay and screams for people to call the cops, an ambulance, anyone.

All I can do is grab at my neck. It feels like my attacker ripped it open but I don't feel any pain. It's cold, though, and my arms feel so heavy.

"Sir, are you okay, sir—oh god."

• • •

The camera lights bother me, but I don't complain. There are seven people in the hospital room. Three behind cameras, one with a microphone, some woman I don't know and Harry—the man who saved my life.

Harry's a little older than me. In better shape. He's got those classic good looks, like something out of *Mad Men*. He's baring his Chiclet teeth at me.

"I'm so glad to see you doing better," he says. His voice is sanitized, not a trace of an accent. He may as well be wearing a white tee-shirt with the word 'generic' printed on it in black ink.

I'm still medicated and the doctors mentioned that I should limit my speaking, so I give a thumbs-up. The screamer, well, he bit a hole in my neck. The wound wasn't as bad as the inevitable infection from being bitten by a guy whose mouth was basically a toilet. One of the nurses actually said it was like a bite from a komodo dragon—there were so many microbes in the guy's mouth that something new snuck on into me and had a hell of a time. Almost rotted my trachea and voice box to nothing. So, that means no speaking. Unless I'm really into the idea of using one of those microphones throat cancer patients use for the rest of my life.

Harry, though. Harry's a natural. He smiles for the cameras, laughs at all the right times, hell, he even pats my hand in a way that convinces me he gives a shit. He doesn't. No, he's moving in and taking all that spotlight that was saved up for me. Not a damn thing I can do about it either.

The weirdest part? I found out a few days after the fact, but Earl, that maniac I stopped was only three doors down from me. He gave up the ghost while I was still being treated and in a fever-induced haze. Part of me feels sorry for him and another part of me wishes I was awake to hear the news in real time. He could have ruined so many lives that day, but it looks like he only ruined mine. Nobody's told me what happened to the assholes that robbed and bit me. I can only assume he ran off to spend my money on God knows what. To be honest, I don't care. Let them rot.

"So Harold, or is it Harry?" the reporter asks.

"Harry, please." He smiles. The camera lights make him glorious.

"What were you thinking when you saw Mr. Givens being attacked?"

Harry leans back, frowns. He's mulls over his next words, but it's an act. I can tell he's rehearsed this answer a thousand times. "I had to help. How could I not help? I mean, his attacker was on him like an animal. It was quite scary."

The reporter nods. "Scary, but you still stopped it."

Harry smiles again. "That's the point, right? Even if we're scared, we have to do something." He places a hand on mine. "And hell, finding out about how Dave helped people so many months ago. I'd call it karma."

I smile weakly. Outside my room, I spot Harry's media consultant. I'd met him the other day. He reminded me that he called me when I stopped that active shooter. That thought can't stop scratching at the back of my head. I should have called him. Should have milked the original save through and through. Now that I'm a victim? Nobody gives a damn. They pity me, but there's no way anyone wants to train a camera on me for longer than five minutes.

The reporter turns back to the camera and smiles. "Absolutely, Harry. Mr.

Givens definitely received the help a man like him deserved. Back to you, Greg."

Everyone leaves the room. No goodbyes or thank-yous. Harry doesn't give me a second glance, no; he's too wrapped up in talking to his media consultant. Me, I stay in my hospital bed—the used prop. IVs stuck in me all over. My throat burning hot—neck's so swollen I look like I should live in the swamp on a god damn lily pad.

Fuck karma.

BOUNTY

Jerry Bloomfield

She was alive. That much she knew. How long she'd been out she had no idea. Somebody had taken care of her though. That sterile hospital smell filled her nose. She tried moving, fingers and toes mostly worked. Finally she cracked open her eyes, glancing around.

It was a small room, with a window on one wall. Besides the bed, there was a small end table and a chair. All simple looking, homemade but sturdy and well built.

She shoved down the quilts that had been tucked in up to her chin, wincing at the movement. Her shoulder was bandaged and the arm in a sling. Lifting hesitant fingers, she carefully ran them over her head. The hair had been shaved away around the gash and stitches closed the wound. She thought it would hurt more.

"Ah, I see we are awake." The woman who spoke was dressed in pants and riding boots, sleeves rolled up on a button-up shirt. Her long blonde hair was tied back in a ponytail. She set a platter down on the end table and fixed the blankets back.

"You must be thirsty." The woman helped her sit up, propping pillows behind her back before handing her a glass of water. "I've got some food too, if you feel up to it."

She sipped at the water, despite the urge to gulp it down. "Thanks."

Cool eyes watched her. "Quite welcome. I'm Sally Donovan. And you are?"

"Nika." She sipped more water. Nothing had ever tasted as good.

"You are pretty banged up, Nika. Do you know what happened to you?"

"I was shot. Trailing after . . . some outlaws. Then someone got the drop on me and clubbed me over the head. Tossed me over a cliff."

"About what we thought. No amnesia, so that's good. You don't know who?"

Nika shook her head.

"Too bad. Ah well, the sheriff will want to talk to you anyway. He likes to keep this a peaceable settlement."

Nika nodded, sipping more water before taking bigger drinks. Her stomach rumbled and she eyed the plate. "Can I try some food?"

"Sure," Sally said, handing the plate over. "You seem to know the drill. Been shot before."

It didn't sound like a question and she didn't see a reason to deny it. This woman had cut her bloody clothes off, after all. "Yeah. Kinda an occupational hazard."

"I see. And what occupation might that be?"

"Bounty hunter." Might as well get it out there. "I won't trouble you for long. I'll be on my way soon as I can."

"Nonsense. You'll leave here when you are healthy enough to do so. My husband and I wouldn't have it any other way."

"He the doctor?" She mumbled around a mouth full of food. Tasted right out of a five star restaurant. Especially after two months of MREs.

"Not exactly, but he is the one who patched you up. I have things to do, so I'll leave you now. Bathroom is down the hall, first door on the left. If you need any toiletries, there's some there and in the end table here. Rest as much as you can."

• • •

Nika spent much of the next few days in bed, with either Doc or Sally bringing her meals. She got her legs under her quickly, walking to the bathroom on her own. Partly it was pure stubbornness and partly survival. Somebody wanted her dead, and an invalid laid up in a bed was easy pickings.

The sheriff came by the second day, inquiring after the attack. She couldn't exactly tell him nothing, being he had the right to know who was in his jurisdiction, so she confessed she had been trailing the Bellamy Twins. Bad dudes. Wanted on planets all over the system for piracy, gun running, murder. At least five bounty hunters had died on their trail.

• • •

Sally stayed closer to Nika, unlike her husband. When she wasn't busy with work she sat with her while she ate, chatted in the evenings. Perhaps she was just hungry for female company. Technology aside, New Laramie was still a frontier town, still being settled and was sparsely populated. Nika didn't begrudge the talking. Truth be told, she sometimes missed having someone to talk to her own self.

"So what's the mark?"

Nika popped her head out of the water, water streaming down her freshly shaved head. Hadn't made sense to have just one side buzzed off.

"On your arm. It's not like your other tattoos. More . . . crude."

They were at the hot spring, perched up in the hills above the Donovan's house. They had a small spread, few cows, some chickens, a garden. Doc did some medical work for the nearby ranchers, taught their children certain times of year. It was Sally did the ranch work.

Nika glanced down at the mark on her arm. Three crude lines forming a shield. It was nestled between the paws of a snarling bear. Her arms, chest, back, most of it was covered in tattoos. Some were cut up by scars and old wounds.

"Oh. A group I did some work for."

"Charles said he recognized it. Stories from Old Earth."

"I've heard that too. No idea if it's true."

"And that one?"

Nika smiled. Sally had pointed to a dragon that was curled around her breast, placed so that its claws held her nipples like the pearls in old paintings. Its match on the other side was partially covered by bandages. "This was done on Terran Five. Little old lady, looked like a stiff breeze would blow her over. Ran the gangs in the whole sector. Descended from the Yakuza they said."

"Did it hurt?"

"Not as bad as getting shot."

Sally grinned. "I don't imagine." She stretched out in the hot water, sighing. "This is pretty much the whole reason we picked this spot."

"Good call, I'd say." Nika scooted up to sit on the rock at the edge of the spring, enjoying the sun on her body.

"Charles told me about the group that used that mark. What they did. Is that why you are here?"

Nika eased her arm back in its sling. It hurt to leave it hanging free too long. She eyed Sally, who looked straight at her, sense of modesty be damned. "What did Doc tell you?"

"Most people didn't think it existed, just some story told to scare criminals. Those that do think it died off with Earth."

"There's some truth to that. And mind you, I don't know the whole story. Hell, probably nobody does. Never was no formal organization. Just people doing what had to be done." She stared down into the bubbling water, kicking her foot around in it.

"Sounds pretty heroic."

"Shit. Says the frontierswoman settling a new planet."

"That's just work," Sally shrugged.

"That does a body good, from the look of things." Nika winked. And laughed at the blush creeping over Sally's face and chest.

"So did that bring you here?"

"Just chasing after the Bellamy Twins, like I told y'all. Nothing special."

"Says the intergalactic bounty hunter."

Nika shrugged and stood up. "Is it lunch time yet?"

Indeed it was. Charles "Doc" Donovan was at the table, plate full of food before him. The circles under his eyes were dark and he chewed slowly, staring off into the distance. Sally hugged him, kissing the top of his head. He pressed into her, body relaxing.

"Long night, honey?"

"Amelia Mercer. The baby was the wrong way."

Nika sat as far away as she could, giving the couple their space. Emotions, comfort, it just wasn't her thing. She filled her plate, shoveled it in. She'd be glad when this sling was gone.

"I keep telling the governor we need medical equipment, but oh no. She says it's too expensive for the population. Has to stay in the capital. Damn her hide!" Doc slapped his hand down on the table.

Sally squeezed and kneaded his shoulders. "I'm sure you did all you could."

"It wasn't enough though, was it?"

"Did both . . ."

"No, thank god. Just the baby."

He fell silent, poking at his food. Sally gave him one last squeeze and sat down beside him to her own meal. He looked up, staring down at Nika.

"So I ran into the sheriff. He was asking about you."

"Is that right?"

"Apparently somebody caught the Bellamy Twins. On Titan Four. A month ago."

"Titan Four," Sally said. "But that's . . ."

"Yes. In the next galaxy. So Nika, you want to tell us why you are really here?" His kind eyes were a lot steelier now.

"I . . ." She looked between them, both staring down the table at her. Reaching up, she rubbed the crude mark on her arm. "I don't know how, but you say you've heard of them. Well it was Protector business. Got word of a crew of raiders, hitting settlements like this. Taking what they could, selling the people into slavery. And not particular to who the buyers were. They been keeping Yawin supplied with fresh meat, if you know anything about that place."

Doc nodded. Sally frowned. "No, what is it?"

"It's, well, everything is for sale there. And everyone," Doc told her. "And it's beyond Federation space so nobody does anything."

"The Neutral Zone, yeah. Doesn't belong to us or any of the aliens. Not a lot there but they make full use of it."

"Oh that's terrible," Sally said.

"How does that bring you here?"

"I got in with the gang. Was hoping to find their headquarters and take them out from the inside. Unfortunately the leader found out somehow. And that lead to all this." She didn't think it was necessary to mention that she'd been sharing a bed with the gang leader, and that the reason she'd been dumped for dead was she had literally been caught with her pants down.

"Why here? Why New Laramie? I suppose it is rather quiet and empty."

"And close to space routes. Nobody to question strange ships coming and going."

"And they are based here?"

"Out in the wastes."

His fingers drummed on the table as he thought over her story. "The sheriff also told me he got an ID back on you."

Nika's head shot up, staring at him. "What?"

"He scanned your prints and retinas while you were out. Wanted to know what he was dealing with."

"Charles!"

He shrugged. "He has a responsibility to the protection of this whole settlement. And I wanted to make sure you were safe. We didn't know anything about her."

"So what came back?" She spoke lazily, fingers rubbing at her thigh. She wished she had her guns strapped back in their holsters.

"I'm sure you'll be relieved to know you aren't wanted for any crimes. However, we did discover your surname. And there are some people interested in your location."

Shit. "When will they arrive?"

"I don't imagine they will. They seemed content with the official documentation of your death and cremation. We didn't think it was too much of them to ask for the urn so we sent it off. I suppose they'll put it in the royal mausoleum on Zxyor."

She blinked, mouth gaped open. She didn't know whether to hug him or knock that shit-eating grin off his face. "I, um, thank you."

"Yes, well. They were rather rude and insistent. Put us off, you know. But this is not good news. Perhaps we should go to the governor. Some of us have been floating the idea of a different kind of police service. Something like the rangers they had on Old Earth."

"That's it? Nobody's here to clap the cuffs on me?"

"You appear to have a guardian angel, Nika. Must have flagged someone's computer when your info was brought up. The sheriff got a call from someone who convinced us you weren't exactly one of the bad guys. Someone from that outfit whose mark is on your arm."

It seemed belonging sometimes paid off after all. "You know, rangers ain't a bad idea on a planet like this. But that'll take time. And who knows what this gang could be up to in the meantime."

"The army . . ."

"Would take even longer."

"You don't suggest we just sit here and do nothing."

"No. I'll go after them."

"You can't! You're wounded." Sally tossed down her napkin. "And by yourself? They left you for dead once already."

Nika smiled bitterly. "Yeah, but I didn't see that coming. This time, they won't see me coming."

"You'll need gear. Maybe the sheriff should deputize you, make it legal."

"Charles!"

"No," Nika said, shaking her head. "I won't be arresting anybody. This will be quick and dirty. Nothing left behind but corpses."

Doc frowned. "We need names. We can't just allow people to get killed without any verification."

"Thanks for the confidence, Doc. But I can assure you these people well deserve this fate."

"So tell us who they are. There could be intergalactic warrants. I'll take the information to the sheriff and maybe we can get something started."

Perhaps. And it would take some time to get outfitted and healed up enough to head out. "Ok, fine. The leader is Lyla Thompson. Her right hand man Dylan Smith. The rest are just your run of the mill outlaw scum."

Doc scribbled the names down. "I'll see the sheriff tomorrow, get in touch with the governor. She'll have to give us a task force, set us up with real police."

"Sure, good luck with that."

"One more question. How'd you end up shot and left for dead?"

Nika sighed, looked down at her plate. "We needed more information," she said in a hurry. "Their numbers, plans, who might be protecting them. Didn't want to just cut off the snake's tail. But they found me out and . . ."

She shrugged.

Doc nodded, looking at her a minute. "Guess spying isn't your strong suit." He stood up, leaned over and kissed the top of his wife's head. "It was a long trip. And I have an early start tomorrow. I'm headed to bed."

Sally squeezed his hand. "I'll be along shortly."

She leaned back in her chair, studying Nika. "The royal mausoleum?"

Nika shrugged. "My sister got lucky with a john."

"That's some luck."

"Yeah. But I'm an embarrassment. At least I'm dead now."

"Should I throw a funeral?"

"Just the wake would do."

The smile fell off Sally's face. "He's a good man, you know. Wants to do what's right. You should let him do that."

"Sally," Nika said with a sigh. "It's not that simple. These are bad dudes."

"And only you can handle them."

Silence was Nika's only answer.

"There are military types in the capital, commandos and special forces. Make them Rangers, they'd do a great job. So why do you have to? Why do you have to be the hero?"

Nika stood up. "Somebody has to."

• • •

She rode out early the next morning, well before dawn. She left the magbike, not wanting to leave Doc without speedy transportation should there be an emergency. Instead she had left on one of the ranch's native mounts, a creature that looked like a cross between a lion and a horse. The settlers, recalling an old Earth word, called them catamounts.

No one had ever met the native people of this planet, if there were any, and no one was sure if these animals had ever been used as mounts before. But they took to it easy enough and even guarded the herds of livestock.

A mount was one thing. Even more imperative was securing weapons. The Donovans didn't have many and she didn't want to leave them unprotected. Nika could just hear Lyla laughing over her sentimentality. Didn't fit her reputation. But then, a rep was easier to get than to keep.

There was a trading post on the edge of the wastes that served the moisture farmers in the area and prospecting miners. It was also used by Lyla's gang. They bought supplies from the trader and sold him slaves. There'd be weapons there, maybe armor. If she just had something to offer in trade. She nudged her heels into the catamount's side, urging it faster. Something would come to mind.

• • •

Smoke rose from the chimney of the small building. Stretching out behind it was the wide expanse of desert they called the wastes. Few people went in there. Few had any reason to.

Nika slid off the catamount and tossed the reins over a post. Poured some water into a small bowl and sat it down before the creature. It nudged her in thanks before starting to drink. Nika hoisted the saddle bag over her shoulder and stepped inside, grateful to be out of the sun.

It was cool inside, the light dim. She stood in the doorway waiting for her eyes to adjust. The counter was at the back, part of it doubling as a bar, some shelves lined up on the floor and a few tables. Long guns lined the wall behind the counter. She walked up slowly, glancing about. Least none of the gang were here.

"Hot out there, eh?" The man behind the counter finished wiping some glasses, setting them back on the shelf. "What can I get you?"

Nika dug out her canteens. "Water. Some MREs. One of them rifles."

He looked her over slowly. "No offence, but can you pay? Water I'll give you, hell it don't cost me nothing. Anything else I gotta see money."

She gave him her hardest flattest stare. "You work for Lyla Thompson don't ya? Want to tell her why you didn't give me what I need? She's waiting on me to get back."

"Oh, I, um, see." He took the canteens and started filling them. "Got into some trouble?"

"An over-achieving lawman. Took a fucking shot at me. Managed to get away, but without my gear."

"Hey, I don't need no details. Lyla's credit is good here. What rifle do you want? Got a few a them laser rifles, some old style ammo guns."

She eased onto a stool, working her shoulder. Maybe she should have grabbed some pills on her way out. "Let's see that one with the scope."

"Ah, that's a fine piece," he said taking it off the rack. "Very old design, but you can't improve on perfection, you know?" He handed it over to her, bolt open and empty.

Nika managed to hide the wince as she fitted it to her shoulder, sighting down the barrel under the scope.

"Gotta work the bolt each shot," the trader said. "Some still prefer it that way. 'Stead of all this fancy automatics and lasers and pulse rays and what have you."

"Ammo?"

He sat two boxes before it. "Made it my own self. Got a reloader in the back. What kind of MREs were you wanting?"

"Whatever you got. Twenty."

"All right, just let me go fetch 'em."

He went through a door into a back room. Nika could hear him rummaging around, cursing as something fell over on him. She opened a box of ammo, thumbed cartridges into the magazine, pushed it home. Worked the bolt, ejected the mag and added another cartridge.

The trader came out, a box under each arm. "I guess you know how to work it okay."

She nodded, lifted the gun. He started to scramble back when she fired. The boxes fell out of his arms and he slumped back against the door, falling halfway into the stockroom. Nika worked the bolt, ears ringing after the loud boom.

She laid the rifle on the counter and rubbed her shoulder. Get this job finished up, she'd go find a spa to lay up in for a month or two, heal up, and get pampered.

She knelt beside the body and rummaged through the pockets. Laid aside a roll of bank notes and a package of genuine tobacco. She took the ring of keys. Found the one to open the cases under the counter and rummaged through the pistols.

She pulled one out, a 1911 .45. The dead bastard really did appreciate the classics. Loaded that one up as well. Seven in the mag, one in the pipe. Nika took the keys and stepped over the corpse, heading straight for the back wall.

When she had been with the gang, she had seen the trader's price for doing business with them. Whenever a new shipment came in, he got first pick. Took two slaves and turned in the old ones. The best kind of lending library, he had joked. She had been at the back of the pack the last time it happened, practically shaking with the desire to shoot him down. She had told herself it wasn't smart, she couldn't help anyone that way, she would've got herself killed for nothing.

Nika yanked a shelf out of the way and peeled back some carpet. The trader kept a hidey-hole. Safe and sound beneath his shop, like a fucking nuclear bunker. Unless one had the keys.

She pulled the hatch open and eased it up. Lights started coming up down the tunnel. Wouldn't want to trip on the way to the harem. Nika tucked the .45 in her pants and dropped into the shaft. She could just hear her old teacher telling her only a complete dumbass stuck guns in their pants.

The tunnel was short, only about twenty steps and ended in another door. Looked like it'd been took off a sub or something, a wheel in the centre of it. She grabbed it and heaved, almost falling over as it turned easily. Of course the man would keep it oiled. Wouldn't want to hinder access to his slaves.

Two young women were huddled together against the far wall. There was a bed and a table. Cuffs and chains on the headboard of the bed.

"It's okay, girls. Not here to hurt you."

They didn't seem to believe her. Just sat, arms wrapped around each other. Nika wished she could kill the man all over again. She laid the ring of keys down on the table.

"The trader is dead. Here's his keys. There's a catamount outside, can carry you both, if you want to leave. There's guns, clothes, supplies. Fuck, run the trading post if you want."

She turned and walked back down the tunnel and climbed up. She wished she could do more, say something that would help them heal, mend. But the only thing she knew to do was what she had.

A quick search of the post and she left atop the trader's prized magbike. MREs and ammo filled the saddlebags. She had a long linen duster, a few handkerchiefs stuck in the pockets, holsters for the guns. The rifle rode on her back. She pointed the bike into the wastes and goosed the accelerator.

• • •

It was hot. The sun beat down, a white hot ball in the cloudless sky. It was a good thing she had the bike, the catamount would've died from the heat hours past. She had the duster buttoned up, goggles and handkerchief covering her face. The wind and sand was almost as bad as the sun.

She had to give the gang credit for one thing. Not many could or would chase them all the way out here. Made her think they had some other transportation. Small aircraft of some sort. Or maybe the rifle butt to the head had scrambled her brain and she would just ride around the desert in circles until she fell off the bike and the heat dried her out until she was nothing but a mummy, the magnets keeping the bike going forever and forever and . . .

There! She slowed the bike near a rock formation. Several pieces of stone piled up and pointing. She shifted direction, following the path laid out. Nika knew she would hit the trail. Some of the other markers must have got knocked over or something. There were strange, large, animals out here.

• • •

She rode until dark. The bike's engine was starting to whine, dust and grit working inside the mag chamber. Didn't matter as long as it got her where she needed to go. She'd just grab another one. Provided she survived.

She had reached the rocks, a sudden mountain in the desert. It covered a large area, there were cliffs and valleys, a canyon with grass and water. None of the settlers seemed to know it was there. Probably had only seen it on fly-overs. Looked like a big chunk of rock.

The canyon was big enough for a small town and over the years a couple buildings had been built. Water piped to them from the pools. One of the gang, a man who had lost an arm and wasn't any good on raids, even grew a small garden.

It was here they brought their goods, and auctioned them over the 'net. Smaller ships could even land close by without the settler government knowing about it, and leave with a cargo hold full of slaves.

She killed the bike and crouched down next to a rock outcropping. There was only one way in or out, which was another reason Lyla liked the place. Easier to defend. And easier to get trapped, Nika thought. If she had any explosives she'd just cave the motherfucker in on them. Unfortunately, this was going to have to be done the hard way.

Unslinging the rifle, she stretched out prone, looking through the scope at the entrance to the cavern. It didn't look like much, just a gap in the rock, but set back in it was a simple wooden door. And there was usually a guard there. More to let the boss know who was coming than any real need of security.

She tried to push down the pain from her shoulder. Steering that bouncing rattling bike hadn't done it any favours. Just letting it hang without a sling was bad enough. Couldn't be helped. She settled the rifle on the door and pushed the pain away, letting out half a breath.

And there was no one there. The door stood open, illuminated by lights inside. Nika frowned. That seemed odd. She lay silently, rifle still. Waiting. Watching.

"Fuck it," she said a half hour later. She slung the rifle on her back and stood up. A few drinks of water and a bite from a MRE and she was ready to go. She wheeled the bike down the slight hill and pushed it inside. Might need it after all.

It was wide enough for about two big men standing abreast and lighted the entire way. She didn't meet anyone as she walked along the tunnel, nor did she hear anything.

She came out of the tunnel and into the canyon proper. Somewhere overhead the whole thing was open to the sky and she could see the moons and stars. It all felt empty. There was no livestock in the corrals and no lights in any of the buildings.

She walked straight to the biggest one, where Lyla lived and had her office. It was upstairs, the second floor. And was just as empty. She stepped into the office and flipped on the light switch. Maybe she could find something that would explain where the gang had gone, a computer, some records, a comm unit or something.

The big man behind the desk pushed the small computer out of the way. He smiled cruelly at her, laser pistol in his hand. Pointed at her stomach.

"Oh, I've been waiting for this."

"Dylan. I didn't expect to see you." This wasn't good. Not only was Dylan Smith a big bastard, he was good. With his fists, guns, blades. Seemingly anything he picked up. Rumour had it he'd been a soldier, but he never said.

"Apparently. What took you so long?"

"Oh you know, us girls take forever to pick out our outfits."

"And the shoulder," he asked with a wicked grin.

She'd hated that grin. Made the big bastard too handsome. "Just a scratch."

"Right. I was behind the scope. Only reason you're alive is Lyla wanted to be fucking fancy. Make an example."

"Where is Lyla? She finally kicked your ass to the curb?"

"Hardly. We're moving our operation to Yawin, and somebody had to stay behind to mop up any loose ends."

She dove to the floor, wincing as she hit on her shoulder. Rolled behind a stack of crates, the .45 in her good hand.

The fucker was actually laughing at her. "Nice landing. Going to come out or do I just walk around and shoot you?"

"It's going to be fun shooting your balls off."

He laughed at her again. She heard the chair squeak as he pushed it back. You've lost your edge, she told herself. Should have shot him soon as you stepped into the room. Nika ran a hand across her brow, wiping away sweat. Too bad that trader hadn't had any power armor.

"You know, I've never seen Lyla so pissed off. She must have liked you."

He sounded a little closer, maybe in front of the desk.

"Jealous?"

"Nah. I like mine less defiant. Tell me who sent you and you won't have to die alone."

She pulled a small syringe out of her pocket. A painkiller. Jammed it in her shoulder and pushed down the plunger. "How comforting."

"This ain't some penny-ante gang, Nika. We got a long reach. Make things easier on yourself for once in your life."

She glanced around. Nowhere else to go. Sloppy, girl. She unslung the rifle and laid it down. No room for it anyway.

"Fine. Time to end this then. I got a shuttle to catch."

Nika gritted her teeth, working the wounded shoulder. The drugs were fast acting, the waves of pain already subsiding. She'd pay later but for now she could move.

She pulled herself to a crouch. Dylan's footsteps approached, boots loud on the floor. She went right, popped around the crates, pistol in both hands. She fired, again and again. He was a wall of black, turning, firing, falling. She heard him curse. Something burned across her thigh. Blood pounded in her ears and she moved closer. No time to take a chance he was wearing armor. She emptied the rest of the clip into his head and kicked the laser pistol away.

She managed to reload her .45 before slumping to the desk. She took a deep breath and knelt by the body, wincing at the pain in her leg. There was no way he had stayed here without some kind of communication. She ignored the blood and searched through his pockets.

• • •

"Looks like you were lucky, girl." Sheriff Cline stood over the body, one hand still resting on the butt of the pistol strapped to his thigh. He was a tall older man, wide shouldered, going soft in the middle. But no less capable for it. Usually.

"I've always been lucky when it comes to killing."

Doc grunted, finishing applying a med cream to the wound on her thigh. "Not that lucky. You keep getting shot."

"Not as bad as him."

"Damn," the sheriff said. "Those old school guns do some damage." He squatted next to the body and pulled a small device out of a pocket. Rectangular in shape, most of it was a touch screen. He selected a program and scanned the dead man's finger prints. Doc glanced over and went back to bandaging Nika.

"Well, we'll find out soon enough." He looked around pointedly. "Only one man. Hardly a slaver gang."

"The rest went on ahead. He stayed behind."

"In case you showed up."

"Case anybody showed up."

He pocketed the device. "But if us yokels were so ignorant of their doin's, then why bother? Just keep goin'."

"Not my department, Sheriff. I just shoot them. But if I were to guess, I'd say Lyla wants to expand. Take a bigger piece of the market. And get off this rock, go somewhere more luxurious."

"That's a mighty specific guess," the sheriff said, crossing his arms. Nika stood up and pulled her pants back up.

"We done here?"

"Those girls did say she rescued them, Jim."

"They did. And another killing doing it. Murder rate's gone up with you here."

Nika buckled her gun back on and slipped the duster on, placing the sniper rifle across her back. "Somebody had to do it, Sheriff."

"Look, I don't want to fight over this. We just want to keep things as peaceful and orderly as we can. Somebody gets killed, we gotta make sure it was on the up and up."

"You can't leave from here anyway," said Doc. "Only spaceships I know of are at New Laramie."

"Then that's where I'm going. This doesn't end here."

Sheriff Cline pulled his comm unit out of his pocket. "Let's see. Mr. Dylan Smith. Quite a few warrants out for him. And bounties."

"Happy now, Sheriff?"

"Looks like he deserved worse then he got but it'll do. I can't hold you on this and the girls at the trading post back you up on what was happening there. I ain't inclined to worry about that very much. You'll have to go to New Laramie to turn your bounty in. But I wouldn't go booking any flights."

"You know something I don't, Sheriff?"

"Probably a few things. We're at the point in this planet's orbit where we're on the wrong side of a meteor field. May have noticed a lot of shooting stars a week or so past? Means no flights. And it'll be another few weeks before they start up again."

"Then where the hell did they go?"

"Well, ain't that the million dollar question?"

• • •

"So where would they go," Sally asked. She looked around the table. Nika was eating as quickly as she could. Doc poked at his plate and Sheriff Cline just stuck to coffee.

"We've been asking ourselves that question," Doc said.

"If we're lucky the wastes swallowed them up and they'll never trouble anyone again," Cline said.

"You don't believe that, Sheriff," Nika said.

"No, I'm afraid not."

"So what do we . . ."

The mobile device on Cline's pocket chimed and he held up a hand to cut Sally off. "Just a minute," he said, stepping into the other room.

Sally got up and started clearing away the dishes, Doc helping out. Nika just leaned back in her chair and stared at the wall. They couldn't count on Lyla and her gang just disappearing, but what? There was nothing to track. Not unless the gang did something and the word spread.

"Wonder what it'll be like when they run the train out this way. Town'll likely get bigger," Doc said.

"It'll be easier to send cattle to market," Sally said, "but it could get rowdier too. There'll be more ranch hands to go to town so there'll be more bars, and maybe worse."

"I do intend to keep pressing the governor on forming that ranger squad. Things are going well and this place will only grow. We need to set up a strong law enforcement agency before it's too late."

Sheriff Cline stepped back into the doorway. "I have to head back to town. Nika, why don't you come along?"

"Is there trouble?" Sally said, a stack of plates in her hand.

"Just a few rowdies. Might be worth a payday, eh?"

Nika nodded and rose to her feet, grabbing up her rifle.

"Just in case, y'all should lock the doors and keep a gun at hand."

"Think something is going down?"

"I really don't know, Doc. I just got a feelin', you know?"

"That's your department, Sally. She's a much better shot than I am."

"At targets anyway," she said.

"I'm sure it won't come to anything. It'll just make me feel better."

Outside, the sun was low on the horizon, moon starting to rise on the other side. Nika shifted her holster and climbed up into the sheriff's vehicle, rifle cradled in her arm. "We should ride the catamounts in. Could eat any bad guys."

"Then how would you collect the bounty?"

• • •

It was dusk when they reached town, the bar lit up and three magbikes out front. Cline pulled his truck up in front of the jail and got out quietly, pulling a shotgun off the rack.

"Let's see what's going on. Could just be rowdy ranch hands."

"That happen often?"

"Once in a while."

Nika nodded and laid the rifle across the crook of her arm, ready to swing it on target in a hurry.

"Could just shoot 'em."

"How bout we find out who they are first?"

"It's your show."

Other than the warehouse, the bar-slash-restaurant was the biggest building in town. Built of local adobe, it had solid thick walls and stayed nice and cool during the hot summers. The doors stood open, letting the evening breeze in. They paused outside, standing to either side of the entrance.

"Just follow my lead."

She nodded and fell in behind him as he walked into the bar. There were few customers other than the three men at the bar, just a few townspeople sitting at tables. The three strangers were as dusty as their bikes. Guns hung from belts and slings.

"Evening, gents." Cline stood easily, shotgun canted over his shoulder. Nika prowled further into the room, widening the possible field of fire. "Mikey, what seems to be the trouble?"

The three men turned around, leaned back against the bar. One was tall, with long curly hair, and had been predictably known as Curly. The other two Nika had never heard names for. They were twins, both short and stocky. Liked to use their fists and were brutal fighters. Rather beat a person to death than shoot them.

"Why, Sheriff, there's no trouble. Just been talking to our new friends here," Curly said. "Ain't that right, Mikey?"

The bartender looked over their shoulders at the sheriff, who nodded. He hesitated, one hand resting under the bar. "They done beat up John over at the store, took whatever they wanted."

Curly smiled. "Oh well that was just a misunderstanding." He glanced over toward Nika, one hand scratching his belly near his pistol. "Interesting company you keep, Sheriff. A dead woman."

Nika stepped forward, swinging the rifle and shooting from the waist. The bullet caught one of the twins, knocked him into Curly, who was drawing his own piece. The bartender ducked down behind the bar and the remaining customers bolted for the door.

"Goddamnit," Cline said, lifting the shotgun and firing. The blast threw Curly back into the bar. He slumped to the floor, gun dropping from his fingers. The remaining outlaw fired his rifle, laser slicing into Cline. He yelled and stumbled back, knocking over a table and taking cover behind it. He shifted to aim at Nika, who had lifted the rifle to her shoulder. They both fired.

The twin's body slumped over his brothers. She worked the bolt and sat the rifle down, drawing her pistol. She walked over and kicked their guns away. Curly was coughing, blood leaking from the corner of his mouth. Nika pointed the pistol between his eyes.

Cline put a hand over the gun and pushed it down. "Don't."

She looked at him.

"He'll be dead soon enough, anyway."

Nika nodded and lowered the pistol. "How are you?"

"Just a graze. I got a first aid kit over at the jail." He looked down at the bodies. "Goddamn. I hate when it goes this way."

"Better them than us. Why don't you go patch yourself up? I'll see if Curly has anything to say."

He nodded, hand clutched to his side. Nika figured it was more than a graze but didn't say anything. He probably knew as much as she did about patching wounds, anyway. She grabbed the bottle of whiskey left on the counter and took a pull. The pain meds were wearing off and she didn't have any more. Too much movement too soon. She wished shoulder wounds were as easy as the action holos made them out to be.

Cline leaned against the wall, looking out the window. Headlights moved over it, they could hear the motors of bikes and transport trucks in the distance. "I think I know where the gang is."

She looked out. The vehicles were coming down the hill above the town. "We got a few minutes. Mikey, you still behind that bar?"

The bartender popped his head up. "Yeah?"

"Go get everybody up and in here. Be the easiest place to defend. There's any guns in that store, have 'em bring 'em along.

"Go," she barked when he hesitated, looking at the sheriff. Cline nodded and Mikey ran out the door.

"I'll go get that first aid kit and any guns you got in that jail, Sheriff."

"Gonna move okay with that leg?"

"Adrenaline's a hell of a drug."

• • •

They loaded and laid out rifles. Pulled in the shutters on the bar's windows. Mothers sat cradling children while older kids stayed with their fathers, swearing they knew how to use a gun. Nika stayed in the background, letting the sheriff take over, talk to the people, calm them. She had her rifle slung over her shoulder, and had grabbed another pistol which she holstered at the small of her back, and took one of the small laser rifles.

Cline caught up to her near the back. "I just got a message from the governor. They've formed the ranger squad and they're sending them here."

"How long?"

"Dunno. But it means help's coming. We just got to hold out until then."

She nodded and opened the back door.

"Where are you going?"

"I'm no good in here. Need to be out there where I can move around."

He nodded and opened the door. "I suppose one person don't make much of a difference if you're just taking off."

"Why would I do that?"

"Bounty hunters aren't known for sticking their necks out for others."

"Trust me," she said and closed the door behind her.

The gang had moved in now, vehicles parked around the town. They were moving through the houses, cursing when they found them empty. Nika crept between homes, sticking to the shadows. The sheriff's office was closest to the docks and warehouses. Coming up from the river was a big clear square, the bar and store and some other buildings all around it.

"Just take what you can find. Money, jewelry, whatever."

It was two of the gang, shoving open the back door of the store.

"Maybe I can find something other than a MRE to eat."

"Psst."

They turned around and Nika opened up with the laser rifle, dropping both. Then she ran past the store into the darkness behind the next building. Shots were being fired at the bar now, and returned from inside. She quickly patted down the bodies, slipping a mobile device into her pocket, and moved on.

There was another group in front of the repair shop. They'd found some beer in a fridge inside and were just watching their buddies firing at the bar. Neither side seemed to have hit anything yet. She leaned around the corner and started shooting. Those that didn't go down jumped for cover. A shot hit the building next to her head, driving splinters into her face.

Nika dropped back, blood running down her cheek. At least it missed her eye. Shots smacked into the building from two different directions and she ran down the side, moving in behind the shop. They knew she was out there now.

She slid down to the ground and cut a strip off the sleeve of her duster, tying it around her head. Crawling to the edge, she looked around. Nika was half surprised the gang just hadn't tried blowing the bar up with everyone in it, but maybe Lyla was figuring on a nice payday selling them all into slavery. How long could they hold out? And how long would the woman's patience and desire for profit last?

Lights were being flipped on now. The vehicles, and some big search lights they set up. Trained right on the bar. Would make it hard to see out, to shoot anybody. And to get any sleep.

"Listen, all you idiots just walk out of there. You're just delaying the inevitable."

It was Lyla, speaking through a loudspeaker on her vehicle. The slavers had stopped shooting so she could be heard, and the defenders inside stopped to conserve ammo. Lyla stood behind the door, one foot on the running board. She was a tall woman, somewhere around six foot. Her black hair was cut short and she was dressed in military gear. Pistol on her belt, rifle hanging from a sling.

"Oh, and Nika, why don't you quit shooting my boys? I know, I know, why should you?" She lowered the mic and said something to the man beside her. He went to the back of the truck and dumped two people to the ground. Hoods covered their heads and their hands were cuffed behind their backs.

"Why? Well, if you don't, I'll just shoot your friends here." The hoods were yanked off and Doc and Sally blinked at the sudden harsh light. "Shame. I kinda like the looks of the blonde. So what do you say? You know how this goes. Tell those folks to put their guns down and step on out. Make it easier on themselves."

Nika pulled out the mobile, watching Lyla. "Go fuck yourself."

The gang leader laughed. "You should have stayed dead."

"Wasn't my choice."

"There's no money in this for you. Just go away and I'll forget how you stabbed me in the back."

"I was the one thrown over a cliff."

"And you know why! You could've ran all this with me and—no. I'm going to finish the job. Who wants to live looking over their shoulder? Drop that sniper rifle and walk down here or I'll shoot Blondie in the head."

"Why should I?"

Lyla stepped behind Sally, shoving the barrel of her pistol into the woman's head. "You want to try me?"

"And get shot for my troubles?"

"Nobody will shoot you." She lowered the mic and raised her voice. "You hear that? Nobody shoots Nika, she's all mine. There, better?"

"No guns. You're always talking about how tough you are. Just fists. I want to knock that fucking smirk off your face."

"You're on." Lyla tossed the mic back in the vehicle and slipped the rifle off and laid it on the seat. Then she unbuckled her gunbelt and sat it next to the rifle. She held her arms out, as if to say come on.

Nika laid her rifle down and stepped out into the lights. She made a show of dropping the laser rifle and the .45 to the ground. "How's that?"

Lyla closed up the distance between them. "Maybe after I've finished you, I'll shoot the blonde anyway."

"So why hit the town? It'll just get the army on your ass."

Lyla laughed and threw a punch. Nika ducked but it caught her right on the wounded shoulder. She yelled out and dropped to the ground, kicking out at Lyla's knee. The taller woman stepped back out of reach then back in to kick Nika in the ribs, back to the shoulder. She grinned down at the writhing bounty hunter.

"Hardly, sweetheart. It's all about money, and I've got protection. There's a lot of ore or gas or some shit sitting under all this land and somebody wants it. Thought it was a job you were going to be helping me on, but well things turned out differently, eh?"

She threw another kick but Nika caught her leg and lifted, tossing the other woman to her back. Jumped on top of her, throwing punches with her good arm. Lyla swung her legs up and pushed her off, grinning.

"You always were fun."

Nika grunted, watching from a crouch as Lyla easily rose to her feet. They crashed together, throwing fists, swinging knees. Lyla targeted Nika's wounded shoulder, Nika trying to deal out as much damage as she could. Lyla had the height and reach on her but Nika outweighed her by a good bit.

The gang was watching as closely as the sheriff and the others from inside the bar. Weapons lowered or even set down. They whooped and hollered, shouted out bets.

"I'm disappointed," Lyla gasped out. She was astraddle Nika, hands wrapped around the bounty hunter's throat. "You have such a reputation."

Nika gripped the other woman's hands, squeezing around them and pushing them off before head-butting her. Lyla slumped to the side, blood gushing from her nose.

"This is the New Laramie Rangers! Hands in the air now!"

A few of the slavers looked ready to jump but thought better. They dropped their weapons and put their hands up high. The townspeople in the bar cheered when the armored rangers stepped into sight.

Nika drew a small pistol from the small of her back. "I was just waiting." She shoved the gun against Lyla's head and fired. She snatched Lyla's comm device as she fell back, staring up at the sky.

• • •

Nika leaned on a cane with her good arm, the other freshly bandaged and in a sling. Doc had patched up the rest of her wounds before moving on to help others. A few of the townspeople, and even a couple of the gang who hadn't died right off. She'd shook her head at that one, but he'd just said it was the right thing to do.

The rangers were busy shackling the gang and getting them ready to travel to New Laramie for trial, gathering up weapons and the like. Nika figured it'd be easier to just shoot them, but nobody asked her.

The captain walked over to her, pulling off her helmet. Long dark red hair fell loose and she ran a hand over her brow. "I'm Captain Stearns. I hear you're responsible for all this."

"Well, I shot a few," Nika said. "The ones who were kidnapping, slaving and murdering people."

Stearns grunted and passed her a small data drive. "That certifies the kills. They pay out in New Laramie. I'm sure you know there's a spaceport there. You can book passage, buy your own ship, whatever you prefer."

"That a hint, Captain?"

"I don't like bounty hunters. Wherever you go, death is right behind you. I want to put these people on trial and send them to prison where they belong, find out who is pulling the strings."

"There's just one problem with that, Stearns. Lyla Thompson had protection from up high. She wouldn't make it to trial. And if you did get her to prison, she'd just be running things from there. The galaxy is better off with her dead."

"Tell me who those people are and we'll go get them."

"Right. You know, I've done things I'm trying to make up for. Figured everybody was always out for themselves. Somebody showed me that wasn't true, helped me out when they didn't have to. Well, now it's my turn."

"And what does that mean?"

"These were bad guys, sure, kidnapping and selling people. But the people who bought the slaves, who visited the brothels. They're even worse. And that's something I can do to help out for a change. Protect people from these scum."

• • •

The bar was a big gaudy place. Half-naked dancers of various sexes and species gyrated on raised platforms. The walls practically vibrated from the loud music. Nika moved through the crowd quietly, finding a table that gave her a view of the entrance.

It's taken about three weeks, and her arm healed up on the journey. The hair's grown out a bit, and she picked up some new clothes. Armored black leather. Supposed to be good in a wreck or gunfight, something about diffusing kinetic energy.

She had barely dropped into her seat before a waitress appeared, placing down a complimentary drink. "Is there any entertainment you're interested in?"

Nika laid Lyla's comm device on the table, glancing over at the entrance. "Oh no. I'm just waiting for someone." A man had just walked in, flanked by two men. He moved to the bar, a path magically appearing. Nika picked up the comm to send a message.

"There's my friend now. How about bringing another drink for him?"

THE LIGHT-BRINGER

Laura K. Curtis

It began with a dress. A white cotton affair with a tight bodice trimmed in eyelet and a full skirt that belled out around my knees when I pirouetted in the great hall at Rockhaven, it was the first newly store-bought item of clothing I'd ever owned. My mother gave it to me for my birthday that March. Fifteen was time to grow up, she said, to learn to be a lady rather than a ragamuffin. Mrs. Smithson, owner of the grand old Victorian ramble where my mother was housekeeper, had laughed at the comment. I think she quite liked my tomboy ways, but she bought me a string of lustrous pearls, the most purely beautiful thing I'd ever seen, to go with the dress.

We were a household of women. Male gardeners managed the small crop of fruit trees that blessed us with peaches and plums in the summer and apples and pears in the fall. Men tended the flowers, too—in the large cutting bed of annuals populated by geranium, snapdragon, larkspur, gladiolus, and zinnia—and kept the lawn and hedges neatly trimmed. But the separation of church and state had nothing on the separation of house and garden. The men rotated through, but the women in the house were my sun and moon.

Mrs. Smithson had hired my mother fresh off the boat to care for her infant son, Matthew. As long as wealthy American women had babies, my Aunt Caítlín used to say, Irish girls would never want for work. But little Matthew Smithson died in a polio outbreak at only three years old and Mr. Smithson was shot in the back six months later walking home from his job on Wall Street. Mrs. Smithson sold their apartment in the city and retired to Rockhaven, their big, empty house in Roaring Brook, New York, an hour and a half north of the city she could no longer stand. She brought my mother with her to serve as housekeeper and companion, and gave her private quarters at the back of the house.

I was born after all those tragedies. After my mother's own tragedy—the death of my father at the hands of Germans in a country so distant that even Mrs. Smithson's money could not bring him home for burial—had bonded the two women in a dark sisterhood. The two of them were my guides, my co-mothers, and they agreed on almost everything except when it came to me.

"Be careful," my mother would warn as I tore through the house on my way outside to dig for the elusive treasure hidden by one of Mrs. S's ancestors. "Remember your place. This is not your house."

"But of course it is," Mrs. S would say. And once, when I was about twelve, she went even further. "One day," she told me when we were alone in the sitting room, "this will all belong to you. You must promise never, ever to sell it; it has been in my family for generations."

Naturally, I promised. For I knew nothing then of taxes, or maintenance, or the responsibilities of my own calling.

It was 1957, the summer of a thousand fires, or so it seemed to us. We were not blessed with rain, and the air raid sirens blared hour after hour, day after day, each blast signaling a new incident. The luncheonette burned to the ground when their ovens malfunctioned. Trains threw sparks into sere grass which could smolder for hours before suddenly, shockingly bursting into flame. A brush fire claimed eight acres before firefighters from six separate townships drove it into the reservoir. Were it not for that aqueous bulwark, the conflagration might have consumed all of downtown.

By mid-July, we were all exhausted. The stream for which the town was named baked in its bed, a muddy trickle rather than a gushing flow. We prayed for relief, for mercy, for the souls of those lost to the ravening flames. We prayed for our neighbors and for ourselves and we wondered—or at least I did—what we had done to deserve God's wrath. For while it was everywhere hot and dry, no other town suffered as we did.

On that Sunday, thunder rumbled in the distance and in our separate houses of worship everyone in town begged God for a quenching storm to break the thick, sulfurous heat that made breathing a chore. We had been fooled before, when heavy clouds darkened the sky and lightning cracked in the air and scorched the land but rain fell only south and west of us, the sky emptying itself into the Hudson instead of upon the desperate soil.

After church, Mrs. S—who attended the Episcopal church the next town over—drove my mother home while I walked over to the library. Already at fifteen I had begun to doubt my mother's God. My heart rested more easily in the stacks than in pews, and the cool darkness of the small brick building provided more of a refuge for my restless spirit than did the grandeur of the spires at St. Jude's.

Perhaps I would not have noticed him elsewhere. Even the young have shields, after all, and for the most part I ignored those occasional, peculiar trickles down my spine. But when he brushed by me there in the stacks, where my guard was down and my heart open, the evil riding him reached out and formed a fist around my lungs. The blood chilled in my veins and my heart halted, then restarted sharp and painfully fast. The thick black glow surrounding him tugged me along in his wake, and I followed him out of the library and across the street to the ruined, condemned luncheonette. He pushed aside one of the boards covering the hole where the plate glass window had stood and slipped inside.

And the world exploded. The spell of his evil broken, I spun around to see the library on fire. Almost, almost I went back. But the air raid siren was already sounding, calling the firefighters from their homes. They would do more than I could and a terrible curiosity held me beside the spot where the stranger had disappeared. I grasped the board in one hand, gathering the skirt of my dress in the other so I would not dirty it, and squeezed through the narrow gap into the gutted diner.

I would not be so careless today, but at fifteen I had no real understanding of my own mortality, of the fragile and pervious nature of the human form. The tickling odor of ash and rot clogged my nose and throat, and I clapped a hand across my mouth to stifle a cough. My eyes adjusted to the darkness, but the man was nowhere to be seen. A moment later, a shuffle and creak above me gave away his location. Marge and Henry Madson, who owned the place, had lived above the luncheonette until the fire stole their home as well as their business, and I set out in search of the stairs.

Before the blaze and those fighting it had done their damage, the Madsons would have had a separate entrance to get upstairs, but the wall between the restaurant and the hallway had fallen victim to axe, hose, and flame. I spotted the staircase, lit by a flickering light from the top, beyond the gaping hole. Crawling across the melted banquette of a booth to get to the stairs, the first doubts began to creep through me, but I was too far gone to heed them and the lure of answers seduced me up the stairs.

The door at the top of the steps hung askew on its hinges and I poked my head inside the large, open room. Light eased in around skimpy boards over glassless window casings, casting flickering, twitching shadows over the space. The stranger knelt, face pressed against the windowspace, arm at a peculiar angle. His body seemed misshapen, and it was not until some breath or sound alerted him to my presence and he turned that I realized why: at his shoulder, he held a rifle. Beside him, the floor was littered with guns both long and short.

Time slowed, dragged, eventually halted as I stood there, assaulted by the images in his mind. His past and his intentions blended together in a burst of flame and gunfire and crippled, dying bodies. Even now the sirens approached, firefighters heading for the burning library. He would kill them all, and there was nothing I could do to stop him.

But his eyes swept over me and the picture in his head changed. Where anger burned, now fear took hold. Fear of me with my pale skin and blonde hair and white dress. In a reflexive action, he crossed himself and backed away from me.

"Eibhlín," he whispered. The syllables ran through me like twin daggers of ice, for it was my name. Eibhlín, the light-bringer. But how could he know?

"*Fan amach ó dom*," he muttered, and I understood. He was not speaking my name, but the language of my mother. *Keep away from me*. How must I appear to him, a pale figure in the ruined darkness? I stepped toward him slowly, deliberately, and he stumbled backward. I herded him—to this day I swear it was unconscious—a step here, a hop there, a delicate dance pushing him back toward the gap where the wall sagged away from the floor.

One final move and the weakened and rotting floorboards cracked and split and splintered beneath his weight. Arms windmilling, he fired two shots as he crashed through the floor, one passing so close to my face its hot breath kissed my skin, the other slamming into the ceiling and bringing down a shower of plaster. He screamed as he fell, a high, whining wail that pierced my eardrums in the wake of the shots. But for all the violence of sound and motion in the room, the ululating wail of the sirens and the crackle and roar of the flames consuming the library held the attention of everyone outside our private universe.

Or maybe the universe was mine alone, for I could no longer see the stranger. He had disappeared through the hole in the floor. The gun had gone with him and I approached with belated caution to peer down into the void. He lay below me on his back, arms outstretched, the rifle mere inches from his fingers. His eyes were open, light falling across them from the cracked boards over the window, but he was too still to be alive.

I scurried down the stairs and made my way toward him. I had seen dead people before—in their coffins, once the mortician had made them up—but still I was surprised at how much color remained in his cheeks. And then he turned his head to look at me. Somehow, he had survived.

"*Go raibh*—" he coughed. It was inconceivable, but he was trying to thank me. It was there in his eyes, too. "*Téigh i sábháilteacht*." *Go in safety*. His eyes blinked, then shut for good. I went, his blessing ringing in my ears.

Out to the sidewalk, where the town had gathered to watch the firefighters work. No one even noticed me slipping out of the luncheonette. And later, much later, when I got home to Rockhaven, the stains on my white dress were forgiven in the excitement of the fire and the relief that I had escaped unharmed. The body was found three days later, but there was never any investigation. The papers never even listed his name. The man was a drifter, a miscreant who had holed up with a bunch of weapons in a condemned building and come to a bad end. The discovery took second place in the papers to the fact that on that very same day the rains finally rolled through, breaking the relentless heat.

• • •

He was my first. There have been many since, and a few have even thanked me. But although several have affected me more deeply than he, I have never forgotten that stranger in the first summer of my adult life, the summer I first heard the call.

THE ADVENTURES OF HERCULES
SPAWN OF THE TITANS

Michael A. Black

Prologue:

It was a time of mythological gods and powerful men ... Tales of epic adventures and titanic legends ... The fantastic deeds of heroes and villains ... These stories were told over and over growing into the myths and legends of the great heroes ... And one such man, who born of mortal woman, but sired by a god, was the most magnificent hero of them all ...

The man who was known as Hercules.

Hercules, whose true father, Zeus, was the supreme god of ancient Greek mythology ...

Hercules, who roamed the lands, righting wrongs, helping the weak and oppressed, and seeking adventure ...

Hercules, the mightiest of mortal men.

It is of his deeds we tell now ...

Of his struggle against the spawn of the titans.

• • •

In the waters off ancient Greece ...

The flaming ball hurtled through the air, the hissing noise sounding like an enormous hornet.

"Hercules," Ulysses said, his youthful voice betraying the sudden fear he felt. "They're using their catapult on us. It's Greek fire."

The woven straw mat next to him stirred and a massive hand curled it downward so Ulysses could see the handsome, bearded face. "The arc is too high to hit us. It's meant to travel overhead. To block us in so they can loot us." He pulled the mat back over his head, and Ulysses watched as the projectile passed over the bow of the *Argos* and exploded on the surface of the water next to them. A wall of flame immediately shot upward from the rough sea, making escape from the approaching vessel virtually impossible.

"You were right, Hercules," Ulysses said, marveling at his teacher's calm demeanor in the moments preceding the impending battle.

"Of course he's right," a second man, Theseus, said. He was under another straw mat, but poked his head out to speak. The man was incredibly handsome. "After all, he *is* Hercules."

Young Ulysses caught the leering stare of the enormous man on the other ship's bow. Metallic bands encircled his muscular arms and an armor plate over his chest. Their eyes locked and Ulysses felt a shiver go down his spine as the man unsheathed his sword and licked his lips. It's the look of a falcon about to descend on a pigeon, he thought, then smiled. But this pigeon has claws, and an eagle beside it. He glanced to his right at the massive figure covered by the coarsely woven straw mat.

"Hercules, the big one on their bow looks like he's anxious to draw blood," Ulysses said.

"The only blood he'll see will be his own," Hercules said. "Now, fit an arrow into that bowstring and get ready to show me that all I've been teaching you hasn't been wasted."

Theseus pulled down his straw mat and muttered another complaint. "Must we endure this ignominious subterfuge any longer? This mat is making me sweat before I've even used my sword once."

Hercules chuckled. "We can't afford to tip our hands by shooting them at this distance. We've spent too long as bait to allow them to turn and run." He pulled the huge woven mat down far enough to expose his smile. "Remember, we want them to be drawn into our trap, and besides, there are no fair maidens around to be upset by your ungainly fragrance."

"Yes, Hercules," Theseus said, his disappointment obvious. "And I suppose you want me to spare the big fellow so you can break him in half yourself?"

Another round from the catapult struck their bow, but this one had not been lighted. Moments later the *Argos* lurched to the side, accompanied by a resounding cracking of wood as the two vessels collided.

"Surrender or die!" the large man yelled as he jumped onto the deck of the *Argos*. He turned and glared at Ulysses with a long look of appraisal. "I like tender young morsels. I shall take you as my personal slave until we get to Oceania."

Ulysses grinned back knowingly as several more pirates jumped onto the deck brandishing swords. "Come and get me then," he said. "If you can."

The leader advanced toward him, cocking his hand back. "I like to sample my meat before I devour it."

Ulysses stood, holding his bow and arrow down by his side.

"You have a weapon and are afraid to use it?" the advancing pirate said. "You must be a ewe instead of a ram." He raised his sword, its thick blade showing the stains of many stabbings.

Hercules threw off the mat and grabbed the man's wrist, spun him around and gave his buttocks a kick. The leader of the pirates recovered well, whirling with sword in hand. His eyes widened as he obviously saw the magnificently proportioned man who was suddenly before him.

"I give you back your ultimatum," Hercules said. "You surrender, or die like the vermin you are."

With a barbarous cry, the leader lifted his sword and rushed forward, as did his other men. Hercules sidestepped and drew his own weapon. Ulysses jumped back to watch the battle's progress. It is not prudent, he thought, to challenge the son of Zeus to physical combat. Hercules was the strongest man he'd ever known. And the most heroic. By all accounts, he was more god-like than man. Ulysses had begged his father, Laërtes, to allow him to accompany Hercules on this adventure. His father had relented after Hercules had assured him that no harm would come to the young man.

An arrow whizzed by Ulysses' head and he crouched down. Hercules and the big pirate leader were facing off about ten feet away.

The two swords clashed at the arc of their respective swings. The pirate leader stumbled back a step, then regrouped to swing again. Theseus, in the meantime, had sent two arrows whizzing into the ribs of the closest pirates. Ulysses watched as the men's swords clashed to the deck and they curled into submission. He turned his attention back to Hercules and the pirate leader. The leader was big, almost as big as Hercules, and the man was obviously an experienced fighter. Hercules blocked the man's thrusting movement as easily as if he were cutting a cluster of grapes from a vine. The big pirate grimaced, then raised his sword high above his head, jumping in to deliver a lethal blow. Hercules caught the man's sword arm in his left hand and smashed his sword's pommel into the pirate's nose, which erupted with blood. Recoiling, the man stumbled backward, his once fearsome leer now reduced to a crimson pulp. Ulysses watched as the muscles of Hercules' arm swelled like huge boulders, squeezing the man's wrist until Ulysses was certain he heard the bones crack. The pirate's sword fell to the deck and he began to slump forward. Hercules then grabbed the huge pirate's leg and arm, lifting him overhead, and hurling him against the mast. The pirate slithered to the deck like a spent snake.

Turning, Hercules raised his arm in a signal to attack the pirate's ship. More Greeks, who had been squatting down against the side railings of the *Argos*, sprang into action, leaping up and onto the pirate's vessel. Ulysses nocked another arrow, pulled back the bowstring, and let it soar. The arrow hit an advancing pirate a glancing blow. The man grimaced, wiped at his torn shoulder, and began running toward Ulysses with an upraised sword. Ulysses jumped to the deck, avoiding the man's charge, and drew his own sword. Their blades clanged together. Realizing the man was far stronger, Ulysses backed away, parrying each thrust and sidestepping the more powerful swings.

"Ulysses, let me take him," Theseus yelled. "He's too strong for you."

Ulysses dodged another blow and this time brought his sword upward in a backstroke. The blade slashed across his opponent's shoulder, opening a huge gash. As the man paused, Ulysses shot forward, his sword held parallel to the deck, going between the pirate's arms and entering his sagging gut. He grunted and fell forward. Ulysses grinned and turned to Theseus.

"See, sometimes strength can be overcome by superior technique."

Theseus parried a thrust from his opponent and whirled, slicing the pirate's neck. As the lifeless body flopped to the deck, he turned back to Ulysses and pointed. "Tell that to Hercules."

Ulysses looked at the pirate's ship. The deck was now a shambles, with the villains jumping over the side as Hercules forced at least twenty of them backward over the edge of the prow by using an oar as a ram. A scant few minutes later, the brief battle was over, with Hercules directing his men to fish the pirates out of the water and chain them to their own oars.

"Their galley is full of captives," one Greek sailor said, opening the grate that led to the underbelly of the pirate's ship.

"Free them immediately," Hercules called. "And bring them onto our ship." He stepped off the pirate's deck and back onto his own. Turning, he watched the progress of the liberation. Hercules stood, his back to them, watching the captives, pale and malnourished, recoiling as they were brought into the bright sunshine. Ulysses marveled at the broad shoulders and tapered waist.

Suddenly Ulysses caught a flicker of movement to the side. He brought up his bow, with another arrow already nocked, in time to see the pirate leader cocking his arm back, ready to throw a knife at Hercules. Ulysses released the arrow, which went through the pirate's neck. The knife clattered harmlessly to the deck. Hercules turned and surveyed the scene, then walked over to Ulysses.

"And so you learn another good lesson," Hercules said, placing his hand on the younger man's shoulders. "In battle, mercy is a commodity to be used sparingly, if at all. Never drop your guard until the fighting is finished."

"In other words," Theseus added, his handsome features taking on a serious look, "save your posing for the sun goddess until you're sure your enemy is dead."

Hercules grinned and swatted Theseus' head. "Laërtes wanted me to teach his son how to be a noble warrior and king, and you fill his head with your ignoble morals." He turned back to the young man standing by his side. "But listen to what I am going to say now. I have taught you the bow and its uses for one reason. Remember these lessons well, for one day, a bow might well decide your fate."

Ulysses smiled. "I will, Hercules."

"And when we get back to Greece," Theseus added, "I'll introduce you to my friend Aesop to complete your education. He can write a fable about it."

They all laughed and watched as the surrendering pirates were lifted onto the deck and placed in chains.

• • •

Hours later, when all the captives had been fed and offered wine, Hercules, Ulysses and Theseus sat with one of them near the mast. The old man was dressed in rags, but seemed mesmerized by the simple act of looking over the side at the sunset.

"We heard them say that the younger ones had been taken to an island," the old man said. As he sat on the bench he leaned forward and rubbed the sores on his ankles. It was apparent he'd been shackled to the galley floor for quite some time. "They always take the young ones there."

Ulysses could see the concern edge into Hercules' expression.

"Where is this island, old man?" Hercules asked.

"I don't know. It's impossible to see the stars when you're locked below and chained to an oar. I would pray that some tempest would wreck us, drown us all, so that I may find peace." He smiled, showing a mouthful of rotten teeth. "And the gods be praised, the tempest came, and now we are free."

Hercules smiled and patted the man's shoulder. "You soon will be. This ship will take you and your fellow captives back to Greece. But I intend to find this island and put a stop to whoever's behind these raids. Who would know the location of the island?"

The old man raised his hands in a look of terror. "It's a horrible place, surrounded by foul mists and guarded by monsters. Please, I don't want to go back there. I couldn't stand it."

Hercules patted the old man's shoulder with a gentleness that belied the power Ulysses knew he had.

"I told you, you and the others will be transported back to the safety of Greece. But is there any of the pirate's crew who would know how to get there?"

The old man's fingers picked at one of his scabs. "Perhaps the navigator. If he survived."

"Would you know him?"

"I would." The old man shuddered. "An evil man with a scar running down his cheek." His finger tapped his forehead, then dropped down to his chin. "His left eye is as murky as mother's milk."

"Hercules, I think I saw that prisoner," Theseus said, standing. "Shall I fetch him?"

Hercules stood and rolled his shoulders, the big muscles dancing like thick ropes under his tawny skin. "Bring him on deck, but be quick about it. While we still have some light left."

Theseus grinned. "I can tell I'm going to enjoy watching this."

Hercules turned to Ulysses. "Now it's time for another lesson. How to ensure hostile cooperation."

Ulysses grinned. "I can hardly wait."

They ascended the steps to the deck of the *Argos*, Theseus going first, followed by Ulysses and then Hercules. When they emerged, Ulysses was shocked to see how dark it had become. The sun was like a far away orange globe, descending into the sea. "Are we really going to send the prisoners back to Greece?"

Hercules nodded. "They've suffered enough. But I gave Androcles my word we'd put an end to these incessant raids on our ships. We'll send the *Argos* back, and take the pirate's ship to their home base." They crossed over to the captured pirate vessel which had been lashed to the *Argos*. Theseus vaulted over the railing of the *Argos* and landed gracefully on the pirate ship's deck. "I'll get our friend from below," he said, and descended the ladder.

After a few minutes, Theseus ascended from the galley of the pirate's vessel, prodding a man with his sword. They approached and Hercules jumped over the rail of the *Argos* and landed on the other vessel's deck. He stood glaring down at the man Theseus held, then grabbed the man's dark beard and pulled his head upward. The man's mouth cocked open in defiance and pain, his left eye murky white, bisected by a thick scar which ran down his cheek.

"What's your name?" Hercules asked. From his tone, it was obvious he expected to be immediately obeyed.

"Notarus," the man said through clenched teeth.

"And so, my friend, I've been told that you were the navigator of this forlorn vessel."

"If you mean to kill me, get on with it," Notarus said. "Or is it your intention to make me beg?"

Ulysses watched as Hercules' face darkened.

"What I mean to do," he said, pushing Notarus' head away, "is find this island everyone is talking about."

Notarus spat on the deck. "You'll find it without me."

Ulysses watched as Hercules looked down at the spittle, smiled, then bent over, grabbing Notarus's ankle. He straightened up, holding the man upside down at arm's length. "You'd rather feed the sharks?" Hercules stepped over to the side, dangling the pirate navigator over the edge. Ulysses folded his arms on the railing and looked down at the darkening water slapping against the hull.

"No, no, please," Notarus screamed. "Don't drop me."

"You'll take us to the island then?" Hercules said.

"I can't. They'll kill all of us because we failed."

"Failed?" Hercules was showing no strain in holding the forlorn pirate. "At what?"

"Getting them the booty of slaves and young women. For he who rules."

"And you fear his displeasure more than mine?" Hercules began to swing the man back and forth, like a vase on the end of a rope. He let him smack against the hard wood of the ship a few times. "Your blood will attract the eating fish."

"All right, mighty one," the pirate screamed. "I will take you there. But please, don't kill me."

Hercules raised his arm up, lifting the man back over the side rail and then dropping him on the deck. "You give me your word that you will not betray your pledge?"

Notarus clasped his hands in front of his face and nodded, struggling to his knees.

"I give you my most solemn vow," he said. "But know this. Your quest is doomed to failure. The island is guarded by a fire-breathing sea monster. It guards the harbor and sinks ships unless you are allowed passage."

"And how are you allowed passage?" Hercules asked.

"Cleatus, the man you killed. Only he knew which signal to give on the horn. There were more than one, and the new one was prearranged by he who rules prior to each departure. Only Cleatus knew the right one."

"A signal," Hercules said. "And if the proper one was given, what then?"

"The monster would allow safe passage into the harbor." Notarus shook with terror. "Otherwise, the ship would be sunk."

Hercules looked at Ulysses and grinned. "This grows more interesting with each passing moment. I'm looking forward to meeting this sea monster who lives in the water, but has captured fire like Prometheus." He laughed.

Notarus cringed again. "You are indeed a powerful man, but he who rules on the island has more than power. He is like one of the gods themselves."

"Then let us meet this evil god who does harm to other men," Hercules said. Ulysses saw his smile widen as he raised his arms and yelled, "Let the challenge for justice begin."

• • •

Ulysses watched as Hercules stood at the bow of the ship with his massively muscled arm around Notarus's shoulders. The pirate navigator was obviously terrified of Hercules, and Ulysses knew that it was prudent to keep the man scared. If he weren't scared, he could lead them into a trap. But Hercules would never let that happen. Ulysses was sure of it. He moved closer so he could hear their conversation.

"We've been at sea for days now," Hercules said. "I'm beginning to think you're telling us the wrong headings."

Notarus cowered as the powerful hand squeezed his shoulder. "No, no, I'm not. I assure you. But the island is protected by the monster. And he who rules there. They are like the gods."

"I'm getting tired of hearing that." The edge in Hercules' voice sent a chill down Ulysses' spine. He could only imagine what the pirate felt.

"There are mists that cloud the island from view," Notarus said. "From the monster's breath. And those ships that pass through the mists are sunk with one flick of its enormous tail. Spikes that can rip through any vessel's hull like it was made of paper. The bottom of the harbor is laden with the remains of many ships, and many more dead men."

Hercules grew quiet, then he pointed. "There in the distance, are those the mists you're talking about?"

Notarus looked and his face became racked with terror. "Yes, yes. Now please, kill me quick. If he who rules finds out I've betrayed him, my fate will be worse than death itself."

Hercules held the man by his neck and turned toward Ulysses. "Find Theseus and take him below. Put him in chains."

Ulysses drew his sword and held it down by his leg, motioning Notarus forward. The man fell to his knees in supplication, his hands clasped in front of him. "I beseech you, please don't go there. You don't know their power."

Hercules grabbed the man by the neck and lifted him to his feet making Notarus look as light as a fallen leaf. "Didn't you tell us there are people enslaved on that island?" Hercules growled.

"Yes."

"Then fear their vengeance when I've set them free, you coward." With that, Hercules tossed Notarus face first onto the deck. Ulysses grabbed the pirate and walked him to the galley where two Greeks took charge of him. After sheathing his sword, Ulysses went back to the side of his teacher and idol. He wondered whether Hercules' decision to have the *Argos* return to Greece with the freed prisoners and majority of the crew was a wise one. Their number of able-bodied fighting men was only a handful now. If they found he who rules on the island to be as formidable as Notarus indicated, would they have enough force to confront him? Ulysses took one look at Hercules and smiled. He'd take those odds, however long they might be, as long as this god-like man was at his side. He was everything Ulysses aspired to be: respected and admired by men, desired and adored by women . . . And the finest teacher Ulysses had ever known.

Hercules looked deep in thought staring at the mist-filled waters ahead of them.

"You think he was telling the truth about the sea monster?" Ulysses asked.

Hercules stared down at him. "Men tell lies to explain what they do not understand. If enough lies are told, it is accepted as the truth."

Ulysses remembered the tales of the gods he'd been told since he was a small child. Tales of supreme beings who controlled the destinies of men on earth. Tales of fabulous creatures, some half-man, half-beast. But . . . Had he ever seen such a creature himself? He took a deep breath and looked at the cloud-like whiteness before them.

"I don't know," Ulysses said. "I understand what you're saying, but I have a strange feeling that something is waiting for us out there."

Hercules smiled. "And I've taught you to always listen to those feelings, have I not?"

Ulysses nodded. "So we should sail onward, heedless of Notarus's tale of a monster?"

Hercules considered the question before shaking his head slowly. "Most legends have some basis in fact." He held up his hand and ordered the prisoners to cease rowing. The command was given and after the oars were raised, the ship began to slow down. Soon, it drifted with the current.

Hercules still stood at the bow, his head bent slightly, eyes closed. Ulysses wondered if he was thinking, then Hercules said in a low voice, "Listen."

Ulysses cocked his head and concentrated. At first he thought it was the sound of the sirens, then the rhythmic beat, methodical and regular, became more distinct. It was the sound of waves hitting a beach. They were drifting close to land. Suddenly the thick whitish clouds that had seemed so distant before came floating closer. Ulysses sniffed the air. It felt heavy . . . acrid . . . hot. He coughed.

"Hercules, the air here—-"

"Some kind of white smoke. Which means these mists are man-made, not from some sea monster." He turned and walked back toward the cabins. "Where's Theseus?"

Ulysses smiled. "Sleeping, probably. Dreaming of one of his girlfriends."

Hercules smiled. "Then go wake him up. And don't ask him about his dreams. That will be a lesson best reserved for another time."

After a few minutes Ulysses was able to rouse his slumbering friend, who'd been snoring as he clasped a pillow against his chest.

"Come on," Ulysses said. "Hercules wants us on deck."

Theseus heaved a sigh, yawned, and nodded. As he rose from the hammock, he paused and yawned again. "A new world to conquer?"

Ulysses laughed. "Something like that." He raced through the door and climbed the ladder to the deck, his eyes flashing over the chained pirates next to the oars. They all had expressions of sheer terror on their faces.

"Please, we beg of you," one called out. "Don't leave us here to die. The monster will slay us all."

Ulysses stopped and looked through the space between the rungs. "We won't let you die. We're better than the likes of you. Now be quiet."

The smoky mists had begun to seep into this lower section, forming a whitish cloud in the air. Two of the closest prisoners exchanged looks, then their faces dissolved into panic. "We must be nearing the island," one said. "No, no, we'll all die a horrible death."

"Shut up," Ulysses said. "I told you. We're Greeks, not pirates. We don't murder people without provocation."

The cries continued as he moved up the steps and stepped back on deck. The foggy mist had enveloped most of the upper deck now. Hercules still stood at the bow, his head lowered, as if he were listening intently. Ulysses rushed to his side.

"Theseus is on the way," he said.

Hercules nodded.

"What are we going to do now?" Ulysses asked.

Hercules still didn't answer. Theseus joined them, his head tilting back in another extended yawn.

"I hope you got enough rest," Hercules said.

"I could use a bit more. Especially if we've got a battle to fight."

"You're going to wait before fighting any battles," Hercules said. "The first thing we must do is find who we'll be fighting against."

Theseus nodded. "Or what, from the sound of that madman's ravings." He looked around, then yawned. "But why don't we simply turn around and sail back to Greece? We can come back with an army of three hundred Spartans and turn them loose."

Hercules frowned. "From all accounts, there are people being held in slavery on that island. I intend to put a stop to their pillaging here and now."

Ulysses smiled. He knew Hercules wouldn't let innocent people suffer.

Theseus lifted his arms and stretched. "All right. What do we do next?"

"You stay with this ship," Hercules said. "Keep it just outside the area where we are now. Once the mists cease, you'll know it's safe to enter the harbor."

"Oh?" Theseus grinned. "You're going to slay this fearsome sea monster by yourself?"

Hercules smirked. "Just remain outside the mists. And once they have ceased and it's safe to enter the harbor, I'll find a way to signal you."

"But how are you going to know that, Hercules?" Ulysses asked.

"First," Hercules smiled, "you and I are going for a little swim. From the sound of the waves on the beach, it shouldn't be that far."

"Swim?" Ulysses said. "Couldn't we at least take a raft? There might be some kind of dangerous creatures in the water."

Hercules flashed a look of concern. "There will be." Then he smiled and picked Ulysses up, tucking him under his arm as he marched to the side and flipped him far out into the sea. "You and me."

• • •

Ulysses twisted in mid-air, positioning himself so that his body cut into the water like a knife. As the water rushed over him, he arched his back, stroking upward until he felt the air on his face. He shook his head and began treading water. Suddenly Hercules was beside him, swimming with powerful strokes.

"Follow me," he said.

Ulysses began paddling after him as quickly as he could, but there was no way he could keep up. The water was colder than he'd imagined. Certainly colder than those of Ithaca, where he'd grown up and first learned to swim, and its salty composition stung his eyes. He looked for Hercules, who was now far ahead. In a few more minutes he'd be by himself. The panic he'd seen in those captive pirates' faces now started to seep into his own mind. What if there really were some kind of monster lurking in these waters? What if Hercules and he got separated? Would he be able to make it to shore? Certainly Hercules would not abandon him out here. He wouldn't let him drown.

But what if he'd become turned around? Maybe he was swimming not toward shore, but farther out to sea...

Another wave immersed him and he struggled to get back to the surface. Spitting out the salt water he yelled. No answer. He yelled again. Still nothing.

Think, he told himself. Don't panic. Remember what Hercules has taught you. Do not fight the enemy. Find your enemy's strength and make it your own. Find his weakness and use that strength against him.

Another enormous wave propelled him forward, threatening to immerse him again.

The waves, Ulysses thought. They're moving toward the shoreline. If I can ride them...

He used a butterfly stroke to stay afloat, and rode the high crested wave forward. At the apex he swam ahead, catching the next incipient peak. It took him a few more times before he had the technique down, but he was able to conserve his own energy and let the rhythmic flow carry him toward land. It was growing almost too easy when his foot brushed against something heavy a few feet below him. Terrified that it was the sea monster the panic returned. Seconds later his foot hit the solid mass again, and this time he felt a sharp pain as something sliced into his leg.

Reaching for his sword, Ulysses somersaulted downward. If he could strike first and strike hard, perhaps he could scare the monster away, convincing it to look for a less ferocious meal.

He squinted through the murky water, watching for movement, but saw none. Yet he could see something... Something dark and extending out of sight beneath the surface. The monster's enormous tail, replete with fearsome spikes.

His heart began to hammer and his lungs felt like they were on fire, and he struck out with his sword. At least he would die fighting the beast. But his sword clanged against something so solid it jolted all the fear and panic out of him. The massive tail didn't move. He thrust his sword again, and once again heard the strangely familiar sound, muffled slightly by the encompassing water: the sound of metal striking metal.

Ulysses kicked upward to the surface, feeling the air caress his face as he broke through. He took a few quick breaths, and then dove downward again, straining to keep his eyes open and focused in the stinging water. He managed a few more strokes downward, then he saw what it was that had brushed against his foot: large metallic coils replete with pointed shards every few feet, had been stretched taut a few feet beneath the surface of the water. It was no sea monster's tail. It was a huge, spiked chain pulled taut beneath the water's surface, placed at just the right depth to pierce the wooden hull of an approaching ship. It would begin to take on water immediately, and no doubt be sunk before it could reach the shoreline. Those of the crew who escaped, would be captured when they swam to shore. The tales of some enormous beast, sinking ships, had spread, twisting into the legend of the sea monster Notarus had feared.

Ulysses kicked his legs, breaking the surface once more, then tried to sheath his sword. Another wave swept over him, and the awkwardness of his position caused him to miss the connection. The sword fluttered out of his grasp. Cursing, Ulysses dived down after it, but the weapon quickly sank out of sight.

If it's not too deep, he thought, I might be able to dive down to the bottom and find it. He took another deep breath and began to swim downward when he felt something clasp over his ankle, pulling him upward. Flailing his arms to get away, he felt the pressure on his ankle grow tighter. But he was being pulled upward, not down into the depths. He managed to twist his head enough to glance backward through the water and saw Hercules tugging at his leg. Relaxing, he arched upward and broke the surface.

"You're slipperier than an eel," Hercules said, grinning.

"I thought you'd left me."

"I wanted to see how you'd fare against the monster," Hercules said, treading water. "I take it you've learned something about the stuff smoke-breathing sea monsters are made of?"

Ulysses grinned. "How'd I do?"

"That remains to be seen."

Ulysses felt confused. He felt he'd done pretty well. Had he let his hero and mentor down? Then he remembered the sword. "I know, it's losing my sword. Wait here and I'll dive again and find it."

"Leave it," Hercules said. "Never waste time searching for a lost weapon. Your enemy will have you at an advantage because you're distracted."

"But it was a gift from my father."

Hercules's dark eyes flashed with a look that told Ulysses he was to be obeyed. "Here's another lesson. Leave sentimentality at home when you're facing an enemy. It's a luxury a warrior cannot afford." He began swimming. "We'll find a new one on the island. Now, come on. We must be close to shore."

Ulysses compressed his lips and swam after him.

• • •

The noise of the waves continued to increase, and suddenly the hovering mists vanished and ahead Ulysses could see the shoreline. He flipped over on his back and looked at the view of the towering rocks they had just swam past. Clouds of white smoke emanated from two outcroppings, one on each side of the inlet.

Hercules pointed. "There's your monster's nostrils."

Where there's smoke, there's fire, Ulysses thought, and if it's man-made, it must be a constant struggle to keep a blaze that size burning.

Ulysses flipped back on his stomach and increased his strokes. Hercules was already several lengths ahead of him. He propelled himself through the water like a fish, and at a speed that was fantastic. Of course, it helped that he never seemed to get tired. The fatigue of the long swim was beginning to affect Ulysses now. His arms and legs felt leaden. Like he would sink if he stopped, even in this buoyant saltwater. The waves crashed onto the sandy beach, and Ulysses rode a big one almost to the shore. His kicking feet felt the soft bottom and he began to walk, the water only up to his knees now. Hercules was already on the beach, standing and waiting. He stood with his hands on his hips, surveying. Ulysses looked at him with admiration, then saw a group of men on horseback riding toward them. Five of them. He ran the last few steps to warn Hercules of the approaching riders, but as he got close, his mentor raised his hand.

"I saw them," he said. "Offer no resistance until I tell you."

Ulysses nodded.

The riders, all clad in black armor and carrying long spears, circled them, holding the spears in striking position.

"Where did you two come from?" one of them asked. Ulysses could see his light colored eyes, the color of the sea, through the slit in the face of his helmet.

"Our ship was attacked by some kind of sea monster out there," Hercules said. "It started to sink. We jumped overboard and swam for our lives."

The helmeted rider glanced toward the fog and grinned. "How many more of you are out there?"

Hercules shrugged. "I'm not sure. Praise the gods that we were able to make it to shore. What place is this?"

"The place where you're going to spend the rest of your lives," the helmeted rider said. He prodded Hercules with the tip of the spear. "You're strong. You'll do well in our service."

"We're no one's slaves," Hercules said.

The helmeted rider laughed. "Keep your eye out for any more stragglers," he said to a second helmeted rider. "We'll take these two to the palace."

The other rider nodded, saying nothing.

The first rider nudged Hercules again with the spear. "Move that way. Do it now."

Ulysses was waiting for Hercules' signal, but instead of fighting back, he merely began walking. It wasn't like the son of Zeus to allow some ruffian to push him around. But that time would come, Ulysses knew, and when it did, he'd be ready to fight.

• • •

"Where are you taking us?" Hercules asked.

They'd walked some distance away from the beach, and were moving toward a dirt and stone road that led between two tall sections of the surrounding mountains. Ulysses noticed that Hercules had been looking around. He'd probably spotted the two peaks from the outcropping of rocks that they'd swum past. The steam and smoke seemed to originate from these two points.

"Just keep walking," the helmeted rider said. "And no talking."

Hercules turned and stared up at the man. "I think I'd rather ride."

The four horsemen laughed. One of them raised his long spear and jabbed it downward, toward Hercules' shoulder. "You need a lesson in manners, slave."

As the spear moved toward him, Hercules grabbed the end of it and tore it from the rider's grasp. The man grunted as Hercules shoved the hilt upward, catching the rider in the throat. He reeled backward, falling off his horse. The other riders immediately charged Hercules, who now held the spear in the middle. He blocked the first rider's thrust, then struck the man with the sharpened end of the spear. Whirling, he brought the other end of the spear upward in a flash of movement, clubbing the next rider's helmet. This man brushed off the blow and circled on his horse. The first rider got to his feet and whipped out a sword, running toward Hercules. The other two riders charged him as well. Ulysses saw Hercules hold the long spear out in front of him. The tremendous muscles of his arms flexed, and the spear broke in half. Spinning between the approaching riders, Hercules stabbed upward with the two ends of the spear, one in each hand, and impaled the two riders, lifting them out of their saddles. He turned and dodged a blow from the man on the ground. Ulysses ran toward one of the downed riders, hoping to grab a sword he could throw to Hercules. The closest rider writhed on the ground, the end of the spear protruding from his ripped gut. The sight and smell of the roiling intestines disgusted Ulysses. He'd never seen such a sight before, but he bent down and gripped the handle of the sword, unsheathing it. Whirling, he called out to Hercules and threw the sword into the air.

Hercules grinned as he caught it, parrying the man's next thrust. The helmeted soldier paused, and for a moment, looked like he might flee. But there was nowhere to go. The man charged again. Hercules reached out, snaring the man's upraised hand with his left hand, and, with his right, drove the sword into the man's abdomen all the way to the hilt. The point of the sword burst through the back of the metallic armor along with a gush of blood. The man slumped forward.

Ulysses watched the man's last breaths, knowing that they would have done the same to Hercules and him if the gods had so decided. Then the sounds of fast moving hooves alerted him. He turned to see the fifth rider, the one they'd left on the beach. Obviously he'd seen the battle and was coming to help his companions. Ulysses' eyes widened. Instead of riding toward them, this last soldier was fleeing, galloping off in the direction they'd been heading.

"Hercules, that one's running away," Ulysses called.

Hercules was already picking up one of the long spears that the dead rider had dropped. The fifth rider was pressing his mount. It would be doubtful that he and Hercules could catch the man with such a lead. He turned to see what Hercules was doing.

Hercules was bouncing the spear in his hand, testing the balance and weight.

"Are we going to let him get away?" Ulysses asked. "If he gets to the palace, won't he alert more soldiers?"

"Let him run," Hercules said. He gripped the spear in his right hand, and held his left arm out in front of him, assuming a classic javelin-throwing pose. Ulysses watched as Hercules remained motionless. The rider was almost out of sight now, a tiny black dot on the road leading between the peaks. "He won't be able to outrun this."

Ulysses felt the brush of wind as the spear sailed upward, out of Hercules' grasp. It arced, like a sent arrow, reached its apex, then began a downward descent. The black dot that was the fifth rider continued to move, so small now that he could barely be seen. The spear had disappeared as well.

Suddenly, in the distance, the rider fell from his horse, which kept going. It was far, but Ulysses could see the long spear sticking straight up, marking the place where the fifth rider had fallen.

"Hercules, that was the greatest shot I've ever seen with a spear," Ulysses said. "If I hadn't seen it with my own eyes, I would never have believed it possible."

Hercules looked grim. "Still, a horse without a rider making it back to their palace will alert them to trouble." He pointed to the two abutments from which the white smoke and steam emanated. "Let's take care of those two places first. Once Theseus has landed, then we'll have some reinforcements."

He kicked over one of the dead soldiers. "This one looks about your size. Try on his armor."

Ulysses smiled. Let the adventure begin, he thought.

• • •

Ulysses, clad in the armor and helmet, pretended to prod Hercules with the spear as they walked down the long corridor toward the tunnel's end. Finally, a few hundred feet away, the bright flickering told them they were nearing the tremendous fires. The heat was almost unbearable, even at a distance. A large man sat eating the remnants of a cooked pig, its skeletal remains a protrusion of bones devoid of meat. He looked up as they approached and grinned.

"What have we here? Another slave?" He tossed the half-eaten leg onto the table and rubbed his hands together. They looked filthy. "And a strong one, too, from the looks of him. He'll keep the fires going round the clock, till he collapses."

Hercules, whose powerful arms looked as if they were secured by a thick staff, looked down at the ground. The man moved forward and grabbed a whip from a peg on the wall, letting it uncurl like a huge snake.

"I like to give them a taste of my whip," he said. "Shows them who's boss."

Hercules moved forward, Ulysses right behind him. As they were a scant six feet away, the man flicked his wrist and the whip split the air.

Ulysses waited, still concerned about Hercules' orders not to give up their ruse until they were sure how many foes they faced. His hand gripped the spear as tightly as he could manage, ready to plunge it into the big jailer at the first opportunity.

The whip shot outward, snapping against Hercules' bare shoulder. When he didn't flinch the jailer seemed surprised.

"Oh, a tough one, eh?" He drew back and started another strike, but before he could bring his arm forward Ulysses stepped forward, jamming the spear into the jailer's overflowing belly. It felt like he were pushing through a giant grape. The jailer's tongue sagged out from between his lips and his eyes showed disbelief. Hercules had the staff in his hands now, and rushed forward, using it like a lance to bring down three more guards who had emerged.

"I told you to wait," he said as he stepped over the last prone guard.

"I wasn't going to let him hit you again," Ulysses said.

Hercules smiled.

Another guard emerged. "Who are you?"

Without answering Hercules jumped forward, grabbing the guard by the neck and the leg. He picked the man up, rammed his head against the wall, and used him as a human shield to enter the large room beyond. Two more guards were there standing over a pit where at least fifty men toiled. Some fed wood and tree branches into several large furnaces while others pushed an enormous set of bellows. The bellows blew the smoke out through some holes near the bottom of the far wall.

Hercules threw the guard he'd been carrying at the other two, knocking them to the ground. Ulysses quickly rushed forward and hit one of the fallen guards on the temple with the end of the spear, then brought the pointed end down against the other man's throat.

"Move and you're dead," Ulysses said.

The fallen guard looked up at him with terrified eyes.

The slaves continued to feed the huge fires and push the bellows. Ulysses watched their rote-like motions. The poor wretches were oblivious to their impending freedom.

Hercules strode among them gently stopping their unthinking movements. First one stopped and looked at the man-god, then another. Gradually, the motion ceased and the men stared blankly at their liberators with eyes more dead than alive.

"It is time to stop," Hercules said to the closest one. "You're free men once again."

The dazed look continued, and several of them tried to resume their tasks. Hercules walked back to Ulysses.

"They're possessed with madness," he said. The grim edge in his voice made Ulysses wonder if his mentor had once known such despair. He decided it was better not to ask.

Hercules walked over to a large barrel of water at the far end of the room. Stooping, he picked it up and carried it to the nearest fire. As he poured, the fire hissed and died with an outpouring of white smoke. Hercules went to the next fire and doused it as well. Perplexed, the army of robotic slaves finally stopped working and stared at him.

"I told you, you're all free now," Hercules repeated, but his words seemed to fall on deaf ears. This time, however, none of the slaves tried to continue their duties. Hercules grabbed the closest one.

"How do you lower the chain in the harbor?" he asked.

The man's mouth dropped open, exposing a gumline of rotten teeth. "Chain?"

"Never mind," Hercules said, and released the man's arm. He grabbed a torch and walked to the far end of the room where a large wheel had been mounted. The structure was perhaps as tall as two men, and wound around the sturdy center were the oversized metallic links that Ulysses had seen under water.

"Hold this," Hercules said, handing the torch to Ulysses. He then grabbed one of the extended wooden spokes and began pushing the wheel in a circle. As Ulysses watched the large chain unwound, lowering through the hole that had been cut into the wall. It was an endeavor that would most likely have to be accomplished by several normal men, but Hercules pushed it alone. "Check the visibility through one of those holes."

Ulysses went to the closest opening and peered out. The smoke was rapidly disappearing and the chain was now slack at the water's edge.

"I think it's passable now," he said.

Hercules pushed the wheel around one more time, then stopped. His body glistened with sweat, but he appeared no more winded than if he'd picked up a kitten. Ulysses glanced at his own stringy arms and wondered if he'd ever have arms as strong as Hercules.

One of the despondent men called out. "Powerful stranger, who are you?"

The voice came from within the ranks of the slaves. One lucid voice among the incessant babbling.

"I am Hercules of Thebes. This is Ulysses, son of Laërtes. We're here to help you."

The man emerged from the crowd. Ulysses saw his body was covered with a multitude of cuts and sores.

"I am Mavros. I come from Athens."

Hercules placed a hand on the man's bony shoulder. "And soon you shall return. Tell me, how many more soldiers guard this island?"

"There are as many as fifty," Mavros said. "But at least half of them departed to abduct more innocents from passing ships. They descend like pox, then rape and pillage."

Hercules frowned. "We've already put a stop to that. We have only to clean out this nest of vipers and take all of you back to the golden shores."

The man cringed. "To be so close to freedom after so long. But there is still he who rules. He is like a god, himself."

Hercules' brow furrowed. "That's the second time I've heard that. I want to make it the last."

The echoing sound of racing hooves, reverberated down the corridor, making Ulysses' ears perk up.

"Hercules," he said. But the man-god was already running back down the long tunnel. "Bring that bow and quiver," he called out as he grabbed a burning torch.

Ulysses grabbed the weapons and ran after Hercules, catching up to him at the mouth of the cave. The smoke was roiling over the water, but it had dissipated so much that Ulysses could see the pirate ship near the entry point of the harbor.

"Hercules, look." Ulysses pointed. A horde of armored riders, perhaps thirty or forty, approached in the distance, pushing their horses at a fast clip. "How are we going to notify Theseus that it's safe to enter?"

Instead of answering, Hercules handed Ulysses the torch and grabbed a long bow and single arrow. He tore a swath of cloth from his tunic, and wrapped it around the arrow's tip, leaving a dangling strip adjacent to the shaft. After nocking the arrow, he held the wrapped end into the burning flame. The cloth ignited and Hercules raised the bow upward, pulling back the string.

Is he aiming for the heavens? Ulysses thought.

Hercules released the arrow and it soared in a high arc, the ferocity of the flame exploding with brightness. Ulysses looked to the pirate ship and saw a similar flaming arrow dispatched in response. He grinned. "It worked, they saw it."

The riders grew closer. It was apparent they would arrive at the cave long before the ship made its way to shore. Ulysses was about to ask Hercules what they should do when he saw the man-god nock another arrow. He raised his arm and adjusted his aim. Another arrow whizzed from the bow. Ulysses watched as it arced and sailed toward the approaching riders. The lead man suddenly reeled backwards and fell off his horse.

"You got him!" Ulysses yelled.

Hercules was preparing another arrow. As he drew back the bow, Ulysses heard a strange rumbling sound. He glanced back over his shoulder at the shore line. His eyes followed it to the point where the huge chain descended into the water. The links were traveling upward now, back into the hole in the side of the high wall. Someone was tightening it.

"Hercules, the chain!" Ulysses called as the second arrow found its mark. Hercules looked back, then handed the bow to Ulysses.

"Take over," he said, and with that he ran down the embankment toward the retracting chain. Ulysses watched his progress as he moved along a series of jutting rocks and then dove into the water. Turning back to the approaching riders, Ulysses nocked an arrow of his own and brought the bow to the ready. Pulling back the string, he aimed and held, then released. The arrow sailed in a far smaller arc than the ones Hercules had shot. Ulysses arrow fell short of its target and seconds later the steeds' hooves rumbled over it.

Have to do better than that, Ulysses thought as he placed another arrow against the string. He took a deep breath, pulled against the tautness, and aimed. This time he remembered the lessons Hercules had taught him: control, aiming, allowing for the wind... He released the second arrow and it flew straight and true, striking one of the riders in the shoulder. The man tumbled down and under the flurry of advancing hooves.

We can expect no quarter from these adversaries, Ulysses thought as he watched the wounded rider being trampled by his own fellows. Turning back, he checked to see Hercules' progress. The man-god was emerging from the water next to the massive chain, which continued to retract. Hercules grabbed one of the oversized links and braced his legs against the rocks. The chain wound inward for a moment more, then stopped. Hercules stood like a pillar, stemming the retraction. The strain was obvious. The veins in his arms and neck writhed like serpents as he began to pull the chain back out of the hole.

Ulysses was amazed at the feat of strength, but went back to his task of firing at the riders. He sent two more men to their deaths by his quick aiming. The group had begun to slow appreciably, but was still advancing. Ulysses glanced back at Hercules.

The chain pulled inward a few feet, then Hercules managed to pull it back. Somehow the group inside the cave must have been recaptured and forced to turn the enormous gear wheel. Turning back, Ulysses fired three arrows, all true to his aim, at the riders. Three more men fell and the group veered off toward the beach.

They're trying to get out of range, Ulysses thought. But at least they've been temporarily slowed down. He wanted to yell to Hercules, and as he turned back he saw that the ship was rapidly closing on the area where the chain was strung.

They don't even know they're rushing toward danger, he thought. Yelling, he tried to warn them but to no avail. The ship continued its forward momentum toward the shoreline, and the jagged teeth of the mythological sea monster. Ulysses saw Hercules turn his head to check the ship's progress. There was nothing they could do. The ship couldn't stop at this point, and if it sunk, they would be trapped on this strange island for all time. Never to see Greece again... Never to see his parents... Never to know the love that his sweetheart, Penelope, had promised him...

Ulysses watched as Hercules let out a growl of anger. His body stiffened and the chain stopped retracting. The muscles of his arms and legs stood out like metallic bands of their own, and for a moment nothing else could be heard but the unceasing slapping of the waves on the rocks, and the grunting roar of the man-god. It seemed a picture painted by a master of an immoveable object confronted with an irresistible force. Then suddenly a cracking sound reverberated from deep inside the cave and the huge chain began to spill outward through the opening. Hercules was carried with it, down the slope upon which he'd stood, and into the water, the giant coils of metal falling on top of him.

Ulysses glanced back to see the riders hovering on the beach, ready to approach as soon as he had left his perch. He couldn't leave, but Hercules would surely drown if he didn't get help. Ulysses began scrambling down the embankment, holding his bow in one hand and the quiver of arrows in the other. Perhaps he could work his way to his mentor fast enough to help and still hold off the approaching hoard if they began to advance again. His foot slipped and Ulysses stumbled, falling several feet before landing hard on his side and then rolling down to meet the expanse of sandy beach. A wave washed up and snatched the quiver from his grasp. He was left with a bow, and no arrows.

Frantically, he searched the deepening water on his hands and knees for the quiver. He remembered Hercules' earlier admonition: don't waste time searching for a lost weapon. The water felt warmer than it had as it lapped about him, but then, from over his shoulder, a voice came that made his blood feel cold.

"Little man, you dare tweak a Titan's beard?"

Ulysses looked up and saw the tallest being he'd ever seen. He was practically two times the size of a regular man, and grotesquely proportioned with huge hands the size of bear's claws. Getting to his feet, Ulysses wondered which way he should run. Fighting this monster was unthinkable, but he withdrew his sword just the same.

The monster's head lolled back in what must have been something akin to a laugh. "I'll feast on your flesh, after I drink your blood." The giant moved forward and Ulysses sidestepped, slashing with the sword. The tip sliced a nick off one of the big fingers, causing the monster to stop. Trying to seize the moment, Ulysses dashed for higher ground. If he could stand even with the creature, perhaps his sword could find a vital area.

Another wave hit the shore, slowing Ulysses' movements and allowing the giant to deliver a swatting blow. Ulysses sailed several feet, hitting the ground with a splash as he came to rest. As he looked upward, he saw a massive foot descending toward his head. Twisting away, the appendage crashed into the sand next to Ulysses' shoulder. Scrambling, Ulysses tried to scurry away, but felt his lower leg being crushed in a powerful grasp. The next thing he knew, he was flying about thirty feet through the air.

Arms flailing, Ulysses tried to twist so he wouldn't land on his head. He struck the ground with his back and shoulder, the breath totally knocked out of him. Another wave of salt water swept over him and as his vision cleared, he saw the monster man standing over him. The huge hands reached out and tore a boulder loose from its perch. Raising it high over his head, the giant stepped forward.

Ulysses didn't think there was any way he could avoid such a devastating blow, but he summoned all his strength to flip to the side. The rock scratched his back and legs, but spared him the crushing injuries had it hit him flush. The giant was quick and delivered another glancing swat, sending Ulysses into a tumble once more. Gasping, Ulysses tried to right himself. In the last fall he'd lost the new sword he'd taken from the dead guard.

Losing my sword twice in one day, he thought, his mind doing a silly little dance with no place to go. Hercules would not approve.

Hercules, he thought. What would he tell me?

Ulysses felt another blow from the giant, harder and better placed this time. He rolled with the force of it, trying to minimize the impact, but he was spent. His arms and legs felt so heavy it was a labor to just try and stand. Still, he struggled to his feet, not wanting to face his doom in the position of a supplicant.

"Ah," the giant said. "You rise for more. But you are so little sport." He rubbed his massive hands together like two Spartan shields.

"Then perhaps I'd be more to your liking," a voice from behind Ulysses said. His ears rung, but the voice was so familiar, he would know it anywhere.

"Hercules," he managed to say.

His head spun like the last wobbling of a spinning top. He saw the water splashing around his arms, then his mighty friend and mentor was next to him, picking him up and carrying him through the water to the safety of the beach. Ulysses heard the snorting breaths of the grotesque monster pursuing them.

Hercules laid Ulysses down as gently as he could, then stepped back into the water to meet the giant's advance. The man-monster's lips curled back, exposing a row of crooked yellow teeth, more like an animal's fangs than a man's.

"Another tender morsel for my stew pot," the giant said. "You've got so much meat, you'll feed me for a week."

Ulysses watched as Hercules held out his arms, beckoning the monster forward. The giant was almost twice his size, and with a body that looked to be all sinew and bone. He extended his hand and grabbed Hercules by the head, twisting and sending the man-god several feet. Hercules rose to his feet, his even features showing no expression. He waited as the creature advanced again, long arms extended.

"This time I'll break your neck," the giant said.

As the man-monster began to bend forward, Hercules stepped inside the giant's grasp and grabbed the massive legs. Lifting, he flipped the giant up and over, causing the monster to land on his back with a tremendous splash. Droplets of the salty water hit Ulysses as he lay on his side watching the battle.

Furious, the giant scrambled to his feet and raised his arms over his head, emitting a ferocious roar.

"Is that the only sound you know how to make?" Hercules asked, once again beckoning the creature to charge. In two long strides the monster was upon him, this time trying to deliver a smashing blow with an overhand fist. Hercules sidestepped and struck the giant's side with a crushing blow of his own. The giant swung again, missing, as Hercules repositioned himself and shoved the monster down into the water. Roaring again, the man-monster rose, his beard frothy with foam.

"I'm going to break you, little man." The creature's voice was a low growl.

"Then come and try," Hercules said. "I'm growing weary of your pathetic attempts."

"You dare to disrespect he who rules?" the giant roared. "I am the spawn of the Titans." He moved forward, his long legs churning the water as he moved, his gigantic hands stretched in front of him ready to grab and strangle.

Hercules brushed the hands away, backing up into the deeper surf. The giant waded after him, his arms still stretched outward. "When I get you this time . . . "

Hercules brushed the huge hands away again, as easily as if he were pushing a branch aside. The giant twisted, trying to lurch forward, but Hercules had caught a wave and his body was rising up with it. As the water rolled over the man-monster, Hercules came down with it, his arm encircling the creature's massive head. Both of them tumbled into the surf, struggling like two serpents locked in a death duel.

Ulysses saw the rest of the battle in flashes as the two combatants surfaced periodically as the water ebbed and flowed. The giant's hands were around Hercules' neck, and the man-god was doing his best to break the choke hold. More water rushed over them. Hercules forced one monster hand away, then the other. They twisted and fell. Another wave washed over the writhing bodies. When it receded, Ulysses saw that it was now Hercules who held the giant's neck in the crook of his arm. Muscles bulged like a rocky shore emerging from a tempest-tossed sea, and Ulysses heard the giant's neck snap with a dull cracking sound. The man-monster sagged lugubriously downward, his body lying twisted and partially buried in the sand as the next wave swept over him and retreated.

Hercules drew himself up and staggered to the beach besides Ulysses. On the far shore Theseus was leading the Greeks from the ship against what was left of the helmeted riders. It was clear, even at this distance, the riders were no match for the trained soldiers.

"Hercules," Ulysses said, "are you all right?"

"More winded than I would have liked," Hercules said. "He was a worthy opponent."

"Do you suppose he really was the spawn of the Titans?"

Hercules shrugged. "It's the stuff from which legends are fashioned." He stretched out, clasping his hands behind his head and smiled. "Now we get to relax while Theseus cleans out the rest of them. Then we'll search the rest of the island. I want to get a look at the slave girls the pirates captured. It's a long journey back to Thebes."

"Slave girls?" Ulysses smiled at the thought. "Do you suppose they'll be grateful to us for freeing them?"

"I'm sure they will be. As well they should. After all, once again, we've saved all of Greece."

Ulysses laughed. All was right with the world.

HOW TO PAINT YOUR DRAGON

Andrew D'Apice

"The problem with you, Pard, is that you're naïve."

Wiping off her blade, Pard paused and looked up. "Yup, that's me, a babe in . . . "

He stabbed his nail into the flesh, and continued. "See? Right there. Acting like you know what's going on, taking chances with your precious gift." He sucked the meat off his finger. "This could've been poison."

Pard pointed to the melon. "But look at the rind, it's . . . "

"Lucky for you, your parents made a wise choice when they hired me." Marv gave his wings a flap, scattering both melon rinds and flesh into the brush. "Now give me that knife before you hurt yourself. And take the bags, we're running late."

Yeah, I'm real lucky, Pard thinks. She remembers the day Marv showed up at the farm. He was the last dragon of the day; he was the *only* dragon of the day. Was that a testament to Pa's spectacular business plan of posting ads inside transit stations that no winged creature would need to frequent? Pa figured that only the most desperate of dragons could possibly have seen their ad. Or was it a reflection of Marv's laziness showing up as late as he did? Judging by how long it was taking them to get to *The Mesmerist Academy for Esoteric Savants*, she had her suspicions.

That day back at the farm, Marv had spent the entire time telling Ma and Pa about his credentials. He listed his experiences escorting esoteric savants, and talked about the sporadic, debilitating condition that, fortunately for all, had grounded him. It had put him in search of a transit depot, and there he found Pa's ad. Except for a few obligatory pats on her head, Marv had barely acknowledged her.

"Sounds like you two have your hands full with this little Pard here. I can tell you with the utmost confidence, you two are making a wise decision to send such a special little thing to *The Mesmerist Academy for Esoteric Savants*. As we all know, control is important." He wrapped his wing around her. "Almost as important as safety." Could've been Marv's natural scent, or the stench coming off what he was shoveling, but either way, Pard could barely breathe.

• • •

Bones are made for rolling, Spirits are made to wrack
I've never cast a spell that didn't answer back
I was born under a conjurin' star

"Now you got me singing that putrid number!" Marv said, as he placed a bulbous finger to one side of his snout. He blew something the size of a small reptile out of the other. By the look of the green and slimy nature of what was expelled, it just might have been an actual reptile. "I don't know how much you understood of what I was saying to your folks, but I wasn't just blowing smoke." He chortled to himself. "You are special. In fact, I don't think you know how special you are. From what I've heard, you don't know just what you have. Of course, most of the young today are oblivious to what they possess. Nothing but impulses and action, no thought of consequences. That's why you need to learn control. Your mother and father did the best they could. Even if he was, shall we say, misguided in his theories, your Pa was trying to help you. I know you don't want to believe that." Marv looked down at Pard walking in front of him, and watched her trace the scars on her arms. "But he did what he did for your own good."

Pard put both hands in front of her, and stretched out her fingers. "My own good? My own good!? If I had . . ."

"Of course, you don't see the benefit. Kids never see what's in their best interests." His tail wrapped around Pard's arms, slowly bringing them down. He pulled her back under his broad shadow, his temporarily out-of-service wings shielding her from the assault of the sun's rays. "No, the young are lost in the chaos of youth. So much noise, so much static. Like a lightning bolt in a tin roof outhouse. Just bouncing around, kicking up . . . What I'm saying is, children need to learn focus. Parents are in over their heads, and sometimes out of their heads; that's when they need a Metaphysical Escort. A professional, if you will. Even better, a *dedicated vocationist*." They walked in silence, the girl trying to step lightly around the subject, and the dragon trying not to put his foot deeper into it. Shadows passed over the landscape. Looking up, they saw a train of dragons flying toward the horizon. Marv said, "There must be a Replenishing Station up ahead. We'll stop and camp there for the night. Just in time, I am exhausted."

• • •

The Replenishing Station looked like all the rest; a cross between a luxury hotel for irregular neurotics and a sanitarium for Onanist invalids. That is to say: beige, bland, and boring. "Very pleasant," Marv said.

• • •

Surveying the area, Pard could only see sensible, rounded pods, not an edge in sight. All of the seats were plush, stuffed to the point of explosion. The intent was extreme comfort, but the effect was claustrophobic. You couldn't go the length of a dragon's tail (and there were plenty of dragons, and plenty more savants bustling about the station) without tripping over a hydration well. Of course, with all the guard fences, replete with padding, no one was tripping over anything. The whole area was like living in a town made of gigantic mushrooms.

"You think so?" asked Pard. "This place is like . . . "

"You need to learn to appreciate all that is being done for you. Do you know that in some places in the world, this area would be no better than a slaughterhouse? No comfort, no plush covered seating; just an open area with chaos lurking around in the shadows." As Marv looked away from Pard to the nearest hydration well, he puffed out his chest and strained, turning his green skin slightly iridescent. Just then two golden dragons walked by with two children marching behind them. Their golden hair was so fair, you'd think they were part of the dragon's wings. "That's right, school her," said one. "It's the least *you* can do," said the other, and the gaggle of four laughed. Marv deflated, his skin going dull and dark. "Come on," he said, as he grabbed their luggage. "Let's find a quiet place to camp."

Pard looked up at the stars, surprised that she was actually able to convince Marv to let her sleep outside by herself. She doubted it was her persuasive speech, (she did take after Pa in some ways), since he barely let her complete a sentence. It must have been how exhausted Marv was. (At one point she saw his translucent second eyelid slide across his iris, like the curtain at the end of a puppet show. A dragon's way of pretending they're listening.) Whatever the reason, there she was, just her and the swirling Universe above.

Was she really born under a conjuring star? Seemed like all the kids she met had the same "gift." Listening to the elders, you'd think they would get tired of saying the word "special," since it seemed to have lost all of its shine. Maybe because the adults had lost their shine, or even their own gifts? She wasn't sure if her parents or any elder ever really had a gift; she couldn't get a straight answer from anyone. Every time she tried to ask Pa, the man with the silver tongue would get all steely, and shut her out. "You're too young to be exposed to such thoughts." The kids she knew all had ideas and theories, but these were the same kids who believed smoking dried dragon turds would give them visions. Considering what they were willing to put into their mouths, she wasn't going to trust anything that came out of them. Her head was a spinning galaxy of questions, with all starlight getting sucked down into the center. She started whistling, and from the huge leather tent came Marv's voice: "Please, anything but that song. I had, WE had, a very tiring day."

Dang it, the lazy slug with wings is still awake. Pard felt bad for thinking that. He wasn't that bad, he was just doing the job Ma and Pa hired him to do. She could take solace in the fact he was only hired to be a Metaphysical Escort to *The Mesmerist Academy for Esoteric Savants*, and no more. She knew some kids whose folks had hired dragons to watch over them all through the "magic years." But those kids started training really early. Pard never had that training, partly because her parents couldn't afford it, but mostly because they thought it was dangerous for her to explore her gift on her own. Of course, that didn't stop her. And now, running her fingers over the scars on her arm, she thought about how after that one night, she never brought herself to explore at home again.

Thinking about that night, her parents, her gift, the sea of stars over her head, and the rivulets of scars on her arm, something started stirring inside. Like all the other times she explored, it began with a small urge that felt like a dull cramp, twisting up into an intense itch. But this time was different. This time there was a pulse, as if from an extra heart. It throbbed just below the surface, churning under the skin, aching to breach through. She stretched her hands in front of her, splayed her fingers, and saw tiny sparks of light dancing across the tips. As she watched the little plasma ballet at the end of her hand, in her palm pooled a glowing nimbus being fed by incandescent rivers running down her arm. She could swear she was touching the stars, pulling their fire into her fingers. This was more than a new territory, it was a new realm. Pard was awestruck by the sensation. Her fingers reached into the Universe, and for the first time she felt, she felt ...

"STOP!" Marv screamed. He reared back his head and spat. A thick green mass landed on Pard's arms, giving her the look of a babe straight from the womb or, in this case, someone a dragon had just spat on. Steam rose from her flesh; dwindling tributaries cooled quickly, and then faded to black. All traces of light had been extinguished by the cosmic slop that festered in every dragon's gut.

"How dare you take advantage of my good nature like that?" Marv spat some more goo on Pard's arm. "Get in the tent, now!" Pard tried to shake the slime from her arms. "Leave it! It's for your own good." Pard slowly shuffled into the tent, head hung low, trying to remember the feeling she just had at her finger tips, trying to make sense of what just happened, trying not to breathe in the noxious fumes from her mittens of spit.

"I was only . . ."

"You were only proving me and your parents right. Showing us that left to your own impulses, you'd damage yourself." Marv followed her into the tent, closing the flaps behind them, keeping the swirling stars and night at bay.

• • •

The sun was high and bright, but Pard wouldn't know. Walking slowly, never able to break out from Marv's shadow, she shivered a bit. "You must be coming down with something," said Marv. "Probably from the stress of your near-death experience." Pard looked down at her arms; the dragon saliva had dried, encasing her limbs like a scab.

"Give it time, it will fall away. I think it would be best that you don't tell anyone at *The Mesmerist Academy for Esoteric Savants* about last night's exploration. We want to start you off on the right foot. Also, when we get to the Academy, please don't call me Marv in front of the Grand Dragon. She's all about formality. Call me Escort Sylvester."

Pard nodded, "Sure thing. Maybe you should . . ."

"We're almost at the gate, once we get inside I will look for the Grand Dragon," Marv said. "And please, try to speak only when spoken to. No interrupting."

Pard waited just inside the gate. The Academy looked eerily like the Replenishing Station: same colors, same structures, and same blandness. The only difference between the Academy and the Station was the fortification. While the school was built well after the area was settled, and there was no threat to keep out, the grounds were ringed with high, intimidating walls. The courtyard was full of savants bustling about. Some were playing music in small groups. Some were playing a game that kind of looked like tag, but with less running, and, by the looks of it, less tagging. On the far end of the courtyard, Pard could see a sizable group of kids playing catch with something that looked like a giant firefly. Her arm tingled.

Pard saw the puffed up Marv approaching alongside a stout, shimmering purple dragon that exuded Grand Dragoness. Trailing behind the two was a tightly coiled haired, barrel of woman who looked like she could take both Marv and the Grand Dragon down if needed.

"So," said the Grand Dragon "this is our newest Savant? I have heard some very interesting things about you, young lady." The Grand Dragon looked at Pard's arms. "What happened here?"

Marv cleared his throat "Well, her father had . . ."

"Say no more. So many parents have some very peculiar ways of dealing with mischievous children. I am quite confident that Escort Sylvester's ectoplasm will repair some of your father's haphazard attempt at control."

Pard nodded.

"Let me introduce you to Miss Higgins, she will be one of your mentors while you are here at *The Mesmerist Academy for Esoteric Savants*."

The robust woman extended her hand. "Pleasure to meet you . . ."

"I've been calling her Pard. Sort of a pet name," Marv said, smiling at the Grand Dragon.

"Madge," Pard said. "My name is Madge. I'm named . . ." Both Marv and the Grand Dragon brought up their translucent lids. Last act, curtain closed. Madge trailed off " . . . after my . . ." Silence rushed into the void.

Miss Higgins coughed and said, "If you two don't mind, I think it would be in Madge's best interest if we got her acclimated to the Academy."

Marv tussled Madge's hair. "Well, Pard, good luck to you. Be sure to tell your parents about OUR safe trip. Remember, little one, CONTROL."

Before Madge could respond, the two dragons were walking away. Marv was going on about how, despite his serious condition, he was able to soldier on. He had dutifully performed the demands of his profession, nay, *vocation*.

Miss Higgins held Madge by the elbow, delicately guiding, and firmly supporting her. She started to sing.

• • •

Bones are made for rolling, Spirits are made to wrack
I've never cast a spell that didn't answer back
I was born under a conjurin' star

Madge's arm started to crackle. Miss Higgins, wide eyed, looked her in the face and said "So, Madge, tell me more about your name . . ."

DON'T FEAR THE RIPPER

Holly West

31 August 1888

The young woman lay sideways atop a rickety metal bed. Her thin cotton shift stuck to her skin, adhered by the sweat of brutal exertion. Beyond that, she was naked, her legs spread open and bent at the knees as she heaved herself forward. She screamed from the pain.

"Hush, now, Mrs. Levy," Caroline Farmer, the midwife, said. "You mustn't yell; it'll only tire you out."

Mr. Levy, as young and inexperienced as his wife, paced from one end of the room to the other. It now seemed ridiculous to Caroline that she'd hesitated to go with him when he'd arrived on her doorstep twenty-four hours earlier, begging for help. Having grown up in the East End, most of her neighbors were well known to her. She kept a running tally of the women who were expecting and called on each of them regularly, knowing that she was their only source of medical knowledge beyond the superstitious clap-trap passed down through generations.

But Mr. Levy was a stranger and she didn't fancy going out into the night with him, especially with the recent murder in Whitechapel. One month prior, Martha Tabram's body was found in a nearby stairwell, stabbed thirty-nine times. Though the district was rife with all manner of criminal goings-on, no one could recall so savage a killing.

Mr. Levy had insisted. "Please, come quick, ma'am," he said. "My wife is dying, I'm certain of it."

"Is she bleeding?" Caroline asked. "Unconscious?"

"Anyone screaming so loudly must be near death."

She nearly smiled. She'd seen this many times before—a young man on the edge of fatherhood, terrified by the powerful forces of labor overtaking his wife. Caroline took up her bag of medical tools, which felt unusually light in her hand. The one she'd used for years, given to her by her mother who'd trained her, had recently been stolen and all of her implements with it. She had yet to replace many of them.

When she arrived at their home, she found his wife was alone and writhing on the bed, her waters already broken.

"Where's your womenfolk?" she asked.

"My wife's mother intended on birthing the baby," he said. "But she died two weeks ago. We've got no one."

"I'll need your help then."

He'd been a worthy assistant, for a man. But the night had been endless, the day eternal, and still, there was no baby.

"Something must be wrong, how could it take so long?" he'd asked several times.

"This is her first child, Mr. Levy. It takes time. Only God can say with certainty when a baby will arrive."

Caroline and Mr. Levy spent the hours ministering to the laboring woman's needs, massaging her feet and lower back, doing what they could to make her comfortable.

Now, finally, the baby was coming. Caroline alerted Mr. Levy: "Hold up her legs!"

The woman hunched forward, straining hard. Caroline counted to ten. "Very good, Mrs. Levy, you may rest," she said. "It shan't be long now."

When at last the baby slid from his mother's body, he was silent and still; his skin tinged a bluish-gray color. Judging by his small size, he'd come early, but Caroline reckoned he'd survive. She turned him onto his stomach, resting him against her splayed palm while she tapped his back. All at once he let out a lusty cry and his nervous parents wept with relief.

"His name is Louis," Mr. Levy said. "After my father."

• • •

It was nearing four in the morning when Caroline made her way home along Buck's Row, content with the knowledge that she'd delivered another life into the world. She couldn't know the child's destiny, but his parents appeared to love him and she hoped he'd thrive in spite of his simple origins in London's East End.

On the far side of the street, a school dominated the landscape and just in front of it, a crowd had gathered. Recognizing several of her neighbors standing on their tiptoes as they tried to see what happened, she hurried over and caught the attention of her friends, Emily Holland and Mary Kelly.

Emily was crying.

"What is it?" Caroline said, grabbing Emily's hand.

"Polly's been murdered!" Mary said.

Caroline caught her breath. "Are you certain it's Polly?"

Emily nodded. "I saw her for myself. Oh Lord, forgive me, I should've never let her go out alone last night!"

Caroline squeezed through the bystanders to where Polly's body lay. In the darkness, she could surmise little about the condition of her remains, but noticed her skirts were raised up around her waist, leaving her bottom half exposed.

"You must let me see to this woman," she said to the bobby standing guard. She knew most of the men who patrolled the area but had never seen this one before. The name "Stubbs" was displayed on his uniform jacket.

"Go on and join the others, missus," he growled. "This ain't no penny show."

"I'm a midwife, Constable Stubbs. I know her. She's—she's my patient."

There was some truth to this, though she'd never delivered Polly of a child. Mary, Emily and Polly were prostitutes, and frequently visited Caroline for ailments suffered as a consequence of their profession.

"Like I said, move along. We're waiting on the *real* doctor."

Frustrated, Caroline returned to her friends. "You must tell me what you know," she said.

"The lodging house deputy turned her away when she couldn't pay the four pence for her bed last night," Emily said. "You know Polly. I saw her at about half past two this morning and she told me she'd earned her doss money three times over but spent it all on drink. I begged her to come home with me but she'd have none of it. Said it wouldn't be long 'till she was back."

"Did anyone see her after that?"

"Not that I know. To think, I might've been the last one to see her alive!"

"Except for the killer," Mary said.

"Oh Mary," Emily said. "Don't say such things!"

The doctor arrived with a second police constable, PC Neil, who'd patrolled the beat for several years. The crowd clamored around the body, hoping for a glimpse of something titillating while Caroline pushed her way forward, wanting to hear what the doctor had to say.

"Get these people out of here," the doctor hissed. As the PCs proceeded to disperse the group, he knelt down and felt one of Polly's legs. "Still warm," he said, to no one in particular. "Couldn't be dead for more than half an hour."

PC Stubbs grabbed Caroline's arm, pulling her back. "You again? Thought I told you to leave."

"And I told *you* that Polly Nichols was my friend. I want to know what happened to her."

"You'll find out when you read the newspapers, same as everyone else. If you don't vacate the area we'll take you in to the station."

She made a final appeal to PC Neil, who knew her reputation in the neighborhood.

"Sorry, Mrs. Farmer," he said. "You'd better do as PC Stubbs says."

Just as Caroline decided it was in her best interest to go home, an inspector had come to take a description of Polly's corpse. As she stepped away from the scene, she heard him say, "My God, doctor. This woman's been disemboweled."

• • •

After Polly's killing, there was much speculation about who'd committed the Whitechapel Murders.

Emily and Mary were adamant that Leather Apron, an obscure character who'd long extorted money from area prostitutes and other vulnerable citizens, was the killer. The name alone was enough to inspire fear throughout the East End, yet nobody seemed to know exactly who he was, or if he even existed. Nevertheless, the gangs that claimed to work for this bogeyman had only to utter his name in order to get results.

Caroline was skeptical. "Why would Leather Apron suddenly come out of the shadows and start killing after all these years?"

"Maybe Martha and Polly owed him money and they couldn't pay?" Mary replied.

"Wouldn't he just send one of this thugs to break their fingers, same as usual?"

Then, in the wee hours of 8 September, Annie Chapman's body was found on Hanbury Street, her throat and abdomen carved open and her intestines pulled out. The killer had removed her womb, taking it with him as a macabre souvenir.

A freshly laundered leather apron was found near her corpse.

The newspapers' disclosure of the leather apron served only to stir the already simmering pot of anti-immigrant sentiment in Whitechapel, heating it to a full boil in the days after her murder. Obviously, the culprit was a Jew—no Englishman could be responsible for such barbaric crimes. Or so thought the British populace.

Caroline, who'd brought many Jewish and immigrant babies into the world, couldn't bring herself to believe that a person's nationality had any bearing on whether they were capable of such savagery. Until someone came up with real evidence pointing to a Jew as the killer, she would look elsewhere for the culprit.

There were other theories, of course. The suspicion that the killer was a member of the medical profession, or at least had knowledge of anatomy, troubled Caroline the most. She hadn't known Annie Chapman, but upon reading the details of her slaying in the evening newspaper, her eyes welled up. How could someone who'd sworn their oath to take care of others betray it in such a horrifying way?

A fierce protective instinct rose within her. These women might've been sinners, but none of them deserved such a brutal punishment. Poverty turned souls desperate and the East End had more than its share of both. Too many of its inhabitants starved in the streets, reduced to selling their flesh in order to secure shelter for the night. Martha, Polly, and Annie were but a few.

In her work, she saw the penalties wrought by prostitution daily: unwanted pregnancy, venereal disease, and assault. Now, murder. She vowed to do something.

• • •

In the early morning hours of 30 September, Caroline received word that Ruth Graves was ready to have her baby.

She set off toward their address in Fairclough Street, not getting very far before a woman's voice broke through the quiet night air. The sound, something between a gasp and a scream, chilled her, and she stopped walking. There was a whisper of movement as a murky figure slipped behind the large wooden gate at the entrance to Dutfield's Yard. She dashed over, and, finding the gate unlocked, she entered the yard, tripping over something in the darkness. She fumbled in her pocket for a match and lit it.

A woman lay on her side, facing the wall. She'd been slashed across the neck. The blood, still pulsing, poured out onto the ground beneath her. Caroline felt her wrist for a heartbeat. Nothing. The match burnt down, flickering out, and she lit a second one, holding it up to inspect the rest of the yard. It appeared empty, but she couldn't escape the peculiar feeling that someone was watching her.

She thought she'd seen someone creeping through the gate and *into* the yard, but had she been mistaken? Had he actually been escaping?

The clop of hooves and wheels crunching across the ground commanded her attention. A cart driver had entered the yard, his pony shying to the right.

"You, there!" he shouted, struggling with the reins. "What have you done?"

The match burned Caroline's fingers and she tossed it to the side. "She's dead," she said. "Stay here with her while I find a bobby."

"How am I to know you didn't do this yourself?"

"Wait or don't wait, I'm going. There's no time to spare!"

She ran into the street, ignoring the driver's protests. She spotted a bobby in the distance, walking in the opposite direction. She started after him and in her haste, nearly collided with PC Stubbs as he rounded the corner.

"Watch it!" he said.

"There's been another murder," she said, pointing. "Over in Dutfield's Yard."

He broke into a run and she followed him. By this time, a crowd had gathered, their lanterns illuminating the scene. There was so much blood that Caroline couldn't imagine there was a drop left in the poor woman.

"I've seen her about," one man said. "Name is Liz Stride."

"Back away, everyone," PC Stubbs said, removing his own lantern from his belt. At his first sight of Liz Stride's damaged body, he shook his head and cursed. He turned to Caroline. "What did you see?"

"I heard a noise—I went to see to it and found her here. I thought I saw someone entering the yard but it was too dark to know for sure. She was already dead when I arrived."

"You're certain of that?"

"Yes." Knowing she could do nothing more for Liz Stride, she continued, "I'm on my way to a birth. If I'm no longer needed here, I'll be on my way."

"You'll do no such thing. You're a witness and you'll remain here until someone can transport you to the station."

"But sir, they're waiting on me."

His only response was to put her in handcuffs.

• • •

As PC Stubbs pulled Caroline toward the Bishopsgate Police Station, the jailor, PC Hutt, was just releasing another inmate, a woman named Catherine Eddowes. "Good night, ol' Cock," she said, waving over her shoulder.

"Pull to it, Kate," he replied, then turned his attention to PC Stubbs. "What 'ave we 'ere?"

"There's been another Whitechapel murder," Stubbs said. "Found this one at the scene, acting suspicious."

"Suspicious?" Caroline said. "I only wanted to help!"

"Put her in a cell to wait for Inspector Abberline."

"Can you at least remove these handcuffs?" Caroline asked.

Stubbs looked to Hutt for guidance and he nodded. Stubbs removed the handcuffs, leaving her wrists sore.

PC Hutt led her to one of the two empty cells located in the far corner of the station. She sat on the hard bench and thought about the baby that was coming. Without her, there'd be no one to deliver it. She hoped that Inspector Abberline would arrive soon so that she could report what she'd seen and be off.

When he finally did come, there were two men with him. To her surprise, he carried a carpetbag in his hands. Caroline recognized it immediately.

"My bag!"

Abberline raised an eyebrow. "We'll get to that later, Mrs. Farmer. These are Inspectors Reid and Drake. We understand that you witnessed the murder of Elizabeth Stride earlier this evening."

"I didn't see it happen," she said. "I was on my way to a confinement and heard what sounded like a scream. I went to see about it and found a woman's body."

"Did you know who she was?"

"No. Only later did I hear someone say her name was Liz Stride."

"A cart driver, Mr. Diemschutz, claims he came into the yard and found you touching the body. Do you have an explanation?"

"I was feeling her wrist for a heartbeat."

"How would you know to do that?"

"I'm a midwife. In fact, I'm needed at a birth this very moment. I've told you everything I know—please dismiss me so that I may see to my patient."

Inspector Abberline raised her bag up. "Where do you think we found this, Mrs. Farmer?"

"I don't know. I'm only glad to have it back."

"When was it last in your possession?"

She thought for a moment. "It was stolen from my person at the beginning of August. I haven't seen it since then."

"You're sure of that?"

"Quite. I reported the theft to this very station."

"Will you see about that?" Abberline asked Inspector Reid. He returned his attention to Caroline. "We found the bag at the scene of Annie Chapman's murder. Have you any guess as to how it got there?"

"I've no earthly idea," she said.

"Is it possible that *you* left it behind?"

She was suddenly apprehensive. How guilty she must appear from his perspective! Not only had she been at the scenes of two of the murders, as a midwife, she had medical knowledge, especially as it pertained to women. And her profession required her to be out on the streets at all hours of the day and night, along side the prostitutes, criminals, and God knew who else.

If her clothing should sometimes have blood on it, it was easily explained—it happened often in the execution of her duties.

Her unease turned to fear as she realized that the murderer himself must've been the thief who stole her medical bag. Had he used the very same tools to kill that she had used to minister to his victims?

Inspector Reid returned to his place beside Abberline. "There's no record of the theft," he said.

"I did not kill these women!" she said. "My life's work is to assist them, to protect them!" Her voice grew quiet. "It's the only thing I'm fit to do."

A great commotion ensued, interrupting Caroline.

"Come quick, Inspector," PC Hutt shouted. "There's been another woman murdered."

Catherine Eddowes, the woman Caroline had seen leaving the police station, had been slaughtered in Mitre Square.

• • •

Just days after the murders of Elizabeth Stride and Catherine Eddowes, the killer began his taunts, sending the first letter to Scotland Yard:

I keep on hearing the police have caught me but they wont fix me just yet. I have laughed when they look so clever and talk about being on the right track. That joke about Leather Apron gave me real fits. I am down on whores and I shant quit ripping them till I do get buckled. Grand work the last job was. I gave the lady no time to squeal. How can they catch me now. I love my work and want to start again.

He'd signed it Jack the Ripper.

Given that Catherine Eddowes' murder had occurred while Caroline was incarcerated—an ironclad alibi if ever there was one—the authorities conceded that she wasn't the culprit. They took their time about releasing her, however, waiting until mid-afternoon the following day. She traveled immediately to the Graves' residence, praying that she wasn't too late.

Mr. Graves himself opened the door, looking haggard. It appeared he'd had an even worse night than Caroline had.

"Mr. Graves," she said. "I'm sorry for the delay. I'm here to check on your wife and child."

"We've no need for you now," he said, his eyes tired and devoid of emotion. "The baby is dead."

He closed the door in her face.

• • •

The morning newspapers reported her arrest and subsequent release, but the damage was done. Her reputation was ruined. The people who'd known her since childhood, whose own children she'd helped bring into the world, crossed the street when they saw her coming. Mothers with babies due refused to admit her when she came to check on them. The prostitutes she'd advised and treated, often at no charge, wouldn't so much as say hello to her. Only Mary and Emily remained loyal friends.

Caroline didn't fear the Ripper. She despised him. He'd taken everything from her—including her cherished medical bag—and had likely tried to frame her for his murders. The only thing that stood between her and the hangman's noose was the Ripper's own folly when he'd murdered Catherine Eddowes while she'd been in jail.

With these most recent killings, she became even more determined. If she couldn't aid and protect the neighborhood's women as a midwife, she would do it by putting an end to this ogre's killing spree.

• • •

Alas, her initial investigation attempts proved unsuccessful. In the first, she approached two women standing on a street corner, both well worn and obviously destitute.

"Pardon me," Caroline asked. "But I wonder if either of you know a man named John Gardener?" It was reported that a man by this name had been one of the last people to see Elizabeth Stride alive.

The fatter of the two women replied, "If you're looking for a man to pay your doss, you'll have to find one on your own, like the rest of us."

"A woman named Elizabeth Stride was murdered a fortnight ago. Did you know her?"

"She asks a lot of questions, doesn't she, Bessie?" the thin one said. "Why d'ye think that is?"

"Liz was a friend," Caroline said. "I want to know how she died."

"A friend, eh?" Bessie. "If that's the case you're the only one she ever had."

"You knew her?"

The thin one said, "Everyone knew Long Liz. She made sure of it."

"How do you mean?"

"She was the most hateful woman I've ever met," Bessie said. "If you were a 'friend,' as you say, you'd known that."

"Bessie!" said her friend. "Don't speak ill of the dead."

"I don't care if she is dead. She was nothing but a common thief. D'ye know she stole my dear mum's pearl brooch? I never did get it back—she probably sold it on so she could drink herself silly."

"You can't prove it."

"Why're you defending her? She was awful and you know it better than anyone. She stole your bloke!"

"I'm better off without him. She did me a favor on that score, she did."

So Liz Stride had been a thief, Caroline thought. Could that have gotten her killed? Could it have gotten them all killed?

"Has she had rows with anybody recently?" Caroline asked.

"You mean like with anyone who might've killed her?" Bessie said. "I ain't no snitch, am I?"

"Even if it might save another?"

She laughed, her round belly bouncing like a child's rubber ball. "You think one of us whores is out here killing our own, is that it? That's a good one, that is."

"Did you know any of the other victims?"

She gave Caroline a hard look. "Wait a minute," she said, her jaw set. "You're that midwife the police suspected of being the Ripper. What're you doing, trying to start trouble? Looking for someone else to blame so you can save your own hide?"

On another such evening, Caroline outfitted herself in one of her dead husband's suits, piling her hair up into a bowler and rubbing coal along her jaw to mimic beard stubble. She went out, looking for women who might attract the Ripper's attention. It was no difficult task; streetwalkers lurked everywhere, beckoning. One gravel-voiced slattern grabbed her by the arm as she passed, startling her.

"Aye, sir, would ye be liking a bit of company?" she said. She appeared to be forty or so, and quite in need of a good washing up. Her eyes were heavy-lidded with drunkenness and she stunk of gin.

"Indeed, I would," Caroline said, her voice pitched low.

"C'mon then," the woman said. "I know a nice private place where we can spend some time together."

She led Caroline to a darkened stairwell. She gathered her skirts and started to pull them up.

"Oh no, there'll be no need for that," Caroline said. "I only want to talk."

"Bah! I've no time for it." She started to walk away.

"Wait," Caroline said. "I'll pay you. How much?"

The woman looked at her with suspicion. "Five pence will do."

Three was the going rate, but Caroline handed over the requested coins with no argument. The woman placed them somewhere amid the folds of her abundant cleavage and said, "What d'ye want then?"

"Do you know anything about the Ripper murders?"

The woman's eyes grew wide. "Why should I know anything about the murders? I mind me own business and it's a good thing I do."

"Did you know any of the victims?"

"I'd seen 'em about. Didn't know 'em to talk to 'em."

"Do you know anyone who might've witnessed something? Seen anything suspicious?"

"Why're you so interested in the killings? What're you, a bobby?"

"Nothing like that—"

Realization crossed the woman's face like a shadow, immediately replaced by an expression of pure fear. "Dear God, you're him, aren't you?"

The woman screamed and tried to run, but Caroline was quicker. She grabbed her arm and covered her mouth. "For the love of God, be quiet or the whole of Whitechapel will hear. I'm a—I'm a newspaperman, looking for a story."

The woman seemed to accept this and Caroline loosened her grip. As soon as she did, the woman broke away and ran, yelling, "It's him! It's the Ripper!"

Caroline made it home that night, managing to avoid another arrest. But if she were to catch Jack the Ripper, there seemed only one way to do it. She'd have to lure him out herself.

• • •

Caroline assessed her appearance in the mirror. It hadn't been difficult to disguise herself as a common East End whore—all it took was a filthy dress and a slovenly manner. She added a black bonnet and veil to help conceal her face and concluded that she looked the part.

She'd studied every available detail of the Ripper killings—the newspapers reveled in publishing every gruesome detail. In each case, the manner of death was strangulation. He throttled his victims first, waiting until after they died to sever their throats and mutilate their bodies. With this in mind, she practiced defending herself against such an attack.

It had been several weeks since he'd killed Liz Stride and Catherine Eddowes, leading some to believe he'd finished his scourge. But the last letter, sent to the president of the Whitechapel Vigilance Committee two weeks after their deaths, was the most shocking of all. With it, the Ripper had included a human kidney. To Caroline, this vile package indicated he'd no intention of halting the killings and it made her more determined than ever to find him.

Armed with a scalpel taken from her makeshift tool bag, she wandered the streets, trying to draw the Ripper out. It was easier to conceal than a kitchen knife, and if necessary, easier to use.

A man on the opposite side of the street called to her. "Is that bonny Ida I see over there?"

Caroline smiled. "It's not Ida you see, sir, but Nellie."

"C'mon over then, sweet Nellie, and give us a kiss."

She laughed and continued on her way, turning up Whitechapel High Street. It was well lit here, illuminated by the interior lamps of the public houses, gin shops, penny show houses, and coffee stalls. Street performers offered every sort entertainment, from singing waifs to wiry acrobats. It was difficult to imagine a killer in the midst of such frivolity.

She walked to the White Hart Pub, intending to stop for a quick drink and a rest. This end of the street was engulfed in darkness, and as she entered George's Yard to access the pub's front door, someone came up behind her.

He grabbed her to him, holding her tightly against his body with one arm and cupping her mouth with the other. Within seconds, he dragged her to the darkest corner of the passage and wrapped a scarf around her neck. Though she'd rehearsed this moment many times, she hadn't known how powerless her panic would render her.

He twisted the scarf tighter. Lightheaded now, she just had the strength to pull the scalpel from her pocket and drag it as deeply as she could along the back of his gloved hand. He gasped and flinched, loosening his grip. She lashed out again, digging the blade in even deeper this time. He backed away and she spun around, swinging it across his face.

He howled in pain and ran off toward the passage's other end. She got her first solid glimpse of him and saw that he wore a police constable's uniform.

"Murder!" she cried softly, for the assault had made her hoarse. "Murder!"

She scrambled after him, knowing there was little chance she'd catch him. After a few steps, she turned back toward Whitechapel High Street to find help.

Then, she stopped short. The man who'd attacked her had been a constable, or at least dressed as one. For all she knew, she'd end up reporting the crime to the very man who'd committed it. Having survived one attack, she had no desire to face another. And having already been a suspect in the Ripper killings herself, she didn't dare go to police headquarters for assistance.

She trudged home, frightened and sore. When she stripped off her coat, she found a torn piece of the scarf he'd used caught on one of the buttons. His effort to kill her had left bruises on her neck.

She spent a sleepless night, wondering at the revelation that Jack the Ripper was either a police constable himself or posing as one. Either way, it was a brilliant ruse—the uniform allowed him to walk the streets at night, concealed as a trusted public official, all the while searching for potential victims.

The following morning, she was still in bed when Emily came pounding at her door.

"Caroline! Caroline!"

She opened the door and found her friend in a mess of tears. "Heavens, Emily, what's happened?"

"It's Mary," Emily choked. "She's been—dear Lord, Caroline—the Ripper killed her."

The significance of Emily's words sunk in as Caroline realized the truth. Mary's death was her fault. If she'd reported the Ripper's attack last night, the police might've laid chase and caught him before he did this to Mary.

Oh, dear Mary, I'm so sorry.

• • •

Caroline steeled herself as the facts of Mary Kelly's slaying emerged. She couldn't allow herself to succumb to grief and guilt, for it would help no one. Instead, she focused her attention on the only thing that mattered: finding the Ripper and avenging Mary. Avenging all of them.

The details were almost too much to bear. Mary's head was severed and placed beneath one of her arms. Her ears and nose were cut off. He'd disemboweled her body and tore the flesh from her thighs. Some of her organs, including her heart, were missing. He'd ripped the skin off of her forehead and cheeks and pushed one of her hands into her stomach.

But the most important detail of all was the photo printed in *The Star* two days after Mary's death: a torn scarf was found on the bed beside the body. Caroline recognized it, for she still had the other half in her possession.

• • •

George Hutchinson, a mutual acquaintance of Mary and Caroline, seemed to have been the last person to see her alive. Two days after Mary's murder, Caroline went to see him.

"I already told the police all this," he complained. "Why's it so important I tell it to you?"

"Mr. Hutchinson, I know how fond you were of Mary. I was, too. I can't rest until I know what happened to her."

"She asked me to lend her six pence and I didn't have it. She said she'd have to get it some other way then and I let her go off. If I'd a known what was gonna happen I woulda stole it for her myself."

"Mary was deep in debt. Your six pence wouldn't have changed anything."

"Maybe not. But I had a feeling something bad was set to happen. She met a man on the next corner and I followed them back to a lodging house. I waited outside for half an hour or more but when no one came out, I left."

"What time was this?"

"About two o'clock, I'd say."

"The inquest revealed that Mary died around four," Caroline said. "Unless you stayed with her all night, you probably couldn't have helped."

He nodded, but didn't seem convinced.

"Do you remember what the man looked like?"

Mr. Hutchinson described a stocky man of average height, quite unlike the person who'd attacked her.

"And did you see any bobbies about?" she asked.

"I suppose I did, but since nothing untoward had happened at that point, I didn't think to say anything."

Before she left, she assured Mr. Hutchinson: "You mustn't blame yourself for Mary's death. There's nothing more you could've done. Let that knowledge bring you peace."

She wished she could believe the words for herself.

On her way home she stopped at a fruit cart to buy an apple for lunch. After she handed the merchant her coin, she turned around and saw PC Neil on the opposite side of the street. He might've been the last bobby in Whitechapel she still trusted, but nevertheless, she had no wish to speak to him. She was about to turn and walk the other direction when she noticed the bandage affixed to his cheek.

No, she thought. It's only by chance. He can't be the Ripper.

PC Neil headed toward her and as he got closer, the truth became apparent. He was the right size and build. He'd been at or near the scene of all the murders. He wore a bandage in the very place she'd wounded her attacker. PC Neil, a bobby who'd ever only showed her kindness, was the man who'd tried to kill her. Which meant, likely as not, he was also Jack the Ripper.

She stood still, wanting to flee but unable to move. Her previous determination to destroy the Ripper now seemed brash and foolhardy. Faced with him now, she gave him the brightest smile she could muster. "Goodness, constable, what on earth happened?"

She searched his eyes for anything that might suggest him capable of the Ripper's savagery, but saw nothing but benevolence. Had she been mistaken? Could the wound on his face be only a coincidence?

He raised his hand and touched the bandage. "It's nothing to concern yourself with, Mrs. Farmer. Just a nasty scuffle last night. All in the line of duty, you know."

"It's weeping through the bandage. Have you seen a doctor?"

"Certainly there's no need for that."

She took a deep breath, trying to bolster her courage. "An infection can be quite serious," she said. "I live just around the corner and have medical supplies at my disposal. If you like, I'll clean it up for you."

"Very well, perhaps you're right. That's very kind of you."

Though it was a short distance, the walk home seemed endless. Along the way, she formulated her plan, understanding the risk. If she failed at her task, he would kill her. If she succeeded, she could be arrested.

She unlocked the door and invited him inside. "Sit down," she said, indicating a chair at the kitchen table. "I'll just go get my bag."

She moved casually in spite of her racing heart. Did he realize that she'd been the one he attacked before moving on to Mary Kelly? Was she playing into his hands instead of the other way around? Thankfully, she kept her bag close at hand in case of emergency; it took only a few steps to fetch it, enabling her to keep her eye on him.

"It must've been a terrible fight," she said, crossing back over to where he sat.

"Working the East End is no easy thing," he said. "But that should come as no surprise to you."

She took out a clean cloth and a bottle of carbolic acid. Using her surgical scissors, she carefully cut the tape away from his face, revealing the wound. She'd cut more deeply than she'd thought, dangerously close to his eye. A half and inch higher and she might've blinded him.

She fought to keep her hands steady as she poured a quantity of carbolic acid onto the cloth and raised it to his cut.

"This might sting," she said.

He winced at the first contact, then relaxed somewhat as she continued dabbing the wound. He settled himself, allowing her ministrations to soothe him. Then, all at once, his hand shot up and grabbed her wrist.

"Stop," he said.

She held her breath. "Did I—did I hurt you?"

"No. It's just that—I'm sorry. It's been many months since I've been touched so tenderly. My wife died in July."

She took shallow breaths as she tried to make sense of his words. July. That was just before the Ripper killings started. Was that what had set him off? Simple grief?

"I'm very sorry for your loss," she said, her voice weak. "My husband died four years ago."

"Then you know how it feels, don't you?" He looked at her now, his eyes showing neither kindness nor sorrow. Just emptiness.

No, she thought. I don't know how it feels. Because I would never turn to violence in order to heal my broken heart, no matter the circumstances.

"I'm nearly done here. I just need to prepare a fresh bandage." She used the bag to conceal her hands while she poured chloroform onto the torn scarf. In one swift motion, she pressed it over his nose and mouth.

"I believe this belongs to you," she said, holding his head against her breast tightly as he struggled. "This is for every one of those women you killed. You will die here, Jack the Ripper, and no one will ever know your true name. That's what the letters were all about, weren't they? Notoriety. Infamy. You'll die an anonymous wretch, but the names of your victims will be known forever."

When he lost consciousness, she eased him off of the chair to the floor, rolling him onto his side. She placed a bucket next to him and using the scalpel, she slit his wrist deep enough to sever the artery. Before she could contain it, it sprayed across her face and onto the wall.

Swallowing back her bile, she cut his second wrist and let him bleed out into the bucket. Within minutes, the ripper known as Jack was dead.

• • •

The next day, the newspapers and broadsheets reported the suicide of PC Thomas Neil of Division H of the Metropolitan Police:

PC NEIL WAS DISTRAUGHT DUE TO THE DEATH OF HIS WIFE IN JULY

East End gossip spread that the constable's wife killed herself when she'd learned he'd given her a venereal disease, rendering her unable to bear children. It seemed that PC Neil enjoyed the company of many of the prostitutes working his beat in Whitechapel, suffering the consequences and inflicting them upon his poor wife. Killing the women he held responsible for his loss was his recourse.

Emily had helped Caroline to drag the Ripper's body out to the street and stage the suicide scene. These women, who'd been friends for so many years, swore on the soul of their dear departed Mary that no one would ever know their secret.

TWO VIEWS

Tim Daly

The sobbing girl, her hysterics finally spent, stops running and collapses onto the grass. Sun drenched yet shivering, alone, wretched and with shaking shoulders, her tears continue to flow. The teacher steps quickly out of the side door of the large Georgian school building and walks across the lawn toward the sixteen-year-old girl. Kneeling on one leg, he gently places his hand on her shoulder. He says something to her, and then stoops his head and attentively listens to her jerkily explain why she is so unhappy. After about two minutes, her crying now over, the two figures stand up and he leads her, his hand still on her shoulder, into the school. Back in the ground floor classroom he had hastily exited only minutes before, his Teaching Assistant and his bemused pupils watch the action through the large sash windows, as do two figures from a first floor office.

This true incident, a fairly normal and unremarkable one in the Camphill School where I interned for six weeks during my teacher training, springs now to my mind as a near-classic example of the way the same scene can be split into two irreconcilable perspectives—both of them true, but in quite different universes.

I first heard about the school when Dr. Stratford, my course supervisor in charge of the Special Educational Needs Department of Trinity & All Saints, where I studied, called me into his room to "ask me for a favour".

He asked me if, as my first six-week teaching-practice, if I would be prepared to stand in for a young friend of his who was the Principal of a Rudolph Steiner Camphill school just outside Wakefield. He coughed into his hand, I remember, and told me how his friend was married to one of the school's "co-workers" and had been having a very tempestuous affair with another.

I got the impression that an emotionally explosive situation had sprung up and that an effective six-week Sabbatical for the errant hubby would be desperately convenient all round.

Now, I'm an amiable and amenable enough soul, but taking over the effective role of a Principal seemed a bit much even for me, and so I hesitated a little before eventually agreeing to take on the challenge with only a few days notice.

As so often, the anticipation was more nerve-wracking than the reality, and once I was at the school, especially in the classroom, I enjoyed my temporary role enormously.

The pupils, in the jargonese of the time, were a mixture of "maladaptive behaviours" (more prosaically thought of as kids off the rails), slow learners and others even less able to cope with mainstream schooling.

Whilst the kids themselves were a joy to teach and to get to know, I found that the staff members were much harder work. A strong religious ethos, based around the Theosophy taught by the Movement's German founder, permeated every aspect of their lives, both on-duty and off-duty. Whilst the man I was standing in for was enjoying his well earned break from Reality somewhere in the Scottish Highlands, both his wife and his mistress had remained.

Tantrums and ill-tempered food fights, whilst rare amongst the kids, were all too common amongst the staff and this, allied to what I saw as a doctrinaire and rigid approach to the way they related to their charges, left me feeling like Alice at the Mad Hatter's tea party whenever I was with them.

Linda, the young Bradford girl who was to break down on the lawn, had struck up a relationship with a boy called Kevin, a likeable enough fellow delinquent who, like Linda, had been pretty much in and out of trouble for most of his seventeen years. Both kids were coping with a host of challenges and problems, not least of which was that none of the grown-ups they knew either from their families or the staff at the school had ever really listened to anything they had to say.

The rapport I established with the pair was thus, for the most part, achieved simply by listening to their view of the world and of each other. The self-absorbed co-workers had little time for them, being far too engrossed with in-fighting and the small-p politics that constituted their chosen milieu.

I was teaching a class one early afternoon when I saw Linda in her distressed state, running from one of the residential buildings towards the main school. When she collapsed onto the lawn I asked the co-worker who was assisting me to look after the class, and rushed towards Linda.

When I got her talking, she told me how one of the co-workers, ironically the same Scandinavian whose affair with the Principal had indirectly triggered my presence there, had been mocking her about her friendship with

Kevin.

The casual cruelty of this co-worker's behaviour had had a devastating effect on the inarticulate teenager, but I listened carefully to her complaints and persuaded her to join my class for the rest of the afternoon.

I thought no more about it until the next morning when the Principal's wife asked me to attend a meeting in the office at the end of morning classes. She gave no indication as to what it was about, but her manner nervously indicated that the matter was grave.

So, at around 12:30, I made my way to the upstairs office where I was asked to close the door once I had entered the room.

I sat down where invited to and looked across the large desk to where three of the senior co-workers sat like a humourless tribunal. I was asked to explain the events of the previous afternoon.

I did so, whilst omitting to mention the name of the co-worker who had upset Linda, but otherwise explained the circumstances in some considerable detail.

As I finished talking, I looked at the three of them and could see that they were not at all happy with my account. If I wondered momentarily if my not mentioning the name of the co-worker was the problem, then their first five words quickly dispelled my doubts and raised a whole bunch of new ones.

"We don't touch the children," they said, as if this truth was really too self-evident to normally mention.

When I pointed out that the "touch" was that of hand on shoulder in full view of the whole school this was quickly brushed aside as an irrelevance. They knew what had touched what as two of them had observed the whole thing, but the mantra of "we don't touch the children" was persistently repeated.

At first I tried to put forward the view that an absolute ban on touching, given how emotionally fragile and needy many of our charges were, constituted a type of abuse-by-neglect, but to no avail. The mantra held sway and I was asked to conform to the absolute ruling as a precondition of my staying on.

I confess that I did agree to their demands, choosing to finish out the next couple of weeks of my teaching practice rather than stand by my sharply differing principles, and to this day I'm not sure I did the right thing.

What I do know is that an innocent and caring touch can be a vital ingredient in any healthy and productive relationship between parent & child, teacher & pupil, friend & friend.

And to demonise touch itself is to make it a gift to the monsters.

A HUNDRED PEARLS

Errick A. Nunnally

A VERY SPECIAL THANKS TO MITCH GRAFF, BRACKEN MACLEOD, AND
JAVED JAHANGIR. WITHOUT THEIR CONTRIBUTIONS, "A HUNDRED PEARLS"
WOULD NEVER HAVE EXISTED.

Halfway to Boise, Clayton Helms pulled into a rest stop. *Stupid name for a bank
of pissers and shitters, but whatever*, he always thought, completely ignoring all
the other so-called amenities provided. He'd spotted the tail two exits back
and knew in his oft-broken bones that this was going to be the best place to
draw them out. The fact that he needed to vent his bowels made the stop a
two-for.

A comically huge mirror in the bathroom startled him when he entered,
giving Helms an extra edge of disgruntled. Not only did he not like being
surprised, but he wasn't happy about seeing his reflection either. It reminded
him of the pain that wracked his body daily and the gut-pounding feeling of
a constipating dam about to break. He ran a coarse palm over his scarred,
crewcut head and noted that there were six urinals and six toilets in two
neat rows on the other side of the privacy wall, as empty as his de-modded
body. His puckered flesh reminded him of what he'd given up, the monster he could've been—almost was. Having the Kevtek sheath removed from
beneath his skin had been the worst of it, but he'd had Pearl at the time, and
she had made it all worth it. Morphine was a shit replacement for her, but it
sure as hell dulled the pain when he could get it.

Helms chose the sixth stall in, dropped his pants, and settled his dimpled
ass-cheeks on the crap-top. Leaning forward, he pulled the Ruger out of its
holster in the back of his pants and waited, elbows on his knees, cursing the

fact that his ass was getting cold and his legs numb. After several minutes of mind-bending pain twisting in his guts, he concentrated on the more urgent business at hand. Sweat beaded on his brow, and withdrawal-induced idiocy started driving the bus.

Other patrons went about their business, coming and going as they do in these places. The clicking of his pursuer's boots on the tile floor eluded Helms while he wiped his ass because the jet-blown winds of the hand dryers drowned out everything. The cacophony cut out, signaling the exit of a bliss-fully ignorant civilian. When a pair of shiny black cowboy boots with chrome tips stopped in front of his stall door, the ex-merc knew he wasn't sitting pretty with one hand on his pants and his bare bottom still glued to the can.

A candy wrapper dropped on the floor, reminding Helms that the energy needs of mods was another pain-in-the-ass he didn't have to worry about. Loud lip-smacking preceded the tin can voice. "Come on outta there, Clay. You ain't got nowhere else you can hide your sorry, wrinkled ass." The drawl on the other side of the stall door emanated from a point six feet higher than the shit-kicking boots under the gap of the weak barrier. The familiar voice chilled him to the bone until the part of him that was still a professional man-aged to take over.

Fucking city cowboy, he thought, *no subtlety, all bravado*. Helms pointed the Ruger up, trying to steady his shaking hands, praying the old acquaintance would open his mouth one more time.

"Hey, pal, you mind? I'm trying to have a moment here with the 2025 Miss March, if you know what I mean." He was starting to wish that he hadn't needed to drop trou for this tête-à-tête, but when you're coming off of mor-phine, you haven't got much of a choice when the bowel beast wants to go for a prowl. His guts trembled and promised a second round of disbursement he wasn't looking forward to. Still, the unorthodox tactical edge of sitting 'helpless' was all he had against this kind of opponent.

"You always had bad taste in women, Clay." The owner of the boots raised a foot to kick in Helms' door. A double blast from the Ruger echoed inside the narrow walls of the stall, ringing in Helms' ears. The stall door slammed open, smashing his shooting hand's fingers into numbness. Cold toilet water splashed up onto his goose-pimpled ass as hot blood sprayed back into his face.

He wiped a glob of yellow from his cheek. It smelled as sulfurous as the rest of the shitty bathroom, mixing with the rush of fluids. Flexing numb fingers, he was pleased he'd managed to hold on to his piece. Helms dried his ass with awkward motions and snapped his pants back on. For a moment, he watched with breathless satisfaction the twitches of Earl "The Mongoose" Whittaker's system crashing. If the bastard had seen Helms had the draw on him, the outcome of this standoff would've been different. Sweet, blessed overconfidence was Helms' angel today.

Mongoose had known Pearl way back when and had been jealous of Helms for the relationship. Only the bad things came back from the past for Helms, none of the good.

The cowboy seized up and froze. Helms smiled, sadistic joy creasing the angles of his broken face—it was the first good thing that had happened all day. You needed a lucky shot to put tinkered mercs like Mongoose down. At least temporarily. Luck and specialized rounds. *Thank the Virgin for unsubtle theatrics.* On a second thought, Helms put a round square into the merc's forehead, buying a few extra minutes, but making even more noise.

A tremble ran down his spine; Mongoose was one half of a nasty pair. Helms needed to move. *Slow, old man, slow on the uptake. Better get thinking and stay in that zone.* He leaned against the busted frame to steady his aim on the door. Precious seconds ticked by as his quivering shook the Ruger's sightline. Satisfied, he stepped gingerly over the malfunctioning freak's torso, watching the last of the yellow juices squeeze out of whatever passed for a heart in the bastard. *Fuckin' Mongoose*—his hairy palms were face up and not even holding a pistol. *Cocky bastard.*

Helms knew there wasn't much time left as the merc's blood pool stopped spreading and reversed its course to begin the march back home. He needed to cut out and hit the bricks because he knew what came next. Mongoose, like any desperate, tinkered mercenary, had sunk a small fortune into a nanotech load that was going to stitch the bastard back together. Only burning or beheading would permanently stop him.

Watching the door in the mirror over his shoulder, Helms knew better than to leave a flank open to Kube, the better of the two mercs on his tail. A prickly fear grabbed hold of his rampaging heart, his skin felt cold, and desperate eyes watched him from the mirror. He did a quick search of Mongoose and palmed a combat knife and sheath from the monster's boot. He considered keeping the merc's pistol, but thought better of it. He wouldn't be surprised if the damn thing were nano-triggered. Helms was no sucker and dropped the weapon into the garbage can. Then he counted the number of steps to the bathroom door, took a deep breath and threw the door open yelling, "Call 911! There's an emergency in the bathroom—oh my God!" The doe-eyed civi slobs stared in soft-brained confusion until he pulled the fire alarm.

Snatching a bright blue trucker cap with "If It Ain't IDAHO It Ain't SHIT" stitched on the front, he ducked into the crowd as it moved, securing the brazen idiot-hat low on his head, and counting his blessings that Kube was nowhere in plain sight.

All the way to his borrowed ride, Helms rubbernecked as stealthily as he could. He spotted Kube's ugly, flattened face cutting a path through the herd. Branislav Kubelko had a mug that looked like it had been raped by a frying pan. The big, modified Serb would be preoccupied with collecting his partner before any cops could get involved.

Helms navigated the parking lot with care, head hunched, eyes forward, neck tight, repeating a mantra in his mind: *don't draw attention, don't draw attention, don't*...Back on the interstate, his head swam and sweat dribbled down his brow. Whether the pounding of his heart was because of withdrawal or the river of adrenaline didn't matter—he was being pursued by a near perfect predator and his pet. What the fuck was Kube doing tailing him through Idaho? As a military-grade, modded merc, neither the Serb or his partner should have even been allowed in the country. That pair was from a lifetime ago, not to mention halfway around the globe. If they were on his ass, then he could expect them to be popping up the next time he was taking a squat or brushing his teeth—especially after giving Mongoose the slip. Kube would be the one kicking Helms' face in and there was no such thing as luck with that beast. His mind struggled with the reality of his situation.

Recalling their time on the Hierophant gig, he hadn't forgotten the bliss in Kube's eyes as the Serb had gone to work with his trusty kukri on their captives. The skinning had been slow, like they were Maltese oranges. Rinds flew like meat confetti. Kube was a pro job, not a back-alley tinker like Mongoose; killing was an art to the Serb, he owed it to his creators.

Could those Latin fucks, the Carradas, have put them on to me? The brothers weren't the only professional smugglers around and it didn't make sense that they'd send a pair like Kube and Mongoose after him. *They're the ones who hired me to do this goddamned snatch, for fuck's sake.* It didn't matter. The only thing that mattered was that he knew they were on his tail. He hoped they didn't know his final destination, but as the screw turns, so did Helms's luck. *Expect shit to go wrong and you'll never be disappointed.*

The package, of course, was his only chance at answers. He understood himself well enough to know that there was no use trying to sort this out; it made no sense no matter how it got sliced. His morphine addled brain couldn't handle the big picture anyway. The important thing would be for Helms *not* to get cut in the process. He needed leverage with the Carradas and protection from the psychopathic Kube and his rat. The only course of action he could figure was to stay alert and stick with the program. Secure the package and negotiate the minefield that lay ahead.

Thoughts of Kube and his ilk tore through his mind again. He supposed he'd been fortunate over the years, finding himself on the right side of freaks like them. Any bits of leftover shrapnel Helms had floating in his body were the dregs of a blast Kube and Mongoose had taken. He'd awoken the next day in a filthy, off-the-grid, basement hospital, unable to feel his legs, with Kube standing over him looking like malevolence in semi-human form. The freak had smiled, blood oozing between his teeth, while he hissed and wheezed: the Kube equivalent of a laugh.

"Say, 'thank you,' Helms."

To which was dutifully replied: "Thank you, Helms."

Kube had hissed again and slid backwards out of the small room. Helms never slept easy again. Not until he could take a blast of shrapnel and walk away. It became a singular goal, saving his money to armor up. It had taken Pearl to persuade him to undo the modification process.

For Pearl, everything for Pearl.

He'd stopped obsessing about the bazillion pieces she'd been sliced into a long time ago, her death was just a death—spectacular, but the end results were no different. It still hurt.

In two hours' time, he was turning onto Eighth Street in downtown Boise. His destination was a joint called the Balcony Club, a former hangout where he'd once been able to take his initial descent into depravity seriously. It was also where his target spent most of his time, according to hard-won intel, and from which this a-hole also apparently ran numbers and moved the occasional kilo of dope.

Santo "Skunk" Bastone. To hear the Carradas tell it, this guy was involved in the robbery of a certain stash house in Tacoma, got away with who knows how much heroin and cash. As well as a certain something that had been en route and of vital importance to the Carradas. By all accounts—including Helms's own shitty research—the guy was small potatoes, just a grunt. Why hadn't the Carradas sent their own men after this clown? Helms may have been a professional once before in their orbit, but was this how low his mangled ass had sunk? Barely a pick-up and delivery. Or maybe the Carradas were losing control of their vast organization? One could only hope. Regardless, they still paid well, even for scut work. The added complication of Kube and Mongoose, however, made the situation a sight more tense.

Helms navigated the rental into a tight spot behind a battered taxi and alongside a porn store, not at all looking forward to the next phone call he had to make. He could see the red and green lights of the Balcony Club up ahead on the right, inflaming nothing but memories of pleasure and pain. From the glove compartment, he grabbed the combat knife he'd gotten off Whittaker and slipped it into his belt. Convincing though his Ruger was, you could never be too careful or too armed. Not when the shit was hitting the fan like it was right now. He'd had no experience with Bastone or any of the boneheads he palled around with, the mutt hadn't been around when Helms circled the drain here.

Achy and more than rundown at this late hour, he slipped out of the rental, glared at a couple of curious porn-store window shoppers, and eased his way toward possible salvation. Goddamn he needed a hit, the pain was becoming unbearable. All of his de-modded joints creaked and every scar prickled murderously. His flesh teemed with dead nanites and microscopic shrapnel.

With far more problems now than when he'd woken up this afternoon, Helms considered the fact that Kube and Mongoose were crawling up his tail. Closing with the unknown Bastone was looking ever more distasteful. It might be better to move sideways rather than straight on. He considered dropping the whole matter and falling off the grid entirely. Hell, that would destroy what was left of his rep but—more importantly—it would reduce his chances of ever getting high again. Helms was an addict with skills and the one thing an addict knows he needs to do is get paid.

It didn't matter if quitting now would be the smart thing to do or not, he couldn't afford to stop. Right now, he needed two things: answers and weapons. With those in hand, he could be up to his ass with hookers and morph in no time—itches scratched, pain assuaged. The hole in his heart, well, that he had gotten used to. In some vague corner of his mind, he knew these were all just the musing of a junkie, ex-merc too banged up inside and out to care anymore.

Helms drifted into the shadows, flipping out his phone for one last look at the photo of Bastone that the Carradas had sent to him. Whoever had set Kube and Mongoose on the warpath may have warned the dipshit as well. Fuck it all, he had to piss too.

To Helms, Boise was a hot spot for the pleasures that kill a man slowly. Bereft of options, he had to try his luck at finishing this gig. If he did quit, then the Carradas would be looking to collect his scalp along with Bastone's. The brothers had enough money to hire God, and he couldn't get far enough off the grid to avoid a holy hit.

Inside, Helms scanned the crowded club. The second level featured a bar and a six-foot wide catwalk that hovered over the room below. A familiar skin-and-bones albino with her back to him stood talking to the bartender. A pair of menacing eyes tattooed on the back of his ex-girlfriend's neck glared until he flashed a twenty dollar bill. One of the neuro-tats winked as Cheri let down her ponytail and leaned in to whisper something to the drink slinger. Helms caught a glimpse of something flash from underneath the girl's tube-dress.

Shit, he thought, *Still got the fuckin' tail*. He shivered, for once not a symptom of withdrawal, but arousal.

"I thought you were gonna get that cropped, Cheri." He had to shout as the albino joined him at an empty table along the wall, pinning him with pink eyes underneath white lashes.

"Yeah, well, I ended up spending the money on getting my teeth pulled instead." The stripper pulled up the front of her skirt, effortlessly kicking a leg onto the table. "You like? It's almost impossible to find an OBGYN with a DDS in this turd state. It cost me a fortune."

Helms held his breath while the pain in his head swelled and subsided. As both a waitress and a stripper, Cheri had fulfilled many of his needs. The hooker part had taken care of the rest until the money ran out and the whole thing became too sour for either of them to stomach. "As much as I'd like to make this a social call, I just need some information," he sighed.

Cheri looked disappointed as she slid into a seat, but the ex-merc wasn't being drawn in.

"I need to find a dumb punk named Bastone. Heard he was dealing up here."

"Bastone? Have you grown a death wish since you left me?"

"Fucking *you* was fulfilling a death wish, Cheri." Helms produced a second twenty. "Where's he at?"

The girl looked quickly around the bar with all four of her eyes and snatched the bills from Helm's fingers. "Whatever. Your money spends whether you live or not. He's at the lower bar, near the Champagne Room." Cheri stood up without saying more and turned to go back to the bar.

Helms moved to get out of his chair, but paused when Cheri bent at the waist, staring at him from between her knees, giving him one more look at her alabaster vulva. "After what they spent on healthcare for your broken down ass, Cheri, your parents would be pissed if they knew." She flashed him an ugly look and sashayed away.

Downstairs, Helms hit the can and hoped he'd find the mook inside. No such luck. Bastone slipped off a stool next to the Champagne Room and chatted up one of the men at the curtain rather than make himself an easy target elsewhere in the bar.

A group of mugs menaced the doorway to the Champagne Room, four freaks with horns that looked more than cosmetic. At a stretch, the ugly crew could be Bastone's, but it was more likely that they were freelance hoping for merc gigs.

Bastone slid into the room with two of the mods at the same time Helms caught a glimpse of Kube's block-like profile on the other side of the place.

Apparently the game was accelerating. Helms followed, sliding off the wall he was leaning on. He had a couple of seconds on Kube, which was all he needed. With not much time on his side, he knew he'd only get one shot at this.

There was a small crowd waiting to enter. UV light lit up the white stains on the walls and floor around the doors. Helms cut through the crowd and made a beeline for the largest of the once-upon-a-time primates in his way. He rubbed sweaty palms on his pants, a nervous energy prickled his scarred skin. He'd only get one shot at this, one chance to surprise the freaks. He was outmatched and they'd know it. Again, it was his best advantage.

"When they come, they rob me twice!" Helms shouted at the large man closest to the door. The goomba had eyeballs like fire to match his red horns and he didn't like being startled by the smaller human.

"The fuck—?" The creature in the pinstriped suit gurgled disjointedly through enhanced vocal cords. A second thug turned towards Helms, equally confused by his banter.

"Where be my hand, the loss of I?" He showed an empty palm to the monster at the door and laid the other on the combat knife's grip. He buried the blade to its hilt in the first monster's throat and slipped the Ruger into his other hand, discharging two hot rounds into the second heavy's crotch. Homo-sap though he was, there was still a rhythm these hybrid machines might never attain. Muscle memory is learned, not programmed.

The crowd peeled back, keeping the other two heavies off his back for the requisite amount of time. As the smaller man went down, Helms shot the first freak in the face and reached inside his victim's jacket where he knew some real heat would be strapped. The modified man carried a fat Magnum— probably loaded with armor piercing—but that was't what Helms needed right now. He shoved the pistol into his waist band and dropped to a knee, thrusting his fingers inside the other man's coat.

"Fuckin' A," Helms said to the whimpering mutt who until recently had a groin. He unhooked an Arsenal Shipka MX from a thigh-strap hidden under the black trench-coat. This weapon he recognized from a border control gig near Bulgaria. He released bursts of fire in two directions, killing the next pair of horned tough guys and spooking bystanders into flight. Helms knew precious seconds had been wasted killing the four men at the door. The path clear, he barreled forward, fired a burst into the black curtain covering the doorway and plunged through firing high on full auto, emptying the magazine at an upward angle.

He couldn't be sure what had happened to Bastone, though he was fairly certain no one would run through the metal storm he had just unleashed above the civilian's heads—a move used to force everyone to go to ground. It was a fool's game, Helms knew, to not be sure of your prey or where the exits were, but the time had come to get the hell out of this joint and he felt reasonably sure that his only option was to spring Bastone from this mortal coil and snatch whatever the target had on him.

The Champagne Room was larger than he'd expected, and silent after the MX clacked on empty. Then he heard the gravel crushing voice behind him.

"Helms, you fucking idiot."

Without looking, Helms slipped the Magnum from his belt and pointed it backwards under his arm. The expected pressure of Kube's thick hand on his shoulder told him when to fire. Explosive rounds thumped underneath his jacket, heat burning his side, as he unloaded the heavy pistol into the deadly Serbian behind him. He'd known Kube would want to spin him around before dealing the death blow, the better to absorb Helms's death through his eyes. Now the modified Serb absorbed .44 rounds instead.

Around him, women melted from the shadows near the walls. "Fuck." Helms muttered to himself, as he tried to comprehend the sight unfolding before him, ignoring the thump of Kube's body hitting the floor.

There was a pinprick at the base of his skull and he didn't have time to unravel the scene. All he could manage was to fall to a knee and go down hard, nodding and seeing at least a dozen women cast in Pearl's likeness staring back at him. They surrounded the slick, well-groomed Carrada brothers who sat calmly sipping wine. Helms had an absurd moment in his fevered dream to wonder why Pearl had decided to go platinum after being reduced to a puddle of biological matter. Then blackness came.

• • •

When Helms opened his eyes, Pearl spoke to him, her muffled commands to wake up coming to his dulled ears. He was lying down and she was above him, bathed in white light. To Helms, she was the most beautiful thing he'd ever see. He'd do anything for Pearl and had made sure she'd known it before she was killed. Which made it all the more shocking when she slapped him hard across the face, turned to Benny Carrada and said, "He'll be ready in a few minutes; the shot I gave him is wearing off. You can talk to him now."

"Clay! I believe Kube has already let you know you're an idiot—"

The cut of Benny Carrada's eyes made Helms glance to his left. Kube stood seething nearby, the front of his shirt stained with the rainbow mix of colors that passed for his blood.

"Now don't waste my time, Clay, I only have one question for you."

Helms's head swam, he was pinned to a table—surgical by the looks of the overhead fixture—he couldn't move anything but his eyes. A sharp current of panic lanced the space between his temples, rivaled only by the confusion. Five Pearls stood around the room in various industrious postures. They checked readouts, flipped switches, adjusted mechanics, and pushed buttons. Helms's buttons, mostly. He sucked in one ragged breath and breathed out one word: "Pearl?" She didn't react. Did she not recognize him?

"Hey, shit for brains, pay attention: that's not your girlfriend. Not anymore. Out of professional courtesy and the fact that she was instrumental in your success during our employ several years ago, you get a choice."

"And then he's mine." Kubelko grimaced, his second set of teeth—surgical steel, sharp as scalpels—dropped into place.

"Kube," Benny warned.

Armand Carrada strolled into the room, his relaxed composure rippling across the tension in the dick-measuring pool. The Carradas were nothing if not confident.

"Armand! I was just about to ask our guest here for the code when Kube interrupted."

Armand fixed Kube with a quizzical look, pinning him to the spot. It struck Helms as a dangerous nonchalance to assume with the maniac Serb. Helms took the moment to survey the room as best he could. Mongoose sat in the corner, his head in his hands, dark glasses on his face. He must have a splitting headache, judging by the puckered hole in his forehead. Something else Helms was sure he was going to have to pay for.

"You're not being paid to interrupt, Kube."

"I don't like being used, Armand. You want a job done, I'll get it done, but this game you play is making me reconsider my employment."

Both Armand and Benny feigned shock, taking offense that Kube would make such a proclamation. They played off of each other, finishing thoughts and sentences, sprinkling in the pidgin language they'd developed as children to further confuse people. A game the brothers enjoyed. Helms occasionally recognized Spanish in the mix, but had no idea what they'd mixed it with.

"We're hurt, Kube."

"*Nia kompobres corakoro.*"

"You make our hearts hurt."

"How could you think so little of us?"

"*Tian pocomulta.*"

"Of course, there's a special bonus prepared for you."

"A bonus, for your trouble, Kube. You've always been a valued asset to us."

"This time is no different at all. Pearl? The package?"

Kubelko looked slightly confused, if a meat grinder with eyes could be interpreted as looking like anything but a meat grinder. With eyes. One of the Pearls in the room slid a wide-mouth, corrugated canister out of a drawer and handed it to Kube.

"An improved nano-load, *mi amikogo!*"

"A little something our Pearl cooked up. Pearl, give him the basics."

Everyone in the room except the Carradas looked spooked. Helms could only imagine the horror being reflected on his horrifying face as several facsimiles of his dead girlfriend spoke at once.

"This a vastly improved nanite delivery, it is far more efficient than your current load and able to be directed in a rudimentary fashion by conscious thought. The nanites will improve your recovery time by over fifty-seven percent and add a thirty-two percent boost to your reflexes when required."

"Hot damn." Kube hissed, his steel teeth retracting. "I like the sound of that. What about Mongoose?"

Pearl responded in disturbing unison again. "At this time, there is only the single load. It will take sixteen days to produce a second, identical load. We are prepared to offer assisted recovery here, for the duration, once the required information is extracted from Clayton Helms."

Kube looked over at his partner who nodded slightly. "Fine, we're good. For now."

"*Excelente!*" The Carradas chorused as Kubelko joined them with a joyful hiss and injected the load into his forearm.

Benny turned back to Helms, securing the captive's wandering eyes. "You were given a code approximately one year after your last job with us. It was a military code, intended as a backdoor hack on a particular level of governmental security. Tell us the code and we won't have to go on with turning your brain into molecular soup for Pearl to decipher. See? Easy as pie." The criminal overlord snapped his fingers, smiling.

Helms struggled on the table, his breath quickened. After all this time, he'd thought he'd given up on life, figured that if he found himself in a situation like this that he'd prefer to be puréed rather than live another day as an addict trying to fill a Pearl-sized hole. Now he was surrounded by copies of his love and he had questions.

"Pearl. Why? I'll talk, but only if you tell me what happened."

"Ah, still clinging to that, eh?" Armand Carrada slid in on Helms's left, and Benny remained on the right as they played vocal tag.

"Love. Nothing else like it in the world. Is there *mia fratomano?*"

"Meh. Money? Drugs?" Armand shrugged.

"I take your point, *fratomano*, there are exceptions to every rule. I stand corrected."

"Shall we enlighten him?"

"*Jestí*, we shall."

"Do you remember Dr. Seminova? About so tall, short gray hair, thick beard? Russian fellow?"

"Somewhat insane? Do you recall what his specialty was?"

Helms remembered the so-called doctor. At the time, he would have ignored the man if the Carradas didn't have a habit of dropping just enough information as an excuse to maybe have someone killed later. "Bio something or other." Helms ground his teeth and saw Kube smiling. The monster stood up straighter, eyes focused elsewhere.

"Biocomputing. He developed a controversial theory combining quantum physics, nanoprocessors, and the human brain."

"It was the human brain part that everyone thought was controversial, of course. Dr. Seminova came looking for us. An organization like ours could use a secure data network. No? He was looking for funding, backing of any sort."

"And human subjects. He was going to need supplies. Expensive supplies. It is amazing how much it costs to break the human body down and reconstruct it several times over."

"We decommissioned his team, collected all the research and set him up."

"Recommissioned, just like that! I think you can see the value in having a wirelessly networked, multi-incorporated, biological computer with the intuition and growth capabilities of the human mind, Clay. As for Pearl specifically—"

Helms's eyes burned, he ground his teeth connecting the dots. "She broke that code I snatched."

"Yes! The mystery. The good doctor recognized an ideal candidate when he saw one."

"Had to have her."

"Had to. So we had to deliver. It was simply in our best interests, Clay. Who would have suspected a prostitute to have her level of intuitive intelligence?"

"And who would miss her?"

"Not much of a prostitute now, eh *fratomano*?"

"Hush, Benny, you'll upset our guest."

"Tsk. I told you she'd be dead meat in the sack. No more passion in that one."

"No more juices either. Meh, it wasn't what we paid for anyway."

They took his Pearl away for a price. Those two dangerous freaks had known Pearl way back when, knew of Pearl and Helms. It made sense to have

Kube and Mongoose do the snatch, they were close and dedicated enough to not be stopped. When Helms had found out Pearl had been taken, tracked her down, when he'd killed his way into the facility in Brazil. Learned she'd been processed . . . It had signaled his descent; the proof of his madness was scattered all over the vats. His Pearl had been deconstructed, but he'd had no idea it was these psychos behind it, nor what they'd planned. Biological matter had all sorts of nefarious value on the black markets.

These bastards needed to die and Helms was helpless to escort them along.

The two of them, Clay and Pearl, both adrift in life. Then they'd found each other, chose each other to be family. Together they'd set about rebuilding their foundation of humanity, removing themselves from their past abuse and subsequent rocky roads. Clay had vowed to protect her, defend her at the cost of his own life, and she'd done the same. Fat lot of good it did in the face of a world they'd foolishly chosen to be a part of before they met. The irony was sharp enough to kill with.

"*Dios mío*, Clay, don't cry! Ay-yi-yi, Armand, he's crying."

"Understandable, I believe. Now, Clay, keep in mind, this is business—nothing personal. We don't hold a grudge against you or your girlfriend. She has been nothing short of phenomenal! All we need is that code to crack a back door open and Pearl will be able to legitimize our access to the world. Even our walking supercomputer has her limits."

"Smuggling never looked so good!"

Helms blinked hard, a decade of sour milk filling his head. He expected the Carradas to high-five over his supine body, they were so pleased with themselves. A movement at the corner of his eye caught his attention. Had Pearl just glanced at him?

"This entire plan to lead you here—we thought it a bit complex—but it got you here in one piece, just as required, sans your blood swimming with morphine or whatever else the shit you put in your body."

"Or on it. An extended adrenaline rush to clear out the toxins, eh?"

"Drugs in your system would screw with the process of blending your brain and we needed you clean on the table."

"Details. You know how they are, Clay."

All the Pearls turned at once. "Everything is ready."

"Last chance, Clay. Code or blender?"

Still burning with hate, Helms considered his limited options: die or die. Memories of being lied to, fucked over, and used formed a puddle of acid that burned every square inch of his creaky, de-modified body. The Carradas were going to get the information they wanted out of his mind whether he recalled it for them or not. They wouldn't have asked at all, however, if manually sorting it out of his brain were quick and easy. Ten years of melancholy thuggishness wrapped around his tortured frame and squeezed the only answer that made sense out of Helms's mouth: "Blender, dickshits, fuck luck with that."

Kube hissed with humor, delighted with Helms's response, no doubt hoping he'd be the one to shove Helms in. The Carradas looked disappointed, but unperturbed. He hadn't pissed them off as he'd hoped. The last failure on his docket.

Armand turned away and Benny said, "Go ahead and get started, Pearl."

It happened all at once. There were so many Pearls in the room, the process began instantaneously. The one closest to Mongoose uncoupled a sharp-pronged power coupling and drove it into the tinker's neck. His eyes lit up and his body convulsed as the voltage burned him from the inside out. Kube looked momentarily confused, then staggered. The monstrous Serb wrapped himself in all of his accoutrements at once: steel teeth, knuckle-spikes, tongue dart muzzle, the works. Then he stumbled, spine bowing outward, collapsing to the floor like a wax figurine in a blast furnace. His beloved kukri clattered to the floor, the flesh sheath melting from his back. His body swam with nanites determined to go in every direction at once. The Carradas barely had a moment to register what was happening when two of the Pearls shot the brothers through their perfect hairdos with sleek, silenced pistols.

Four of the women rushed over to Helms and started unbuckling his straps while one cradled his face and stared into his eyes. "I've missed you so much, Clay. It took so long, but here you are."

When his arms were loose, he pulled her close and they kissed. After a gasp of release he had only one question. "Pearl, how?"

She clenched her jaw once and spoke with tight lips. "The Carradas have been using me to improve their operations. I've been able to legitimize most of their assets over the last few years. It was a slow process to remember who I was. But I remembered you, Clay, remembered *us*. Now we're set for life—the Carradas had their fingers in a lot of pots."

Helms tensed. "Guards?"

"I've been running their network as a proxy for years, they don't question me."

"You put this whole thing in motion." Helms' head swam with skeptical relief.

"I took advantage of the situation." All the Pearls in the room helped Helms to his feet. "Kube, that heavy-mod bastard, was the hardest to maneuver. I had to arrange things so that he'd allow me to get under his skin, nothing else would do. Mongoose was a loose thread, I expected to get messy handling him, but you softened him up quite a bit."

Helms took in her smile, her beautiful smile. "My God, how—how many of you are there?"

She hesitated, blinking rapidly, unsure of how Helms might take the information and answered quietly: "One hundred."

Helms licked his lips and turned the number over in his mind. The idea that Pearl was alive again banged around his hard head like a loose marble in a dryer. That there were one hundred of her, well, that was a lot of marbles in the chamber.

Helms took her into his arms and touched her platinum hair. "Pearl, I'd take a thousand of you, if I could." And he would. Everything for Pearl— always for Pearl, every gorgeous one of them.

SNAPSHOTS

Christopher Irvin

The fresh eviction notice mocked Nick from across the street as he made his way back from the rental he'd parked two blocks away. There was plenty of room in the oil-stained driveway beside his father's old Buick, but he had to be careful now. Couldn't take another chance. One more careless mistake and ... He didn't want to think about it.

He winced as he hopped the curb, slipping a backpack off his left shoulder, taking the full weight on his right. The stress of the short walk had reopened the wound in his side and he'd broken out in a sweat despite the breeze. He felt a length of clear tape beginning to pull the bandage from his abdomen and pressed it back down through his t-shirt, revealing pink stains.

Of course it would be Lenny, the worthless old man who'd stumbled in half-cocked as usual, looking for a place to lay low after his wife locked him out. The shop was supposed to be empty, the guys nursing hangovers on their day off. Nick had known the code to the safe for years, seen the stacks the boss was placing inside and knew it was much more than a roadside auto body shop should be pulling in. It was true some of that money might have found its way into his pocket on occasion as a little bonus for his hard work. But as Lenny had said earlier, thumb hugging the clip of his pocket knife, "When the chips are down, you turn to your friends, eh?" Nick should have loaded the gun.

As much as the pain weakened his legs, he felt a growing sense of relief at the sight of the worn house and its unkempt grass threaded with last year's dead leaves.

"Keep it together, man. You're almost there." He felt the pull of the back-pack and prayed that it would be enough—at least to get her where she needed to be. Once she was in, they couldn't get rid of her. Not like the banks and their predatory loans, eating away at his mother like an unstoppable cancer. The Home would be different. It had to be, because he promised her it would. A naive promise he'd made before he set up an appointment. Learned about waiting lists and the high cost of keeping someone you love alive and well cared for. Neither of which they could afford.

He let his doubts hang, opened the Buick and dropped the backpack on the floor of the driver's seat beside the groove his father had worn between the pedals with his heel. The hole in the floor mat had widened over the years, so much that it made it difficult for Nick to drive. In the time following his father's death, nothing seemed to fit quite right.

He tore the eviction notice from the door, crumpling the single sheet of paper between strong hands. He hadn't bothered to read the previous, and the latest wouldn't tell him anything new either. What was it the debt collector had told him? There's no shame in starting fresh. No shame . . . if only it were that easy. The men he dealt with had no concept.

"Ma, let's go!" Nick raised his voice over the sound of the screen door slapping at his back. Held his side again as another wave of nausea ran its course. He palmed the door open wide enough for his head to fit through and spit a wad of crimson phlegm into the rose bushes. Thought of his last visit to the dentist when he swallowed the rest.

Two medium-sized black suitcases sat idle in the wood-paneled entryway, giving off that new car smell. Nick cursed as he reached for one, instincts telling him they were both empty upon first glance. His mother had possessed an aversion to all things "new" since Nick's father had passed, though in truth it was always in her nature. Even forced Nick to find a way to "return" the stolen big screen television he'd bought to replace her old box when it went out, instead opting for costly repairs to keep her six basic channels running. Given her disease, he quickly learned it was better to keep things as they were, as best he could. Didn't mean he couldn't go down swinging, though.

"You were supposed to be ready," Nick whispered to himself. The neglected suitcases added a level of panic to his voice. He crossed the dark living room, floor boards creaking beneath his boots. The light was on in the bathroom at the end of the hallway, broken ceiling fan generating a low hum. He grabbed an Orioles hoodie hanging from the door knob of his bedroom and grit his teeth as the cotton material stuck against his sweat-soaked skin, twisting to pull it down around his waist. Careful of the trigger, he removed the cold piece of metal from the rear of his waistband by the grip, and set it on the bedside table. He found the full magazine he'd left behind underneath his mattress. Slid it into the weapon until he heard a soft click, and tucked the pistol back into his belt. The difference in weight felt good.

"You know I don't appreciate cursing inside my house, young man." Nick heard the faint voice of his mother as he approached her room, kitty-corner across the hall from his own. "You and your brother, always letting that screen door slam. Thought I raised you boys to pay attention."

The door to his mother's room was open, as it often was since the sickness had gripped her mind. Closing it, even as she slept, made her feel cut off and alone. The soft, late afternoon sun filled the room through the open blinds, highlighting the gaps in the dust where her picture frames and knickknacks used to rest. And for a moment, the emptiness of the room gripped him with a peaceful sadness, and part of him was glad the day had turned south hours before. That his last memory of his mother's room would be filled with the strong scent of her perfume.

His mother's ancient flowery set of pastel green suitcases were laid out side by side on top of her bare mattress and packed to the brim. The old beauties as she called them, had visited more skylines than Nick would ever see. One suitcase was crammed full of her odd and ends, stuffed between an assortment of clothing for safe keeping. The other appeared to contain the dumped contents of the medicine cabinet. A haphazard sea of orange bottles, prescriptions old and new. Nick heard a clatter at the sink and turned the corner to find his mother.

She stood facing the bathroom mirror bordered with photographs of family and friends. A hairdresser in her youth, when Nick was born, she'd quit her job and brought the tradition home with her, taping memories of her coworkers to accompany her on long days as a stay-at-home mom. Nick's father despised the clutter, but relented when he saw how much the photographs meant to her. The originals were long gone, but those that took their place were more important than ever. Now the faces and names filling the mirror helped his mother retain her identity.

"Almost ready. You know I like to look my best before I leave the house, Jimmy." She uncapped a light red lipstick and twisted the end between her thumb and forefinger. She wore a pale yellow dress, a favorite that in recent years she'd saved for Easter Sundays. Her graying black hair was matted in places as if she'd woken from a nap, but the woman looked remarkable for having barely crossed into her sixth decade. She capped the lipstick and dropped it into a small peach-colored bag on the counter. "Never know who we might run into."

"It's Nick, Ma," he said, with a sigh. It was a trivial mistake, one that occurred daily without Nick so much as batting an eye. Sometimes, when she was adamant, he even played along. But on today of all days . . . it was his turn to make the sacrifice and he wanted her to know that it was he who had stepped up to the plate, taken charge like an eldest son should.

His mother stared wide-eyed at him through the mirror in slow recognition of her error. Her face softened as she turned to face her son, eyes blinking back sorrow.

"Oh, silly me," she said, adjusting the sides of her dress, busying her anxious hands. "You know I get a little mixed up sometimes. Come here, Nick." She extended her arms out wide for a hug and Nick took her hands in his.

"It's okay, Ma. But we have to go. I told them we'd have you checked in before dinner." He tried his best to smile. His mother looked away from his face for a moment, squinting into the fading light, her features scrunched in a look of uncertainty.

"In a hurry to ditch your own mother now? Leave me out in the pasture to graze with a herd of old cows until we've had our fill and keel over?" She couldn't hide a tight-lipped grin. "Oh, I'm just kidding. You know—"

"I know, Ma, but we do need to leave. Get your photos together while I take your bags to the car. We can put them right back up when we get there."

"After dinner."

He chuckled. "Yes, after dinner."

She took a step backward, craned her neck a bit to see the mirror, eyes tracing the layers of photographs as if estimating the job and longing for more time. "Okay, dear . . . "

Nick gave her a light peck on the cheek and turned his attention to the suitcases, pressing them shut to zip them fully closed. He took a deep breath and dragged the pair to the floor, clenching his teeth through the roaring pain and lifted both through the doorway. Heavy as they were, Nick used his knees to help propel the awkward bags down the hall and out to the car, wincing when they scuffed against the walls. By the time he reached the Buick he'd resorted to dragging the weight behind him.

Over the past week he'd filled every inch of the trunk with boxes of his mother's things, so he placed the two suitcases in the empty back seat. After the two were snug within, he unzipped the latter, running his fingers over half-empty bottles of medication until he settled on expired prescription painkillers. He unscrewed the cap while working up a bit of saliva and popped two into his mouth. The bitter taste was awful, but he managed to get them down, nearly choking at the sound of the sirens spinning up in the distance. Took him a few seconds to recognize the pattern—that it was EMS and not police closing on the neighborhood. Some things are more discernable with age; even so, the high-pitched wail gave him another start as he turned to head back inside.

Nick took his time shuffling back up the walk to the front porch, shoes tugging at weeds that sprouted through overgrown cracks in the pavement. He could do little to hurry his mother. If he kept up the pressure, he'd only give her more cause to worry. Back inside, he cupped water from the kitchen faucet, draining the cold liquid from his hands to clear his throat, feeling the intense throbbing in his abdomen begin to fade.

Down the hall, he licked his thumb and wiped away the scuff marks left by the suitcases on the walls. He waited in the doorway until he heard a sniffle. His mother stood hunched over at the sink, a pile of photographs on the counter beside her, a single photograph in her hands.

"Jimmy died in the war, didn't he?"

"Afghanistan. We buried him at First Baptist. Dad was there."

"Why can't I remember?"

"Come on, we're going to get you help."

His mother shook her head and wiped her nose with a crumpled tissue. She kept the photograph of her son in her hands and left the rest behind on the counter as Nick put his arm around her hunched shoulders. She said little as they walked together through the empty house.

He held the door for his mother like the gentlemen she'd always hoped he'd be, and she thanked him, though he knew as she wiped away her tears that her focus was still on the crinkled photograph of his brother clutched in her hands. He pressed the door closed, dialed The Home and apologized for keeping them late, and said they were on their way. He gave his mother a wink when he started the car on the third twist of the key and her face wrinkled with joy. A little smirk at the end of a long day. Lifting her spirits was the one thing he could do better than anyone else, even if it wasn't as often as he'd liked.

• • •

The drive across the city was uneventful. Nick stuck to back roads and took his time. He thought about striking up conversation, but couldn't think of anything to say as his mother sat there, hands still in her lap.

Her touch startled him as he began to drift off, causing him to jolt and tense his grip on the wheel. She wiped a bit of sweat from his brow and felt his head with the back of her hand.

"You feel warm."

"It's nothing, just a little cold."

"Promise me you'll drink plenty of fluids when you get home."

"Don't worry about me."

"Promise."

"I promise."

They drove.

• • •

The tan-skinned man dressed in baby blue scrubs waited for them near the side entrance to The Home. Nick waited for him to finish his cigarette before opening the door for his mother and helping her out.

"Don't be silly," she said, pushing past him toward the suitcases. "I might be getting old but these arms are still good for something. Besides, it upsets me that you're not feeling well and I won't be there to take care of you." She managed to pull both from the backseat, only then letting Nick carry the heavier of the two after attempting a step with both. "Ah, who am I kidding?" she laughed. "Make yourself useful." And together they crossed the small parking lot to the man in baby blues.

"Welcome, ma'am," said the young man as they approached. "Set that bag down and I'll be right with you to take you inside. You're going to be very happy here." His smile grew from ear to ear as he spoke.

Nick squeezed her left hand. "Martin is going to help me with a few things at the car. We'll be right back."

When they were out of earshot, Martin dropped the charade. "You got the money, no?"

"Of course I got the money. Think I'd just dump her on you and leave?"

"You never know with people, man. Not many in your position would do that same. You should see some of the kids I have to deal with these days."

"Not like I had much of a choice."

Martin shrugged. Nick handed him the backpack, pressing the weight against his chest. Martin peeked through a gap between the zipper pulls at the top and nodded.

"Take care of yourself, Nick. You're looking a little rough—"

"Don't worry about it."

"I don't want none of this coming back on me now."

"I said don't worry about it." Nick brushed a forearm against his face, wiping sweat from his forehead and nose, dampening his sleeve. "We good?"

"We good." Martin slung the backpack over a shoulder. "Paperwork is all set. Room 435 in East Nunnally. Bring the rest of her stuff around tomorrow. I'll make sure we're squared away."

"Thanks, man." Nick hesitated, placing a hand on the top of the open car door. "Say goodbye before you take her in?"

"Sure," he said, checking his watch. "But make it quick. None of that half-hour goodbye shit."

Nick closed the door and walked back toward his mother, keeping his eyes on the smooth asphalt beneath his feet. Martin followed behind, busying himself with his cell phone.

"Martin's going to take you inside, Ma. I'll be back later with your things." He struggled to swallow, his voice faltering as he struggled to hold back the tears he knew would find him.

"Thank you, son." She took him into her arms.

"I love you, Ma."

"I love you, Jimmy." She pulled him tight, embracing him with all her strength as he began to sob. "Thank you. Thank you for everything."

He tried to return her smile through the tears when he pulled away, but a glimpse of the red stain on her dress caused him to quickly turn and head for the car. He felt the dampness extend to his thigh and pressed a palm against the hurt.

Slouched in the driver's seat, he watched Martin retrieve the suitcases and lead his mother inside. He couldn't muster the strength to return her wave.

The sun began its descent along the tree line. Nick stared out into the twilight, wondering what he was looking for. The ignition caught on the first try.

With a bloodied hand he reached up and flipped down the overhead visor. A pair of old movie tickets fluttered to his lap. A photograph of his family huddled together around his brother was taped to the underside. Jimmy looked good in uniform. It was the last day Nick saw his brother whole, his family whole, before the IED.

Is this what it feels like, Jimmy? He thought, trying to imagine what it would feel like to be carried by his brothers. The pressure of the air against his skin as the helicopter approached. Shouts of, you're going to be okay, man, just hang in there. To look into their eyes and *know*.

Is this what it feels like to be a hero?

DECEIT

Joyce Carol Oates

Not by email but by phone which is so God-damned more intrusive the call comes from someone at Kimi's school—*Please call to make an appointment urgent need discuss your daughter.*

No explanation! Not even a hint.

Candace has come to hate phone calls! Rarely answers phone calls! If she happens to be near the phone—the kitchen phone—quaint old soiled-plastic that has come to be called, in recent years, as by fiat, a "land phone"—she might squint at the ID window to see who the hell is intruding in her life, for instance the ex-husband, but rarely these months, could be years, does Candace *pick up.*

Cell phones she keeps losing. Or breaking.

Cell phones are useful for keeping in (one-way) contact with Kimi—*Crummy substitute for an umbilical cord*—and a pause, a beat, the signature wincing laugh that crinkles half her face like pleated paper, then—*Ha ha: joke*—if the assholes don't get Candace's wit.

And more it seems to be happening, assholes don't *get it.*

Well, the cell phone. Unless she has lost it, she has it—somewhere. Could be in a pocket of a coat or a jacket, could be on the floor of her car beneath the brake or gas pedal, or in the driveway; could be in a drawer, or atop a bureau; could be, as it was not long ago, fallen down inside one of Candace's chic leather boots; the cell phone is a great invention but just too damned small, slight, impractical. Could be sitting on the God-damned thing and not have a clue until the opening notes of Beethoven's *Fifth Symphony* come thundering out of your rear.

Not that Kimi answers Mom's calls all that readily—the docile-daughter reflex seems to have atrophied since Kimi's thirteenth birthday—but the principle is, getting voice mail on her cell through the day at school, text messages from MOM, Kimi at least has to acknowledge that MOM exists even if MOM is no longer one of those desirable individuals for whom Kimi will eagerly *pick up*.

• • •

"Your daughter."

"Y-yes? What about my daughter?"

Cool-calm! Though Candace's voice is hoarse like sand paper and her heart gives a wicked lurch in her chest despite that morning's thirty-milligram Lorazepam.

"Has Kimi spoken with you, Mrs. Waxman, about—yesterday?"

"Y-yesterday?"

"Kimi was to speak with you, Mrs. Waxman, about an issue—a sensitive issue—that has come up—she hadn't wanted us to contact you first."

Weedle, Lee W.—"Doctor" Weedle since there's a cheesy-looking psychology Ph.D. diploma from Rutgers University at Newark on the wall behind the woman's desk—speaks in a grave voice fixing her visitor with prim moist blinking lashless bug-eyes.

Why are freckled people so *earnest*, Candace wonders.

"Your daughter has been reported by her teachers as—increasingly this semester—'distracted.'"

"Well—she's fourteen."

"Yes. But even for fourteen, Kimi often seems distracted in class. You must know that there has been a dramatic decline in her academic performance this semester, especially in math . . . "

"I was not a good math student, Dr. Wheezle. It might be simply—genetics."

"'Weedle.'"

"Excuse me?"

"My name is 'Weedle,' not 'Wheezle.'"

"Is it! I'm sorry."

Candace smiles to suggest that she isn't being sarcastic, sardonic—"witty." Though *Weedle* is a name for which one might be reasonably sorry.

" . . . have seen your daughter's most recent report card, haven't you, Mrs. Waxman?"

"Did I sign it?"

"Your signature is on the card, yes."

Weedle fixes Kimi's mother with suspicious eyes—as if Candace might have forged her own signature. The woman is toughly durable as polyester—like the "pants suit" she's wearing—short-cropped graying hair and a pug face like an aggressive ex-nun.

"If my signature is on the card, it is my signature."

Candace speaks bravely, defiantly. But this isn't the issue—is it?

Hard to recall, in the Lorazepam haze, what the issue *is*.

"You can't expect children to leap through flaming hoops each semester. Kimi has been an A-student since day-care—it's cruel to be so *judgmental*. I don't put pressure on my daughter to get straight A's any more than I'd put pressure on myself at her age."

Since the ex-husband is the one to praise their daughter for her good grades at school, as a sort of sidelong sneer at Kimi's mother whom he'd taken to be, even in the days when he'd adored her, as an essentially *frivolous person*, Candace takes care never to dwell upon Kimi's report cards.

Now the thought comes to Candace like a slow-passing dirigible high overhead in the Lorazepam haze—she hadn't done more than glance at Kimi's most recent report card. She'd had other distractions at the time and so just scrawled her signature on the card having asked Kimi if her grades were okay and Kimi had shrugged with a wincing little smile.

Sure Mom that smile had signaled.

Or maybe *Oh Mom. . . .*

For this visit to the Quagmire Academy—i.e., Craigmore Academy—which is Candace's first visit this term—Candace is wearing a purple suede designer jacket that fits her tight as a glove, a matching suede skirt over cream-colored Spandex tights, and twelve-inch Italian leather boots; her streaked-blond hair has been teased, riffled, blow-dried into a look of chic abandon and her eyebrows—recklessly shaved off twenty years before when it had seemed that youth and beauty would endure forever—have been penciled and buffed in, more or less symmetrically. Her lipstick is Midnight Plum, her widened, slightly bloodshot eyes are outlined in black and each lash distinctly thickened with mascara to resemble the legs of Daddy-long-legs. It's a look to draw attention, a look that startles and cries *Whoa!*—as if Candace has just stumbled out of a Manhattan disco club into the chill dawn of decades ago.

Weedle is impressed, Candace sees. Having to revise her notion of what Kimi Waxman's mom must be like, based upon the daughter.

For Candace has style, personality, wit—Candace is, as the ex-husband has said, *one-off*. Poor Kimi—"Kimberly"—(a name Candace now regrets, as she regrets much about the marriage, the fling at motherhood and subsequent years of dull dutiful fidelity)—has a plain sweet just slightly fleshy and forgettable face.

Weedle is frowning at her notes. Which obviously the cunning psychologist has memorized that she might toss her dynamite material, like a grenade, at the stunned-smiling mother of Kimi Waxman facing her across the desk.

"... at first Kimi convinced us—her teachers, and me—that her injuries were accidental. She told us that she'd fallen on the stairs and bruised her wrist—she'd cut her head on the sharp edge of a locker door, in the girls' locker room, when she was reaching for something and lost her balance. The more recent bruises—"

Injuries? More recent? Candace listens in disbelief.

"—are on her upper arms and shoulders, as if someone had grabbed and shaken her. You could almost see the imprint of fingers in the poor child's flesh." Weedle speaks carefully. Weedle speaks like one exceedingly cautious of being misunderstood. Weedle pauses to raise her eyes to Candace's stricken face with practiced solemnity in which there is no hint—not even a glimmer of a hint—of a thrilled satisfaction. "I am obliged to ask you, Mrs. Waxman—do you know anything about these injuries?"

The words wash over Candace like icy water. Whatever Candace has expected, Candace has not expected *this*.

And there are the moist protuberant eyes which are far steelier than Candace had thought.

The Lorazepam, like the previous night's sleep medication, provides you with a sensation like skiing—on a smooth slope—but does not prepare for sudden impediments on the slope like a tree rushing at you, for instance.

Warning signs are needed: SLOW. DANGER.

"Excuse me, w-what did you say, Dr. Wheezle?"

Weedle repeats her question but even as Candace listens closely, Candace doesn't seem to hear. In her ears a roaring like a din of locusts.

"Then—you don't know anything about Kimi's injuries? Neither the older ones on her legs, nor the more recent?"

Candace is trying to catch her breath. The oxygen in Weedle's cramped little fluorescent-lit office is seriously depleted.

"'Kimi's injuries'—I j-just don't . . . I don't know what you are talking about, Dr. Wheezle—*Weedle*."

"You haven't noticed your daughter's bruised legs? Her wrist? The cut in her scalp? The bruises beneath her arms?"

Candace tries to think. If she says *no*—she is a bad mother. But if she says *yes*—she is a worse mother.

"Mrs. Waxman, how are things in your home?"

"Home? Our *home*?"

"Do you know of anyone in your household—any adult, or older sibling— who might be abusing your daughter?"

Abusing. Adult. Candace is sitting very still now. Her eyes are filling with tears, her vision is splotched as if often it is in the morning, and in cold weather. In order to see Weedle's scrubbed-nun face clearly Candace has to blink away tears but if Candace blinks her eyes tears run down her face in a way that is God-damned embarrassing; still worse, if Candace gives in, rummages in her purse for a wadded tissue. *She will not.*

"N-No. I do not—know … I don't k-know what you are talking about, I think I should see Kimi now …" Wildly the thought comes to Candace: her daughter has been taken from school. Her daughter has been taken into the custody of Child Welfare. Her daughter has falsely informed upon *her.*

"Mrs. Waxman—may I call you 'Candace'?—I'm sorry if this is a shock to you, as it was to us. That's why I asked you to come and speak with me. You see, Candace—we are obliged to report 'suspicious injuries' to the police. In an emergency situation, we are obliged to use the county family services hot-line to reported suspected child abuse in which the child's immediate well-being may be in danger."

Candace is gripping her hands in her lap. Why she'd chosen to wear the chic suede skirt, matching jacket with gleaming little brass buttons and the leather boots, to speak with the school psychologist/guidance counselor, she has no idea. Her heart feels triangular in her chest, sharp-edged. Despite the Lorazepam and last night's medication she'd had a premonition of something really bad but no idea it could be—*this bad.*

Eleven minutes late for the appointment with Weedle. Taking a wrong turn into the school parking lot and so shunted into the adjoining parking lot for the high school and so routed by one-way signs onto a residential street—God damn!—returning at last to the entrance to the middle school lot which she'd originally missed impatient now and would've been seriously pissed except for the Lorazepam—(which is a new prescription, still feels experimental, tenuous)—and a hurried cigarette simultaneously first/last cigarette of the day, Candace vows—and inside the school building which looks utterly unfamiliar to her—*Has she ever been here before? Is this the right school, or is her daughter enrolled at another school?*—bypassing the front office in a sudden need to use a girls' lavatory at the far end of the corridor—praying *Dear God dear Christ!* that Kimi will not discover her mother slamming into one of the stalls, needing to use the toilet and yet, on the toilet, cream-colored Spandex tights huddled about her ankles like a peeled off skin, there is just—*nothing.*

God-damned drugs cause constipation, urine retention. If excrement is not excreted, where does it *go?*

Once a week or so, Candace takes a laxative. But sometimes forgets if she has taken it. Or forgets to take it.

Candace recalls another lavatory she'd hurried into recently on a false alarm, at the mall. This too a place where girls—high-school, middle-school—hang out. She'd been shocked to see a poster depicting a wan adolescent girl with bruised eyes and mouth staring at the viewer above a caption inquiring ARE YOU A VICTIM OF VIOLENCE, ABUSE, THREAT OF BODILY HARM? ARE YOU FRIGHTENED? CALL THIS NUMBER. At the bottom of the poster were small strips of paper containing a telephone number and of a dozen or more of these, only two remained. Candace wanted to think that this was some kind of prank—tearing off the paper strips as if they'd be of use.

Weedle is inquiring about Kimi's father: does he lose his temper at times, lose control, does he ever *lay hands* on Kimi?

"'Kimi's father'—?"

Candace has begun to sound like a deranged parrot echoing Weedle's questions.

"Yes—Kimi's father Philip Waxman? According to our records, he is your daughter's father?"

Some strange tortured syntax here. *Your daughter's father.*

"Well, yes—but this 'Philip Waxman' no longer lives with us, Dr. Weedle. My former husband has moved to Manhattan, to be nearer his place of employment in which he occupies a sort of low-middle-echelon position of shattering insignificance."

"I see. I'm sorry to hear that. . . ."

"Sorry that he has moved to Manhattan, or that he occupies a low-middle-echelon position of shattering insignificance? He's in the insurance scam—I mean, 'game'—should you be curious."

Candace speaks so brightly and crisply, Candace might be reciting a script. For very likely, Candace has recited this script concerning the *former husband* upon other occasions.

Usually, listeners smile. Or laugh. Weedle just stares.

"The question is—does Kimi's father share custody with you? Does she spend time alone with him?"

"Well—yes. I suppose so. She is in the man's 'custody' on alternate weekends—if it's convenient for him. But Philip is not the type to 'abuse' anyone—at least not physically." Candace laughs in a high register, a sound like breaking glass. Seeing Weedle's disapproving expression Candace laughs harder.

Once it is *dialogue* Candace is doing, Candace can do it. *Earnest conversation* is something else.

Weedle asks Candace what she means by this remark and Candace says that her former husband has refined the art of *mental abuse*. "But indirectly—Philip is passive-aggressive. It's as if you are speaking to a person who does not know the English language—and he is deaf! He becomes stony-quiet, he will not *engage*. You can speak to him—scream at him—clap your hands in his face, or actually slap his face—only then will he acknowledge you, but you will be *at fault*. It is impossible for the man to lose at this game—it's his game. And if you stand too close to him you're in danger of being sucked into him—as into a black hole." Candace laughs, wiping at her eyes. *Black hole* is new, and inspired. Wait till Candace tells her women friends! "'Abusive men are 'provoked' into violent behavior but my former husband can't be provoked—*he* is the one who provokes violence."

But is this a felicitous thing to have said? With Weedle staring at Candace from just a few feet away, humorless, and slow-blinking?

"What do you mean, Candace—'provokes violence'?"

"Obviously not what I said! I am speaking figuratively."

"You are speaking—in 'figures'?"

"I am speaking—for Christ's sake—analytically—and in metaphor. I am just trying to communicate what would seem to be a simple fact but—I am having great difficulty, I see."

Breathing quickly. Trying not to become exasperated. Her hands have slipped loose of their protective grip and are fluttering about like panicked little birds.

"What I mean is that, through his extreme passive-aggressive nature, the man provokes others, his former wife for instance, to rage."

"*You* experience 'rage'? And how does this 'rage' manifest itself?"

This is coming out all wrong. It's like Weedle is turning a meat-grinder and what emerges is *wrong*.

"It doesn't! Not me."

Candace's voice is trembling. Tiny scalding-hot bubbles in her blood, she'd like to claw at the imperturbable freckled-nun-face.

"It doesn't? Not *you?* Yet you seem very upset, Mrs. Waxman—Candace...."

"I think I want to see my daughter. Right now."

"'See' her? Take her out of class, for what purpose? So that the three of us can talk?"

"No—take her home."

There is a pause. Candace is breathing quickly in the way that a balloon that has been pricked by numerous small puncture wounds might breathe, to keep from deflating.

"Take her home! I think that—yes. Take her home."

More weakly now. For, having taken Kimi *home*—assuming that Kimi would agree to come home in the middle of the school-day—what would follow next?

Imperturbable Weedle does not advise such an act. Imperturbable Weedle is telling Candace that taking Kimi out of school—"interrupting her school-routine"—would be "counter-productive"—especially if Kimi's friends knew about it.

"Yesterday Kimi was quite defensive—she insists that the injuries are 'accidental.' It was the girls' gym instructor Myra Sinkler who noticed the leg bruises, initially—this was about ten days ago—then, just yesterday, the shoulder and upper-arm bruises. Then Myra discovered the head injury—a nasty-looking little wound in Kimi's scalp, which should have been reported at the time, if it took place, as Kimi claims, in school—in the girls' locker room, after gym class. But no one informed Myra Sinkler at that time and no one can verify the account that Kimi gives—so we are thinking, Myra and I, that the 'accident' didn't happen when Kimi says it did, but at another time. And somewhere else. When Kimi was questioned she became excited, as I've said 'defensive'—it's never good to upset a traumatized child further, if it can be avoided." Weedle paused. *Traumatized* hovered in the air like a faint deadly scent. "Kimi promised us that she would tell you about the situation, Candace, but evidently she didn't. That was about the time I'd called you and left a message. In the interim—you didn't ask Kimi anything?"

"Ask her—anything? No, I—I didn't know what to ask her. . . . "

"You don't communicate easily with your daughter?"

"Well—would you, Dr. Weedle? If you had a fourteen-year-old daughter? Do you think that mothers of fourteen-year-old daughters and fourteen-year-old daughters commonly communicate *well*?"

Candace speaks with sudden vehemence. The moist protuberant nun-eyes blink several times but the freckled-nun-face remains unperturbed.

"Well—let me ask you this, Candace: what is Kimi's relationship with her father?"

"Dr. Weedle—is this a conversation, or an interrogation? These questions you are firing at me—I find very hard to answer. . . . "

"I understand, Candace, that you're upset—but I am obliged to ask, to see what action should be taken, if any. So I need to know what Kimi's relationship has been with her father, so far as you know."

"Kimi's relationship with her father is—the man is her father. They are 'related.' I was very young when we met and arguably even more naïve and 'optimistic' than I am now—obviously, I wasn't *thinking*. The two look nothing alike and have very little in common—Kimi is clearly my daughter—one glance, you can see the resemblance—though Kimi is just a few pounds overweight, and a much sweeter girl than I'd been at that age. Is she ever! Too sweet for instance to say she doesn't much want to spend time with her very dull father—but she isn't, I think, *frightened* of him."

Was this so? Candace never asks Kimi about her weekends with Philip out of a sense of—propriety, you could say.

Or dignity, indifference. Rage so incandescent, it might be mistaken for an ascetic purity.

But mostly boredom. Candace is *so bored* by all that—enormous chunk of her "life"—like a clumsily carved male-likeness on Mt. Rushmore—the features crude, forgettable.

You can't just erase me from your life. How can you imagine you can do such a thing. . . .

Easily. Once Candace makes up her mind, breaking off relations with certain people, it's like an iron grating being yanked down, over a storefront window. And the store darkened, shut up tight.

"She sees her father, you'd said, on alternate weekends? Does she seem happy with this arrangement?"

"'*Happy*'? For Christ's sake, no one I know is '*happy*.' This is the U.S.A. Are you '*happy*'?"

Candace is perspiring—something she never does! Not if she can help it.

Relenting then, before Weedle can respond, "Well—yes—frankly yes, I think Kimi *is*. Happy, I mean. She's happy with her classes, her teachers—her life.... She's an only child—no 'sibling'"—(with a fastidious little wince to signal that, in normal circumstances, Candace would never utter so tritely clinical a term)—"therefore, no 'sibling rivalry.'"

Weedle allows Candace to speak—fervently, defiantly. Hard not to concede that what she is saying mimics the speech of the mother of an adolescent who doesn't know what the hell she is talking about—hasn't a clue. Can't even remember exactly what the subject is except she's the object of an essentially hostile interrogation and not doing so well—Lee W. Weedle, PH.D. is one of those individuals, more frequently female than male, to whom Candace Waxman is *not so very impressive*.

When she escapes back home she will take another thirty-milligram Lorazepam with a glass of tart red wine and maybe go to bed.

Except: what time is it? Not yet 11:30 AM. Too early for serious sleep.

"And what about boys, Candace?"

"No—no boys. Kimi doesn't hang out with boys."

"She doesn't have a boy friend? She says not."

"You've seen Kimi. What do you think?"

A sharp crease between Weedle's unplucked brows signals that this is not a very nice thing for Kimi's mother to say, however frank, candid and adult-to-adult Candace imagines she is being. Quickly Candace relents: "I'm sure that Kimi doesn't have a boy friend—even a candidate for a boy friend. She's—shy..."

"And what about other boys? In her class? Or older boys, from the high school, possibly?"

"Kimi never mentions boys. The subject hasn't come up."

"You are sure, Candace?"

"Yes, I am sure."

Poor Kimi! Candace is embarrassed for her.

Grimly Weedle says: "Of course, there are boys even at Craigmore who intimidate girls—harass them sexually, threaten them. There have been—among the older students—some unfortunate incidents. And there is this new phenomenon—'cyberbullying.' Has Kimi ever mentioned being upset by anything online?"

"No. She has not."

"It's a strange new world, this 'cyberspace' world—where children can 'friend' and 'unfriend' at will. We are committed to protecting our students here at Craigmore from any kind of bullying."

"Committed to stamping out bullies. I like that."

They will bond over this—will they? Candace feels an inappropriate little stab of hope.

"But Kimi hasn't mentioned being harassed? Bullied? 'Teased'?"

"I've said *no.*"

But Candace is remembering—vaguely, like a photo image coming into just partial clarity—something Kimi mentioned not long ago about older boys saying *gross things* to the ninth grade girls, to embarrass them; pulling at their hair, their clothes; *bothering* them. On the school bus, this was. Candace thinks so.

Candace asked Kimi if any of these boys were bothering her and stiffly Kimi said, "No, Mom. I'm not *popular.*"

Candace knows that terrible things are said about the behavior of some of the middle-school students—both girls and boys—at Craigmore. Oral sex in the halls and beneath the bleachers, girls younger than Kimi exploited by older boys with a hope of becoming "popular"; boys bragging online about girls' lipstick smeared on their penises. Not at this private suburban school perhaps but at nearby public schools—boys physically mistreating girls, sexually molesting them in public; grabbing and squeezing their breasts, even between their legs. Some of this behavior is captured on cell phones—and posted online. From the mothers of Kimi's classmates Candace has heard these things—she'd been so shocked and disgusted, not a single joke had occurred to her. Where Candace can't joke, Candace can't linger. It is very hard for Candace to do *earnest*.

She'd been upset at the time. Seeing poor sweet moon-faced Kimi, a shy girl, with not-pretty features, hair so fine it sticks up around her head like feathers—among such crude jackals.

"If Kimi says she hurt herself accidentally, then Kimi hurt herself accidentally. My daughter does not lie. She is not *deceitful*."

"I'm sure she is not, Candace. But if she has been coerced, or threatened—"

"Kimi has always been accident-prone! As a small child she had to be watched every minute, or..." Candace has a repertoire of funny-Kimi stories to testify to the child's clumsiness though the stories don't include actual injuries, of which there had been a few. Just, Candace wants this hateful suspicious "school psychologist" to know that her dear sweet daughter is *prone to self-hurt*.

"And Kimi's friends are all girls. They're all her ninth-grade classmates. She's known most of them since elementary school. Great kids, and I don't think they 'hang out' with boys."

As if unhearing, or unimpressed, Weedle says: "Adolescent boys can be terribly predatory. They can sense weakness, or fear. At almost any age, however young, if there's a ring-leader—an 'alpha male'—with a tendency to bully, he can manipulate the behavior of other boys who wouldn't ordinarily behave in such a way. These boys can harass girls like a pack. And girls can turn against girls...."

Candace protests: "Kimi has never said anything to me about any of this! I really don't think what you are saying pertains to my daughter and I—I resent being...."

Candace feels a sensation of something like panic: really she doesn't know what Kimi is doing much of the time, after school for instance upstairs in her room, with the door shut; frequently Kimi is at her laptop past bedtime, or texting on her cell phone, as if under a powerful enchantment; sometimes, one of Kimi's girl friends is with her, supposedly working on homework together, but who knows what the girls are really doing on laptops or cell phones.

If Candace knocks at the door, at once the girls' voices and laughter subside—*Yes Mom? What is it?*

A careful neutrality in Kimi's voice. So Mom is made to know that this is not *little-girl-Kimi* at the moment but *teenager-Kimi*.

The interview—interrogation—is ending, at last. Weedle shuffles papers, slides documents into a manila file, glances at the cheap little plastic digital clock on her desk. Candace sees a pathetic little array of framed photos on the desk—homely freckled earnest faces, in miniature—Weedle's parents, siblings, little nieces and nephews. Not one of Weedle with a *man*.

"You will call me, Candace, please, after you've spoken with your daughter this evening? I hope she will allow you to examine her injuries. We didn't feel—Kimi's teachers and I—that the injuries were serious enough to warrant medical attention any longer. But you may feel differently."

Feel differently? Meaning—what? In a haze of eager affability Candace nods *yes.*

Yes she will call Weedle—of course.

Yes she is an attentive, vigilant, loving and devoted mother—who could doubt this?

(Wondering: is this interview being recorded? Videotaped? Will Weedle use it against Candace as evidence, in a nightmare court case?)

(Is the former husband Philip Waxman in some way involved? *Is Weedle on Waxman's side?*)

Faintly now Weedle manages a smile. As if to mitigate the harshness of her words:

"I will wait until I hear from you before making a decision about reporting your daughter's injuries, Candace. Kimi is certainly adamant that they were 'accidental' and we have no proof that they are not. But, you see, if I don't report 'suspicious injuries' to a child, and there are more injuries, that are reported, I will be held to account and I may be charged with dereliction of duty."

"Well, Dr. Weedle, we wouldn't want that—would we! 'Dereliction of duty.' Absolutely not."

Candace bares her beautiful teeth in a smile to suggest—to *insist*—that her words are lightly playful merely. But Weedle reacts as if stung:

"Mrs. Waxman, this is not a joke. This is a serious matter. Anything involving the well-being of a vulnerable child is serious. I would think you might be grateful that the staff at Craigmore is alert to a situation like this, rather than reacting defensively."

"I am grateful—very! The tuition I pay for Kimi's education here suggests how grateful! But I warn you—and Kimi's teachers—if you over-react about something harmless—if you call the 'Hot Line' and involve the police—I promise, I will sue you. I will sue you, and the others involved, and the school board. I will not allow my daughter to be humiliated and used as a pawn in some sort of 'politically correct' agenda."

Feeling triumphant at last, Candace is on her feet. Weedle struggles to her feet. With satisfaction Candace sees that Weedle is shorter than Candace, and at least a decade older; Weedle is a homely woman, exuding the sexual allure of one of those inedible root vegetables—turnip, rutabaga.

"Goodbye! Thank you! I know, Dr. Weedle—you mean well. In fact I am impressed, the school staff is so *vigilant*. I will talk with Kimi this afternoon—as soon as she returns from school—and clear all this up. Shall I make an appointment now to see you next week—Monday morning? At this time?"

So brightly and airily Candace speaks, it seems she must be making a gesture of reconciliation. Such abrupt turns of mood are not unusual in Candace but Weedle is slow to absorb the change. Warily she tells Candace that Monday is a school holiday—Martin Luther King, Jr.'s birthday. But Tuesday morning—

Candace laughs almost gaily. Something *so funny* about this.

"'Martin Luther King, Jr.'s birthday'! Every month there's a 'great man's' birthday! Sometimes there's 'Presidents' Day'—three for one. And how many 'great women' birthdays do we have? Is Eleanor Roosevelt so honored? Emily Dickinson? Amelia Earhart? What about—Circe? Circe is a goddess—that's big-time. Or was there more than one of her? Is 'Circe' the singular—or the plural? Is there a 'Circ' and the plural is 'Cir-say'? Like goose and geese—ox and oxen?"

Weedle stares at Candace with an expression of absolute perplexity.

"All right! Tuesday, then. Same time, same place—I promise, I will be on time."

Candace thrusts out a glittery-ringed hand to shake Weedle's pallid hand—one of those warm-friendly-intimidating gestures Candace has perfected, like a sudden parting social kiss to the cheek of someone who has been entranced by her, yet guarded.

Strides out of Weedle's office. Already she is feeling much, much better.

At the front entrance of Craigmore Academy Middle School Candace has her cigarettes in hand and by the time Candace locates her car, on the far side of a lot she doesn't remember parking in, she has her cigarette lighted.

• • •

It's so: Kimi's friends are all girls she has known since grade school. A small band of not-pretty/not-popular girls of whom at least two—Kimi and Scotia Perry—are invariably A-students.

Friendships of girls unpopular together. Candace hopes that her daughter's friends will remain loyal to one another in high school which looms ahead for them next year like an ugly badlands terrain they will have to cross—together, or singly.

Scotia is not Candace's favorite among Kimi's friends—there is something subtly derisive about the girl, even as she politely asks Mrs. Waxman how she is, and engages her in actual conversations; Scotia is stocky and compact as a fire hydrant, with a ruddy face, deceptively innocent blue eyes and thick strong ankles and wrists—a girl-golfer!

(Candace has never seen Kimi's friend play golf but she has been hearing about the golf-"prodigy" for years.) Scotia is an all-round athlete who plays girls' basketball, field hockey and volleyball with equal skill, while poor Kimi takes aerobics for her phys-ed requirement—Kimi shrinks from sports and has difficulty catching balls tossed to her so slowly they seem to float in mid-air. Though not a brilliant student, Scotia so thrives on competition that she maintains an A-average in school; she also takes Mandarin Chinese at the local language immersion school and she has been a savior of sorts for Kimi, as for their other friends, helping them with malfunctioning computers.

(Scotia has helped Candace, too!) From a young age Scotia exuded a disconcerting air of mock-maturity: Candace recalls when, after Kimi's father had moved out of the house in the initial stage of what was to be, from Candace's perspective, an ordeal like a protracted tooth extraction, both painful and intensely boring, Scotia said with a bright little smile, "Hope you had the locks changed on the door, Mrs. Waxman! That's what women do."

(In fact, Scotia's parents are not divorced. This droll bit of information must have come to Scotia from other sources.)

Last year, in eighth grade, Kimi's closest friend seemed to have been a girl named Brook, displaced over the summer by Scotia Perry. Now it's Scotia who spends time in Kimi's room as the girls prepare class projects together, or work on homework; watch DVDs, do email, text-messages, MySpace and Facebook; snack on cheese bits, trail mix, Odwalla smoothies which Candace keeps stocked in the refrigerator—*Strawberry Banana, Red Rhapsody, Super Protein, Mango Tango, Blueberry B Monster.* Often Candace is out—with friends—for the evening and returns to discover that Scotia is still on the premises, though the hour is getting late—past 9 PM. She can hear, or half-hear, the murmur of their girl-voices, and their peals of sudden girl-laughter; she's grateful that Kimi has a friend though Scotia Perry seems too mature for Kimi, and too strong-willed; and Scotia's mother hasn't made any effort to befriend Candace, which feels like a rebuke.

Once, Candace thought she'd overheard Scotia say to Kimi in a laughing drawling voice—a mock-male voice, was it?—what sounded like *fat cunt*—but Candace hadn't really heard clearly for Candace *was not eavesdropping* on her daughter and her daughter's friends. And afterward when Scotia had departed and Kimi came downstairs flush-faced and happy Candace had asked what Scotia had said and Kimi replied, with averted eyes, "Oh, Scotia's just kidding, teasing—'fat cow' she calls me, sometimes—but not, y'know, mean-like. Not mean."

"'Fat cow.' That girl who looks like a young female twin of Mike Tyson has the temerity to call my daughter *fat*. Well!"

Candace pretended to be incensed though really she was relieved. Very relieved. *Fat cunt* was so much worse than *fat cow*.

Conversely, *fat cow* was so much less disturbing than *fat cunt*.

Another time, just the previous week, after Scotia came over to do homework with Kimi, next morning Candace was shocked to discover that, in the refrigerator, not a single smoothie remained of six she'd bought just the day before.

"Kimi! Did you and Scotia drink *six smoothies between you?*"

Kimi's face tightened. The soft round boneless face in which large brown eyes shimmered with indignation.

"Oh *Mom*. I hate you counting *every little thing*."

"I'm not counting—I'm recoiling. I mean, it was a visceral reaction—pure shock. I just went shopping yesterday and this morning all the smoothies are gone. No wonder you're overweight, Kimi. You really don't need to put on more pounds."

This was cruel. Unforgiveable.

Kimi made a sound like a small animal being kicked and ran upstairs.

• • •

"Kimi? May I come in, please?"

This is a tip-off: something is seriously wrong. For Mom is behaving politely—almost hesitantly. Instead of rapping briskly on the door and opening it before Kimi can reply.

Kimi's voice lifts faintly—whether inviting Mom in, or asking Mom not to interrupt her right now, she's working; but the door isn't locked, and Mom comes in.

"Hiya!"

"Hi."

Candace's eyes clutch at the girl—sprawled on her bed with her laptop opened before her, a shimmering screen that, as Candace slowly approaches, vanishes and is replaced with drifting clouds, exquisitely beautiful violet sky. Candace wonders what was just on Kimi's screen but has decided she will not ask, even playfully. Kimi bristles when Candace is too inquisitive.

Kimi is lying on top of her bed surrounded by the stuffed animals of her childhood: Otto the one-eyed panda, Carrie the fuzzy camel, Molly the big-eyed fawn. Since returning home from school Kimi has changed into looser-fitting clothes—sweat pants, sweatshirt. Her feet are bare and her toes twitching.

Last summer Kimi painted her toenails iridescent green, and still flecks of shiny green remain on her toenails, like signs of leprosy.

On the pink walls of Kimi's room are silly, lewd rock posters: Lady GaGa, Plastic Kiss, Raven Lunatic.

There is music in Kimi's room—some sort of chanting, issued out of her laptop. Kimi brings a forefinger to her lips to silence her Mom who nonetheless speaks: "Sweetie. . . . "

When Kimi, frowning at her music, doesn't glance up, Candace says she'd been summoned to Kimi's school that morning—"D'you know Dr. Weedle?—she has some sort of psychological counseling degree."

Kimi's surprise seems genuine. Her eyes widen in alarm.

"Dr. *Weedle*? What's she want with *you*?"

"She said that you were going to speak to me about an issue that came up at your school yesterday. But you didn't."

"Mom, I *did*. I mean, I certainly tried."

"You did? When?"

In a flurried breathless voice that is an echo of Candace's girl-voice Kimi tries to explain. She'd started to say something to Candace but Candace had been in a hurry and on her way out of the house and now belatedly Candace recalls this exchange but details are lost—crucial words are lost—Kimi had drifted away, and later that evening Candace heard Kimi in her room laughing, on her cell phone with a friend.

Candace has changed from her designer clothes into pencil-leg jeans, a magenta silk blouse, flannel slippers. She sits on the edge of Kimi's bed with less abandon than usual. Bites her lip ruefully saying, to enlist her daughter's sympathy, "I'm not good at whatever this is—a TV scene. If I can't be original, I hate to even try."

Kimi smiles to signal *yes*, she knows that her mother is a funny woman, and clever, and original; but Kimi is tense, too. For Mom has let herself into Kimi's room for a purpose.

"Kimi, I have to ask you—is someone hurting you?"

Candace is hoping that this will not turn out to be the horror film in which the perpetrator of evil turns out to be the protagonist—or maybe, on a somewhat loftier plane, this is Sophocles' *Oedipus Rex*.

Though knowing—*She has never touched her child in anger still less has she abused her child. Or any other child.*

Kimi sits up, indignant. Kimi tugs her sweatshirt down over her fleshy midriff. "'Hurting me'? You mean—making me cry? Making me *feel bad*?"

"Yes. Well—no. I don't mean 'hurting' your feelings—exactly—but 'hurting' *you*. Physically."

Kimi squirms and kicks, this is so—ridiculous! Candace sees a paperback book on the bed—Kimi's English class is reading *To Kill a Mockingbird* and this is consoling, to Candace.

"Mom, for God's sake! That is so *not cool*."

"Sweetie, this is serious. You are saying that no one has hurt you? No one at your school? Or—anywhere?"

"No one, Mom. Jeez!"

Yet Kimi's voice is faltering, just perceptibly. You would have to be Kimi's Mom to hear.

"Will you—let me examine you?"

"Examine me!" Kimi laughs hoarsely, an uncanny imitation of her mother's braying laugh. "What are you—a doctor? Psychiatrist? Examining me?"

Nonetheless, Candace is resolved. The roaring in her ears is a din of deranged sparrows.

"Will you let me look, Kimi? I promise that—I—I won't be—won't over-re-act. Dr. Weedle said something about a head injury—"

Kimi is scuttling away, crab-fashion, on the bed. Stuffed animals topple onto the floor with looks of mute astonishment.

"You hit your head on a—locker at school, and cut it? Did you go to the school nurse? Did you tell anyone? Did you tell *me?*"

Kimi would swing her hips around to kick at her mother but Mom has captured her, kneeling on the bed. The mattress creaks. Another stuffed animal falls to the floor, and the paperback *To Kill a Mockingbird*. Candace is panting gripping Kimi's head between her spread fingers—not hard, but hard enough to keep the girl from wresting free—as Kimi hisses, "Mom, you *smell!* Disgusting cigarettes, wine—you *smell!*"—as Candace peers at the girl's scalp through a scrim of fine feathery pale-brown hair at first seeing nothing, then—"Oh! My God"—Candace sees the dark zipper-like wound, something more than a simple scratch, about four inches long, at the crown of Kimi's head.

Candace is stunned, staring.

Feebly Kimi protests, like a guilty child.

"I didn't mention it to you because it's *just nothing*, Mom! I was stooping to get one of my shoes, in the locker room, after gym, and banged my head on the edge of a locker door—it didn't even hurt, Mom. It's *just nothing*."

"But it must have bled, Kimi—head wounds bleed...."

"Well, sure—but I didn't just let it *bleed*. I had tissues in my backpack and some girls brought me toilet paper, I just pressed it against the cut. After a while it stopped bleeding. Scotti had some kind of disinfectant, we went to her house after school, and she put it on the cut with an eyedropper." Kimi smiled, recalling. A guarded look came into her face. "Scotti's going to be a doctor, she thinks. Neurosurgeon."

"Is she! I wouldn't doubt, that girl could do it..."

But Candace doesn't want to get sidetracked into talking about Scotia Perry, whom Kimi hero-worships. Not right now.

Staring at the dark wound in her daughter's scalp, that had existed for how many days, without Candace knowing, or in any way suspecting, beneath the feathery child's-hair, Candace feels a sensation of utter chill futility—emptiness: the way she'd felt, just for a moment, in the women's restroom where she'd seen the poster with the photo of the bruised and battered girl—ARE YOU A VICTIM OF VIOLENCE, ABUSE, THREAT OF BODILY HARM? ARE YOU FRIGHTENED?

How awful the world is. No joke can neutralize it.

She has failed as a mother. She has not even begun to *qualify as a mother.*

Maybe just, oh Christ—cash in your chips. Tune out.

Suicide: *off-self.* Candace has always wondered why more people don't do it.

Candace is stammering—not sure what Candace is stammering—drawing a forefinger gingerly along the scabby cut in her daughter's scalp—"Not to have a doctor look at it, Kimi—it should have had stitches—I should have known..."

Not even begun to *qualify as a mother.*

Kimi pushes Candace's hands away. Kimi is flush-faced as if her soft smooth cheeks have been slapped.

"Mom, I told you—it's *just nothing.* If there'd been stitches—they'd have shaved my head, think how ugly that would be." Kimi makes a fastidious little face, in unconscious mimicry of her mother.

"But, Kimi—not to tell me about it, even...."

Kimi scuttles away drawing her knees to her chest. Candace is surprised as always by the fleshiness of her daughter's thighs, hips—the swell of her breasts. And now the hostility in Kimi's eyes, that are red-rimmed, thin-lashed as if she has been rubbing at them irritably with a fist.

You don't know this child. This is not your child.

See the hate in her eyes! For you.

"That really bothers you, Mom—doesn't it? That you were not *told.*"

"Yes of course. Of course—it bothers me. I was summoned to this terrible woman's office—in your school—'Lee W. Weedle, Ph.D.' it was an occasion for your school psychologist to terrify and humiliate me—and to threaten me."

"Threaten you? How?"

"She might report your 'injuries' to—some authority. 'Abuse Hot-Line'—something like that."

"But—I told them—my 'injuries' are *accidental*. They can't make me testify to anyone hurting me because *no one did*."

"This cut in your scalp—does it hurt now? Does it throb?"

"No, Mom. It does not *throb*."

"It could become infected...."

"It *could not* become infected. I told you—Scotti swabbed disinfectant on it. And anyway it doesn't hurt. I've forgotten about it, actually."

Candace lunges—clumsily—*this is what a mom would do, impulsively*—to hug Kimi and to kiss the top of Kimi's head, the ugly zipper-scab hidden beneath the feathery hair as Kimi stiffens in alarm, then giggles, embarrassed—"Jeez, Mom! I'm O.K."

Candace shuts her eyes, presses her warm face against Kimi's warm scalp, disheveled hair. She is fearful of what comes next and would like to clutch at Kimi for a little longer but the girl is restless, perspiring—resisting.

"Mom, hey? O.K. please? I need to work now, Mom—I have homework."

"Yes, but—it can wait for a minute more. Please show me your shoulders now, and your upper arms. Dr. Weedle said—you're bruised there ... "

"What? Show you—*what*? No!"

Now Kimi shrinks away, furious. Now Kimi raises her knees to her chest, prepares to use her elbows against Mom.

Candace is trembling. Is this abuse?—*this*? Asking her fourteen-year-old daughter to partly disrobe for her, to submit to an examination?

Candace is in terror, for maybe she is to blame. In her sleep, in an alcohol-ic-drug blackout, abusing her own daughter and forgetting it?

Kimi is more fiercely protective of her body beneath her clothes than she was of the wound in her scalp. Panting, crying—"Leave me alone! Don't touch me! You're crazy! I hate you!"

Candace kneels on the bed, in the twisted comforter, straddling the resist-ing daughter. Kimi is shrieking, furious—Candace is trying to pull Kimi's sweatshirt up—has to pull it partly over her head so that she can see the girl's shoulders and upper arms—oh this is shocking! frightening!—the bruises Weedle described, on Kimi's pale soft shoulders—ugly rotted-purple, yellow. In order to see Kimi's upper arms, Candace has to tug the sweatshirt off Kimi's head as the girl kicks, curses—"I hate you! I hate *you!*" Kimi's fine soft hair crackles with static electricity—Kimi's eyes are widened, dilated—like a furious snorting animal Kimi brings a knee against Candace's chest, knock-ing the breath out of her. Candace is disbelieving—how can this be happen-ing? She, who loves her daughter so much, and Kimi who has always been so sweet, docile . . . "You fat cunt! I hate you."

Candace stares at the bruises on her daughter's shoulders and upper arms—beneath her arms, reddened welts—and on the tops of her breasts which are smallish hard girl-breasts, waxy-pale, with pinprick nipples just visible through the cotton fabric of her bra—(Junior Miss 34B: Candace knows because Candace purchased the bra for Kimi). For several seconds Candace is unable to speak—her heart is pounding so violently. It does look as if someone with strong hands—strong fingers—had grabbed hold of Kimi and shook, shook, shook her.

"Your f-father? Did he—is this—? And you're protecting him?"

"Don't be ridiculous, Mom! You know Dad would never touch me," Kimi says scornfully. "I mean, Dad never even *kisses* me! How'd he get close enough to 'abuse' me?" Kimi's laughter is awful, like something being strangled.

"Then—who? Who did this?"

"Nobody *did anything*, Mom. Whatever it was, I *did to myself*. I'm a klutz—you always said so. Always falling down and hurting myself, breaking things—my own damn fault."

Kimi's eyes shine with tears. *Damn* is out of character, jarring.

Klutz. Such words as *klutz, wimp, dork, nerd* are just slightly more palatable than the cruder more primitive and unambiguous *asshole, fuckup, fuckhead, cunt.* Or maybe the equivalent would be *stupid cunt.*

So to call your daughter a *klutz*, or to conspire with others, including the daughter herself, in calling her *klutz*, however tenderly, fondly, is to participate in a kind of child molestation.

This seems clear to Candace, like a struck match shoved into her face.

"Kimi, you are not a 'klutz.' Don't say that about yourself."

"Mom, I am! You know I am! Falling, tripping, spilling things, ripping my clothes—banging my damn head, my legs"—with furious jocosity Kimi speaks, striking her ample thighs with her fists. "And a *fat cow-klutz* on top of it."

Family joke was that Kimi was a little butterball, chubby legs and arms, fatty-creased face like a moon-pie, and so *eager*—spilling her milk glass, toppling out of a high chair, spraining wrist, ankle in falls off tricycle, bicycle, down a flight of stairs.

Philip! Our baby daughter is a piglet. Cutest little piglet. With red eyes, red snub nose like a miniature snout, funny little pig-ears but—too bad!—no sweet little tail.

Young mother high on Demerol, entranced with her baby. *Oh Jesus it is a—baby! But—mine? Not mine!*

The horror washing over her, even as she felt love for the little piglet so powerful, could scarcely breathe and even now—fourteen years later—a muscle constricts in her chest, in the region of her heart—*Can't breathe can't breathe love comes too strong.*

And it was so—nursing started off so wonderfully—*Peak experience of my life*—then something went wrong. Little Kimberly ceased nursing as a baby is supposed to nurse, spat out precious milk, tugged at Candace's sensitive nipples and the nipples became chafed and cracked and bled and now, not so much fun. More, like—ordeal, obligation. More, like—who needs this. Milk turned rancid, baby puked a lot, cried and kicked at the wrong times. Young mother *freaking God-damned depressed.*

Fourteen years later not that much has changed. Except the baby's father is out of the picture even more than he was then.

That day returning home from Weedle and yes, Candace took another thirty-milligram Lorazepam reasoning that she will not be engaged in *operating heavy machinery* for the remainder of the day and yes, Candace washed down the capsule with a (only two-thirds full) glass of tart red wine but no, Candace did not sleep but spent headachy hours at her computer clicking onto *abuse, girls* drawn to read of *abuse, rape, female cutting, slaughter in Africa* until she became faint thinking, where were the girls' mothers? how do they bear living? Thinking, jokes cease when little girls are raped, strangled, left to die in the bush.

Exactly as Weedle said: you can see the imprints of fingers in Kimi's skin.

"I'm asking you again, Kimi—who did this to you?"

Kimi grabs her sweatshirt back from Candace and pulls it furiously over her head.

"Please tell me, was it a boy? I hope not a—teacher?"

Candace hears herself beg. Candace wants to gather Kimi in her arms for another hug but knows that the girl will elbow her impatiently away.

"Mom, for God's sake cool it."

"But honey—I want to protect you. I want to be a good mother. It isn't too late—is it? Don't push me away."

Kimi yanks the sweatshirt down over her breasts, as far as it will go. Kimi is exasperated and embarrassed but seeing the expression in Candace's face, Kimi says: "Well, see—what happened wasn't primary. It was, like, a secondary factor."

"What do you mean—'secondary'?"

"The cut in my head wasn't on purpose. Nobody actually hit me. I was slow doing something and she pushed me from behind and I stumbled and hit my own damn head myself on something sharp—not a locker door but a chrome table edge. And she stopped the bleeding, and put disinfectant on it, and kissed it, and was sorry. So—it's okay. It's, like, nothing."

"Who did this? She?"

"Scotti. Who've we been talking about?"

"Scotia? Scotia did this to you? What do you mean?"

"Oh, Mom. Jeez! Just forget it."

"But—what did Scotia do to you? Pushed you? So you fell, and hit your head? Why?"

Kimi shrugs. Kimi's eyes shine with a sort of defiant merriment but her skin is flushed-red, smarting.

"Why would Scotia do such a thing? What were the circumstances?"

"Probably some stupid thing I said. Or didn't answer fast enough. Scotti has a problem with *slow*. Half the kids in our class, Scotti says are *retards*."

"That terrible cut in your scalp—Scotia caused? But why are you protecting her?"

"Yes, my scalp. Mom. And my damn arms—you're so excited about—Scotti was helping me on the bars. Gymnastics."

"Scotia did that, too? 'Gymnastics'?"

"We were fooling around at her house. She's got all this Nautilus equipment her dad bought for her. You're always telling me to lose weight so I'm doing exercises at Scotti's. There're these, like, bars you hang on—Scotti was showing me how. No big deal, Mom—will you stop staring at me? I hate it."

"I'll call Scotia's mother. This has got to stop."

"It's *stopped*, Mom. I told you—it wasn't anyone's fault."

"It was Scotia's fault. And it isn't going to happen again."

"No! Don't you dare call Mrs. Perry! Scotti is the only thing in my life that means anything—the only person who gives a damn about me. If you take Scotti from me, I will kill myself."

Kimi begins crying, sobbing. Her swollen face seems to be melting. When Candace moves to embrace her, Kimi shoves her away as Candace expected—which doesn't make the hurt less painful.

• • •

Candace stumbles downstairs. Rapidly her mind is working—thoughts fly at her, through her, like neutrinos—can't quite comprehend the significance of these thoughts or what they are urging her to do—for a Mom must *do*, a Mom must more than simply *be*—until she's in the kitchen peering into the refrigerator: no Odwalla smoothies? *None?*

But there are ingredients for smoothies, Candace can make her own for Kimi, and for herself; strawberries and raspberries, banana, a dollop of orange juice, the remains of a container of yogurt blended together in Candace's shiny, rarely used twelve-speed blender. She is thrilled to be preparing something *homemade* for Kimi which she knows Kimi will love, and she knows that Kimi is hungry for Kimi is always hungry at this time of day, after school and before dinner which isn't always on the table until—well, after 8 PM. Or then. The blender yields two tall glasses of strawberry-tinged smoothies, rich with nutrients, and delicious. Candace thinks *But more.* She goes to a kitchen drawer where there's an old stash of pills, pre-Lorazepam, a handful of anti-anxiety meds, with tremulous fingers she empties one of the tall brimming glasses into the blender, tosses in a pill or two—or three—and whips the liquid again, grinds the pills to a froth, repours into the glass; then, who knows why, a neutrino-thought has pierced her brain with the cunning of desperation, she empties the other glass into the blender, tosses in a pill or two—or three—and whips the liquid again into a strawberry-hued froth.

Upstairs there is Kimi sprawled on her bed still wet-faced, panting and indignant—under the pretext of squinting into *To Kill a Mockingbird* she's been texting on her cell phone, which with clumsy childish deceit she tries to hide beneath the book so that Mom can't see. Of course Mom can see but Mom smiles radiant and forgiving as if not-seeing, carrying the glasses of strawberry-raspberry-banana smoothies—"For you, sweetie. And for me." Kimi is sullen but surprised and pleased—Kimi can't resist of course. Mumbling *Thanks Mom* for truly Kimi is a very well behaved and polite girl and always hungry.

Without waiting to be invited Candace sits cautiously on the edge of the badly rumpled bed and both Kimi and Candace drink their smoothies which are in fact delicious—"Better than what you get in the store, isn't it?"—and Kimi has to concede, yes.

"Just so you know I love you, honey. You do, don't you?—know this?"

Kimi shrugs, maybe. Yes.

Soon Kimi is yawning and blinking in a futile effort to keep her eyes open and Candace says yes, why don't you have a nap before dinner sweetie, a nap is a very good idea as Kimi whimpers faint as a kitten sighing and curling up to sleep unprotesting amid the stuffed animals which Candace has retrieved, to arrange on the bed around her daughter; as Candace, grunting with effort, beginning to be light-headed, straightens the comforter, fluffs up the flattened tear-and mucus-dampened pillow. Kimi's face is still puffy, flushed—her lips are swollen like labia—there's a babyish glisten at her nostrils Candace wipes tenderly with a tissue. With her new caution Candace takes away the smoothie glasses, makes her way swaying into the hall into the bathroom to wash each glass thoroughly in hot water, rub her fingers around inside the glasses and again hold them beneath the hot-gushing water and then returning to Kimi's room making her way carefully now knowing it is crucial not to slip, not to fall heavily onto the floor Candace returns to the white-wicker girl's bed where Kimi is now snoring faintly, lying on her side with her head flung back and her fine pale-brown hair in a halo on the pillow, beads of sweat at her forehead; the sweatshirt has been pulled down as if to flatten her breasts, showing a soiled neckline. Carefully Candace climbs onto the bed and gathers Kimi in her arms, her heart is suffused with love for her limp unresisting daughter, sweet little piglet, Mommy's own piglet, she has forgotten to switch off the light, the God-damned light is in her eyes. But what the hell.

THE PERFECT WEAPON

Zak Mucha

EXCERPT FROM *EMOTIONAL ABUSE: A MANUAL FOR SELF-DEFENSE*

"...there is no real difference between physical, sexual, and emotional abuse. All that distinguishes one from another is the abuser's choice of weapon."

—Andrew Vachss

If you feel this is an overly dramatic description, then your response is not uncommon. We have been socialized to believe emotional abuse is not serious. We have been taught without evidence of physical damage or physical contact between the aggressor and the victim, the abuse itself is nothing more than "hurt feelings" and there is no "real" evidence other than the victim's complaints. And if the only evidence is the victim's complaints, we wrongly justify, there is no way to verify whether these are valid. The victim of emotional abuse is dismissed precisely because he or she cannot "prove" their feelings. Here is the viciousness of emotional abuse—no one can prove their feelings.

Emotional abuse creates a vicious circle where the victim is taught his or her feelings do not count and any aggression suffered is, somehow, their own fault. Emotional abuse becomes the perfect weapon, one which the victim self-imposes long after the aggressor is gone.

Like any other abuse, emotional abuse is about power. Whoever can define reality has the ultimate power. In emotional abuse, the aggressor attempts to define reality with statements like, "You're too sensitive," and "I couldn't help it. You made me mad." Each statement is an attempt to shape how another person perceives the relationship and themselves. Telling another person they are "too sensitive" is nothing more than saying, "Your feelings have to be approved by me. I will tell you how to be . . . " The other side of that coin—the aggressor justifies his behavior, saying, "I did this because you made me mad. Therefore, the fault is yours, not mine. You are responsible for my behavior."

Emotional abuse changes our reality. We learn to blame ourselves for being hurt and we learn to blame ourselves for being targeted. We learn to redefine ourselves in the hopes that we do not get attacked again. In redefining ourselves we retreat to new, constricted boundaries for where we can go, what we can say, and how we "should" feel. We do this in an effort to avoid pain. When we do feel this emotional pain, we try to tell ourselves, "It's not that bad," which is another way of telling ourselves we are wrong for how we feel. We minimize our own pain, criticizing ourselves for even feeling it. We imitate and incorporate the aggressor's accusations, repeating the same things they told us about ourselves.

Physical and sexual abuse does not exist without emotional abuse. Emotional abuse is a component of any act where the aggressor hurts or uses another person for their own gains. All forms of abuse can be boiled down to a simple statement the aggressor says, silently or aloud, consciously or unconsciously: "I hurt you because it makes me feel better." The abuser will present layers of excuses and justifications while the unstated truth continues, "I will continue doing this as long as there is no cost."

A young man named Tyler Clementi was videotaped having sex with a partner in the privacy of his own room. When he learned his roommate and another accomplice were behind this, live-streaming the video on the internet, Clementi took his own life. When the roommate and accomplice were arrested, their first response was to deny any involvement. Once the police refuted that lie, the roommate and accomplice said they did it, but did not mean for Clementi to commit suicide. It might be true they did not expect Clementi to commit suicide, but their justification that they meant no harm does not stand scrutiny. What did they mean to do? Show their support? Love? Respect? Friendship? How did they expect the young man to respond? Did they honestly think he would enjoy the prank? Did they think he would sue them, or get a gun and shoot them? Or did they think he would not respond in any way dangerous to them? Consider what kind of response they were expecting—if they thought the young man would retaliate in any way, would they have destroyed his privacy? They did what they thought they could get away with.

The perpetrators claimed they were not responsible for the behavior of the victim. They also attempted to avoid responsibility for their own behavior. They only meant to demean the victim, not kill him. This is a common response from the abuser—they say they never meant to hurt him.

As observers we can end up collaborating when we accept the aggressor's excuses. The aggressors justify: *If someone is hurt, they must be overreacting. They must be too sensitive. They didn't get the joke.* If the victim commits suicide, the general consensus created by the media and social networking implies that the victim must have been emotionally unstable. No one notes that a steady diet of emotional abuse makes a person more susceptible to further, and escalating, abuse. No one notes that a steady diet of abuse is a factor contributing to emotional instability.

As a society, we remain willing to accept the abuser's minimizations. It is easier to blame the victim. The righteous indignation and efforts to stop the abuser in cases of physical and sexual abuse does not exist when the abuse is emotional or psychological. Instead, we accept the abuser's excuses: *I didn't say that; You misunderstood me; I was angry; You made me mad; I have a right to say what I want; I couldn't help myself; You're too sensitive; It was a joke; let's forget it and start over.*

This is why emotional abuse is a weapon equal to, if not more damaging than, physical or sexual abuse: We have been taught to accept these justifications. Emotional abuse becomes the perfect weapon when the abuser's excuses are accepted by the victim and by the community. The perfect weapon is one no one sees. The perfect weapon is one the aggressor can hand over to the victim to use against their own self. The perfect weapon is self-perpetuating. The perfect weapon leaves the victim believing they deserved the attack. The perfect weapon changes the victim's view of the world, of himself, and expectations for relationships.

Here's the simple definition of emotional abuse:

Emotional abuse is the systematic diminishment of another. It may be intentional or subconscious, but it is always a choice of conduct, not a single event. It is a pattern of behavior in a relationship, designed to reduce a person's self-perception to the point he considers himself unworthy . . . This perceived unworthiness manifests itself in the victim's belief they do not deserve respect, love, safety, caretaking, or choices.

• • •

As children, we are dependent upon adults for everything. Food, shelter, clothing, warmth, love, and empathy are all requirements. Children want these things without even understanding what they are. Children absorb whatever is presented to them. Dependent upon adults, children create definitions of themselves, their relationships, and the world, based on each interaction. Children are not resilient, they are completely malleable.

Watch the young boy who struts, imitating his father going out for the evening, or the adolescent who gets out of a chair, imitating the hitch in his father's back after a long day of work. Listen to the tone of voice a daughter picks up from her mother, expressing joy or exasperation. Children play, imitating the adults, practicing for their own adulthood and trying on different roles. At a quick glance, these behaviors may appear genetic, but these lessons learned are passed along both consciously and unconsciously, even when there is no DNA connecting the child to the adult.

As children we learn definitions for the world we inhabit. Not just concrete nouns, verbs, people, places, and things, but we learn to name emotions ("This feeling is...") and diagram how relationships operate ("If I do this, they do that..."). Most of this is so subtle, we do not notice the process. A child's world is colored by the experiences and the lessons the adults impart. We learn the importance of work, education, food, family, money, racism, ethnicity, religion, gender, and sex from the people around us. We are not born with any sets of beliefs, behaviors, or emotional connections. No children are born wanting to join the Klan. No children are born wanting to be a preacher or a doctor. No children are born believing love must include a degree of verbal abuse. We are taught such things, directly or indirectly.

Children learn in such a way it almost feels like osmosis. There are thousands of little messages children pick up every day. Some they accept immediately, some they discard, and others they hold on to until they can figure out what they mean. Some messages are too terrifying to consider for very long. All these messages stay with the child and contribute to who the child can become in adulthood. In a household where emotional abuse is normalized as a component of a relationship, the message learned by any victim is: *Your pain does not count. Not as much as mine. In fact, to prove you are a good person and a part of this family, you will have to carry more pain than others. If people act badly, you caused it. If you are hurt or offended by the behavior of others, it is your own fault...*

Because of these messages, the child learns he or she must do whatever it takes to avoid the displeasure of others. It becomes the child's duty to never make other people mad or angry or depressed. Taking on this responsibility, the child also accepts the blame for any conflict and any pain anyone might suffer. If others are in pain or angry, the child says, "It must be my fault. I am bad." If the child is in pain, the child says, "It's not that bad. I shouldn't be hurt." And the child learns to feel guilty or shameful for all those things beyond his or her control; the emotional abuse victim feels responsible for everything and in control of nothing. At fault, no matter what.

This is a responsibility no child should have to shoulder, but this responsibility is one the child volunteers for as a survival tactic in order to try to minimize their own pain. In doing so, the child can spend her life trying to make sure she doesn't do whatever she did in the first place, even though she doesn't know what that was. She doesn't know what she did wrong, but feels that she was wrong because she is in pain, uncertain of herself, uncomfortable. She is willing to change herself in order to maintain relationships. Things that prompt her anger go unacknowledged because she been taught she's "too sensitive." She learns how to be very careful of other people's feelings while also ignoring her own.

One young woman presents a common set of concerns, doubting herself while fighting to not recognize the aggression from her mother.

• • •

I remember my mother was like two people. Sometimes she would be really sweet and other times she would explode in my face. Food was always an issue. I was too fat, too thin. Ever since I was a little kid, the rule in the house was you had to eat everything on your plate... But she was perfect, I mean physically, there was not an ounce of fat on her. If I was eating anything outside of a meal, she would ask if I really needed that. If I didn't get the hint, she would start calling me any variation of fat. I felt like a lumpy, misshapen little kid. I was 11 years-old... She ended up being right—the more she said it, the more I ate. I would hoard food and eat it in secret. I wasn't like her, I felt like I needed the food. She told me no boys would ever be interested in me if I kept it up, the eating...

Sometimes she would scold me for eating, sometimes she would buy me diet books and help me cook special meals. Other times, she would use initials or little nicknames that sounded cute and harmless, but they always referred to my weight. I'm embarrassed even thinking about the specific names. If I got upset, she told me this was how she and her friends always teased each other and they never got mad.

By the time I went to prom, my mother said, "Well it was nice of any boy to ask you." This was a boy I was dating for two months and she made it sound like he was just being nice. She told me if my boyfriend ever saw me eating, he would break up with me.

In college, I gained the "freshman 15" and my mother clucked her tongue at me—just that noise was sickening. I knew that meant she was disgusted. Before I could leave the room she told me, "At least you won't get pregnant." When I got mad, she told me that wasn't what she meant. She only meant that I had so much to look forward to and a child would get in the way. She told me how much she had to sacrifice when she got pregnant with me.

Jennifer felt she could do "nothing" right. She felt "everyone" scrutinized her every meal and judged her weight, her hair, her complexion, her grades, her clothes... The criticism her mother presented, Jennifer assumed were shared by the rest of the world. Even when her accomplishments were applauded by others, Jennifer felt uncertain of herself. People were "just being nice" if they complimented her. They didn't mean it. She distrusted compliments, but assumed criticism was always true. Jennifer had no consistent measure of herself, but felt dependent upon her mother's approval. Her mother defined reality.

The only way to protect herself from her mother's disapproval was to be "perfect" in every way possible. Perfection as a goal is always self-defeating, a guaranteed failure. Perfection is inhuman. Jennifer placed herself in competition with an impossible fantasy. She would always lose. She even criticized herself in the second-person, as if she were addressing another person: "*You will never be...*" Not until Jennifer saw her own self-admonishments were literal recitations of her mother's criticisms was she able to see that she had adopted her mother's definitions and internalized her mother's voice.

Cruelty disguised as motivation is one of the basic tools of the emotional abuser. Many victims learn that diligent self-criticism without relent is a way of being a "better" person. This also allows the victim to avoid conflict with the aggressor, and to deny any pain or distress in the relationship. The victim of emotional abuse is forced to deny their own pain in order to "save" the relationship with the abuser; the victim of emotional abuse internalizes the aggression and accepts the fault to be her own.

Emotional abuse, by definition, has to be committed by a person we trust to some degree. The aggressor in emotional abuse cannot be a distanced stranger. To hurt another so deeply, the aggressor has to be important to the victim. Friends can hurt us, family can break our hearts. Strangers cannot. The cop who pulls you over and the landlord who never returns your calls can insult, intimidate, and disrespect us, but emotional abuse is dependent upon the relationship between the aggressor and the victim. The aggressor has to get close to plant the seeds, gaining the victim's trust, and creating a relationship the victim wants to preserve. Emotional abuse is a stealth attack that comes over time, testing boundaries while demanding loyalty to the aggressor. It is the only weapon that becomes a part of the victim long after the attack, like a time-release bomb going off over a period of years.

The more desperate the victim is to maintain the relationship, the more pain they are willing to absorb. The more pain you have to absorb, the more you have to tell yourself it is "normal" to feel like this. The more you have to try to convince yourself that this is not pain. To do this, you learn to redefine your own pain and your own emotional responses. You become susceptible to other emotional attacks across life. And this becomes, "How life is . . . "

Without a caretaker's empathy and compassion, a child will re-label the next best thing to be just that. This becomes the definition. This becomes *how the world is* . . . If emotional abuse is a part of that "love", the child will still define that behavior as love. If this "love" does not feel like enough, the child blames himself for wanting more. When that "love" is intermittent: "On Monday he's wonderful and caring, but on Wednesday he might call me a whore," the child decides the bad days are simply the price you pay to have any good days at all. If this is not satisfactory to the child, the child scolds himself that he should not want so much from others. He grows to adulthood believing happiness will always be out of reach because of his own imagined faults. He takes a piece of his parents' misery into his own adulthood, feeling as if it is a family curse or genetic predilection. These are the results, the damage, of emotional abuse. They are not hard-wired or Karmic. We can protect ourselves from this pain.

Emotional self-defense is a skill we each need to develop, either as children or as adults. When this skill is learned in childhood, the lessons are carried over into adulthood. If the skills are not learned in childhood, the fault is not that of the child. Emotional self-defense—the ability to say "this hurts"—is not a lesson children can teach themselves. Examples have to be provided, behaviors have to be modeled. The possibility of emotional self-defense has to be allowed rather than forbidden. Any child has to feel safe enough to acknowledge their pain without fearing the punishment of being abandoned or labeled "bad."

Victims of emotional abuse grow up to become hypervigilant to these threats and are willing to do anything to avoid that pain. The reference points a child learns from adults contribute to that belief system which contributes weight and severity to those threats as he or she grows to adulthood. Adults create the child's worldview. Opinions and cultural standards absorbed in childhood become unchecked and unverifiable "truths." The emotionally abused child, having felt the threat of abandonment or diminishment, learns it is too dangerous or "wrong" to be angry at, or hurt by, the people who are supposed to love her.

In an effort to protect the self and those vital relationships, the child alters definitions. The people who love us are not supposed to act like this, so we tell ourselves those hurtful behaviors are not hostile, aggressive, mean, or bad. The problem, we justify, "Must be me . . . I must be too sensitive." We make that decision because the relationship is needed. We have little choice in this. Our literal survival depended on these adults. As our knowledge of the world expands through adolescence and we see the difference between "them" and the rest of the world, we tell ourselves "they" must be "crazy" or "can't help themselves." And we put their emotional needs first, because they told us that's what we have to do to be strong, good, and earn their approval. What we learn at home, we take out into the world. Those lessons become generalized. We are taught to be strong only in socially acceptable ways:

• • •

Keep the peace.
Don't make waves.
Be nice.

The message behind those statements is: *Bury your feelings. Ignore your pain.*

If you stand up to the aggressor, they always respond with another variation of the instructions to ignore or diminish your pain. They say:

• • •

It's not that bad.
You're too sensitive.
I had it worse, don't complain.
You deserve it.
You made me do it.
That shouldn't hurt.

We are told such false mantras until we internalize them, dismissing our own pain and making the aggressor's excuses become the truth. As those excuses become truth, reality shifts and we are praised and rewarded for accepting it: When you swallow your pain, you can maintain the relationship. You learn to consider your own discomfort to be proof that you are "good." The abuser's behavior and excuses create the lie, but it's a lie we feel forced to accept. We feel the threat—spoken or silent—that the relationship will end, the partner will leave, the others will shun you if you do not accept the lie. In self-defense, we teach ourselves to become numb.

But wanting a relationship, wanting to be loved and cared for is normal and healthy. We humans are pack animals. We want to bond with others. We need to. From the moment of birth through to the end of our lives, we need other people. Food, shelter and clothing alone are not enough. We are not meant to live in solitude. This essential need for warmth is what makes us susceptible to emotional abuse, but it is also what makes us caring and empathetic humans.

This need makes us willing to accept the accusation, "It's your fault…" Adult victims of emotional abuse learn this dynamic early in life. No child independently has the ability to refuse the terms of a relationship with adult caretakers. So the child victim accepts the responsibility.

And this becomes more confusing when there are moments of affection from the abuser. In the previous example, Jennifer said of her mother, "It would be easier if she were a jerk all the time. Then I could make a decision. But sometimes she's really nice and being with her feels really wonderful. I wish I could get her to be nice all the time. Not even 'nice', but 'not-vicious' would be enough for me. I've tried everything I can think of to get her to be nice."

Jennifer spent years avoiding the acknowledgment that she is incapable of making her mother behave decently or that her mother will not behave decently. One of them, she suspects, is *bad*. One of them—either she or her mother—is making the other miserable. There no need for confrontation if Jennifer blames herself. But this decision forces her to endure and absorb more abuse.

As one woman explained of her abusive husband, "Maybe it's a trade-off that if I want him to love me I have to accept he's going to scream at me and have a girlfriend on the side." This woman notes that her boyfriend did not act like this when they started dating. If he did, she would not have tolerated it.

In becoming accustomed to the abusive behavior, we re-label their aggression as something else (love, concern, etc.). Then, having relabeled the aggressive behavior, we blame ourselves and our own perceived deficiencies for the pain that stays with us. This is one of the inherent aspects of emotional abuse—we do not recognize the pain as a specific result of interactions with the abuser, but perceive it as a part of us, a fault of our own character.

When the norm for any relationship includes a degree of victimization and blindness to one's own feelings, anxiety and depression become a constant to be coped with, rather than an illness to be eradicated. One day we notice we are not how we want to be. We do not feel like ourselves any longer.

For reassurance, we ask others how we "should" feel.

No one else can answer this for us. Any emotional self-defense techniques will rely on our ability to self-reference our own feelings. We have to know what actually hurts before we can learn how to deflect pain. Once we are better able to self-reference our own feelings, then we can identify our own needs and recapture the potential we have lost or had taken from us. No one else can decide whether we are in pain, or dictate the degree of our emotional pain. Too often, our own pain has been dismissed by other people and we have had to agree because they had the (real or perceived) power in the relationship and they were the ones who hurt us.

Acknowledging emotional pain is an act of bravery. It is a step in our healing. Emotional self-defense, like any self-defense, starts by looking at the question, "What hurts?" We have to be able to identify our own pain in order to eradicate the suffering. We will have enough normative pain in our lives—heartbreak, grieving, disappointments—but we can learn to eliminate the suffering and protect ourselves from aggression.

We can learn to defend ourselves emotionally.

Many of us have learned to ignore our own feelings or mask our emotional responses in order to deny the people we want to love, to like, to respect, are hurting us. Self-referencing our own emotional responses is a path that will vary from person to person. Often, that path doubles back on itself, broadening our own self-definitions. We become stronger, more confident, and more capable.

We learn to see our true potential and our true selves.

Emotional abuse is a part of the world, but it does not have to define "how the world is." Only if we accept cruelty and abuse as a part of our lives does it become a part of life.

If emotional abuse teaches us to ignore our pain, then the first step in defending ourselves from emotional abuse is to be honest with ourselves and acknowledge emotional pain. In this, we begin defining our own boundaries.

FREAK

Charles de Lint

—*1*—

"Do you understand the charges as they've been read to you?"

"Yes sir, I do."

"How do you plead?"

"Guilty, your honour."

—*2*—

"Get your head outta them comic books," Daddy'd say. "They're gonna rot your brain."

And I guess they did.

Or something happened to me that don't have any kind of an explanation that makes a lick of sense 'cause there's a mess inside the bones of my head that's been giving me a world of grief pretty much ever since I can remember.

I hear voices, see. Sometimes they're only pictures, or a mix of the two, but mostly it's them voices. Words. People talking. The voices show up inside my head with no never you mind from me and I can't shut 'em out.

They come to me about the same time I learned how playing with my pee-stick could be a whole lot of fun. I never knew it was good for anything but peeing until I woke up one night with it grown all big in my hand and I never felt anything near as good as when out comes this big gush of white, creamy pee. I felt bad after—like I was doing something dirty—but I couldn't seem to stop.

But when I finally did, the voices didn't.

For the longest time, I thought I was imagining them. I didn't have me a whole lot of friends, living out by the junkyard like we did, so it makes sense how maybe I'd get me an imaginary friend. But they was just voices. They didn't talk to me; they talked at me. Sometimes them voices used words I couldn't tell what they meant—they'd be too big or in some foreign language. And sometimes the pictures that come to me were of things that I'd never seen before—hell, stuff that I couldn't even start to imagine on my own—and sometimes they were of things I didn't *want* to imagine. People doing things to each other. Mean, terrible things.

I figured maybe the voices were punishment for all that playing I done with my pee-stick. You know, instead of growing hair on my palms, I got all this noise in my head.

But because they wasn't telling me nothing personal—they wasn't talking *to* me, I mean, like telling me I'd been bad or something—I come to realize that maybe I got something broke in my head. It was just something that happened, no accounting for it. Like I'd become a kind of radio, tuned to a station only I could hear, and these voices was just coming to me outta the air.

I can't remember when I finally worked out that they was other people thinking, but that's what they are, sure enough.

Funny thing about 'em is how they come with a smell. Like, take Blind Henry, lives on the street, same as me. His thinking's like the tobacco juice usta build up in the spit pot in Daddy's office. It was my job to dump it. I'd take it out to that cinderblock building at the back of the junkyard where we been dumping all manner of things. Oil and dirty gas, yeah, but other stuff, too. You'd go into that building and your eyes'd start to sting something fierce and the taste of puke'd rise up in your throat.

I remember the first time I saw the pirates come—I knew they was pirates because they had the Jolly Roger on the side of the barrels they brought in that big truck of theirs and they come late at night, secret-like. I looked hard but I never saw no one with a peg leg or a parrot, still they had the skull and crossbones, so I knew 'em for what they was. That first night I snuck outta the trailer and followed Daddy and them pirates to the cinderblock building and stared in at 'em through the window. But they wasn't hiding any treasure. Them barrels with the Jolly Roger on 'em only had some kind of watery goo that Daddy dumped into the pit.

Anywise, I was telling you how every voice's got its own smell. Daddy's was sweaty leather, like that old belt of his he used to whup me whenever he got in a mood. Mama's was like fruit, rotting on the ground. Kinda sweet, but not right.

The best voice is Jenny Winston's. It smells just like she looks, fresh and kind, like apple blossoms and lilacs when the scent of them comes to you from a few backyards over. Not too strong, but you can't mistake it.

I learned pretty damn quick to hide the fact I could hear what a body was thinking. People don't like it. It don't make no never mind that I can't stop from hearing it. They just assume you're a-doing it on purpose.

But I'd give anything to make it stop.

I can't never make 'em go away completely, I guess, not unless I went to live on some desert island where there was nobody else to do any thinking, but how would I live in a place like that? I can't do much for myself 'cept look for handouts as it is.

But I can tune 'em down some by listening to music. I don't know why it works, it just does. That's why I always had me spare batteries for this little transistor radio of mine—I'd make sure I got batteries afore I saw to getting me enough to eat.

It's hard in here without that radio. The voices that fill my head are cold and mean and hurting.

But better 'n the radio was live music.

Sometimes, afore they put me in here, I'd go in back of The Rhatigan, that little jazz club over on Palm Street. I'd sit in the alley by the back door and listen to the house bands play. It was best in the summer when they got the door propped open and them cool, moody sounds come floating out—they don't just take the voices away; that music makes me feel good, even when the band's playing a sad song, or the blues.

—3—

"Bernie—can I call you Bernie?"

"Sure. That's my name."

"You know I'm here to help you."

"Sure."

"The court may have appointed me to represent you, but that doesn't mean I don't care about winning this case."

"Sure."

"I think we need to send you in for psychiatric evaluation."

"I'm not crazy."

"Bernie, copping an insanity plea is the only chance we're going to have to save you from long-term incarceration or worse."

"I'm not crazy."

"This state still has a death penalty."

"I know that."

"If we don't do something, Bernie, you could end up on death row."

"Maybe that's the best place for something like me."

Daddy died first of the cancer. It just started growing in him one day and afore you'd know it, it was spread all through him. He was in a lot of pain by the time it finally took him, which made him real hard to be around. My head was filled with the screaming of his thoughts the whole time. That was an ugly time.

Mama died not long after—cancer took her, too—but she went quietly. Like a long, drawn-out whimper.

Cousin Henry took possession of the junkyard and become my guardian until I turned sixteen. Then he sent me packing with hard words and meaner thoughts.

That's how I come to be living on the street this past couple of years. I tried to find work, but nobody wants something as ugly as me to look at, day after day.

See, I never had no chance at a normal life. It's not my hearing the voices—I learned pretty damn quick to keep that to my ownself. It's that I look like a freak. Got no meat on my bones, but I got a head big and round as a damn pumpkin, and my skin's all splotchy with big red marks like I got me freckles on steroids. It made the kids laugh afore I dropped out of school, but now people just stare, then look away, like I turn their stomach or something.

I always had that big head and I never did grow into it. There's times I wish it was even bigger so that I could get a steady gig in a sideshow or something. People'd still make fun of me, but it wouldn't be the same, would it? It'd be like my job. I'd be getting paid for being a freak.

In them comic books I used to read, I'd've been a hero, what with being able to read people's minds and all. I woulda got myself some fancy clothes and a mask and I'd go out and save people's lives 'n stuff. It wouldn't matter if I looked like a freak 'cause I'd be part of some gang of superheroes, saving the world 'n stuff and people'd admire us and like us, even me. In the comic books, a freak like me can still live a good life. Hell, sometimes they even get them a girl.

But I don't live in no comic book and the only time I tried to be a hero is what put me in here.

I ain't saying I didn't mean to do what I done. Hell, I'd do it again if the situation come 'round same as it done before.

How it happened was I was panhandling outside the gates of Fitzhenry Park. It's mostly women give me money. I guess, ugly as I am, they still want to mama me. Or maybe they're mamas themselves, thanking God their own kids didn't turn out like me and they drop a couple of bills in my cap like they would an offering of thanks in church.

I don't ask. I just keep my head down and say thank you ma'am, earphones in my ears and the music from my radio keeping me from hearing too much of what anybody's thinking.

The day it all went down, Jenny Winston comes by like she often does. She's one of Angel's people, them sorta social workers who help street people 'cause they care, not 'cause it's some job.

Jenny's good on the inside and out. I should know. She's the prettiest woman I ever saw, but anybody can see that. But I hear her thinking and there's not a bad thought in her head. She can look at me and all she sees is a person, not some freak with an oversized head.

This day she gives me a sandwich and a little carton of milk, asks me if I need anything, so I take the 'phones outta my ears to answer her properly. That's when I hear the thinking of the guy standing behind her.

The look of me turns his stomach, but that's no big surprise. It's what he's thinking 'bout Jenny that makes my blood run cold.

Lotsa people think bad things. The difference between bad people and good is that good people don't act on 'em. If you didn't know better, you might get confused as to which a fella might be, but I've got so's I can tell the difference.

And I can see in his head, he's done this afore. Courted a pretty gal and then done away with her. He's got him a whole set of graves, laid out in a nice little row, way back up in the mountains.

How come he never got caught? You'd think somebody'd have figured out he's got all these girlfriends disappearing on him. But there he is, standing behind Jenny, not a care in the world, just kinda daydreaming of the day he's gonna do her in, too, so I guess he's got something working for him.

There's folks like that. There's folks get away with pretty much anything. It's like common sense just turns its head away from them, don't ask me why. And the more I listen to him, the more I see he's a sly one. Not many folks know how serious him and the gal's getting. Usually he pretends he's getting a divorce so they can't let on how it is between 'em until the paperwork's done. So this gal, she's got herself a true love, they're gonna get married and all, but she can't tell anyone just yet.

I see all that in his head. It's something he thinks 'bout all the time—these are the things that make him feel good.

And this time he's gonna do it to my Jenny.

I don't mean I ever thought she'd be interested in the likes of me. Hell, I'm just an ugly freak; I ain't stupid. But she's been kind to me. She's kind to everyone. She's not like some of the others who work with Angel to help us street people. Most of the others come up offa the streets and it's their chance to give something back. But Jenny wasn't like that. She's helping 'cause she's got her too big a heart. She wasn't hurt as a kid. She didn't live on the streets. The thing is, she just can't stand by when others are in need. It's as simple as that.

So she's ripe for the plucking of a man like the one standing behind her now, accompanying her on their rounds afore they go to dinner, pretending to care so much for her. She don't see through him 'cause she can't read what's inside another's head like I can. 'Cause she only sees the good in people. While he, oh he's a-glorying in what's to come.

How come somebody as good as her attracts that kind of person?

I don't know. Same reason that people like my parents are allowed to have them kids, I guess. There's no sense to it, not unless we were really bad people in some other life and this is payback time. But I don't buy that. Life's just the way it is. Kids get born into families that don't even want 'em, never you mind love 'em. And good always attracts evil. The strong feed on the weak. Guess if there's any rule to living, that's what it is, and it's up to each of us to put what charity and kindness we can muster back into the world.

So I get up off my feet and I walk over to him. I reach under my coat to where I got me a sheath hanging under my armpit and pull out that old Randall knife I stole from my Daddy's office afore Cousin Henry sent me packing. It's got an edge sharp enough to shave with, which I've done a time or two. I don't say a word. I just whip the blade across his throat and cut him deep.

People mistake me. They think 'cause I'm so skinny, got this big head, that I can't move fast. But it ain't like that at all.

It's over and done afore anybody can make a move. Then he's falling, blood spurting outta his neck. Jenny's screaming—oh what she thinks of me hurts something fierce. There's other people on the sidewalk screaming and rushing around.

I try to tell Jenny what he was thinking, how I can read what's in people's heads, but she won't listen. She can't hear me. And I realize it don't make a whole lot of difference anywise.

I just drop the knife on the pavement and stand there, watching the real freak die while I wait for the cops to come and take me away.

—5—

"Do you have any last words?"

I look through the plate glass window to where the witnesses are sitting, staring back at me, all strapped down and waiting to die. There's a lot of dark thoughts coming my way, but I can pick out Jenny's real easy. I just follow the scent of apple blossoms and lilacs. She's sad, but there's a hardness in her, too. She's looking at me, thinking there's the man who killed the fella I loved. He deserves to die for what he done. But she's not easy about this business of a death penalty. It feels too much like revenge to her. And though there's a part of her wants revenge, she knows it's not right. Trouble is, she's not strong enough to stand up and say it's wrong neither.

Do I have any last words?

I could tell back what Jenny's thinking right now so that she'd know I was telling the truth. I could go right into her head and pull the thoughts out, word for word. But then she'd have to live with her part in putting to death the man who up and saved her and I can't let that happen.

She's safe now. That's all that matters.

"Yes sir," I say. "I ain't sorry for what I done. Best you give me that injection now."

And they do.

AN OPEN LETTER TO THE CHILDREN OF THE SECRET

C. Dionysios Dionou

Tortured far apart
Children of the Secret are
Alone until love

—Andrew Vachss
from the dedication to *Born Bad*. © 1994 Andrew Vachss.

I'm a child of the secret. I have been my entire life. I come from a large tribe. My tribe has no borders, knows no race, religion, or ethnicity. Yet we cover every continent. Who are we? We're the *children of the secret*. Our secret is the pain we carry deep within us. The pain of neglect, abuse, torture, humiliation, that has been our lives. Most painful for us is the knowledge that we suffered at the hands of those who were supposed to protect us. Those who were supposed to nurture us, support us, laugh with us, cry with us, and should have instead been grateful for us, and proud of us. This was not our lot. We wished it was, we raged for it, cried for it, and prayed for it. We never got it. What we *did get* were the scars, the many scars we all carry. Some can readily be seen, other run deep. They cannot be seen with the eye, but we feel them every day of our lives. It is these deep scars that hurt us the most. The ones you cannot *see* but we children of the secret can *feel*, and we live with the cost. This is an open letter, a public essay for all. But most importantly, it is for my brothers and sisters of my tribe. It's for them, and to them, that I write this letter. Many will read this essay. My tribe will *feel* this essay. For them my words may open wounds, and that's alright. Wounds heal but not always properly. The scar tissue though healing leaves other types of damages. When this occurs sometimes the wounds need to be reopened, like an orthopedist needing to break and reset a bone, in order for a better healing to occur.

• • •

Anyone can survive an event or a trauma in their lives. People regularly survive illness, accidents, combat, personal, and financial loss. However when it comes to the *children of the secret* there is a major difference. Survival is only half the battle won. The other half sadly too many of my brothers and sisters never fight nor win. Yet it is the most important part of our struggle. It is the battle to transcend. This I have done, and it is to this topic, for people who came up like me, that I'm addressing. How did I accomplish this? What difference did it make in my life? What difference will it make in *your* life? The following is my response. Let's go back to my beginning.

• • •

I'm a sold child, sold for Judas' purse. My purchasers (certainly not qualified to be parents) bought me and took possession of their *purchase* when I was 5 months of age. Both of my purchasers were mentally and emotionally ill-suited to be parents irrespective of how they had a child. For much of my developing years I was emotionally and at times physically abused. Often I was referred to by my purchasers as "dog", "Baby Huey" (think cartoon character of the 60s), "louse", "dope", "son of a bitch", I needn't go on, you get the picture. Beatings were sporadic but intense, and occasionally plates were slammed on my head. Though most painful to me was the verbal, and emotional abuse. This combined with the total blackout of my origins, which I was told often to simply forget. "Just be like us" is all I was told. That alone was horrific for me. To be like them, for sure would have been what Victorian era novelists called, "A fate worse than death." My life was chaotic, and dismal. I had a quick mind and intelligence far beyond my age, and as such became the butt of other kids, who had only the most superficial knowledge about anything, and seemed to have no interest in changing their status. I excelled in all school subjects except for math. This brought a torrent of abuse upon me from unsympathetic teachers, to the neverending rantings of my purchasers. They were convinced there was something very wrong with me, and dragged me to several shrinks in order to "find out what's wrong with you." Meaning you're not turning out as we wanted, this was not a good *business deal*. They were convinced that they didn't get *their money's worth*. What then to do? Well just as you would do with a dog that you bought from a shelter, that's not behaving as you would want it to, you're left with two options. Either you return the dog to the shelter, or you beat the animal into submission. Since it was impossible to *return me*, beating me into submission seemed the only option available. Breaking and crushing can be done emotionally, and verbally, leaving plenty of scars, but none to the eye.

Those of you from the secret know exactly what I mean. Don't you? Of course you do. Tell a child they're fat, stupid, an idiot, a moron, their teeth are crooked, they should just fall down and die, you're nothing without us, you're a loser, and you will do more longterm damage to that child than a kick to the ribs, or a vicious pulling of the hair. Most importantly the pain from the verbal abuse will last longer, and run deeper, than any beatings they receive. Why is this so? Many have asked us this question, as if a tongue lashing hurts any less than a cat o' nine tails. When you're hit you feel the pain, and you understand why you have the pain, you have been hit, struck, assaulted. But when you're cursed, insulted, humiliated, mocked, you cannot understand why. Especially if you're a child, or young adolescent, for you this becomes even more disturbing. Why would your *parents* call you these things, say these things to you? Aren't they supposed to *build you up* not *tear you down*? The pain and confusion you feel, and feel deeply inside your core is devastating. Growing up is not easy. The outside world is cold, mean and unforgiving. To the young child, to the teen, their home should be a haven of comfort, support and safety. The home should be a place to go when the outside world gets too heavy, too intense, and you need a place to relax, reset, and find support, love and caring. When this is not to be, when the outside world is pressing, and your home is equally pressing, then you find yourself caught in a vise grip, that can, and will, crush the spirit out of you. Not necessarily the life out of you, though it can do that too.

Worse is to leave you a broken shell, and like Humpty Dumpty you need to put yourself back together again. If you cannot put yourself back together, then your abuser will fit the shell back into the shape that suits them, though this may leave you very cracked, and an empty human being. Know what I mean? Yes of course you do, you too have felt it, as I did, so many years ago. What was worse for me was on top of this avalanche of abuse, was the nagging, the longing, to know exactly who I am. Where did I come from? Who are my people, my ancestors? For it sure as hell wasn't my purchasers' culture or religion. Theirs left me as cold as a side of beef hanging in a walk-in ice box. Eventually in my early teens I learned my true identity, by accident. I was born in Greece. I was baptized Dionysios in the Orthodox Church. This hit me like Vulcan's thunderbolt. I came from a great heritage, a great legacy that I had read about, and studied on my own, and in school. Now to my shock and happiness I learn that it's mine, I'm a Hellene! Now I knew my legacy, and now I had to claim it as mine.

This wasn't so easy.

• • •

My purchasers were hell bent on making sure that I would neither know nor desire anything of my life or birth culture prior to being bought by them. They tried to impose their own religion and culture on me. That backfired louder than a tailpipe! My identity papers were left in a metal box in a closet. Like Pandora's, I opened it and let their worst nightmare out. Now they had to set about crushing me any way that they could. I resisted with all my heart and soul. I fought them back like a wild beast in a cage. The verbal and physical violence in my *home* reached explosive proportions. In a rage the male of my purchasers raised a knife to me, but I was too fast for him, and I escaped until he calmed down.

My purchasers weighed in on me like a wrecking ball. To destroy me, tear me down and rebuild me as they wanted me to be. To escape, I began to run with a very bad crowd, got into much mischief and trouble. Eventually, I focused. Various events in my life caused me deep pause (read my memoir to find out what had happened). Suffice to say I knew in my heart, in my soul, that I was better than them, and better than their miserable respective families. But what could I do?

I decided to do what I call *inner migrate*, I went inside myself and I lived there. Outwardly, I gave the impression that I had given up, that my purchasers, that the two freaks had broken me and won. They didn't win a damn thing. In my heart, in my soul, I was Dionysios the proud Hellene, while to the world I was whatever brought me the peace I needed to continue to work, go to college, and establish myself.

This was only half the battle. I fought and I fought hard. My entire life I was a fighter, in one sense of the word or another. I fought and I won. I survived. But this was not the brass ring. Survival wasn't the key, all this meant was that I fought it out, wore them out, outfoxed my purchasers and I'm here. I married and I had two children. Now I would face the real challenge, the final battle, the battle to transcend. If I lost this battle, then all of my earlier victories were Pyrrhic in the extreme, empty and hollow. I had to transcend, to be the father I neither knew nor had. How did I do it? I will tell you. Though explaining this is not as easy as you might think.

• • •

You see, when you don't transcend, you don't heal. Or you heal broken. Liken it to a broken arm that isn't set properly. The arm heals, but it doesn't function properly, doesn't function to optimum condition. It's the same with a child of the secret who never heals. We function, but not healthfully, nor do we have a high level quality of life. Some of these members of our tribe *think* they're healed, because they may have had commercial success, and this brought them a high living standard, or a luxurious lifestyle. As such they *think* "Well, I turned out alright, I overcame, look at me. Today I'm a business man, doctor, lawyer, plumber, general contractor, actor, singer, musician. I have a great house, sharp cars, I shop in boutiques not outlet stores, I go on vacations, the theatre, dine in top restaurants. Obviously I transcended."

No you didn't. Why? It's because you drink heavily, you use cocaine or are heavily into weed, you verbally and/or physically assault your spouse, your children, and though you never knew it, your friends find you either weak and without independence of thought, or nasty and irritable. Or you're hyper vigilant, overly critical, and always have to be right. Recognize yourself? Yeah, *you know who you are*. Pretty soon your friends tire of you if you're the hyper vigilant, I have to always be right type. Or if you're the weak-willed type, they take advantage of you, and then they dump you.

While you go through life lamenting, "Why do I attract such assholes into my life?", it's because you never *broke the link* between the damage that was done to you (and damage was done, accept it or not) and as such, you continue the patterns and the resulting behavior. Maybe not always in the same way as your abusers, but you carry it with you into your adulthood. No amount of university degrees, 4,000+ square foot homes, Benz, BMW, Porsche, Rolex or Movado watches, Mikimoto pearl necklaces, orchestra seating on Broadway, or dinning in high-end restaurants will change this. Add children into this equation and it's even worse. Unless you transcend you are going to *continue the abuse* that you experienced, and *pass it on* to your kids. When your kids reach adulthood, they too will pass it on, the links in the chain of abuse having never broken.

• • •

The Danish pioneering psychotherapist Erik Erickson coined the concept, "the child as father to the man." Now at first glance, reading this statement, it might sound strange. How can a child be a man's father? Shouldn't it be the reverse? Biologically yes it should, psychologically, and mentally no. As Erickson understood, and we transcended children of the secret *understood and experienced*, all childhood conflicts, pains, traumas, and issues, not resolved will continue on into, and acted out, in the behavior of the adult. The child's life *creates* the life and behavior of the adult. When one of our tribe doesn't transcend, then he or she will be in continual conflict and battle within themselves. Still trying to fight the abusers, looking for the love they never had in all the wrong places, or a combination of both. Emotionally, behaviorally they are like the incorrectly set broken arm, or a malfunctioning clock. They are the assembly line that creates more broken clocks and malfunctioning arms. The only way to break the link is to transcend. Although forgiveness could be a part of it for *some* of us, it is not a universal requirement for transcendence. Until you understand this, my brothers and sisters of the secret, you will never transcend. No amount of drinking, drugs, financial success, or empty gestures of forgiveness will do it.

• • •

This of course then begs the question, *How do you transcend?* My answer might shock you, I don't know! I know how *I transcended*, you might have another route. All of us children of the secret traveled the same highway. We just got off at different exits. Here's how I transcended. Perhaps as you read you'll recognize some of your own thoughts and conclusions. For me it was to recognize what I call offsetting the damage, or tipping the scales. What does all of this mean? For years I suffered systematic emotional and physical abuse. I was regularly cursed and called practically every insulting and humiliating name imaginable. What did I do? As a young child I fought back, threw temper tantrums, rages, screaming, crying, I ran away and rode the New York City subways for hours, often at night. But this wasn't aimless wandering.

While I rode the IRT and the BMT lines I would become focused. Focused on everything around me, I would observe each subway station, its design, the mosaic tiles, that told me at one time this was a very impressive subway system, until political neglect let it become run down (this was in the mid-to late 1960s). I would stand in the front subway car looking out of the window and in my mind I was the motorman. I would observe the tunnels, the switch tracks, and figured out how they operated. In the hot summer when the motorman would keep his cab door slightly ajar, I would start a conversation with him. Most were very friendly, and I would ask them questions about operating a subway train. I learned about how subway trains operated. Powered by electricity, I learned about air pressure, how to start and brake the train. I learned about the dead man's handle, and how it was a safety device. If the motorman's hand let go of the handle the train came to an immediate, sudden halt. I learned about the chuck key and how its positioning determined if the train ran forward or backwards. I learned how the motorman knew when the doors of the subway train were closed: a small light went on in his cab. I was, and still am a quick study. I learned all of this quickly, and once I mastered it, I would talk to other motormen *with authority*. I had the *power of knowledge* and they were all impressed how a kid barely ten knew so much about the subway system and trains. I felt good, I felt strong. I felt like I was *important*, I actually *mattered*.

I then struck up conversations with the token booth salesmen. (No swipe cards in those days. How many of you remember *tokens*?) One of them actually let me inside the booth to work the token counting machine! I went to Coney Island, bought a crab trap and caught crabs off of Steeple Chase Pier. I met a kindly fisherman who showed me how to use his fishing rod. I could fish, I could eat my catch, I could *survive*. When not riding subways or hanging out in Coney Island, I was in the library. Reading book after book in the library, and not just kid's books, fancying myself a *crab fisherman,* I studied all types of crabs and crustaceans. Even tide pools and break waters. I could name the various crabs and lobsters from memory and *discuss each one of them* in depth. I even bartered some of my crabs for a free lunch on the Coney Island boardwalk. I could do commerce and negotiate too! It was these bits and pieces that gave me the strength to endure, to handle the chaotic miserable existence that was my so-called home. I thought *maybe, after all, there was nothing wrong with me.* Even the shrinks I was dragged to by the freaks, to find out what was wrong with me, seemed to like me, and had no problem with me. Maybe, I started to think, *there wasn't anything wrong with me.*

• • •

But the abuse continued, and as I entered my teen years it got worse and worse. I had to get away, but where to go? In my mid-late teens I took to the streets. I got involved with a cast of characters that were a playbook cross of Damon Runyon and Nicholas Pileggi (think *Guys 'n' Dolls* and *Goodfellas*). I ran for a while with a very bad crowd. I got into all kinds of mischief (to say the least). I was heading down a very dark path. I got picked up by undercover NYPD, and landed in a holding cage. In the cage this older Chinese guy started talking to me. He was like the *I Ching* on legs. He told me that I would be all right in life, that he could tell that I suffered much, but I could handle it, and the key to my life was deep within me.

I had to look inwards and not outwards, to find my answers. We were soon released from the holding cage. We left the precinct, we shook hands, and went different ways. I never saw him again, but he made me think, and I soon quit *the life*. Back to my so-called *home*, and back to my books, now including much Asian reading: *Sun tze*, *The I Ching*, and *The Book of the Tao*. I also read the books of my ancestors: Herodotus, Plato, Aristotle, Thucydides, and Plutarch; the famous Romans, Livy, Tacitus, Cesar, Suetonius, and Cassius Dio. I searched and searched for knowledge. Many of these works, I had skimmed as a young child; now I read them closely and seriously. I read Adam Smith, Marx, Machiavelli, Nietzsche, and Clausewitz, and I took something from every one of them.

I even read medical dictionaries. When I injured my knee badly at age 16, I cleaned, closed, and treated the laceration myself in my bathroom. My doctor afterwards wanted to know who worked on it. He told me the repair was done well, but why weren't stitches used? When I told him I did it, but didn't know how to stitch a wound, you should have seen his face of shock, surprise, and admiration. He told me I'd have a scar. (Like I didn't have plenty already? I thought to myself.) His expression told me he was impressed. *I impressed him. I could impress people, even doctors.*

By the time I was studying for my B.A., I was more and more focused. I still had to deal with the neverending barrage from my *purchasers*. I knew how to play them. There's a Russian proverb, "When you live amongst wolves, you learn to howl like one." I learned how to *howl* and blend, but all the while I inner migrated inside myself. I presented to my *purchasers* what they wanted to see. But inside I was someone very different, and that someone was incubating, waiting for the right moment to come out and strike. Still, it was not easy. The stress was intense, and it often brought me to the point of sporadic but intense panic attacks. I fought through them and continued on my path. During my university days, I met several men, and a woman who took me under their wings, and like the guy in the holding cage, they made me think. They introduced me to famous well known people in many fields. I graduated college with a Bachelor's Degree in the Arts with honors, and won a summer school scholarship to Greece.

• • •

In a moment, in a flash the sword of Damocles that hung over my head for most of my life was gone! I was like Archimedes, who screamed *I'VE GOT IT* and ran screaming from his bath naked into the streets of Syracuse, so excited to tell everyone what he had discovered. Well I didn't run bare-ass through New York City! But I understood everything clearly. All my life I was told I was stupid, an idiot, a dog, a louse, a bastard, I should just die, I'll never amount to anything, just a dope, a loser by the people who were supposed to do the opposite. The ones who should be building me up were always pulling me down. Yet while I'm being emotionally torn to shreds at home, other people, in some cases *strangers,* are telling me I'm smart, well read, very erudite, intelligent and worldly beyond my years, I have a great sense of humor, very handsome, great dancer, amazing cook. . . .

Who do I believe? Do I believe my *purchasers,* the freaks, *or* do I believe others who have nothing to gain from all their many compliments of me? I know in my heart, in my core, in the depths of my soul, I'm *not what the freaks and their relatives say I am, to my face, or behind my back.* Strangers, yes, strangers see in me what I always knew in my heart I had within me. I wasn't what the freaks said I was, and now I knew it and I could *feel* it. This was my *transcending moment and from then on it just got better for me.*

Not perfect, I still had a motherlode to deal with. But now I dealt with it differently. Everything changed: my goals, dreams, the direction of my life, even most of my friends. I still howled with the wolves. I had selfish reasons for doing so. But I howled *on my terms* now. This is what my brothers and sisters of the secret must do, you must decide, you must self-reference: Were your abusers correct? Were your tormentors justified in their actions? Or were those who gave you compliments and support correct? They saw something *in you.* Isn't it about time that *you see it, feel it,* and *acknowledge it?* You must decide. It's the highway all of our tribe traveled. You see these exits? Which one will you take? One exit will take you off the highway and then put you right back on it. The other exit will take you off the highway of pain and broken dreams *for good!* Do this and you will be able to achieve the greatest feat any child of the secret can do: be the father or mother that you never knew, nor had, and break the cycle of abuse forever.

I did it. Now let me tell you how I became a transcended father, so *you* can do it too.

• • •

Our traumas taught us much about ourselves and about life. We're in tune to our feelings, and understand that others often are not. When my first child, my daughter Sophia was born, I swore to myself that I would be the father I never knew nor had. Never for a moment was I concerned that I couldn't be. Why? My horrific early years and abuse enabled me to understand much about childhood and child-rearing. In effect, I had a negative education. I *knew what not to do*. I *knew how to behave* and *how not to talk* to my Sophia. Three years later my son Paul was born, and it was not even an issue.

I knew my job as Dad to my kids was to guide, nurture, and create for them a home where the vibe was one of love, strength, frankness, and focused determination. I understood that my kids needed not just guidance, they also needed discipline. Homes where too many kids are growing up in chaotic situations, where anything goes, and parents try to be buddies with their kids. They are afraid to discipline their kids. They worry that they will go too far, imitate their own abusers. Such of our brethren are not transcended. Discipline is *not abuse* however *abuse* can be confused with discipline. How can we tell the difference? The answer is already within you. *You* know the difference, because you experienced it! You *lived* it. Didn't you? You *felt* the difference. You knew there was no need for you to be beaten because you spilled a glass of something. You knew you didn't deserve to have your head hit because you were not good in a particular school subject, when you shined at all the others. You knew that a helping hand, not a striking hand would have made all the difference in the world. Then why I ask you would you raise the same hand to your child or children? You don't know better? Come on, you know you do. You can't help it? Unless you're a full blown psychotic, then *yes you can help it*. Or maybe it just makes you feel good? Maybe you *like hurting* your kids? Does this question make you recoil as you read it? Congratulations, none of the excuses apply to you. *You have no excuses!*

• • •

You can discipline without abusing, I know, I have done it. You can do it, too. It's the same with emotional abuse, which I'm firmly convinced leaves us more longterm suffering and damage than any beating can provide. When I got hit, either by the freaks, in street fights, and years later in sparring matches, I knew why I'm hurt, why I'm in pain. It's because someone *hit me*, in one form or another. Justified or not, I can absorb it, counter it, and heal from the initial trauma.

But emotional abuse is very different. The weapon is the tongue, and I remember a dear departed friend of mine, who was also a mentor to me used to say, "Be careful what you say. Your tongue is a weapon, and when you attack someone with your tongue, it's the same as if you punched, kicked, or body slammed them. The words that fire off your tongue wound as painfully and seriously as any 9mm or .45 ACP. Once you fire them you can't take them back." Whatever physical abuse we've had to endure, all of us children of the secret know nothing hurts more than the words. They echoed in our ears, they burned our hearts, they vivisected our souls. Some of us believed the words, the verbal torture. Others (like me) didn't believe them, but still felt the wounds, we were hurt, we were injured, but there was no clinic to go to that could make you heal. You had to heal yourself.

I used to be told all the time as a kid, that I was too short. I was told to stand in the doorway and stretch and hang from a cross bar. When I didn't want to, I was told I was lazy. No I wasn't lazy, I just wasn't overly concerned about my height. But the freak was very, very *freaked* about it. Maybe because *she thought* it made *her look bad*? So in order to bolster her feelings of insecurity, I was torn down. I felt terrible until I began to study historical figures in libraries. I learned that many famous people were my height. *Wow! Kings, emperors, czars, generals, sultans, industrialists, U.S. presidents, and entertainers were my height. Screw that bitch, I'm in seriously good company.* It was like magic! My height never bothered me again.

You see the truth is, my brothers and sisters of the secret, there was *nothing wrong with us*, but there was *a lot wrong with our abusers*. You know how their words hurt you. Why use those words on your kids? This does not mean that your kids won't frustrate, annoy, or irritate you. They will at times. They're kids. But there is a way for you to address this: explain, demonstrate, lead the way for them by example, and help them when they're in a jam. This is how you address issues and problems in their lives. You also learn to pick your battles. Not everything is worth making a big deal about.

Another thing you can do in such a situation is to take a breath and walk away. Cool down, relax, refocus, and then address the issue with your kids. Your kids will see you in another light. They will *come to you* for answers, and discuss their issues with you, just as my Sophia and Paul often do with me. When you experience what I have just described there is no better feeling on earth. Because you *know* in your *heart*, in your *gut*, in your *soul*, that you made a difference in your kid's lives. You've *transcended*, you broke the link with the abusers, with the freaks. They are gone. They won't come back. They won't hurt you any longer. You don't need to drink, to snort, become prey to gurus and cults, political hucksters, to demean yourself looking for the love and acceptance that your abusers never gave you.

You're getting that love, that affection from your kids (amongst others) freely, and openly. For those who came up like us, trust me, there's *nothing better!* You'll see the results of your transcendence as you watch your kids soar to greater and greater heights in all that they do. You'll marvel at their maturity, their self-esteem and focus, and how they stand out amongst their peers. In your heart you'll know you've got the brass ring and you broke it, and the link in the chain of abuse and pain is now broken *forever!*

• • •

Regardless of our individual situations and circumstances, our futures, and our kid's futures, in fact the future of our society and civilization all boils down to *choice*. You choose how to ingest, interpret, and respond to your life, and your life's experiences. Certainly we are all influenced in a variety of ways, as to how we understand, react, and process the reality of our lives. No one person lives in a vacuum. It doesn't matter where you live or what your experiences have been, all of us are influenced by cultures, schools, books, media, and our life's experiences. However, irrespective of this, regardless of our circumstances my brothers and sisters, *all* of us children of the secret ultimately have to make the *choice*.

This choice, the most important choice that you will ever make, will determine which way you will go. Will you go onwards triumphantly towards transcendence, or will you stay chained to your past, to your abusers? They may no longer be in your life, (they may even be dead), but nevertheless they still haunt you. *Through the choices you will make your abusers will live on through you.*

• • •

The great martial artist Bruce Lee, founder of the martial art system Jeet Kune Do (Way of Intercepting Fist), used to tell his students who had difficulty mastering a technique, "I've shown the way to you. But you haven't taken it, it's still mine. When you master it you've taken it from me. Then it will be yours." My brothers and sisters of the secret your abusers took something from you. Transcend and *take it back from them!* I have transcended. I have triumphed. I'm free.

BEHAVIOR IS TRUTH

Gwyndyn T. Alexander

"BEHAVIOR IS TRUTH" GETS ITS TITLE FROM A HAIKU BY ANDREW VACHSS AND FRANK CARUSO, WHICH FIRST APPEARED IN *ANOTHER CHANCE TO GET IT RIGHT: A CHILDREN'S BOOK FOR ADULTS,* PUBLISHED BY DARK HORSE, © 1990.

1.

He's great at a party,
says all the right things,
smiles all the right smiles.

You trust him
to get you tickets to the game
to watch your house when you're
away.
He makes a great bloody mary.

He's your neighbor.
He's your friend.
He's a great guy,
always good for a laugh.
He knows all the best jokes.
He smiles and smiles and smiles.

And he goes home
draws the curtains
and rapes his daughter.
Again.

You avoid seeing the bruises.
You don't register the possessive arm
on his daughter's waist.
You don't translate
the fear in her eyes.

Because he smiles
and tells you
what you want to hear,
what you want to believe.

He lies.
And you help him.
He lies.
And you believe him.
He lies.
And you invite him
into your home.
He lies.
And you want to believe him.

2.
That little girl
with the bruises
hauled along at the end
of her parent's arm.

She's cowed.

She's small.

She's invisible.

But her heart is huge
and she knows
that she does not have to become
the monster.

That monster lives next door.
The one that you aid and abet
because he lends you his lawnmower.

She does not have to do
what is done to her.

He lies.
He destroys.

She makes a choice
to love
to fight
to protect.

He does it because he can.
He does it because you help him
by believing his empty words
and his empty smiles.

She is not the victim.
She is so much more
than her abuse.

You say he can't have done it.
Such a nice, quiet man.
Such a good friend.
Behavior is truth.
Believing the monster,
denouncing his victim,
your behavior shines through.

She reaches out her hand
not in anger
but in love.

She knows
behavior is truth.

The monster next door
is reflected
in your mirror.

And she can see the monster
in you.

PIGEONS FOR PROTECT!

Linda Sarah

Heroes

ABOUT THE
CONTRIBUTORS

Linda Sarah wanted to be a firefighter, but being massively short-sighted and claustrophobic, ended up inventing stuff with words and pictures instead. Her children's books *Mi and Museum City* and *On Sudden Hill* came out in 2014, with more to follow. Other illustrated story-poem things can be found here: travelandsing.com. Oh, also, I adore pigeons and all negative myths about them are completely untrue!

New York Times Best Selling author of *Confessions of a Prairie Bitch: How I Survived Nellie Oleson and Learned to Love Being Hated*, **Alison Arngrim** is best known to viewers world-wide for her portrayal of the incredibly nasty "Nellie Oleson" on the much loved, long running hit television series *Little House On The Prairie*, and continues to amuse audiences through her film, television, stage and multi-media appearances. She currently serves as California Chair, National Spokesperson and Founding Board Member on the National Advisory Board of The National Association to Protect Children, aka PROTECT.

Allison Glasgow is a bookseller and longtime editor of the magazine *ThugLit*. Her stories have been published in *Shotgun Honey, Literary Orphans, New World Writing, Brev Spread* and *The Red Line*, and occasionally under the pen name Nellie Aberdeen.

David Morrell is the author of *First Blood*, the award-winning novel in which Rambo was created. His numerous *New York Times* bestsellers include the classic spy novel, *The Brotherhood of the Rose*, the basis for the only television mini-series to be broadcast after a Super Bowl. An Edgar and Anthony finalist, a Nero and Macavity winner, Morrell is a recipient of three Bram Stoker awards and the prestigious Thriller Master award from the International Thriller Writers organization.

P.J. Ward is from the Midwest and writes stories about climate change. She enjoys reading works of speculative fiction and magical realism, as well as the obituary columns and the opinions of people she disagrees with. She is from Washington State, and she occasionally misses the ocean.

Andrew Vachss has been a federal investigator in sexually transmitted diseases, a social-services caseworker, and a labor organizer, and has directed a maximum-security prison for "aggressive-violent" youth. Now a lawyer in private practice, he represents children and youths exclusively. His many works of fiction include the Burke series and two collections of short stories (with a third to be published in 2013). His books have been translated into twenty languages, and his work has appeared in *Parade, Antaeus, Esquire, Playboy*, the *New York Times*, and many other forums. His latest novel, *Signwave*, is the third in the Aftershock series. For more information, visit www.vachss.com

After growing up on a Nebraska farm, **Richard Prosch** worked as a professional writer and artist in Wyoming, South Carolina, and Missouri. His western crime fiction captures the fleeting history and lonely frontier stories of his youth where characters aren't always what they seem, and the wind-burned landscapes are filled with swift, deadly danger.

Susan Schorn writes "Bitchslap: A Column About Women and Fighting" for McSweeney's Internet Tendency. Her work also appears on such websites as *Jezebel*, the *Hairpin*, and *The Rumpus*; her memoir *Smile at Strangers and Other Lessons in the Art of Living Fearlessly*, was published by Houghton Mifflin Harcourt in 2013.

Gary Phillips's crime novels include *The Jook, Bangers* and *Warlord of Willow Ridge*. He also writes other stuff including graphic novels such as *The Rinse*, about a money launderer, which was optioned for TV. *Occupied Earth*, a hardboiled sci-fi anthology he co-edited, is out now. His website is: gdphillips.com

New York native **SJ Rozan** has won multiple awards, including the Edgar, Shamus, Anthony, Nero, Macavity, and Japanese Maltese Falcon. She's written fifteen novels and fifty short stories. Her newest book is *Skin of the Wolf*, written with Carlos Dews as the writing team of Sam Cabot.

Scott Adlerberg lives in Brooklyn. He is the author of the Martinique-set crime novel *Spiders and Flies* and the genre-blending noir/fantasy novella *Jungle Horses*, from Broken River Books.

Rachael Acks is a writer, geologist, and dapper sir. She's written for *Six to Start* and been published in *Strange Horizons, Lightspeed*, and more. Rachael lives in Houston with her two furry little bastards, where she twirls her mustache, watches movies, and bikes. See her website www.rachaelacks.com

Terrence McCauley's new acclaimed techno-thriller *Sympathy for the Devil* is published by Polis Books. Polis is also republishing e-book versions of his other two award winning crime novels: *Prohibition* and *Slow Burn*. A proud native of The Bronx, NY, he is currently working on his next work of fiction.

Linda Rodriguez's Skeet Bannion mystery novels, *Every Hidden Fear, Every Broken Trust*, and *Every Last Secret*, and books of poetry, *Skin Hunger* and *Heart's Migration*, have received many awards, such as St. Martin's/Malice Domestic Best First Novel, Latina Book Club Best Books 2014, Midwest Voices & Visions Award, Thorpe Menn Award, Ragdale and Macondo fellowships. She is Chair of the AWP Indigenous/Aboriginal American Writers Caucus.

Bracken MacLeod has worked as a martial arts teacher, a university philosophy instructor, for a children's non-profit, and as a criminal and civil trial attorney. His short fiction has appeared in *Shotgun Honey, LampLight, Beat to a Pulp, Splatterpunk*, and *Shock Totem Magazine*. He is the author of *Mountain Home, White Knight*, and his next book, tentatively titled *Stranded*, is coming soon from Tor/Forge. You can follow him on twitter at @BrackenMacLeod

Rios de la Luz is the author of *The Pulse Between Dimensions and the Desert*, and she is an editor for Redfez.net and Ladyblog (Ladyboxbooks.com). Her work has been featured in *Vol.1 Brooklyn* and *Entropy*. She currently lives in Portland with her Partner and beautiful beast dog.

Graham Wynd can be found in Dundee but would prefer you didn't come looking. An English professor by day, Wynd grinds out darkly noir prose between trips to the local pub. Wynd's novella of murder and obsessive love, *Extricate*, is out now from Fox Spirit Books; her short stories appeared in Otto Penzler's KWIK KRIMES, *Noir Nation, Spinetingler, Shotgun Honey, Pulp Metal Magazine* and more. Visit GrahamWynd.com for more.

C.R. Jahn is a hook-handed biker who provides security and investigative services to the private sector in the Denver metro area. He is the author of *The Outrider* and *FTW Self Defense*. He rode with the Rocky Mountain Chapter of Bikers Against Child Abuse for two years and supports their mission to empower abused children to feel safe in the world in which they live.

After years of online RPGs and community writing, **Karina Cooper** eventually decided that she'd take her real life and make it all about fiction. She is the author of the award winning *The St. Croix Chronicles*, an avowed gamer, a borderline hermit and occasional Outer God. Find her abyssal domain at @ karinacooper and www.karinacooper.com.

John A. Curley was born in Staten Island, New York. He began training in martial arts in 1980 and teaching martial arts in 1985. He has worked in varying capacities as a private investigator and security agent since 1987. He is currently the president of J. Curley & Associates, LLC. The dedicated website is jcurleyandassociates.com.

Chad Eagleton is a hardboiled writer and unrepentant leftist working on the style of his soul. He is a Spinetingler Award nominee and a two-time Watery Grave Invitational finalist with work available in print, e-book, and online. An obsessive Shane Stevens fan, he's spent the last several years compiling a biographical portrait of this forgotten master. He's also busy plotting more Coffin Boy Occult Investigations. Join the fray at dimestoreriot.blogspot.com

Dyer Wilk is a writer and graphic designer living in Northern California. His work can be found online at aseasonofdusk.com.

S.A. Solomon has published crime fiction and poetry in *New Jersey Noir* (Akashic Books), *Grand Central Noir* (Metropolitan Crime), and the *5-2 Crime Poetry Weekly*, and has fiction forthcoming in *Jewish Noir* (PM Press). She is a regional board member for the Mystery Writers of America, New York chapter. You can find her on twitter @sa_solomon

Jyl Anais Ion is an artist and writer who works within the intersections of a variety of media. Originally from the Caribbean, she currently resides in the United States where she nurtures orchids and faces the blank page. Connect with her on her website www.jyl-ion.com.

Reed Farrel Coleman is the New York Times Bestselling author of Robert B. Parker's Jesse Stone series and of the Gus Murphy series debuting in January 2016. He is a three-time winner of the Shamus Award for Best PI Novel of the Year and a three-time Edgar Award nominee.

Joe R. Lansdale is the author of numerous novels and short stories, screenplays and comic scripts. He has written for Batman the Animated series, and his story "Bubba Hotep" became a film of the same name. He has won many recognitions for his works, including the Lifetime Achievement Award from the Horror Writers Association, The Edgar Award, and nine Bram Stokers and the Grandmaster Award from HWA. His latest novel is *Paradise Sky*.

Teel James Glenn has been a stuntman, fight choreographer, swordmaster, jouster, illustrator, bodyguard, actor and haunted house barker. His stories have been in *Weird Tales, Mad, Black Belt, Fantasy Tales, Sixgun Western, Tales of Old, Another Realm, Blazing Adventures* and other publications. He has over thirty books and anthologies in print in many genres. You can find him at theurbanswashbuckler.com

Hilary Davidson has won the Anthony Award, the Derringer Award, the Crimespree Award, and two Ellery Queen Reader's Choice Awards. Toronto-born and NYC-based, she uses her background as a travel journalist in her Lily Moore mystery series, setting stories in places such as Peru and Mexico. Her latest book is the hardboiled *Blood Always Tells*, her first non-series novel. She is also the author of 18 nonfiction books. hilarydavidson.com

Harlan Ellison® has written or edited 75 books; more than 1,700 stories, essays, articles, and newspaper columns; two dozen teleplays, for which he received the Writers Guild of America most outstanding teleplay award for solo work an unprecedented four times; and a dozen movies. He won the Mystery Writers of America Edgar Allan Poe award twice, the Horror Writers Association Bram Stoker award six times (including The Lifetime Achievement Award in 1996), the Nebula three times, the Hugo 8½ times, and received the Silver Pen for Journalism from P.E.N, The World Fantasy Award, the British Fantasy Award, the American Mystery Award, two Audie Awards, the Ray Bradbury Award, and a Grammy nomination for Spoken Word recordings. In 1990, Ellison was honored by P.E.N. for his continuing commitment to artistic freedom and the battle against censorship. He lives with his wife, Susan, inside the Lost Aztec Temple of Mars, in Los Angeles.

Thomas Pluck is the author of the action thriller *Blade of Dishonor*, several story collections, and the editor of the PROTECTORS anthologies to benefit PROTECT. His work has appeared in many magazines and anthologies, including *Dark City Lights: New York Stories*, edited by Lawrence Block, *McSweeney's Internet Tendency*, and *The Utne Reader*. He also trains in mixed martial arts and powerlifting, hosts *Noir at the Bar* in New York City, and is the social media editor for PROTECT. Find him online at thomaspluck.com and on twitter as @thomaspluck

A former delinquent wrangler, **Neliza Drew** grew up as a boring Southern girl who still hates sweet tea. She has spent way too many hours entertaining herself because everyone else assumed she'd crash-landed from Mars. Her stories have appeared in *Needle*, *Noir Nation* and *Feeding Kate*. She lives in Florida with her husband and furry minions (okay, they're cats).

Laird Barron is the author of several books, including *The Croning, Occultation*, and *The Beautiful Thing That Awaits Us All*. His work has also appeared in many magazines and anthologies. An expatriate Alaskan, Barron currently resides in upstate New York.

Elizabeth Amber Love is the author of comic stories published by Red Stylo Media and Northwest Press and a prose short story in the Dark Horse Sequential *Pulp Athena Voltaire* anthology. Her podcast Vodka O'Clock and website are intended for mature audiences. Follow at amberunmasked.com and @elizabethamber on Twitter.

Albert Tucher is the creator of prostitute Diana Andrews, who has appeared in more than sixty short stories in such venues as *ThugLit, Shotgun Honey*, and *The Best American Mystery Stories 2010*. Diana's first longer case, the novella *The Same Mistake Twice*, was published in 2013 by Untreed Reads. Albert Tucher's colleagues at the Newark Public Library talk a lot about retirement—whose, he's not sure.

Clare Toohey is a story junkie who'll bogart anyone's stash. She's the Executive Editor of CriminalElement.com and *The M.O.*, an award-winning collection of short crime fiction, as well as other anthologies. Having presidented, programmed, and been empaneled for various writers' organizations, now, she mostly writes, works freelance, indulges her taste for the uncanny, and blogs for WomenofMystery.net. Tweet her @clare2e.

Will Graham is the pseudonym of a professional investigator specializing in computer forensics and electronic evidence exclusively. His musical tastes pretty much stopped with The Rat Pack, and he still reads Leslie Charteris, Sir Arthur Conan Doyle, Dame Agatha Christie, and Ellery Queen. Keep current with events at: grahamwm.com

Wayne D. Dundee lives in the once-notorious old cowtown of Ogallala, on the hinge of Nebraska's panhandle. To date, he has had over two dozen novels and nearly thirty short stories published. Most of his early work featured his PI protagonist, Joe Hannibal, whose appearances in stories and novels comprise one of the longest-running, still-active series (over 30 years) on the fictional PI scene. Titles in the Hannibal series have been translated into several languages and nominated for an Edgar, an Anthony, and six Shamus Awards. Dundee is also the founder and original editor of *Hardboiled Magazine*. He is the recipient of three Peacemaker Awards from Western Fictioneers: *Dismal River* (best first Western novel 2011); "This Old Star (best Western short story 2010); and "Adeline" (best Western short story 2012). You can learn more about Big Wayne and his writing at: fromdundeesdesk.blogspot.com

Joelle Charbonneau has performed in theatrical productions across Chicagoland. She is the author of the *New York Times* and *USA Today* bestselling *The Testing* trilogy as well as two adult mystery series. Her YA books have appeared on the Indie Next List, the YALSA Top 10 books for 2014 as well as state reading lists across the country. Her social media thriller, *Need*, will hit shelves November 3, 2015.

Alex Segura is a novelist and comic book writer. He is the author of the Miami crime novel *Silent City*, the first in a series featuring Pete Fernandez. *Silent City* and its sequel, *Down the Darkest Street*, will be out via Polis Books in 2016. He has also written a number of comic books, including the best-selling and critically acclaimed Archie Meets KISS storyline. He lives in New York with his wife. He is a Miami native.

Dennis Calero is an award-winning writer and artist who helped developed "X-Men Noir" for Marvel Comics, as well as having worked on DC and Dark Horse Comics. Calero has also worked on entertainment projects for CBS Films and Weed Road Pictures and famed horror writer Stephen King. He also adapted *The Martian Chronicles* by Ray Bradbury as a graphic novel for Hill & Wang as well as "The Tell Tale Heart" for Stonearch books.

Gill Hoffs is the author of *Wild: a collection* (Pure Slush, 2012), *The Sinking of RMS Tayleur: The Lost Story of the 'Victorian Titanic'* (Pen & Sword, 2014, 2015), and numerous articles and short stories. Find her as @GillHoffs on twitter or via gillhoffs.wordpress.com

Martyn Waites is the author of ten crime novels under his own name, eight thrillers as Tania Carver and Great Lost Albums, a comedy music book. He's been nominated for lots of awards, won one, had a Guardian book of the year, and been a bestseller. He lives in South London with a famous cat.

KL Pereira's fiction, poetry, and nonfiction appear in *Shimmer Zine, Lightning Cake, The Golden Key, Innsmouth Free Press, Innsmouth Magazine, Mythic Delirium, Jabberwocky, The Medulla Review, Bitch Magazine* and other publications. Her chapbook, *Impossible Wolves*, was published by Deathless Press in 2013. Find Pereira online at: klpereira.com and @kl_pereira.

Josh Stallings grew up in the shadows of NorCali, down where the lamps have all been shot out with pellet guns and no one asks questions they don't want to hear the answers to. Author of the multiple award winning Moses McGuire crime novels, and the Anthony Award nominated memoir, *All the Wild Children*. His '70's glitter-rock disco heist novel *Young Americans* will be published fall 2015.

Angel Luis Colón's fiction has appeared in multiple publications. He writes book reviews for *My Bookish Ways* and is an editor for *Shotgun Honey*. He's been nominated for the Derringer Award and has won a writing contest or two. His debut novella, *The Fury of Blacky Jaguar*, is out now.

A transplanted Kentuckian, **Jerry Bloomfield** lives on the east coast of Canada with his wife and children, some of the feline persuasion. When not writing, Jerry is losing at video games and ferrying kids around. He has previously been published at *Beat To A Pulp* and *Beat To A Pulp: Superhero*.

Laura K. Curtis has always done everything backwards. As a child, she was extremely serious, so now that she's chronologically an adult, she feels perfectly justified in acting the fool. Published in crime fiction, romantic suspense, and contemporary romance, she lives in Westchester County, New York with her husband and a pack of wild Irish Terriers.

Michael A. Black is a retired cop and the author of 25 books and many short stories and articles. He has a BA in English, an MFA in Fiction Writing, and writes the Executioner series as Don Pendleton (*Dragon Key, Desert Falcons*, and *Uncut Terror*). Black's latest novel is *Chimes at Midnight*.

Andrew D'Apice is an unrepentant crap artist. He is proudly from New Jersey (which may explain some things) where he lives with his wife, son, their five cats, and too many books and bad thoughts for his own good. This is his first publication.

Holly West is the author of the Mistress of Fortune series, set in 17th century London and featuring Isabel Wilde, a mistress to King Charles II who secretly makes her living as a fortuneteller. Her debut, *Mistress of Fortune*, was nominated for the Left Coast Crime Rosebud Award for Best First Novel. When Holly's not wandering the captivating streets of 17th century England, she lives in the Sierra foothills of Northern California with her husband and dog.

Currently living in Tree Frog Farm with his wife and two children in a Florida wood, and formerly chairman of the West Cork Writers, 66-year-old **Tim Daly** started out as a political performance poet who found himself with a very active career as a lyricist cum lyric doctor throughout the '80s. Nowadays he just writes whenever the words dance too loud.

Errick Nunnally was raised in Boston, served in the Marine Corps, and graduated from art school. *Blood for the Sun* is his first published novel and he has several short stories in anthologies and magazines.

Christopher Irvin has traded all hope of a good night's sleep for the chance to spend his mornings writing dark and noir fiction. He is the author of *Federales* and *Burn Cards*, as well as short stories featured in several publications, including *ThugLit, Beat to a Pulp, Needle*, and *Shotgun Honey*. He lives with his wife and son in Boston, Massachusetts.

Joyce Carol Oates is the author of the memoirs *A Widow's Story* and *The Lost Landscape: A Writer's Coming of Age*. Her most recent novel is *The Sacrifice* and her most recent story collection is *High-Crime Area*. She is a member of the American Academy of Arts and Letters and is currently Distinguished Writer in Residence in the Graduate Writing Program at NYU.

Zak Mucha, LCSW is a psychotherapist in private practice. He is the consultant for the PROTECT H.E.R.O. Corps as well as a mentor at the Chicago Center for Psychoanalysis.

Charles de Lint is a full-time writer and musician who makes his home in Ottawa, Canada. The renowned author of more than seventy adult, young adult, and children's books, he has won the World Fantasy, Aurora, Sunburst, and White Pine awards, among others. Modern Library's Top 100 Books of the 20th Century poll, voted on by readers, put eight of de Lint's books among the top 100. De Lint is also a poet, artist, songwriter, performer and folklorist, and he writes a monthly book-review column for *The Magazine of Fantasy & Science Fiction*. Visit his web site at charlesdelint.com

Dionysios Dionou was born in Greece, orphaned, sold in a black market, and raised in a nest of pythons. He is the author of the memoir *Twentieth Century Janissary: An Orphan's Search for Freedom, Family, and Heritage*, and the novel *Daniel's Message*. This year Dionou will release a collection of short stories, a cookbook, and a co-authored book on martial arts. He is a proud member of PROTECT and the Greek Adoption Reunion Registry. www.dionou.com

Gwyndyn T. Alexander was born in San Francisco, but moved to New Orleans and never looked back. In 2005, she lost her house and job and her library to the Great Levee Failure. She survived her abusive childhood, Katrina, and ten years in exile in Texas. Back home in New Orleans, she lives happily with her husband and her feline overlord, Scout.

Suzanne Dell'Orto (print design and cover design) earned her BFA from the School of Visual Arts, and her Master's Degree in Studio Art from NYU's Venice Program and has been exhibiting her work since 1995. She is a practicing artist, curator, and designer, and she is a design educator at Baruch College/CUNY in New York City. She specializes in book design and designs for artists. Find her art and design on www.modomnoc.net

JW Manus (ebook design) of QA Productions specializes in producing digital and print-on-demand books for independent author/publishers. Donating her skills to this book is far more personal than being able to work with some of her favorite writers. She adopted three "special needs" teenagers, and JW's proudest achievement is helping them end the vicious cycle of abuse.

Printed in the USA
CPSIA information can be obtained
at www.ICGtesting.com
LVHW020812311023
762532LV00024B/386